CARTHY FAMILY SECRET

BOOK 1 OF 4 PART 1

Very Special thanks to:

Carol McLean

for her incredibly inspiring Red Pen!

Adrian von Ziegler

for his amazing musical compositions on YouTube and for
allowing the world to listen to his music, use his songs and
enjoy his creations. His music has been an inspiration in
my ability to write and I cannot thank him enough!

Scotweb Store

for their McCarthy fabric I will use to make
my bookmarkers for my books
This is their Address:
Units 3-4
14 Spring valley Gardens
Edinburgh, Scotland
EH10 4QG
UNITED KINGDOM

CARTHY FAMILY SECRET
BOOK 1 OF 4 PART 1

THE BEGINNING

K. M. M.

CARTHY FAMILY SECRET BOOK 1 OF 4 PART 1
THE BEGINNING

iUniverse books may be ordered through booksellers or by contacting:

iUniverse
1663 Liberty Drive
Bloomington, IN 47403
www.iuniverse.com
1-800-Authors (1-800-288-4677)

ISBN: 978-1-5320-5750-2 (sc)
ISBN: 978-1-5320-5751-9 (hc)
ISBN: 978-1-5320-5749-6 (e)

Library of Congress Control Number: 2018912895

Print information available on the last page.

iUniverse rev. date: 11/06/2018

CONTENTS

NOTE TO MY READERS

This book, Carthy Family Secret, Book 1 of 4, Part 1 is the beginning of my pursuit to reconnect my family's delegated posts of the world known within as the Whole of the Green Isles.

Each story was intended to be a separate book but due to my need to complete them and get them to you, I have combined them into four books. In addition, I have added a Part 2 to Book 1 and Book 4 that hold Information and Stories that will educate you on the World Within.

This book is the first of the four.

GRANDFATHERS TALE

A FAMILY SECRET REVEALED IN A DREAM

Grandfathers Tale

A Family Secret Revealed in a Dream

By K.M.M.

Editor: Kimberly O'Brien Young

For My Daddy
Justin H. McCarthy Jr.

His eyes hold the history of our ancestry.
They glisten with the richness of the lives that have gone before us.
We are honored and proud to be of their line.

His arms hold the strength of our family.
They are powerful and solid yet they are
a place that we can call home.
We are happy and content to be of their kind.

He taught us to stand tall among the many.
He taught us to be glad with life's simplest joys.
I am honored and proud to be of his line.

Justin's line Cluster L

Diamond Forest

Introduction to my Dream

I hold a memory in which I overheard a story about a family secret. The teller of the story was my grandfather Justin H. McCarthy Sr. and he was telling the story to my eldest brother Jim.

In some ways, I believe this memory to be only a dream, as to this day I do not recall ever meeting my grandfather. He, I have been told, died the summer before I was born. Yet this memory of him sitting beside my brother Jim and explaining our family's secret is as real to me as any of my own true-life memories.

My grandfather was a solid framed man with a firm jaw and a gentle smile. He had dazzling blue eyes that brightened with each word he spoke. In this memory of him, he appears tired and slow. Nevertheless, he sounded determined to pass his story on to my brother Jim, who sat captivated in his gaze.

Jim is for true, a round faced chubby cheeked redhead with matching bright blue eyes like our grandfather. He was three years old in this memory, I know this because, as this memory begins I could hear my grandfather asking Jim a question.

"How old are you now my boy?"

"I'm three." Jim answered clearly proud of himself.

Jim's mention of his age makes me question whether this memory is a dream? You see my brother Jim turned to the age of four, the day before I was born. How could I remember Jim at age three when I was not yet born? This bit of knowledge from Jim's own lips, is what I struggle with as I understand this memory. Is it a genuine memory or is it a deep irrational delusion I have made up?

To add to the discrepancy, my next remembrance of my big brother Jim was the moment he was pushing my face down into a puddle of murky sludge! The sludge had collected in the back yard of our home in Endicott, New York. Jim was eight years old and I remember being four years old. It was the first time my mother allowed me to go outside by myself in the snow and play with my older sister Noreen, who was five.

In this recollection, Noreen was crying from inside her overstuffed pale pink snowsuit as she tried to pick me back up without falling into the gunk herself. Jim then stood over us laughing as my recollection of him faded.

Why would I remember Jim at three years old and then not again until he was eight? The questions of what I believe I have seen, and experienced make me doubt the reliability of my mind's memory and trouble me deeply. None the less, I have been haunted by this scene of my grandfather and brother so often throughout my life I must attempt to explain it in hopes of making some kind of sense of it, if only for myself.

As I cue up this memory of my Brother Jim sitting with my Grandfather Justin H McCarthy Sr., I see: a cloudy edged moment like an old-fashioned snapshot, only it moves before me and there is a sound about it that hums softly. My grandfather and my brother are sitting next to each other on the front marble steps of a cottage home. Jim is sitting a few steps higher than my grandfather is and their heads are nearly the same in height.

The screen door behind the pair snaps shut and I hear my grandfather begin his story.

Grandfather's Story

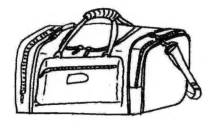

As my grandfather leans towards my brother Jim. I can see a slight grin appear on my grandfather's face as he begins . . .

"Well my boy, do you want your old pop to tell you a secret?"

Jim bobbed his head in a way that I can only assume was a 'yes' as my grandfather continued his story.

My grandfather's grin faded into an amazed look, his gaze intensified upon Jim' face as he spoke in a compelling whisper.

"Now Jim, what I am about to tell you is something our family has kept secret from the world for a very long time. This secret only Clan Carthy's, like you and I, can hear. It's important you remember this!"

Jim settled down and leaned in close to my grandfather. His eyes grew wide as he listened carefully to grandfather's words.

"You can keep the family secret, can't you?" Grandfather asked as his hand drifted over the neck of a large tan duffle bag that sat between his legs. He clutched it firmly in his fist as if he were checking to make sure it was still there.

Jim nodded his head slowly twice.

"Well, that's good, because it will be up to you, our family's inheritor, to keep the secret and protect our post. When it's time, you too must pass it on to your son or grandson, just as I am passing it to you."

Grandfather then glanced back over his shoulder. His eyes narrowed and his facial expression developed into an annoyed stare as he noticed me standing behind the screen door.

I am startled in the moment as the fear that I have heard something I was not to know filled my being. The scene then goes dark for me but I can still hear my Grandfather as he continues his story.

"In the time of the beginning, and I mean the beginning of all things, there was Magic! Magic that became the spark of all life. It swirled through the heavens and space generating worlds including this Earth we stand upon. The people of Earth know this but what they are unaware of is what our family has kept hidden from them for generations. We must continue to keep this knowledge concealed to protect what I am going to show you, for if we fail the people known as members of the Isles will be doomed."

Grandpa cleared his throat slightly. "As magic created life, life and creation sometimes encircled magic, capturing it inside its grasp. Holding it like a delicate bubble filled with smoke."

"What Grandpa? We have magic?" Jim' whispered.

"No, my boy, unfortunately in our world the magic has for the most part escaped us. The majority of the magic was used up during the creation of Earth. Some of it evaporated back into space traveling out into the vast heavens to create life and planets once more. We here in this world have only the embers of magic left but there is something that I am holding that holds the purest magic. That is why we McCarthy's have vowed generation after generation to protect this. I speak of the Secret of the Isles."

At that moment, the darkness I had been shrouded in slips away and again I could see my Grandfather and Jim sitting on the steps.

Grandfather then pulled from the tan duffle bag that sat between his legs an enormous pure white crystal with several smaller white and orange pristine crystals surrounding it. The base of each crystal was encased in a blue rock that sparkled with traces of gold. The top of the crystals and full lengths stood up and sparkled in the sunlight.

"There are fifty-five Crystal Isles to be exact that we have grouped into thirteen Cluster. Each crystal Isle is different and houses a portion of the world within known as the Green Isles. Within these crystals magic has survived." Grandfather explained as he placed the large Crystal Isle into Jim hands.

"Wow, it is beautiful Grandfather. Where did you get?" Jim inquired in awe.

"Our ancestor Florence Jr. of Dunmanway had been entrusted by his father Florence Sr. with five of the Crystal Isles in a cluster known as 'The Diamond Forest.' They have been kept safe by our family here in America ever since Florence's son Cornelius with his sister Catherine carried them here hidden in a wooden trunk in 1852 on the ship called the Constantine."

Jim gasped, "That's like 100 years or something!"

"Oh, it goes back a lot farther then that my boy, a lot farther than that. However, what we know about the very beginning is somewhat hazy. I do know that it all started with a man who went by the name of Oiloll. And later in Oiloll's life just before he died he told his son Cian the truth about his life, where he had come from and why he had traveled to Cork to die."

The Change

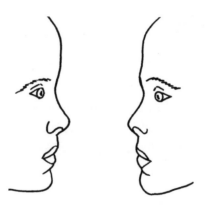

During this part of my dream, I could see my grandfather and Jim sitting nearly head-to-head and almost eye-to-eye. The sight of them sends a queer shiver through me as if a wave of cold air was suddenly released over me, and for an instant, they are a reflection of each other. They have transformed into the same man. Their bodies were altered so much that there is no difference between them and I could not tell which one is my brother and which one is my grandfather.

The moment passed quickly and I find myself standing on a hill. A vastness of trees, foliage, and unusual rock formations lays before me. The Earth at my feet was cool and lush. I could feel the grains of soil between my toes and I was energized by touching them.

Suddenly I was light, and free. My body vaporized into tiny drops of moisture that hover just beyond the misty scene of my brother and grandfather who were no longer sitting on the marble steps of the cottage.

They were still in front of me but they were no longer similar to each other or themselves. They were older, much older. My grandfather's hair is longer, grayer and thinner on the top. His face has aged; thick carved wrinkles branch out from his eyes and reach across his forehead. He seemed weak and tired. His clothing was extremely odd to me. He looked like he is dressed in a long green costume like that of one of the Three Kings from a Christmas nativity play. The gown richly embellished with gold embroidery that obviously indicates the elderly man was of wealth.

My brother's form was now much taller and stronger. He held my grandfather's form with a sturdy grip. Their heads still turned towards one another and their words were still meant to be heard by only each other but I in a mist and air, could hear them as clear as if they are speaking to the world.

As I listened to their words, I realize they are no longer my grandfather and brother; they were memories from the past. My grandfather's form was that of Oiloll, the man of my Grandfather's story and Jim was now Oiloll's son Cian.

Oiloll's Story

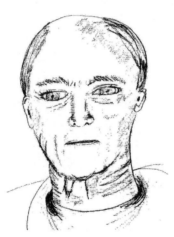

Oiloll's voice echoed in my ears, it is strangely weak and I draw to his desperation.

"My Son," he whispered, "I must tell you . . . I must explain . . . everything to you. It is important that you understand what I need you to do. I am too weak, too old. I have waited too long to come back and make things right. I was so wrong . . ." his voice breaks.

"Father don't, not now, you should rest. We have traveled so far, it is late, and you are tired," Cian urged.

"No!" Oiloll shouts angrily. "I am not tired, I am dying, and you must listen before it is too late for me to set things right. It is important that you know it all, that you understand what happened from the beginning. Where I came from, what I did and what you and your sons must do for me."

"Yes father." Cian answers.

Oiloll took a deep breath and then began his tale.

"The land I come from is surrounded by a dreadful sea. The waters there are perilous to our kind making transportation off the isle impossible unless you have strong magical powers, which I do not. The isle I speak of is the Isle of Carthy; it sits as land within this Crystal."

Oiloll explained as he struggled to pull to his side his old odd shaped carpetbag. He opened the bag and tried to pull out the top of a tall green crystal. It was larger than the old man's two hands and it took the help of his son for it to be removed from the bag.

Cian's eyes grew wild as he held the crystal in his hands. He said nothing; he merely sat back and allowed his father to continue his story.

"When I was a child, the Isle of Carthy became inhabited by the most violent Ubil Clan ever known. Ubil members were those who did evil magic and they were feared throughout all the lands. Before I was born, the Isle of Carthy was peaceful. My mother, a good-natured soul, told me of days filled with song and children dancing in the fields of flowers they called Christy Toes. The smallest members of the Isles, known as Eties, lived spreading cheer. Our kind known as Feldens enjoyed collecting Missy Grass to press. Life was simple and unmarked by evil, the magic of the land was clean and used for only goodness. Then it all changed when they came, the evil Ubil. They came from a far northern isle known as The Blue Isle of Sorrow, a Clan that called themselves Sherideens of Spalding. The Sherideens used the clean magic of Carthy to do evil magic. Before long the peaceful members of Carthy were being kidnapped, cruelly tortured, mutilated, and murdered."

"My mother feared for my safety and worked tirelessly to find a way for me to escape the island, because it seemed that all the land of the Carthy Isle was overrun with Sherideens. The Sherideens had attacked the Rickstown and Kyle town on the isle we were on. They had taken all the tiny Eties, collecting, killing, drying, and grounding them up for their magical dust, giving them more magic power. It seemed that once they gotten all the Eties, they then came for our kind, the Feldens. We Feldens within were given gems in the palms of their hands, the gems called Palm Gems give us our luck. The Sherideens wanted the Palm Gems and beheaded our kind to get them."

Oiloll moved his left hand and placed it before Cian, and then he pulled off his glove, revealing the palm of his hand. There in the center of his hand was a large green emerald stone that sparkled and glistened with a little glow from within.

Cian gasped. "Father, I have never . . . seen . . . such."

"That's because I have never shown anyone. But you can now understand why my mother was afraid for my life. She knew they would come for me and she had to get me off the Isle of Carthy. However, to leave Carthy and travel to a distant isle seemed even more risky for our kind because the sea is dreadful just beyond the shore of the isle. The Isle of Carthy sits far above the normal sea and to travel away from it, it takes you to a death-defying drop only members with strong magic can survive, and I so young, limited in my learnings, I could never survive the fall. My mother, herself strong in magic and skilled in such things could survive but she would not risk my life in such a way. So it seemed there was nothing we could do to escape."

"For many passes, years to you, my mother and I hid in Jamestown, deep within the coral hollows of the coastal caves with other members of my kind. I was schooled there in the art of potions, wand works, and swordsmanship, even though a sword was not much use against the strength of the Ubil magic. My mother's only hope was to give me at least a fighting chance."

"Later we fled to Florence where my mother had heard of an old knowledgeable Lassie they called a Kathrie, who had ancient documents containing spells. My mother hoped to find the missing lines to a spell she had heard once when she was young. She believed it would save me. So, we ventured there only to find the Kathrie was gone, her home was undisturbed, and her ancient books were still upon her shelves. My mother believed the Kathrie had left Carthy in a hurry to get away from the Sherideens just as we wanted to. That is why she had left her home as it was. In doing so, the Kathrie had given us hope that we too could leave. My mother, a Kathrie by birth, knew how to read the documents but it still took her many days to find the words she knew would finish the spell that would save me."

"It seemed however, that the very day my mother found the lines she was looking for was the very moment the Sherideens found us. I don't know how they found us, but they did and there was nowhere to hide. My mother sacrificed herself for me, to give me time to cast the spell upon myself. I was still so naive I had no idea what my mother was doing for me. I spoke the words of the spell, sprinkling my head with a bag of magical dust known as saddle dust, just as she had told me to do. As I spoke the last word, I was propelled upwards flying far above my mother and the attacking Sherideens. I was still holding the bag of Saddle Dust as I sailed into the open vastness above all. My last glimpse of my world was that of my mother falling backwards, her wand flashed green as a bolt of energy engulfed her."

"The next thing I recall I had landed face down in a dark musty emptiness. The soil beneath me smelled strange, like nothing I had ever smelled before. It was damp and stale; the fragrance of it swelled in my nose and filled my lungs. It was all I could do to just breathe, let alone think. My mind was filled with the most horrible thoughts that kept playing round and round in my head, spinning endlessly. My mother had died before my eyes, the world I knew was gone, and I was now alone, frightened and surrounded by a feeling of nothingness."

"I did not know where I was. I did not know what I should do next. I struggled to my feet and stood in the dank darkness trying to collect my wits. What should I do, where should I go? I didn't have an answer. I only knew I wanted to go back to help my mother. But I did not know how. I did not truly understand where I had come from. Then I noticed a twinkling of light slowly appearing at a far distance ahead of me. The longer I stood there the stronger it seemed to get. Soon it was giving off enough light for me to get my bearings. My eyes searched the space and I realized I was in a cave; a damp limestone cave with a tiny stream trickling through it. Beside me laid a huge crystal. The base of the Crystal was encased in stone. I would later learn the crystal was an emerald and the rock at its base was a bright blue stone call Lazurite. Still I knew the moment I picked it up, it was where I had come from, and I knew the crystal held the Isle of Carthy. I don't know how I knew but I did. In my hands, it sparkled faintly in the frail light. Its beauty blinded me from my senses. Oh, how it blinded me. My concern for my mother faded from me and I was consumed with the desire to control the Isle. My body tingled with hatred and all I wanted was to run from that cave."

The Family Promise

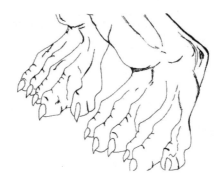

O iloll cried out. He threw his head into his hands and cried, "It was somewhere here that I stood and held my homeland Crystal Isle in my arms. The cave is somewhere around here but it all looks so different now, so much bigger and I cannot find it,"

Oiloll sobbed as he pointed at a strange rock formation covered with rich green plants.

"Father, it is alright I will help you find it. Together we will find it, and all my sons will soon be here to help. If you hadn't run off so suddenly from the camp they would be here now." Cian said, for he and his sons had come with Oiloll to help him find the Cave. It had taken several days and they had not found it yet. So, on this day Oiloll was dying, he ran out in hope of finding it before he died, but he still had not.

"I do not have any more strength to search, my son, I thought I did but now I am spent and there is little time to wait for your sons. You alone must help me; you alone must listen and understand my urgency to find the cave; my urgency to return the crystal to its rightful place." Oiloll's face grew desperate. "And then you must promise me, Cian that you and your sons will protect the place in which it belongs with your lives."

Oiloll grabbed Cian by the collar of his tunic and held it. "Promise me," he whispered.

"Father of course, I promise, I promise we will protect it."

Oiloll released his son and collapsed to the ground.

"Father!" Cian shouted as he watched his father's lifeless body rebound from the impact of the ground. Cian bent over his father and pulled him into his arms.

"Father please, do not die."

Oiloll gasped, his eyes sprung open and he began to breathe.

"Cian!" Oiloll huffed between awkward breaths. "I was wrong to take the crystal from the cave, I was so wrong to have disturbed the balance here."

"Father please don't talk, you should try and rest."

"No, there is no time." He choked. "You must listen."

Oiloll pulled himself up to a sitting position, his face showed his pain as he continued.

"When I stood in the cave holding the crystal I was filled with anger, so much anger. Anger I had no control over, I can't explain it. I was not myself and in my anger I did something that I now realize was terribly wrong."

"What did you do, Father?" Cian asked breathlessly.

"I stole the crystal from its dwelling place. I ran from the cave, clutching it under my arm. But even more horrible than that, I slaughtered the protector of the dwelling," Oiloll confessed.

"Protector! What protector?" Cian asked turning his head in a most odd way.

"There was an enormous bright green, eleven toed dragon lying at the mouth of the cave. He sprung on me as I attempted to escape. I had no weapons to defend myself. I tried a spell that would have worked if I had still been inside the crystal but the magic I uttered did nothing in this outside world. I had only a sachet half-filled with magic saddle dust left over from my cowardly escape from Carthy. Having nothing else, I threw it at the beast hitting it square in its scaly green forehead. The sachet burst open and the dust covered the beast's head, shoulders, and front legs. Almost instantly, the dragon froze and stiffened into rock. It's once shiny green scales were now gray, only its eyes remained unchanged. They sparkled like two giant yellow orbs filled with liquid fire. Cautiously, I approached it and looked into its eyes. I could sense the magic that surrounded it; I could see the wizardry of spells swirling in its eyes. It had been spellbound to this place, to this crystal, to protect it and I had killed it. I had slaughtered the protector and now there is no rightful defender or guardian. I was so wrong to have done what I did." Oiloll explained

"Now I hope you understand why I must find the very place where it came from. I must put it back and set it right. And then you, your children and their children must stand as the protectors and guardians; it is what we must do for the wrong I have done. I have no right to bind you to my wrong but if I do not, the future inside the crystals and the world of my forefathers, your forefathers is doomed."

Oiloll lowered his head, the shame of his actions flooded over him and he sobbed. "All I have accomplished in this world, I achieved selfishly. The anger of that moment served to propel me ruthlessly though my life, eating away at my soul and turning me into the very thing I had run away from. It was as if the evil from the Isle seeped out from within the crystal and filled me."

"No father, that is not true, you have done great things, and you are a great man. The people of this land would not have made you their king if you did not deserve to be," Cian said.

"No, my son, I took what I wanted and set forth my hand upon this land with an evil dominance. A force that now chases me in my weakness and plots against me to gain possession of this most sacred item." Oiloll said as he clutched the green crystal in his arm.

"Lughaid Mac Con?" Cian asked.

"Yes, your brother is filled with my anger, though I tried to keep it within myself, it escaped me. And now he is what I was, and I am clear of mind to do what I must to set things right. That is if I can find the cave and you will help me to keep it from him."

"Grandfather."

Several new voices filled the air and suddenly Oiloll and Cian were not alone. Cian's sons had finally caught up with them and joined the two men encircling them.

"Is this why we left the north so suddenly?" One of the sons asked as he knelt beside Oiloll.

"Yes." Oiloll admitted lowering his head. "Lughaid Mac Con has attempted to seize the crystal. He wants to destroy it and absorb its pure magic. I cannot allow this to . . . "Oiloll gasped, his body jolted with a quiver and then his eyes closed.

The group of men moved in closer to Oiloll and I could no longer see his frail body. Cian then emerged from the group holding the crystal in his hands. The other men turn and face him; they lower their heads and the scene around them changed.

The Finding

Suddenly I was no longer outside among the rich foliage. I was now inside what looked like a small, dusty hunting lodge. There were uneven stones on the floor and rocks form the base of the building. The walls and ceiling were made of wood and all along the walls were tools for digging. On the far side of the one room lodge was a large hearth, burning fiercely with a flame so hot I could feel it drying my vaporous form. The light of the fire was blinding and I could not see the face of the man's voice that now shouted loudly through the air.

"We have found the cave. Come brother. It is not far from here," the voice echoed.

A swirl of colored lights hit me, and I was propelled from the heat of the fire into the cool of darkness. My eyes were still blinded, this time from the lack of light but I could still hear the man's voice calling out before me.

"See brother, this is where the beast once stood, all that remains are his feet. You can count the toes, eleven, just as Grandfather said."

"Yes!" A second man's voice confirmed.

"Come Cas, there is more." The first man beckons from beside my vaporous form. Then suddenly the first man lights a torch and I can make out his face. He is one of sons of Cian. I remember seeing his face alongside his dying grandfather, Oiloll. This son is young and strong, he has long blonde hair, his eyes shimmer in the close radiance of the fire and I cannot see what color they are. But his face is very similar to the man he is calling to, Cas.

Cas is taller and older. He has long gray hair and in the more distant glow of the torch, I can see he has bright blue eyes as he looks through my misty form to his brother. "Lead the way, Kerry." Cas says.

"Once we broke through the wall of rock, here, the cave was revealed to us." Kerry explained.

The light from the torch allowed me to make sense of what is happening around me as the brother's maneuver through the damp cave. They are moving away from me, going deeper into the cave. I follow.

Ahead of us was another lit torch. I could see the light from it blazing and I realized that it is held by another son of Cian who is standing in the center of a wide cavern. He is standing alone; his face is licked with flame. He is motionless like a statue, his eyes are wide, and there is a strain of worry over him as if the ground he stood upon was cursed.

The brothers I had been following suddenly stop and stand up right. Both turn with astonishment as they look at their surroundings. I then turn and looked for myself at the walls of the musty cave but I was so overwhelmed that I cannot hold my place in the dampness. My vaporous state becomes uncontrollably weightless and I ascend to the calcite-covered ceiling of the cave where my perspective was like that of a god.

Below me in the vastness of the cave walls was an awesome sight. Dazzling in the flame of the torch are hundreds of finely developed crystals. There were emeralds, rubies, opals, diamonds and many more rare minerals all in pristine symmetry with the base of each crystal set down in a stunning blue rock, with the tops of most crystal standing upright. The blue rock, lazurite glistens and seems to gently sway as if it were alive, like a sea of solid rock that flows around the bases of the crystals. Yet the blue rock held its form and did not stray or drip from its position on the unusual shelf like foundation in which the massive crystal and lazurite creation exists.

I was struck by the impressively delicate world below me and I was filled with a sense of calmness and serenity. There is silence as I drink in the importance of the moment and I wished for my dream to end knowing this place was safe.

But suddenly the stillness is broken as Kerry, steps forward. His actions are swift and direct as he moved in towards a small gap at the edge of the massive blue rock where the blue rock is uneven and broken. On the edges there is a portion that seems to be missing and only the rich damp Earthly soil remains.

In Kerry's hands he carries the emerald stone that Oiloll, their grandfather had removed and stolen from the cave. The very stone they have sworn to protect and return to the cave.

"When Grandfather Oiloll told us of this cave in which he had taken the Emerald crystal from he never explained to us that there would be so many more here!" Cas expressed in shock.

"It is possible he never knew that such a world like this existed and now that we know that it does, we must insure the protection of not just this one, but The Whole!" Kerry said as he held their Grandfather's Crystal forward. He then pointed it towards the empty space: the single break in the brilliant blue stone. "Do we all agree that this is the place, here, in which it belongs?"

"Yes." the brothers agreed.

"And do we agree that our vow to protect this one stone is now extended to include The Whole of the Isles?" Kerry asked.

"Yes." the brothers agreed.

With that, Kerry placed the emerald into the gap. Instantly a rush of energy and light gushed from the space, first sealing it and then exploding forward extinguishing the torches and hurling the brothers to the floor of the cave.

The energy then flexed upwards ripping through my molecules and propelling them through the cave. My being was stretched throughout the world of the crystals. Each tiny shard, each shiny mineral, I touch and in that moment I know every island. I know every city, every town. I know their members and their history. I understand the importance of protecting the crystals and I was given the understanding that I was a Kathrie, one with connection to the world inside.

CHAPTER 7

Blarney Fortress

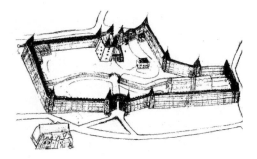

T hen all was still and I felt as if the dream was finished. I felt as if I drifted off to a deeper sleep but the calmness of the moment did not last and I was wearily awakened to another foggy-edged scene.

This time the cloudy edged moment was ancient and dusty. I was in a room, an old wooden walled room that looked like a banquet style hall from a bygone era. There were huge furs hanging heavily on all sides of the room. An antler and bronze candle chandelier hanging from the ceiling. In the center of the room, under the chandelier was a long and narrow birch wood table.

There was a fire burning at the far end of the room in a marble framed fireplace with the carcass of a deer slowly roasting over it. The deer's juices were dripping into the flames causing a scent of burnt flesh to saturate my nose.

The room was filled with men, but I did not recognize any of them. For a moment, I believed that this was not related to the story my Grandfather was telling my brother Jim. It didn't seem connected to Oiloll and the crystals. After a moment my assumptions were swept away when the man at the head of the table rose and began to speak.

The man whose face was gentle, skin was pale, seemed familiar to me? He had a look about him that was similar of someone I felt I knew? His clothing was of a period I did not recognize. He had a long tunic, brightly colored with a golden cloak draped over it. It was pinned with a pearl-headed brooch at his shoulder. I would swear he looked just like my father. But this man was much too old to be my father. This man's hair and beard were platinum white with tiny sliver highlights. Still he had those familiar bright blue eyes of my father and grandfather. Eyes that I know well, and they brightened as he spoke, there was however a seriousness about his words, and it worried me.

"Brothers of Clan Carthy, I Dermot, King of Cork, son of Carthach and descendant of Oiloll, am humbled by your swift attention to the matter at hand in this year of 1177." he began. "Much in the past days has occurred to place worry upon our vow, our promise to our forefather Oiloll, to protect the crystals. Ever since the third century, our lines have secretly protected the crystals here at Blarney. We have established boundary patrols throughout Cork to stop intruders who wish to seize our post. With the help of the descendants of Cian, sons of Duhallow in the Northwest, sons of Reagh in the southwest and sons of Kerry along the border of Cork and Kerry we have been able to keep our vow. In addition, we have surrounded the cave that houses the wondrous world of the Crystals with this mighty wooden structure which supported us through the invasion of the Normans just two days ago spent, but brothers look around you. The structure was nearly breached during the Norman's attack and we must now face the reality that this structure may not be enough of a stronghold in the future."

"What then should we do?" a younger man uttered without restraint.

"I propose the construction of a solid stone fortress that extends to include the entrance of the cave, a wall and tower should be placed in four corners, and a castle like structure should stand in the place of this wooden fortress." A slender man sitting at the table to the right of Dermot said with a commanding voice.

Dermot turned to the slender man and nodded his head to him. "My son has a very good point but is there anyone else that might have a suggestion?"

"I say we should remove the crystals from the ground and lock them up within the wall of the fortress." came another voice from across the table.

"Break the Crystals into manageable portions and assign each of us who hold a true Carthy line to Oiloll, a section of the crystals. Each head of the line will then be in Charge of protecting their share with their own rendition of strategy. Strongholds can be built throughout Cork to aid them and then as a whole we can continue our vow and yet ease the stress in this one given location." Said a man who stood to the left of Dermot.

"Thank you brothers for your suggestions but I must admit I consider my son's proposal to build a stone structure and reinforce the grounds here at Blarney, to be our best defense at present. As for the suggestion of removing the stones from the ground, I believe that is hasty and ill-advised at this time. Although the call of a "Rendition" of strategy per line should most certainly be considered as our last resort to protect them and it shall not be dismissed from our options. It is something we will plan and plan hard." Dermot said with a slight nod of his head towards the group.

The group of men at the table agreed with Dermot as they all nodded their heads, he continued to speak.

"Still I fear we are overlooking the true answer to our dilemma. It has become clear to me that we cannot tolerate another possible invasion. We must do all that we can to discourage such hostilities. By this I mean we MUST befriend all those whom are essential to our protection, even at times forsaking our own." he said lowering his head shamefully.

The men in the room became agitated and they began to question their leader.

"What do you mean, Dermot, forsaking our own?"

"We must extend a hand of friendship to all, even our enemies. Those of the family in great positions of power, it will be essential that you understand why we must do so and I must beg you all to overlook and forgive such actions when and if they occur." Dermot explained.

"But our enemies?" The group called out in shock. A roar of conversation began to build but Dermot clapped his hands and stifled their objections.

"Yes brothers, our enemies. We must become skilled in the art of weaving our tongues, so that all who hear us hear only what they wish to hear, while we remain neutral."

The men in the room go silent and I felt myself spinning. Within seconds, I could see below me the wooden fortress growing in width and height while changing into solid stone. In addition, a stronger fortification of walls branched out to the west and to the east. At the end of the walls, towers spring up, and to the south was a gateway.

The air around me grew cold and I was suddenly on the roof of the massive stone Structure. The structure is a reinvigorated Castle and from where I stood, I could look out over the vast expanse of the castle grounds. Two men stood below me. Both had the same familiar bright blue eyes of my father and grandfather. One of the men also had my grandfather's distinct smile and he is young, clean-shaven with shoulder length strawberry blonde hair. His clothing is that of the Renaissance period and it becomes clear to me that several hundreds of years had passed before me since I saw Dermot speaking to the men inside the wooden fortress.

The second man is older and taller. His face slightly winkled around his blue eyes and his long brown hair braided down the back of his head with a hollow golden ball tie at its end.

Both were dressed in tight fitting leather jackets and traditional Irish Truis type pants.

The younger man leaned over the edge of the castle wall and shouted down to another set of men below.

"Ready the hoist and pull." The young man shouts.

I watched as a giant slab of marble is raised to the roof of the castle and slid into a ready-made shaft. It was placed as if it were a crowning touch or a special ornament meant to be seen by all.

I then heard the men in conversation. Although it is low like a hum in my ear, I can clearly understand their words.

"A Scotsman's peace stone on Irish soil, I never would believe such a thing. Your father, Cormac Laidir, surely knows how to calm the Irish foe." The younger man says to the older.

"Aye, my father's tongue, your grandfather has danced many a sweet plot of assenting favor. But it was our ancestor Cormac McCarthy, King of Muster that supported Robert the Bruce of Scotland at the Battle of Bannackhom over one hundred years ago. In doing so, he sealed the two families in a relationship of harmony. Thus, half the Royal Stone of Scone was presented to the McCarthy's and now it will sit on top of our newly constructed stronghold, Blarney Castle, as an ornament of peace, Luck for the Castle and for the Crystal Isles a gentle kiss of protection." The older man explained with a thrusting pat upon the marble stone.

With his final word, I felt myself spinning again, although slowly . . . .

Rendition

Many years were passing before me. The vision I saw was like that of an old black and white time-lapse movie. The scenes of the Blarney Castle were similar to pictures that clip by one at a time and there is only a slight change in each one as the Blarney Castle aged. To me it seems the castle is quiet and unhampered by war in 1646. I sensed that the Crystal Isles were intact and safe here below the castles structure. I also sensed that Clan of Carthy had been successful in securing and protecting them.

I felt calm and sleepy once again. Floating and peaceful. I hoped for the vision to end here in this feeling of solitude, but it did not! I was dropped like a weight into the next heated scene.

I was back in what looked like the banquet hall and yet it was surely not the same one from the wooden fortress? This one seemed smaller and clearly made of solid rock. There was the same long and narrow birch wood table, set in the center of the hall but it is marked with age and most certainly well worn. Above the table the antler and bronze chandelier had been replaced with a three-tiered iron rack, jammed with candles and a blazed with light. The fur skins that had hug on the wooden walls were gone and, in their place, hang intricate tapestries with scenes depicting the sea. There is a beautiful marble faced fireplace at one end of the hall but no fire burning. The aroma of something sweltering lingers in the air. There were so many men squeezed into the hall I could hardly see all of their faces.

The man at the head of the table stood. His face was drawn and pale. His hair was white and his eyes are as blue and clear as the sky. They sparkle and again I was reminded of my father and grandfather. I am certain that the man is of my Irish family's lineage, and yet his clothing stood out as an English 17th century design. It seemed custom-made, with intricate details on the velvet jacket and matching breeches. It screamed nobility. It was quite obvious to me that this nobleman was the leader of the group in this room.

When he spoke his voice was coarse, and tired as though he had done much negotiation and verbal maneuvering. I sensed it was to no avail, judging by the forlorn and serious tone he now spoke with.

"Sons of the Great Oiloll from Carthy, I, Donough, Lord Muskerry, hail thee. For more than one thousand years, our family has maintained our promise here at Blarney. We have kept safe the Crystal Isles in their native soil. A task we have accomplished, together. I do not need to remind any of you of the delicate circumstance we now face. But with the knowledge that Lord Broghill and his Cromwellian army, well equipped with the new formidable weapon they call the cannon, sits ready to attack us tomorrow. I beg you brothers to agree to my plan. It is our only hope to uphold our promise. We cannot allow Lord Broghill to take possession of the cave." Donough paused for a moment and steadied himself before continuing. "Broken, there are 13 clear cluster sets of Crystals Isles."

"Broken!" a voice breaks the heat of the moment.

"Yes, they are broken," An enormous red-haired man answers as he stood beside Donough. The enormous man then lifted his chin as if he is looking for someone to confront him, but no one else spoke. There is complete silence in the room.

"Thank you, Charles." Donough said as he placed his hand on the enormous man's shoulder and motioned him to sit.

"Yes Father." Charles replied as he sat back down while his blue eyes remained firmly inspecting the crowd of men.

"It is a desperate day, and all we have left is our call for Rendition!" Donough stated with apprehension.

The room gasped. "No, that is a last resort."

"Have we no other way to keep this from happening?"

"I'm afraid our gift of Blarney has worn out its ability to disguise our true selves and we are now with no other choice but to split up the Crystal Isles into groups of clusters that can be easily transported away from here and hidden." Donough uttered as he weakly sat down in his chair.

The men around the table began to talk between themselves. Their tone seemed uneasy with the decision to remove the Crystal Isles from the soil of the cave and break them into groups of cluster sets.

"Quiet brothers, can you not see how my father has fought to do all that he could to prevent this. He has side-stepped so many a foe, well he has protected us, but there is now no other choice but to remove the Crystal Isles and hide them as far away as we can." Charles stated firmly.

"It will only be for a short time. When all is well again, we will return the Crystal Isles back to the cave. Once all has subsided, we will give you a sign to return but if it lingers longer than one year we will set now a meeting to take place on this date next year at St. Finbarr in Bantry." Donough conveyed to the room.

The roar in the room continued and neither man could seem to calm the horde. Then suddenly a voice cleared the roar and all went deathly silent.

"Calm your tongues!" the voice declared.

For a moment I did not know where the voice had come from but then I saw her. She was like a vision floating down the wooden stairs. Her gown is a rusty brown taffeta, simply styled with a pulled in waist and tight fitted sleeves. She was the first and only Lassie in my vision. My mind raced. "Who is she? Why have I not seen any other women?" But before I could make sense of it she turned to me in my vaporous form and she saw me. She alone saw me. Her eyes were angry with me; her lips moved as if she wanted to speak to me but she did not. Instead, I heard her in my mind.

"Why are you here? Only first-born daughters are Kathries and only Kathries are allowed to see this!" she barked at me.

She was right. I am not a first-born daughter, I am a second. I am my father's second daughter in a line of three. These are visions for my elder sister, Noreen, who is asleep beside me. I was confused, am I seeing what is meant for Noreen to see and I am not supposed to know. I was fearful of the woman's anger, I was afraid of what I will learn but still I remained in the room and watched as the woman took control of the men.

"Sons of Clan Carthy, I, Justina, daughter of Donough and Kathrie of The Whole, I am in need of your alliance once more. Thirteen Cluster sets of Crystal Isles now lie in your hands for safekeeping. As you, all know from the beginning when this plan of Rendition, our last resort, was established we had linked each cluster to one of you, the sons, or grandsons of Cormac Laidir, King of Muster and builder of this Blarney Castle. Listen well, as I call to you to come forward and accept your Cluster set and confirm your post as Inheritor or Devotee. Once in hand, you will be expected to travel as far away from Blarney as you are able and follow your plan of rendition. You are to hide the crystals and live quietly while you wait for the time when we can put them back together. Do not draw attention to yourself or to them. If necessary, you will train your sons to guard and protect the crystal with their lives."

"Each of you will need your eldest daughter to remain with you and your sons as you guard your Cluster set. Your daughter will then become the Kathrie for your post. Part of my power will pass to her and with my power, she will be your visionary of the future, as well as your ability to communicate back to me. Once you are settled in your new home and all is well, I will be able to sense your position and when necessary communicate through your daughter. I and the other additional Lassies of the Family will travel to Bantry where we have already begun a sanctuary at St. Finbarr; it is protected by the Roman Catholic Church and those in robes there are bound to our secret by blood. In Bantry, we will store all the knowledge of our family's secret. It will be sealed and kept undisclosed until the time when we can return here to Blarney."

Justina waved her hand and thirteen young boys appeared each struggling with an enormous burlap sack. Slowly she called out each name of the sons of Cormac. After each new name was called, a descendant of that son stepped forward and collected his sack as well as confirmed his vow to protect it. There was an un-calming silence in the room when she finished with her task. A nervousness that even filled me, it was like the end of something huge; the feeling that you would never see your parents again; never see your home again. They were agreeing to leave their lives behind in order to save a world within the crystals. A world some had only heard of, they were giving up everything for a vow, a promise made by their ancestor Cian over a thousand years ago. Yet, none of them fought their path, they simply parted ways. I watched as the room grew empty and then dark.

Blarney is Lost

T here was a pause, and within that silence, I started to feel as if the dream was concluding, that the end was near, this had been the final scene. Just as I was ready to drift off to sleep, a thunderous noise crashed through the silence. I hear the sound of footsteps, screams and the excruciating sound of metal clashing and grinding together.

I knew with certainty that the English army leader Lord Broghill, with his cannons had broken through the last of the defenses. He was now threatening to overthrow the castle. My heart beat rapidly, and my mind raced with thoughts of the crystals and their safety. Did my family have enough time to get away? I prayed that they did!

The sound started to die off. It grew quiet again. I Felt that I was once again floating and at peace.

I was surrounded by flickering lights, and what I saw next was like flashing black and white snapshots. The snapshots were like still photos of what had taken place, and they quickly rushed past me. In the first set of still photos, I can see Lord Broghill. He was victorious in his endeavors, and had broken through the castle's defenses. He now sat in the very hall that once held the Clan.

The next set of still photos, I could see Broghill and his men as they were tearing through the floor of the castle. As the photo's clip by, it showed the men as they stripped the wood, plank by plank. It was clear that they were desperately trying to find something. The end result was the wooden floors of the castle were gone and this once magnificent building stood stripped of all its valuables.

The next images showed Broghill's men smashing the walls around the mantel of the marble hearth. They were cutting away the wall plaster scraping at the sides as if they believe something was hidden there.

A bright light suddenly flashed and in the next set of still photos the most disturbing scene of all was revealed. It is Broghill's men. They have found the cave below the castle. Broghill was enraged. I could see his fury escalate as the still photos quicken in speed, flashed faster before my eyes.

In an instant, I was filled with the shocking knowledge, that all along Broghill had been looking for the crystals. He had come to Ireland to take possession of them! My family had been right to break them up, disperse them among the Clan, and move them. I don't know how Broghill knew about the Crystal Isles or how he knew where they were hidden but it was obvious to me that his actions against Blarney were clearly to obtain the Crystals for his leader Oliver Cromwell, Cromwell was the Commander and Chief of the Commonwealth of England, Scotland and Ireland.

How had Oliver Cromwell known about the crystals? Perhaps the English had captured one of my family and they had told of the secret? But in my visions, I did not see Cromwell or the English holding the crystals, nor do I see them with my family members. Surely if they had been caught, my vision would have shown me? So, I fee; certain that none were captured, all must have escaped undetected. Nevertheless, it is apparent that Broghill, Cromwell, and possibly all of England know about the crystals and the Castle at Blarney is no longer safe.

My spine tingles.

The next still photo showed Broghill leaving Blarney. In this image, he appears to not be angry any more, he seemed content, almost happy. His face holds a smirk, his eyes a shifty glance . . . . . .I am ill at ease because it is clear from that smirk that some diabolical plan is festering in my mind. Then he is gone and so are the jerking flashing still photos.

Almost instantly, the visual perspective of my dream changes and it is as if a live action movie has started and I again have a front row seat.

Now I was in the entranceway to Blarney Castle. Two determined men march towards me. Their costumes are similar to the group that had met in the banquet hall just before Broghill sieged the castle. I now know that not much time has gone by and we are still in the same 17th century.

The morning light casts shadows over the two men as they enter and I cannot see their faces. Yet I sense that they were family, somehow, I knew they are members of MacCarthy Muskerry who had bravely remained at Blarney.

They brush past me and enter the Great hall. Their urgent pace was cut to a dead stop as they behold the horrible sight of the castle's wrecked interior. The taller man turns to look at the other and I see those familiar blue eyes again, this time they are filled with tears and his voice echoes with their emotion.

"It is true. Broghill knows!"

"Yes," the other man confirms, "and he is not the only one. They will be back and they will have the Crown of England on their crest."

"Without a doubt, brother, my worry that this handing back of the Castle is a trap, is now valid. They have restored us to a false position, cloaked in a glorious title of Earl. All to bait us into a fake sense of security. They hope we will fall for their deceitful plot and give the Clan the clear to return. While our sanctuary here has been destroyed and we stand now with a fateful decision, a decision that will mark the generations to come, and yet if we do not, and instead trust the English, we condemn the Isles of Clan Carthy to Peril."

"Brother, we can take no other path but the one laid down for us that will protect the isles, only a fool would trust the words of Cromwell." The second man agreed.

"Send word to Bantry," the taller one whispered, "Blarney is lost."

Was this a Dream?

With that the two men evaporated into the mist of the room. Their essences swirl in all directions, breaking off into tiny whirlwinds that spin gently in the air and then one by one they grew bright. Behind each brightness a group of men appear. Separately the glowing visions move closer to me and I can clearly see each group has a cluster of crystals in their hands. It is quite apparent that the crystals have survived to modern day. For each group of men are dressed in 20th century clothing.

I heard myself calling out each Crystal Isle by name as they are revealed to me and then disappear. Each group of men stands protecting their crystals in their own way, in their own part of the world. Some are shown with many men and some with just two or three. Some are teaching the next generation to guard and protect. Some are handing them down to the next generation and there suddenly before me is one very familiar to me.

I cannot say that I noticed it at first but after a moment or two I was drawn to the scene of an old man and a young boy sitting on the front marble steps of a cottage. The old man was placing a huge white crystal into the young boy's hands.

This sight became the focus of my dream, the castle disappeared, and the foggy edged moving snapshot return to me. I then felt myself being pulled into the spot just behind the screen door. My body tingles as I realize I was no longer vapor. I was once more whole and I back to the beginning of my dream.

My grandfather's voice was cheerful as he spoke to my brother. "Remember my boy; it will be up to you now. Your father and your uncle will help you but it will be your task and the task of your sons."

Then, as if they were there all alone, my father and his brother Charles appear standing just in front of the steps. They were both happy and welcomed my brother as an equal.

They shook his hand and patted him on his back. Their conversation continues as I heard the screen door behind them open. My placement and view from behind the door slowly moves forward in the direction of my brother and grandfather. My brother Jim jumped to his feet and turned towards me. He threw open his arms and reached up to me.

"Mommy!" He called out as I felt his grasp around my space.

I can see the side of his face pressed up against the barrier that surrounds me. His eyes were closed and he is happy in his embrace. Then suddenly the edges of the snapshot like vision of my brother grew thick until all goes black.

Sleep then hit me with a vengeance, and when I awake, the memory of the crystals haunts me. I tell myself it is only a dream. A dream, nothing else. But why does it seem so real and why have I had this dream so many times over the past fifty years of my life?

I have had the dream so many times I can remember every part it. I remember every Crystal Isle, every name, every place, every city, and every member therein placed. I know the story of the Clan Carthy's, the history and the truth.

And why, if this was just a dream, how did I know every inch of the Blarney Castle grounds and buildings when I traveled to Ireland this past April for the very first time in my life? Why did I have the overwhelming feeling I had been there before, walked the grounds, the halls and finding a room I thought was my bedroom? How did I know exactly where the cave was and how did I dream that there would be the stone remains of an eleven toed beast guarding the entrance?

Anyway, this is my online post of my dream from my heart. I am sorry my writing may seem odd because my mind is stuck in the visions of Ireland. I am doing this because it has been in my mind all my life and I need to find someone else who has this same dream and I hope they will help me understand all this.

All I can do, is confirm, that I can't stop until I have all the answers of what I am supposed to do.

THE END

Note: To readers of my post, this is also information that is held in my brain. Therefore, I have made a list of all the information. I hope it helps you.

CARTHY TERMINOLOGY
FOR OUTSIDERS

TERMS REFERRING TO THE CRYSTAL ISLES:

Below you will find a list with descriptions of many of the terms used when referring to the Crystal Isles. There are several ways the term Crystal Isles can be used. For example, the term *Crystal Isles* can be cut down into two separate uses. The first being *The Crystals* and the second being *The Isles*. Both Members and Carthy's use this shortening of the term in day to day conversation.

A Cluster- When the whole of the Green Isles was broken; it was separated into thirteen groups called Clusters. Each Cluster has between three and six individual Isle groups known as Crystal Isles and each Cluster has a rulering Regan that is with the Main Kingdoms.

Crystal Isles / The Isles / The Crystals: Crystal Isles are a grouping of gemstones in a solid sea of lazurite. The gem stones inside form islands. The islands or Isles, depending on your native tongue, form a territory that is generally governed by a predominant breed of Members. Each Crystal Isle has one Capital city. There are 55 Crystal Isles also called Isle Groups.

Gem Stone- Each Gem Stone houses a single island. The gemstones to the outside world are rare and valuable precious stones. There are diamonds, emeralds, opals, rubies, amethyst, garnets, and sapphire, just to name a few. The inside of the gemstones retains an atmospheric habitat in which life exists.

Individual Isle Group/ Isle Group- Isle groups are a grouping of gemstones in a solid sea of lazurite. There are 55 isle groups also called Crystal Isles.

Insiders- Is a term referring to the members who live inside the Crystals.

Outsiders- Is a term referring to people who live on the outside of the Crystals.

The Land of the Green Isles/ The Whole/ The Green Isle- All three terms refer to the world of all 55 isle groups. It is known by its members as the Land of the Green Isles. It is also referred to as the Whole.

The Seven Major Kingdoms of the Green Isles- There are Seven Major Kingdoms of the whole above ground; Sterling, Seymour, Hurley, Donavan, Dwight, Keagan and Hawkins. Each includes several Clusters and varies in rule depending upon the strength of the given Regan who can give each Cluster a leader that is connected to their Major Kingdom. Note: the word Regan means ruler.

The Realm of the Dark- The Realm of the Dark is below ground and ruled by the Caved Ones known as Ullden. This Realm stretches between many of the isles but has been cut into sections due to the call of Rendition.

Post/Charge/Charges: The Cluster of crystals given to a McCarthy family member to protect.

The World Within: Refers to the living world inside the crystal isles.

TERMS REFERRING TO THE SONS OF CORMAC

Sons of Cormac: Refers to the builder of the Blarney Castle, Cormac Laidir, King of Muster. It is his line of sons and Grandsons who have been entrusted to the vow and promise made by Cian to his father Oiloll.

Before the Blarney Castle was built, the family's rule was only that the direct descendent or single inheritor had to confirm his vow with protecting the Crystal Isles as a whole. But once Cormac Laidir took on the task as Holder and Guardian of the whole, he established the plan of last resort known as Rendition. He instituted the action of O.I.'s (The name of the Original Inheritor) and developed a core of Carthy Devotees which he dispersed throughout Cork. These men became the eyes and ears of their Guardian and the reason why the family of Carthy's have spread throughout the world. There is no town, city, or village that exists out on Earth that doesn't have a McCarthy family member keeping watch for the Whole. . . . . . Oh wait I was not supposed to tell you that.

Brothers of Clan Carthy/Brothers of Carthy/ The Brethren of Carthy/ Clan Carthy/ Sons of Carthy: All these terms refer to the descendants of Oiloll.

O.I.- The name of the Original Inheritor once the whole is broken. The O.I. names are the names of Cormac sons and grandson who had agreed to take on the post of one of the clusters if Rendition was called into effect.

Holder /Guardian/ Owner: These terms refers to the male Carthy who is in charge of the Cluster.

Inheritor: Is generally the first-born son of the Holder. The Inheritor is the next in line to inherit the responsibility as Holder of the Cluster.

Secondary/ Secondary Inheritor/ Second Son/ Stepper- These terms refer to the male Carthy, usually the son of the Inheritor, who will become the inheritor once his father is the holder. This is generally only used when there is a period of illness with either the Holder or Inheritor. The term "Stepper" is used when positions change unexpectedly.

<u>Devotee/Protector:</u> Usually refers to the brothers of the Holder of the cluster. However, it can include any other male family member who is devoted to the safety of the Isles and is willing to pledge their devotion.

<u>Family Secret:</u> The secret of the world inside the Crystals that has been protected for over a thousand years by the Carthy family at Blarney Castle. The Crystal Isle now broken into 13 clusters that are being hidden and protected secretly throughout the world.

<u>The vow/ The Promise/ The Pledge:</u> A promise made to Oiloll by his son, Cian, that he and his sons would protect the crystal that housed the Isle of Carthy for the rest of their lives, as well as the generations that followed. When Cian and his sons gave their promise to Oiloll they did not know that there was more than just the one stone. Once they discovered the whole of the isles in the cave at Blarney, they all **vowed** to extend their promise to include the whole.

<u>Rendition/ Rendition of Strategy-</u> Rendition is the execution of a drastic strategy to save the Crystals Isles from being discovered. The Call of Rendition is the last resort for the Carthy Clan when all else has failed to save their stronghold at Blarney Castle. The Crystal Isles had been protected under the Castle in their native soil for over one thousand years. From the moment, the family had created this option it was put into place as only the last possible action. It means taking the crystals out of the ground and breaking them into small enough groups so that they could be easily carried away. The O.I. lines had been preparing for this from the time the Cormac Laidir was the King of Munster. Each line having its own plan set and passed down from inheritor to inheritor, in case that time ever arose the course of action that each line would take was their rendition, their version or their execution of an action to protect the isle.

<u>The Gift of Blarney/ weaving thee tongue</u>- The ability to speak in a favorable manner in which all sides believe in compatibility.

It was Queen Elizabeth 1 who, in 1586, after commissioning the Earl of Leicester to take the land and castle at Blarney from the McCarthy clan and failed due to, too much delay in negotiations, remarked that the McCarthy's had a gift of Blarney. Yet it was Dermot, son of Carthach and King of Cork, in 1177, who instituted the family's focus on their talent of verbal execution.

<u>M.O.M.</u> – Monitoring Of Many- agency in Bantry at St. Finbarr Church. A.D.C.s – (Additional Daughters of Cormac) are the females who work the M.O.M.

<u>Rootle Underground Dormitory</u> – Is the structure built under the thatched Chapel in St. Finbarr for all A.D.C.'s. Rootle meaning the third party of the Family.

CODES OF CARTHY

After establishing, a core group of devotees that eventually spend throughout Cork to become the family's eyes and ears. Cormac found it imperative that his family develop a method of communication, which could not be detected by outsiders. Therefore, the Carthy Code was cultivated. Through the years, the use of technology has been a major benefit to the usage, upgrade, and stealth ability of the family codes. Through time, much of the family's original secret codes have been developed into historical symbols and integrated into abbreviations for technical subject matters in Math and Science.

Below is a list of some of the Original body movements, markings, and written text used by the family for centuries.

BODY MOVEMENTS

1) Interlocking the fingers of both hands, and then pulling both hands over the head and resting them on the back of the neck. This action means: It is not safe. Do not stop here.

2) A left arm reaching across the front of the body and touching the right shoulder or arm with fingers unhampered and then with the right arm reaching forward to shake hands. This action is the Carthy Family signature hand shake. It means I am of Carthy, all is well.

3) A left arm reaching across the fount of the body and touching the right shoulder or arm with fingers in a fist like grip. A hand shake may or may not follow. This action means: Be prepared to fight. The griping of a fist can also occur without the use of the arm across the front of the body. The gesture merely needs to be seen by the person for which one is trying to communicate to.

4) The crossing of two fingers. This action means: "Bad" or "no". Over time an additional meaning was added to this movement. "One can only hope that not all will go bad."

5) The extension of one's pinky finger. This action means: "Yes" or "good".

6) The resting of one's head on their hand while allowing the thumb to touch the throat. This action means: We must kill.

7) The resting of one's head on their hand while allowing the thumb to touch the temple of their head. This action means: Take rest.

8) The crossing of the right ankle over the left. This action means: The Kingdom is well.

9) The crossing of the left ankle over the right. This action means: The Kingdom is not well.

10) Arms crossed with the showing on fingers. This action means: All is well.

11) Arms crossed with no sight of fingers. This action means: go into hiding, or hide evidence.

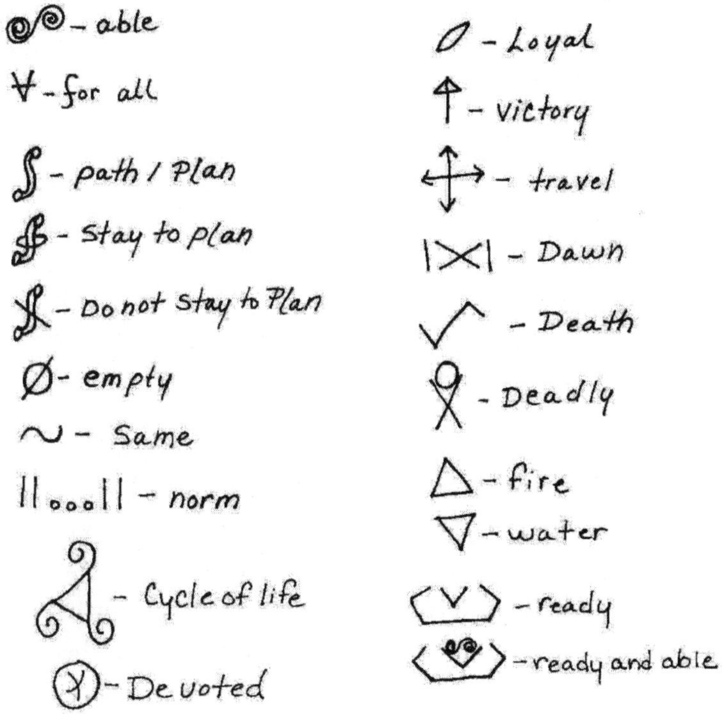

@@ – able

∀ – for all

∫ – path / Plan

∬ – Stay to plan

∬ – Do not Stay to Plan

∅ – empty

∾ – Same

||∘∘∘|| – norm

⟁ – Cycle of life

(Y) – Devoted

𝟘 – Loyal

⬆ – victory

⬌ – travel

|✕| – Dawn

⋁ – Death

φ – Deadly

△ – fire

▽ – water

⟨ ∨ ⟩ – ready

⟨ ◉◉ ⟩ – ready and able

MARKINGS AND SYMBOLS

There is an extensive amount of coded markings and symbols that have been developed by the Carthy clan. So many that we cannot list them all. Below you will find the most common markings used. These symbols are the earliest known codes used by the Carthy Family. They were used in all forms of communications including print.

1) **The Four-Leaf Clover**. To the Carthy's the four-leaf clover symbolizes the union of the original four sons of Oiloll who declared that they would protect the whole of the Crystal Isles. Each son represented a gift of Positive energy; Cas represented Luck- Kerry, represented Faith- Duhallow, represented Hope and Reagh, represented Love.

Before this, the three-leaf clover or Shamrock was viewed by many as a sacred symbol, meaning rebirth and eternal life. Its three leaves creating a sense of balance and the beginning of the passion for the number three in Irish history and religious beliefs. It is said that is was used in the teachings of St. Patrick, who used the shamrock to explain the Holy Trinity. Whether or not this was made up to help protect the Carthy's I cannot say, but it is very possible for I recall a vision of the three-leaf clover being held as a sign that the Carthy's were in agreement with another group of members.

As for the four - leaf clover, the Carthy's adopted it as a tribute symbol to the first sons, in order to honor them without the world knowing officially what it meant. The knowledge of Oiloll's four sons representing the four leaves of the clover was kept from the world with the help of the Catholic Church. The Catholic Church when realizing the symbol had been exposed covered for the family by retelling the stories of St. Patrick and his interpretation that the clover embodied the Holy Trinity. When asked about the fourth leaf, it was explained as a blessing of luck to the finder and to this day both the shamrock and the four-leaf clover are still used as pronounced symbols for the Irish.

2) **Celtic Triquetra**- The Celtic Triquetra is created by three arching cuts. The arching cuts when equal and finely placed form three intersecting lines that form delicately extended "x's" and at the same time creates three perfectly tapered ovals. The "x's" mean Devotion, the Tapered Ovals mean loyalty and having three of each means balanced. Because of this the devotee members of the Carthy clan use this as their symbol of Never Ending Devotion.

3) **(V)**– The (V) means: Join.

4) **(^)** – The (^) means: Meet or meeting.

5) **(*)**- Means Energy. The energy to the Carthy's stood for the Bad energy coming from their Ring Theory. The ring theory states

that Oliver Cromwell possessed a broken shard set in a ring from Oiloll's original crystal. This symbol (*) was used when any mention of the Ring or Cromwell was under discussion.

6) (:) – The (:) means: extend, over or inner product. This was used in the coding system in letters. Placed before the date on the top of a letter this would tell the reader to take their count from the start of the letter. When placed at the end of the date the reader was to begin their count from the end of the letter. An example will follow below.

7) (+) The marking (+) means: Move from one side to the other, remain balanced. It is also the first letter of the Celtic alphabet. To the Carthy's, if one stands in the center, then one can easily step from one side to the other and still remain balanced.

8) The marking (.) means: Time.

The marking (/.) means: with.

The marking (.\) means: without.

The marking (!) means: Not.

The marking) (means: Engage

The Marking (-) before (:) means to count lines by the numbers in the letter do not use the date on the note and read the first letters of each word on that line.

WRITTEN TEXT CODED

As technology and Christianity developed and spread, much changed with the coding of the Carthy's messaging. During the centuries when written letters were used, the following terms were christened among the coders with more literal meanings.

<u>Starting Letter phrases:</u>

1) I am writing in reply to . . . . This phrase literally means that the letter is a responding letter to a message that the receiver had sent out requesting an answer as quickly as possible.

2) Good to see you again. -This phrase means the information in this letter is of major importance. Please read and destroy immediately.

3) I hope all is well- This phrase is used in a letter meant for testing an area or a delivery service. It literally means the writer hopes that all is well with the delivery of the letter. This kind of letter is watched and followed extremely closely to ensure the loyalty of the person making the delivery.

4) Sorry it's taken me so long to write. - This phrase means that the letter contains updated information.

5) I would be grateful if. . . . – This phrase means the letter contains an issue that needs an immediate response.

Ending Letter phrases:

1) May all be well! – This phrase is used on coded letters to mean that the letter coding was done in the normal pattern.

2) God Bless. – This phrase means to "keep a watchful eye". Most likely, there have been reports that the enemy are in your region and the note is to inform its recipient of the reports. If the word "You" is added to the phrase, it means the enemy is extremely near you.

3) God speed. - This Phrase means your hard work has paid off and all has been made safe.

4) May our God be with you. - This phrase is used when there is a major issue with a family that is in need of help from Bantry. An example would be that the family Kathrie has become extremely ill and the family has no replacement.

5) Sincerely yours – This phrase is the response from Bantry to the family that they can help. An example would be that they have a replacement Kathrie available and she will be sincerely yours.

6) Kindest regards- This phrase is a response from Bantry that they cannot help at this time. But they will continue to try.

7) Best regards- This phrase is used when reporting a death in the Family.

8) Best wishes- This phrase is used when reporting a death of the enemy.

9) Cordially- This phrase is used on coded letters to mean that the letter coding was done in the secondary pattern.

10) Respectfully yours- This phrase is used to allow an individual the ability to make their own call on a pressing issue.

11) Yours truly- This phrase is used to give the go ahead.

12) Yours always- This phrase is used to state that the sender will not make a move until given the word to do so.

~4-14.1254:

Dear Ann,

I was so happy to see you this Summer holiday at South Beach. I truly couldn't believe how much you had grown. You have grown into such a lovely young women just like your mother. By the way, I hope she enjoyed the fifteen lovely flavors of saltwater taffy I had you take to her.

I hope you enjoyed your stay and will come back next Summer to visit. I so look forward to spending time with you. Perhaps you too could stay four weeks next visit.

Please give your parents my love.

May all be well

Auntie Mary

EXAMPLE LETTER:

^ 4-14.1754:

Dear Ann,

I was so happy to see you this summer holiday at South Beach. I truly couldn't believe how much you had grown. You have grown into such a lovely young woman just like your mother. By the way, I hope she enjoyed the fifteen lovely flavors of saltwater taffy I had you take to her.

I hope you enjoyed your stay and will come back next summer to visit. I so look forward to spending time with you. Perhaps you too could stay four weeks next visit.

Please give your parents my love.

May all be well,
Auntie Mary.

Above is an example of a Carthy coded letter.

First take note of the first phrase of the letter. *I was so happy to see you.*

This phase is a take-off of - Good to see you again. That means the letter is of major importance. It will have information in it that will be crucial. So, the receiver needs to read the letter quickly and then destroy it.

Next read the closing part of the letter. *May all be well.*

May all be well means the letter is coded in the normal pattern.

Now that you know that the letter is coded in a normal pattern you would then look at the date written at the top of the letter.

^4-14.1754:

The (^) means: Meeting. This letter will be providing information about a necessary meeting.

The (:), at the end of the date, means the count will start from the end of the letter. If the Letter was in a secondary code pattern, the reader would do the opposite and count from the start of the letter.

The (.) after the 14 and before the year 1754 means that the 1754 numbers will be a time.

With this information, you now take the first number in the date and count from the end of the letter back four words to the word *May.*

The 14th word = *four.*

The 17th word= *too (translated into a number is two)*

And the 54th word= *fifteen*

Translation: May 4th at 2:15

There is one more piece of information to extract from this letter and that is where the meeting will take place. In order to find this out the reader must reread the letter and take note of the true numbers mentioned. The important thing to remember is, to jot down the numbers from the direction the dated code told you to read. In this case, it was from the end of the letter back to the beginning of this letter. So, in this case, the first number was *four* and the second number was *fifteen.*

Now to solve the question of where, you take the numbers and count from the opposite direction of the letter, meaning for this you count from the start of the letter. Count the words and collect the first letter of that word.

Fourth word = *Happy* = *H*

Fifteenth word = *Truly* = *T*

The family has several designated meeting places most of which I cannot reveal, but I can tell you that the initials H.T. stand for Holy Trinity Church in Cork.

So, the meeting will take place May 4th 1754 at 2:15 at Holy Trinity Church.

Thank you for reading my post.
I hope I have written will enough to purely explain the dream in my mind and find someone to help me.
Have a nice turn!
Caitlin Mary McCarthy

The Great Green Isles

The story of an Outsider
Who has Fallen In

THE GREAT GREEN ISLES

The story of an Outsider who has Fallen In

Written from Marypat and her son's recollection
of their experience within
By K.M.M.

Editor: Save Laura
Fiverr.com/tricia_craig

For Haley Robinson

Her joy for life and vivid interpretation
Her delightful enthusiasm and spirit so passion
Her electrifying eagerness and meaningful devotion
Teleports my visions and intensifies my writings

CLUSTER

Kerry's line Cluster N

The Golden Mountains

Crystal: Pair Mountain #50

The Great Isle

FOREWORD

My story "Carthy Family Secret" posted on my website in June of 2013 with my hand drawn pictures to go with my story. In August, I saw that it was only viewed by one person, a lady who I shall call Marypat. Marypat also lived in Jamaica and had a home just up the road from me and my Family.

She seemed to have many questions for me about my dream for which I could not answer over the phone, so I invited her to my home for coffee the following day.

When she arrived, I was shocked at how much we looked alike and there was an aura about her, which made me feel as if I knew her. It was so amazing, instantly I felt as if she was my sister. Oh, and she loved my Seahawks shirt I was wearing, all though she called it an Osprey and told me she had a connection with ospreys as well.

Anyway, the questions she asked about my dream, and the crystals I had written were the same questions I myself had but the most surprising of all was when she told me she too had had a similar occurrence, and that was why she had to find me. She too needed to tell someone about what she had seen, she too needed to make sense of all that was going on inside of her mind and finding me and being able to talk to me was finally a comforting happening in her life.

She told me her encounter was connected to my dream in a very strange way. In her experience, the crystals were real, she had held one, she had felt the energy and power within. She had not only seen that there was life within but that she had been there. She had walked on the soil of an Isle, spoken to the members and suffered through several Ubil moments. All of which, she confided in me was not a dream and she could prove it.

Her words brought tears to my eyes that all of what I had thought was a dream, and struggled to come to terms with, could be true. Finally, there was someone else, who believed in my vision.

I begged her to tell me her entire story, but she would not unless I agreed to write it for her like I had written my own. She hoped and believed that our connection would be the solution to what she felt was her life's purpose, to bring all the crystals back together as they were meant to be.

I agreed to her request and so the following is my attempt to tell Marypat's story of what happened to her and her son Blaze, within.

The Find

T he surf foamed with salty bubbles onto the sandy beach of Maiden Key, Jamaica. Gently it rolled back into the sea and rose again to bubble once more.

Young Blaze trotted through the moving water splashing about. He was a boy of 13 years and 4 months old. He had dark brown hair that curled slightly at its ends. His eyes were green, and they glistened in the sun light. He had lived a carefree life with his mother, Marypat, the whole of his life in Jamaica. He was a happy child, who loved adventure and was always looking for excitement.

This day was no different. Marypat watched her son as he drove into the water acting like a giant sea creature attacking the innocent sea life at the bottom of the sea. He dove and splashed trying to catch them, but they were always too fast for him to catch. But then suddenly Marypat saw her son's head break the surface of the water as he yelled with excitement.

"Mum, look what I found."

Marypat, who had been sitting on the tiny beach on the key, stood and ran to him, somewhat afraid that something had happened to the boy.

"What is it son, are you all right?" she shouted, pulling her bright red hair from her face and holding it on her head.

"Look, mum, look what I have found, isn't it the most beautiful thing you ever seen?" Blaze said holding up his find.

His hand glowed as the sun's rays touched the object and bounded outward.

"Yes!" She answered almost mesmerized by its glow. "It is."

"Can I keep it?" He asked jumping up and down in the water.

"Bring it to shore and let me see it first, and then I will let you know whether you can keep it." She said with a grin. It looked familiar to her, but she had to look at it more closely to be sure.

Blaze sat down beside his mother on a blanket. He pulled his brown hair out of his eyes and then opened his hand. There in his palm laid the most remarkable thing, a perfectly formed green Emerald. It was about six centimeters in height and two centimeters wide. It was set in a hunk of lazurite that had tiny pyrite crystals running through it. The pyrite glistened like gold. Beside the large emerald sat a nearly perfect prismatic crystal of yellow citrine. It stood four and a half cm tall and was 1 cm wide.

In front of the emerald was a single small flat torbernite stone that was right beside a lovely large red ruby. The red ruby's tip was chipped, and it sat in the lazurite at an angle. The fire red color reflected onto the emerald producing an orange case on the rock. Beside the ruby was a tetragonal shaped quartz crystal, that was nearly perfectly clear with only one tiny inclusion. Lastly, on the hunk of blue lazurite sat twin tetrahedral shaped chalcopyrite crystals. They were golden yellow with deep blue, purple, and black streaks.

Marypat took the stone from her son and looked at it. She had seen one before and knew of its Magic.

"Could there actually be more than one?" She thought to herself. *"Could more than just her own exist?"* This she truly did not know, and she wasn't sure whether her son was ready for the knowledge of the Green Isle nor did she believe she was ready to tell him. She had kept it from him all these years but now with him finding one, she should have to prepare him. She would have to tell him; it was the moment.

"Have you ever traveled through the eye of the emerald?" She asked her son.

"No" he answered in a whisper. "Have you?"

"I have taken a journey there." She answered." It is a wondrous place, which can test your strength of mind as well as your soul. The fire green emerald with the eye of treasure is rare and is true. To find one you must believe with more than just your mind. It takes your heart. A genuine emerald has a precious crystal form which is a delicate reminder of its fragile existence. A human can hold such an emerald in the palm of his hand unaware of the magic it holds. Deep within lies it's meaning and its true beauty."

Blaze listened to his mother in awe. "What do you mean mother." He asked.

She handed the stone back to her son and asked," The Green Isles are a great responsibility, are you prepared to take it on?"

"What are the Green Isles?" Blaze asked.

"The portion of the very stone you hold in your hand my son." She whispered.

"The Green Isles?" He asked looking at the stone.

"Yes." she said "But never stare into the eye or you will find yourself inside." she said with a smile.

"Really, mum." He said smiling back at her. "Oh, you're just pulling my leg."

Marypat turned to him and grinned "Or am I?"

Later that night as Blaze climbed into bed, he asked his mother to tell him more about the Green Isle.

"Tell me mum." he inquired as he held the emerald stone in his hand. "Tell me of your journey."

She smiled at him with a thoughtful look. "Are you sure you want to hear an old tale of mine. It's not a video game, ya know, me have no pictures and flashy lights to keep ya interested." She said in her thickest Jamaican accent.

"Yes mum, me wan ear." He replied.

She sighed loudly and then said "Alright, but I warn you, the Green Isle is like no place you have ever seen, things there are different, Magical." her voice trailed off as she thought back to the beginning of it all. When it first happened, to when she had found her Green Emerald. . . . . .

It was the summer of 1986; Marypat had just turned 14 at her families' country home in New Castle, Jamaica. The house sat on what seemed to be the very top of the world. Above her was only sky and below were rolling mountains and jagged cliffs of the Blue Mountains. The air was thin, and cold, but the sun shone brightly every day and there was always plenty to do. There were trees to climb and animals to chase but best of all there was the Mammee River that ran just below the landing of the property. She visited the river every afternoon. There were frogs and crayfish that lived in the small pools that collected on the sides of the rippling river. She would stay there for hours catching them and letting them go.

One bright afternoon Marypat had made her way down to the river. The water level of the river was low; there had not been rain for several weeks and the side pools that she normally played in were nearly empty of water. There was little water to play in and yet she still pulled her red hair up and tied it tightly behind her head, so it wouldn't get in her way when she would begin to dig in the damp river sand.

She was wearing her favorite pair of clam digger pants. They were tan and had large deep pockets on each side, perfect for carrying frogs in. She wore a striped blouse that was fitted at the waist and it had a tie in the front that often came untied and hung at her sides. She wore a backpack on her back, which was full of "Foolishness." according to her grandmother, Miss Lora. It was the way Marypat always looked when she headed on an adventure down at the river.

When she reached the river, she right away began to investigate the driest of the pools. There was no telling what interesting thing or creature might be buried there. After digging in the pool for quite some moment, she noticed something in the nook of one of the large boulders that blocked the rivers flow and created a portion of the enclosure that helped form the pool. The object was green and shiny. She picked it up and looked at it. It was a beautiful emerald about 10 cm tall, it sat in a bed of blue stone and it sparkled like it had gold in it. Beside the emerald, also set in the blue stone was a blue opal with a pink fire.

It was so lovely Marypat could not take her eyes off of the stone. She starred at it. She turned it slowly gazing into it. Deeper and deeper she looked at the crystal. Suddenly without warning, she found herself falling into an open space that seemed to have no end.

Then without warning, she landed on her back in a field of grass, which grew along a gentle river. The fall was shocking but the way she landed on the soft grass prevented her from injury and she was able to sit up and look around with little discomfort.

Nothing looked familiar to her. The sky was a pale green and the grass was so rich in color it didn't seem real to her.

"Where am I?" Marypat said out loud thinking she was speaking to herself.

"Grassy Point!" A tiny voice answered with a giggle.

"I never knew Dandy Sprites could fly.," said another tiny voice with excitement.

"Amazing she must have been flying a very long moment for she doesn't know where she is." The first voice commented.

"YAH." the second voice replied.

"Who is talking?" Marypat said most frightened for she could not see who was speaking to her. "Where are you?"

"Here we are, down here." The two tiny voices called together.

"Ya, know ya almost squashed us." The first one continued.

"That's right, that wasn't very polite." The second one added.

As Marypat began to apologize, she looked down into the grass and
saw to tiny little people. She jumped back, and looked at the two little
people starring up at her. They were dressed in fitted cotton skirts with
white knit sweaters; each one wore a hat, which covered their short red
hair. One of them had a tiny straw basket that seemed to be filled with
seeds.

"What are you?" Marypat squealed.

"She must have bumped her head on that fall." The second one said
turning to the first.

"Yes, sister it probably affected her memory." The first said nodding
her head, then she turned and looked up at Marypat again. "I'm Rose
and this is Daisy.

"We're Flower Sprites!" the second one added. "And who are you?"

"I'm Marypat." Marypat said with a very uneasy look on her face as
she stared at the sprites. "You. . . you're. . . you're tiny!"

"Yes, we're Flower Sprites, not a Dandy like you." Rose said, "Haven't
you ever seen a Flower Sprite before?"

"NO." answered Marypat nervously "We don't have Flower Sprites
where I live."

"Oh" said Daisy with a frown. "Well it's nice to meet you."

"Oh. . Yes, nice to meet you as well." Marypat replied trying to
compose herself. She was trying to understand where she was and what
had happened to her.

"Now could you please tell me where I am? I believe that I am lost."
Marypat asked again this moment very politely.

"We told you, this is Grassy Point." Daisy replied.

"Yes. . . but where is Grassy Point?" Marypat asked.

"You don't know where Grassy Point is?" Rose asked a bit shocked.
"You really did hurt your head on that fall."

"You stand upon the Isle known as the Great Isle. It is only one of
the many Isles that make up the Whole of the Green Isle's, you have
heard of Great Isle, haven't you?" Rose continued.

"No, is that in Jamaica?" She asked.

"Jamaica?" Rose laughed, "I have never heard of Jamaica."

Daisy leaned into her sister and whispered, "Perhaps she's under a spell, or may-be she's been tricked by a Jinxie."

"Yes, sister, but in any case, we should keep an eye on her, in this condition she could get hurt." Rose whispered back to Daisy.

"You say you are lost?" Rose asked.

"Yes, I don't know how I got here, but I do know who I am and where I am from, I just don't know this place. I mean I was standing beside the Mammee River, the river that flows beside my home. It is very similar to this river here and then . . . I fell. I fell here. I fell here to this place. Everything seems so different, so strange. Even the sky, has the sky always been that green here?" Marypat remarked in a breathless voice.

"No. It was very dark right before we saw you falling. We have lived in darkness for so long; I hear it has been more than 35 passes. So, it was wonderful to see the light this morn and then down you came almost on top of us." Rose answered.

"Oh, I am very sorry about that, I didn't mean to harm you, I promise." Marypat said quickly." But if it was so dark here before, how did you see and get around."

"With our glow of course, we all have an inter fire. You couldn't have forgotten that, could you?" Daisy said with a questioned look on her face.

"I'm afraid I didn't know that." Marypat said sadly. Then she stood up and looked down at the sprites. "Again, I am very sorry if I scared you; please know I meant no harm."

Marypat began to walk away but turned back one moment and said "Thank-you for your kindness." Then she continued on her way. To where she did not know, but she had to try and find her way back home, back to Jamaica.

Before she could get very far, she heard a voice calling to her.

"Wait. We will help you!" called Rose.

Marypat knelt down and smiled at the sprites, "You will?"

"Yes! We will take you to the Great Loralac that lives in the mountain cave; he will know what to do."

"Thank-you, you are very kind. Because of your kindness I shall carry you, would that be alright?" Marypat expressed gladly.

"Yes." They answered climbing aboard Marypat's out stretched hand.

Then she carefully placed them on her shoulder and began walking in the direction of the mountains.

The Fall

The lush dark green grass gently swayed as Marypat made her way through its thick undergrowth. The tiny bladed heads blossomed as she passed and made a path of yellow buds that followed her all the way to the edge of the tall grass.

Soon she entered the forest. It was heavy with broken branches and foliage. She had to climb over logs and thicket, which she soon grew tired of.

"I need to rest. I'm afraid I cannot go any farther, I am tired and hungry." Marypat relinquished.

"Then you should rest, leave the food to us." Rose giggled cheerfully. To her they had traveled a great distance and she was very happy with their progress. So, for Marypat to need a rest was certainly acceptable. Beside she and her sister were hungry too and they knew just where to get some delicious food.

"Te-ly-ly." Rose called in a song. "To lou lee."

Suddenly from out of nowhere, there came a vision, darting in and out. Little balls of glowing dust flittered past, all around Marypat's head. The little vision stopped for only a moment to set down their heavy load then they flittered away again, to bring another. Before long there was a pile of fresh sweet berries on a leaf that lay on Marypat's lap.

"How did you do that?" Marypat asked.

"I didn't do it, the Etains did, and they are very friendly." Rose admitted.

When the Etains were done, they appeared to the trio. They had slight little faces. Somewhere pink and some purple, there was even a tiny slender yellow one. Each one was dressed in a modest little dress that was so light and airy that it flouted. Their hair was left long and flowed around their faces. Their wings flapped endlessly as they stopped in midair and spoke.

"Good travels, fare ones?"

"Yes, Forest Etains, great thanks to your brewed for your kindness," Rose spoke very politely.

"To where do you haste on such a fine bright morrow," The Etain asked still hovering in the air above the sprite.

"We are off to the Great Loralac, which lives in the cave just beyond the forest," Daisy answered.

"Then safe be, for there is a Grundle asleep in the wood, take heed cousin, he will be hungry, he should." Said the Etain.

"Thank- you.," said Rose before the Etains flew away just as quick as they had appeared.

"Shall we feast?" asked Daisy.

"We shall." Answered Rose and they began to devour one of the juicy berries.

"What are you waiting for?" Daisy asked Marypat. "You do remember berries, don't you?"

"Why yes. . . I do. . . I love berries." She said with a smile. Then she scooped up two and began to eat them. "mm they are delicious."

Rose watched Marypat as she ate the berries, and Rose's face grew worried. She turned to her sister and gave her a nudge.

"What is it, Rose, I'm eating." Daisy replied quite annoyed.

"Look sister, she is not a Dandy, she must be a Colleen." Rose whispered with her eyes very wide, for the sight she had seen of Marypat, had given her a scare. A Colleen who ate berries was not a great sight for it would give to all who had seen it, a fright.

"What's wrong, why do you stare at me like that?" Marypat asked as she noticed the two sprites staring at her.

"Now my dear do not be alarmed, but Colleens can't eat berries, they swell." Rose stated as calm as she could.

"But I'm not a Colleen, my name is Marypat. And what do you mean, swell." Marypat asked nervously. She reached her hands to her face and felt her bulging checks. Her forehead tightened, and she became frantic. "What is happening to me?"

"Hum" Rose sighed, looking away. "You didn't tell us you were a Colleen."

"But I'm not." Marypat screamed.

"Yes you are, a Colleen cannot eat berries, or. . " Daisy's voice trailed off

"Or what, what will happen to me? Tell me!" Demanded Marypat.

"Well you turn into gremlin." Daisy said shielding her face.

"That is if you don't get her help in a moment, Daisy, how could . . . you tell . . . her." Rose shouted and squeezed her sister's arm.

"Help, what kind of help?" cried Marypat. Tears slipped down her face. "How much time do I have?"

Rose looked at Daisy and then back to Marypat. "Time?"

"How long do I have before it happens?"

"About six sweeps, I think."

"Six what, what is a sweep?" Marypat asked still very nervous.

"A sweep, you don't know how long a sweep is." Rose asked.

Marypat shock her head no.

"Well, it took us 2 sweeps to get here from Grassy Point, does that help?" Answered Rose.

Marypat looked at her watch. "About 2 and half hours have gone by, that means I have about 9 hours to get help but where, where can I find help in this crazy world of this Green Isle?"

Marypat looked through the tall trees of the forest and into the green sky. The brightest part of the sky was to her far left. If this was her world, the left would be the west and it would soon be dark and difficult for her to travel. She looked at her watch again and it was 4:30 in her time.

"How will I find help, if it gets dark?" She began to cry.

"Why do you think it will get dark, it only just got bright?" Daisy asked.

"In my world, it would start getting dark about now; if it does I won't be able to find help, besides who can help me?" Marypat began to sob. "And I shall become a gremlin."

"Don't cry Marypat, I'm sure we will find a Balm, we just have to find someone to ask." Confided Rose.

"What about the Etains, wouldn't they know?" Marypat asked as if a light had gone off in her head.

"Why yes, the Etains might know." Said Rose excitedly. She stood and called out to them. "TEE-LEE yah."

Soon the fluttering balls of light were back floating all around them. "Good morrow, again, fare ones." Their tinny voices echoed.

"And to you good Etains, of the wood." Rose called back. "We are in need of your help once more."

"Help. . Help? How may we help?" Their voices resounded again.

"Our friend the Colleen has eaten the berries and now is in need of a Balm. Pray tell us is there such a Balm who lives near this wood." Begged Rose in her most gracious voice.

"Oh my!" The Etains gasped. Some of the Etains flew away but there was one little Etain who did not fly away, she instead appears in fount of Marypat and spoke sweetly to her.

"Oh, you poor dear. I wish that I could help but I do not know of a Balm in this part of the forest. The forest is very very large, and I have not traveled the entire wood. I am sorry." The Etain lowered her head.

"Do you know any creature that might know the entire forest, perhaps a Gulden, who flies in this wood, or a Jinxie who lives in the trees?" Daisy begged the Etain for any help she could give.

"Yes, perhaps we can find a creature that can help, but not a Jinxie. A Jinxie will play a trick on us and send us in the wrong direction. I shall call the Gulden's." The Etain answered, but before she could open her mouth to call, there was a frightening roar that came from the bush.

The Rose and Daisy disappeared leaving Marypat alone with the Etain.

"What was that?" Marypat whispered.

The Etain flew up to Marypat's ear and whispered back. "I'm afraid it's the Grundle, I warned you of earlier."

The two watched as the Grundle stepped out from the bush and growled at them. He had four huge paws that sunk in the rich purple soil as he stepped. His head was a massive structure of bone covered with orange and green hair that circled his face like a lion. But he was not like any lion Marypat had ever seen before. His fur was long and nearly dragged on the forest floor. His tail was short and stuck straight up in the air. But the strangest thing about him, Marypat thought, was the horn in the center of his head. It looked like a horn from a rhino, it was wide and short and very sharp.

The growling frightened the little Etain and she shook as she hovered in the air.

"He wants to know . . . what you are doing in his forest." The Etain said with a quivering voice.

"You can understand him?" Marypat said in shock. She couldn't imagine that the little flying Etain could talk to a beast.

"Yes, I can speak to all the creatures." The Etain answered.

"Well, tell him, I am his friend, I will give him a stretch behind his ear if he will help me find a Balm." Marypat said as she smiled. For she did not find him scary at all, to her he looked like a big house cat, who would love a good stretch.

The Etain spoke to the Grundle and he agreed, he would help them, but first he wanted his scratch. So Marypat approach the Grundle very slowly, she reached out her hand, for him to smell her. Just like she would if he was a strange cat, she was trying to befriend. The Grundle smelled her hand and then closed his eyes. He accepted her scent. So, she glided her hand through his long hair and began to give him the best scratch she had ever given a kitty. The Grundle's body went limp and he lay down on the ground and began to purr.

"Why you're just a pussycat!" Marypat said with a giggle, continuing to stretch the Grundle behind his ears, and then she slowly moved her hand under his chin. He rolled his head up and let her scratch him on his neck.

"OH" he groaned with his eyes closed, and a smile on his face.

A little while later Marypat was done giving her scratch leaving the Grundle on the ground seemingly content with himself.

"Thank-you "he purred and the Etain translated. "There is a Balm at the edge of the forest; I will lead you there if you give me another stretch when we get there"

"Of course, I should love to give you another." Marypat answered with a smile then she patted the Grundle on his head while he continued to purr.

The sky was darkening as they approached the edge of the forest where a small cabin was set among the wilds. There was still enough light for Marypat to see, thanks to the Etain and the Grundle's inner flame. The pair glowed like candles in the night and Marypat understood now how they had survived in darkness for so long.

"Good bye" The Grundle said with a meow when they approached the cabin and then he began to walk away but Marypat had promised him another scratch, so she ran after him and gave him another.

"Thank-you, you have been a very big help to me. I shall call you, Tiger, my friend." Then she scratched him one last moment before stepping up to the cabin door and knocked.

The cabin was old and dusty, it had a wooden frame built out of green oak logs and laid together with mud and tar. The roof was made of straw that had been weaved together. There were two windows in the front of the cabin that had very simple curtains hanging in them. The curtains blocked the view inside but did allow the light from inside to escape between their layers. This gave a clear indication that someone was inside.

After a moment, the door cracked open. A very old man peered from the opening. He had white hair. His eyes were blue, and he had a gentle look about him.

"You must be the Colleen who fell through the sky and brought the light back to the Green Isles and it looks like you got here just in moment." The old man stated with a thick Irish accent.

He opened the door wide and gestured for Marypat to enter.

"But how did you know?" Marypat asked in amazement as she entered the cottage.

He laughed, "A little sprite told me, or should I say two."

Marypat looked shocked then she turned and looked at the table in the middle of the room and there sitting in the center of it and eating a feast was Rose and Daisy.

"I wondered what happen to you two, but I thought you didn't know of a Balm in the area?"

"When the Grundle spoke of this balm we were able to appear to him."

Marypat shook her head at them she didn't understand how just speaking of something could allow them to come to it. It was all so confusing to her, but she didn't have time to question them any farther she needed help for her illness, so she turned to the Balm and extended her hand. "I am Marypat, and I do hope you can help me." she said.

"I believe I can. I am Doctor Cornelius McCarthy, pleased to meet you my dear." He answered.

"And you sir." She replied shaking Cornelius hand.

"Please sit, dear." The old man said. Then he walked over to his cupboard and pulled out a jar of cream. "I must get straight to work; you wouldn't want to become a gremlin, would you?" He laughed.

"Why do you laugh?" Marypat asked.

"It's just a myth. I have never seen it happen, but then again I have only been here for 37 passes or as you might say years and anyone who has come to me for help in this matter, I have been able to help." He answered applying the cream to her face.

"You've been here for 37 years, where were you before here?" She asked shyly.

"Earth, like you." he stated with a smile. Then he turned away to put back the cream in the cupboard.

"Where did you find the crystal?" He asked.

"How do you know that I found a crystal?" Marypat asked in shock.

He smiled at her and spoke very slowly. "My dear child, you are within its mystical center, you have fallen into its eye. Now tell me where you found it." His voice was so rhythmic and relaxing that it put her into a trace like state.

"In a pond of muck alongside of the Mammee River in Jamaica." She answered without emotion.

"Well that explains it then, you must have dropped the emerald onto open ground when you fell into the eye, for us to get the light back, and for that I must thank-you. It has been slightly difficult for me to live here without light; we outsiders have no inner light and soon after I came here the light from our world outside vanished causing this world for the past 37 years to be in darkness. While I have been here, I have been studying the members, which I couldn't have done without the help of the Pixies and the Frandies sharing with me their inner light. Yet, I still miss the sun."

Marypat started at Cornelius. Could everything he said be true, could he really be from her world? Could this really be the world inside of the emerald? He didn't glow like the others; he had a fire burning in the fireplace for light. He looked human, but he had a strange accent and his cloths they too looked strange. He had on a tweed jacket with patches over the elbows and checked knickerbockers with tan hose and linen gaiters.

"You look as if you don't believe me well let me explain. At the age of 62, I inherited the crystal, you just found, from my father. I promised to protect it. But I didn't understand what I had." Doc. McCarthy said sadly. "I was mesmerized by it and I couldn't take my eyes off of it, most likely just as you just did. Then suddenly I found myself falling. I had fallen inside, and I have been here ever since."

"Have you ever tried to leave, to go home?" Marypat asked.

"NO, why would I go home, I love it here. I have so much to keep me busy. I have been writing all I can remember of our world and putting it in these books." He answered with a smile as he waved his hand at the endless shelve of books that lined the walls.

"Not only that but I have been researching the creatures of this world and putting them down on paper, I have sketched just about every creature known to the Green Isles and I have put together a book of spells and incantations as well as my own book of remedies and cures. Life here is filled every day, and it is so easy living here. I would never go back up there."

"I see, then you wouldn't know how I could get back, would you?" Marypat asked sadly.

"No, I wouldn't. But I think I know who could?"

"You do?" She asked.

"Perhaps the Loralac would know." He answered.

"That's what we told her." The sprites giggled.

"Well then, we shall head to the Loralac's coming morning and you are welcome to stay here with me, for you look to me as a daughter." Cornelius Replied, and then stepped back to Marypat side and gave her a hug.

Marypat accepted his hug and felt naturally connected to him.

The March

T he morning opened with glorious rays of light dancing in the green sky. Marypat awoke and went to look for Cornelius. She found him outside staring at the sky.

"Isn't it beautiful? It is just as it had been when I first came here. It's an incredible sight." Cornelius said with a joyful smile.

Marypat looked into the sky; it was truly something amazing to see. "Yes. Yes, it is." she said.

After a moment Cornelius spoke. "Well, let's get going, we shall grab some berries on the way." He joked, laughing as he strolled back into the cottage.

Marypat shook her head, he was a nut, and she knew why he wanted to stay here, because he fit right in.

Suddenly in the corner of her eye she saw something in the bush, it rustled around and then sprung at her.

"Tiger!" she screamed with delight. "I thought you had left me, come let me get you some milk, you like milk don't you boy. You're such a good boy." She said scratching his head.

Tiger followed her up to the cabin and she gave him a saucer of milk.

"Put butter on his paw and he will never leave you." Doc. McCarthy laughed.

Marypat just shook her head again, "He's a nut, don't play him any mind." she said to tiger as she stroked his fur.

A moment later, Cornelius was ready to go. He had a backpack on his back and a rifle cracked open at the breach and hanging over his left arm.

"Let's march!" he called.

Marypat looked about and wondered to herself how did she get into this mess. She's taking the advice of clearly a mad man, who now thought she was his army. But as she looked around the cottage there came: out of the walls, the books and the cupboards, a troop of small men all dresses in military uniforms and standing less than a foot tall. They formed ranks and began to march in lines straight out the door.

"To the general's outpost." Cornelius called.

"Yes sir!" Came the answer from his troop.

Marypat was left behind with only the Etain that had helped her the day before.

"Is this the norm here?" Marypat asked the Etain.

The Etain only smiled.

"What are those?" Marypat asked as she pointed at the marching men before her.

"They are Frandies, original called "Pattie Dies", they are very strong militarily." The Etain answered.

"Thank you, by the way thank you so much for your help last night, you have been so very kind to me and I don't even know your name." Marypat said.

"Oh me, 'tis I who should have exclaimed my notation, I am Zeta, Guarantee of the Forest Edging 'tis my duty to make safe all who enter my endowment."

"We won't wait all turn on ya, so close the door and get in gear." Cornelius yelled back to Marypat interrupting the Lassie's conversation. "Let's get a move on."

The troops of Frandies lead the way, with Cornelius following at a good pace.

"I suppose we better get moving?" Marypat said to the Etain, Zeta who knobbed in agreement.

Marypat strolled behind Cornelius with the Etain and Tiger.

"Are you planning to stay with me?" Marypat asked Zeta.

"Yes, 'tis my duty." Zeta answered as she landed on Marypat's shoulder.

"I appreciate that very much, but I don't want to make trouble for you."

"No trouble my dear Colleen. It is my joy in life to aid others and I look to this as my chance for an adventure. Imagine I have never been out of the Forest and now I have an opportunity to see the whole. I will be pleased if you should allow me to stay with you, at least until you find your way to get home."

"Oh, I will, that's awesome of you, by the way what happened to the Rose and Daisy?"

"The pair of them had to get back to Grassy Point to do their work as Flower Sprites. Once you were in safe hands they knew they could leave you."

"I didn't get to say goodbye and thank them."

"It shall take 2 sweeps to get there, so look alive back there Marypat, stay sharp and keep your eyes out for the enemy." Doc. McCarthy shouted at the top of his lungs interrupting their conversation again.

"Enemy?" Marypat questioned the Etain.

"Oh yes, I had heard that the Frandies and the Hedlens had been having a dispute over something, but I don't remember what it was all about. I do know that the head Eties in this region had been brought into negotiate a settlement but that was some moment ago. I had no idea it had gone this long. I don't believe that we are in any danger though, the Hedlens usually are a very scared breed and run away if there is any conflict." Zeta stated calmly.

Before long they had entered the foot hills of the Emerald Green Mountains. The terrain was more difficult for the Frandies and the pace slowed down enough that Marypat and Cornelius were able to take a break and sit down.

He offered her a water cracker and a hunk of cheese from his backpack.

"Is it safe or will this turn me into a gremlin too?" she joked.

Cornelius smiled, "It is safe. Marypat, you said you found the crystal in Jamaica, is that the island in the West Indies?"

"Yes. Why do you ask?"

"Hum, I just wondered how the emerald came to be in Jamaica that's all." He said.

"I don't know how it did. Where was it supposed to be?" Marypat asked.

"Cork, Ireland." He said taking a deep breath before continuing.

"I have always felt somehow responsible for the emerald falling into darkness, perhaps if I had been guarding it. It would have been safe." He said softly.

"Oh, you can't blame yourself for that." Marypat said realizing for the first time that she too had put the emerald into jeopardy, by dropping it along the river's edge. What if it dropped back into the muck she had pulled it out of or if it broke? She had to get back, she had to, not only for herself but for the safely of the Great Isles.

The two sat quietly for a moment, it was a lot to think about. It was almost too much to speak of. So instead, they sat waiting for the Frandies to give the call that they were ready for them to follow.

"Ready, sir." The head Frandies called down to Cornelius. The Frandies had cleared the face of the mountain and were now marching through the pass. For Cornelius and Marypat it would take them only a moment to catch up and before long, they had passed the troops and were entering the underbrush of the Loralacs cave.

The Frandies dispatched into small groups that sat along the underbrush and began to set up camp. Tiger, the Grundle, made a bed in the bush and curled up for a nice nap while Zeta excused herself from Marypat's side.

"I shall meet up with you later; I must find myself some proper food for dinner. I cannot eat what Loralacs eat." Zeta grinned and then disappeared for Marypat's sight.

Meanwhile Cornelius made his way through the bristle bush and bur-thorns that filled the cave. Finally, he came to a huge wooden barricade that sealed one end of the cave off completely. It stood three men tall and four wide. It was constructed of what seemed to be red wood but on closer inspection, it was fire birch, which burned to the touch. Only the Lachlanns and the Loralacs had no trouble with its burn and so Cornelius took great care to only touch the large metal knocker in the center of it. He grabbed hold and knocked on it loudly. "Bang, Bang, Bang."

Within the entrance to the Loralacs cave, Marypat and Cornelius waited for an answered. There wasn't much light except from the Frandies glow. All was quiet.

Then sudden the large opening in the barricade screeched open and a very tall creature emerged. His skin was green in color and his hands were covered in thick burly hair. The hair on his head was black and worn long and straight, but the strangest thing about him, Marypat thought, was that he had only one eye and it sets large in the center of his huge head.

"Greetings, Commander McCarthy." The one-eyed creature said with a baritone voice that echoed through the dark cave.

"General Gillian." Cornelius saluted.

"It is most good to welcome you to my dwelling." Gillian, the one eyed, declared as he opened the door wide. "Please come forth and we shall celebrate this occasion."

Marypat looked up at Cornelius. She was somewhat confused at the Loralacs words. *Was there to be a party?*

"Don't worry my dear, we will get to your dilemma, but first we must show our gratitude to the Loralac and eat with him and his horde." Doctor Cornelius said with a smile.

"The Loralac broods are known for their ability to see things that others cannot, they are gifted with visions and have the power to heal. Their greatest flaw is that they enjoy a good time and a good time can always be found no matter what else is happening on the isle. Although they are quiet members, who never ventured out into the sunlight or give trouble to any other being of the nation, they do have a reputation of getting carried away with a celebration, they do like a good party.

General Gillian is no exception, he loves having guest, and one of his favorite guests is me. We seem to have the same outlook on life and so we have enjoyed a longtime friendship." Cornelius explained as they entered the home of General Gillian.

The narrow entrance way was made of a white marble stone that was clean and smooth and led into a small dusty cave like space. Once they had all entered the cave they were greeted by another one-eyed creature who Cornelius introduced.

"Marypat this is Gillian's Mate Jillian."

"Favorable duration to you our honored guests. It has been ever so long since you beckon at our door and gave visitation to our humble souls." Proclaimed Jillian with a bowed then she turned to Marypat with open arms. "You are of special venture my lovely Colleen; to whom we now celebrate your coming."

"Thank-you. I am grateful for your words of kindness." Marypat replied with a curtsy.

"Let the celebration begin." Shouted Gillian.

Then suddenly the dusty little cave that seemed no bigger than a cabinet came to life with dozens of creatures. Their glow filled the cave and illuminated the interior. Marypat was then able to see her surroundings and the creatures that had entered the now large space. There were several tall Loralacs, who entered carrying trays of food. They placed the trays on one of two huge banquet tables and then began to eat. They stood around the table gobbling down handfuls of fruit and meat. They never said a word or even stopped to take a breath. They eat until the platters were empty. Then they picked up the trays and left the room only to return a few moments later with more.

There was also a group of very well-dressed men, who were too busy drinking and laughing to notice the little Colleen, who stepped past them, looking for a place to sit down. Marypat found a comfortable chair in the corner of the cave beside a table. She sat down and watched as a group of short men marched in dragging stools. They pulled their stools up a long side of the Loralacs that were eating at the table. They then nudged at the Loralacs until there was space for them to push their stools beside the table and climbed up. Happy for the company the Loralacs laughed and gave way to the short men, who settled in for their meal. Side by side, the Loralacs and the short men eat until the platters were empty once more.

Jillian and another group of Lassie Loralacs took up the empty trays and offered still more food. This moment the Lassies joined the group which seemed to change the eating habits of the Patties. Marypat took notice of how the Patties actually became social when the Lassies entered the group. Was it because the women were more interesting than food or was it that the Patties were now full after three huge trays. She thought about it but her thoughts were interrupted suddenly when she heard a little voice calling to her from the table.

"Have a drink, won't you." called a tiny figure dressed in tights. He smiled a great big grin and held up a mug. The mug was larger than he was but still he presented it to her as if it were his very own.

"That is very kind of you. But I had better not." she smiled back at the tiny man and then turned back to watch the crowd.

The tiny man squinted up his face and shock his head. He didn't seem pleased with her reply.

"Hum" He hummed as he put down the mug of tonic. "If she won't drink, maybe she will eat." He said with a grin.

Then he jumped off the table and on to the floor, where he bounced back up and landed onto the banquet table. He slipped in between two Loralacs. He grabbed up something and then took something else out of his pocket. He looked around causally and then he sprinkled something over the object he had pickup off the table.

"Berry merry tick and thrive, be only a morsel in her eye." He whispered.

With that, he bounced across the room once more and landed beside Marypat on the arm of the chair.

"You must be hungry my dear, Have you a bit?" He called to her again with a smile and holding up what looked to her like carrot.

"You are very kind, little sprite. I have to wait for Cornelius." Marypat answered bending her head down to look at the little man. She had seen what the little man had done and said and she was certain she shouldn't take the bit of food from him.

"Oh" The tiny man groaned with a sour face. He stomped his foot and shook his head once more. "This Colleen thinks she so smart, well I will get her, she will see." Then he bounced off the arm of the chair and up into a tiny opening in the cave ceiling, where he disappeared into the darkness.

Marypat shock her head at him with a giggle. "Does he not realize I can hear him?" she laughed to herself.

A few moments later, he returned carrying a large velvet sack. "If she won't drink, and she won't eat, perhaps she will accept a gift." he giggled almost uncontrollable.

He bounced right on to her lap and took her by surprise.

"Oh, hello there again. You are so kind and friendly to me, no one else has even. . . ." Her voice trailed off as she frowned slightly and then continued." had time to say hello to me, expect your cute little tiny sprite." Marypat smiled then and asked "What is your name? I should like to call you by your name."

The man stood straight up he looked quite annoyed at her. "Arrrrr." he groaned in frustration then he dropped his bag and stepped right up to her face. "First of all, I am not a sprite. I'm a Jinxie." He said quite angrily.

"Oh, I am very sorry, I'm afraid I have not been here that long and I ...." she humbly tried to explain but he interrupted her by waving his hands in the air and telling her to "hush."

"Do you want everyone to hear you talking to me, well do you?" he said shouting at her.

"You're the one shouting. You don't have to shout!" Marypat said with disgust.

"Oh, you watch yourself, Colleen; you think you're so smart, ya think you're so clever. Me going to run your foot, me little Colleen, yours beware." He said pointing his finger at her nose and pocking the end of it.

"I'll beware, but you still didn't tell me your name? What do you have there is that something for me?" She smiled again quite amused by the Jinxie. She recalled Rose and Daisy mentioning a Jinxie yesterday and how you couldn't trust them and all of what this little man was doing made sense to her that Jinxie's were jokers. So Marypat thought she should have some fun with him.

The Jinxie smirked a sincere grin. "Oh yes it's for you alright." he laughed and then jumped away leaving the velvet sack on her lap.

"Well, how nice! Thank- you. Bye little Jinxie I hope we meet again." She shouted after the little man.

She scooped up the velvet sack and held the tiny strings in her fingers, then she pulled it tightly closed and looped the end of the strings tying them into a knot.

She believed he had put something in it that was a joke of some kind, so she knew she shouldn't open it. Especially because the velvet sack wiggled as she held it up.

"A Jinxie is a Jinxie in any world." She giggled. Then she placed the sack into the deep pocket of her clam diggers for safe keeping and laid back in the comfortable chair and fell to sleep.

The Vision

Marypat sat relaxed in the chair that sat in the corner of the Loralacs cave. She had only just drifted off to sleep and then awoken by Cornelius.

"It's moment my dear." He said.

Marypat woke up and followed Cornelius to one of the large banquet tables. There were chairs placed all around and Gillian was already sitting in one of them. Cornelius took his place across from Gillian and then offered a seat to Marypat.

Marypat sat down but could not see above the table. She had to climb up on to her knees in order to be seen while Zeta hovered above her.

The cave went quiet as Gillian began to speak.

"Welcome, Marypat, visitor from above." he announced.

The others in the cave gathered round to hear and suddenly Marypat found herself surrounded. A short man had pushed his way up beside her and he sat on his stool patiently listening while two Loralacs stepped in behind her.

"You have come a long way and you have many questions?" Gillian asked.

Marypat nodded "yes." as two little Etains flew near her and gently pulled her red hair from her face and interweaved it on the back of her head away from her ears, so that she might hear every word that was said.

"I will try to answer them, but first take hold of this quartz crystal, clear your mind and allow all that clutter it to be held within the stone." Gillian said handing her the crystal.

Marypat took the crystal and held it in her hand.

"Now let me tell you of my vision.," he said spreading his hands out in front of him.

"The eye is wide, and I spy a clear glowing rainbow with sun beams as pure as light. I view a river flowing to the south, it bubbles unblemished, it moves in your world. I hear voices, language foreign to me, but somehow, I believe that they wish to help. I observe a figure un-winged yet in flight. A soul that is pure and meek, with a heart that is true and strong." Gillian paused for a moment and then continued. "I perceive, regard, and understand that the being is one chosen, selected, and called to our homage, our respect for she shall be the answer to our despair, disorder, and distress." With that, he closed his eye and held his hands up into the air. His vision was over, his recollection complete.

Marypat sat kneeling in her chair, looking all about at the faces of those around her. She didn't understand what Gillian had said; she was confused and searched the crowd for someone who could explain it to her.

Her eyes meet Cornelius. "What does that mean?" Marypat whispered to Cornelius.

Gillian put down his arms and opened his eye; he looked directly at Marypat and said. "You are here to save us from destruction."

"How can I, little me, save you?" She asked quite shocked.

"We believe that all answers are found within one's own being. You must strive to unleash your vast knowledge, expose your eternal wisdom, and uncover our unfortunate flaws. You alone are our only hope." He answered.

Marypat shock her head "No." Then with a slight giggle, she turned back to Cornelius. "Is this for real?" she smiled nervously.

Cornelius said nothing. His face was serious as he nodded his head yes.

Marypat looked back at Gillian her brow turned down and her voice was sharp.

"I came here for **you** to help me get home. All I want to do is go home."

"Indeed." Gillian answered as he stood from his seat. "The path home has many turns." Then he stepped away from the table and said good night leaving Marypat with Cornelius.

Most of the guests disappeared into the darkness only Cornelius, Jillian, and Zeta remaining with Marypats.

"What do I do, he says I must study to find my way home? If the answer lies in a book, then everyone here must know how to leave, why they don't just tell me."

Marypat began to cry. She had been among the Green Isles for two days already and the longer she stayed the more of a chance the emerald had to fall back into the rivers murky silt, back into darkness.

"If I am their only hope to save them, then I must get back. The longer I am here the more danger the emerald is in." Marypat expressed to Zeta and Jillian.

"I do believe you are right, that is to the fact that you must get back and protect the emerald. But on the matter of knowing how to leave, I'm afraid it is not in any book. It is something you must discover on your own." Cornelius said reassuring her.

"Is there anyone else who can help me?" She asked sadly.

"I do not know of anyone else, I am so sorry my dear." Cornelius said softly placing his hand on her shoulder.

"What about the Regan?" Said a tiny voice floating in the air like a whisper.

"Yes! The Regan, what about the Regan?" Echoed several little voices coming from the walls.

Marypat looked about. "Who said that?" She asked.

"I did." Answered the tiny voice as he floated pasted and landed on the table.

"Who are you? I don't remember you." Asked Cornelius.

"I am Aden," he said with a bow. The Etie floated before Marypat and Cornelius much like Zeta only this one wore light brown pants, a green feather shirt, and a black cap on his head.

"An Etain?" Marypat said with a smile.

"I am not! How dare you say I look like an Etain? Am I not strong?" Aden shouted flexing his muscles. "Am I not Handsome" He held his head to the side and puckered his lips. "How could you mistake me for an Etain?" Then he turned his back to Marypat and folded his arms as if he were mad at her.

Cornelius nudged Marypat's arm and she looked up at him.

"He's a Laddie, not an Etain. They don't like it when you mistake them for Lassies. You had better apologize." Cornelius said quite seriously.

Marypat stood up straight and cleared her throat. "Well . . . please forgive me. . . Aldan was it. . I . . . didn't mean to hurt your feelings. . . . I am . . . well . . . I am new here and I haven't learned . . . all the types of . . . people there are here." Marypat said with a stutter.

"What are people?" He asked jumping back around as to look into Marypat's face.

"You know people, I'm a person, and you're a person, people?" She said with a questioned look on her face.

"People are called Members here. There are three types. The smallest groups are called Teeny's. Teeny's have two categories: Eties that include Etains, Laddies, Pixies, Jinxie's, Naxies and Daxie's and Dies that include Frandies, Krysdies, Kandies and Andies. The second group is commoners they include Feldens, Ullden's, Lachlann's and Hedlens. The Regan is a Lachlann. The third group is the biggest of the members, known here as Vasters. We're Vasters." Cornelius added.

"Oh, I suppose I do have a lot to learn. I am very sorry." Marypat said sadly as she sat down in the large chair. There was so much she didn't know, and it began to make her head hurt. She was never good at school her average grades were "C's" and to think she would have to study and learn things here in order to get out made her sick.

"Now then little Laddie, what was it you were saying?" Cornelius asked with a smile.

"I suggested that your Colleen goes to the Regan, he is very wise, and perhaps he might have an answer for her. If she is nice I will show her the way." Aden said with his arms still folded over his chest.

"That's an excellent suggestion. Very good, Laddie, you must take us there, we will leave in the morning." Cornelius announces with joy.

Night had fallen on the Isle and the darkness of the Loralacs den had increased by two. Marypat could no longer keep her eyes open so Jillian showed her to a bedchamber, where she could sleep.

Jillian lead Marypat up a large staircase carved out of the Mt stone. The stone was green with sparkling white rivers of quarts running throw it. Marypat found it quite an amazing sight to see, as Zeta's inner glow reflected off the stone creating a light show all around her.

The staircase seemed to go on forever, bending round, and round. Soon they came to a landing and Jillian turned off the staircase and walked down a long narrow hall. The hallway was also carved out of the mountain stone and arched high above Marypat head. There was intricate caving throughout the hallway, on the walls and ceiling. Marypat took a moment and asked Zeta to light it up for her to see. The Etain did and to Marypat amazement, the carvings were delicate portraits of Loralac children playing in a field of flowers. It took Marypat's breath away, it must have taken centuries to carve, and it was remarkable.

"Right this way, my dear." Jillian replied as she opened the tall door to a bedchamber and entered.

Inside Jillian lit two lanterns and set them on either side of the room. "May this help you?" She whispered setting the second lantern down on a table. "There is clothing here for you and a nightgown. Cornelius told me you might need some, so I have had them made for you. Are you in need of anything else?" She asked.

"No, but Thank-you, you have been so kind." Marypat answered.

"Good evening then, till morrow." Jillian said with a smile before leaving the chamber and closing the door behind her.

Marypat looked around the room, three of the walls were just as the hallway and the stairs. They were carved from the marble green mountain stone. But the fourth wall was not like the others. It was smooth like glass and the edges of it seemed to melt into the marble walls in an uneven pattern. She slid her hand down the wall and examined it closely. How unusual it was she thought.

Then she turned to Zeta as she reached for her nightgown and asked. "Who is this Regan that the Laddie spoke of?"

"He is a wise Lachlann. He is greatly respected in all the lands; you must be very humble when you go before him." Zeta answered.

"I will." Marypat replied and then asked, "Is he your king?"

"What is a king?" Zeta asked back with great curiosity.

Marypat giggled to herself, how silly it was to her that this little Etain knew not what a king was. "Alright, a king is one who is greatly respected by the people of his nation and he rules the lands he owns, he wears a crown of jewels on his head and is called something like your grace or your majesty. Some people call their king by other names like Emperor, Shake, or Ruler. Or yes and in some places, they don't have a king they have a "President or where I come from we call our leader the Prime Minister, they rule the land but they don't own it, or wear a crown."

Zeta flittered in the air looking a bit confused.

"Is your Regan anything like that?" Marypat asked as she made herself comfortable on the big fluffy bed.

"I suppose he is like a king, he wears a ring of jewels through his hair, and he keeps peace throughout the lands, he is great and powerful." Zeta answered.

Marypat nodded and smiled at Zeta. "Then I shall meet your king, your Regan."

"I only hope that he may help you." Zeta mentioned.

"Me too!" Marypat replied. "Me too!"

Before long, Marypat had drifted off to sleep, beneath the thick covers of the Loralacs comfortable bed sheets. Zeta too was sound asleep and lying on one of the fluffy pillows beside Marypat. All was quiet, all was still.

As the two slept, a tiny figure crept from a small crack in the wall and slipped onto the bed. He stepped up to Marypat's face and blow into her eye.

"I told you I would get you, you evil Colleen." The tiny figure said. But Marypat only squinted her eyes a bit until he was out of breath and had to stopped, and then she sighed a large sigh and turned her head, knocking him over. The tumble rolled him down the fluffy pillow and into the sheets where he was trapped and unable to move.

"Blasted! She's got me again." He shouted.

Unbeknown to Marypat, the little Jinxie lied there all night, trapped by her grip. In the morning, she arose to a most glorious sight. The glass wall she had only felt the night before was now plan to see as the sun light radiated through it. The glass covered ceiling to floor and side to side in an incredible shade of green. The shape of the window gave an edged cut appearance as if someone had carved and shaped it to fit the room.

Marypat sat up in bed and waited as the sun light danced through the glass and showed across the floor and bed.

"Isn't it beautiful?" She remarked.

"Yes!" Zeta answered as she floated up toward Marypat's shoulder. "It must be the wall of the crystal."

"What?" Marypat questioned. If this were the wall of the crystal, then perhaps she could see outside, and see her world. She jumped from the bed, exposing the Jinxie hiding now under the covers. Marypat noticed the Jinxie and scooped him up into her hand.

"So, we meet again, Horatio?" Marypat giggled. But she had not the time for him, so she stuffed him into the pocket of her pants and trapped him with the button cover.

"I shall deal with you in a moment." She said, and then she ran to the glass. She pressed her face up against it and stared through it, trying desperately to see the world beyond. What she could see was repetitive do to the edges of the crystal. She seemed to be able though to make out a tree and a bush and when it was very quiet, she could hear the river flowing by. Then suddenly she heard someone calling her.

"Marypat, Marypat, Mary Patricia." The voice called again and again.

Marypat listed as the voice became louder and louder. Marypat soon realized it was her grandmother calling to her from the outside.

"I'm over here grandma, I am here, down here." Marypat shouted with all of her might, she jumped up and down, but her grandmother did not hear her. Marypat began to sob.

"Grandma, Grandma, help me, I'm in here, I'm in here." Marypat slide down the wall of the green crystal until she sat in a heap on the floor. She cried, and she cried, oh how she missed her grandmother and her world.

"Grandma help me I wanted to go home."

She sat there on the floor unaware that the crystal had been moved.

"LOOK! A great shadow has consumed us." Zeta shouted.

"What?" Marypat sniffled. She looked up and it was true a giant shadow had reached across the crystals face and left its mark. The mountain began to tremble, and it was all Marypat could do to hold on. She pushed her face once more to the crystal and searched the world outside for an answer. Her eyes made their way across the shadow and soon discover it wasn't a shadow at all, it was a finger, a human finger.

"It's ok; I think my grandmother, Miss Lora, has found the emerald. The emerald should be safe now."

Marypat continued to search the world outside, she recognized the stone steps that lead to the top house where she lived with her grandparents. She could even see the porch on the back of the house. Her grandmother had taken the emerald to her home; she took it straight inside and sat in a chair beside the fireplace. There she sat, and she began to sob. She held the crystal up to her face and rubbed her own tears away with the back of her hand. Then she spoke as if she were speaking to the crystal.

"Please bring my Marypat home safely, I miss her so."

Marypat could see her grandmother's face very clearly; her eyes were filled with tears as she stared into the crystal. Marypat composed herself and took the opportunity to try and reach her grandmother.

"Grandma!" Marypat shouted with everything she had.

"I'm in here!"

Marypat's grandmother sat back her face became quite serious as she looked around.

"I must be hearing things." She said with a slight laugh.

"Grandma it's me." Marypat continued to shout.

"Marypat, is that you?" Miss Lora asked.

"YES." Marypat began to laugh with relief, she had gotten through to her grandmother, she had heard her.

"Where are you?" Miss Lora asked nervously holding the crystal in her hand.

"I'm in here, look in the crystal, here I am." Marypat answered as she waved her hands in the air.

Marypat's grandmother lifted the crystal to her eye and gazed into the side of the crystal. A huge eye appeared in front of Marypat as she continued to wave and jump.

"Here I am, can you see me, I'm trapped in here."

Marypat's grandmother's eye went wide as she caught sight of her granddaughter inside the crystal. Her hand began to shake, and tears slipped from her eyes.

"How did you get in there, how will I get you out?" she questioned.

"I don't know but I am going to find someone who might know." Marypat answered.

"You must be careful dear, oh how I miss you." she sobbed.

"I miss you too grandma, and I am trying to come home to you, but I need your help." Marypat called to her grandmother.

"What can I do? I would do anything, anything to help you my dear, to help you come home." Miss Lora said quite sadly.

"You must keep the emerald safe. Promise me you will keep the emerald safe." Marypat pleaded with her grandmother.

"Of course, I will. I love you dear, come home to me." Miss Lora promised, and then she kissed the crystal.

"I shall, but now I must go if I am ever to get back to you. Soon come!" Marypat called with tears in her eyes. Then she kissed her fingers and laid it against the glass. A moment later, she turned away and headed for the door.

CHAPTER 5

The Journey

Marypat ran down the hall and quickly made her way down the stairway. She entered the Loralacs dining room where the two large banquet tables stood. There she found Doc. McCarthy and Gillian having tea.

"Doc!" She shouted, "Doc you won't believe what just happened!"

"What is it my dear?" He asked as he stood quickly.

"I saw my grandmother. She has found the crystal and has agreed to keep it safe." Marypat answered with tears in her eyes.

"Why that's splendid, my dear, girl. We are safe and in good hands." He smiled a reassuring grin. Then he reached out his hand to her and invited her to sit.

"Now, that leaves us with how to get you back to her, doesn't it." He said calmly.

"Yes." She answered.

"Then we should start out right away. I shall ready the troops! But first, we eat!" Cornelius said with delight.

Jillian brought in a huge tray of food. There was a strange looking fruit that looked like pears, but they had yellow spots all over them. There was a plate of bread that looked like pancakes and a bowl of something that looked like oatmeal, but it was green in color. Marypat looked up at Cornelius and turned up her brow. Cornelius understood and replied.

"Rule number one: Don't eat pear unless you want to grow hair! Rule number two: berries make you scary! Rule number three: Potato cakes with a speck, can make your tummy hurt like heck."

He smiled at her again and then gave her a lump of porridge.

"This is safe, it's what I am eating!" he said.

Marypat nodded and eat every drop even though it didn't taste like any kind or porridge she had ever had before. She was very hungry.

Later she feed Tiger and gave him his morning scratch. She was quite happy to see that he was still waiting for her outside the Loralacs cave, and that he hadn't made breakfast of any of the Frandies. She sat in the bristle bush and scratched his head while the troops broke camp and ready themselves for the day's march. It was going to be a treacherous walk to the Regan's dwelling. They were going to have to cross the Caboonee meadow where there had been an ongoing war between the Lachlann and the Frandies.

"This mission will not be an easy one and I will not harbor any resentment against any member, here, who feels he cannot proceed with me. We have seen many a good fight and we have been through many a dark mission, but this one goes far above the call of duty. So, I must allow each of you to choose for himself whether or not you will assist me in my obligation. Those of you who choose to support this cause must ready yourself as we march on the sweep." Cornelius announced to his troops.

When Cornelius finished his speech, he turned to the tiny Laddie, Aden who was hovering just above his head and said. "We should check the map one last moment."

The Laddie agreed and the two went inside the Loralacs cave.

A few moments later Cornelius, Gillian, Jillian, Aden, and Zeta emerged from the opening ready to go. Cornelius turned back to Gillian and thanked him one last moment for his help and then he kissed the hand of Jillian.

"You have been most kind my dear friends; we shall visit again in more Jubilistic Turns." He said with a bow and then he turned and called to his troops. "Forward."

The Frandies formed ranks and soon had cleared out of the underbrush well on their way down the side of the mountain leaving Marypat and Tiger behind.

Marypat looked up at the Loralacs. She smiles and said sweetly. "My deepest gratitude to you most humble members."

"Safe travels young one. Lead with your right foot and it shall never lead you wrong." Gillian replied.

Marypat waved good-bye then and she and Tiger headed down the Mt. following the Frandies.

After a while, Marypat felt something moving in her pocket.

"Oh my, what is that?" She called out.

She carefully opened the pocket and peeked inside. There at the bottom of the pocket sat the little Jinxie, just stirring from his slumber. "Oh, it's you, Horatio; I forgot you were in there. Is all well?" she giggled with glee.

"How can you ask me that after you shoved me into your pocket. No, I am not well, you have broken my feelings. Feelings that can never be repaired," he said quite angrily. He tried to stand but the pocket was too narrow, and he toppled over onto his side.

"Here let me help you," Marypat said as she held him around his waist and pulled him from the pocket. She held him up in front of her face and spoke to him softly.

"Is that better?" She asked.

"No, put me down." He shouted at her.

"Are you sure you want me to put you down?" She asked.

"Yes, put me down this instant!" He demanded.

So Marypat did what she was told and bend down to put the Jinxie on the ground.

But before Marypat could release him, she spotted Tiger beside her licking his lips while the Jinxie's eyes bulged from his head in what looked like pure fear.

"Jinxie's hate cooses, it's one of the only creatures in all of the Green Isles that Jinxie's are afraid of." Zeta laughed from Marypat's shoulder.

"Pick me up, pick me up!" The Jinxie exclaimed.

Marypat quickly stood up with the Jinxie still in her grasp. "But you just said to put you down, you don't even know what you want!" she said pointing her finger at him.

"Oh! Ya well you have some nerve cohering with a Grundle and caring me about as if I were his lunch. You're despicable." The Jinxie shouted.

"Despicable! Me?" Marypat questioned shaking her head at him. "Just for that I should feed you to him for lunch." She dangled the Jinxie over Tiger's head, as the Grundle continued to lick his lips and purr.

"NO, all right then you're not despicable, just don't feed me to your coose, I beg you." The Jinxie cried.

"I won't feed you to Tiger under one condition." She stated.

"What's the condition?" He asked with a frown.

"You have to be nice to Me," she said.

"That's all?" He asked with a sly little grin.

"Yes, you have to be nice, no more tricks, do you hear me, I'm not kidding, be nice or you're the Grundle's lunch." She said quiet convincing "Agreed?"

"Agreed," he answered, shacking Marypat's hand to seal the deal.

With that, she placed him on her shoulder and continued on following the Frandies as they entered the forest.

"By the way, where are we going?" The Jinxie asked.

"We are headed to the Regan, in hopes he can tell me how to get home." She answered.

"Oh, I have never met the Regan, I should like to go. It should be fun to play a prank on the Regan." The Jinxie stated with a devilish grin.

"No pranks on the Regan, Horatio!" Marypat stated.

"But why I only promised to be nice to you," he giggled.

The bright green sky had nearly gone to dark and yet the sky still had a luminosity glow to the east. The rays from the glow penetrated the crystal in an unusual way, unlike any light had before. Marypat glanced at her watch it was nearly 7:00 pm so she speculated that the usually light coming through the crystals was her grandmother leaving a light on for her. The thought that she was safe at home made life inside the crystal a bit more bearable. Knowing that the crystal was safe was one less thing for her to worry about and gave her more moment to think about how to get home.

"Halt, we make camp here." Cornelius commanded, with that, the Frandies broke up into groups and began setting up their tents. Some of the Frandies made fires to cook over while another helped Cornelius to set up his tent for himself and Marypat.

Soon all were settled in and night fell over the camp. The Frandies made a large fire for Cornelius to keep him warm and they cooked a pot of "Pash Dash" for all to enjoy. Marypat looked to Cornelius for the big "ok", to eat it and when he nodded yes, she dove into it hungrily. She was so very hungry, and it tasted so good. She gobbled down every bit and then asked for more. With her second helping, she feed her friends Zeta, the Jinxie, and Tiger.

"What is Pash Dash? I don't believe I have ever had such a delicious stew." She asked the Jinxie, who was busy eating.

"Oh, well that's because it made from. . . . . Billy Bat wings." he paused then swung his head down. "Sorry it's not made with Billy Bat wings; it's made from very tender Huff meat. It has beans in it too, they are my favorite. Do you enjoy beans?"

"Honestly? No, beans are not my favorite, but these were delicious." Marypat could tell he had wanted to try and trick her but because he had promised he wouldn't play any tricks on her, he had to come clean.

"You know you still haven't told me your name; how should I call you?" Marypat asked.

"What was the name you called me this morn. . . . . Horatio was it? That is what you should call Me." he answered.

"But that is not your name. Horatio is just a name I made up." Marypat said with a silly grin.

"It is now," he answered solemnly.

"How can that be?" she asked.

"Because Jinxie's don't have names, do they Horatio?" Zeta taunted with a laugh.

"That's right they don't!" He replied with a frown.

"But if by chance someone calls them by a name, they are forever beholding to that name and that member. So little Horatio, are you beholding?" Asked Zeta.

"Zeta! You should be ashamed of yourselves. How can you make fun of him like this?" Marypat asked.

"I am very sorry, Marypat, but you see a Lassie of the wingless Pixie can't keep a trickily Jinxie around for long. So, they have this tiny little curse on them which keeps them trustworthy to their beholder. Do you understand?" Zeta looked at Marypat.

Marypat nodded her head," yes."

"Pixies choose a Pattie and call him by a name; once he is named he must stay true to her. No tricks, no pranks, no silliness. Otherwise those Jinxie's would never settle down and Pixies would be extinct." Zeta said very seriously.

"I see, but what is so funny?" Marypat asked.

Zeta smiled and looked at Horatio. "He's now beholding to you." She giggled.

Marypat's eyes went wide. "But I am not a Pixie." She announced quite shocked.

"That's what is so funny!" Zeta exclaimed still giggling.

Marypat shook her head; this world was very strange indeed. She had eaten a berry and nearly been changed into a gremlin. She had named a Jinxie and made herself a beholder. What could happen next?

She turned to her new little friend and spoke to him with respect. "I do apologize to you; it was not my intention to disrupt your life. Perhaps we may need to think on this for a moment and come up with some way to release you from this curse."

"You are most kind, but I am afraid that there is no hope of that. Instead I shall be a true friend and help you find your way home, that I pledge." Horatio proclaimed.

"And I pledge to you my friendship and my loyalty." She announced.

Zeta looked at them in disbelief. "I cannot believe this I have never seen a Colleen befriend a Jinxie. It is unheard of; this is not right." Then she flew away.

Marypat and Horatio stayed behind and sat by the fire for quiet sometime later. He explained many things to her that she had had no idea about. There was much she needed to learn and he was willing to teach her. After a while, she grew tiered and bid him goodnight. She kissed him gently on the head, "Good night, Horatio, till morrow." Then she stepped away and entered the tent.

Horatio sat alone by the fire. "Goodnight fare one," he whispered softly.

He didn't feel a need to play a joke or a prank. For some strange reason he didn't want to jump into the trees and run on the tree tops or eat Jay Berries till his stomach ached like he normally wanted to do. But no, not now, now he wanted to help this Colleen, he wanted to be her friend. Was it the curse? He had no way to tell, but he knew he wanted to stay right here with her.

The War

T he morning opened with a multitude of light, it was sudden,
and it was bright. It was as if the entire world was surround by
the sun. The beams of light reflected off one another causing
an incredible arch of rainbows. A spectacle that lasted in the sky the
entire day.

Marypat found it astonishing and magical. The day of marching
was filled with the sounds of singing and of members celebrating. All
along the way she met Pixies and Etains who were very happy to see her,
she met Colleens and Wardeens who greeted her with waves and smiles.

"Why are they so happy?" Marypat asked Horatio as they walked
through a village filled with happy members.

"They are happy because our world is set back right, don't you see the rainbows?" He asked, pointing to the sky.

"Yes! But what does that have to do with your world being set right?"

"When our world fell to darkness, there were no rainbows and we haven't seen one till this very day. In fact, I have lived my whole life in darkness, this is the first I have ever seen such a sight. All is well, and all the members see the rainbows as a sign that the world is right." He said.

"Safe." She whispered to herself. The rainbows came because the world was safe in her grandmother's home. She smiled because she knew her grandmother was watching over the crystal and keeping it safe. She knew that the rays of sun light were actually light from light bulbs her grandmother had turned on around the crystal. She took the rainbows as a sign too, but a sign from her grandmother that everything was going to be ok.

Later that day the troops approached an open field. They had cleared a forest and continued through the tall grass of the field.

"Beware, Goblin Moss." Called the point man, from the front of the company.

"Goblin Moss." The Frandies called back one after another until it reached Cornelius and Marypat.

"Is it new?" Cornelius called back forward.

The Frandies then began to call the message forward again one after the other until an answer to Cornelius's question came back to him.

"No, well dry!" The answer was.

"Hum. I need a fresh batch; I may take this opportunity to collect some." Cornelius mentioned.

"What it Goblin Moss?" Marypat asked Cornelius.

"Oh, it is quite dangerous; you don't want to step on goblin moss. Excuse me dear but I think I am going to go collect it." Cornelius said before quickened his pace and headed for the front of the regiment. His step equaled five of a Frandies and he was soon at the Goblin Moss. The troop continued marching on while Cornelius bent down to take his sample. Before long Marypat had caught up to him and he showed her the plant.

"If these thorns scratch you, they will put you to sleep forever. They are very powerful!" he explained.

"Why then do you want it?" She asked shyly.

"I use it medically, to help me patience." He said with a smile. He stood up then and put his sample away in his pack. "We better keep up with the troops."

But before they could move there was a loud commotion at the front of the line. It sounded like members shouting at one another but Marypat couldn't make out what was being said. Quickly Cornelius took Marypat's hand and they ran to the front of the line.

"Attention." Cornelius shouted as he approached the point man. "Lieutenant, explain to me what is going on here."

The troops were spending out throughout the tall grass, with their muskets readied. It appeared as if something serious had taken place.

"Yes, sir." The Lieutenant shouted back as he saluted Cornelius. "The enemy, sir they were hiding in the grass. When we approached, they ran off."

"I see. Any of our men injured?" Cornelius asked.

"No, sir." The lieutenant answered.

"Good, what direction did they head?"

The lieutenant pointed straight ahead and then looked at Cornelius.

"Ready the men, Lieutenant. We pursue!" Commanded Cornelius. He turned to Marypat and whispered. "Stay hidden here in the grass dear, you will be safe."

Then he headed off with the Frandies in pursuit of the enemy.

The peaceful afternoon march had suddenly turned into a war. A war Marypat could neither see nor understand. So, she sat in the tall grass and listened as the tiny bullets popped from the Frandies muskets and wondered why.

Horatio jumped from Marypat's shoulder and bounced off the ground. He hopped into the air, trying to see the battle.

"What are you doing?" She asked him.

"Don't you want to see what's going on?" He answered.

"Not really," she said scratching her head.

"Well I do, and I can't see anything from here." He shouted as he sailed through the air. "I need more height."

Then he bounded away from her and caught onto the branch of a nearby tree. Up the tree he bounced till he was at the top.

"What do you see?" She asked Horatio.

"Thought you didn't care," he commented.

"Don't be a wise guy, just tell me what you see," she said pointing her finger at him.

"Alright. The Frandies are in the grass line right ahead of us. I can see a group of Hedlens just on the other side of the river. It looks like 20 or more, can't be sure." He reported more seriously.

"Do you know what they're fighting over?" Asked Marypat.

"No." Horatio answered.

"Horatio, is there a safe place to cross the river?" She called up to him. She had an idea but she would need to get to the other side of the river in order to pull it off.

"Are you mad, there's a battle going on." He shouted.

"No, I am not mad, just tell me." She shouted back.

"Yes, but I'll have to show you." He answered.

"Good, I'll get Zeta." Marypat said then she turned and called "tulla lou."

Suddenly Zeta appeared and Marypat explained what she wanted to do. Zeta agreed and the three set off. They crossed the river at some distance away from the struggle and found their way to the where the Hedlens had made camp. The camp seemed to be abandoned as all of the Hedlens had gone to the battle.

Yet there was one small Hedlen hiding behind a barrel. He stood only 2 feet tall. He had green skin and a bumpy, baldhead with small bits of hair that stuck out like weeds in a garden. He was frightened and Marypat could see that. So, she asked Zeta to translate.

"I'm a friend, I want to help."

Zeta spoke to the boy in a language that sounded like French. Marypat was amazed she understood what Zeta had said.

"You are not with the Frandies?" The young Hedlen asked.

"We want to help you; can you tell me why the Hedlens fight with the Frandies?" Marypat asked in French.

"We do not fight with the Frandies; it is the Frandies who fight with us." The Hedlen shouted quite angrily.

"Yes, yes, please excuse my Colleen she is new here. Tell me why they fight with you." Zeta said softly in a calming voice.

"We had to move from our home in the bog, there is no more water there. We came here for water. But the Frandies don't let us stay on this land. They chase us away. I miss my home; I miss my lovely bog." The young Hedlen cried.

Marypat approached the child and put her arms around him. "Don't cry little one, we shall find a way to help you. Can you take me to your bog?" she asked.

The young Hedlen nodded his head, yes. Then he showed Marypat paths that lead through the forest. The walk through the thick forest took 1 sweep and ended at the foothills of a large green mountain. To the west lay the bog, it's blood red soil was dried and cracked, Marypat poked the soil, there was no moister at all. She picked up a handful of soil and twisted the dry grains through her figures until all that remained was a single hard rock. She stuffed the rock into her pocket when she suddenly noticed that she seemed to be standing in a dry narrow riverbed that lead back to the east and up the side of the mountain.

"Was there water here before?" She asked the young Hedlen.

"Yes," he answered. "It was a very small creek that ran all the turns."

"I want to see where this river bed leads." Marypat said to Zeta as she bent down and picked up a dust covered red stone. She busted it off and noticed some kind of red gem so she slide it into her pocket, thinking she would look at it later.

Marypat then started to climb the side of the mountain, following the narrow riverbed. She followed it to a place where the land leveled off and the bed continued to the east. Sometime later, she came to the mountain face again but this moment there was a running river flowing from it. The water rushed down the face causing a beautiful waterfall. Then the water followed across the flat land and down another incline to finally flow across the grasslands below, down where the battle was taking place this moment.

Marypat could see from where she stood that the war was still ragging. She could see the Hedlens attacking on the right flank while a troop of Frandies ran across the river, shouting at the Hedlens. Three of the Hedlens tried to run away but several of the Frandies jumped on to them. They screamed at the Hedlens and stabbed their tiny bayonets into the Hedlens tuff skin. To the Hedlens the tiny knives gave only moderate pain. They were more afraid of the Frandies themselves than their weapons.

One of the Hedlens spun around and around grabbing at the Frandies and tossing them away. Another ran into the forest, while the third one dove into the river and splashed at the Frandies until they fell away.

Marypat just shook her head. "Foolishness! Grown men, they act more like children."

She then stepped away from the cliff and walked back to the waterfall. She studied the dried creek bed that once flowed to the bog and she discovered that a bolder blocked the path of the river. All she needed to do was move the bolder and the water would return to the bog as it once had.

She tried to move the bolder, but it would not budge, she would need help. So, she stepped over to the cliff once more and she throw up her arms and shouted first in English and then in French.

"I have the solution!"

Both the Hedlens and the Frandies stopped what they were doing and looked up at her. She waved her hands at them and then shouted again. "Peace is at hand, yet I shall need your help."

Cornelius stood up straight and stepped out from behind a tree while he answered back. "What are you doing, there's a war on."

"Come doctor, I need your help." she yelled back.

Cornelius commanded his man to stay on ready while he and several others made their way up the cliff to where Marypat stood. A group of Hedlens also made the climb, to investigate the claim of peace.

Marypat quickly explained to all that the solution was clear, move
the bolder and the water would return to the bog. Then the Hedlens
could return to their homes and the Frandies could have their land back.

Cornelius agreed and with help from several from both sides, the
bolder was pushed from the bed and the water instantly began to flow
again into the bog.

The Hedlens cheered, the Frandies cheered and Cornelius smiled
at Marypat. "Good job." he said to her.

The young Hedlen jumped for joy and hugged Marypat.

"You are a friend. Thank-you," he said in French.

Peace was at hand, it had been in Marypat's and with a simple move
she had shared it with all. There was peace once more in the valley for
the Hedlens and the Frandies, but still it had not brought her any closer
to home, her quest would have to continue.

The Whimple

As night fell over the bog, the Hedlens celebrated their homecoming. On the bank of the bog the Frandies joined in, with dancing and singing. Several Frandies shot off their pepper powder as fireworks, lighting up the sky with fluorescent explosions. It was a night of elation, of merriment. The war was over, and life could go back to normal, to peace.

Marypat and Horatio enjoyed the party, dancing on the bogs edge. She had never seen such a sight in all her life. There were hundreds of Frandies dancing about with members she had not noticed before. Surely, she would have taken note of such tiny members. But funny enough she had not. These new members were about half the size of a Frandies and yet they were not children. They were fully-grown and mature. She stared at them with a questionable look until she was interrupted by Horatio.

"Don't stare at them, they don't like that," he commanded.

"Oh, was I staring? They are so small, what are they?" She asked, still looking at the tiny members.

They were dressed in leather loin clothes of green, that were ornamented with breads. They had large eyes that glowed in the night like a cat's eye and their ears were large and flat and pointed.

"They are Andies and Kandies, rarely seen by you Vasters. They prefer it that way." He answered.

"Andies and Kandies! How remarkable. I should like to meet one." She whispered.

Horatio only wobbled his head and replied. "You do have a lot to learn."

Then he bent down his head and asked, "Do you still have the velvet sack I gave you?"

"Yes!" Marypat answered. "Why?"

"Give it to that Kandie, right there." He said.

"Horatio, there's a spider in that sack, isn't there?" She asked

"Yes." He answered.

"Why would I give her a spider?" She asked.

"Because Kandies love to eat spiders." He answered with a frown.

"No tricks!" She said waving her finger at him.

"No tricks, I swear," he responded sadly.

"Good!" She said, then she turned back to the Kandie and slowly approached her.

"Hello." Marypat called in her sweetest voice. But the Kandie didn't find Marypat all that sweet and disappeared without an answer.

"Hum!" Marypat huffed.

"Need some help, call for that Laddie, Aden he speaks their language." Horatio said in a mean voice.

Marypat called to the Laddie, Aden and he soon came to her aid.

"I wish to speak to a Kandie and make her acquaintance. I have a delicious spider to offer in friendship." Marypat explained to the Laddie.

"Very good!" Aden answered. Then he flittered away heading towards a group of Andies and Kandies. When he returned one of the Kandies followed him.

"She wishes to see the spider, before she will make any deal." Aden explained to Marypat.

Marypat opened the sack and the Kandie peered into it to find a big fat juice spider wiggling inside. The Kandie nodded her head and then motioned to the other Andies and Kandies that the deal was on. A few moments later Marypat found herself surrounded by Andies and Kandies. Their tiny little hands and faces reminded Marypat of her dolls at home. But these were not dolls, these were real. Fascinated by them she asked them many question and Aden translated. Soon she had made friends with all of Andies and Kandies in the group and Marypat was pleased. At the end of the evening Marypat handed over the spider to the lead Kandie and bid them all goodnight. Then she stuffed the empty sack back into her pocket and went to bed.

Mourning came with a sudden burst of light. The camp was illuminated. All around the ground laid lifeless Frandies. Their bodies still positioned as they had collapsed the night before. Some groaned as the light aroused them. Others simply rolled over and covered their faces. It had been a late night of ritualized events that took their toll and now as the bright light beckons their attention they all struggled to get up.

Cornelius was the first to call order, and soon with little protest, the troops were mobile once more, this moment heading towards, Grand's pass and the Regan's estate.

They entered the pass, which was cut out of the green marble like mountain. The sides stood taller than three Vasters. They were cut smooth and clean as if they had been polished by hand. About half way up on each side of the pass was a delicately carved inscription. "Those who enter in peace leave in Harmony. Those, who enter hostile, leave alone."

"WOW! This must have taken centuries to complete." Marypat exclaimed in awe at the sight.

Horatio shook his head. "No. They say it took the Lachlann's fifteen turns to complete the passageway, and two more to do the engraving."

Marypat shook her head, she couldn't believe it. She understood now that a turn was like a day to her and it seemed impossible for something so perfectly cut and carved could have been completed in only seventeen days.

Once through Grand's Pass the group made their way through the Petrified Forest. The trees of the forest stood like stone in the ground and there was no grass or leaves about.

"Stay on the path. We would not want to leave any of you behind." Cornelius called out to the group. Then he laughed as he turned to Marypat and whispered. "Teeny's believe the ground here will turn them to stone but it will not." Then he smiled and turned back to complete his orders. "Let's quicken the pace!"

The Frandies did just as Cornelius ordered and began to run down the path that bent through the Petrified Forest, as quick as they could. They did fear the forest and had no reason to want to stroll through. The quicker they were through it, the better.

The path ended at the edge of a roaring river, which swirled past them like a mighty wave. To the right stood a wooden dock, quite weathered and gray, but reliable just the same. Its sturdy posts lined the river's edge and housed a cabin at the far end. Yet there were no ships of any kind at rest there, only the dock.

"Doctor, May I suggest that Zeta and I fly ahead of the group and announce your coming. The Regan and his family are not very social members and I feel some warning might ease the Regan, to accept your visit." Aden advised.

"Agreed, Aden, you and Zeta take flight and we shall meet you there as soon as we can." Cornelius answered then he turned to his troops. "At ease men, we shall wait for the dingy."

The Frandies dispersed and made camp while Cornelius approached the cabin and knocked. No one was inside so he returned to Marypat.

"We shall have to wait my dear. Satisfaction awaits those who keep faith." He smiled.

Marypat stood on the river's edge and gazed out into the open vastness of its water. It was crystal clear water that rushed by with great force. The bed was bright blue stones of lazurite with tiny glistening flecks of what looked like gold.

She was mesmerized by their shine and reached over to touch it. She bent down and plunged her hand into the cold water. She grabbed up a handful of stones and looked at them. They were so very pretty, she couldn't resist putting her other hand in and taking another handful.

She was so taken by the shiny stone that she hadn't noticed that the river boat, Scorpio, had returned to port. The ship blew its horn, startling Marypat and throwing her off balance. She lost her footing on the soft bank and toppled into the river. Her hands still clutching the stones made it difficult for her to swim, and before long, her struggle to stay afloat was over as she sank like one of the tiny stones she had held so tightly in her fist. Down she went without even a notice from anyone on shore.

Cornelius and the Frandies were busy packing the riverboat, they hadn't seemed her fall. Horatio had gone back into the forest while they were waiting for the ship to arrive to collect some Jay Berries for the trip. Alden and Zeta had flown ahead of the group to announce their arrival on the Regan's island leaving Marypat all alone. There was no one on shore that noticed she was missing, no one to help her.

Poor Marypat was now caught by the powerful curtain so not only was she sinking but she was being pulled farther and farther from shore, even if she could get back to the surface it would be impossible for her to reach the shore where she had once stood.

Her eyes blinked twice as her last bit of air was released from her lungs. She thought it was the end and then suddenly like a vision she saw a most handsome creature approaching her under the water.

His face was trimmed in flowing green hair, his eyes glowed a bright aqua. He smiled at her and then placed a shell over her lips as it covered her mouth he tipped it up causes a huge bubble of air to fill her mouth and lungs. He held the shell over her mouth and with his other hand gently pulled up on her arm. Soon they were moving towards the surface of the water.

As they broke the surface, Marypat took a big breath of air and opened her eyes wide. She turned and looked at the creature holding her, and he looked back at her. Again, he smiled. Then with his powerful tail he maneuvered them through the water and back to the shore where she had once stood. He placed her on shore and then handed her the shell. He winked at her before he turned and swam away.

Marypat stood on the bank of the river-soaking wet. Her brain was in shock; only moments before she was drowning and now, she was a live stand back on shore. She couldn't make sense of it all. All she could do was stand and watched as the creature disappeared beneath the water.

After a few minutes, she realized that her left fist still clenched the stones from the riverbed. So, she looked down at her fist and opened it. The lazurite stones and an Azurite gem glistened in the sunlight. She took out the velvet pouch Horatio had given her and opened it. It dripped droplets of water onto the ground, so she squeezed it once to release the water then she placed the stones in the bag and pulled it closed with its string. She stuffed the velvet pouch back into her pocket. She picked up the shell and started back to the dock.

When she reached the dock, she met up with Horatio. He bounced up to her and hopped onto her shoulder.

"What happened to you, you look like a drenched rat." Horatio said with a giggle.

Marypat turned her head so that she could look at him standing on her shoulder. She smiled at him and said, "I fell into the river."

"What? How did you survive?"

"Some creature saved me!" She announced.

"A creature you say? Did it have a tail and was it as big as you?" He asked.

"Yes, how did you know?" She said quite surprised that he knew of the creature.

"You were saved by a Whimple. You are very lucky one was about and willing to help you."

"Yes, he was very nice to me; I had never seen one of them before! I should like to thank him." She whispered.

She looked back out over the water and wondered if she would ever see him again, she owed him her life. She regretted not having the sense at the time to thank him and she now wished she could see him again so that she could thank him. She wanted him to know how grateful she was to him.

CHAPTER 8

The Regan

"All abroad" The Captain called as he waved his hand in the air from the top deck of the Scorpio. Captain Edmund Clayborne had been born on the sea and was an experienced sailor. He wore a beard that covered his face and neck, leaving only his bright blue eyes and long slender nose exposed. He commanded his ship like a filibuster and expected his workers to take every order without reproach and with respect.

Quickly the dock cleared leaving two sailors to stand ready at either end of the ship. Captain Clayborne then gave the signal and they were underway. The Scorpio turned away from the dock and headed out across the river. The water swirled past her sides and splashed over her bow. All inside her hull remained dry as they pressed on throw the mighty surf.

Marypat sat near a window and gazed out over the water, there was a very fine mist that hovered on the horizon. The mist glistened in the sun light in a magnificent blue, but it also hides from sight all that lied ahead. It was somewhat spooky, not being able to see where they were going, and having to put your trust in someone, you didn't even know. Yet Marypat still sat calmly as she watched out of the window. She was not afraid. She did not worry. Perhaps it was because she felt safe knowing the Whimple was in the water, or that she had already defied death in these waters. Whatever it was she was silent, she was still, and she was at easy traveling on the Scorpio.

After some time, the mist suddenly broke and Marypat could see clearly, what lie ahead of her. To the right was a spectacular waterfall that fell into the lake in which they traveled. Its mighty force was the reason for the great mist and the unending current.

To Marypat's left was an island composed of rich green stone. High atop the stone was a bright green castle. It glowed as if a very bright light sat right behind it, shining out for all to see.

Marypat stood when she saw it. She could not believe how beautiful it was.

"It is quite a sight!" Horatio remarked and Marypat agreed.

Soon the Captain gave the order "All hands ready," and the Scorpio glided into port alongside her sister ship the Virgo. Quickly the hands had tied off the ship and Marypat found herself standing at the base of an amazing staircase.

The stepping was carved out of the clear green crystal base. Each step looked like glass, shiny and polished. A long the stairs grew vines of Pigberries, that were juicy and red. Beyond the vines grew peppermint beans and vanilla buds. Their lovely delicate flowers filled the air with a most delightful sent.

Marypat and the group climbed the stairs and finally came to two large arched doors that adorned the entrance. Cornelius knocked once, and it opened without hesitation.

"Welcome. The Regan awaits you." Called the guard to the group.

Two very well dressed Wardeens escorted the group through the main entrance and into the receiving hall. As they walked, Marypat noticed that the entire castle was carved from the rich green crystal of the island's base. The walls were like glass shimmering in green tones. The floor was clear and reflected her image. The ceiling eliminated as it bounced the glow of the members that past. It was quite a sight and Marypat could not help herself but look all around the magnificent castle.

As they entered the receiving hall, Cornelius took off his hat and all of the Frandies followed doing the same. Then slowing he advanced forward until he stood in the front of the hall facing the Regan. Marypat was more cautious and took a bit longer to reach Cornelius side, but soon she stood beside Cornelius as he began to bow.

"I present Doctor Cornelius McCarthy and his ward Miss Marypat." The announcer beside the Regan proclaimed.

The Regan raised his hand. "'Tis good to see thee, fine doctor. Your Teenys bring word of your troubles and of your deeds."

Then the Regan stood and stepped forward. He was only about four feet tall and to Marypat he looked like a dwarf who had stepped out of one of her favorite novels, the Hobbit. Only this dwarf like Pattie was dressed in a rich blue tunic trimmed in red and accented with diamonds. The tunic draped over red tights that were tied at the knee with black velvet and he wore a golden crown on his head.

"You should be commended for your work in solving the crises between my brethren the Hedlens and the Frandies. Many thanks for your insight." The Regan said.

"I am afraid, Regan, that it was not I who solved the crises, but young Marypat here, who did." Cornelius corrected the Regan and then bowed again.

"Yes, I have heard of this flying Colleen. She has come to the Great Green Isle from the outside world?" He asked with a smile.

"Yes, that is so. Can you help me to get back?" Marypat blurred out.

The Regan went silent; he turned away for a moment and then looked back at her.

"For every cause, there is a purpose." He quoted.

Marypat did not understand and turned to Cornelius for an answer.

"What does he mean?" She whispered.

"What I mean! Is that you are here for a reason, one unknown to you or I. A reason perhaps not urgent, but none-the-less, a reason to being. To that you must wait, look, and study this great kingdom, and you shall discover the reason you have been sent here and then only then will you find a way back to your world." The Regan replied

Marypat was numb; she had hoped that the Regan would help her, that he would have the answer for her to get home. But he had not. Instead, she again was told to study, learn and wait. She did not wish to wait; she wanted to go home now, more than ever. The lack of help made her begin to cry.

"But . . . I did stop the war; couldn't that be why I'm here? Isn't that a good enough reason for me being here?" She asked. Then she stood there waiting for an answer, but she received not a word.

"I want to go home, why someone can't just tell me how to go home?" She cried out loud.

"One can never tell another, how to go home. One must find it on their own." The Regan quoted.

Marypat sobbed as the Regan took his seat once more. Then the Regan whispered these worded that still echoed in Marypat's ears.

"You must solve it yourself, you must put it together, you must put the pieces together, Marypat. . . Put the pieces together . . . Together. . . . . . Together."

The Regan's voice echoed over and over inside Marypat's head.

"Put it together."

Marypat's thoughts began to whirl around her; she became dizzy and like a bolt of lightning from out of the blue, his words shot her thoughts back to the present.

"That's it! I know what I have to do "She shouted to her son, who was sitting in his bed and listening to her story of long ago.

The Purpose

Marypat drove up the steep twisting road that lead to her family's home in the Blue Mountains of Jamaica. Blaze had fallen asleep as they turned past the Blue Mountain Inn and followed the road to the left. It was 10:35 in the evening and it would take approximately a half an hour for them to reach, so Marypat left her son to rest in the back seat while they drove.

It was just about 11:00 then she pulled up to the gate to her family home. She rolled down her window and reached her arm out to the gate controller. She put in the code and the gate opened. The headlights of her car bounced through the front windows of her grandmother's house, awaking the guard who was asleep at his post.

"Miss Marries?" He called out in the dark. "dah yuh?"

"Yes, Henry. It's me." Marypat answered as she opened her car door. "Me mumma hup?"

"Naa missy, shi go-dung long moment! Dat pickey yuhs halright?"

"Yes, he is good. But Henry I need Miss Lora, can yuh ring er."

"Right way." Henry called as he turned back to the house and buzzed the door.

A moment later, Miss Lora called out from the top floor of the house. "Henry, is everything alright?"

"It's Miss Marries, she came to call." he yelled up.

"I'll be right down." Miss Lora replied.

When the door opened, Marypat was standing on the landing holding Blaze in her arms. Miss Lora face looked panicked and she gasped. "Ha."

Marypat read her grandmother's face and was quick to calm her. "No grandmother he is fine, he's just a sleep." With that, Miss Lora opened the door wider and motioned for Marypat to come in.

Marypat stepped inside the house and headed for the couch. She laid down the boy and then turned to her grandmother.

"The crystal, I have to see the crystal." Marypat whispered.

"Oh, course dear. Is something wrong with it?"

"No grandmother! I just have to set it right."

"I don't understand, I thought you were done with It." Her grandmother questioned nervously. "That's what you said when you came back this last time, you promised me you wouldn't go back." Tears filled Miss Lora's eyes. "I can't watch you go again!"

Marypat turned to her grandmother and held her hand and said. "I meant that, Grandmother, believe me. The last trip was enough. My life is here with you and Blaze, everything is alright."

"O.K., well you know where it is." Miss Lora replied nodding her head.

Marypat went quickly to the room where the crystal was kept, she turned on the light, and the room was a glow. Six bright floodlights were set all around the room each one fixed with its beams directed onto the crystal's showcase that set it the center of the room. The clear glass showcase stood as tall as Marypat. Within the case stood a pillar that gently held the Emerald.

Marypat went to the showcase and opened the glass door; she reached inside and grabbed a hold of it. She paused for a moment and glazed at her grandmother. Then she reached into her pocket and removed a piece of cloth. Wrapped in the cloth was the emerald her son had found that mourning at the beach. She unwrapped it and the cloth fell away to the ground.

Marypat stood in the center of the room and held the two crystals in front of her. She looked carefully at each of them and then turned the new one slightly to the left exposing a small notch. She looked up at her grandmother again and smiled.

"It looks right." She whispered.

"What does?" Blaze asked from the doorway as he rubbed his eyes.

"You're awake, good, come and see." Marypat called to her son. "Your crystal is a match to mine."

Blaze looked at the two emeralds his mother held in her hands.

"Wow, so it's true, you really did go to the Green Isle? You saw all those things? It really happened?" Blaze shouted with excitement.

"Yes!" Marypat answered with a smile. "And now I can tell you the end of the story, I know now my purpose, as the Regan had said, it is to put the Green Isle back together. Your emerald and my emerald were at one time one."

With that, Marypat placed the two pieces together. They fit perfectly. Their bases melted back together as one and as it melted together a bright light emerged from the crystals and danced across the room. It glowed a bright piercing green and after a moment, Marypat could hear sounds coming from inside the crystal. It was the sound of rejoicing; it was the sound of joy. The nation had been repaired, it was together once more.

Marypat placed the connected emerald back on its base and then hugged her son.

"Now their world is ok, right mommy."

Marypat nodded "yes"

"Good, now I heard great grandma say that you've been there more than once, can you tell me what else you did there." Blaze said most eager to hear of his mother's adventures to the Green Isles.

"I'm afraid it's late, young man, and that will have to wait till another Time." Marypat said with a grin.

The following morning Blaze slipped into the front room just before the sun rose. The room was dark as he closed the door and then stepped up to the pillar. Standing in front of the crystal's pillar was his mother, Marypat. She stood in the clothing she had been wearing the night before. Her head was down, and her hair hung over her back and it moved when she turned to look at him.

"Morning" She whispered to him. Then she put out her hand to him.

"Morning, mom." He answered, stepping closer to her.

"Did you sleep well?" She asked.

"Ok, I couldn't stop thinking about the emerald." Blaze said with a smile. "It's so cool!"

Marypat just smiled back at her son. She too thought it was pretty cool that they had found the other piece. It was now together, back together the way it was supposed to be. The way it should be.

"Mom, can you tell me more about the Green Isle? I want to hear more." Blaze asked.

"Perhaps! But let's first greet the day."

Marypat stepped over to the wall panel. There were three switches on the wall and she turned all three on at the same time. Suddenly the room was a glow. Six giant floodlights beamed from all around shining directly at the crystal sitting on the pillar.

A brilliant green glow emerged from within and bounced on to the walls of the room.

"Listen!" Marypat whispered as she pulled her son close to her. "Can you hear it?"

Slowly they moved closer to the pillar each with their ear leaning towards the crystals.

"Oh, I hear it.! I hear them." Blaze exploded with excitement.

The members were cheering as they felt their world set right once more. Marypat felt great, she had finally fulfilled her destiny, and she had solved their woes. And now all was well.

"So, you want to hear more do you?" She questioned the boy.

He nodded his head yes and she reconfirmed to him, "There aren't no flashing lights, no great sound effects, it's just a simple tale about your old mother. Are you sure you want to hear it?" she asked.

"Yes, mother, tell me more. Tell what you did next, what did you do, what did you see, and mother how did you ever get home?" He asked with an eager breath.

"Alright then, I shall tell you what happened to me next."

"Do you remember where I left off?"

"Yes, the Regan had told you, that you would have to find the way yourself. I do say, mother, he wasn't very nice." Blaze commented.

"Yes, that's right, he had told me to put the pieces together, and that's what brought us here now, wasn't it?" She smiled remembering how the crystal had glowed so brightly when she put them back together. And how great she felt when she had fulfilled her destiny. She stood for a moment taking it all in, how good it felt but her moment was interrupted by a very impatient young boy.

"Mother! I thought you were going to tell me."

"Oh yes, but first come and sit, for I have much to tell, and many strange and wonderful members to report of. Some you have already heard of and others you shall learn of now but all with their own mystery and magic, all of them helping me in their own little way to get back here, back home." She called back to her son as she left the glowing room and entered the parlor.

There were two huge comfortable couches in the center of the room facing one another. Between them set a large mahogany coffee table with a clay dish setting near the center. The room was dim for it was still quit early, the rosters hadn't even crowed to mark a new day. She climbed in to one of the corners of a couch and curled up her knees. Blaze followed and bounced up beside her.

"Comfortable?" She asked her son.

"Yes." Blaze answered as he sat back and waited for his mother to begin.

A Story

"My heart sank." She began. "I felt as if my life was over, I had put all my hopes into the Regan and his knowledge. That he would be able to tell me how I could get back, back here, back to my world."

Marypat's mind flooded with the memories of that time, she felt the pain and loneliness she felt then as she told her story. . . . . . .

The Regan's once bright castle had suddenly seemed so dark and miserable to her. All she wanted to do was run away. Sanding in the Regan's presents, she turned to Cornelius and burst into tears as the Regan's voice echoed in her ears.

"You must discover your own way; it is the only way. No one can tell you how to get home, only you can do this for yourself." The Regan's voice continued babbling away as he sat in his high back chair that set on a raise beside his wife.

His wife nodded her head in agreement with each passing word. Her simple voice confirming her husband's declaration.

"Yes, yes." She whispered.

Cornelius seemed unmoved by the Regan's unwavering decision not to help. His face unchanged, his manner unconcerned. He stood there beside Marypat and finally after much time of unwavering stillness, bowed and gave his thanks to the Regan for his time and for sharing his vast wisdom.

Marypat was shocked, how could Cornelius thank him? Thank him for what? What had he done? Nothing! Nothing except to tell her again, that she must find her own way home. Thanks for nothing! She shouted in her head as she ran from the Great Hall.

She ran without knowing where she was going, without even thinking. She ran in a daze down a very long hall that turned into a foray. The foray's walls were made of yellow stone and they stood two stories high. There were painting of the Regan and his family hanging on each 1/8th turn of the wall, under which sat crystal pots filled with large yellow flowers.

It was obvious to her that it was not the way they had come in. She stood on the bright yellow tiles in the center of the foray floor and turned around slowly; the scent of the flowers filled the air and was almost over powering. There were more hallways heading out from where she stood like spokes in a wheel. Again, without thinking she choice one and ran off.

This time the hallway ended at a great green glass door. She pushed through the door. It swung open easily. She run through it and stepped on to a stone pathway. The pathway looked old and unused. There were weeds growing between the stones and on either side of the path growing wildly were pigberries and vanilla buds. They were not as manicure as the plants had been in the entrance to the grand castle. No these were untidy and left to their own discourse. Yet there was stillroom for her to pass between the wild plants. Staying on the path she slowly made her way along carefully ducking under a large branch now and again. The path twisted and turned through the dense bushes of the forest and ending at the river's edge.

Marypat stopped and stared at the water, she looked out at its vastness and watched the untamed water rush from the cliff top and crash into the surf below. The thundering wake created a sparking mist, which hovered in the air around her. It was cool and refreshing and it somehow calmed her down. She took a deep breath and sat down on a stone that laid beside the river's edge. Although now a bit calmer, she still was torn inside. She wanted to go home, oh how she missed her Grandmother. She began to sob again; tears filled her eyes and collected until slowly a large tear fell from her eye and landed in the river. Instantly the tear froze and formed a diamond. It sank in water undetected by Marypat.

Below her in the water, tiny bubbles began to raise to the surface. These bubbles caught Marypat's attention and she sat astounded by them. Soon they dispelled and there in the water appeared the face of the creature that had helped her earlier that day. His green hair flowed around his face, moving with the ripples of the water. Effortlessly he rose up through the water until his face broke the surface and he faced Marypat, nearly nose to nose.

Marypat jumped back and gulped. Where had he come from, how did he know she was here at this moment? She had so much she wanted to ask but was unable to speak.

"Good morrow, fare lassie!" The creature spoke almost in a lullaby. His voice was like that of an angle, smoothly, gentle and yet strong.

"Good morrow to you, creature of the water." Marypat stuttered.

"I be, Atlas." He proclaimed with a slight bow to his head. "How might you be named?"

Marypat was dumbstruck for the moment as she tried to remember who she was. It was as if the mist from the waterfall had drained her mind and she was left struggling to regain herself.

"Take moment, lassie." The creature whispered to her as he touched her softly on her knee. Instantly the fog was lifted from her mind and she was able to think once more.

"The mist of the Froymin can fill one's mind if one has not the will. Pray tell me, lassie, thou name."

"Marypat and I was. . . I mean I want to. . Thank you for saving me today!" She blurted out.

"'Tis not to mention, for I am on watch for just such an event. My only despair is reason for one so bright to be in such sorrow. Such deep sorrow that her sadness could break the soothing mist of the Froymin." He said softly.

"Do what, what did I do?" She said with a sniffle.

"The mist of Froymin is a magical vapor of calm. It has the power to fill the mind and subside all pain and sorrow, yet you young Marypat have the deepest of sorrow, sorrow so deep your tears have frozen in its waters. I have never seen such a deep sorrow." Atlas mentioned.

"Yes, I am very sad indeed." Marypat admitted with tears in her eyes.

"Sad? Why is one so sad?" He asked.

Marypat could hardly speak for just as he asked the sadness stuck her again and tears filled her eyes once more.

"I. . . . I. . . want. . .. I want to go home, and no one can tell me how to get there." She stammered.

"No help was the Regan?" Atlas questioned.

"No. He only told me that one cannot tell another the way home, one must find it on their own." She sobbed.

"He is very wise." Atlas nodded.

"Wise? You call that wise, how is that to help me?" She continued to cry.

"It was not meant to help you, Mary, but to remind you, we all must follow our own path no one should disrupt another's way. My dear lassie your path is yours to take, you must have your hand in it, YOU must be in control. There are many worries in each one's life, one cannot prevent them, but one can be willing to take them on, reveal in them, and surpass them. It is your path. Make it what you will. Take in only pain and sadness, or move above it, take hold of it and find your way home."

His words were clear and sure, they reached into her heart and placed within it a seed of hope and for the first time she smiled.

"Yes, you are right. I had not thought about it that way."

"What will Mary do from this turn? Will ye drown or will ye swim?"

With great thought, Marypat sat up. This was a turning point for her, a moment that would decide her fate. She chose her words carefully, and then she spoke.

"I shall step up to my path and I shall follow it where ever it leads me."

"All well, then I shall give you something to help you keep your mind on your route." He smiled and then raised his hand out of the water. He held his palm out to her and in the center of his hand was a huge tear shaped diamond. He offered it to her.

"Oh no, I cannot take that, it is too beautiful!"

"But you must, it is yours." He whispered as he slowly slid back into the water. "Good travels, fare lassie, till our paths meet again." With that, he disappeared below the surface and was gone from her sight.

She watched from the river's edge until Atlas was out of sight, then she stood and ran back to join the others.

A Room

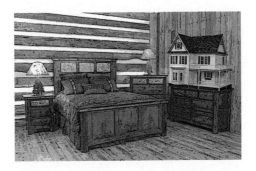

Marypat had taken a new look at her situation. Atlas had given her an opportunity to regain herself, her control, her being. What she did with it was her choice.

When she reached, back with the others Zeta and Aden were bidding their farewell to Cornelius and Horatio.

"Where are you going?" Marypat asked in disbelief. She was shocked that Zeta was leaving her. Not because Zeta owed it to her to stay, but because Marypat felt Zeta was one of her only friends here and now knowing she had to stay much longer then she wanted too, she would at least have Zeta's friendship to help her through. At least that was what she had hoped but now even that small bit of hopefulness was washed from Marypat's courage to continue.

"The Regan has offered us positions at his side. Zeta as his translator and I as his Primer" Aden answered with an air of superiority.

"Can you imagine Marypat all my life I have hoped for such a placement, a chance to experience the Whole and now thanks to you, my dream has come true?" Zeta asked Marypat as she fluttered merrily in fount of Marypat's eye.

Marypat again felt a want to selfishly cry, but Zeta's words held her warmly and she realized she was being completely self-centered. Sad that she was loosening a friend Marypat still gladly smiled at Zeta.

"Congratulations, to you both. That is awesome!!" Marypat announced with as much joy as she could come forth with, for she was truly happy for Zeta seeing her dream come true.

"Your friendship has been and will be forever cherished by me. Take not to sadness but to glee, hold this and call 'tis thee ever need me." Zeta whispered in Marypat's ear as she handed Marypat a tiny Blue topaz stone.

The tiny Blue crystal touched with yellow glistened in Marypat's hand. It was the same color of the flowers that grew around the border of the forest where Marypat had first met Zeta. Marypat smiled at her friend. I shall keep it for always and remember, you, my dearest friend.

The next few days were uneventful as the group made their way back to Cornelius's cottage at the edge of the forest. A long the way Marypat had taken more interest in the members she met. Somehow now their existence was more absorbing, more exciting. Marypat did all she could to learn about each and every one of them.

When they returned to Cornelius's cabin the Frandies disappeared into the woodwork leaving Marypat, Horatio and Cornelius alone. The first night back at the cabin was like starting a new for Marypat. She was excited and questioned everything she saw.

"It will all come in turn, my dear." Laughed Cornelius.

"You can't learn it all in one eve." Added Horatio, as he hopped up to her shoulder.

"We shall start in the morrow, you may look over my books, but until then, . .Hmm . . . . Where shall we put you? An eve on the couch will do for now but it will not do for long. . . . I know. . yes . . . don't you worry yourself, sleep here tonight and I shall take care of it in the morrow." With that Cornelius disappeared into his bedroom and was not heard from again until early the next morning, when Marypat awoke to the sound of his voice outside shouting orders.

"Take it out, the window. . . No. . no. . .the window. . . yes I want a door, but put it where the window is now!!!!" Cornelius shouted.

A few minutes later, he stumbled through the front door with a short man following him, huffing as he went. Marypat and Horatio watched from the couch peeking around its arm.

"The creature can't hear a bloody thing, why is he at his post, can't you find one of you who can take an order without me having to shout, oh for good ness sake." Cornelius rambled.

"My humble apologies Good Doctor, my father is very old and has run our business for many passes. I am afraid it is very hard for him to let it go. I will see to it that your addition is carried out to the letter." The short little man mumbled as he bowed excessively." But I must urge you to bring your concerns to me personally."

"Very well, Harry.... tea then?" Cornelius asked as he poured out a cup of hot water. The short fellow nodded and the two sat down to tea.

"Excuse me. Would there be enough for me and Horatio?" Marypat whispered from the couch.

"Heaven yes, dear, come forth and meet my friend Harry, he is in charge of building your room." Cornelius proclaimed.

"My what?" Marypat asked in astonishment.

"Why we can't have you sleeping on my couch all eve, every eve. Where will I throw my parties late into the break, where will I rest in the evenings to read and relax, no we can't have you sleeping on my couch any longer, it is just not right." He announced waving his hand at her. "You shall have your own room, where I can send you to bed when you get on my nerves. A place where you can keep all your things, and I won't have to look at them anymore." He said pointing at her backpack.

Marypat thought to herself, "*I don't have that many things!*"

"Now come have your tea, there is work to be done."

Marypat approached the dinette and sat beside the little man, who now had finished his tea. He was dresses in a green work suit, complete with tie and cap. There were pockets on the breast on the suit and on the legs. Around his waist hung a tool belt filled with strange metal objects. His eyes were green, and his skin was slightly pink while his hair was dark brown. He worn it long in the back pulled into a braid. When he finally stood he was the same height as Marypat. They stood eye to eye for a moment and then he was off.

"Back to work, work every sweep, and never sleep, 'tis happy one will keep!" Henry said in a rhyme.

Marypat watched the man until he was out the door.

"He is a Lachlann. They live to work, building, and hammer. Best at wood but if it's back braking, they are good at it." Cornelius explained.

"And work fast too." Horatio said hopped onto the table to have his tea.

"That's right, Horatio, they should finish your room by the morrow, but I told them that they couldn't work in the eve. I need my sleep, so it won't be complete till the turn after. There isn't a problem with that is there?"

Marypat nodded her head no. That was alright with her, who could expect it sooner? She thought. After all, Cornelius was doing so much for her when he didn't even have too. He owed her nothing and it surprised her at how much he was willing to do, and had done for her, a person he didn't even know. Worst of all over the past week he had taken her in to his care as if she had always been there and SHE hadn't even thanked him.

"Cornelius, sir, I want to tell you how much I appreciate what you are doing for me. I don't know what I would have done without you, or what I will do, I mean I don't want to make trouble . . ."

"Oh, now stop that right now, no need, no need to go on like that. You are no trouble, no trouble at all. You belong here with me; I believe that is why they brought you to me. Together we will find a way home for you, which I promise and once you are back, you will pay me back by keeping the crystal safe as I was meant to and failed." He lowered his head.

Marypat saw the agony in Cornelius face and realized why he was so helpful to her; he needed her as much as she need him. Together they could make right both of their paths. She stepped over to his side and hugged him, he hugged her back.

"Together we shall see this through." Cornelius said with confidence. Then he stepped over to the shelves where he stored all of his research. He pulled out a long thick compellation, a large volume, and a small thin binder. He brought them back to the table. Once there he set them down beside Marypat.

"So, for your part in all this, you better get started with your studying. You may begin with these three books; two of them have much of my own research in them. They are not professional, as you may be accustoming to. I have had to do with only my own abilities to complete them, yet still they should be some help to you. Remember Marypat they are still working in progress and the other is an educational publication for Kathrieens and Maurieens."

He left the books with her and she looked at the first one, *The Green Isle, Patrimony Edition of Incantation's and Spells. Complied by Nnon Frothper the 2ⁿᵈ and Ailbhe Urson.*

"How interesting." She thought turning the book so that Horatio could also see. Horatio waved it away with a non-interested motion as he sipped his tea.

"pee ome hen li un jay." She whispered with a giggle.

"Just watch what you repeat from that book, you might find yourself in trouble. Good thing that phase is harmless. I wouldn't say anything else out loud, if I were you!" Horatio barked

"OK." She said thumbing through less eagerly. Then she noticed the verse the Lachlann had said. *"Work every sweep and never sleep 'tis happy one will keep."* She found it under verses of the Ells. She also found. *"One can never tell another how to get home, one must find it on their own."* The words from the Regan.

How strange it was to see the quotes in the book. She put the book aside and picked up the large compellation, it said on the leather cover, Book of Nations, by Dr. C. McCarthy. The paper inside was thick parchment and on each page was a name on a group, a detailed drawing and description. The first was a Pixie, also known as a Flower Sprite. Marypat had met two of them when she first arrived on the Isle, Rose and Daisy. She read about the Flower Sprite and then moved on until she reached the members group called a Maurieen.

The heading was written in large letters, MAURIEEN daughter of Maurieen. *What is a Maurieen?* She thought, she had never met one or seen one that she knew of and there was nothing much on the paper except for a very light penciled sketch of a women covered in a cape. It wasn't colored in as the other pages had been. There was no description or information. It seemed the book was incomplete just as Cornelius had mentioned. As she continued to flip, the pages there were some that were completely blank except for the names, Sherideen, Ubil, Torideen, Whimple, and Gulden. On the last page the Loralac was complete and full, but why weren't the other pages? Why hadn't he completed his research? She wondered.

Before she could muster up her willpower to ask, there was a strange noise outside. Marypat ran outside to find a huge crane moving into place. A moment later, it had crashed into the house, taking out the window. Instantly several Lachlann's jumped into the mess and began scurrying about until there wasn't a speck of debris left.

Marypat found the Lachlann's amazing to watch. She could not believe their speed and accuracy. She spent the rest of the turn watching them, while tiger purred at her feet and Horatio bounded and laughed playing pranks on the Lachlann's.

When darkness fell on the cabin, the Lachlann's had completed the floor, put in a door where the window once was, put on the roof and the frame of the new room.

Cornelius was pleased with their achievement but still he ran around shouting. "Go home, go home, see you in the marrow, now go home."

He chased them all away and then invited Marypat inside for a quite meal.

"Doc. McCarthy, I know you said the books you gave me were works in progress but why haven't you completed them?" She asked before sipping her soup.

"Haven't had moment I suppose, to be honest I got side tracked with the war and everything, now that it is over I imagine I could get back to work right away." He spoke crunching on a piece of bread.

Marypat could barely understand him.

"Perhaps that's what we should do then . . . yes! . . . and it just might help you at the same stretch . . . how does that sound?"

A bit lost, Marypat had a little idea of what she was agreeing to as she nodded her head, yes.

"Good then, we shall leave in a fort night." He declared.

"To where?" She asked.

"Good question, perhaps we should consider this more closely . . . where did I leave off?"

"Maurieens, it has a drawing, but nothing else." She answered.

"Well then that's where we start!" Making another declaration, he slammed his fist on the table. "Now ask me no more as I am weak from all this babble, I shall see you in the marrow!"

Then he stood and went to his bed.

The morning came with a slam and jilt. Marypat jumped from the couch and ran to the door. She could see the same team of Lachlann's working busily to put up the walls. One of the Lachlann's spied her as she peeked from the door and suddenly she was surrounded by six tiny Lachlann Lassies, each holding swatches of cloth in their hands.

"You must choose, yes choose. Need to know, just what one likes." They cheered and hopped.

"Many colors, many choices, you can choose. Want me to help?" Asked one of the Lachlann Lassies.

Marypat was over whelmed, they each wanted her to choose something, but she didn't know what she was choosing the cloth for. Confused and wanting of the Lassies Lachlanns to leave her alone Marypat shouted. "I like yellow."

With that the group of Lachlann Lassies took a step back as if they were processing the information and then in unison as if planned, they exclaimed.

"Yellow, good choice, yellow is just perfect, yes good choice." With that, they disappeared into the forest without another sound leaving Marypat all alone with Tiger.

She gave him a scratch and a saucer of milk. Then they sat and watched the Lachlanns work another turn. When darkness fell again, Cornelius chased them away and it was quiet once more.

The next morning the final wall was to go up but before it did there was a parade of fabrics that passed by and entered the room. When all had passed, two Lachlanns hammed it shout. A few moments later Marypat was surrounded again this time, she was dragged to her new room's door and told to open it.

She did and inside was like a dream. Bright yellow curtains on the windows flowed onto a bright yellow woolen rug. On which set a full-size redwood bed covered in an overstuffed yellow comforter and yellow flower printed pillows. Beside it was a nightstand made out of the same red wood and a dresser that was filled with yellow dresses, shirts and pants. There was even a little house made to look like Cornelius cabin, it was just the right size for Horatio. Tears came to Marypat's eyes as she tried to take it all in.

"You don't like!" Stated one of the Lachlanns who was standing beside the door.

"Oh, no, I do like, I like it very much, thank you." She whispered.

It was the sweetest thing she had ever seen. Marypat was so touched by their work that she could barely contain herself.

"Thank-you. Thank-you all so very much." Then she turned to Cornelius and hugged him. The old man blushed three shades of red before he announced.

"No need for all that, come on now we must prepare the goat. We party tonight!"

And so, it went, the Lachlanns, the Frandies, Marypat, Horatio, Cornelius and even the Loralacs came to celebrate the new addition to Cornelius home. Goat blood was smeared over each window and at each corner, blood was spilled. A blessing was said by Gillian and the party began. It went late into the eve, so late that Marypat was grateful for her nice new room where she could get away, find quiet and sleep.

Marypat loved her new room it was comfortable and pretty. It was bright and cheery. Making it a place, she enjoyed spending time in.

Horatio enjoyed his miniature home just as much and they had many sweeps together just talking and playing in her room.

But if they weren't in her room they were off to the Flower River, to splash in her majestic clear water, play in her quartz sided caves with their opal veins, dive into her deep caverns or warm themselves on her glistening moss filled boulders.

The flower River was so named for the moss quarts that made up her bed. Each boulder was clear crystallized quartz surrounding a portion of soil with a growth of vegetation. Each boulder was different from the next. Some had beautiful flowers in them that were still as wondrous as they had been when they were growing wild on the hillside. Still in a phase of forever beautiful, forever young, never to grow old wither and die.

The river was unlike any place Marypat had ever been. The riverbed was crystal clear and the colorful flowers showed through to the surface providing a colorful spectacle. In addition to the colorful flowers caught in the quartz there were opal stones of brilliant red and green fire scattered about adding to the immense beauty.

Marypat loved it here and she wanted to always remember her precious time here so she took an opal from the water. A brilliant red flamed opal and put it in the velvet sack with her other stones. She would take these stones home with her when she went so she could always have a part of this world with her. That was if she ever made it home.

She wanted so much to go home. She knew that she would spend her whole life here if she didn't work to find her way home. So, she read Cornelius books every evening, studying the spells and phases, reading through the book of nations, and inquiring information from Cornelius himself. It was not long before she had memorized most of the spell book and was able to recite the members of nations with ease.

But whatever it was she needed to learn in order for her to get home, she did not find it in these books. She needed to look elsewhere, and she pressed Cornelius to arrange a journey to study the Maurieen.

"When can we leave; I am anxious to get started." She said to Cornelius one night a dinner.

"The trip to Great town will take us 3 turns, there is still much I need to arrange."

He said as he shoved a spoon full of stew into his mouth. "Morrow after next could be possible if all goes well."

That evening Horatio and Marypat packed their thing into her backpack and talked about the trip to Great Town.

"Great Town is a wonderful town. There's no other place in the isle like Great Town. The streets are paved in gold." Horatio said excitedly.

"You've been?" Marypat asked quite curiously.

"No, but a cousin of mine once went there, and he told me all about it." Horatio bragged "Great town sits like a vision on the shores of the lake of whispers. The buildings are carved from stone and are painted brightly. They are as tall as the eye can see, with roof tops that stretch like daggers into the mystical green sky."

Marypat laid back and thought about how wonderful it must be. She could hardly wait to see it for herself. In her mind, she pictured the vision of Great Town as Horatio continued his description.

"More grand then the Regan's castle, more spectacular than the rainbows of Doodle Falls. Great Town is a marvel, a delight for the eye." Horatio went on as if he was dreaming.

Marypat could only imagine how it must look and inquired about the falls. She had been to the Regan's castle and had seen for herself it's magnificent beauty, but she had not heard of Doodle Falls and had no way to judge its spectacular form.

"Horatio, what is Doodle Falls?" She asked him as she laid on her bed and imagined the sight.

"You've never seen Doodle Falls? Why I can't believe that! It's not far from here, ya know, we could go there one turn. It is a most unusual water fall indeed; there is no other in all the isles." He said standing with his hands on his hips.

"On either side of the falls flows a steady stream of crystal clear water, but when it reaches the floor, the center of the water is propelled straight up into the air. From the end of it a rainbow stretches beyond one's eye. The Feldens have claim to it and use it to catch sunbeams, the sun beams they spin into gold. It is a remarkable sight." He explained as he passed across the small patio of his tiny house.

"I should like to go there! Perhaps when we return from Great Town." She yawned.

"That will be the plan, dear Mary, we shall set out for Doodle Falls on our return from Great Town." Horatio declared. "Now off to sleep you sweet one and I shall see you in the marrow."

An Adventure

The next morning Marypat rose to find Cornelius giving orders to his troops. Marypat thought for a moment that perhaps the war was back on and they wouldn't be able to travel to Great Town a planned. But as it was Cornelius was not preparing for war but preparing to make to trek after all.

"There is much to do my dear, provisions and such, make ready yourself as we leave at wake of the marrow." He proclaimed stomping his foot in the mud as he marched off looking for the lieutenant.

Marypat turned to Horatio in surprise. "Did you hear? We leave tomorrow!"

"Then make ready yourself dear." Horatio joked as he marched on the ground making fun of Cornelius.

Marypat laughed out loud at the sight. But the fun soon ended as Cornelius spotted the spectacle and terminated it with a single. "Attention!"

Horatio and Marypat ran off heading for the forest, laughing all the way.

Before long they came upon Tiger who was just about to pounce on his breakfast, a nice juice purple Lofty Zort. He had positioned himself just right and with a single jump, he grabbed the Zort in his teeth and flung his head side to side as if he were fighting with it. Then he chewed it for a moment before swallowing it, gulp.

Horatio screamed at the sight in pure terror. He jumped to highest tree breach possible and stood motionless, while Marypat approached the Grundle.

"Good morrow to you, Tiger. Want a scratch, do you?" She asked.

Tiger responded with a gentle purr as she slipped her fingers into the thick fur around his neck. She scratched him just the way he liked it, right behind his ears while she spoke to him about the trip to Great Town.

"You should come with us; it will be an adventure to remember!" She said to him as he purred loudly. Tiger followed her back to the house for his milk and stayed the night on her doorstep.

The following morning broke early and it didn't take them long to get under way. Fifty Frandies lead the march caring their bundles as well as driving two cattle carts full of provisions, that were pulled by two wee-colts. Each solid specimen was well trained for such a journey. The wee-colts stood knee high to Marypat and she found them to be an unusual breed. They were very similar to a pony, yet these had a much stronger hind leg, more like a Clydesdale. They had gentle faces and were easy tempered. It took two Frandies to steer them but because of their mild manner, they moved with simple gestures.

Behind the Frandies followed Cornelius and Marypat with Tiger. Horatio still unsettled by the Coose, Tiger coming with them he bummed a ride on one of the cattle carts.

The course was set and off they went, following the Flower River through the forest to Grassy Point then on to Bolder Town where they had planned to camp for the eve. The trek was easy, and time passed quickly, before they knew it they were pulling into Bolder Town just as the darkness fell.

Boulder Town was not really a town at all. It was only a run-down shack on the side of the river. The Shack was a rickety structure that lend slightly to one side. Its total height was about twelve common hands in height and seemed only large enough for one large member to stand in. And yet this was Bolder Town there first stop on their way to Great Town.

The Frandies spread out and pitched their tents all along the grass where the shack sat. Almost instantly they had fires stared and food being cooked.

"Where is our tent?" Marypat asked curiously, as she looked around. Normally the Frandies put up Cornelius tent first and it was easy to spot because it was much larger than the rest but this eve they had not put it up and Marypat grew concerned at where she was to spend the night.

"Oh, we are not sleeping in my tent tonight I have made reservations at the shack." Cornelius said with a smile.

"The shack? But there is hardly room in there for one of us let alone both of us." Marypat said in shock.

Cornelius shook his head and replied. "I'm sure there will be plenty of room, you'll see." Then he hurried away calling over his shoulder. "Just wait for me here a moment and then we'll go get checked in."

Marypat looked down at Tiger and wobbled her head. "Sometimes Tiger I think he's nuts!" Then she screeched Tigers chin and decided to find Horatio.

Marypat found Horatio tending to the wee-colts.

"How was your ride?" She asked Horatio.

"Splendid, wish I could always travel this way. These wee -colts are such fascinating creatures, and can they sing, I tell you they are wonderful." Horatio said with a grin. Then he looked up a Marypat and saw something in her eyes.

"What's the matter with you, did you have a bad ride?"

"No!" She said shaking her head. "It's just that Cornelius didn't bring our tents and we have to stay in the shack. . ."

"The shack, really! Oh, say I can come. Please! I've never been to the shack and I hear it is amazing." Horatio begged.

"But it's just a shack!" Marypat said waving her hand. She couldn't understand why he was so excited to stay in a shack.

"Please!!" He begged her again.

"Sure, why not." She answered. Why not if there was enough room for herself and Cornelius in that little shack then there must be enough room for a Jinxie.

"Yes! I'm staying at the shack." He jumped up and cried with delight.

"Well then come on, we better find Cornelius, we haven't checked in yet." She said shaking her head again. *They are all just crazy! Wanting to sleep in a shack."* She thought to herself.

Marypat caught up to Cornelius as he was just preparing to enter the shack.

"There you are dear, are you ready?" He asked.

"Yes, Cornelius, may Horatio stay with us?" She asked.

"No point leaving him out here with Tiger, bring him along." He said in his usual tone then he turned to the left and stepped into the old sack. It was dark inside and Marypat was quick to pull Horatio up into her hand so that she could see around, while Cornelius didn't seem to have any trouble finding his way to the back of the run-down shack.

In the back of the tiny enclosure was a very tiny desk, on the desk was a bell. Cornelius rang the bell once and instantly the room was a glow with tiny Etains flying all about. Another moment pasted before a short bearded Felden stepped up to the desk and bowed to Cornelius.

Marypat's chin fell as she watched the little Felden as he began to speak.

"Welcome Sir! I'm a Carrick. Will yer be staying with us this evening?" He said with a bit of an Irish accent

"Yes! We have reservations, McCarthy."

"Oh, yes, very good." Carrick said as he glanced down the list in front of him. "Here we are. That was for a riverside view?"

"Yes."

"Very good, then. Chuck, Chad you're up!"

A few moments later Chunk and Chad appeared out of the darkness, wearing little red informs with matching bell caps. They were the same size as Carrick behind the desk, but they were not bearded, instead they were clean-shaven.

"Take their things to room 307, on the double!" Carrick said in a commanding voice. Then he turned back to Cornelius and said. "Please enjoy your stay with us, Cornelius, if there is anything else I can do for you please call me, I am at your service."

"Thank you, Carrick." Cornelius answered with a slight bow.

Instantly Carrick disappeared and Cornelius, Horatio, and Marypat left standing with Chuck and Chad.

"This way please!" Chad said stepping into the farthest corner of the shack.

"All the way in." Commanded Chuck from behind pushing Marypat until she was squashed into the very corner.

Marypat looked worried as the small man pushed even harder on her thigh. What was he doing, couldn't he see that she couldn't get any smaller or move in any tighter, but then suddenly the floor began to move, and they were traveling downward at an amazing speed. Then just as suddenly as they began, they stopped.

"Right this way, right this way." Chuck ordered them. He leaded them down a dark musty hall that seemed to have been carved out of the soil. The walls were rich, dark, and damp, but that didn't seem to be any concern for any of them so Marypat just followed as she was instructed.

"107, 207, 307, here we are." Shouted Chuck as he took out the key and opened the door.

Chuck ran inside and set down Cornelius bag then he ran to the far side of the room and pulled back the excessively long drape that hung the full distance of the room. Marypat entered the room and stood and watched as Chuck struggled with the fabric, before long he had succeeded in revealing the riverside view the doc had requested.

Marypat stood amazed. In front of her was a massive wall of Moss Quartz, beyond the quartz flowed the Flower River. The same Flower River that Horatio and she had swam in many times, only this section of the river was much deeper and wider. She could see the force of the river as it bubbled by the enormous window of Quartzes. The water was crystal clear and brilliant and as it moved it reflected off the flowers suspended in the quartz and caused a flicker of light and shadow all around her.

"Isn't in splendid?" Marypat asked Horatio, who had just emerged from her pocket and who had just gotten his first glance at the sight.

"Yes!" he whispered most in awe.

"Two rooms, two rooms." Called Chuck. "This way."

Chuck showed Cornelius to his room while Chad grabbed Marypat's arm and urged her into the second. This room also had a view of the river on the far wall, but the bottom half of the wall was blocked by what looked like two large, blue lazurite boulders captured by a glass flack, keeping them from entering the room. The other walls and the floor of the room seemed to have been carved out of soil just like the hallway. In the center of the room, hanging from the ceiling was a single framed four-posted bed. It's four posters were long and stretched upwards through the ceiling. Holding the bed midair, its legs were three common hands off the floor. The nightstand and chest of draws all matched the bed, with none of their legs touching the ground.

Marypat found the design quite peculiar and yet Chad made no reference to its oddness. He merely continued to shove her through the room until he had showed her around. Then he bowed to her and placed out his hand.

Not aware of what he wanted Marypat stared at his chubby hand. It was a slight green color but what caught her eye was the magnificent orange gem that glowed in his palm.

Marypat reached forward to touch it, it was so beautiful. Only Chad didn't find her curiosity very innocent at all and instead he was insulted.

"What do you want to do, steal me luck, do ya! Well, I won't have no luck stealer in my mist, no sir." He hurried back away from her and shook his hands in front of himself as he shouted at her. "Steal me luck from me very own palm. Evil will take ye, never leave ye calm." Then he turned and ran out of the door, only to run into Cornelius and Chuck who had heard every word Chad had shouted.

"What happen here?" Cornelius asked with his arms folded across his chest.

"She was trying to steal me luck, she was." Chad shouted heatedly at Cornelius.

"I was not. He held his hand out to me, I thought he was offering me the gem, I had no idea it was his luck. Besides, if I wasn't meant to touch it, why was he offering it to me?" Marypat answered.

Cornelius turned to Chad and apologized. "Dear sir, please excuse my charge she has no knowledge of our members, and I assure you she had no intention of stealing your luck, on the contrary she was only curious about your most radiant gem, which I must add is one of the very largest and unusual shades of Felden gems I have ever had the honor of viewing. Please take this." Cornelius placed a gold coin in his hand. "And our most humble apologies for any discomfort we have caused you, dear sir."

Chad accepted the gold and then turned to Marypat with a curious look as if he was weighing in his mind, what Cornelius had told him. Then he nodded his head and headed out the door with Chuck on his heels.

Cornelius closed the door and then turned to Marypat.

"He was looking for a tip, my dear, here take this for the future." Cornelius said in a gentle and understanding tone as he handed her a few silver Verts with the impression of a hammer and nail pressed into the center of their silver blob.

"We have dinner reservation in two sweeps at The Blarney Stone, down in the Main Town. I'm going to take a rest, if you decide to venture out in to the town, be sure to take Horatio with you; he may help you avoid another incident." Then he smiled softly." I'll meet you in the main lobby."

Cornelius turned away from her and entered his room, closing the door behind him.

"Did he say there was a Main Town?" Marypat asked in astonishment. How could there be a whole town under here, it seemed a bit too much for her to comprehend but then on the other hand she was after all underground in a hotel room with a view of the Flower River. Anything was possible. And if it did exist she wasn't going to miss it, no sir.

She looked down at Horatio and they both smiled. "To town!" They cheered and out the door they went.

The Town

Back into the strange lift that had brought them to their room, Marypat asked Horatio how he thought it might work.

"Perhaps there's a button or something." He said looking around.

"But how will we know we are on the main floor even if we get it to work?" She asked as she now thought she should wait for Cornelius. She had not thought that it would be so difficult to find the main floor and get to the town.

But before she could step away, the lift started to move again. They traveled downward for a few moments and then stopped. Marypat stepped off the lift and searched the vast dark room they were now in. She picked up Horatio and put him on her hand, his inner light lit enough of the room so that Marypat could see her way forward. Soon she noticed in the distance a light in front of her, so she headed towards it. Surprisingly it was the lobby.

Huge circular pillars stretched the full height of the room. And they seemed to be cut from the same green marble that the Loralacs home was carved from. The floor on the other hand was white and there seemed to be small glowing cracks running through it. The glow from the floor lit the room so much so Marypat didn't need Horatio's light any more to see, so she placed him on her shoulder.

Once in the main lobby of the Shack Hotel it took Marypat only a moment to find her way out into the Main Town. Both her and Horatio were excited to step out of the Hotel's lobby into the openness of the underground town.

The town lay out before them; huge stone building carved out of the stone that formed the base in which the Great Isle laid within. There were Cottages and shops each with their very own distinct style and design.

The pair walked through the town, lit by thousands of tiny Etains and Laddies that flew around the vast soil celling of the town and hovered among the tree trunks that protruded through the town. It was magical.

"Marypat! Loan me a Vert, would ya, I'll pay ya right back." Horatio called.

Without even thinking Marypat handed Horatio one silver Vert and he bounced off her shoulder into the crowd.

Marypat tried to follow but the crowd seemed to be moving at a snail's pace, while Horatio bounced over them with ease and went off into an establishment called "The Lucky Wager."

After a while, the crowd dissolved and Marypat was finally able to follow him. The name, Lucky Wager, made her wonder a bit, "Did Horatio come in here to gamble?"

There was a Loralac at the door, who gave her the once over with his eye, before allowing her to enter.

Inside she found row upon row of what seemed to be slot machines. Dimly lit except for the member's inner light and the fluorescent light coming from the machines. Marypat found the Lucky Wager to be a dismal place there was garbage on the floor, an unpleasant scent, and members passed out on stools.

"This place is a Casino?" She said aloud to which she was immediately "SHHHHED"

She walked down one row and up the next looking for Horatio. She saw many Small members intensively working their machines, but she wasn't sure whether they were Lachlanns, Hedlens or Feldens, to her they all looked the same.

They were dressed so strangely in their bright colored pants and matching jackets. Each of them stood only to Marypat's shoulders, like little children, but she could see they were adults. She was fascinated by them and stopped to watch one until he noticed her watching and shoed her away.

"I won't let you get me luck, ya nasty Kathrie, now run from me, or I'll turn ya to stone." Shouted a fat little green member with pointed up ears.

Quickly Marypat turned away and started back, looking for Horatio.

She found him finally as she came around a corner. But to her dismay he was being held by the throat by a short member that kept calling him a theft. Poor Horatio, his legs dangled in the air, his voice unable to sound, all he could do was wiggle and squirm in his own defense.

"Unhand him!" Marypat shouted at the member. "Let him go."

"I'll do nothing of the sort, he is a theft, he stole my gold. Jinxie's they're all the same. Always trying to Steal a Feldens gold. For shame you!" The small Felden shouted causing a seen.

"I did nothing of the sort, I put in my Vert, and you were nowhere near this machine when I pulled the lever." Horatio barked.

But this only made the Felden madder. He pulled out what looked like a butter knife and held it to Horatio's throat.

"Cut out ye gizzard I will!" The Felden shouted but before he could act on his threat, he was pulled into the air with a great wave.

To Marypat's delight the Loralac that had been at the door, had heard the commotion, and arrived on the scene just in time.

The Loralac held the Felden by the ear and pulled him up so he could speak to him eye to eye.

"Drop the Jinxie, Forbes Flynn. I told you if you cause any trouble I'd throw you out on your ear." The Loralac said without emotion and the Felden did as he was told.

Horatio bounce off the ground and landed in the coin tray of the machine. Quickly he grabbed at the Verts in the tray and tried desperately to shove them into his pocket.

The Loralac grinned at the sight of a tinny Jinxie trying to carry four Verts at once.

The Verts were bigger then Horatio and he soon fell over from their weight.

"Here. This might help." Laughed the Loralac.

The Loralac flung down a blue velvet sack with the Lucky Wager logo on it. Then he turned and walked to the front door of the establishment, where he tossed Forbes out the door and on his ear.

Horatio didn't seem the least bit phased by what had transpired his only concern was his coins. Marypat watched as he slipped every last Vert into the velvet bag until the bag stood taller than him.

"Ready?" He asked her with a big grin on his face. He was holding the ties to the bag in his hands and he flipped them around as if he was going to haul the bag himself on his back. But as he leaned forward to hoist the bag on to his back the bag merely stood still. It wouldn't budge. Horatio flipped around again and tugged and pulled. But the bag would not move. Several moments passed before he looked up at Marypat, he was exhausted, his efforts fruitless, the bag had not moved.

"Care for some help?" She asked with a smirk on her face not realizing how bruised Horatio's ego was after failing to budge his winnings.

Horatio hung his head down, he was beaten.

"You owe me a Vert. Pay me now and I'll transport your bag for you, deal?"

She said. She had realized his position and decided to help him out.

"Deal." Horatio beamed holding out his hand to shake hers.

They shook hands and then Marypat coughed.

"The Vert."

"Oh, yah." He said jumping on to the bag and opening the top. He pulled out a single Vert and handed it to her with a grin.

She put the coin in her pocket and then lifted the velvet sack up and held it in her arms. It was heavy even for her to carry but she managed it and they were soon on their way out the door.

The Loralac bowed to them as they left the Lucky Wager and said graciously, "Luck is a foot and yours is soaking in it."

Marypat stopped and looked at the Loralac, she smiled up at him and said. "An eye wide open sees all, and yours is worthy of our deepest thanks." She bowed.

The Loralac tilted his head to the side as if he was trying to figure her out. As if what she said was not expected of her.

"You are very wise for a mere Colleen; how do you know that Loralac saying?"

He asked curiously.

"I'm a student of Cornelius, he has taught me many things and I have meet your kind before in fact I have stayed in their home, Jillian and. . . " She said being interrupted.

"Gillian, he is my Brother!" He said in surprise, "It was not common for Colleens and Loralacs to mix. Most Colleens and Wardeens find Loralacs too strange and avoided contact with us at all cost."

"Well I am not your normal Colleen and I am very pleased to meet you Gillian's brother, I am Marypat." She said with a curtsy.

"And you. I am called Thaddeus." He answered with a bow.

"Pleased Thaddeus." She smiled.

"Lead with your right foot and it shall never lead you wrong." They said in unison and then Marypat said good-bye.

Horatio and Marypat strolled outside the Lucky Wager and headed back to the Shack. They passed a few shops and then came to a glowing sign that read.

"Miss Honey's Sweet Delights and Scrumptious Confections."

Marypat turned to Horatio who had already bounced off her shoulder and landed beside the sign.

"Even the sign smells of Honey! Can we go in?"

Marypat didn't answer she only smiled the broadest smile he had even seen her make and then she turned and open the tiny green door to the shop. Marypat had to bend down low to make it through the door, but once inside the ceiling rose high enough for her to stand at her normal height. The walls of the shop glistened like shinny drops of golden honey, in the center of the shop as a clear tube that ran the full height of the shop. The top of it went through the ceiling. Inside it, Marypat could see thousands of bees, they were moving around in a busy fashion unaware of their spectators.

In the front of the shop set little round tables each with two chairs. There were a few customers enjoys their purchases at the tables and Marypat glanced over their confections, looking to see what was popular and good, all of the items looked most delicious.

To one side of the shop stood a large glass wall and beyond it she could see a huge waterfall, only it wasn't water that was cascading over the quartz boulders on the other side, to Marypat it looked like chocolate. Suddenly Marypat saw four short Feldens shoot out of a door on the other side of the glass. The four Feldens were dragging a huge cauldron. They pulled the cauldron up to the lake of chocolate that had collected at the base of the falls and began scooping the chocolate into cauldron, when it was full they dragged it away and scurried through the same door they had only a few moments before burst through.

Marypat looked at Horatio. "Look at all that chocolate? Let's go buy some."

To the back of the shop there stood a long glass counter. Marypat hurried towards it with Horatio in toe. Inside the glass case were so many sweet things that Marypat's mouth dropped open and Horatio sighed.

"What to get." Horatio uttered in a dreamy state.

The two just stood there gazing into the glass case, the smell of sugar was intoxicating the sight of so many delicious confections were criminal.

"That'll cost you two Pie-it's if you don't stop drooling all over my case. Looking is not free, ya gotta buy something." A plump Lassie Feldens from behind the counter shouted at them.

"Of course. . sorry!" Said Marypat as she quickly stood up and looked at the Felden.

"I would like to get some things for my friends."

"Very good, I am Miss Honey and I am at your service. What would ya have then?" Asked the Felden as she pulled out several empty boxes. "Fill this one for a Pie-it, this one for 5, this one for 10 and the largest one for a vert."

"Well I'll start with two of the ones for 5 Pie-it's" Marypat said slowly.

"What ya want in um?" The Feldens slurred.

"Might you suggest something a Frandies would like?" Marypat asked shyly.

"A Frandies? They would eat everything!" The Feldens laughed.

Marypat looked annoyed and the Felden suddenly changed her approach.

"Chocolate, anything with chocolate. May I suggest the chocolate covered rat tails or the chocolate covered kox pear, Frandies love pear."

"Very well then, I'll take the pear. Now the other one is for a group of Kandies. . . ."

"What! Where, where are the Kandies, close the door sound the alarm, there are Kandies!" Shouted the Felden is a crazy state.

Three more Feldens ran from behind a door and stood like armed guards in front of the glass case. Their eyes search the small crowd of members in the shop, but they found no Kandies.

"Must have been a false alarm!" One of them said to the other.

"Better check the stock."

Then they ran back behind the counter and declared. "All clear." To the plump Lassie Felden who had a look of frantic shock on her face.

She whipped her forehead dry and turned to Marypat with a serious look on her face, "Why would you scare me like that, don't you know we were overrun with them just a few turns back, ate every last bit of stock we had, nearly drank the chocolate river dry, those things are crazy, crazy I tell you." Her voice fell off as if she were trying to regain her composer.

"I am so sorry if I formed my words wrong." Marypat realized she hadn't better mention, again, that the box was indeed for the Kandies that were camping just above them so instead she decided that she had better think fast and cover herself.

"What I was trying to say, dear lady, is any candy would do nicely in that one."

"OH" Said the Felden in a relieved voice. "An assortment then?"

"Yes." Answered Marypat.

Once the box was full, the Felden asked with an inquisitive look. "Will there be anything else?"

"Yes, two more, one for Cornelius and the other for my friend here Horatio."

The Felden was delighted and took down two more boxes. She filled the one for Cornelius with an assortment of chocolate caramels and creams; they were very simple nothing unusual in the lot, as far as Marypat could tell. For Horatio she instructed the Felden to fill the box with an assortment of chocolate cover Jay Berries, Jay Berry creams, Honey cone cups filled with Jay Berry juice and Jay Berry taffy.

Horatio was jumping up and down they were all his favorite.

"Now what about you dear, what can I get you." The Felden suddenly seemed so nice, it was as if the more Marypat bought the nicer she became.

"I don't know, there are so many delicious things, I can't decide!" Marypat said sadly. Not only could she not decide but she was still afraid of eating anything without Cornelius O.K.

"Why allow me!" Said the Felden and she ducked under the counter and went through a trap door, a moment later she reappeared holding a gold box wrapped with a pink satin ribbon. "This is from our special house stock; it's for our very special customers. They're called heavenly treasures and believe me they are just that."

Marypat nodded her head. "O.K., I'll take them, thank you."

"Very good, dear, I'm sure you won't be disappointed with them!"

"Will there be anything else?" The Felden said with a smile.

"No, I think that's it!" Marypat said with a grin.

"OH, well. That will be one Vert and 10 Pie-it."

Marypat handed the Felden two Verts and she gave Marypat her change. Then the Felden handed Marypat her purchase. The Feldens eyes looked at Marypat's arms and then said. "Would you like me to have these delivered to your hotel dear?"

"Could you? That would be such a big help."

"Certainly, where are you staying?" The Felden asked.

"We are staying at the Shack room 307." She answered.

"Very good then." The Felden said jotting down the information. "Cormack, front and center."

A young Felden shot from behind the door, he was half the size of the Lassie Felden behind the counter, and Marypat assumed he was very young. He wore a tan pair of overalls and a yellow shirt. His hair was pulled up in a net and his face was smeared with flour.

"Yes, mother." He said as he stepped through the door.

"I need you to deliver this to the Shack, room 307." She said handing him the parcel.

The Sherideen

After tipping Cormack 2 pie-it's for delivering the parcel and thanking Miss Honey for all her help, Marypat squeezed back through the green door at the front of the shop and continued her stroll along Boulder Town. She still had by her watch fifteen human minutes and she didn't want to waste a minute rushing back to the Shack.

The shop next to the sweet shop was a pharmacy, in the window hung advertisements for Trortle moss and a poster for, Timothy O'Hara's fine drip cream in a can or in a bar, along with a huge pile of cans displaying the O'Hara's name in green and gold. There was also a display of Himan's ale root-rice and two large piles of Swamp Mash that seemed extremely old to Marypat.

In the next shop there were cauldrons piled up in the window, so many that you couldn't see inside. The sign read. "The Ready Kathrie."

"Let's go in!" Said Marypat curious to see what was in a Kathrieen shop.

"Yes, perhaps I can buy a good trick or something."

The door creaked as they pushed it open. There was a green mist in the air that slowly pasted Marypat and then circled back as if it was watching her. It hovered right behind her head, which she didn't seem to notice or mind.

Once well inside she and Horatio investigated every isle. They found parcels of Etie dust, Saddle dust and Pixie dust; there was a full isle of mosses, another of love potions. Marypat saw strange tools, nails, hammers, and pins. There was an isle dedicated to containers, jiggers, bowls, vats, and more cauldrons.

The store was packed full of equipment, Kathrieens needed, but nothing Marypat found useful. She had read most of 'The Green Isle's Patrimony Edition of Incantations and Spells', but still she had no need to do magic. Maybe it was because she knew she wasn't magical, after all she was only a Colleen and the fact that anyone who did bad magic had to pay the price with the Hisue made doing magic not something Marypat wanted to do. So soon she became board in the store and was ready to leave. Horatio on the other hand was ready to purchase several different items, Pixie Dust, a crystal feather, two vials' that read love potion # 4 and a vial that looked like blood.

Marypat didn't interrupt him she only left him his bag of Verts beside him at the counter and continued to browse. Without realizing it, Marypat had mistaken the dark floor in front of her for a dark tile and stepped forward. She fell forward into dark hole and landed on her right knee.

"Crack."

Pain flew through Marypat's body and all she could do was lie back and cry.

"Help!" She cried. Without Horatio she couldn't see a thing, she had no idea how far down she had fallen, she had no idea where she was.

"Someone please help me." She cried a bit louder. In so much pain and feeling as though she were going to pass out, she gave one more cry for help, this time she was heard and a moment later she could feel someone beside her.

"Let me see your leg, oh yes, that's bad." A young man's voice said. He too had no glow to him, but he could certainly see in the very pitch-black room where she lied.

"Let's see if I can get you out of here. Grab my neck, that's it." He said as he grabbed a hold of Marypat and then suddenly jumped. They flew up through the hole in the shops floor and he landed softly beside an old withered Kathrie. The boy's long black cape pitched wildly as they landed and then circled the pair.

"Well done, Donovan. You have her." Cried the old Kathrie Gretel.

"Oh, but mother, she is wounded horribly, her leg. Look!" He said without hesitation. He pulled his cape away to the side to reveal the ugly sight. Marypat's bone had broken through the skin and now protruded outward. Blood gushed from the wound and yet the Kathrie seemed unconcerned.

"No worry. Bring her to my case." Gretel told her son.

The boy did as he was told and again grabbed a hold of Marypat. He followed his mother to the rear of the shop while Horatio bounced after them quite concerned shouting. "Marypat, speak to me, speak to me."

The Kathrie opened an old musty door and let the boy through, but she quickly shut it again trapping Horatio outside.

"Prepare a crunch and heat the spinders." Horatio heard the Kathrie shout.

"No don't, don't hurt her. Let me in, let me in, I'm beholding to her, you must let me in." Horatio cried.

Suddenly the door opened again and a thinner uglier Kathrieen stood in the doorway.

"Be quite Jinxie, or my sister won't be able to work. Just wait here and she be as good as new." The thin Kathrieen said curtly and then she slammed the door.

Suddenly Horatio thought of Cornelius, he must be waiting for them lobby at the Shack; he would know what to do. And he surly wouldn't want Marypat to be in the arm of Kathrieens.

Quickly Horatio throw pixie dust on his bag of Verts and call out. "Trick thick blink." The bag disappeared from sight. Then Horatio bounded off and headed towards the Shack.

Meanwhile behind the musty door, Donovan, had laid Marypat into a small wooden box that had the appearance of a coffin. Her leg was still bleeding, and she was now unconscious.

"Will she be alright, mother?" Ask Donovan quite concerned. But his mother was too busy preparing a flesh crunch to answer. Donovan watched her tiny body lie there unchanged. Her bright red hair fell over her face and he pulled it back gently to reveal her pretty face.

"Mother, she's beautiful so beautiful, like a dream." He whispered. He had never seen a Colleen with such a lovely look about her and he was fascinated with her.

His mother Gretel didn't answer him she was still so busy. Then without warning, she turned around madly dripping something on the floor. A moment later Gretel's two sisters Gritty and Gretta entered the room and quickly came beside the case where Marypat laid.

"Donovan, hold her head, Gritty you take her arms, Gretta you take her legs, everyone ready? This is going to hurt." Gretel announced urgently.

Then the two other Kathrieens grabbed tightly to Marypat's arms and legs, while Donovan held her head. He felt terrible for Marypat that she was injured and in pain and he wanted to try and comfort her so he bended down close to her face and whispered in her ear. "It's alright; mother knows what she's doing."

Gretel poured the boiling spinders solution into Marypat's injured leg. The solution covered the wound and then poured out filling the case. Once the injury was well covered Gretel pushed with all her might, a bunch of Trortle moss into the wound. She pressed it together as the other two Kathrieens held on tight. Marypat gave out a deafening shriek and passed out again.

At the Shack Cornelius had just entered the lobby, when he was jumped by Horatio.

"They're killing her, Doc, ya gotta hurry, it was all I could do to keep them from her. Oh Doc, I failed, I failed, and they dragged her away, through the huge Iron Gate, they put her into a casing, oh Doc. They're torturing her." Horatio sobbed uncontrollably.

"Horatio, get a hold of yourself, what are you talking about?" Cornelius shouted angrily as he grabbed a hold of the Jinxie and pulled him off of his arm like he was peeling off an unwanted large bug that had just landed on him.

"The Kathries have her, they took her away and it's all my fault if I hadn't wanted to. . . . " His voice trailed. "Ya gotta hurry Doc. before it's too later. Please follow me. I'll take you to them."

Cornelius followed Horatio back to the shop. They went inside, and Horatio lead him back to door where they had taken Marypat.

"In here?" Cornelius asked Horatio.

Horatio nodded, "Yes, the coven of Kathrieens are in there."

Cornelius knocked once and then turned back to look at Horatio, but Horatio had dropped out of sight into a cauldron a moment before. Fearful the Kathrieens would catch him too.

The door squeaked open and one of the Kathrieens pocked her head out. The Kathrieen was thin and old. Her long hair was grey, and it fell over her face covering her left eye.

"Gritty?" Cornelius said with a smile. "I hear you are torturing my charge is this true?"

"Oh, does she belong to you, Cornelius, dear, I had no idea. She's a lovely lot, she is. Come on in Dear, she's doing much better now." Gritty said as she let Cornelius inside and slammed the door again.

"She had quite a fall, but as you can see she's just fine". Gritty added as she showed Cornelius to the case where Marypat lie still out cold.

Cornelius knelt down beside her and listens while Donovan explained what happen.

"You're a good lad, Donovan, thank-you for helping her." Cornelius said solemnly to the boy then he turned back to Gritty and asked when she thought Marypat would awake.

"Gretel thought it best that she stays asleep while the spinders were still working, let me have her come now and take a look see." Said Gritty, then she disappeared in front of Cornelius and an instant later, she was back with Gretel.

"Cornelius, how good to see you." Said Gretel giving Cornelius a hug. "How long has it been nine passes, I bet."

"Yes, that would be about right, Gretel. I remember Donovan was about 3 the last moment I saw him. He has grown fine, just fine Gretel, you must be so proud." Cornelius said tapped Donovan on his shoulder.

Cornelius watched as a tear slide out of Gretel eye. She whipping it away and then bent down beside Marypat. "Let me see how far along we are."

Gretel examined the leg. "Looks good as new, it might be slightly weak and stiff but that will go away before long."

Gretel leaned over Marypat then and snapped her fingers saying. "Greet". Instantly Marypat woke up.

"Cornelius, what happened?" Marypat exclaimed. Then she grabbed her leg remembering she had hurt it but it wasn't broken or cut or anything.

"It's alright dear, Gretel here healed it for you." Cornelius said with a confident voice. "Do you think you could stand?" He asked.

She nodded her head and he helped left her out of the case. He placed her legs on the ground and she wobbled at first but soon was standing on her own.

"Oh, Gretel how can I ever thank you for helping Marypat like this." He said turning back to face his dear friend.

"Not a word, you would have done the same for my Donovan, in fact you have." She giggled.

"The least I can do is take you lovely Kathrieens and Sherideen, out to dinner this eve at the Blarney Stone." He said beamingly.

"Oh Cornelius, we would be soooo honored." The three Kathrieens giggled in unison.

Marypat stood a bit shaky on her newly fixed leg. It was stiff, but strong. She looked down at her yellow knickers and realized they were ruined, the pant leg had been ripped nearly the full length of the leg and they were covered in bloodstains and spinder liquid.

"I can't go out to dinner in this." Marypat whispered to Cornelius. Who looked at her clothing and agreed.

"We must do something about that." He grinned and quickly turned to Gretel.

"Have anything she can slip on." He said pointing to Marypat's slacks.

"Oh my, yes we can't take her to the Blarney Stone looking like that, come with me dear." Gretel said pulling Marypat's arm.

"Right in here, this is my dressing room." Gretel pushed Marypat into what seemed to be a large closet. Inside was brightly lit and Marypat could clearly see large bits of fabric, all folded in piles through the room. There was a large mirror that hung against the far wall. The mirror had an enormous frame that was carved out of wood; the pattern suggested it had been carved by an expert craftsman, most likely a Lachlann, Marypat assumed. At the top of the frame carved into the center was an eye shaped sphere.

Gretel pushed passed Marypat and handed her a red piece of cloth.

"Now when you're ready put on this cloth and turn to the mirror. Then point to the eye and call out 'fin frie fix!' All Right, any questions?" Gretel said.

Marypat didn't quite understand what she was doing in a closet with a red sheet; she looked down at it and frowned.

"What's the matter dear?" Gretel asked.

There was silence and then Gretel exclaimed. "Of course, wrong color, red will never do with your red hair."

Gretel touched the sheet with her wand. "Green then?" Gretel beamed, then she stepped out of the closet and closed door leaving Marypat standing in fount of the fancy cut mirror not sure what she was to do. She took off her torn outfit and pulled the long green sheet over her head as she was told.

"I look like I'm going trick or treating." She said aloud, but no one heard her. "Ok now what am I supposed to say?" She thought for a minute looking at herself in the mirror. She pointed to the eye and tried

"Tick Mick Flick, no that's not it, Trick me sick". She laughed as she tried to remember what to say but as she stood there trying to remember she hear the mirror speak . . . .

"Ya ya. You're supposed to say, Fin frie fix!" The mirror laughed sarcastically.

"What! You can talk?" Marypat said falling over.

"Of course, now let's get on with it, I don't have all day!" The mirror shouted at her.

"All right you don't have to be so mean. . Fin Frie Fix." She said. Instantly the wooden eye opened and thousands of tiny winged creatures flew forward from it striking the green sheet that covered Marypat. The sheet shrunk onto her body, she could feel the creatures moving and turning, all around her. She tried to touch them but something pushed her hand away. Marypat looked into the mirror all around her, was a blur. Then just as suddenly as they had started they stopped and flew back into the eye. Marypat stared into the mirror; her green sheet was now a lovely green dress.

"Wow, that was neat, thank you so much mirror, and please tell those . . . well you know thank you too, I love it." Marypat said excitedly.

"Why do you thank the mirror when I'm the one that help you?" Came the same voice.

"Ah. . but. . I . . Where are you?" Stammered Marypat. Her mind raced there was no one else in the room with her and if it was not the mirror who was it?

"I'm down here. . No here." The voice called as Marypat searched the ground through the piles of fabric. "Oh, never mind I'll get up".

From behind a small stack of purple fabric stretched a black and white striped coose. He was as large as her house cat back home and he had bright blue eyes that sparkled in the light.

"It's moment for my milk anyway, so don't think I'm doing you a favor." He said.

"I can't believe it, you can talk!" Marypat explained kneeling down in front of the coose. Without thinking, Marypat reached forward to give the coose a scratch but he pulled away in anger and growled.

"What are you doing?"

"I was just going to scratch you; don't you want one?"

"Oh, well if that's all."

Marypat scratched the coose and he began to purr. "See isn't that nice?" she said.

"Oh yes." The coose said with a sign.

There was a knock at the door and it was Gretel. "Are you all right dearie?"

"Yes, you may come in." Marypat called back.

Gretel open the door to find Marypat scratching the coose. "I see you have met Jack! Come Jack, moment for diner." The coose scooted off without even a bye, leaving Gretel alone with Marypat.

"Thank-you so much the dress is perfect, I love it." Marypat said as she stood up and walked out of the closet.

"Not a word." said Gretel.

"Please." Marypat said as she turned to look at the Kathrieen. "Please tell me how that coose can talk?"

"OH, it's a simple potion really I believe I still have a vile in the shop, it's called coose-gotta-tongue, works great on most coose's. Why do you ask?" Asked the Kathrieen.

"I would like to talk to my friend Tiger, would it work on a Grundle?" She asked innocently.

"A what?" The Kathrieen said with surprise. "You have made a friend of a Grundle, my dear, I had no idea, all along I thought you a simple Colleen, but I think not. No, a Colleen would never go near one. You certainly surprised me not many members have ever gotten close enough to one to say for sure that they exist. I really must say you are a unique member, perhaps you are a Kathrie, Kathries are very special, you know."

"Yes miss, but would the potion work on a Grundle?" Marypat asked again.

"Well a Grundle is in the coose family, so I don't see why not."

"Then I'll take a vile, thank you." Marypat sang with glee.

The Blarney Stone

The sign outside the huge cave read, 'THE BLARNEY STONE' established 1120, watch your step.

Marypat read it with a bit of surprise the year seemed strange, but Cornelius found nothing wrong with it and he proceeded inside as if he had eaten here many times. The three older Kathrieens followed with Gretta's three Kathrieen daughters in toe with Horatio, Marypat, and Donovan in the rear.

"This restaurant was built in 1120? Is that the same years as we have outside?"

"What is years?" Asked Donovan, with a deep look of inquiry.

"She means passes, and Marypat I don't know. What is your pass numeral out there? Ours is 6853."

"Oh, my we are only 1986, and here I thought 866 years of establishment for this place was a long moment but it's far greater than that. This is one OLD restaurant, I hope the foods not that old." She laughed out loud and Horatio laughed with her while Donovan stood unmoved by her humor.

"Good evening, Cornelius, good to have you with us again, it has been so long." Said the Maître d' as Cornelius approaching his desk.

"Good to see you to Henry." Cornelius said stepping up to the man.

Henry was a short thin Felden dressed all in green except for his yellow pinstriped shirt. He had brown well-trimmed hair and long side burns that came across his checks and ended with a mustache.

"I have you down for three, is that correct?" Henry asked.

"I'm afraid we're 10 now, Henry, hope that's not any trouble?" Cornelius answered but just like the Lassie Felden in the candy store, Henry seemed to be much happier when he had more to do.

"Not a problem at all, 10, that's splendid, just splendid, oh my yes 10 is a good number, it is lucky you know, I must say it is very lucky indeed."

He fussed around very excited and then finally said. "Please follow me, I have just the right table for all of you, our best table you'll see, grand view of the Blarney Stone, right up close I dare say, perfect seats for the show too. Well come alone this way, stay together I wouldn't want to lost my lucky number 10." He laughed.

Henry showed them a path that lead deeper into the cave. It was dark and damp, stalactites hung from the ceiling stretching their long fingers toward the stalagmites on the ground. Shinny patches of calcite grew all along the walls and occasionally some parts of calcite glowed purple.

After walking down what seemed to be quite a distance, to Marypat, of steps carved into the soil, they came to a landing. Marypat could hardly see anything; she could feel however, Donovan's breathe on her neck.

"Sorry. Why have we stopped?" He asked.

But before she could answer him they were moving again, and she could see a light a head of her.

"Here we are." Shouted Henry. "*Nottron!*"

With that a large bolder blocking the entrance moved away. Inside was cool and damp, so Henry went straight to work to start a fire in the center of the room, under a very large cauldron. "STRRRAT!"

Once the fire was lit he replaced the cauldron and pulled two half-moon shaped tables around the fire.

Marypat could now see the cave they were in, it was very large and musty, the walls were sold calcite, and they glistened in the firelight. On the far side of the cave, hug a huge velvet curtain. Henry didn't touch the curtain; he only brushed against it and said under his breath "We'll open you after dinner." Then he continued in a clear voice.

"Fred will be your waiter, and he'll be right with you, enjoy your stay, and thank you so much for choosing the Blarney Stone." He said. Then with a snap, he disappeared for sight.

Right away the Kathrieens sat down; they were talking among themselves in a buzz, giggling with excitement.

"They do that all the moment, the coven, you know." Donovan said numbly to Marypat.

"No, I don't know? Can you explain it to me?" She answered looking at Donovan. He was a handsome young boy, jet-black hair and purple eyes that sparkled with flecks of red. He had milky white skin that looked as if he had never been outside in the sun

Donovan gave her a sideways glance. "Why don't we sit down, you look cold and the fire should warm you. There now, I will answer any questions you want?" He said sweetly.

So, the pair sat down across from the six Kathrieens and Marypat began her questions. "What is a coven?"

"Well when you say a coven, there are two types, a regular coven is a cauldron placed in the ground, and they use it in making potions. The other is a coven of Kathrieens, 9 or more."

"But there are only six with us and you called them a coven?"

"True, six is called a circle but let me try and explain more better. Kathrieens are born in sets of three, there must always be three, or their magic strength is broken. Take my mother and her two sisters, born together in a set. My auntie Gretta is the third sister, she bores the Lassie. She has had this first set with us now." Donovan pointed to his side where Gretta's three daughters sat talking to each other in whispers. "And she is expecting a second set any moment now, this makes them a coven even before the second set is born, that's why my mother can't leave and take me to my Sherite Extolel." He said sadly "Any way Kathrieens always come in sets of threes while we Sherideens arrive as one, rarely two."

"So, you are a Sherideen?" Marypat asked in awe she had not met a Sherideen before this was her first one.

"Yes!" Donovan answered.

"What is the Sherite Extolel?"

"When a Sherideen turns 13, he must be received into the Sherite Tribune before he turns 14 or he will be dejected by the other Sherideens. My mother doesn't want me to go because she thinks that they will change me, but I want to go. My father is there, and he has sent for me to join him. The Sherite Extolel is my right of passage; I just wish my mother could see that." Donovan said with an angry tone as he stared at his mother.

"I'm sorry, Donovan." Marypat said softly trying to comfort him but not knowing exactly what to say. So, she changed the subject. "Tell me, if there always has to be 3, what happens when one of the Kathrieens die's."

"Well with any luck, the other two will find her a good host to transplant her soul into or the other two will die too." He said with a grim look.

Marypat wished to inquire more about this host thing but she was interrupted by the waiter who bumped into her spilling water on her new dress.

"You fool!! Look what you have done to me lady!" Donovan shouted at the waiter.

"So sorry, my lady, so very sorry. It was all my fault, please forgive me."
The waiter bowed over and over again.

"Move on." Shouted Donovan as he shoved the waiter out of the away then he pulled out his wand and hummed something in a strange language all the while he made tiny circles with his wand. Once he finished his incantation, Marypat's dress was dry.

"It's dry! How did you do that?" Marypat exclaimed.

Donovan just smiled and sat down as the waiter entered again with more water. He carefully put the mugs down on the moon shaped table and then began taking orders.

"What do they have, is there a menu?" Marypat questioned Donovan in whisper.

"Everything, what do you like? Foul, hoof, or swine, they are all good. I am going to have the foul, roasted with haps." He answered, slightly showy.

"I'll have the same." Marypat answered shyly it sounded good to her and she thought foul, must be some kind of bird, and bird must be good, perhaps it was like chicken.

Once the orders were taken and Cornelius assured Mary that her order was safe. So with that Marypat turned back to Donovan and asked her next question.

"What do you mean by host?"

"A Kathrieen set can't live if there is less than three, so the other two will find a willing host, another body for the spirit of the third to enter." Donovan said matter-of-factly.

"Like what?" She asked a bit nervously. It all sounded a bit evil to her, taking over another person's body.

"The best host for a Kathrieen is a coose." He answered as the cauldron in front of them began to boil.

"Oh, that's dinner!" one of the young Kathrieens called out.

Marypat sat and watched as the cauldron sparked and burped. Abruptly the waiter entered again and this moment he handed out large brown plates and skewers to each member. Then he clapped his hands twice and blue sparks shot out of the cauldron.

"Bon appetite." He said. Then he disappeared out of sight.

Gretel and her sisters were the first to stab their skewers into the hot cauldron and pull out their dinners. Cow foot in gravy. Cornelius followed skewering a large pork chop looking piece of meat.

Marypat was stunned as each member stuck their skewer into the sparking cauldron they pulled out their dinner.

"Here!" Donovan said with a smile, taking Marypat's skewer from her. He stabbed the center of the cauldron and pulled out her dinner for her. He placed it on her plate and then turned back to his.

The waiter entered again and hurriedly set out two empty platters. Gretel took the first and tossed it in the cauldron. The Cauldron bubbled again and throughout purple sparks. After a moment, the sparks subsided, and the tray shot out of the cauldron and landed back on the table beside Gretel. On the platter was a heaping pile of rice which Gretel quickly helped herself to and then handed it to her sister. The second platter was thrown in next and it reemerged with several types of greens piled on it.

Reluctantly Marypat began to eat and found the foul delicious. She smiled to herself with relief, she was so hungry, and it was nice to eat something other than Frandies stew and potash.

After dinner, Fred entered again and cleared away the mugs and plates. He hurried around the cave tripping twice before he was done. But when he finished he turned to the large curtain and said. "Have you fallen asleep? Well then, it's moment!" With that, the curtain shook and then began to open. Fred ducked through it as the Blarney Stone was reviled to the group.

All conversations stopped while the attention of the group turned to what was beyond the curtain. Marypat could see a huge green stone that sat in the center of a large pool of water. The stone glowed from within and sparkled in the flowing water.

Beside the pool stood a stout Felden, dressed in an orange robe that was trimmed in green. He raised his hands and shouted.

"Let the show begin!"

With that, he pulled off his robe to reveal his sequin covered suit that shimmered in the glow of the huge stone. Trumpets blew and suddenly the air above the stone was a whirl of activity. Tiny floating balls of florescent colors swirled around in intricate movements. Their ballet continued until the stout Felden lowered his hands and held them out to his side. Then the floating lights swooped down and surrounded him. They picked him up and flew him into the air, straight to the top of the huge Blarney Stone. Gently they set him down and then went back to their dance.

The stout Felden sat down on the top of the stone and hung his feet over the edge. He smiled from ear to ear and looked around at the floating lights. After a while, he clapped his hands and all the illuminated creatures dove straight down into the water.

"May I present the Blarney Stone Dancers." He called from the top of the stone. Just as he finished his last word, the surface of the water began to swirl about. Then suddenly Water sprayed upwards in to the air, lit by something below the water. Gradually each spray lessened and from each entry emerged a single Lassie Felden dressed in what looked like a rubber body suit. 24 in all, thin lassies exited the water until they stood on the very surface with their tippy toes dangling in the water. In rhythm, they splashed, kicked and moved in a beautiful arrangement. To which the audience clapped their approval.

When the dancers reentered the water, the stout Felden stood up on the boulder the called out "It is my great pleasure to introduce at this moment, Geraldo the Great."

The audience went crazy clapping and shouting with delight. Even Donovan sat up in his seat to get a better look.

"He's one of the most famous Sherideens ever." Donovan said to Marypat excitedly all the while never taking his eyes off the stage.

"Kathrieens and Sherideens, Colleens and Wardeens, all Lassies and Patties alike, I thank you for your wonderful applause. Allow me to make your view of this evenings magic a bit easier on your eyes." Geraldo said with a dramatic voice.

Instantly each member of the audience was fitted with a pair of binoculars. Good trick, Marypat thought to herself but what was even better was that each set was just the right size for that member. Horatio's was Jinxie size, while Cornelius's were large, just his size. Everyone at the table had their proper size.

"In addition, I should like to make it even better by. . . " Geraldo said with a snap of his fingers. Instantly his body separated into 12 equally parts, that just as quickly formed 12 Geraldo's. The 12 Geraldo's bowed and then marched around the boulder until they were equally dispersed on all sides of the stone, making it quite easy for his audience to see at least three of his forms.

In unison the 12 Sherideens performed a battery of tricks to which Donovan's Mother and aunts were impressed with. After some wild hair rising tricks involving apparitions, Geraldo called to his audience.

"May I have a volunteer to assist me with my next trick?"

Each Geraldo moved forward into his viewing audience and selected a member to aid him. The one in front of Marypat's group step into their cave and quickly looked about. He pointed at Marypat and asked. "Would you be so kind, my dear."

Marypat looked around at the others, who were all smiling and nodding their heads 'yes'.

"Go on dear!" Cornelius said with encouragement.

Horatio bounced to her side and cheered. "Go Marypat it will be grand!"

The Geraldo's image jumped back slightly at the sight of the Jinxie and quickly called again to her. "We must hurry my dear."

With still a bit of apprehension Marypat finally stood and went with the transparent Geraldo. The other Geraldo's and volunteers were already standing in position when Marypat emerged from the cave and approached the bolder.

When she was finally in place, all the Geraldo's called. "Dom me a sue!"

Out of the thin air, setting on the ground in front of them, appeared a wooden box for each volunteer.

"Vot to." Geraldo called out and the boxes open to reveal a large red stone.

"Cinerin!" He called then, and audience gasped.

"I will ask the volunteers to assure the stones are real, by asking them to attempt to pick them up." He announced. Again, the audience gasped. Cinerin was a harmless stone, but an impossible stone to just pick up. Only someone with great magical powers could even attempt such a feet.

Each volunteer slowly attempted to raise the stone but as they touched it, they were flung upwards, their feet over their heads, their hands glued to the stone like a magnet. The audience laughed. But Marypat hadn't moved she watched the others with their legs flying in the air and did nothing.

"Go on now, try and pick it up!" Geraldo said to her with an annoyed tone.

Marypat looked over at him, his transparent face slowly filled back in solid as she continued to not move. "Go on!" he said.

She looked down at the stone, she didn't want to pick it up, let alone touch it she was worried it would cause her another illness. Hesitating she finally bend down and rapped her arms around it. Squeezing the stone to her chest she stood up, holding the rock in her arms. The entire restaurant gasped and then began to whisper loudly.

Geraldo's face went red, his eyes bulged. "Why you have soiled it, you stupid . . . . . . " Then he grabbed her arm as all the other Geraldo's disappeared.

"What spell have you used, tell me you Ubil beast." Geraldo glared at her.

Marypat stuttered breathlessly as she dropped the stone at her feet. "I did nothing, nothing."

"Nothing?" He stared into her eyes and she watched as the tiny veins in his eyes slowly began to rupture.

"Go away! You wicked Ubil." He angrily said to her under his breath so that the audience couldn't hear.

Then he disappeared in a puff of black smoke, which smelled to Marypat like rotten eggs.

The stout Felden on top of the boulder didn't seem to mind the abrupt end to Geraldo's show. In fact, he simply stood and proclaimed the end of the program. The swarm of lighting creature filled the air again and carried the stout Felden back down to the floor of the cave, where he shooed the volunteers back to their seats.

Marypat sat down and looked at Donovan with a frown.

"He said I spoiled it." She said next to tears.

"How did you do it?" Horatio asked jumping from his seat to stand on the table in front of her.

"I don't know. I just picked it up like he told me to."

"I wouldn't worry. I understand he has quite a bad temper." Gretel said as she stood up.

"He's not very well liked!" Announced Gretta.

"Horrible disposition." Added Gritty

"Still I didn't mean to spoil it!" Marypat said sadly.

"Never mind. I don't think you spoiled anything, I had a great moment!" Donovan said with a smile.

Everyone nodded in agreement. Then they all stood and left the Blarney Stone.

The following marrow, Cornelius rose early and woke Marypat.

"The stay has been nice, but we mustn't delay, for we are off to Great Town this very turn." He said with a smile and a skip. Then he disappeared out her door.

Marypat rose dressed and shook Horatio from his sleep, then she followed Cornelius out to the sitting room where she found him eating a tea cake.

"Come dear, I had them prepare a few little bits before we head off on our journey."

Marypat approached the small table that sat just beside the huge crystal wall that shielded them from the Flower River. On the table were several different types of teacakes, a pot of porridge, bread, jam and a pot of tea.

"Not a pear or a berry in the lot, I assure you!" He said with cake still in his mouth.

She sat and ate, while Horatio joined them.

"What a spread! They sure do know how to take care of ya in this place." Horatio said with joy.

Cornelius knobbed his head in agreement but continued to eat his cake.

"By the way, dear, you had a delivery. They're over by the door." Cornelius said as he sipped at his hot tea.

Marypat looked shocked for a brief moment but then she jumped to her feet.

"Oh yes, I forgot all about them!" She ran to the door where they sat a large bag. She searched through the bag for a moment and then she turned back to Cornelius.

"I bought this for you, I hope you like them. . . I wanted to thank you for everything you have done for me. . I mean you didn't have it. ."

"Nonsense, don't say another word. . ." His voice trailed off as tears welled up in his eyes. She meant more to him then he could ever say, it was as if she represented everything and everyone he had left behind, his daughters, his wife, his mother. She was very special to him and he would do anything to protect her and help her even if it meant helping her to go home. And That he knew when the moment did come was going to be the hardest thing he'd ever have to do, let her go. It had been only a short moment, but he had grown to love her like a daughter.

She handed him the box and he accepted it with a smile.

"Well enough with all this blubbering, we have much to do!" He announced holding tightly to his box of Miss Honey's finest confections.

Later that morning Marypat and Horatio emerged from the crooked old shack that stood precariously at the edge of Flower River. The Frandies, Andies, and Kandies were already packed and ready to roll when they approached them.

"Good Morrow!" Marypat called to the leader of the Frandies who was sitting at the reins of a wee cart.

"Good morrow, to you too fare one." The Frandies called back.

"Have you any sight of the Grundle I call Tiger?" She asked worriedly knowing how much Frandies disliked cooses.

"The Kandies have him in the wood, just yonder." The lead Frandies said unconcerned.

"Hence ye balm, one called Doctor?" One of the Frandies asked.

"Ye Balm soon come, him make stop and be right with us." Horatio answered bouncing on to the back of the wee cart where the two Frandies sat. There was one place he didn't want to go and that was in the wood with a hungry Grundle, he preferred to stay behind on the wee cart with the Frandies.

"To your honor regal Frandies may I offer my gift to you and yours." Marypat said with a curtsy, handing the lead Frandies the box of Miss Honey's fine confections.

The Frandies face turned for unconcerned to great surprise.

"Is this truly a box of Miss Honey's?" He said dripping with want.

"Ya, she got one for the Kandies too!" Horatio said with a yawn.

"Oh, no. . no.. no. You mustn't give it to the Kandies. . . at least not until we are far away from Boulder town. If they discover there is a sweet shop below. . . they will . . . Oh I can't even think what they would do. . . It would be . . .just horrible!" The Frandies said quite disturbed.

"Why don't you leave it with me and I'll see to it that they receive it when it is safe."

Marypat remembered what Miss Honey had said about the Kandies, destroying all of her stock just a few turns ago. And Marypat wouldn't want these Kandies to do the same thing so she agreed and handed the Frandies the second box of confections.

"Perhaps you know best." Marypat relented with a halfway smile. "I'm off to find Tiger then, Horatio, are you coming?"

"Won't test me toe near a hungry beast! Better I stay here!" He said lying back on a sack of flat beans and yawned.

"Suit yourself, but you'll miss the surprise I have for him." She said somewhat annoyed.

"Oh, yes! That's right, surprise!!! I'm breakfast." Horatio said with a sarcastic burst that only irritated Marypat even more.

She snubbed her nose into the air and walked away from Horatio and the two Frandies to look for Tiger.

"Tiger, here kitty kitty." Marypat called as if she were calling her house cat, back at home. "There you are." She spotted him rolling on the ground. His four paws reaching for the sky, his head back, and his tail curled. He was contently basking in all the attention the Kandies had been giving him. But as she spied him the Kandies darted off into the wood leaving him lying on his back all alone.

"I see they've been taking care of you. I have something for you." Marypat said with a grin.

Tiger jumped to his feet and slowly stretched as he walked towards her, purring.

"I don't know if you want it though, it could change everything, so you must decide, boy. Do you want to speak . . . do you want to communicate with me?"

Tiger looked up at her.

"Well this is it." She said taking out an ordinary bun. She held it in the cup of her hand and showed it to him. Then she took out the vial of "Coose-gotta-tongue", pulled out the cork with her teeth and pour the liquid out into the center of the bun. The bun absorbed the liquid easily, not a drop dripped out. Then she presented it to the Grundle.

"If you eat this Tiger, you will be able to speak to me, in the language I speak."

The Grundle smelled the bun and then he ate it. Gulp! It went down in one bit.

Marypat waited for something to happen, for something to change. But Tiger only stood there starring at her with his big green eyes.

"Oh well, it was made for house cooses any way!" She said with a frown, she had really hoped to be able to speak to Tiger. "Well I better get out to the front; we'll be on our way soon."

Then she turned and stepped out of the wood and headed to the front of the line.

Cornelius was waiting there with Donovan when Marypat reached.

"Donovan? What are you doing here?" Marypat squealed.

"Donovan will be travelling with us to Great town." Cornelius said sweetly to Marypat then he turned to his troops and with a commanding voice shouted.

"Ready troops and we are on!"

Suddenly the line of Frandies, Andies and Kandies moved out across the grass and then over the small wooden bridge that spanned the Flower River, leaving Marypat, Donovan and Tiger still standing beside the old Shack.

"I thought your mother wouldn't let you go?" Marypat said as they started to follow the caravan of Frandies.

"Cornelius talked to her and she changed her mind. His going to take me all the way to Cimmevian City. I can't believe I'm finally going. Cornelius is the best, just the best." Donovan said with a smile.

Marypat nodded, he was the best, and she was happy for Donovan. She was happy because she knew it was something Donovan really wanted and because this meant she had someone her age to talk to for a few days. So, for the next few sweeps the two talked about everything, and Donovan filled her in on Kathrieens and Sherideens. It was like they were old friends, just seeing each other after a long separation. Catching up, talking, laughing, and enjoying each other's company.

Meanwhile somewhere above Cimmevian City a cloaked figure appeared in a cloud mist and hovered over a small stone balcony. Below him, another figure steps forward and motioned to him to come closer.

"I can't believe you would show yourself back here again after what you did!" The figure on the balcony whispered into the cloud.

"Handrew, please I have to see him, I have information that could change everything!" The cloaked figure pleaded.

"It had better be every impressive, or he will kill you. He is still not over your last . . . mishap."

Silky Flats to The Pond Sprite

The wayward caravan traveled quickly along Silky Flats. A flat piece of land used by ranchers for grazing cattle and for growing crops. It stretched between the Flower River and the Cinerin Mountains. It was easy going as the land had only a few rolling hills and flat prairies covered with grass, a few trees and even fewer ponds.

Silky Flats was legendary for its Wardeen Cowboys, saloons, and shootouts over just about anything one could think of. But for the moment all was peaceful as the group made their way along.

Evening set in as Middleton City came into view and marked the half-way point between Bolder Town and Small Town. Middleton City was a western style settlement with wood framed buildings that faced one small main street, called Middleton Alley.

Marypat thought she had entered the wild wild west of North America. It had all the same look and style of an old black and white movie western. The buildings had huge false fronts that made them look two times the size they actually were. There was a saloon, with two Colleens in brightly colored dressing gowns welcoming members to enter; there was also a barbershop, a depot, a hotel and jail. But Cornelius didn't seem interested in the western town at all, instead he marched his troop straight through Middleton City without stopping. Once they had reached the out skirts of the town, he instructed the Frandies to make camp, which they did instantly. Again, Marypat discovered that there was no place for her in the tiny tents that popped up all over the ground.

"Where are we to stay, then?" She asked Donavan with concern, but Donavan seemed unconcerned about where he would sleep, it was his first time outside in the wide open, without his mother.

"'Tis not my care, you helpless twit. Tonight, I am my own member, no one especially you, is going to keep me down." He answered with a grin and with that, he flew into the warm turquoise sky and landed in a cloud.

Marypat shook her head at him, granted she hadn't known Donavan for that long but surely this was not the Donavan she had just spent the last two turns with. All of a sudden, he was fresh and ill-mannered, not at all his usually kind self.

"Donovan is rapidly now, you should stay away from him, Sherideens they are such curt creatures, creatures of pestilence and plague." A voice from behind her rang in her ears like a gentle purr. It was a voice she didn't recognize and yet it didn't frighten her.

Slowly she turned around to find Tiger sitting proudly staring up at her.

"Tiger was that you?" She asked dumbfounded.

"Were you expecting that wimp of a Jinxie?" He answered coldly

"Tiger, how rude, perhaps you are the curt one?" She replied.

"Perhaps, but at least I shall never put on a mask and hide my true heart. A Jinxie is that of a trickster and a Sherideen is that of evil. I as your only true alliance must caution you of the friends you make of these."

"I appreciate your concern my friend." She said bending down to face the Grundle and give him a scratch. "But I must disagree with you."

"Then I shall leave it at that and leave you to make your own mistakes. Oh, yes there behind the ear!"

Marypat scratched the Grundle behind his ear while she asks. "When did it happen?"

"When did what happen?"

"When were you able to speak?"

"I have always been able to speak, you just haven't listened." He answered swooshing his tail.

She grinned at him and nodded her head." Perhaps you are right. I can hear you now anyway; do you know where Horatio has gotten to?"

"That trick of a Jinxie has ridden off towards the canyon with those Frandies, those delicious Frandies." Tiger said licking his lips and purring quit loudly.

"That will be just about enough; I don't want you to trouble not one Frandies." She scolded.

Tiger closed his eyes as if to tune her out, then he changed the subject by calling out with a big yawn. The yawn was so high pitched that Marypat could not hear a sound but a troop of Kandies did and rushed to Tiger with several Lofty Zorts on their wooden spears.

"I see. You have plans, so I bid you good night." She said unruffled by the commotion around the Grundle.

"See you in the morrow." The Grundle murmured with a full mouth of Lofty Zorts.

Marypat turned away from the Grundle and began to walk towards the front of the camp when she spotted Doctor Cornelius.

"There you are dear, come I want you to meet our host." Said Cornelius as he rushed by Marypat on his way to the other side of camp.

Marypat nearly had to run to keep up but soon they were at their destination, in front of a large campfire. Around the fire and on wood logs sat several very brawly Wardeens dressed in leather slacks with woolly cotton shirts and Stetson looking hats.

"Marypat dear, this is Wild Lee Granger and his son Ace." Cornelius said introducing a tall thin Wardeen and a younger version of the first. Both wore their hair pulled back in a ponytail and both had long mustaches that curled on their ends, the only difference Marypat could see was the first had a bit of gray streaking through his hair while the other had no gray at all.

"Pleasure to meet you." Marypat said with a curtsy.

"Pleasure to meet you, little Colleen." The Wardeen's replied.

"We've got a pot of beans, if-in your hungry like." Wild Lee said through his mustache.

"The Huff won't be done for a half a sweep yet, but ya can start on the beans." His son added.

"Very well." Cornelius said with a grin. "Bring on the beans!" Then he trotted off following Wild Lee to a table that was set up on the far side of the campfire.

Marypat took a seat on one of the logs that encircled the fire. The air was calm but cool and the fire was hot. She stretched her arms out to the fire, it felt good against her hands and it warmed her. The cracking fire reminded her of home; her grandmother often lit the fireplace on a cool Blue Mountain night. It was strange, she hadn't thought of home so much lately but all of a sudden, she missed it very much. She missed her grandmother, her cat and even school. Tears filled her eyes, she felt so alone.

"Why my lady crying?" Came a familiar voice from beside her. It was Horatio and he was carrying a large bag over his shoulder. He dropped the bag when he reached Marypat's side then he jumped up onto her shoulder. "Oh Marypat, has someone hurt you, I shall hex them for you!"

"No, Horatio, no one has hurt me; I just miss my home so very much."

Horatio wrapped his tiny arms around her neck and hug her. "I am so sorry, you are sad but this just means we need to work harder to get you home. I shall do all I am able to help you."

"I know you will, my friend." Marypat said with a half way smile. She knew, despite what Tiger believed that Horatio was truly a good friend to her and he more than anyone she trusted with her feelings. Slowly she tried to regain herself as she asked. "What do you carry in your bag?"

"Oh that!" Horatio shouted, bouncing over her shoulder and landing beside the bag. He pulled the tie open and flashed its condense. Inside the bag were tiny yellow leaves.

"Sweet grass, it makes a delicious beverage! The Frandies and I had to travel all the way to the canyon to find enough, the Huffs in this area love the stuff. But we got what we need to make a huge batch." Horatio explained.

He looked at Marypat who was smiling back at her friend with tear-stained cheeks.

"I'll just be a moment." Then he hopped away with his bag and returned as he said he would. Together the two friends had a filling meal of huff and beans and then sat around the camp fire drinking the Himan's ale root-rice that the Frandies had made from the sweet grass while listening to the Wardeens tell stories about: Careless Conway, Lefty MaCkinley, Rippen Rudie, Little Johnny G and Maxie James the want-a-be Cowboy.

Later when Marypat couldn't keep her eyes open another moment, Ace approached her.

"One is ready to rest?" He asked.

"Oh yes, but I have no bed, no cot, nothing." She said sleepily.

"Nonsense, you have a log roll." Ace said with a tilt of his head.

Marypat looked up at the Wardeen with a confused look, she had no idea what a log roll was.

"Here allow me." He said grabbing a hold of her arm and pulling her to her feet. Then he called out,"Vock to," as he tapped the wooden log with his hand.

Instantly the log rolled forward unraveling a sleeping bag complete with blanket and pillow.

"Ah, how incredible, thank-you!" She said quite delighted.

"No mention, fare one, now rest, for morrow will come in heed."

Marypat climbed into her bed with Horatio sharing her pillow. A moment later they both were fast asleep.

Morning came with a flash of light and all was suddenly bright. The sound of a roaster crowing flooded Marypat's ears as she tried to remember where she was. Then it came to her and she sat up. She could still smell the Himan's ale root-rice in the air from the night before as well as the scent of beans. The fire had died down to a small flame amongst a heap of ash, but still it warmed the air.

"Good morrow, Colleen. Did ye sleep most favorably?" Wild Lee asked as he approached her.

"Yes, thank you."

"Fine to hear, there is grub on the fire and the Doc asked me to tell you, they'll be moving out in a sweep." Wild Lee said with a tilt of his hat.

Marypat past on the breakfast of flat beans and found a piece of dried bun instead while Horatio ate his fill.

Soon they were on their way again. Horatio caught a ride on the wee cart with the Frandies; Tiger strolled along with the Kandies followed by Marypat who was watching the cloudy sky for signs of Donovan.

A few sweeps out the sky cleared, and Donovan had no choice but to rejoin the group on the ground. Still he avoided Marypat and concentrated on his flight technique.

At mid turn, the troops stopped beside a watering hole to give the Wee-colt's water and a chance to rest before heading on.

"It will be very late when we reach Small Town so take moment to rest." Cornelius shouted to his troops.

At the stop Marypat saw plants she had never seen before, there was one tall plant that looked like corn, but their pods were full of seeds instead of a corn cob. She picks one of the pods to show Cornelius and then she saw another plant almost as tall as the first, but it was bright green and had yellow hair sprouting out of the top of it. She also found near the edge of the pond in the very shallows the most remarkable creatures. They were transparent two-headed worm, with a head at each end, which allowed them to only wiggle from side to side.

Oh, may what be those." Marypat whispered.

"Spinders Lie, they are great at mending bones." Said a soft little voice.

Marypat looked around but saw no one. She thought for a moment and then realized that there could be a tiny member anywhere around her. In this world, anything was possible, so she decides to act nonchalantly, as if it were common place for her to talk to herself.

"Spinders Lie, you say, they are very unusual." She said.

"Very" Said the voice.

"You seem to know quite a bit; would you happen to know the name of this?" Marypat asked holding out the strange pod she had picked from the stalk like plant.

"Yes, that is Flirter rye, we grind it and eat it. But we can't always reach it so mostly it goes over ripe on the stack and falls to the ground spoiled."

"Why that's terrible, is the one I hold over ripe?"

"No, it is just right to use, you should make sure to use it soon though, flirter rye spoils fast once it is off the stalk."

"Oh, well, I have no use for it as I am traveling to Small Town. Would you like it?"

"You would give me such a gift, when I have nothing for you?"

"It is not a gift, if you don't take it, it will only spoil and what good is that?"

"Indeed. You are very wise. I accept your offering but say to you in heed: One must not pick what one is not willing to consume!"

"You too are very wise, and I shall remember your advice. Now where are you so I may give you the rye?"

"Just below you in the pond moss."

Marypat looked down, on the edge of the pond growing in the water was a thick patch of blue-green pond moss. With the mosses, blades held high and their stems having little space between them, there hid a tiny member perfectly from sight. It took Marypat a few moments before her eye picked up the sight difference in shape and color between the figure and the plant.

"I have never seen a member like you before, what are you?" Marypat asked as she stared at the cone shaped head of the member.

"I am a pond sprite, or Naxie. My name is Lilly." Said Lilly

"It is a pleasure to meet you, I am Marypat." Marypat said handing Lilly the pod of rye. The pod was just about the same size as the pond sprite, but Lilly managed it very well, as she stuffed the pod between two stems of the moss.

"You are very kind for a Vaster, perhaps you would accept this as my gesture of friendship?" Said Lilly holding out her hand with her offering in it.

Marypat extended her hand and accepted the charm. "Thank-you." She said.

Marypat looked in her hand and saw the pretty green crystal she had ever seen, it was as big as her smallest finger nail and was perfectly shaped on all sizes.

"Oh my. I could not accept this, it is just too precious." Marypat said in disbelief. She couldn't believe that the pond sprit would give her such a beautiful stone for a mere piece of rye.

The little pond sprite began to laugh. "'Tis not precious, there are many of those deep in the pond there are orange ones too." She said holding up an orange crystal almost the same size. "Since you like that one so much you may have this one as well."

"Are you certain?"

"For true, please take it." The pond sprite smiled.

Marypat took the gem from the sprite and then said. "I shall keep it for always and remember you, my friend."

"Indeed." Bowed the pond sprite then she dove into the pond and swam away to get help with the rye pod. Marypat watched her for a moment before she heard the Frandies trumpet, the call that they were moving out again.

It was very late in the turn when the group reached Goose Path, a narrow road that lead directly into Small Town. The path had two well-worn tracks, which the wheels on the wee cart fit into perfectly.

Making travel somewhat easier then when they were moving through the thick grass of silky flats. Still it was quite dark when they came upon a change in the path.

"We're here." Cornelius called out bringing the troop to an immediate halt.

Marypat looked around but saw nothing at all that resembled a town, not even a small town. There were no buildings no signs, no lights, not even a bench, there was just wide-open space and at her feet a black tar road that lead into the distance.

The well-worn path they had been traveling abruptly came to an end as it was covered over by what Marypat considered a modern road. But what was a modern road doing here? She starred at it and wondered, if they had a modern road, could they have cars and if they had cars why were they walking everywhere?

She turned to ask Cornelius but before she could even utter a word she was distracted by a most horrible shrieking sound.

She turned to the sound to find a huge green bus like contraption coming towards her. She shrieked with dread but in vein as it stopped precisely on the edge of the pavement missing her by a hand. A moment later the front of the thing swung open and a short member stepped down the embankment and out onto the pavement. He was dressed in a dark green plaid jacket with solid yellow slacks and a matching cap. In his hands, he carried a clipboard that had so many pages clip to it that the board had two double clips. The little member never took his eyes off his clipboard as he stood before them flipping his papers back and forth. After a while, he flipped the board over and finally spoke.

"McCarthy and party?"

"Yes!" Cornelius answered.

"Delivery Port Fin?" The member asked in a commanding voice.

"Right." McCarthy answered again.

"Well then let's get ya loaded we have to travel, all the way in there, all the way in." The Lachlann called and the troops started up the ramp into the bus.

First, the wee carts with their Wee-colts entered then the Frandies on foot followed by the Kandies and the Andies. Marypat looked down the side of the bus and thought to herself "*Surly they all couldn't fit in this one vehicle, the trail of Frandies a lone stretched longer than the bus itself.*" But strangely as she watched from the side of the thing, it gradually grew longer and longer to accommodate each group that entered.

Once the entire party had entered the Lachlann called out. "All a board for Port Fin, step it or be left."

Marypat jumped, she realized he was talking to her, and she was the only one still outside.

"Coming." She cried and with a hop, she was up the ramp. The door closed, and she was left in near darkness. All the other member had made their way to their places and no one was close enough to her for her to use their glow.

"Horatio?" She whispered as she stood there in the darkness. The contraption then began to move, and she could feel it vibrate through her feet. She put her hands out in front of herself, so she could feel her way. Just in front of her she felt a solid wall. The wall stretched the full length of the vehicle. She felt around it for a way to open it. She found a latch and pulled it. It was a door. As she opened it the compartment she stood in was instantly lit up as the next compartment was a live with members enjoying their ride. Some members were stretched out on comfortable benches, while others were laying in the bed hammocks that were strung on the ceiling. To one side of the compartment the wee carts and Wee-colts were put in stalls lined with hay. Even Tiger had found himself a comfortable place surrounded by a batch of Kandies.

Marypat came to the end of the compartment and found another door. She opened it and went inside. In the next compartment, she found Cornelius, Horatio and Donavan sitting at one of the booths that line both sides of the compartment.

"There you are, Marypat dear." Cornelius called to her as she emerged from the door. "We have already ordered, but I'm sure the waitress will be right back."

Marypat made her way past several booths filled with hungry Frandies devouring their meals, before stopping beside Cornelius. She sat down and picked up a menu.

"What's good?" She asked.

"Everything." Said the short round waitress who seemed somewhat annoyed with Marypat's question. "What will it be?"

"Foul?" Marypat asked nervously.

"And...?" The waitress questioned with a wide eye.

Marypat looked at the short member and quickly conclude that she must be a Felden. Then just as quickly she remembers Miss Honey, she remembers how rude she was until Marypat ordered a lot of sweets from her shop so Marypat decided she should do the same here and perhaps the Felden would soften up.

Marypat read the menu quickly and then turned to the waitress and order. "I'll start with Filters soup and bun, then I would like 2 crack couches with butter and for dinner I'll have the foul, baked with creamed pots and cabbage followed by a large slice of Carmel ice cake."

As Marypat spoke, she noticed the waitress's face go from a frown to a beaming smile.

"Yes, now that is an order my dear, I'll bring it right away." The Felden sang sweetly then she rushed away towards the very front of the compartment.

"I had no idea you were so hungry!" Cornelius said with a smile.

"Neither did I." Marypat answered.

After dinner, the four made their way forward to the very front of the vehicle. Immediately Marypat Noticed as they entered eight small areas were cordoned off with long velvet curtains. Beyond there, there was a huge open space filled with many large comfortable couches also covered in velvet. The couches where placed so that one may enjoy the view through the huge glass window at the front of the bus.

The group took a seat in one of the couches and watch as Small Town flashed by.

To Marypat the town seemed quite modern compared to Middleton City. Small Town had modern roads and cars, it had lighted streets, and homes that looked like houses Marypat had seem in Jamaica. There were sidewalks and street signs, fences and playgrounds. It almost looked like home, but it wasn't. Marypat suddenly felt home sick again, as for an instead she thought she might be home on the streets of Jamaica, but then she realized she wasn't. Horatio hopped up to her.

"Thinking of home?" He asked.

"How did you know that, but then again you always know, don't you?"

"I am beholding to you." He answered with a hug.

The two friends hugged for a moment and then the bus thing came to a jilting stop.

"All out for Port Fin!" Cried the driver.

The Lake of Whispers

Port Fin was no bigger than a single dock that had one pier stretched out several lengths into the Lake of Whispers. There was however a small hut that served as the dock house, where the dock captain stationed and controlled the fares to Great Town.

"Ya booked passage on the Lady "K, she should be here in the sweep." Said a tall breaded member who stood in the dock house. He had long gray hair and he wore a navy-blue captain's cap with a gold anchor embroidered in the center of it.

His clothes were weather beaten, and it looked like he was used to being wet and wind blow. His voice was rough when he spoke, but he seemed nice to Marypat.

"The Colleen may wait under the cover here but the rest of ya stay off the dock till the Lady "K" is docked and ready!" He told the group.

Then he scribbled something down on his note pad and slammed the window. Leave Marypat and Cornelius to smile at one another.

"Friendly Wardeen, wouldn't you say." Said Cornelius sarcastically.

Marypat giggled and then looked up at Cornelius. "Doc, it's getting late, when will we stop for the night?"

"Are you tired, dear?"

Marypat answered with a nod.

"Well there are accommodations on the Lady 'K', you can rest when we get aboard. For now I better go see to the others, you can stay here." "He said with a smile then he stepped away.

Marypat found a weather-beaten bench and sat down. She could see the water below the wooden planks that made up the pier. It was the deepest green she had ever seen; still it allowed the light from the lamppost to go through it and illuminated the fish that swam within. With her attention on watching the tiny fish, she had not noticed Donovan approach her.

"They say the Lake of Whispers can answer your hearts true desire. I don't believe them though; it's probably just the Whimples in the mist." Donovan said more to himself then to her. "It will take the whole night to get to the other side, ya know, the whole trip in the dark!" His voice was eerie when he said 'dark' as if he was trying to scare her but she wasn't afraid of the dark.

"Sounds grand." She said with a smile.

As she answered the Dock Captain came out of his hut, locking the door behind him. Marypat watched him as he limped across the dock and then down the long pier. When he came to end of it he picked up a large rusty rope and tossed it into the air. To Marypat it seemed completely strange to throw a rope to no one, but in truth it wasn't no one, she just couldn't see the Lady 'K' that was hidden in the lake of Whispers Mist.

The Dock Captain then hobbled to the next rope and throw it up where it seemed to just hang in the air. A few moments later the Lady 'K' was pulled snuggly to the dock where she came into view. Another moment pasted, and a gangplank was flipped from the ship onto the dock.

"All aboard for Great town!" The Conductor announced from the Lady "K's deck.

Slowly the caravan loaded on to the Lady K. The Wee carts and Frandies headed below carefully guiding their cargo into the huge storage rooms of the ships belly. The Kandies and Andies slipped aboard and disappeared into the woodwork leaving Tiger alone for the first time during the journey.

"What are you looking at Jinxie, afraid I might get hungry?" Tiger purred from the gangplank as he sauntered aboard.

"That will be enough, Tiger." Marypat quickly scolded as she greeted him with a stretch behind the ear. "There is no reason we can get along."

"Right." Tiger purred with a slight grin and a glance up to Marypat's shoulder where Horatio sat with a worried look on his face.

"Leave that thing and come and see the view from the upper deck." Shouted Donovan from a set of wooden steps that lead upwards.

"What thing!" Tiger turned with a growl. "Are you speaking to me?" Tiger pounced landing direct in front of Donovan. The coose moved his lip just enough to show off him fangs.

"Coose-gotta-tongue, great! Just what I need." Donovan said crouching down to the beast. "You may be a beast of the wood, but to me you're just a house coose with a big mouth." Then he tapped the coose on the end of his nose with his wand. A spark of light struck Tiger sending him into pain.

"RRRREEEEE." Tiger growled in agony. "'Tis warned are you fair Marypat, this Sherideen has no merit in your world and is more trouble than one as dear as you should have to bear." Then the Grundle hurried away to lick his wound.

"Tiger!" Marypat shrieked as she turned to run after him, but her arm was caught by a force much stranger then herself and she was held back.

"Leave him, I didn't really hurt him, it was only a little spark, besides what should you have me do? You saw for yourself how he practically attacked me. I was only protecting myself." Donovan spoke so convincingly that even Horatio couldn't resist his explanation.

"Now let's go have a look, shall we." Donavan said leading Marypat towards the stairs. It was very strange how she didn't resist him; his words were like a soothing warm bath and she had no power over leaving. It was so relaxing, so nice.

On the upper deck, Cornelius was already standing beside the wooden railing that rapped around the deck and he was overlooking the misty waters of the lake.

"Mary, dear, come and take a listen, if you're quiet enough you can hear her whisper to you right in your ear." Cornelius said with a grin.

Marypat walked over to the rallying and held on while she looked out at the darken waters of the lake.

"Quiet now and listen." Cornelius said in a whisper while the three new comers eagerly listened to the gentle wind that whispered around them.

What Cornelius heard:

Cornelius ear perked up as he listened to the same refrain he always heard when he traveled the lake.

"Ride safe in my water for you know, you live your life well, in happiness you go."

It always satisfied him to hear that he knew his direction in life, that he was still living, as he believed all members should, happy and good.

What Horatio heard:

Horatio worried his decision to help Marypat was not his true desire, perhaps it was tricking and tree jumping he should be concentrating on. So apprehensively, Horatio leaded slightly into the breeze and turned his head so his right ear had the best advantage to hear his verse.

"Stay the path in which you've embarked, for true a friend is your mark."

Relieved he looked down at his friend and watched her as she listened.

What Marypat heard:

At first, it seemed to Marypat, that there was no voice to the wind but then it came as true to her heart as any words.

"Steady be as steady go, when you find it you will know, that home and heart is one in the same, doodle not, the way you came."

The verse came as reassurance to her that she was indeed on the right path; she looked up at Horatio and smiled. He smiled back all was well for them.

What Donovan heard:

For Donavan the verse that played in his ear was not what he had expected at all. And to some degree it cut to close and he had to hide his face as the words repeated again and again.

"Your true heart stands beside you, see it clear, and yet too close to you I fear."

The verse angered Donovan; he turned away from the railing and huffed.

"Wimple's, I tell you, it's all a game to them. They laugh at our expense; I will not have any part of it." With that, he pulled his cape tightly around himself and disappeared.

Later Marypat found a small room for her, Tiger and Horatio to get some rest in. It had a short little cot, a porthole, stool, and simple desk. Nothing else, but it was just what Marypat needed. She was asleep the moment her head hit the pillow and the next thing she knew she was awaked by the Great Town bell announcing the morrow.

Timothy O'Hara's Fine Drip Cream in Cans and Bars

O n the deck of the Lady K, Marypat could see in the distance the wonderful Golden panoramic view of Great Town; she understood now why Horatio's cousin had said it was a city of Golden Streets.

Even the dock that stretched as far as her eye could see was immaculate and pristine, a sharp contrast from Small Town's dock. Every piece of wood, every small detail was spit and polished; there was nothing less than perfect anywhere. Which seemed to Marypat, to be one very difficult task to keep up as she watched from the upper deck as the wee carts were off loaded pulled by the Wee-colts who were more than excited to be finally free of the ships hold.

Their tiny huffs bucked and jumped strapping the finally painted dock, sending the elaborate dressed Dock Captain into a frenzy.

"Move them along, quickly now, move them, that's right, keep it going. You there move, MOVE." Cried the captain.

Before long the Frandies, Andies, Kandies, and wee carts were all off on to dock, leaving only Marypat, Horatio and Donavan remaining on the ship.

"Right then. You Vasters, off with ya now." Called the captain as he pulled off his blue cap and rubbed his forehead of the moister that had collected there. "

The three turned and walked down the plank and across the dock. With the last of them gone the Dock Captain pulled out his wand and could be heard shouting, "Pen tre brok grette grock!" Instantly the dock looked like new again.

At the end of the dock and to the right, they found Cornelius and the Frandies had corralled the Wee-colts and carts into a huge warehouse, were the goods that they had brought with them were being off loaded on to scuffling.

"We meet back here in two turns. Troop dismissed." Shouted Cornelius and instantly the Frandies, Andies and Kandies flashed out of sight leaving the warehouse staff of Wardeens alone to off load the goods.

"What is all that?" Marypat questioned Horatio. She hadn't realized that they had been transporting goods all the while.

"Dried foliage, rare stuff like bog rose and pepper moss. Cornelius sells it to this plant and they distribute its isle wide." Horatio announced proudly pointing to the top of the warehouse.

"No finer products then O'Hara's."

Marypat looked up over the warehouse door and there was the insignia, O'Hara's in sparking green and gold letters. She had seen it someplace before but couldn't quite remember where.

"For best results use Timothy O'Hara's, fine drip cream in cans or bars." Horatio began to sing and then she remembered outside the pharmacy in Boulder Town, the O'Hara advertisement and the can's stacked in the window.

"Marypat, Donavan." Cornelius called to the youngsters. "Come meet Timothy O'Hara's great grandson, Tiomoid O'Hara. Tiomoid may I present my ward Marypat and you must know Kathrie Gretel's son Donovan."

The very tall Sherideen turned sharply turns Donovan his piecing red eyes danced as he ignored Marypat completely and reached forward to greet his fellow Sherideen.

"Donovan Drake Gazpalding, of course you have your fathers dominate hairline and dashing look about you. It is my pleasure to meet the great one's heir." He said with a bow. "But where is your mother?"

"She was unable to make the trip; Auntie Gretta is to have her second set at any turn. Cornelius here was kind enough to bring me so as I may make it to my Sherite Extolel." Donovan answered.

"Yes, s s s. How kind of you Doc. . . . ." The Sherideen hissed turning back to Cornelius. "And this is . . . " He asked turning towards Marypat. He's eyes blazed at her as if they were sucking the very energy for the air around her.

"Marypat." Cornelius finished the Sherideen Tiomoid's sentence as the Sherideen Tiomoid slowly approach Marypat and slide his hands over her hands.

Horatio then appeared on the fence post that divided Marypat from the Sherideen.

"And I'm Horatio, the JINXIE, and I'm her friend." Horatio said with a beaming smile across his face. He pumped his arms as he pressed his fisted into his waist.

The Sherideen Tiomoid jumped back with a disgusted look on his face.

"So, tell me Cornelius, when you were in Boulder Town did you have a chance to catch my cousin's performance at the Blarney Stone?" Sherideen Tiomoid asked with a slippery grin.

"That was your cousin? He was sensational, just grand I tell you; I enjoyed it very much but Marypat. ." Donovan said flipping his hand at her. "Spoiled his last trick with the Cinerin stone. Such a shame really, it was going so well."

Marypat couldn't believe her ears. How could Donovan be so mean? The evening of the show he had been so nice to her after it happened, so sympathetic, so reassuring, this wasn't the same boy, this wasn't the Donovan she knew.

"Really, spoiled it did she!" Tiomoid slithered enjoying every word. "How did she spoil it?"

"She picked of the Cinerin of course." Donavan answered with a strange expression on his face.

"Impossible!" Tiomoid replied glancing back at Marypat with a sharp cast of his eye. "She's a mere Colleen is she not? How could she move a Cinerin stone, it must have been a plant, a fake? Geraldo must have spoiled his own trick and put out the switch too soon."

"Perhaps, but he wasn't very happy about it, claimed she used a spell and when she told him she had not, he disappeared in anger." Donavan explained.

"Sounds like my cousin, quick tempered, leaves little room for failure. Well never mind dear." Tiomoid said sweetly as he turned back towards Marypat. "It wasn't your fault; my cousin has always been one to over react when things don't go his way." Then he reached forward, cautiously passing Horatio on the post and gently patted Marypat on her shoulder. "You shouldn't allow it to get to you!'

"I won't." Marypat answered with half a smile. She looked up at the tall Sherideen and thought to herself. *"He's nice."* At first, he had frightened her but really, he wasn't all that bad.

"Well, I must get back to work, may you have an eminent stay in Great Town." Tiomoid said with a wave, and then he turned away and strolled back into the warehouse.

Once he was inside, and safe from their view, he called in a whisper. "Com-mor om do mos so, sider jet, jet no."

"Tell me, what do you know." Came a voice, it echoed around him in the air.

"What Geraldo said is true." Tiomoid answered in a low tone.

"Does she travel still with the Jinxie?" Came the voice again.

"Yes, Horatio is his name, and . . ." Tiomoid hesitated. "She travels with your son."

"Donovan!" The voice hummed. "I am glad for that news, but we must keep our thoughts on the task at hand and we can do nothing while that Jinxie is around her." Came the voice.

"What would you have me do, Supreme Master?"

"Stay close to her; I have something in the works. I will let you know when it is ready." Then the whispering voice ended, and the air went quiet.

CHAPTER
19

The Maurieen Palace

Travel in Great Town was an easy measure. Now that the huge troop of Frandies, Andies and Kandies had taken a two turn leave and the group was reduced to three Vasters, one Teeny and a Grundle. The only difficulty lied with the Grundle, few Vasters had ever seen a Grundle, and none had ever seen one walking through the streets of Great Town. This sight was more than unusually and caused quite a stir as the small group moved along Regal Avenue.

Several members shocked at the sight fled into shops, there were more that ran away squealing while even more popped out of sight with a puff of smoke. Meanwhile the Grundle noticed none of them and merely walked along following the group minding his own business. It was Marypat though that felt uneasy, the gazing stares and mournful shrieks were unsettling. Though she tried to put it out of her mind, it just seemed to her that someone was watching them more than just for the Grundle.

Still she tried not to think about it and instead enjoy the beautiful town. It was just as Horatio's cousin had described. Tall stone carved buildings that stretch to the sky. Brightly colored roof tops with intricate accents. There were shops for everything you could think of, restaurants and elegant homes. The name Great Town certainly fit!

At the end of Regal Avenue Cornelius hailed a carriage drawn by two handsome Hackney Trotters. Both brown in color while their forelock, crest, and tail were metallic emerald green. The carriage they pulled was silver and reflected the green of their tails in a sparking display.

"Maurieen's Palace." Cornelius said.

"Right." Said the driver and they were off.

A few moments later the group had left the busy town and were now riding along smoothly on what seemed to be a country road. Tall grass grew on both sides of the road and it looked to Marypat that they were back on silky flats. But then suddenly in the distance the palace came into view. Huge sparking sliver towers surrounded five lilac structures, each topped with dark purple tower caps, roof tiles, and accents.

It was an incredible sight, even Donavan sat up in his seat as it can into view.

The carriage brought the group straight up to the front door where they were greeted by two well-dressed Colleens. Both were wearing purple dresses that fit tightly in the waist and then flared out and down to the floor. The bodice fit snuggly, yet it looked comfortable. It had short puffy sleeves and an open neckline that revealed their white corsets. Pinned to the corset was their name embroidered on a badge, Doreen and Careen.

"Greetings to all, will thee being staying or just here for a look see?" The two ask in unison.

"Greetings and yes I have booked three rooms." Said Cornelius as he climbed out of the carriage.

"You are Cornelius?" Doreen asked while Careen helped Marypat out of the carriage.

"Yes, that I am." Declared Cornelius with a chuckle.

"This way then." Doreen instructed. She guided Cornelius into the main lobby. Where the rest of the group meet up with him a few moments later.

The lobby was a huge room, the walls, ceilings and supports were all covered in mirrors, giving the illusion that the room went on forever.

There was a counter to one side where Doreen had taken Cornelius and on the other side, there were several stone benches with large purple pillows tied to the top of them. But the most interesting thing about the room was that in the center of it was a huge well lite water fountain. It was cut from white marble and it stood three tears high. On each tear and fixed to the side in equally distance around the tear were four huge tusked triptoephant heads pointing their trunks high and spraying water into the air. On the very top of the fountain stood one complete, opal bellied, tusked triptoephant with his trunk in the air, spraying just like the heads. The fountain reflected in the mirrored walls and ceiling creating quite a sight drawing the group to its side.

"Wow a tusked triptoephant, their extinct you know." Donovan said with sarcasm.

"Really, they look like elephants to me." Marypat said calmly.

"Oranous Phantaneous Triptous, easily recognizable by its distinct tusks, note the swirling twist of the tip and its large opal belly." Cornelius said from over Marypat's shoulder. "Quite similar to our Asia Elephant, except for that amazing opal belly. Wouldn't you say Marypat dear?"

Marypat nodded her head in agreement while Donovan had no comment.

"Well our rooms are ready, why don't we get settled. We have lunch with Iola, in two sweeps. We can meet back here then." Cornelius replied.

Careen and Doreen showed the group to their prospective rooms, Donavan had a single with a splendid view of the gardens. Beside him was Cornelius's room again a single with the same view while Marypat's room on the other hand was two floors above the others with a view of the mountains and instead of a single, she had two rooms with an open balcony. The rooms included a bedroom that had a plush pink canopy with matching miniature for Horatio and a sitting room. The balcony was stuffed with beautiful plants and full of green soil, as if it had been plucked out of the very garden in Donovan and Cornelius's view.

Tiger made himself at home among the foliage and instantly pounced on a stunned Lofty Zort.

"Gulp" He swallowed it with ease and then strolled over to a patch of light and curdled up to take a nap.

"I take it you won't be going to lunch." Marypat said as she watched the Grundle lay his head down on his paw.

"Meals are not to be eaten in groups, besides I prefer the solitude of this patch to the crowding of Vasters and the scent of boiled flesh." Tiger said with a yawn. "A warm fresh catch was all I needed, now go away so I may nap."

Marypat left Tiger in the balcony garden and went inside her room. "What shall we do Horatio, Explore the tower, the garden, the library, or the sweet shop?"

"I hear the view from the tower is spectacular." Horatio answered as he bounced to her side.

"Then shall we be off."

"In deed."

Down the hall and up the main stairs the pair went with ample speed. The interior walls and ceiling of the castle was a gorgeous glossing pale lilac with deep rich purple accents on the moldings and carpet. There were statues of animals at every corner and nock, made of crystal or clay, there was even one made from pyrite in the shape of another Triptoephant.

The route to the main tower was not a direct one and so it seemed to take some time before they reached the foot of the steep spiral staircase that lead up to the tower room. Once there though they slowed their pace and started up. The tower walls were made of what seemed to be seamless silver mirrors and the steps themselves were the same pink marble they had seem in the lobby. Every few steps or so was a window cut outwards, enabling a view of the countryside and allowing in needed light. The windows were narrow and tall, and the light they let in was cast lengthwise on the mirrored center wall, causing an unusually glow. None the less it was enough light for the pair to see, so they continued on.

After a bit they came across a strange painting hanging on the center wall. It was shades of purple from light to dark, nothing more. Yet it glistened in the light as if it was made of glass and Marypat could hardly resist touching it.

"It's so shiny." She said to Horatio, who had already hopped past her and wasn't interested in the painting.

She slid her hand over the painting, only it was not a painting at all instead it was a huge slice of an amethyst crystal. Marypat could feel the cuts and ridges all along it, yet it was smooth and polished. The light bounced through the crystals causing it to glow and shimmer. It was a beautiful sight.

As Marypat glided her hand off the stone painting, she felt one of the crystals braked free in her hand.

"Oh no." She explained looking around expecting someone to see that she had broken it. But there was no one there so quickly she pulled out her velvet sack filled with all the other stones she had collected and placed the amethyst crystal into it. She pulled the sting tight and shoved the bag back into her pocket and then followed after Horatio.

A few steps later, she came across another large painting hanging on the center wall, but this time it was a lovely painting of a cliff side with a view of the ocean and rocks below.

"You can feel the sea mist from here." Called Horatio's voice.

The sound of his voice stopped Marypat in her tracks. She looked around but saw no one.

"Horatio? Where are you?" Marypat called out nervously.

"In here, look." He said hopping up and down in the painting. He was on the cliff's edge behind a large plume of yellow flowers.

"Come and see, it's so beautiful from here."

"How did you get in there?" She asked.

"Just climb in, it's a Realagraph." He answered.

"A what a graph." She asked as she climbed into the painting.

"A Realagraph, see it looks so real." He answered pointing out over the cliff.

"It does look real." Marypat answered as she stood up in the painting and looked out over the cliff to the rocks below. "A little too real." She added as the rocks below her feet crumbled slightly and several small stones rolled down the face f the cliff and then into the water below.

"Slash!"

"I think I have seen enough." She said. Then she turned to step back out of the painting but suddenly her foot slipped on a loose rock and she fell. Her hands scrambled to catch hold of something as she felt herself going over the edge, but there was nothing strong enough to hold her weight so over the cliff she went.

Horatio screamed as he hurried to help her. "Marypat, NO!"

At almost the same instant that he screamed, she was swooped up by a caped figure that had been hiding on the beach below. The figure caught her just in time, brought her back to the beach, and set her down.

"You're all right, you're safe now." Said a familiar voice.

The fall had frightened her so much that Marypat had closed her eyes tight and now they were red and teary. She opened them slowly and found Donovan standing in front of her. The sight of him brought fresh tears to her eyes as she began to cry.

"Thank you, Donovan, that's twice you have saved me, you must be my Emperador Salvador." She spoke through her tears. Then without thinking, she put her arms around his neck and kissed him on his lips.

At first Donovan didn't move, he wasn't used to this kind of affection, Kathrieens and Sherideens never acted like this, it seemed strange to him. But then something happened, her warm salty tears touch his cheek, they slid down slowly warming him and touching his very soul. Instantly the cold crust of his cursed Sherideen heart cracked and it began to beat freely in his chest like it had never done before.

It made him feel warm; it made him feel her affection for him deep within his being.

He looked down at her, their eyes meet, and for the first time in his life, he wanted to hold someone in his arms. So, he put his arms around her and they hugged. It felt so nice he didn't want to let her go. He knew that instant he was in love with her, and he would always love her. Yes, it was true from the moment he had set eyes on her he was attracted to her but this now was something more than that.

"Oh Donavan, you shaved her." Chirped Horatio as he bounced down beside the pair.

The sudden sound of Horatio's voice separated the two from their embrace, but Donovan managed to keep hold of her hand as they stood on the beach. For some unknown reason he couldn't bear to let her go. It was as if beside her, touching her, embracing her filled him with something wonderful, warm and irresistible, that he couldn't tier himself from. It was as if he were under a spell, or a love potion, only he was not.

"How will we ever get back up there?" She questioned.

"Don't worry." Donovan said squeezing her hand and smiling at her. "I'll take you."

Then he gently pulled her in front of him and for an instant let go of her hand. Then he scooped her up into his arms and jumped up into the sky of the Realagraph. As they flew, Marypat wrapped her arms around his neck, and tucked her head towards his. The senses of her grip around him made him feel free and alive something he had never felt before. It drenched him with a power that made his action of carrying her effortless, he was so exhilarated they flew straight out of the Realagraph in a flash and before he knew it they were at the landing on the marble stairs of the tower.

A moment later Horatio bounced out landing beside them.

"A shan't never want to let you go, for fear you may come to harm once more." Donovan whispered into Marypat's ear so that only she could hear. It was spoken from his heart and he meant every word.

Marypat giggled as she wiggled free from his hold.

"I am so lucky to have you as my friend and my Emperador Salvador." She said with a bow and a giggle.

"If you still want to see the tower, we must move a long, moment is nearly spent." Called Horatio from several steps above the pair.

Marypat hurried after Horatio with Donovan on her heals. A few strides later they had reached the main tower room. It was a huge circular room with large arched windows and a high arched ceiling. In the ceilings still resting in the rafters were several huge nests. Old certainly, yet still whole they were a reminder of the mighty specter that once haunted the tower. Known then as Ferrara Fortress.

"Long before the peaceful Maurieen took over the grounds, an Ubil Sherideen known as Carson Ferrara tortured and killed thousands of innocent Guldens for their golden feet. Which he melted down to create his fortress towers and buildings." Horatio said with a dramatic voice.

"He was a dreadful member feared by many, but one young doomed Gulden had the foresight during his end to curse the Fortress with his own dire soul. Later as a specter the Gulden appeared to Ferrara and tricked him, causing him to lose his life as he fell from the tower window." Horatio bounced to the windowsill and hopped twice before continuing.

"Still the Gulden roamed the tower, until a Maurie set him free by releasing all the gold from the Palace, thus the walls and towers turned silver."

Marypat and Donovan looked around the room in awe. There wasn't much to see but the thought of a specter living in that very place was fascinating.

Marypat step to the window and looked out at the view it was even more extraordinary. She leaned out of the huge silver frame window and felt a soft breeze on her face, it filled ears and then she suddenly heard someone whispering to her.

"Beware, beware, beware, beware, for there is Ubil everywhere." The soft whisper said. But strangely the gentle voice was not soothing but frightening. Marypat jumped back inside the tower.

"Did you hear that?" She said nervously.

"Hear what?" Donovan asked as he peered back at her from his position at the window.

"Nothing I guess." She answered.

"Perhaps it was the wind." Horatio said with a bounce. "You know from up here I can see all the way to the Pert and the Kert of Cinerin."

"Can you really?' Asked Donovan excitedly as he knocked into Marypat to get a better look.

"Sorry." Donovan said as grabbed her arm.

"What are they?" she asked not knowing what the Pert and Kert were.

Horatio bounded to her shoulder and pointed to a cut out section of the Cinerin mountains.

"That area, there, where it looks like a building on the mountains peak is called the Pert." Horatio explained.

But then Donovan took over as he placed his arm around Marypat and softly spoke to her with his lips close to the side of her face. "It's there that the Supreme Master rulers the Ubil land known as Cimmevian. Just beyond the building is a tunnel carved through the mountains; it is the only land entrance into Cimmevian. They call it the Kert. Can you see them?" He asked.

"Yes" she answered as she looked out of the huge window.

From the tower window to the north and east, she could see the Cinerin Mountain range with its red crusty soil, Huge Birch and enormous cherry green kettle post trees growing wild along its vast stretch of land. She could see the Pert and the Kert just as Horatio and Donovan described. To the south she could see, the lake of whispers with all of its boundless variations of color. To the west she could track the Darling River as it traveled through the Raye Raye Forest and into the Lake of Whispers.

It was a spectacular sight but one they had to leave as lunch was to be served in only moments.

On the north, side of the Maurieen Palace was the Principal Balcony. The balcony was used for grand events, it was large enough for 200 members, and yet still it was quite enough for a gathering of 5 for lunch. Its huge tiled floor and railings were made from pink marble stones, each cut and fit, precisely together. The darker shades of pink stones were used to form a complicated pattern of a tile in a symbol of peace, on the center of the floor.

Beyond the balcony and down the huge marble stairs was the Principal Gardens. Viewed easily from the balcony the gardens were an array of green foliage most so rare that Marypat had never seen before. Like the waxy green flower of the Callimim plant and the purple threaded Tandy tree, which was carefully transplanted from Peacock Isle, and was one of only two knowns to have survived the journey.

When Marypat, Horatio, and Donavan arrived at lunch on the balcony, Cornelius was already sitting and sketching, her Quizment the Maurie, Iola Frothper the 3rd, their hostess. Iola was a 3rd generation of Maurieen with master achievements in magic and commerce. Her husband was, The Exalted Grand Torideen, Orida Nnon Frothper the 2rd, Governor of Great Town.

"Sorry we're late. We were in the tower looking at the view." Marypat said with a curtsy.

"No tears on me, my dear, lunch can always keep when there are better things to do." Said Iola with a smile as she glanced at Cornelius through her long white toga trimmed in purple. Her eyes were large with bright golden flacks that sparked as she spoke. "Oh, to be un-aged, free to run about without restrain and care. 'Tis passing our enemy, this. Not?"

"So right you are, Iola. They know not what they possess." Cornelius said smiling back at Iola.

Marypat tried to understand what Iola was talking about. *Passing our enemy? Did she mean death?* Then it hit her. *No not death but moment, moment was their enemy!*

"Come forth young one and let me see thy face." Iola said reaching a hand out from her robe towards Donovan.

"You are the Kathrie Gretel's son, not?"

Donovan nodded yes.

"Good natured Kathrie your mother be, I know true to fact, but on thy father's, breast take heed my words, young Sherideen, trust not every tasked held to thee and think more with thee own head. Remember a Sherideen ye are from birth, an Ubil is ye choice, choose wisely." She looked him deeply in the eye and then smiled at him.

"Sit dear Donovan, while I inspect my next guest, Horatio, might it be, a Jinxie with a cousin I may know, not?" Iola asked grinning from ear to ear.

Horatio too only nodded his head in answer.

"Fear not dear Horatio, for ye is not among foe, I see thee is true and good, to which I open home and hearth."

Horatio bounded to the table just in front of Iola and bowed. "Quizment, I am humbled by thee wisdom and kindness ye show a common Jinxie." He said.

"'Tis not to mention, but now I must receive my finally guest, fare Marypat from above. I wish to know this place ye fall from, is it as fare as the Green Isles?"

"The Whole of the Green Isles are fare, but not as grand as your Great Isle." Marypat said softly.

"An answer worthy of a Regan, I dare say. Perhaps I shall see this place one day and judge it for myself. But in the meanwhile, we shall eat and speak of many things."

After lunch, Iola turned to Marypat and asked. "Ye question thy membership?"

"I beg your pardon?" Marypat asked back.

"One may wonder, are ye a Colleen, or other. Not?" Iola asked again.

"Yes, I wonder, but if I am from above, perhaps I am not a member here at all, but only a mortal from above?" Marypat said more asking then telling.

"Perhaps, but as ye claim to have fallen in, you must have been from here, and ye must be a member of one group." The Quizment Maurie Iola said quite matter of fact.

"What? You think my world came from here?" Marypat asked in disbelief.

"Ye must understand that when Ubil members ran thick many many passes ago, many members wanted to get away from them so they ran to the high place, where magic could not be used. Those who could not dream of losing their power, they stayed here."

"Then you know how to leave don't you!" Marypat shirked jumping to her feet "Oh tell me please how can I go home?" She was so excited she was going to learn how to go home, there was a way out!

"I'm afraid that that knowledge was lost many passes ago, I believe it was a memory spell proclaimed by the Regan, to stop the flow of

members leaving. Whatever it was, I know not the secret, I'm sorry."
Iola said softly. "But I can indeed assist ye to discover ye membership."

Marypat sat down quite sad, for a moment she thought Iola might
hold the key to how she could get home but then, puff, it was gone. Her
insides felt as though they were crumbling, and she wanted to scream
and cry, but her energy was drained. Her being was exhausted. Now all
she had was the consolation prize of knowing what she was. So, she sat
back, and half heartily listen as the Maurie Iola, quiz her.

"Let me begin by eliminating those you are not." Iola stared at
Marypat with a careful eye. "Naxie, Pixie and Etain you are not.
Krysdie or Kandie you are not Felden, Ullden, Lachlann, Hedlen,
Gulden, Loralac, or Whimple you most certainly are not. What remain
are the four most difficult to determine with one's eye and they are
Dandy, Kathrieen, Colleen and of course Maurieen."

Iola moved her toga slightly so that her hand was exposed. She
reached forward and placed a seed on the table.

"Take this seed and plant it in the garden." She said.

Marypat did as she was told and took the seed to the garden where
she placed it in the ground. Nothing happens so she returned to her seat.

"A Dandy you are not. Now pull back your hair so I may see your
hair line." Iola said with a smile."

Again, Marypat did as she was asked and pulled back her bangs so
the Maurieen Iola could see her hair line.

"Straight and round, a Kathrieen you are not! That leaves a Colleen
and a Maurieen. Now I have one final test, it will tell us what ye are, but
I must ask are ye prepared for what it will be?" Iola said in a reassuring
voice.

Marypat's mind was still reeling from the knowledge that her world
above had all come from here. It just didn't seem possible; her head was
full of confusion, so she really didn't hear the Iola's question. She only
nodded yes without a thought.

"Good, I must have a look at your neck." Iola said as she stood up.
She pulled her toga away from her face unveiling her long hair. Then
she stepped around to Marypat and touched her shoulder. A slight

spark emitted as they touch but nothing strong enough to stop the examination.

Iola pulled Marypat's collar away from her neck and exposed her fare white skin and 8 tiny freckles that encircled her neck perfectly.

"I thought ye my sister, and now I have proof." Iola sang as she lowered her face to Marypat." 'Tis moment to be gemmed." She whispered into Marypat's ear.

But Marypat had no idea what she was saying.

"I believe you carry them in ye pocket my dear, bring them forward, and allow them to make whole your membership as a Maurieen."

Marypat was even more confused, a Maurieen? She was a Colleen wasn't she, that's what everyone called her when they first see her, a Colleen, not a Maurieen. But without thinking she pulled out her bag of crystals and poured them on the table.

There were nine gems, a green Beryl, a red corundum, an opal, a purple amethyst, a blue azurite, a large clear quartz, a Blue topaz, a green Emerald and a tear shaped diamond.

The Quizment Iola examined the crystals, "Yes they are all here, but this one." She said holding up the tear shaped diamond. "This one is for something, yet to come, you should put it away for now."

Marypat stuffed the diamond back into the velvet pouch and waited while Iola arranged the other crystals into a circle.

"When a Maurieen is born of this world her gems are born within her, but when a Maurieen is born outside, she must recover them on her own. Only when she has done this, she worthy of her place and so now because ye have done so, I can restore ye to your place as a Maurieen. However, know this; the gems will appear around the neck of any Maurieen when they want them to appear and when they need their power to help them. So please, once I have them to you, give your body a want to show them, so we can see them and confirm you are a Maurieen. "Iola picked up her wand and touched the center of the circle of crystals, and then she said,

"A dark green Beryl to chase any hex's away
a blood red Corundum to clean the Hisue due to pay

a red fire opal for its passion and endless flame
a rich purple amethyst for its power to heal and tame
a deep blue azurite to calm, give peace and open the mind
a rock crystal Quartz for its purity, clarity for all kind
a topaz of Blue for a kind-heart and gentleness
and last a green Emerald for virtue and goodness."

With the spell complete, the gems rose and encircled Marypat neck. Then gently one at a time each gem took its place around her neck in bedding themselves in her skin. At first it felt strange but then the odd sensation went away, and all was normal.

"My sister!" Iola exclaimed with her arms extended. Her toga had fallen away and now Marypat could clearly see her eight gems around her neck and it hit Marypat that she belongs. They hugged but not for long, because Horatio excitedly jumped between them and cheered.

"Beheld to a Maurie, who would ever guess!" Horatio shouted with glee.

"Jinxie what is this you say. You are beholding to Marypat?" Iola gasped.

"Yes." Answered Marypat shyly.

"But why, when there is a removal spell that can relapse you both, it is quite simple really I can do it for you." Iola said with a strange look on her face.

Marypat looked at Horatio and then back to Iola. "Will it free him to have a normal life with a Pixie?" Marypat asked.

"I cannot promise that at all, once the beholding spell is removed he cannot be beheld to another. It just can't be done but he will be free from a commitment to you." Iola said.

"All right then." Marypat said sadly.

"Come with me we will need it quiet, as not to break any others who might be in ear shot, what trouble that could cause." She giggled slightly as she stood and lead the pair away leaving Cornelius and Donovan alone on the balcony.

Iola took them into a small dark room inside the palace. Then she pulled a huge crimson drape down to seal the opening and offered them each a stool.

Horatio was very quiet, to break the beholding spell meant to him that he would be free again to do whatever he wanted, but that also meant he would leave Marypat and he didn't want to do that. He could hear the voice from the Lake of Whispers repeating in his head.

"Stay the path in which you've embarked, for true a friend is your mark."

Perhaps it was only the beholding spell that made him feel this way but for one brave moment he decided he couldn't go through with the removal spell, no matter how free he would be.

"Wait." He said, looking up at Marypat. His eyes were sad and droopy.

"The removal spell is not what you want either, is it?" Marypat said with tears in her eyes.

"No!" He answered

"Neither I, but it is your decision, Horatio. It could mean your freedom."

"Freedom? Do I not have freedom? Do I not jump in the trees when I want, and chase clods if I want to? Is there ever a moment that I can't do what I want to do?" Horatio shouted at her.

"No." Marypat answered smiling.

"Then the only thing this removal spell will do is tear us apart, and I can't let that happen." He said bravely standing on his stool and holding a butter knife at Iola.

"Well I see, 'tis not my way to dispute a merry life, it is by all means ye own decision, I cannot make it for you." Iola said with a bow.

"Then leave it as it is." He commanded.

"Left it is." Replied Iola.

ornelius stood on the Principal Balcony talking with Donovan about the following turn's events, when Marypat and Horatio rejoined them.

"Well, how did it go?" Asked Cornelius when he saw her approaching.

"Let's just say we are happy with our decision." She answered with a smile to Horatio. To her no one needed to know that they hadn't gone through with it, it was after all their choice and no one else's.

"Good." Cornelius said with a smile. "Right then who wants to go into town with me, I need some ink to complete my work and there's a lovely shop in town, called 'It's all Write', where I know I can find what I need. Anyone interested?"

All three members cheered. "Indeed."

"Fine then the only question that I need reply is how shall we travel, by Spit cock, Huff or rail?"

"Spit cock?" Marypat question in her mind, what was that? She wondered if she didn't really want to find out. She could only hope that it wasn't chosen but she was so busy worrying that she hadn't noticed that Donovan and Horatio had chosen Rail.

Somewhat relieved she agreed, and they were off.

Unbeknownst to the group, a shadowy figure stood below the balcony and overheard the groups intentions.

"Com-mor om do mos so, sider jet, jet no." Commanded the figure in a whisper.

"Tell me, Tiomoid, what news have you?" Came an eerie voice in an echo.

"The Maiden is of the Maurie lines her membership is renewed."

"I see, that would explain many things!" Replied the echo.

"Master, there is more. The Quizment has released the Jinxie and he is no long held to the Maiden."

"That is truly good news, with that we may now act. Find out where she might be this turn." Commanded the echo.

"Master, they travel to town, this moment, to a shop called, it's all Write." Answered Tiomoid.

"Good, it may occur there then. Stay close and report back only if there is any distraction." Directed the voice.

"Are you sure he will fall for it?" Asked Tiomoid.

"Yes, I have put a very strong allurement spell on it, the Jinxie will be sure to want it." Answered the voice.

"Very well." Replied the figure and then all went silent.

Meanwhile, Cornelius lead the group through the main lobby and back towards the front of the palace. But before he came to the main door he turned left and headed down a side passage. After a few steps, Marypat noticed that the purple walls were becoming black with soot. The air too smelled of burning coal.

Was the train inside the palace? She thought, how strange. And yet as strange as it was she continued to follow Cornelius as he ascended a narrow staircase that went several lengths under the ground. The stairway was dark and the walls thick with ash. The smell of coal became almost over whelming. Finally, the staircase ended. Marypat looked around, there was nowhere to go. The stairway had ended, yes, but now they stood walled in, three solid black walls blocked their way forward. Still Cornelius seemed unconcerned and reached casually for his hanky. With his hanky in hand he stepped towards the forward wall and began to whip it down. Before long Marypat could see a Realagraph hanging there. But to her surprise it was not only a painting of a train but an entire train station.

Through the Realagraph the group went. The air at the station was clean and fresh unlike the air in the staircase. There was a patch of clean grass in front of the station to which the group marched through and stepped up to the short wooden platform. The train was not there but they were greeted by a short Lachlann dressed in a navy-blue suit and conductors cap.

"Greetings to all, and welcome to Middle Station. Will you be traveling to Up or Bottom?" he asked.

"Greetings to you my fine member, we plan our travels to Up." Cornelius said with a bow.

"Fine choice, as I can hear the Mag Tag rounding the flick right now, if you hurry you may have enough moment to buy your passage." The Lachlann said as he pointed to the tiny shed beside the platform.

Cornelius stepped over to the shed and bent down to the vender window beside the shingle that read "Middle." He booked 4 tickets to town, but before he could return to the group the Mag Tag puffed and creaked pass the platform and screeched to a halt. A huge cloud of smoke engulfed the station and swept out of the Realagraph and back up the narrow stairs. A moment later the doors of the train swung open and several members emerged and walked off the platform, heading for the opening in the Realagraph.

"All aboard. To UP station Great Town, All aboard." Called the Lachlann in the blue suit.

The Realagraph in Great Town was an exact duplicate to the one hanging in the Maurieen Palace, except for one tiny thing, the name painted on the shingle read Up. When the group stepped out of the Realagraph they found themselves standing in an alley way, there wasn't much around but again just as it was at the palace the walls of the alley were covered in ash and soot. The group made their way out of the ally and on to the main street of Great Town.

"Stay close, and don't get lost. Remember we are heading for a shop called 'It's all Write.' it should be up here on the right" Cornelius said as he hurried along.

The main street was a buzz of activity. Colorfully dressed members filled the streets and the air as they traveled from shop to shop. There were banners on posts that advertised, Himan's ale root-rice. The banners exploded every few moments with a flash of streamers and firelights. There were beautiful colored carriages running up and down the cobble stone streets, and venders waving their wares.

Huge tall buildings lined both sides of the street, the massive structures pressed up against each other as if they were muscling out every speck of soil. Somewhere brightly colored while others were made from what looked like solid crystal. But none the less they all were open for business and completely ready to provide every member with their needed wares.

After struggling through the crowded street, the group finally came to the building that housed the shop Cornelius was looking for.

"It's all Write," The large black sign read in front of what looked like a gigantic book that had been left open, facing the street.

Cornelius pulled back the enormous flap of the book and reveled the opening into the shop.

"In we go." Cornelius called, and the group stepped in.

The flap swung back with a snap and seemed to shut out all the noise of the street. Inside the shop, all was quiet, and still. Cornelius and Donavan headed for the stairs and the second floor leaving Marypat and Horatio standing alone in the mitts of thousands of old leather bond books.

"Have you ever seen so many Chronicles?" Horatio said as he bounded towards a stack of dusty legislative binders.

"Yes, my library at home has many books, but I must say they are not as OLD as these." She replied as she walked along the aisle reading the titles.

"Lawful acts of The Green Isles, Sanctions: A Narrative, Allegations: Both Wide and Narrow."

Strange books to have in a shop, Marypat thought, then she turned a corner and the tiles seemed to change and grow more interesting.

"The Green Isles Patrimony Edition of Incantations and Spell's." She had heard of this one in fact she had been given this one by Cornelius.

"Magical Misfits through the passes, Magic for the beginner, Mastering the Wand, and Learnings of Beasts, Lands and Emotions." This section was very interesting to her but she was quickly interrupted when Horatio peered over and enormous stack of books and calling to her.

"Marypat come look at this one." He said waving his hand at her.

She stepped around the table and there in the center of the next table in striking color was, 'Legends and Tale's, A Complete Account of the Most Legendary Events to Date.' There was no other book in the shop that looked like this one. The cover glistened and glowed a blue hue. Marypat picked up the book and held it in her hands it was larger than her forearm and she had to struggle to keep it flat on her arm so that she could open it. But when she did finally manage to open it she was surprised to find that there were no words in the book only pictures.

"It's a book of Realagraphs." Horatio shouted with excitement.

"What?" Marypat asked quite shocked

"You must step into the picture and see the tale played out before you." He said as he popped into the book.

"Horatio!" Marypat shouted as she watched him disappear into the page with a picture of a very sad Hedlen on it.

"Horatio come back this instant!"

But he didn't, so nervously she closed the book, held it tightly in her grip and headed for the stares. *"Doc will know what to do."* She said to herself as she marched up the steep steps.

On the second floor she found rows of pens and other writing utensils but no doctor. She glanced about the floor and found one member sitting at a booth, who was surrounded by hand written art work. Large woven looking tapestries with names and emotions written in bright colors and accented in gold and silver. There were tiny flowers and swords intertwined in the pieces. Each one very different from the next, each with its own unique design.

The member behind the booth was dressed in tan slacks and a white cotton shirt with his sleeved rolled up to his elbows, over it he wore a white smock that was splattered with several colors of ink. His hair was a mess and he seemed to be hard at work. Marypat approached the member, she really didn't want to bother him but she was hopeful that he had seen Cornelius and that he might know where Cornelius had gone.

"Excuse me fine sir, I mean not to bother you, but may I inquire. . . ." Marypat tried to ask but the Wardeen seemed uninterested in what she was really trying to say and he interrupted her.

"Where you might order a Name Tapestry? Why yes, my dear, I can do one for you in no moment at all, yes indeed, I can see.. . . ." He said with his fingers on his temples." Your name is Mary isn't it . . . no. . no. ., Marypat, yes a Maurie, no doubt, just let me make a note. ." The Wardeen fumbled through a stack of scrap paper, before retrieving a clear sheet and then began to scribble on it as names flooded his head.

Marypat was numb, she didn't want to hurt the Wardeens feeling but she also wanted to find Cornelius to help Horatio. She didn't know what to do or say and for that instant she did nothing but listen as he went on.

"Cornelius, Cornelius is it and Horatio." He said scribbling again on the paper and then he looked up at her. "Oh, my dear you worry so about him, but no matter, the story soon over and he will be back." Then he went back to his scribbling. "Tiger, how strange, Grundle is it, yes well and then Donavan, good name, here here, now let's see, Thought Post RN, that of friendship of course, Now what of your threads. . . . . Abundant, remarkable, trusted, heroic, reliable."

Then he stopped for a moment and looked up at Marypat with wide eyes. "Protector." His eyes slid back to the paper where he made one more scratch then he put down his marker and proclaimed. "I shall have it sent to the palace in the marrow."

Then he handed her a slip of paper and said. "Give this to the cashier down stairs."

Marypat took the paper and said nothing.

The Wardeen looked at her a little strangely and then smile. "Wasn't there something you wanted to ask me about your friend Cornelius?"

Marypat looked up at him queerly and said. "How did you know?"

"Oh, I knew all along, I can read your mind, but it doesn't mean I can't sell a tapestry first. It is after all how I make my living. Cornelius was here, he went upstairs to fetch a parchment he should return momentarily." The Wardeen grinned.

Marypat was relieved to hear that Cornelius would soon return but was put off by the Wardeen's trick.

"Now don't hold a grudge dear Marypat, the tapestry will be something you will cherish you will see, a friendly thought, a trusting bond is all in your tapestry." Said the Wardeen with a snap of his finger and with that he disappeared into a puff of smoke.

Marypat stood all alone beside the booth. She was surrounded by word tapestries, samples of thought posts and thread styles and suddenly she felt strange. She felt as if someone were watching her. It burned at her from a distance and yet she could not find the source or even what direction it was coming from. She searched the entire second floor with her eyes but there was nothing.

"There you dear, are you ready?" Cornelius asked startling her.

"Doctor, Yes I am quite ready."

The pair headed for the cashier where they met up with Donovan, who had just purchased a stack of books on magic. When it was Marypat's turn she handed the Colleen behind the counter, the small slip of paper for the tapestry and the large colorful Realagraph book.

"Well." Said the Colleen with a gasp. "I have never seen this book before, it's so lovely." She opened the cover and there in side was the shops stamp and the price 100 pie-it. "Your total is. . ."

But before the Colleen could read the amount the Realagraph popped open and out jumped Horatio.

"What a story." He shouted.

"A Jinxie, oh no, how did you get in there?" Now the book is spoiled. I must get you another." The Colleen shrieked in fright.

"No, No. The book is not spoiled, I will take it as it is." uttered Marypat with a laugh." So, with that the cashier wrapped up the book and the group headed back to the train.

Moments later on the Kert of Cimmevian a dark figure emerged from the clouds and lightly set foot on the out stretched perch of the Pert Balcony.

"What news you bring, has she taking possession of the book?" Asked a Sherideen dresses in red, from the balcony floor.

"Yes! And the Jinxie seems quite pleased with it." Remarked the figure on the perch.

"Then my plan goes into effect once the calling is complete. Go now and set the wheels." Said the Sherideen in red.

"Yes, Supreme Master."

The Calling

As the light of morning slowly crept back into the Great Isle it was the moment for Donovan to leave on his journey to his Sherite Extolel. The Sherideens rite of passage held each pass to invite all young Sherideen to a place in the Sherite Tribune. At 13 all young Sherideens were brought into the fold and made welcome. This was Donovan's chance to be accepted by his own kind, taught to be a great Sherideen and perhaps one day take the place of his father the Supreme Master himself.

Donavan was so very excited as the carriage approached the palace. Two copper sturn colts pulling a bright orange carriage that came to a halt in front of him. Cornelius and Marypat had asked to escort him and he had not turned them down. Any last chance for him to see Marypat was reason enough for him to allow them along. But what he did not know was that Horatio had secretly hidden in Marypat's backpack and was also coming.

The carriage brought them all the way to the Kert, where a tunnel in the Cinerin Mountains created a passage to Cimmevian Town on the other side. But the Sherite Extolel was not held in Cimmevian Town, it was up on the high top of the Cinerin Mountains at the Pert. The very place the First Bagree, Supreme Master Gazpalding sat and ruled. Bagree 1, lived many passes ago and he is the great great-grandfather of the current Drake Gazpalding, Donavan's father. It was here that Bagree 1, lost his bangle and it was trapped in the Cinerin mountain. Because of that, it is here that all Sherideens are washed of their Hisue and lead to the Sherite Tribune. Here to which evil has a foe, willing and wanting. Here where the unnatural is desired and suffering of others granted as just. All these things to which Donovan now held in his path as what he wanted for himself. Though not his to tell but his to refuse, if that he so desired.

To get to the pert, the group had to climb the solid marble stairs that cover the Cinerin Mountain. Built so many more passes ago that no member can date when the marble was laid into the Cinerin or how the stairs and patio flooring above were carved out of the Mountain. The patio of the Pert was constructed of solid beams of Cherry Green Kittle Post that laid over the marble stone to create the floor for the Pert. The pert itself was not a grand statement at all for that was left to the Grand Castle of Cimmevian. No, the Pert was not a castle but the Masters Lookout point on the isle. It was someplace he could watch and rule without a nervous twitch, it was comfortable, protective and an advantage.

Up the stairs the group marched. Donovan in lead with Marypat a step behind and Horatio in her pack and then Cornelius in the rear.

But as they walked along it seemed that their group grew, for behind Cornelius was two more young Sherideens and their families.

After a few moments they finally reached the balcony of the Pert. There before them stood several Sherideens dressed in long orange robes trimmed in a gold woven rope. Beside them sat an ornate copper chair. The chair was empty but Marypat thought that that was where the leader sat, and she was right. As a moment later, the group of Sherideens lowered their stance and welcomed a Sherideen dressed in solid copper gowns. The Sherideen entered the patio and sat down.

When the enter group had filled the balcony, one of the Sherideens dressed in an orange rope rose into the air and began to spark, suddenly the air above the balcony was swarming with Guldens. With their huge orange wings, they flew around swooping above the onlookers. Then without any command they began to call aloud.

"Bring forth, bring forth for all to see, for all to see, the one they call Birkey." Then the Guldens went wild with squawking noises as Birkey's name echoed in the air.

Horatio wiggle in the bag to get a better look, while Marypat herself searched the crowd to get a look at the one they called.

There was a rustle of bags towards the back of the crowd and then a young dark faced boy emerged from the group and stepped forward. The Sherideens in orange cheered in unison.

"Brother Birkey is welcome."

Then the Guldens began to call again. "Bring forth, bring forth, and let him stand, and let him stand, the one they dubbed Conan." Again, the birds went wild calling Conan's name until the red-haired boy step through the crowd, pulling his mother from him like an old wet coat.

"Mother, stop, let me go." Conan commanded as he slipped from her grip and managed to stagger up to Birkey and stand beside him.

Once in place the Sherideens cheered again. "Brother Conan is welcome."

Again, the Guldens sounded a call "Bring forth."

Donovan nervously turned to Marypat and grabbed her hand. "They call me next and I am gone, please do not forget me, as you, I am most fond." He said with a tear in his eye. He suddenly realized that this was perhaps his last chance to tell her how he felt for her, it may be the last moment he saw her. How final it all suddenly seemed and he for the moment wavered in his wanting to go.

"I will never forget you. You are my Emperador Salvador, I could never forget you." Then she kissed him on his cheek and their eyes met and held for several moments. It was like a band of electricity held them together and nether one could move. The air between them grew heavy and it was difficult for either of them to breath. Donovan reached forward then and kissed her mouth, it was sweet and soft, nothing more, but enough to brake the bond.

Meanwhile in Marypat's backpack, it was all Horatio could do to keep himself under control, he despised Sherideen tricks and felt that his dear Marypat was being spell bond by Donovan. He wanted to burst from the bag and sock the rogue, to his knees but he knew if he did it would cause such a state that it would only hurt his fare Marypat. So instead he stood listening while his blood boiled hotter at each word the enemy spoke.

Donavan held Marypat's hand and she did not protest as they listen for his name, but it was not his name that was called.

"The one they named Rowan." The Guldens called "Rowan." The name echoed through the air but there was no Rowan to emerge from the small crowd on the balcony. After a long stint there was still no Rowan and the Sherideens grew annoyed, their call was a sheik of pain that echoed for a great distance.

"Ro-wan, deep the pain you cast on your fellow Sherideens, for thirty passes we call thou name and still you do not claim, so now we wash your name from our post, our hearts and our lineage." Then they throw their arms in the air and a thunderous cloud rose in the place where Rowan should have stood beside Conan. It built with rage until it burst into rain and poured down on to the balcony. It continued to rain as the Guldens went back to their calling. "Bring Forth, bring forth and let him stand, and let him stand, the honorable Donovan."

There it came, his name and all he could do was stand still. He so wanted to go and join his Sherideen members, but he also couldn't bear to leave the fair young Marypat, which now as he stood beside her was more convinced of his love for her. It was a love that even as he was so young he knew that there would be no other that would mean so much to him.

"They await your stand, my Dear, but take heed in the knowledge that you take my heart with thee." She said.

He turned to her in surprise as if he was reborn in her smile. Had he heard her right had she said what she had said, did she mean those sweet words? If yes, then he was truly free from the anguish of not knowing her heart and it was now his to keep and cherish. This made things, though, not any the easier in leaving her side but it did give him opportunity to kiss her one last time before letting her hand go and taking his place beside the rain cloud.

He lowered his chin and closed his eyes as he moved his lips to hers. They kissed again, and this time Donovan felt his chest crunch. There was a slight throbbing pain from the crunch, but he pushed pass the ache believing it had happened because he did not want to leave her. But still knowing he had wanted to be accepted by his father and that his father was watching he stepped away from Marypat and finally took his place.

With that the Group of Sherideens cheered "Donavan is welcomed."

"Welcome all." The Sherideen in the copper chair proclaimed as he stood. The group of Sherideens behind him bent in honor and then stood straight.

"I am Drake Gazpalding Supreme Master of the Sherite Tribune, and it is my honor to lead these three fine Sherideens on their Sherite Extolel." Said the Copper dressed Sherideen as he gazed at the large group that was before him. Then he changed this position and looked only at the three young Sherideens.

"You may enter now." Drake Gazpalding said with a sweep of his hand and the long curtain behind his chair rose so that the three some could pass and then it closed again.

"To the rest of you I bid thee good Turn." Then he swept his hand at the crowd and they seemed to disappear, leaving Marypat alone in his presents.

"You are Marypat." Drake Gazpalding said coldly.

Marypat ears drummed as she looked around in shook, where had everyone gone? Why was she alone with him? She grew frightened and couldn't answer him.

"Dear, you are the fare one, my son Donovan has lost his heart for are you not?" He smiled at her but still she did not answer. "Yes, me think you are. I am not here to hurt you, dear Marypat, but instead to give you something from Donovan." His voice was sweet and gentle. "Come."

She obeyed him and stepped forward. Beside him stood a thin pillar. He guided her with a slide of his hand towards the pillar and told her to take the tiny stone box, cut from Cinerin that set on the pillar.

"It's a gift from Donovan." He said.

Hesitantly Marypat reached forward and retrieved the stone box from the pillar. She held the box with easy, to which the Supreme Master showed no evidence of his excitement.

"Open it dear." He said quite pleased.

She did and inside the box and a beautiful crafted gold bow pin with three rectangular diamonds on the end of each wing. It was a remarkable piece and Marypat felt strange accepting it.

"My dear Marypat, if you don't accept his gift it will crush him, do take it and wear it for him." Then he rose and took the pin from her hand, he pinned it to her blouse and then smiled at her.

"The symbol of innocents, how sweet. Now off with you before Cornelius gets worried." Then he snapped his finger and she was back with the group on the balcony as if nothing had happened.

She looked around at the crowd and wondered how she could have left the group and no one noticed. But then she thought it really didn't matter, she had her pin from Donavan and no one else needed to know anything about it.

Back in her room, Horatio emerged from the bag quite vexed. His feelings crushed, his heart trampled. Yet Marypat didn't seem to notice his mood. Instead she headed for the garden balcony to check Tiger, who was napping peacefully in a patch of light.

"Greetings, Tiger of the wood." She said happily.

"You have some nerve. Am I not a sleep? Do I wake you in your slumber? This was the first descent nap I have had in a round and you must disturb me?" Tiger snapped.

"So sorry Tiger, I only wanted to show you my gift from Donovan." She said shyly.

"Fine, I see it, now go away." He growled. Then he laid down his head again and closed his eyes.

"Well I guess they are right when they warn you about giving a voice to someone." She said sarcastically.

"I can still hear you." Tiger moaned.

Marypat tiptoed back inside her room and laid back on the bed, she looked happy and joyful. To Horatio she looked to be in love. Horatio was crushed and in such a bad mood he wanted to scream at her for being so naive when it came to Sherideens. *They trick you, play with your mind, and do anything to control you, they want control everyone*! He shouted in his head, but he didn't say a word to her.

"How did he do that thing, where everyone disappeared but us? That was pretty neat wasn't it?' She asked Horatio innocently.

Horatio was annoyed at her; how could she be so simple minded. It was too much, and he couldn't hold it in any longer. He exploded.

"It's a trick of the mind, a phase spell, don't you know anything. They were playing with your mind."

"Playing with my mind? What makes you say such a terrible thing, Donovan loves me." She shouted back at him.

"Loves you, what does he know of love." Horatio yelled, knowing in his heart that he loved her, and it was a love more powerful than a desire. Stronger than a spell and truer than anything Donovan could ever understand. Yet he could do nothing more than be her friend. He was only a teeny, a Jinxie. Never could he hope to be a vaster size member, though that is what he so wished. He had to be satisfied with what he had with her, her friendship and that was all.

There was silence in the room.

"How can you say that?" She asked with tears in her eyes.

"Because, Marypat, a Sherideen cannot love, his heart is cursed and what they do feel is not love but dominance, control. They thrive on control." Horatio's voice trailed off as he knew his words would hurt her.

"I don't understand, he said he loved me." She cried.

"No, Marypat, I never heard those words from his mouth." Horatio pleaded.

"Yes, he said it over and over I heard him say it." She demanded.

"It was a trick, you heard it in your mind."

"No" She sobbed

"Marypat, look at me, Marypat." Horatio demanded. "You must try very hard right now and clear your mind, and remember who we are talking about, Donovan. The Sherideen who is rude and curt. Donovan who has no occasion for you until this turn. Marypat! He has put a spell on you and it is up to you to shake him out of your mind. Think about it, do you really love him?"

Marypat's tears rolled down her face it was painful for Horatio to watch as his words opened up her mind.

"No, I don't love him, how did he do that, why did he do that to me?" She shouted.

"I don't know, a Sherideen is not a trusting member, he was only being true to his kind." Horatio said softly.

"Now I see, he has some kind of power over me, whenever we're together." She said.

"But now he is gone, and you are free from his hold." Horatio said patting her hand gently.

"And I have only you to thank, my friend, my dear friend." She grabbed him up and hugged him.

"Well don't overdo it now." Horatio squeaked from under her grip. She put him down and they both giggled.

"Horatio, what do you know about the curse on the Sherideen heart?"

"Only that they are, it's one of the reasons a Kathrieen prefers the company of a Wardeen over a Sherideen. But if I recall there is a tale in that book you bought." Horatio said with a bounce over to the bed table where the book laid unopened. He opened the book and read the index.

"Yes, there it is, 'The curse of the Sherideen Heart.'"

"I should like to know the tale, would you come with me Horatio." She asked softly.

"No need to ask, I wouldn't let you go alone." He answered.

Marypat took the book from Horatio and laid it on the floor, she turned to the page with the heading, 'The curse of the Sherideen heart' and stepped inside. Horatio followed.

The Tale

The seen on the page was a cottage on the edge of a dark forest. Marypat found herself dressed in a long pastel gown and standing in a field of flowers just in front of the cottage.

"Horatio, where are you." She called out.

"Down here, among the weeds." He sneezed

"Well get up here. Now what do we do?" She asked with a wave of her hand and he bounced to her shoulder.

"I'd head for the cabin." He said sneezing again.

So straight to the cabin they went. Marypat knocked on the door but there was no answer, so she went inside.

There was a fire going inside and the cabin was warm but there was still no one around.

"Is this the way it starts?" She questioned Horatio.

"I don't know there was a Commoner in the other one, I just followed him around." Horatio answered still standing on her shoulder.

The pair waited quietly then suddenly there came a great crash and a thump, outside the door.

"Dom me a gron." Shouted an old voice from outside the door. Then the door swung open and there in the door way stood a long hair Kathrieen in a dark red dress.

"Oh, there you are, sorry I'm late but I got stuck over in the tower that Gulden sure can squawk a lot. Anyway, on to our tale." The Kathrie said pushing her way into the tiny cabin.

"Ya think they could have painted this thing a bit bigger don't you." She hollowed as she struggled into a chair beside Marypat.

"Now dearie since there's the two of you, what do you say we play out the story together, I see you're already dressed for the part." She said smiling at Marypat, "But I'm afraid the Jinxie will need a bit of a change, do you mind?"

Horatio nodded his head "No"

"Well then off the shoulder, I wouldn't want to miss and have something happen to our maiden." The Kathrie said with a toothless grin.

Horatio bounced onto the floor and the Kathrie pointed her wand at him and said, "Pix six height and moon, Quee atee ben mol a doon."

Suddenly the Kathrie's eyes went wide as Horatio began to grow, he grew as tall as any Vaster and to Marypat's surprise he was taller than she.

"Horatio, you're so tall." Marypat replied with glee.

Horatio himself looked amazed. He stood before Marypat and held his hand out to her. She took it and stood in front of him eye to eye. They smiled.

"Well enough of that, on with the story." The Kathrie interrupted.

"Now as the tale goes, You." She pointed at Marypat. "Were to marry thy true love." She pointed at Horatio. "Notice the white gown." The old Kathrie hurried the story along.

It seemed apparent to Marypat that they were getting the abridged version and not the original. But none the less Marypat looked interested as the old Kathrie continued.

"But there came a rival, a Sherideen from the dark wood who challenged the groom to a duel." The old Kathrie stood and pushed open the door.

"Outside now." The Kathrie motioned to the pair.

Hand in hand Horatio and Marypat stepped back out in to the field of wild flowers. This instance though Horatio could see above the flowers and they didn't bother him. Together they stood dressed in white bridal clothing as they awaited the next installment of the story.

The old Kathrie continued the tale explaining the details of the wedding. As she spoke she encircled the pair and magically spellbound them to their place.

Meanwhile from the dark wood rode a masked figure who rode up to them and pulled out his sword. Without warning the dark figure thrust the sword at Horatio and Horatio fell to the ground.

"NO" Shouted Marypat as she watched Horatio fall with the sword in his chest. She tried to reach for him but the old Kathrie grabbed her.

"It's alright dearly it's only the story, he's fine." Then she whispered two words that Marypat could not hear and with that the beautiful bow pin that was still pinned to her gown began to spin. Instantly Marypat's mind was taken over by a power stronger than her own and she was in a trance.

In horror Horatio watched from the ground, unable to help, as she was stripped of her mind by the pin and then carried away by the masked figure.

"Now that is how the story should have gone." The Kathrie said with a strange laugh.

"What do you mean should have?" Horatio groaned in pain. The sword had gone straight through him and he was pinned to the ground with a powerful blanket of magic.

"Oh, you fool, in the true legend the dark Sherideen losses to the dumpy little magician, and in his anger at the loss, he the dark Sherideen curses all others of his kind, of ever truly feeling love. A curse to which even Kathrieens are affected this Turn. Well I hope you like your final resting place, it is quite lovely here, if you like that kind of crap." She spat.

With that she disappeared from his sight.

Horatio laid on the ground, the pain was unbearable, he could feel the warmth of his blood dripping from his body and he could do nothing to help himself, then he thought of something. The Kathrie had claimed to be visiting the Gulden in the tower of Ferrara, if she could move between the pictures so could the others.

"Shamus, I have need of you. Shamus hear my cry, Oh Shamus friend come with thy tools and help me or I die." Horatio called out as loud as he could bear.

"Who calls like that, so loud, on such a fine turn, to disturb me so." Mentioned a tall fellow from across the field.

"'Tis me, Horatio, here with in the flowers, please help me."

The gangly fellow strolled up to Horatio and looked down at the sight of him.

"What a fine mess, my friend, but what would you have me do?" The fellow said quite calmly and unconcerned.

"Is there a balm with in this book that could heal my wounds?" Horatio asked in pain.

"Perhaps but I have no period to go and do your bidding, good turn." Said the fellow and he walked away.

Horatio had all but given up when he heard a very strange buzzing sound above his head. He opened his eye to find a flower sprite riding on a big fat bug.

"Conway has no sense, Me think, for you are in great need. I am Maxie James a flower sprite of the wood, but I hear that a Maurieen is being born just a page ahead. Would thee wish for me to seek out the healer of that page and bring her back to thee and repair thy injuries?"

"Yes, please Maxie, I would be in thy dept." Horatio uttered in pain before blacking out.

The Masked figure rode through the dark forest with feverous speed. Marypat body was drape over his sable, her body lifeless, and her will gone. At the edge of the forest, hidden slightly by a thicket of birch, stood a simple wooden frame and a painting of the Main room at the Pert.

The masked figure stirred the sturn colt and through the painting he jumped, landing in the main room with precision. There were several Sherideens in the room, still dressed in their orange ropes that had to move as the colt landed. Beside the orange robed Sherideens stood Conan, Birkey and Donavan, now dressed in grey robes and ready to hear their masters great plan.

"Supreme Master, I have her." The masked figure said as he pulled the Colt to a halt.

"Take her down and bring her to me." The Supreme Master Gazpalding commanded the Sherideens in the room.

Donovan watched as the older Sherideens pulled the lifeless body of a maiden from the colt. Her head hung down and her hair covered her face. *Who was she?* He thought.

But as they brought her in front of Gazpalding, Donovan's eyes widened as he realized who it was. It was his Marypat, his dear Marypat.

Why had his father brought her here, why was she in this state? The questions rolled in Donovan's head as he stood among the others. He just stood there and said nothing, nor did he do anything to help her.

He watched as she was unable to stand for herself. She was heavy in a trace and that angered the Supreme Master Gazpalding.

"She is too weak, the spells too strong, remove it at once." The Supreme Master Gazpalding shouted at the Kathrie who was hiding behind one of the other Sherideens.

The old Kathrie slithered up to Marypat and shyly answered her leader. "'Tis not to strong, only to fast, my lead."

"Whatever it is, deal with now as I am of need, NOW." He commended.

"SO, BE." The Kathrie smirked then she turned to Marypat and whispered a single word. The pin began to slow and as it did Marypat regained some of her strength, but still her mind was not her own, it was controlled by the Supreme Master Gazpalding.

"There now my dear I have a job for you." The Supreme Master Gazpalding said softly.

"Job for you." Marypat restated as if she was heavily intoxicated.

"That's right." The Supreme Master Gazpalding smile broadly as he sauntered over to the young maiden Marypat. He put his arm around her and guided her to the very spot where Bagree Gazpalding himself lost his life. The place where the Magic Bangle had been buried all those passes ago. There under their foot, with in the Cinerin stone, only a Vaster length below them laid the Gazpalding birthright.

"You, Marypat are the one being that can retrieve from this cursed stone, my family's Bangle for me. How great this moment shall be, how enormous the position I shall hold and you shall be of my honored, if you can do this task for me." He said so gently and sweetly as if he were tucking in a child at bedtime, like a loving father to his dearest child.

"Bring her the tools." The Supreme Master Gazpalding called to his followers and a moment later there were many devices used for digging at her disposal. He grinned as he watched her start to work, breaking the Cinerin and placing the stones in a tube that rested on the side of the Pert. The tube then transported the Cinerin stone to the base of the mountain where the stone was then out of the way of the Sherideens.

The Observer

Meanwhile in the Maurieen Palace dinner had been called, yet Marypat and Horatio did not appear, to the worried eye of Cornelius and Iola.

"I shall check their room." Cornelius confirmed with Iola who insisted she must go with him. She had a strange feeling about Marypat and needed to be relived of it by assuring that she was fine.

They came to the room, and all was bare, excepted for a hungry Grundle.

"Is dinner passed?" The Grundle, Tiger asked.

"YES, and Marypat has not come down for hers'. Might you know where she is?" Cornelius asked Tiger with a concerned voice.

"She has gone within that silly book over there, with that horrid Jinxie." Tiger said with disgust. "And she has not come out as yet and I still wait for my evening cream."

"What book is that?" Asked Iola with a strange concerning voice.

"A book of Realagraphs with legends and tales, she bought yesterday at the shop in town." Cornelius answered as he stood over the large book.

"A book of Realagraphs?" Iola replied nervously.

"Why?" Cornelius asked not understanding the concern about the book.

"Realagraphs can be very dangerous, if in the wrong hands. We must take the book to Orida; he will know what to do." Iola said grabbing up the book instantly she felt something Ubil about the book. She feared the book was cursed and if she opened it she too would be sucked into its evil. So, she held it tight and running out the door hoping to get to her husband before it was too late.

"Bring me some cream, won't you!" Declare Tiger as the two Vasters left him behind.

Down the staircase Iola flew, across the lobby and into a huge library, where a heavily breaded member stood glancing into an orb. He was very tall and thin and had long gray hair that still had flecks of black through it. He wore a long crimson Stola pulled in at the waist with a long rope made of stars.

"Something has happened to Marypat." Iola replied urgently to her husband.

"Yes, I see it too." He said still staring into the orb. "That is that you carry."

"A book she bought yesterday in town." Iola answered as she handed the book to Orida.

He took the book from his wife and held it.

"There is a strange heat coming from the book, I can feel the evil seeping from its pages. This is not good, there is Ubil a foot."

"Yes. I felt it too." Iola agreed.

"What should we do?" Cornelius asked in fear.

But they had no chance to act, for in the Pert at that very moment Handrew was calling out to his master.

"They have found the book." Handrew announced.

"Then it is the interval for our next step, bring forth the observer." The Supreme Master Gazpalding shouted out loud.

Several Ubil members suddenly appeared pushing a hugely heavy observer. The observer was casted from solid gold and formed a triangular frame which held a perfectly circular crystal face. In the very center of the face was a blood red ruby also cut perfectly round. Within the ruby was in a six-rayed star that shone through the ruby and glistened into the crystal. The ruby moved ever so slowly in a round causing the rays to rotate around the huge face of the crystal. At the very top of the observer sat a dial which counted the rays and revealed the instance of the turn, each ray equaled 3 sweeps and 6 rays completed a turn.

The Supreme Master Gazpalding stood before the Observer and held out his wand. He used a trectacular moment with his wand and called aloud. "Zee on spin ion so grime, hee jert frim toe, breek, me a re!" (Stop the dial, still in moment, no movement make till broken be mine.)

With that the center piece of the Observer stopped dead and with The Supreme Master Gazpalding's words all that surround him including his own followers and his son, Donovan, were stopped frozen in their tracks. The Supreme Master Gazpalding looked out over the balcony and out over the land. Nothing moved, not even a foul, or a Lofty Zort. All was still, dead still. He turned back to Marypat who also was charmed by the Observer spell. He touched her on the hand and whispered low so only her ears would hear the braking tone of his removal spell.

"Tec way, do."

Instantly the spell was broken from her and she could move. Back to work she went removing Cinerin stone from the floor of the Pert. While all of the Great Isle sat still as moments moved only for the Master and his slave. Iola and Orida too had been frozen in their study at the palace. Cornelius and Tiger, all were now at the mercy of the Ubil Supreme

Master Gazpalding, no member upon the land was unaffected, none were able to save the Isle.

However, there was one member who was not upon the land of the Great Isle and he was not under the spell of the Observer but he was trapped within a cursed book of Realagraphs.

The Bangle

A sliver of light fluttered in Horatio's eye as he struggled painfully to see his surroundings. He lay motionless, broken, draped with pain. His will was gone from his life and he was now wishing for it to end. But that would have to be another turn for he had no stint now to die, his Marypat was in need of him, he was all that was left to save her. He had to reach deep down with in and pull from the depths of his being the will to fight his pain and awake.

"Why there you are. That's it dearie." Said a very old Kathrie voice and for a moment Horatio thought it was the same Kathrie that had tricked him early. But as he opened his eyes he realized it was not the same ugly Kathrie, but a light brown skinned sweetly looking old Kathrie. Her hair was cut short around her slender warm face. She wore a light blue flowing gown with a yellow apron tied around her waist and her form seemed to glow in a passionate light like that of a vision. Horatio could tell the glow was of a good-natured Kathrie and with her he was safe.

"Marypat, the dark Sherideen has taken her into the forest. I must. ." Horatio struggled to sit up but pain shoot through his body like a tremor and he was forced to lay back still.

"Please, your wound will never heal if you do not lay still. But to your worry I must inform thee, hurtful and strained as it may be to hear, that yes, something wicked is a foot. The pages of this book are reeking with an odor to which I have never known. I fear that the world outside is foul with Ubil stench and we have little measure to haste in making our attempt to set things right. Still we of the book are no help to you outside these pages, we only can exist within. You, Dandy, are the hope of all."

Horatio sat quiet on the small cot within the cottage of the painted Realagragh. The same cottage the Ubil Kathrie had changed him into a Dandy, the very spot he had held Marypat's hand for the first time as a Vaster. How great that moment was, yet how long ago it seemed now.

"Good Kathrie, if what you say is true, what hope do I have in setting things right. I am only a Jinxie, not a Dandy as you say. The Ubil Kathrie of this tale change me big as to play the part of the groom. So, I too will be of no use once I set foot outside. Will I not be small again?" Horatio said soberly.

"A Jinxie you say, but how can that be. A Kathrie couldn't change you as such; no magic I know can do this. You must be or have some Dandy power of your own. She could have only opened you to the change." The good-natured Kathrie explained.

"There, try it now . . . well change." The good-natured Kathrie said.

"Change? How?" Horatio asked.

"A Dandy changes with his will, just tell yourself you want to change!"

Horatio concentrated with all his mind, but nothing happened.

"You're going about it all wrong, don't try so hard."

Horatio tried again this time he calmed his mind and thought of Marypat's face so close to his as he sat upon her shoulder. With that he instantly shrank into his normal small self.

"See, she didn't do anything you didn't already have the power to do yourself." The Kathrie said proudly. "Now you know when you leave the book you will be able to fight the dark Sherideen."

"How will I know what to do or where to find him?" Horatio asked.

"Maxie, Rudy, and Johnny G are searching the forest as we speak, I expect them back any moment with news. For now, though you rest and let the spinders lie do their work." The good-natured Kathrie said softly.

But as she said the words the door of the cabin flew open and Johnny G, the Andie, burst through with his spear in hand.

"An Ubil Sherideen guards the portal on the edge of the dark forest." Johnny G exclaimed breathlessly. He ran across the wooden floor of the cabin and hoisted himself up onto a chair that sat near Horatio's bedside.

"He has a maiden under a spell from a spinning pin upon her chest, she digs through stone of a Magical burden for an object the Ubil Sherideen entitles a Bangle." Johnny G continued soberly.

"Is only he alone. All others stand still, solid, unmoving, like fresh dong on a cool morning warm and firm yet misty around the edges." Maxie interrupted as he flew in from the open door on his bug.

"yes, 'tis true what he says. It seems an Observer sets unmoved by sweeps, it's dials not in counting." Johnny G replied.

"A phase spell must." Maxie added as he landed his bug on the bed sheets. "Our fellow seeker, Rudy, waits and watches for the tell. What does ye wish us to do for ye as yet?"

"Where is the sword the Sherideen used on me?" Horatio asked the Kathrie.

"There." She answered pointing to the wall. The sword sat with its point laid down and handle leaning on the wall with Horatio's blood still fresh upon its blade.

"Tell me Kathrie is it real or is it of paint?" Horatio inquired.

"It is surely not of paint, its touch is solid, it must have come from your world outside the book." The Good-Natured Kathrie answered as she placed her hand on the blade of the sword.

"Then I shall need it, help me to stand." Horatio commanded bravely as his mind became engulfed with the thought of rescuing his love, Marypat from the Ubil members. His body became energized and his want to live and fight radiated his will and transformed his size back to the height of a Dandy.

At the Pert the air stood still, a rotting stench of Ubil odor was building as the Observer held its post. All around and slowly growing was the mist that rose from the spell bound Sherideens. As at the pert, as everywhere on the Great Isle the life mists rose from the phase captured members, yet not as vile as that on the Pert.

It would not be long before the Isle was covered by the reeking mist and suffocated all life for one so greedy. So greedy for his bangle the Supreme Master Gazpalding could not see the way in which he too had to pay for his evil phasing spell. The Hisue that came his way could not be absorbed by the bangle for it was one hundred times the normal amount and it was striping away his flesh ever so slowly.

Within the stone cavity, Marypat worked with devilish determination until she glimpsed a speck of something other than rock. Gently she cleared the rubble from around it and uncovered the pyrite bangle. She turned it over and rubbed it slightly as she did the intricate designs that once sparkled all around it came into view. She noticed that five of the six diamonds were intact but that one of the prongs was empty. Looking at the empty spot on the bangle, she smiled. She placed it down gently and reached into her pocket where she kept her velvet bag. She opened the bag and poured out the tear shaped diamond that the Whimple had given her from the Mist of the Froymin. Then she took the diamond and placed it into the Bangle.

Like a magnet the bangle grabbed hold of the diamond with its prongs and with that that bangle was whole once more and ready for its possessor.

Slowly, like a drone Marypat climbed out of the pit. She sat at its edge and held the bangle up to Drake Gazpalding. He accepted the bangle and quickly placed it on his left arm. Immediately the Bangle glowed white and the tear shaped diamonds vibrated in their prongs. The bangle inhaled every speck of Hisue that had come to him and gradually his skin rejuvenated throughout his body. Then the bangle set to work on the obeah stench which it absorbed quite quickly as well. Before long Gazpalding stood afresh Sherideen, with new power and new strength. He was truly the Supreme master of the Isle.

"Now all members shall kneel before me and I shall judge them worthy to live." Gazpalding shouted for all the land to hear. "And you my dear . . . shall be the first."

Gazpalding reached for Marypat with his hands around her throat and he began to strangle her. She did not resist or struggle, she merely closed her eyes. But his hand had only begun to tighten when he was struck from behind. A devastating blow hacked off his right arm.

Gazpalding turned around to face his adversary. It was Horatio. He had come from the Realagraph on the wall, the one that was magically connected to the Legends book.

"You, Jinxie?" Gazpalding stumbled. His voice was pained but not finished.

"Pen tre brok greete grock." Gazpalding whispered and his arm was back on in a flash. "You cannot fight me Jinx you have not my power." He said showing off his left arm with the pyrite bangle already on it.

Horatio looked shocked, he was too late. He lowered his sword in defeat. There was nothing he could do.

"Kill him Horatio. He is one alone, you can defeat him, and you must for Marypat." Came a voice from behind Horatio. It was Rudy, a Realagraph Wardeen, still standing in the Realagraph and unable to step out. All he could do was encourage Horatio not to give up. "Kill him!"

Gazpalding heard the whispers of Rudy and quickly acted to protect himself. He grabbed Marypat around the neck with his left arm and pulled her head up to his chest. Gradually he applied more pressure around her neck until she gagged.

"So, is this why you came?" Gazpalding asked with slithering voice. "You came to save this maiden, well." He shouted as he rose up above the flooring. "I shall save you the embarrassment of her seeing you die by killing her first." Then he squeezed her neck and Marypat gave out a shriek her eyes flew open and she grabbed at Gazpalding's arm.

Her hands clasped the bangle and as she did the bangle began to glow blue at her touch. Her entire body glowed an unnatural hue. The bangle accepted her, perhaps it was her innocents, or was it her tear shaped diamond she had placed in the bangle, but whatever it was the bangle did not repel her, instead it surrounded her warmly. It evaporated any slight imperfection to her body and absorbed her pain. She hung from the bangle like an angel, floating gently, calmly, peacefully. All the while Gazpalding clutched her even harder under his arm, slowly choking her, while he laughed at Horatio, who stood below watching in horror.

Horatio in a panic, throw his sword into Gazpalding's chest. The blade went straight through his Sherideen heart causing a shower of sparks to fly outwards. A moment later, the hinges of the bangle gave way and opened. Marypat fell away from Gazpalding and landed on the cherry green kettle post floor with the bangle still in her hands.

Gazpalding's body still hovered with the sword protruding out of his chest. With the bangle removed from his arm the pay of Hisue escaped the bangle and emptied into Gazpalding's body causing it to swell and boil. Then the liquids from his vile body began to drip from him and melt the flooring below him. The melted floor grew into a pit and the Cinerin Mountain began rumble. Horatio ran to where Marypat had fallen and grabbed her, she was still in a trance and holding the bangle. He remembered Johnny G saying that Marypat was under a spell by a spinning pin so quickly he located the pain and removed it from her dress. He threw it into the vast pit that had developed under Gazpalding's whiling and drip body. Then he took the bangle from her, as he did her tear shaped diamond dropped off, of the bangle and slipped into her pocket. Horatio then throw the bangle in the same direction of the spinning pin.

With bangle reentering the Cinerin cavity, the mountain shook violently causing everything on the pert to move uncontrollably. Finally, Gazpalding liquefied body exploded and fell into the pit sealing it once more. Meanwhile the Observer continued to shack violently until it fell over with an incredible crash, releasing the Great Isle of its spell.

At once, the orange gowned Sherideens and the three young Sherideens came back to life, to find Horatio and Marypat scurrying back through the Realagraph.

Once the pair was safe on the other side Rudy, and Johnny G destroyed the frame on the book side, to prevent anyone from following them. Then they helped Horatio carry the still dazed Marypat back to the original opening in the tale.

"Many thanks to you. It would not be as it was, if I had not had all of your pledges." Horatio said to the four brave members of the book.

"No mention, we would not be if there was not your world." Said Rudy honestly.

"But might I inquire what will become of us once you return?" Asked the Good natured Kathrie

It was a bold question, for the book alone had proven itself to be dangerous in the hands of Ubil, and it should be destroyed. What was to keep it from happening again? And yet these members, Realagraphs as such, had proven themselves worthy to be alive even if only in their Realagraphs. Would it be right to destroy them? Horatio could not answer these questions, there was far more knowledgeable members then he and it would not be far for him to answer as it would not be his decision.

"I cannot answer what will happen once I step from your page, I can only give you my solemn vow that I shall do all that I can to plead your case." Horatio answered solemnly.

"That is all we can ask of you, friend." Rudy said with a smile. "Now out with you."

Rudy and Horatio kicked open the book, knocking it to the ground of the Maurieen Palace's library and study where Iola, Orida and Cornelius were themselves still waking from the Phase spell.

Horatio then carried Marypat in his arms and stepped through the Realagraph. He then laid Marypat on the wooly carpet of the library floor before changing back to his original Jinxie size.

At the sight of the pair, the quite study suddenly was a burst of commotion.

"What happen?" Iola asked shacking her sleepy head.

"Where have you been?"

"What happen to Marypat?"

Horatio did his best to answer all the questions, telling them the whole sorted story. Including how the members in the book help him and how he felt the book should be put away safely, guarded perhaps, but not destroy. There was only one part of the story he didn't tell them and that was that he was a Dandy Jinxie, and that he could grow large. He feared if Cornelius knew he would not allow him his friendship with Marypat, and that he could not bear. So he left out that tiny bit of information and kept it to himself.

Orb Sight

O rida after hearing the tale went directly to his orb, where he found conformation of Gazpalding demise. The scene was reeked in panic as the Ubil world swarmed in disbelief. Their Supreme Master Sherideen had been slayed by a mere Jinxie. Now even the slight thought of a Jinxie brought sheer terror to those of Ubil.

The orb also showed the isle's members slowly recovering from the Phase spell. Many members were weakened by the spell, but it seemed that no real damage had been caused and they would all soon be back to normal.

Unfortunately, the same could not be said for dear Marypat. She had been under a much stronger spell in the form of a mind control amulet. She was still dazed, and it would take quite some time before she could regain her mind.

Orida knew this and was very concerned, that if what Horatio said was true, and he believed it was that the amulet was in the Cinerin Mountain with the bangle. Then Marypat needed to get as far away from it as possible in order to recover from it.

So, it was decided, Marypat needed to leave Great Town and go back to Cornelius cabin in the quiet forest of Finster. The long slow route, as they had come, was out of the question. Marypat was much too delicate, there was only one way to travel, Spit cock.

After a long eve of nightmarish screams and panic-stricken moments Cornelius and Horatio were convinced that Marypat needed to leave the palace at once. Cornelius arrange for an appointment of Spit in the Palace receptacle directly after their mourning meal and he sent word to his troops to make their way back to Finster on their own.

In the morrow, they packed all of their thing, and sent them down to the receptacle. Then they took Marypat down to the Principal Balcony for breakfast. Iola was there with news from the counsel.

Horatio sat on the edge of the sugar bowl intensely listening to Iola's report. He feared that the counsel would destroy the book and all the brave Realagraph members. To which he was greatly indebted to.

"It seems the book was created by an artist, the Kathrie Penny of Pinewood. It was commissioned by the Regan for his Granddaughters 3rd birthright. But it was stolen before it could be delivered, 5 turns past. Penny did not report the theft. She was apparently under a memory spell, which was broken when Gazpalding was slain." Iola mentioned calmly.

"What will happen to the book, Iola?" Asked Horatio nervously.

"The council has decided to leave it here at the palace under guard as you requested, Horatio." She looked at Horatio and answered with a smile. "They will all by safe, that I promise you."

Horatio sighed with relief; the Realagraph members would be safe.

"But why did they, I mean why listen to me?" Horatio questioned shyly.

"Because my Brave, Horatio, your opinion is greatly appreciated among the council and they have asked me to give you this." Iola said as she unrolled her hand to reveal a gold medal with an eight-point star in the center of it.

"For bravery above and beyond the summons of obligation." Iola said proudly.

As she said the words, trumpets began to play, and the tiny group was surround by the enter council, cheering Horatio's bravery.

"Hurray Hurray. Horatio." They called.

"But wait." Horatio called out as he jumped from his seat onto the sugar bowl.

"I was not brave, I was scared. I was filled with hate. Gazpalding had dear Marypat. I couldn't bear it, so I killed him. That's not bravery . . . that's. . . Oh I don't know what it is, but the ones that were truly brave where the Realagraph members, without them I would still be trapped in that book, I would be dead. I'm not brave."

He lowered his head in shame, but Iola made no change to her declarations.

"Horatio. The Green Isle is forever after indebted to you . . ." In a whisper she said to Horatio.". . . and those of the Book. ." Then her voice went loud once more. "And so, we honor you with the pristine award for Bravery. Please accept this with our most gracious Thanks."

She placed the medal around his neck and then kissed him on both cheeks.

Horatio blushed at that but then cleared his throat to say. "I will accept this honor, not because I deserve it, but because I am humbled by your gratitude."

After a little breakfast, Cornelius thanked Iola and Orida for their hospitality. It had been a long two turns and he was looking forward to getting home and settling Marypat on her road to recovery.

"Allow me to help." Iola offered aiding Cornelius with Marypat down the long staircase to the basement of the palace.

There under the brightly colored romantic palace was in sharp contrast, a Dark dusty room filled with hay to which they called the Spit cock Receptacle.

Spit cock had long since been the fastest way to travel. It was however unfortunate a return if one did not have a return receptacle. In other words, Spit cock could indeed get you where you wanted to go in a blink it could send a member anywhere they wanted to go on the Great Isle, all one needed was a zone type, or address but unless where you were going also had a Spit cock Receptacle; you could not return the same way.

There were only five receptacles that had ever been built on the Great Isle. There are three in Great Town; one at the palace, one at the Chief Counsel's Post and one in the town itself. The other two belonged to the royal family of Regan's, one at the Crystal Castle and the other at their summer palace on the beach at Out bend.

With so few receptacles Spit cock, although fast, had never quite caught on. Still it would be the easiest way for Marypat to travel given her delicate state and there was no worry about the need to return quickly as she would need a long recovery in the quiet of the forest.

"McCarthy, it's you." Shouted a very short Lachlann dressed in navy-blue pull over, that had his name embroidered on the chest, Lester, and a bright yellow tie. His hair was quite curly, and it bounded when he spoke. He had a pencil and chipboard and he pocked the pencil into the arm of Cornelius as he rattled on.

"That's four with luggage, one balm, one young Maurie, ... a Jinxie?. . No way is a Jinxie riding this spit. . . I got to check this out."

The little Lachlann tried to run away but Iola caught him by the collar and turned him around.

"Listen hear, Lester, Horatio is no common Jinxie, you let him ride or I'll have your job." She said. Then she let the Lachlann go, he pulled on his collar and straightened his tie before continuing.

"So that's one Balm, one young Maurie, . . a very special Jinxie and a WHAT?" The Lachlann eyes went wide. "Oh no you don't know Grundle's are not allowed in here, what if he goes for the cock. No, No, No!" The Lachlann shouted so loud his tiny face turned red and steam welled up in his hair.

Iola caught him one last time and whispered softly, "Let the Grundle travel."

With that the Lachlann turned back slowly and knobbed his head as if he was falling asleep. "Right this way then."

He led the group into the center of the room, where there sat a very large circular drain. Their luggage had already been placed on the drain and they were asked to wait a moment while they sent the luggage ahead.

"Wait right here." The Lachlann said pointing to a large blue square off to the side of the drain.

"Remain in the safely zone until I give you the all clear." He commanded then he ran up the embankment to the control center.

Cornelius and Iola carried Marypat into the blue zone, while Tiger and Horatio followed. Iola hugged Cornelius, gave one last scratch to Tiger, and then kissed Marypat and Horatio.

"Righteous turn to you I plea, that I may glance again upon thee again." She said.

A moment later, there was a loud strapping sound that came from above them. The floor above them rattled and small bits of dust and hay fell through the cracks on to their heads. The sound stopped, and a voice called out "Dom dee pat."

With that, a new sound was heard. It was like giant footsteps coming across the floor above. Again, the ceiling shock. With each step, more dust fell down on them.

Then came the voice again. "Hoc to!"

There was a great scratch to the floor above, a hack and then silence.

Horatio looked around, but nothing happened. Then without any warning there came a most disgusting sound, it was a "ho" just a "Ho" but the way it "Ho"-ed. It was slippery, it was wet, and it was big.

The thing shot out from above them, it hung in the air for longer than a moment. Then it splashed down covering the luggage like a blanket. It was wet and milky, thick and heavy. It dripped over their boxes and bags, slowly slipping until the substance touched the drain.

Once every speck was covered by the goo, the luggage disappeared and all that was left was the wet substance which slowly slipped down the drain.

Two little Lachlann ran in then with giant squeegees and helped to hurry up the process when they cleaned the drain they hurried off out of sight.

"All right then, McCarthy, would you step forward?" Called Lester as he ran back down the embankment and stopped beside the drain. "Hurry now the cock won't sit for long. Make sure your well inside the drainage area, we wouldn't want an accident."

Horatio was horrified. That spit was not going to touch him, he bounced around nervously trying to find a good place to keep dry.

"Set yourself down you, fool, a bath is all you will need. Think of what I'll have to go through with some disgusting foul's spit messing up my fur." Tiger said as he sundered over to the drain and sat down next to Cornelius who was already in the center and was still holding Marypat.

"It's just too awful." Horatio gasped as he jumped onto Marypat's lap. "Is there any other way?" He pleaded with Cornelius.

"Oh Horatio, it's not all that bad you'll see." Cornelius said with a wink.

Horatio didn't buy it, he was convinced that having a Spit cock on you was pretty bad and he wanted no part of it. So, he scooted under the blanket that held Marypat and covered his head.

"Good morrow, Iola." Cornelius called loudly to Iola who was still standing in the blue zone. "Thank you."

She nodded her head and gave a wave as the sound of the "Ho" filled the room.

Just like the luggage the four were covered with the spit, it dripped slowly thickly, warmly. Until it began to slide through the holes in the drain and instantly they were home, standing in the middle of Cornelius living room. All were there, all were as well as they were and all were dry.

Doodle Falls

S everal turns passed before Marypat was actually able to communicate and understand what had happen to her. She was weak, but she was gaining strength every turn, and she was soon wanting to go outside and sit in the light with Tiger.

Horatio who had never left her side, was her constant companion. Lively and fun he made her laugh. Their stint together was happy, simple, and natural.

On the return of the Frandies, Andies and Kandies, Marypat was excited to hear that she had correspondence. Two parcels from Great Town. The first was a flat heavy bundle. She opened it first, to discover the Name Tapestry she had bought from the Wardeen in the bookshop. She looked at it with searching eyes; her name was on the center of it in big green letters. Her M decorated with feathers symbolizing, reliable and cockleshells symbolizing friendship. Through her A and R ran Horatio's name, with Cornelius running through Horatio's first O. Tigers name ran through Horatio's, I and lastly Donovan's name clutched on to Horatio's final O. All around the letters were vines of green with red cherry snips symbolizing abundant. Above the names and showering over them was the symbol of unselfishness and lastly under Marypat's name was a staff that was the symbol of the Protector. The tapestry was beautifully framed in silver. It was lovely and Marypat couldn't take her eyes off of it. She rolled her finger over Donovan's name as tears filled her eyes.

"What will become of him, Horatio?" She asked.

"One cannot predict an others path, Marypat, he has choices to make, and they are his alone."

"Yes, but we killed his father and I worry he will hate us for it. I never wished him such pain, I never wanted this." She sobbed.

"Nor I." Horatio said hugging Marypat's neck. "Well shall we see what more treasures lie?"

Marypat was still very weak but she could tell Horatio was trying to change the subject for he thought it best if she didn't dwell on such sadness right now. So, she opened the second parcel. Inside was a small but thick package with a note attached to it that read.

"Esteemed friends, merriest morrow this might be sent and well it finds thee. To maiden Marypat, a note of good cheer for this replacement for thee to study. Make note of page 14. Greetings Iola."

Marypat opened the parcel. It was a book of Tales and Legends, not a Realagraph book but a common old used book with words and ordinary drawings. Nothing special, nothing out of the ordinary, just a regular book of Legends and Tales.

Marypat smiled.

Horatio giggled. "Do you think this one is safe?"

"Only one way to tell." Marypat said bravely and she opened the book. She thumbed through a few pages until she came to page 14 as

Iola had noted. The tale was entitled, *"The Lofty Legend of Lucky Lucas."*
And she began to read:

Lucas McConahay was the luckiest Felden to ever be.
It is said his that luck started ever since he was conceived.
His mother, a meager pet,
And father, grossly penniless
Both were doomed unlucky and completely without relief.

But that soon ended when young Lucas bounced in
Changing their world forever with his tiny little grin.
Happy as a lark bee
And as easy as can be,
Lucas found his riches came abundantly.

Once young Lucas tripped over a mound of dirt
He scratched his knee and was only slightly hurt
Yet, the twist of the tale
The head of the nail
Was that the mound was covered by some rotten hale

On another occasion, young Lucas fortune was blessed
When he found the Regan's ring in a Quivells nest
Delighted was the Regan,
Ecstatic was the Da
For in The Regan's glee, he granted them some land.

A patch of rock just above the Flower's Water run,
Not much of anything but there was more to come,
A fall of water,
A pond of stir
Etched for a place where more luck would come for sure.

On the turn that Lucas turned an 18 count,
His mother gave him a sturn colt and a mount

Gleeful was the Felden,
For riding he was fond
So off rode the pair, towards the water pond.

As they reached the water, Lucas told the colt to jump,
But the poor animal instead collided with a bump,
Down came the pair,
Down through the air
Straight over the waterfall as if they just didn't care.

For a moment, they sat silent as they realized their Good luck,
But then they noticed something in the waterfall was stuck
A boulder quite great,
Bridged like a gate
Caused the waterfall to spit back its cascade at an alarming rate

Lucas climbed the falls to take a better look
He had never seen water do this in a brook
Strange was this sight,
Awesome was its might
And when he tried to jump in side, he went straight for a flight

The water took him high beyond the Emeralds Eye,
Higher then his world below into a very blue sky

Marypat's face went white, she read the words again.

"The water took him very high beyond the emeralds eye
higher then his world below into a very blue sky"
and again "BEYOND THE EMERALDS EYE, INTO A VERY
BLUE SKY."

"That's it Horatio, the blue sky, that's my world, where is this place?"
She had to find out she had to read on. Shacking she pulled the book
closer to her eyes, so she wouldn't miss a word. While Horatio face
went blank.

Up to the top,
He prayed not to drop,
And wished for his frighten ride to come to a stop

Then suddenly, the water came to an end
He was sitting on a rainbow right at the bend.
Happy to be,
He clapped three
And with that sunbeams, were his plenty

He took the sunbeams home quite urgently
For his MA and DA to see
Swiftly they were spun,
Into gold rungs
Making them richer than anyone else

Now Lucas became the Luckiest Felden ever to be
Yet, the falls still remain in his family
Sunbeams they harvest
Open to tourists
Doodle Falls is a National legacy.

"Doodle falls, Horatio, it's Doodle falls. Can you believe it, the way home is so close, it's so close? I can be home for dinner!" She was so excited she didn't notice Horatio's frowned. She read the passage again and then called to Cornelius. He too read the tale and smiled wide.

"If this is true, and I know the falls exist, you may indeed be on your way home. But my Dear you are still very weak, and you can hardly walk the falls in your condition. Once you are strong enough I will take you. But for now, chase any thought of getting home this turn out of your head." He scolded her and then walked back into the house, shutting the door behind him.

The turns passed and Marypat grew stronger. It had taken her more time than the average member, but that was because Cornelius used no magic, no spell, or amazing remedy to heal her. He felt that if she was going home she stood a better chance of staying well once outside without the use of magic. He imagined that if he used magic on her that the magic might not be effective out there. So, yes it took longer to heal naturally, but once she was well, she wouldn't have to fear a relapse. In addition, Cornelius was very sad to let her go. She had become so important in his life he wanted her to stay.

For Horatio, he was quite happy with the lengthy recovery. He enjoyed every moment they had together. Marypat in turn realized that Horatio was feeling sad about her eventually going home but she reassures him that she would be back. She promised to return for summer break and they would have 10 rounds to enjoy themselves. Even with her convincing tales of return Horatio, dreaded hearing the words Cornelius used one morrow . . . .

"Looks like a good turn for a walk." Cornelius said with a grin.

"If we leave after breakfast you can be home before dinner."

Marypat looked at him with surprise. "Do you mean it? You think I'm ready?"

He nodded his head yes and turned back to his pot of tea.

"Say your good byes and be ready once I finish my tea." He said sternly. He had tears in his eyes as she darted out of the house and headed for the forest under brush.

Horatio's eye welled up as he made eye contact with Cornelius.

"It's for the best, we can't keep her here." Cornelius told Horatio.

Meanwhile out in the forest Marypat had caught up to Tiger.

"Tiger, I'm going home today." She told the Grundle with glee.

"Good, great." The big coose said sarcastically.

"What's wrong with you? I thought you would be happy for me?"

"Oh, I am so happy for you, you give me a voice, you give me a scratch, and then you leave me behind like an old shoe, just go, go get out of my forest, leave me." The coose shouted.

"Tiger I had no idea you felt that way, you never seem to care much for company, your very independent, I just thought you. . . well. . . why don't you come with me?" She said with a spark of excitement, "I'm sure my mother won't mind, so long as you don't try and eat the house cat."

The big coose purred loudly. "For true?"

"Yes, oh but to get there you'll have to get wet!" Marypat added.

"How wet?" The Grundle asked cutting his purr off completely.

"Oh, pretty wet, soaking in fact." She said.

"O.K. Then have a great trip and I'll see ya when ya visit." The Grundle said with a change of heart. Then he rubbed up against her one last time and scurried away after a Lofty Zort.

Marypat stood shaking her head at the coose, "He certainly has a mind of his own."

Back at the house, Cornelius was packed and ready to go. Horatio was waiting for her at the door and they went in together. She took a moment in her room and packet a few things, the book from Iola, the name tapestry, and her book of incantations and spells.

"When I come back in the summer I hope to get my wand, will you be here when I come back, or will you go back to live with the Loralacs?" Marypat sadly question as she looked at her dresser. Horatio was behind her and she was unable to make eye contact with him. Because for the first time it hit her that she was leaving and that meant leaving Horatio behind.

"I should like to stay here, if Cornelius will have me." He answered.

Tears filled her eyes and she was overcome by sadness.

"Oh Horatio, come with me, you can live with me and my mother." She cried flinging herself on to the bed. "I don't want to go without you."

"I will see you in the season." He said.

"The what?" Marypat laughed. "You mean the summer!"

"Yes, this summer we will be together. I promise!" He smiled, being brave.

The hike up to Doodle falls was a bit more than they expected and they needed to take a break now and again so Marypat could gain her strength. But after a while they reached the narrow path that lead to the falls.

From a distance, they could see it. A spectacular sight. Clear clean beautiful water flowed over the flower captured boulders. It stood only three members tall from downward flow to river base but the center flow that repelled from the river's base and into the air went higher then Mary's eye could see.

"It's true, look!" Marypat crying, "The center of the waterfall goes straight up into the air."

They quicken their pace and were standing at the park entrance in no time. A very pretty Lassie Felden dressed in a green Leprechaun like outfit, was at the gate, and stopped them as they approached.

"Wel-sta yar be flying or spying." She asked with a heavy Irish accent to which Marypat made a face as she tried to comprehend the Lassie Felden's words but also Marypat imagined she could be a Leprechaun.

But Cornelius had no trouble and answered for the group. "One flying, two spying."

"That will be 50 pie-it" The Felden said. "But if the flyer brings back beams ya get your payment back."

"Very good." Cornelius said with a raised eyebrow.

"Take this up to the peak and hand it to the guide." The Felden said handling Cornelius one flying ticket to ride the falls.

As they approached the falls the air seemed to get quit damp with mist, there was so much water being forced back up into the air that moister seemed everywhere.

At the top of the falls was a narrow bridge that only went as far the center. There on the bridge was a second Felden again dressed in a green Leprechaun like outfit. He was well wet and seemed annoyed each time he was approached with a ticketed flyer. A head of Marypat were two young Wardeens, both were ticketed to fly but nether wanted to go first. It seemed that they were there on a bet and in truth nether wanted to do it.

Finally, after a time of arguing, and realizing the line the two Wardeens were causing by their hold up, the Felden came to the rescue. He approached the two fellas calmly and instructed them what to do.

"When you reach the rainbow, clap three times, caught the sun beams, and ride the rainbow down. Got it?" He said it as if he had said it a trillion times and probably he had. After a moment longer and still neither one would go, the Felden pushed the two of them in at once and off they flew into the air.

"Next." The wet Felden called and there stepped a grown Lachlann and his son. The Felden took their tickets and the son jumped in.

Marypat turned to Cornelius and hugged him, "I guess this is it, thank you for everything.

"Not to mention my dear, but do come in the summer, I shall be very pleased to have you." He said kissing her forehead.

"And you Horatio, I shall never forget you." She kissed him softly on the cheek and then turned away quickly handing the ticket to the Felden. The Lachlann had already jumped after his son and was gone, so without any farther to do, Marypat jumped into the water fall and was flown up into the air.

Home

It was an amazing ride, she could almost see the enter Great Isle from where she laid in the water. Down below she caught her last glance of Cornelius as he stepped off the bridge and headed away from the falls. So, with that she concentrated on the task at hand. She swung her feet underneath herself and waited for the moment her head would be above the emeralds eye, that's when she would jump and just as the legend had said "Into a very blue sky", it came the top of the eye. Marypat stood and jumped. Out she fell onto the floor of her grandparent's front room.

Marypat stood, she was soaking wet, the windows of the house were open, and the room was cold from the cool Jamaican mountain air. She grabbed her shoulders and shook a bit before calling out. "Grandmother, grandmother I'm home."

"Marypat." A startled voice called back from the kitchen. "Is that you?"

Marypat ran from the front room and headed towards her grandmother's voice. In the hallway they met with tearful smiles.

"Grandmother!"

"Mary, dear." The two hugged for quite a long time before Lora spoke again.

"Mary you are so cold come warm yourself by the kitchen fire."

They went into the kitchen and Marypat sat down in front of the fire. Lora fixed her a plate of food and a hot cup of tea then she sat down beside her granddaughter.

"I have missed you so much, I'm so happy you are home at last. Tell me what it was like in there?" Lora said with a grin.

Marypat told her grandmother all about her adventure, about Cornelius, Horatio, the all the Teenys she had meet. She told her about meeting the Regan, and the Whimple. She told her everything except about what happen at the Pert. She didn't want to frighten her grandmother or give her any reason not to allow her to return for the summer as she had promised Horatio. She explained how Cornelius had once lived on the outside like them and how he had fallen in over thirty years ago.

"Tell me again the name of Cornelius?" Lora question strangely.

"Doctor Cornelius McCarthy." Marypat answered before stuffing her mouth with her grandmother's homemade sweet potatoes.

"It just sounds so familiar." Lora replied, she excused herself for a minute and then returned with an old family album. She dusted it off before she opened it and then whisper to herself. "My maiden name is McCarthy, my father's name was Cornelius, and he was a doctor. The last moment I saw him was the day of my wedding to your grandfather in Ireland. This is a picture of him at my wedding the day before he went missing. I wonder if it's him, it would certainly explain what happen to him so long ago, anyway. . . this is the picture, do you recognize anyone." Lora said as she handed the album to her granddaughter.

Marypat searched the photograph it was old and in black and white but there was no denying who the man was standing beside the groom. It was Cornelius.

"That's him, that's Cornelius. Cornelius is your father? That's so awesome!" Marypat's mouth fell open.

"You're sure?" Lora asked as tears dripped from her eyes.

Marypat nodded her head yes, "I'm sure, he looks the very same."

"The very same, no older?" Lora asked.

Again, Marypat nodded her head yes.

"This picture was taken forty-five years ago, and he was 67 years old when he went missing. I can't imagine that your great-grandfather could be alive and not look any old then he did 45 years ago. It's all a bit too much for me to understand perhaps tomorrow we can talk about it again, for now I am just so glad to have you home, all is well."

"So, grandma wrapped me up and put me in bed. I think I slept for a week after that but then school started, and I was back to the grid of school work." Marypat said as she sat on the couch of the grandparents' home and told the story of her adventure on the Great Isle to her son Blaze.

"That reminds me did you do your homework." She said poking him off the couch.

"Yes, I did it on Friday remember!" Blaze answered with a giggle, landing on his feet in front of her.

"Well it's getting late and you have school tomorrow, we better get down the hill and home before dark." Marypat replied.

"But mum, you didn't finish the story." Blaze pleaded.

"Well that's enough for now." She scolded.

"What about when you went back for the summer what happened then?"

Blaze jumped up and down. "I want to know all about your trips within, I can't wait for another moment I wanted to know now." He demanded.

"Listen here young man, I promise I will tell you more but at another moment, now off to bathe and change, it's already getting dark and it will be bed moment by the moment we reach." Marypat said sternly as she guided her son in the direction of the restroom.

"Alright, but you can tell me more on the drive home then!" Blaze insisted with a smirk and then he ran off to bathe.

Marypat shock her head and whispered under her breath. "Sometimes he is just like his father."

Marypat turned to me then and said. "And he still is to this day a son of a Sherideen, but much has happened to him, to change him."

"Your son is a Sherideen?"

"Well, 'tis another long story."

"Well if you are willing, it would help me understand more about you. Please tell me how a Maurieen could have a Sherideen for a son. My ears are open."

Return to the Great Isle

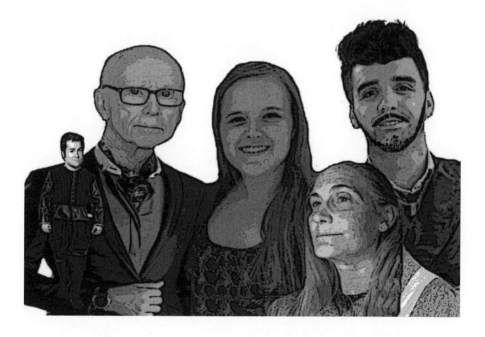

CHAPTER
1

The Conspiracy

"For the next three summers my grandmother allowed me to go and visit her Father, my great-grandfather within. He was so happy to know I was his great-granddaughter, I don't think he was surprised, it was as if he knew it from the first moment he meet me. He is an amazing man. Anyway, over those summers I learned a bit of magic as well as earned my wand, the Predom Excell. But that again is another long story I can tell you at another moment."

"The summer of 1990 I headed off to college and let me see, it was the summer I returned home from college that this . . . . happened it was June 1993. I remember it so clearly. My grandfather had picked me up from the Kingston airport; I hadn't seen him in two years. I hadn't been home the last two years, what with summer classes and work. He looked so tiered and old to me. I just wanted to hold him and have it last forever." Marypat said with a sign as she remembered her grandfather and the last few days she had with him.

"He was ill, I knew it, he knew it but we went on as if nothing was wrong.. . ."

"We spend the next four days together quietly. Then it all seems like a blur, it happened so quick, I didn't even had a chance to say good bye." Tears welled up in Marypat's eyes as she recalled he grandfather's death.

"He had been so brave, so strong; he never wanted us to know how much pain he had been in. If I had only known I could have done something to help him. . ." Her voice trailed off as she described the moment it happened.

The sun had just begun to rise from the farthest reach of the sky, when Trevor, Marypat's grandfather, was found unconscious on the kitchen floor. Lora hovered over him desperately trying to revive him as Marypat stood in the darkness weeping.

"Trevor, don't, no. Come back to me." Lora shouted.

But Trevor didn't move. His lifeless body lay limp across Lora's lap. She grabbed him up and held him as she sobbed.

Marypat watched in horror as her grandmother grabbed her deceased grandfather and wondered why she hadn't helped him. Surly there was something she could do for him. She was a Maurieen after all. Had she forgotten that? But now it came back to her in a flood of knowledge. She ran to her room and grabbed her opal tipped wand and her Patrimony Edition of Incantations and spells.

Then she returned to the kitchen where her grandfather laid. She through the book onto the floor and knelt down beside him. Franticly she whipped through the book looking for the right spell, but there wasn't one to help him.

"A brew!" She thought, but no there wasn't time to make one.

"What can I use?" Marypat finally shouted as her grandmother's eyes closed with shame at the sight of her granddaughter's selfish attempts to save her grandfather.

"Yes an incantation." Marypat whispered as her eyes caught the sight of Incantations for good.

"RA TON DO PON RE." Marypat called a loud as she held her wand over her grandfather's chest and waved it in a circular motion. "RA TON DO PON RE!"

"That will not work here; you know that, put it away!" Lora scolded her granddaughter.

"Yes it will, it has to, if only I had studied more, if only I had taken my gift more seriously, worked hard, I could help him, I must help him." She cried.

She jumped to her feet and with all the grandeur, she could muster; she waved her hands and shouted again. "RA TON DO PON RE!" With the last word, she pushed her wand point towards her grandfather and held the "RE" until it echoed through the Mountain air.

Suddenly the room darkened, the windows blow open, and gust of wind pushed by Marypat and encircled her grandfather. The sound of her voice still echoed in the room.

"DO PON RE."

Faster and faster, the wind swirled round him. The force of the wind pushed Lora backwards against the cupboards, causing her to lose her grip on Trevor. With that, the swirling wind turned into a funnel and swallowed up the body like a hungry beast. Then it pushed pasted Marypat and flew into the front room.

Marypat ran after it and watched in horror as his body knocked into the pillar that held the Green Emerald. The crash dissolved the pillar and then his body into nothing.

"What have you done?" Screamed Lora as she pushed past her granddaughter and ran into the front room. "What have you done?" She sobbed uncontrollably as she searched for a sign of Trevor's dead body.

"I don't know." Marypat whispered in shook. That was not what she had planned to happen at all. The incantation was for good, it was to restore good health. What had happened was not intended and she was just as upset as her grandmother was.

"I told you, you can't do that stuff out here." Lora shouted all most in a panic. She placed her hands on the emerald it felts warm and soothing to the touch. Fresh tears rolled down her face as she uttered, "What do we do now?"

"I don't know." Marypat replied again.

"Is that all you can say, I don't know! Well you better find out, I won't allow your grandfather to be in limbo just because you don't know what to do now. Do you hear me, missy?" Lora yelled.

"What would you have me do?" Marypat bravely questioned.

"There must be someone in your Great Green Isle that can tell you what to do, think of someone." Lora proclaimed.

Marypat thought for a moment she had met many wise members during her visits to the Great Isle, but now to recall one that could help her out of her very delicate situation was another thing all together. There was of course Iola and Orida at the Maurieen Palace, Great Town. But Marypat feared that what she had done was against the laws of the Isle and that she may get into some trouble if she approached them. So she thought a moment longer, Dr. McCarthy her Great-grandfather, would do all he could to help but he was not an expert at magic. The Loralacs again would try and be helpful but again they were not experts in magic. Then it came to her, the perfect member to help her.

"The Kathrie Gretel. Yes I can ask Gretel to help me."

Gretel would be the right one; she was indeed a Master Kathrie and Good-natured one as well. Marypat knew Gretel would help her and she would ask no questions.

Without another thought, Marypat clutched hold of the Great Isle and stared into the eye. With that, she was gone from the front room, leaving her grandmother alone still holding the emerald and crying.

"Be safe my dear Marypat, be safe and bring your grandfather home."

The sound of her mother voice vibrated in Marypat's ears as she sat up and found herself in the familiar ground of Grass point. Quickly she got to her feet and began running in the direction of her great-grandfather's cabin on the edge of the wood. As she entered the wood, however she had to slow her pace as she dodged under branches and stepped over low brushes.

"What is thee haste, fare maiden." A blue blur of light called out as it pasted Marypat's face.

For a moment, Marypat jumped in surprise at the sound. She had forgotten about the small members of the Isle. Her mind was only on her situation and not her surroundings. But then she remembered she quickly replied.

"Forgive my haste dear Etain but I am on a timely mission to get on the other side of the wood. I did not mean to disrupt your turn." Marypat said as she darted under a low branch.

"No, harm, but thee only take hark that there is a Grundle in the wood, and he speaks of hunger." The little blue Etain warned.

Marypat stopped in her tracks and turned to the Etain. "Did you say he speaks?"

"Yes, a tongue of a Vaster." The Etain answered.

"I don't believe it, could it be my Tiger? TIGER, TIGER, HERE BOY, HERE BOY." Marypat shouted into the quiet wood.

The Etain fluttered her wings in horror. "What have ye done, he will hear ye for true, take heed, take heed." She said franticly.

Marypat looked at the Etain and smiled. "No worry dear Etain, this Grundle you speak of is my friend and I have long since missed his presents. Take heed if you wish but I will not."

Then she turned to her left as a sound of rushing leaves were heard in the bush there.

"Tiger is that you?" Marypat questioned the bush.

"And who might want to know?" Came a rough and angry voice.

"I would, Marypat."

"The one called that, has been gone to long for me to remember and I have long since given up hope of ever seeing her again, indeed she gave a mighty fine scratch as I recall, but of any other point I have no memory." The voice said with a snobby yawn.

"OH really! I am sure that it will all come clear once you have had one of my good long scratches." Marypat said with a giggle as she pulled back the bush to uncover the greenish red furry Grundle stretched out in the under growth.

The Grundle picked up his eyes and blinked them at her. Then he rounded his body to the side and welcomed her touch. She scratched him vigorously for several moments as he began to purr.

"Does that bring back any memories?" She asked the Grundle.

"Perhaps, but . . ." He yawned.

Marypat continued her course and soon the Grundle gave in.

"Many a pass has come, Marypat, what has kept you from this wood?" Tiger asked.

"So you do remember me, you beast? But it has been a very long moment, and I am sorry for that, but I have been away at University, studying." Her voice fell off, as she thought now for the first moment how unimportant her moment had been used studying History. When she could have been studying with the Maurie Iola all about magic and Medicine and if she had she would probably not be in the situation she was in now. With this in mind, she quickly changed her position on the forest floor and stood.

"I am sorry for my hasty departure dear friend, but I must travel with brisk foot to the balm Cornelius on the edge of the wood. There is much I must do and not a moment to waist."

"Then I shall be as swift as ye and travel as always at your side." Tiger said with a blink.

With that, the two friends headed off in the direction of the small familiar cabin. But before Marypat stepped out of sight she called back to the Etain.

"Good morrow fare one and many thanks to ye for reuniting me with my friend."

The Etain shook her head in disbelief and flew away.

It was not long before the small green cabin came into sight. It looked just as it had the last time Marypat had been there, only in some ways it seemed smaller and older. The mossy roof was brightly alive with green hatch ferns and jingle toes. The Filtch weeds were in bloom and they were almost as tall as the windowsills. The house looked like a dream and it was more than comforting to see it still as she remembered it.

She ran up to the cherry green kettle post door and knocked twice. The sound echoed in the air as she waited for a response. And then it came the door creaked open and there in the candle light stood the familiar foam of the Good Cornelius himself.

"Great grandpa." Marypat called with relief.

"Mary, dear girl, come in come in." He roared happily, as he waved his arm to motion her in.

"My eyes have been lonesome for your sight, my dear girl."

Marypat crossed the threshold and hugged her great-grandfather as tears filled her eyes.

"My dear what is it, tell me." He confronted her. He closed the door and led her over to the couch where she told him all about what had happened outside the isle and how she needed the Kathrie Gretel's help.

"Yes, I agree she would be the best one to help you, my dear. We shall head to Boulder Town then in 2 turns." He announced.

"No, you don't understand I must leave in the morrow, right away, there is no moment to waist."

"I see, yet I am afraid that I have a previous endeavor that will prevent my accompanying you, on the marrow. You see I am head conceal for the Frandies in their land dispute with the Hedlens. They have arranged a meeting between both parties, which has been planned for many rounds and I must not allow any farther delay in settling the matter. Still if you can wait. . . I would be able to assist you in 2 turns." He said as he held her hand.

"I understand, but I cannot wait. I will go alone; I believe I remember the way. "She said hopeful that he would not insist that she wait for him. She knew she could find her way and although it would have been nice to have her great-grandfather with her, she felt it was not necessary for him to go as she was after all a grown woman now.

"If you insist on going alone, then I must insist that Horatio go with you in my steed."

"Horatio! Is he here?" Marypat said with excitement.

"Yes, indeed. He has never left, he has become like a son to me." Cornelius said with a nod.

"Where, where will I find him?" She asked looking about.

"He is more than likely in his room."

Marypat jumped from the couch and ran to the door of her old bedroom; she pulled open the door and stuck her head inside. There on the dresser was Horatio's little house and through the window Marypat could make out the glow of one single member.

She stepped up to the dresser quietly and knocked on the door. The glow in the window jumped with fright at the sound.

"Cornelius is that you?" Horatio called loudly.

For a moment, it did not sound like the familiar voice of her friend to Marypat. So consciously, she called back. "No, I mean no causes for alarm; I am only looking for a friend."

"A friend you say, what kind of friend are ye, to go freighting members such. Beside no friends have I, to visit in this place, so explain ye self or I will curse ye post." Angrily he shouted back.

"Please, there is no reason to weave your curse, for I was told that Horatio, my friend resides here." She said smiling.

Not a sound came from inside the small house.

"Horatio?" Marypat called in a whisper.

"Yes." Came the reply finally.

Then the door of the house opened and Horatio stepped out. He was taller and larger than she remembered. His soft rounded cheeks had thinned and his chin had squared handsomely. His shoulders were broader, and his shape was well formed. His features had certainly matured. He had grown up just as she had. But somehow it seemed strange to her to see him grown because she remembered him as a youngster.

"Marypat is that you?" He asked shyly.

"Yes, Horatio, I'm home!"

The reunion for Horatio was a reason to live again. His Marypat was home and after hearing all about what had happened to her grandfather, he was ready to leave with her for Boulder Town immediately.

When morning broke, the two longtime friends were still chatting and catching up. Marypat realized how much she had missed Horatio's company. But soon it was as if she had never left at all. They were like two comfortable shoes, a lone they are incomplete, worn and empty, but together they had the will, the soul and the strength to cover great distances, and they proved this on their jaunt to Boulder Town. They made good time and had checked into the Shack by mid-turn.

A sweep later Marypat found herself standing in front of "The Ready Kathrie."

Without wasting another moment, Marypat pulled the door to The Ready Kathrie open and stepped inside. There was a musty familiar smell in the air that Marypat almost found comforting. She closed the door just as Horatio landed on her shoulder and whispered in her ear.

"No harm in shopping while ye plead ye tale, no?"

Marypat smiled at her friend and nodded. To that, Horatio bounced off in the direction of the potions aisle, leaving Marypat standing in the front of the store with Tiger.

Beside them, they found the checkout counter and behind it was an old Sherideen who seemed to be nodding off to sleep unaware of their presents.

"Good morrow, sir." Marypat called to the Sherideen. But the Sherideen seemed to be in a very deep sleep and continued to sway as he sat precariously on his stool.

"Excuse me, can you please. . ." Marypat's voice slowly rose louder with each word as she realized he still did not hear her. "SIR!" she finally shouted as she slapped the counter with a boom. Her patience was gone. "Kathrie Gretel is she in?"

"No need to shout fare Colleen, I am not deaf." The Sherideen said with a yawn.

"My sisters in the back, let me raise them for ye."

Then with that, he disappeared and reappeared in a flash, back on his stool and back a sleep. In the same instant, Kathrie Gretel appeared beside her, grinning from ear to ear.

"My eyes are blessed, you have come home. We have sorely missed your sight." Kathrie Gretel cheered with a hug. "How long, my dear, is the pleasure of your visit, for I must let Donovan hear of this news, he so pines for your sight and speaks of you often." She smiled.

"I would so like to see Donovan." Marypat confided in the Kathrie. "but I am cautious of my moment, you see, it is not pleasure, my visit but instead a pressing task to which I am in need of your expertise."

"Oh dear, of course I am at your aid. Tell me then what is so urgent." Kathrie Gretel spoke in a most concerned voice.

Marypat explained what had happened to her grandfather. She told Kathrie Gretel which spell she had used and how it all went so wrong. Tears filled her eyes as she retold the events and she could hardly keep herself together as she asked if there was a reversal spell.

"I have never heard of such a thing. This is a most unusual happening, one I am not familiar with, but rest-a-sure my dear, my sisters and I will find you what you need. Now don't worry yourself."

"When will you know?" Marypat asked solemnly. She worried her answer would be many turns and she felt she could not wait that long.

"I will send word when I have the answer. Are you staying at the Shack?" Kathrie Gretel asked.

"Yes." Horatio answered as he bounced on to the counter beside the Kathrieen.

"Good, then worry not. My sisters are very knowledgeable and I am sure by the morrow we will have your answer. Go now and enjoy the town, visit Miss Honeys. I know how much the both of you enjoy her confections and relax. Let your mind be at ease. Take this with you if nothing else, the situation is unusual but it is not unsolvable, and that you have my word." Kathrie Gretel said with a smile at Marypat.

Marypat felt a little better as she and Horatio exited the shop. But still she did not feel much for shopping at Miss Honey's and so the pair headed back to their room at the Shack.

Meanwhile Kathrie Gretel disappeared from the shop and reappeared in the kitchen where she found her sister Gritty, attending to a brewing lesson with Gretta's second three set. The girls were preparing a batch of shrinking potion and were just about to add the jay berry juice to the scolding pot when Gretel appeared and startled the lot.

"No moment for potions, sister dear, Miss Marypat's in trouble and she needs our help."

Gritty immediately dismissed the three young Kathrieens and call for Gretta. Without a moments delay the three elders held hands and vanished from sight.

While in the front of the store, the old Sherideen, blinked open his eyes and took a glance about in the shop. He steadied himself on the stool, sat up straight, and closed his eye. Then he called in a whisper, as if to himself, "Com-mor om do mos so siber jet, jet no."

A hum filled the air around him; he opened his eyes then and nervously glanced around the shop again, and worried that someone might over hear him.

"Uncle Leopold, do you have news." Came a voice through the hum.

"In deed. She is here and she has confided in your mother just as you predicted." The old Sherideen smiled.

"This is good news uncle. Where is she now?" The voice echoed again.

"She awaits word from your mother at the Shack, but Master, she travels with the feared one." The Sherideen snarled.

"You mean the Jinxie, Horatio?" The voice replied.

"Yes, and he is more formidable then I recall."

"No worry uncle, you forget, he and I have history, and I know all of his weaknesses. Take the amulet I gave you and see to it that Horatio is in possession of it by dark. Do this and the rest on my plan will not fail." The voice echoed in the air one last moment.

A Note

L ater that same turn a knock was heard on the door of room 707. It was Chuck, the bellhop.

"Greeting, Maurieen. I have an urgent correspondence for ye." Chuck said with a slight bow of his head. Then he raised his hand up towards her and presented a bright red parchment on a small white lacey pillow.

Marypat took the parchment from the pillow and placed a silver Vert in its place.

Then she thanked the Felden and closed the door.

"What is it? Could Kathrie Gretel have the answer already?" Horatio asked excitedly.

Marypat held the note in her hands and took a deep breath. "Oh Horatio, I do hope so."

She looked down at the parchment; it was rolled up like a tube and tied with a blood red silk ribbon. She untied it and handed the ribbon to Horatio, who curled it up and tied it around his waist. Then he bounced to her shoulder, so he could get a better look at the note.

It read:

Fare Marypat,

Meet me at the Blarney Stone on the 6th ray.

I have good news.

That was the entire note; there was no signature, no other mark, no indication of the sender. So Marypat assumed it was Kathrie Gretel.

At the shop however, Kathrie Gretel was in her room, busy studying over a stack of reference books, entitled Magical Mishaps the series. She was currently browsing letter "F" when her door swung open to reveal an enormous cloud of smoke. The distraction did little to break her concentration, instead she ignored the apparition and continued to read, Flatulence gone wrong.

"Are you not pleased to see me, mother, that you don't even rise your borrow?" Came the voice from the cloud.

"Oh Donovan!" Kathrie Gretel huffed. "I have no moment for your antics, Son. But of course I am pleased to see you; I just have other things on my mind..."

"Yes, uncle Leopold has told me." Donovan said calmly. He stepped into the room; his bright red cape swirled behind him and neatly folded into place. He was dressed in a charcoal black suit, with a red vest and gold necktie. His hair was neatly combed, and his beard was trimmed perfectly. He looked quite handsome and Kathrie Gretel noticed this with a raise of her eye to her son.

"How handsome we are this eve. I can only imagine why." She said sarcastically smiling at her son. She knew how her son felt about Marypat; after all, she was all he talked about. Still Kathrie Gretel never took it for more than a crush and found it amusing that her son could be so taken by one, as she saw it, so plain.

"Oh, mother, I have only come to help." Donovan replied with an air of duty.

"Of course dear, why else would you come so quickly, I do believe it has only been a sweep since she arrived. How faithful you are, son." Gretel remarked.

"Mother do you not want my help?" He asked turning his back to his mother as if his feelings were hurt.

"If you can, I would want nothing else." she answered.

"Then worry not, mother, all will be right. I will take it from here." Donovan announced, pausing as if he were sacrificing himself in the line of duty.

"Oh really, and you know just what to do, do you?" Gretel asked with sarcasm. She suddenly grew suspicious of her son, and felt an eerie shiver go up her spine.

"Yes, it's simple really, a beginner could do it." He said with a wave of his hand.

"Oh, really that simple? How would you know? Unless. . ." Kathrie Gretel began to suspect that her son had something to do with it. And if that were the case then he was certainly up to something more despicable then just wanting to get Marypat back to the Great Isle. *But what was it?* She thought and then it came to her.

"What will be the cost to Marypat for your services?" Gretel asked as she rose from her position on the lounge.

"Cost? There is no cost" Donovan laughed at his mother.

"Somehow I do not believe that." Kathrie Gretel alleged as she faced her son and looked him in the eye. "You know that magic can't be used that way, love potions and such never last, they never work out the way one would want. Don't do this, son. If she means that much to you, you would not want to win her with trickery, for if you did, it would only spoil any real chance at true love."

"Oh mother, why couldn't you just keep your nose out of it. Just step away as I am asking and allow me my path." Donavan stated angrily as he turned away from her.

"I won't stand here and allow you to do it. It is wrong, wrong I tell you." Kathrie Gretel shouted at him. She grabbed his arm and only wished to shack some sense into him but he took her aggression with haste and escaped her grasp with a lung backwards. In the same move he grabbed for his wand and with a Dacular movement he called, "Quantom Bee Q ee."

With that, his mother fell silent as if frozen in time.

"You gave me no chose, really. I didn't wait to do it this way. I had hoped you would not interfere, but you have and I cannot afford for you to spoil my plans, it has taken me so very long to get her back here and I can't, no I won't let her leave me again." Donovan whispered in his mother ear. "All my efforts now lead me to the finally moment, this eve when I shall finally have her. She will be mine. Can you see it, Mother? She will fall into my arms, after I resurrect her grandfather. Yes, she will be so grateful to me, I will have saved her again. I have it all planed, a candle light dinner at the Blarney Stone, magical nuptials on the Cascades and an eve raped in the clouds. I have dreamed of this since that turn we first meet remember, when I saved her from the fall here in the store? She was a vision, and now I will have her for my own. You will not stop me."

His voice suddenly sounded evil and it echoed as if his powers were escaping through his voice.

He stepped away from his mother and tapped her on the shoulder with his wand. Then he pointed the wand at the closet and with one pavular movement, instantly he placed his mother inside of it. Lastly, he approached his frozen mother and with one last sweep of his wand, he recited, "Tell oct um me." Whipping his mother's memory of the incident clean from her mind.

Then he shut the closet door and disappeared from sight.

Below in the shop a young Colleen dressed in crimson blue dress entered. She was a fare yellow faced maiden with lime green hair that she wore in ringlets that hung on the side of her face and were tied with tiny blue bows. As she entered, she smiled at the Sherideen sleeping behind the counter and then continued her stroll through the store. She stopped on the isle filled with containers and reached for a clay jigger. She inspected the jigger and was just about to put it back when her ears were filled with a strange sound.

"Atee om ree,om wen jay. . ." The clay jigger dropped from her hand and crashed into pieces on the floor.

"Om kole hert rut- in re hem -op trol."

The shop shook franticly, bottles drop to the floor, cauldrons rolled and a burst of hot red light engulfed the Colleen.

At 2 sweeps past bend, Marypat and Horatio exited the Shacks main lobby and entered the underground streets of Boulder Town. The streets were nearly empty except for a few shopkeepers closing up their front windows and locking up for the eve. Yet strangely, the streets were no darker now than they had been earlier in the turn. As the Etains and Laddies that lit the streets were still hovering about, living in the roots and leaves of the tree like structures that grew in the soil of the ceiling.

It was an ideal existence for the Eties, living in the safety of the underground, and providing light to the town. There was little conflict or worry about being eaten, and so it was a ceiling of Etie light that guided Marypat and Horatio down the now empty street.

Marypat's mind was on one thing and that was solving the problem that brought her here and nothing else. Even Horatio seemed uninterested in anything else that was until they spotted a young Colleen crying horribly as she sat in the middle of the lane. Her crimson blue dress was muddied and soiled. Her lime green hair was tossed and untidy. The sight was enough to bring anyone to her aid. Yet there was no one else on the street.

"Marypat, we must stop and help her." Horatio insisted.

But Marypat was torn, she just wanted to get on and see Kathrie Gretel. She wasn't interested in the poor maiden, but still she knew she must stop. So, they did.

"Please tell me, Colleen, to what would bring such tears to one so fare." Horatio asked as he landed in front of the Colleen.

The Colleen jumped with fright at the sight of the Jinxie but managed to control herself as she explained her dismay.

"I have done a terrible thing and now I must pay for my deeds." The maiden sobbed. "You see I borrowed my mother's diamond bracelet and it has fallen deep within the catch pit of the street, I shall never retrieve it, though I try with all my might."

"Is that all, dear Colleen? Say not another word, I shall retrieve it for you in an instant." Horatio declared with a bounce, then he disappeared into the catch pit and a moment later, he was back on the street carrying one end of the bracelet. Easily the Colleen pulled the rest of it through the hole until the entire thing rested her hand.

"Oh! How can I ever thank you!" she cried.

"No need." Horatio answered bouncing up and down.

"But I must do something for you. I know. . Please take this token."

The Colleen reached into her tiny purse and turned out a small lump of silver that was pressed into the form of a clover. "It has been a lucky keepsake of mine; please take it with my deepest thanks."

Horatio accepted the token and pushed it into his vest pocket. "Be well Colleen."

"And you." The Colleen said with a strange crack to her voice, but Horatio never noticed as he bounced away quite pleased with himself. He landed on Marypat's shoulder and they were off once more.

A moment later something strange stuck Horatio in the chest, nearly knocking him off Marypat's shoulder.

"Are you all right Horatio." Marypat asked as she watched him sway slightly as if he were drunk.

"I'm just fine, mind your own business." Horatio barked rudely.

Marypat was shocked Horatio never spoke to her like that.

"Horatio, how rude, what is wrong with you?" She blasted.

"Nothing a little bet at the Lucky Wager wouldn't cure." He laughed as they approached the old wooden sign hanging in front of the musty shop. Quickly he bounced forward and hopped through the Teeny's entrance in the door.

"Horatio, there isn't moment for that now, oh Horatio!" Marypat called after him. But he didn't hear her.

Marypat shook her head, she was angry with him; he knew how important it was for her to get to the Blarney Stone. He could make his bet later; she might even make one with him. But not now.

She opened the heavy wooden door to the Lucky Wager and stepped inside. The place was dark and dingy just as she remembered. She glanced around shyly, until she saw a familiar face. It was Thaddeus, the Loralac.

"Good eve, Thaddeus." Marypat said.

"And good eve to thee fine Maurie Marypat. 'Tis been long your feet from this deepened soil, I have missed the pleasure of your word." He said with a bow.

"What brings you in to this dreadful place, on such a late ray?"

"I am in search of, Horatio the Jinxie. He came in here only a moment ago. Did you see where he went?" Marypat answered the Loralac.

"Yes, in haste I do believe. He has found a place in the back; he plays a hammer game, two slots in." He reported with a nod of his head.

"Thank-you friend, as always, an eye wide open sees all." Marypat remarked with a curtsy and then ran off towards the back of the establishment where she found Horatio glued to the very machine Thaddeus had told her.

"Horatio! We don't have moment for this, we have to go now. Kathrie Gretel is waiting!" Marypat said breathless.

Horatio did nothing to answer her. He only studied the machine as the dial came to rest on three hammers in a row. It was a win, a big win, but still he made no attempt to answer her.

"Horatio! That's enough you won, let's go!!" She shouted.

But Horatio didn't move or blink, he only placed another Vert into the machine and pull the lever. The dials spun again and he watched them until they stopped on two nails and a pigberries. A lose.

"Let's go." Marypat became angry now, Horatio was being foolish, and she couldn't stand another moment. "Horatio, now."

But still he did not move.

"Horatio, I have to go, this means so much to me, and if you can't see that, then you are not the friend I thought you were." Tears slipped out of the corner of her eyes.

"Please Horatio, I need you to come with me, NOW."

Still he did not move.

"Then I go, with OUT you." She sobbed.

She turned away from him and ran for the door. She didn't even stop to wish Thaddeus fare well. No, she continued to run until she stood in front of her destination, the Blarney Stone restaurant.

The Blarney Stone front entrance seemed quiet and dark. Marypat wondered to herself whether it was even open at all. She approached the podium and glanced around nervously.

"Where is the head waiter or Host? He's probably seating someone, oh, be patient, Mary, be patient." She thought to herself.

Then from out of the darkness stepped a tall figure dressed in orange. It was not Henry the Felden, the usual host of the Blarney Stone. No this was a Wardeen, a dark skinned Wardeen with bright blue eyes and long black hair.

It seemed strange to Marypat to be greeted at the Blarney Stone by a Wardeen. Something wasn't right, but when the Wardeen bowed to her and began to speak, all of her doubts were set to rest.

"Greetings, I am Ragnar. How may I assist you?"

"Greetings to you, Ragnar. I am to meet Kathrie Gretel Gazpalding at rest." Marypat said nervously.

"Oh yes, the tower, very good." Ragnar said with a slight smile. Then he shuffled a few things behind the podium and said. "Please follow me then."

The Wardeen turn to the right and entered the long dark tunnel Marypat remembered from the first moment she had been there, but then he turned left after only a few steps in and started on a path that went up. This path was narrow and steep. It was poorly lit and at one-point Marypat could see nothing at all.

"Try and keep up." The Wardeen call down to her as she struggled to pull herself up the embankment.

"Some light would quicken my pace." Marypat said out loudly, but the Wardeen continued on without any response.

The soil around her was soft and smelled freshly dug, and as she thought about it she did not remember this pathway being here before. Perhaps it was new. Perhaps it hadn't been used very often but which ever it was, it certainly needed work.

By the time Marypat reached the Wardeen and turn around the second spiral, she was exhausted.

"Is this the usual path?" Marypat asked the Wardeen breathlessly.

"'Tis new." Ragnar answered without emotion.

"Well you can tell the management it needs work." She said as she stood beside the Wardeen and tried to straighten her blouse.

"I shall." The Wardeen spoke with a turned up brow and an air of snootiness.

Marypat looked around her, then and realized that they were no longer in the narrow tunnel. They now stood in an entranceway that was carved out of the blue lazurite. Four stunning archways stood in a round and were lit from above by a huge crystal chandelier. The floor was made of gray marble and in the center of it sat an enormous silver cauldron filled with pink and blue flowers.

"Oh, it so lovely." Marypat gasped.

"Indeed." Ragnar replied unmoved by her genuine awe.

"You may wish to wash up before . . . ." His voice trailed off, as he looked her up and down with disgust.

She was a muddy mess, her blouse and jeans showed signs of struggle and her hands were black with soil.

She looked down at herself for the first time and was shocked at her appearance.

"The management really needs to do something about that tunnel." She said trying to remove Ragnar stares from her.

"Perhaps you could point me in the direction of the ladies room?" she asked.

"You will need more than a room for Colleens I'm afraid." Ragnar stated as he stepped forward towards a door on his right under one of the archways. He put his arm out and the door swung open, then he turned back to Marypat and said. "You may however find everything you need in the laboratory." Then he snapped his fingers and the small room on the other side of the door lit up.

"I will leave you now, but when you are ready you may meet your party behind the blue curtain." Then he tilted his head and disappeared.

Marypat hesitated for a moment before entering the brightly lit room, but when she finally did the door slammed shut behind her. The noise frightened her and she went quickly to find the doorknob, to open the door once more, but there was none. Frantically she searched the door for a knob or a switch but again there was none.

After a few moments, she gave up on the door and decided to look about in the room. To one side was an overstuffed chair, a stool and a small round table draped in yellow lace. On the other side of the room, Marypat found the enter wall was covered with mirrors. Six thin panels of mirror, stretched from ceiling to floor. They were exactly the same size and width, the only difference between them was that each was framed in a different style. The first had bronze colored flowers weaving all around it and when she stood in front of it she saw herself clean and dresses in an overly fluffy yellow gown with flowers in her hair. Somewhat shocked at the sight of herself, she stepped back away from the mirror and realized what the mirrors did. They were like the mirror in Kathrie Gretel's house, back on her first trip here. When she had fallen in the shop and messed up her clothing.

Cautiously she stepped up to the second mirror. The second mirror had a very thin frame of gold, it was delicate and classy. Her reflection in the mirror made her wonder if she could really look that good. In the mirror, her hair was pulled up tightly and held in a French knot. The gown she wore was long, tan, silk and it gently fit her in all the right places. She was lovely and she could not believe her eyes. Still she didn't think it was what she should be wearing at a time like this, so she moved onto the third Mirror.

The third Mirror had a wide blue clay like frame that looked like tiles. When she stepped up to the mirror, Marypat saw herself in a bright pink sleeveless sun dress, and her hair pulled up in pig tails.

"Certainly not." She squealed as she is stepping away from the mirror and quickly moving to the next.

The fourth mirror was framed in silver that seemed to have no pattern to it at all. She stepped up to it bravely and saw herself in a simple knee length gray gown, with her hair in a French braid. It was perfect, but she still wanted to see what the other two had to offer, so she quickly moved to the next one.

The fifth mirror was framed in cherry green kettle post and dressed her in the same outfit she had come in only it was clean.

The sixth mirror was framed in gray marble and dressed her in a low-cut gown that made her look like a 1920's flapper girl.

After viewing all of her choice's she was torn between, her same outfit, cleaned or the simple gray knee length gown. "What would grandpa tell me to do?" She thought and then it came to her. "Why not, it's only a little magic."

She stepped back up to the simple silver frame and called " Fin Frie Fix."

Suddenly out of nowhere came the tiny glowing creatures. They flew around her so quickly that all she could see in the mirror was a blur of activity. They zipped in and washed her hair, then drying it, and then pulling it into a braid. They tickled her fingers while they scrubbed the mud from them. They moved with ease around her and only a few moments later they had all flown away and she stood dressed in the simple gray knee length gown with her hair pulled back in a braid.

Marypat emerged from the laboratory like breath of fresh air. Her cheeks rosy and her mind hopeful that all would be well for her grandfather, once she met up with Kathrie Gretel.

Quickly she walked past the huge silver cauldron in the center of the floor. She spotted the long navy blue velvet curtain hanging in the center archway and went to it. She pulled it to the side and step in, expecting to find Kathrie Gretel waiting for her. But she was not, instead Marypat found an empty room, with a fire place to one side, burning warmly. In front of the fireplace were a love seat and a chair. Beyond the fireplace was an open balcony, with a small round table and two iron chairs in the center of it. The evening sky was dark and the only light came from the fireplace, nervously Marypat took a seat on the love seat and waited for her Hostess.

A few moments later, the curtain flew open and a small green fellow burst into the room.

"Need light, yes, I told, ye not with sight, I forgot, please make pardon while I set things right." The Felden said as he rushed about lightly numerous candles that were scattered throughout the room. When he finished the room was a glow. In the light Marypat could make out the Feldens face. It was Henry the main host of the Blarney Stone Restaurant, but he did not seem to be himself.

"Thank-you, Henry." She said.

"Make no mention I beg, or it will surely be my head." He said with a nervous twitch. "Now tell maiden, your delight and I shall bring it in the light."

Marypat was just about to answer when the air suddenly turned around and several of the candles were blown out. She turned and looked out at the balcony just as a shadowy figure landed effortlessly on the ledge. His huge wingspan nearly blocked her view of the night sky and she frantically stood and grabbed Henry.

"What is that!" She shrieked.

"It is the Master." Henry answered without fear or emotion.

Marypat watched in horror as the figure folded up his wings and made his final descent onto the balcony. He stepped forward slowly and entered the light.

His face was calm and familiar, yet Marypat didn't recognize him.

"Mary dear, did I frighten you? Tell me not, as it would be the last thing I should care to do." The figure said facing her and holding out his hand to her.

She hesitated for a moment.

"Do you not remember me?. . . oh the sharp sword of forgotten love, ye must not pain me any farther, dear one, and recall my name."

Marypat searched the face of the one Henry called Master. But she could not recall ever meeting such a handsome Sherideen, the only Sherideen she ever knew close enough to call a friend was Donovan.

"Yes, it must be Donovan." She thought.

"Donovan? Is that you?" Marypat asked.

Donovan bowed with a swoop of his cape. Then he approached Marypat and reached for her hand. With easy she placed her hand in his and he kissed it with a gentle caress.

By now, Henry was busy relighting the candles that had been blown out. He stumbled around until Donovan called him to bring a jigger of wine and glasses. With that, the Felden flew out through the curtain leaving the pair alone.

"How lovely you look this eve." Donovan remarked as he sat down beside her on the love seat.

"Thank-you, Donovan that is very nice of you to say." Marypat answered nervously. She had not expected to see Donovan, and wondered where his mother was.

"Donovan, I am so pleased . . . ." She began with a smile and nervously touched his hand.

He smiled back at her and took her hand into his and held it while she continued.

". . . to see you again, but I thought I was to meet with your mother, you see I. . ."

"Don't utter another worried word, my dear. It was my mother who insisted that I help you. You see I am quite experienced, more so than my mother and when she told me what had happened to you, why, how could I not come to your rescue once again." He smiled at her. "Am I not your Emparejar Salvador?" He replied as he reached his right hand forward and touched her face gentle cupping her head in his hand.

She smiled back at him. He was right; Donovan had always been there for her, saving her, keeping her from danger. It made sense that he should be the one now to help her.

"But there is something I must ask of you." Donovan said staring into her eyes.

Marypat's mind raced, what could he want from her, he was after all a Sherideen of Ubil and evil was one of his virtues. He could want anything and she was afraid to ask but she had to.

"What?"

"That you will stay and dine with me once the deed is done." He smiled.

Relived Marypat nodded "yes."

"Then we should get to work, come my love." He commanded as he stood. He pulled her with him and guided her out of the room and through the long navy blue curtain. He turned once he was through the curtain and entered the first archway. Then he stopped for a moment and kissed her hand again before pulling back the long gray velvet curtain that covered its entrance.

Inside the room was pitch dark and Marypat could not see. Donovan stayed very close to her wrapping his arms around her gently and guiding her along until they reached the middle of the room. Once there Donovan snapped his figures twice and a small bulb of light floated upwards allowing Marypat to faintly see her surroundings.

In the center of the room, Marypat could make out a waist high pillar that flared out at the top in a circular shape and held two vats of purified water. Donavan placed the tip of his wand in the water and swirled it around slightly causing a wake. With that it was as if he had turned on four huge TV screens, for on all sides, bouncing off the rock walls, Marypat could see the inside of her house in Jamaica.

Stunned she turned around and slowly took it all in. It appeared to her that it was the front room; the only thing missing was the emerald, which would have stood exactly where the pillar stood now. Then suddenly from the wall, stepped Marypat's mother Lora. Like a ghostly figure she walked up to the pillar and stared at it. Marypat reached forward to touch her but her hand slide through her like she wasn't there.

"It's merely a specter, dear, she's not here, she is still in her world." Donavan reassured her calmly. "Now I will need your help."

Marypat nodded yes and then turned back to look at him.

"We need to hold hands and repeat the spell, alright?"

Again, she nodded yes. "What is the spell?" She asked.

"Jak turn poe." He answered. "Ready?"

With one last nod of her head, she reached her hands across the water and held his.

"JAK TURN POE." They called out together.

"JAK TURN POE."

Suddenly the air in the room became thick and heavy. "JAK TURN POE." they called again, this time the air around them began to blow freely as it spun through the room.

"Donovan what's happening!" Marypat cried out, fearful that something had gone wrong.

"Marypat, concentrate, say the spell with me. JAK TURN POE." He shouted back as he held tightly to her hands.

"JAK TURN POE."

The wind continued to spin and on the room began to shack. Marypat became even more afraid that something had gone wrong, especially when she watched the same effects happening in her mother's world.

"We are almost done concentrate, Marypat or we will lose him for good." Donovan shouted through the wind.

Marypat closed her eyes and called one last time. "JAK TURN POE." With that, the two friends were through apart and what appeared to be Marypat's grandfather bobbed upwards through the purified water and was swiped away into a funnel of air. It tore through the room and then smashed back into the pillar where it disappeared into nothing.

Marypat screamed, "We failed, I failed."

Donovan was quick to his feet and even faster to her side.

"No Marypat, we did not fail look." He pointed at her mother's specter and there beside her stood Trevor, a little weak but alive.

"OH, Donovan." Marypat screeched with joy, tears streamed down her face. It was over and the giant weight that had been sitting on her chest had finally gone away, she was free of the gilt, free of her torment. She grabbed Donovan into her arms and kissed him on the mouth.

Donovan grabbed her too, and kissed her passionately before making his move.

"Marypat, how I dare speak to you now, as I see you feel as I. Bind with me, darling and I will make you happy beyond your dreams."

Dinner

The air sat still, the moment in time an eternity to Donovan as he sat with the woman of his dreams in his arms and his heart revealed. He held her waiting and wanting to hear her answer, but it would not be what he had hoped it would be.

"Donovan, I have just returned . . .and although I certainly have feelings towards you I could not at this moment agree to marry you. . ." She said searching his deep purple eyes. "I need moment; we need moment to get to know each other again."

Donovan was crushed at her words; he had so hoped that it would be genuine love that brought them together. But it was not to be, so he tried to recover from his blow as best as he could.

He rose from his position and rested on his knee. He looked her in the eye and smiled. "Of course you need occasion."

Then he tapped her gentle on her nose, causing her eyes to close for an instance. It was only an instant but in that instant the memory of his proposal was whipped from her mind.

When she opened her eyes again, he was still knelling before her and she had no memory of the kiss or his words.

"You promised to dine with me." He declared, with an outstretched hand.

She took his hand and they stood together. Then he led her out of the room and through the Navy blue curtain where their dinner was waiting for them on the Balcony.

The small table was draped in yellow silk over which was heaped a fine white organza that gave the appearance of a cloud resting on the tabletop. The meal was an exotic mixture of raw chockles on the half shell, rose moss salad, stuffed huff fillet, sage bread with pansy jelly and Andree caps sautéed in Jay berry juice. It was a meal fit for the Regan.

After dinner, Donovan invited her to sit by the fire and have dessert. While they waited for the waiter to bring the scrumptious tidbit, Donovan poured Marypat another glass of wine and sat down beside her. He thought that he would make one more attempt to win her without the use of magic.

"Dear Mary, I know we have not seen each other for some span, but I must know your heart on a matter so sacred, that I am breathless to ask." He said with a most earnest heart.

"What is it, tell me, you can tell me anything." She affirmed with a touch of her hand to his cheek.

"Could you. . . ever find it with in you. . . to care for. . . me?" he whispered.

"Donovan, I do care for you." She answered with a smile.

"As a friend? Not a lover?" He asked bravely needing to know his fate quickly. As if a dagger was stuck halfway into his chest and he wished for her to either take it out or slam it all the way in. Oh how he ached to hear her say the word, lover.

"You pose a devil of a question. But a friend you have always been, though in moment who could say." She smiled nervously.

"Then there is hope?"

"There is always hope, and we have plenty of instances." She replied still holding his face in her hand.

But to Donovan he had waited long enough and could wait no longer. Her words of hope only made his next move easier. Why wait it was obvious that they would be together, that they should be together and if all she needed was another phase, he could give her plenty more, by magic.

"You have made me so happy, we should celebrate." He declared. He stood then and stepped back to the table where the jigger of wine sat. He poured her another glass and then one for himself. As he sat down the jigger, Henry entered with their dessert, distracting Marypat for a moment while Donovan worked quietly at the table. He pulled a thin vial that was filled with a blue liquid, from his vest pocket. He pulled off the cork and poured it into her glass of wine. The wine sizzled for a moment and then settled back down.

"Here's to getting to know you!" He proclaimed as he turned away from the table and handed the glass to Marypat. "Bottoms up!"

He drank down his glass and then encouraged her to do the same. She did and when she was done she seemed too slipped off to sleep yet she could hear Donovan when he spoke to her.

His voice was gentle and comforting. "We have spent the last 3 sweeps together, with each passing moment you have fallen deeper and deeper in love with me, and I with you. Tonight we met to celebrate our love and now I wish for you to open your eyes and look into the eyes of your one true love."

Instantly she opened her eyes and looked deeply into Donovan's. "Now I want to ask you something, darling." he paused for a moment as he focused his power on her.

"Will you bind with me?"

Marypat's eyes blink as if she was awakening, as if he had lost control over her. Her head shook once and her eyes closed again. Then she sprang to life with a beaming smile.

"Bind to you? Oh yes, Donovan Gazpalding, I will marry you." She cried.

They kissed.

"We should hurry, everyone is waiting. Come my dear and I shall take you to the altar." Donovan said scooping her up into his arms.

"But wait." She stuttered.

And for a moment Donovan feared she was in need of still more of the potion. Nearly frustrated he barked. "What now?"

"My dress, I should like to wear a more appropriate dress, it will only take a moment I know just the one. You will wait for me won't you darling." She said holding his face in her hands.

"YES, but hurry, everyone is waiting." He relinquished.

Marypat rushed from behind the navy blue curtain and ducked quickly into the laboratory. She stood in front of the thin gold framed mirror and watched as her image changes from her short gray gown into the delicate tan long form-fitting gown. It was just perfect.

"FIN FRIE FIX." She called and again her image in the mirror was transformed to a blur as the tiny creatures worked to change her. When they finished she ran back to the curtain stopped, poised herself, and then entered.

Donovan was amazed, she looked as he had always seen her, she was a vision, an angel, and now she would be his.

He walked over to her and complemented her. He started to hold out his right arm for Marypat to take, but a small sharp pain shot threw his hand causing him to step back and offer her his left. She took his arm and he guided her to the balcony where he threw open his cape and told her to hold on.

"But I don't know how to fly?" She uttered.

"No worry my dear, I won't let anything happen to you, just hold my neck and we shall be off." he answered warmly.

"Where are we going?"

"To the cascades, it has all been arranged." He declared as he jumped from the balcony and the couple flew up in to the evening sky on their way to the cascades.

The deep green sky of the great isle seemed magical as Marypat flew in Donovan's arms. Below them, she could make out the flowing Flower River glowing in Etain light. Then the terrain changed to what seemed like flat land, where every so often she could see a small cabin or a campfire with cowboys stretched out for the eve.

After some time the landscape changed again, this time to a wide flat span of water. On either side of the water, standing on the banks where members dressed in long orange robes and carrying large lanterns. The glow from the lanterns lit up the river and enabled Marypat to see where they were heading.

There before them, at still a distance, was a spectacle of light. Donovan changed course only slightly as the river turned to the left and then back to the right. But still they headed towards the exhibition.

Soon they neared the bright show of lights that were pointed into the evening sky. The multicolored beams swayed with excitement as the couple came into view.

Below them, Marypat could see, in the center of the river was an isle of blue lazurite. The isle sat in the river and caused the roaring water to slit suddenly, forcing the water to shoot around it on both sides before it fell the length of 20 Vasters, into the Lake of Whispers below.

The isle was known as the Cascades, its huge boulders had created behind them a flat area, which was used by all members for sacred ceremonies. The High Sanctifier's of the Cascades were given the rights to perform, Nuptials, Bindings, Blessings and Birth rites for any member of the isles, regardless of size, rank or temperament, so long as said member was courteous and mannered.

On the flats stood 8 hooded Sanctifier's all a glow with light around a statue of a Pattie and Lassie in each other's arms. The hooded Sanctifier's were as Marypat realized the bright beams she had seen in the evening sky. Each pair was a different color and swayed as they chanted in song to the Obligorical. While at the head of the group, the ninth Sanctifier dressed in solid white knelt at an altar that was just in front of the statue and covered with flowers.

Donovan gently maneuvered the pair as they landed on the beach end of the isle. He put away his cape with a flick on his hands and then turned to Marypat.

"Are you ready?" He asked, offering her his left arm while the pain in his right hand persisted.

She took his arm and they stepped forward passing between the first pair of Sanctifier's. They continued along until they reached the Sanctifier kneeling at the altar.

This Sanctifier then stood and turned around to face the couple. With that, the glowing Sanctifier's stopped chanting.

The white robbed Sanctifier stepped up to the couple and pressed his hands on to their hands.

"Peace!" Shouted the glowing Sanctifier's.

"Peace." Whispered the white dresses one.

He then placed his hands on the couple's shoulders and the glowing Sanctifier's shouted," Kindness!"

The white Sanctifier moved his hands to their heads and the glowing Sanctifier's shouted, "Respect!"

Then he stepped back, leaned over and placed his hands on their feet, with that the glowing Sanctifier's shouted, "Understanding!"

The white Sanctifier stood, and looked the couple in the face.

"All of these things we give you to take with you, it will be your duty to enable them to grow strong between you. Weaken any one and you may kill the love."

Then he stepped backwards away from the couple and held his hands over them.

"This eve it is the wish of Donovan and Marypat to take one another in love and trust. To be here after, bond together. Is this accepted by the core."

The glowing Sanctifier's shouted again, in unison, "The core accepts their wish!"

With that the white Sanctifier turned to Donovan and asked, "Do you come here of your own free will?"

"Yes." He answered.

"Does your heart speak Marypat's name and her alone?"

"Yes."

"Will you promise to be affectionate, truthful, understanding, and respectful with her always?"

"Yes."

"What is your wish of me this eve?"

"To bond my heart to Marypat." Donovan proclaimed.

The white Sanctifier then bowed to Donovan and turned to Marypat. He asked her the same questions he had asked Donovan.

"Do you come here of your own free will?"

"Yes." She answered.

"Does your heart speak Donovan's name and his alone?"

"Yes."

"Will you promise to be affectionate, truthful, understanding, and respectful with him always?"

"Yes."

"What is your wish of me this eve?"

"To bond my heart to Donovan." Marypat answered softly.

With the questioning, complete the white Sanctifier stepped back again and called out for all to hear. "With these answers and the requests made I ask all here to bear witness that on this eve, this couple, Donovan and Marypat are so bonded by their own order and from this turn forward are to be as one. Joined by the heart, the soul, and the body."

The glowing Sanctifier's cheered, "Forever true!"

The white Sanctifier then moved forward one last time and whisper to the couple.

"Sweet is the vow when it is true, you may taste of it, both of you." He smiled at them but when neither moved forward so the priest nudged Donovan and motioned to him to take his wife.

Marypat smile and whispered to Donovan, "You're supposed to kiss me now."

Instantly a huge smile appeared on Donovan's face, he had done it, he had won. He scooped Marypat into his arms and kissed her. As he kissed her his Ubil heart was cleaned of evil. Then he turned to the

Sanctifier and wished him well before flying away with his bride in his arms.

His red cape opened and flapped out wide.

Donovan expertly guided them upwards, heading straight for a large grayish white cloud where he spun out his cape on to the cloud as he and Marypat hovered above. Once the cape was settled and spread out smooth Donovan lowed Marypat down on to it. He gently sat her down and then sat beside her.

The view from the cloud was amazing. Marypat could see all the way to the beaches of Hapton. She could see the cliffs of Cliffdale and the Cinerin Mountains. Below her were the Lake of Whispers and the lights of Great Town. It was a beautiful sight.

"Are you tired dear?" Donovan asked his bride. It had been a long turn and it was very late.

"Yes." she whispered.

"Then to bed." He said with a wave of his hand and with that, the soft cloud rolled in on them like a big warm comforter.

Soon they were fast asleep.

The morning light came as always with a sudden wave of light. From all sides of the isle the rays glowed through and caused a sensation of rainbows on the horizon. From their vantage point, they could see 18 separate rainbows all arching high into the bright green sky.

"It's so lovely up here, now I see why Sherideens prefer to live here." She said to Donovan as she stood in the light high above the isle on the soft white cloud.

"Yes, but 'tis the last stretch I shall venture here." He replied painfully. The pain he showed was not for giving up his freedom of living among the clouds as Marypat might have thought but instead was for the Hisue he had been paid in his hand for giving Marypat the love potion. The Hisue had left him with a burning scare on the back of his hand and it was growing slowly up his arm. His right hand was now excruciating and it was all he could do to keep it from Marypat. He even tried covering it with his black leather glove as he listened to his wife.

"Why!"

"There is only one place I shall ever want to be, and that is beside you." He stated as he looked into her eyes. It was an honest answer yet one that would bring him relief, he thought, behind the wall of Cinerin. The longer he remained away from the wall the worse the Hisue would burn. He needed to get to Cimmevian, to their home.

"Now if you are ready, I shall show you the home I have made for you."

"Yes, my love, I am ready." Marypat answered with a beaming smile. "Take me home."

Donovan's wicked Sherideen heart melted with her words, to reveal his genuine heart and with it came such gilt he could hardly stand. If only he could have heard her words untouched by his spell, but now he would have to live with his lie. Knowing it was not her true heart.

He took a moment to remind himself that he was after all a Sherideen and that things like this shouldn't affect him. But what he did not know was that ever since his Sherideen heart had cracked those many passes ago, when Marypat's tears had warmed his face, he was slowly changing inside. He was changing from the traditional Ubil Sherideen, causing him now to fight his instincts as Ubil and struggle between good and evil. Still on this turn, he choose Ubil and with it choose the lie of a life with Marypat.

"Then we are off." He called with a jump into the air, while Marypat held on tight.

The couple flew with ease through the air towards the Cinerin Mountains; they flew passed the Maurieen Palace, the gardens and the Raye Raye Forest. Next, they passed the Pert as the Kert came into view. They sailed over the Kert and straight into Cimmevian town.

Below them was a village there was a cobble stone path that lead out from under the mountain and forward until it reached a great tall pillar made of stone. The pillar sat in the center of the town and was surrounded by a knee high stonewall. It stood perfectly rectangular with the top capped off with a solid pewter roof. On two sides of the pillar, were identical crystal Observers with matching black moon stones in their centers.

The Observer Tower sat like the center of a wheel while the stone path spread around it and then out in 8 different directions.

Four main spokes lead away from the observer, one to the mountain tunnel, the way in which Marypat and Donovan had just come. One straight ahead which lead to the pier and the rich red sand of Fire Beach. The other two ran in opposite directions, perpendicular to the first two paths and lead up into the surrounding mountains.

The remaining four spokes were spread out one after each main spoke, filling the gap between. These spokes disappeared into archways and then broke into three separate paths that lead again into the surrounding mountains. Each archway was carved from selected colors of marble and formed a cove at each spoke.

The coves housed the four elements of life, which were denoted by the Order of Tradition's in which all of the Green Isle members held dear. These elements were respected here and it showed in the fine detailing of the monuments created in each cove.

Beyond the coves and lining the pathways to the mountains where stone carved shops and buildings each in the color of their designated element.

The pathways themselves finally ended as they reach the mountains and disappeared into elaborately carved doorways made of Quartz, pewter, pyrite or Sphalerite. Behind the doorways were where the members of Cimmevian Town lived. They borrowed deep within the Cinerin mountains below the untouchable Cinerin rock, where rich soils was easy to move and made it possible for them to build their dark domiciles. While at the same time keeping them close to Bagree's Hisue absorbing bangle. It was an ideal place to live for the Ubil.

But these styles of building was not what Donovan had had in mind when he designed his wedding hearth. No, below the rock was no place for his beloved, Marypat. Her brightness and beauty would not be kept in such a hollow. Instead, he wanted to build her a brilliant dwelling above the town overlooking the sultry waves of Fire Beach and nestled among the tall Lange trees that lined the mountaintop. It was here in a place they called Cinerin's cliff that he commissioned a grand residence, carved from sheets of solid pick marble and accented with red-flamed opals.

Two great circular towers stood at each end of the house, while the face curved in creating an interesting entranceway that leads to three round steps and the polished arched opal door. Around the door, fanning out and upwards was an enormous stain glass window with the symbol of the hearth as its focal point. Rich red and yellow flames framed the door in the glass and slowly grew larger as they reached the cauldron that sat on its log base just above the door. The flickering light from inside the home gave the stained-glass life, creating a look that there were flames in the glass that were truly burning around the door.

Inside, the home was simply decorated with lightly weave furniture that complemented the look of the marble walls. In the center of the main entrance was an enormous flame pit, a blaze. It lit up the room and warmed the cool air of the cliffs. Beyond the main room was the sun porch that over looked the cliffs themselves and Fire Beach below. To the right of the main room was the dining hall and kitchen. While to the left were the bedrooms and loft. Each room was decorated with Marypat in mind using soft shades of pink and yellow in the tapestries and fabrics, a complete contradiction to the inhabitance of Cimmevian town that generally used bright hues and dark stone tones in their homes.

In truth the entire idea and construction of the home was against all that the members of Cimmevian town who were Ubil, stood for. Some members of the Tribune had even thought that Donovan had lost his mind, to have made such an unusual testimony to his bride. A Maurieen after all, one not even worthy of their mention let alone the measure of a Master Protector.

But Donovan with his heart so overtaken by want, for Marypat, had not heard the whispers of those Sherideens who plotted against him. The Sherideens who felt his weakness and his withdraw from the Ubil ways, the same Sherideens who seemed sure that Donovan had no place in the tribune and were working to have him denounced.

No, Donovan didn't realize his position among the tribune, he moved with his own agenda much like his father had, when he sot the bangle and even that was part of the reason for Donovan's deep burning desire for Marypat, it stemmed back to that turn, when his father had her under his power. That very turn when he stood, powerless, unable to help her. Such gilt had grown around his heart, so much so it spread through the crack and weave its way in to his desires, strengthening his resolve and driving him to this moment where he now stood with his bride on the sun porch of their home.

"Oh, Donovan, this is such a beautiful place." Marypat whispered into Donovan's ear as she hugged him happily.

"You are pleased then?" he asked.

"Oh, yes!" She answered. "Thank you."

The coupled embarrassed, both hearts at that moment in sink, both happy, both complete, though one bewitched and the other bewilder.

CHAPTER 4

Looking for Marypat

The rustle of foots steps filled the dark and dusty air of the small room. There was only a sliver of light from the old wooden doorway, thrown forward like a vale through the center of the room. But it was enough for the dark figure to make his way to the back of the room and find what he was looking for.

"Bing." The sound of the small pewter bell echoed off the walls.

With that more rustling foots steps scuffed the floor, there was the sound of a slamming door and then a horrible groan rose up from in front of the figure.

"Urrrrrr."

"Slam!"

"Carrick! Me thinks it's moment for a new book that one grows to heavy." called the dark figure to the glowing smaller member that now stood in front of him.

"'Tis true, wise Balm, 'tis moment." The Felden answered with a grin as he pulled open the huge book he had just placed on the counter. The dark figure was an old friend of the Felden and he found no harm in his words. "Tell me my friend, what brings you to Boulder Town, this trip is not one planned, 'tis not?"

"'Tis not, my ward is in Boulder on a pressing quest, I have hopes to meet her and give council." Answered the figure.

"You speak of the Maurieen, who travels with the Jinxie and the Grundle?" Asked Carrick as he placed his finger on the book and slowly pulled it down the page until he arrived at her name. "Room 707" Carrick replied as he raised his eyes to his old friend. "Would ye like young Chad to light your way?"

"That would be most fine."

"Very well." Carrick answered before turning to his left and chapping the bell trice, instantly another small Felden appeared and stood at attention while he awaited his orders.

"Chad, take Cornelius McCarthy to room 707." Carrick ordered.

Chad nodded his head and then turned to Cornelius and said. "Please follow me."

Before long, the two stood outside the door of room 707. Cornelius McCarthy knocked twice and waited for a response, but there was no answer. He knocked again but still there was no answer.

"I possess the key." Chad said pulling the gold instrument from his vest pocket. "Would one want to enter?"

"Yes!"

Chad unlocked the door and allowed Cornelius to enter. The room was dark, so Chad lit the room with a wave of his gem hand over a sliver crystal beside the door. Instantly the room was a glow with the light of thousands of tiny Etains.

With the light, Cornelius could now see the room with ease. The large cherry green kettle post bed was undisturbed, Marypat's pack still laid in the center of it unopened. The smeller's cot on the dresser beside the bed was also undisturbed. There was no sign of Marypat, Horatio or Tiger.

Cornelius stood in the center of the room and slowly turned, looking at everything in the room, hoping to find some clue of where she might be. Then he noticed a piece of parchment on the small round table beside the river wall. He quickly picked up the parchment and read it.

It read:

Fare Marypat,

Meet me at the Blarney Stone on the 6th ray.

I have good news.

"She's gone to the Blarney Stone? 6th ray?" Cornelius said allowed.

"Evening be, the maiden is quite early, wait she must!" Replied Chad.

"Perhaps, but if this note was from last eve, that would explain why the beds are not disturbed." Cornelius answered as if a light had gone on inside his head.

"She did not return here. . . . . . . .Chad, thank-you much."

Without another word, Cornelius headed out of the door and down the hall.

Moments later, he emerged from the lobby of the shack and entered the main street of Boulder Town. His foot was swift as he hurried towards the Blarney Stone in search of his granddaughter.

But he did not get far when his thoughts were broken by a sudden pain in his left elbow. It wasn't a hurtful pain but an awakening pain just the same. It shock Cornelius from his deep concentration and brought his mind back to the world around him.

"Cornelius, friend, is your mind ill of reason, I have been calling to thee, yet ye do not answer." Thaddeus the Loralac said coldly as he held tightly to Cornelius elbow.

Cornelius's eye fluttered for a moment as he looked about; trying to locate the face of the voice, he now heard speaking to him. Upwards his glance turned and he found finally the familiar face of his friend Thaddeus, as he stood in the doorway of the Lucky Wager.

"Good fellow, I apologize for my ignorance, but I am in a great hurry to find my ward. Forgive me now I must make haste." Cornelius replied with an uneasy voice. He turned away and tried to move on but the Loralac held firm to Cornelius's elbow.

"It is I that must make haste for two, friend, for one known as Horatio is unmoved from my post, and his duration is well spent. He makes no attempted to budge from his sport, though I have made many an attempt to vacate him. It is as if he is under a spell and then the second a Grundle with tongue sit watching Horatio while threating to kill him." Thaddeus declared. "Ye are their friends, are ye not?"

Cornelius nodded his head, "YES"

"Then I implore ye, thou assistance in removing them from this station." Stated Thaddeus irritably.

Cornelius nodded again. "YES." He would help, but even before, he agreed to assist the Loralac, his mind filled with questions to why Horatio would be in the Lucky Wager with Tiger and Marypat.

After ducking throw the door, Cornelius and Thaddeus made their way to the back of the establishment where they found Horatio still feverously playing the slot machine.

Cornelius turned to Thaddeus and asked. "Marypat, is she here as well?"

"No, she left him here last eve, when he first arrived. She was not glad to leave him, yet he did not seem to care." Thaddeus answered.

"Might you know where she was heading, when she left?"

"No, it is not my way to ask such things." Thaddeus replied.

"And the Grundle?"

"He arrived just a sweep ago also looking for Marypat."

Understanding the Loralac ways Cornelius accepted Thaddeus' response and said not another word about Marypat.

Cornelius approached Tiger who looked up to Cornelius with anger.

"Tiger what is happening?"

"Him not move one flick and he won't give me my fare, even when I threaten his Teeny-ness he stays on his play. I tracked him here at first light and no Marypat in sight." Tiger growled.

Tiger had no more information so Cornelius turned his attention to Horatio. The first thing Cornelius tried to do was speak to Horatio, to reason with him, but Horatio did not respond. He did not even acknowledge the good Cornelius. He seemed only interested in the machine, locked in its neon glow.

"Ye eye sees how queer one remains, almost spellbound." Thaddeus remarked to the good Cornelius.

Cornelius agreed.

The sight of Horatio was enough to convince Cornelius that something strange was causing Horatio to stay fixed to his position at the machine. There was only one thing he could do, he would have to intervene. Quickly Cornelius made a plan with Thaddeus and a moment later, they set off in action.

Cornelius made his move, grabbing Horatio from the back with one hand, around both shoulders pinning down his arms. At the same time with his other hand, he grabbed, Horatio around his legs. Then with a swift flowing move, he lifted the Jinxie away from the machine and tossed him into an awaiting open sack, held by Thaddeus himself.

Thaddeus pulled the drawstring closed with a jerk and handed the wiggling sack to Cornelius.

"'Tis not my way, but I am however certain that it is for his own good." Thaddeus remarked as he passed the bag. "May clear sight be yours?"

"And yours too good friend." Cornelius added as he accepted the now cursing sack. It jiggled a bit as well, as Horatio tried desperately to escape, but Cornelius paid him no mind. Instead, he wrapped the tie once around his hand and held the mouth of it firmly with his palm. Then he bid Thaddeus fare well and headed out of the Lucky Wager with tiger following, both were now even more determined to find Marypat.

It seemed to take Cornelius and Tiger forever to reach the old wooden sign that read "The Blarney Stone." But finally, there it was and he felt partly relieved when he saw Henry's familiar face.

"Good Morrow, Henry, 'tis good to see thee." Cornelius exclaimed as he approached the podium that sat out in front of the restaurant.

"'Tis fine indeed to set mine eyes on thee. To what occasion brings thee here at this early sweep, perhaps an early brunch, I shall have the kitchen up at once." Henry beamed from ear to ear.

"No, dear friend, although I am hungry it is not the reason I have come so early to your establishment." Cornelius said with a gasp. "I am in search of my granddaughter, Marypat. It seems she was to …"

Cornelius tried to explain but Henry had his own ideas and quickly quieted Cornelius by instructing him to follow.

"Right this way." Henry said as he ordered Cornelius into a small dark room just beyond the podium. "Str r r r at." He called out and a fire blow up in two fireplaces that sat on opposite walls of the room providing much light.

Within the room sat several small tables with three chairs to each. In the center of each table was a small cauldron, similar to the big dining rooms, but these sat on small metal frame and had small pieces of coal and crystals under them.

"Sit, eat and we shall speak." Henry ordered.

Cornelius did as he was told and sat down in one of the chairs, then as though he had forgotten what he was carrying in the sack he tossed Horatio on the table with a "thud".

"Hay, watch it! Yarn Vaster ye have no manners." The sack squealed.

Henry turned to Cornelius with a strange look on his face. "Ye have much to be concerned with this morn. Best we get a nosh, before ye start." He tapped the cauldron then with a metal fork and it began to bubble with tiny bright green foam.

Henry waited for the foam to change colors before he stabbed his fork into the center of the cauldron. When he did, his fork emerged with a large sugar bun covered with pigberries. After a few more stabs, there was quite an assortment of sugary rolls and buns for Cornelius to choose from.

"A meal, me like." Purred Tiger as he rubbed up against Henry and accepted a sugar roll from the Feldens hand.

Cornelius finally settled on a sweet cinnamon and prune twist, Henry turned to him and asked. "What great matter brings ye to this horrid plot? To seize a little? I cannot harken to ye parallel."

"Yes, it is quite a plot, by the look of it. But I assure you it is innocent by all course." Cornelius replied with a solemn voice. "The little in the sack is Horatio, who seems to be bewitched, I am certain he is not himself so I have had to restrain him until a removal can be done."

"Restrained? Try kidnapped!!" Shouted Horatio in the sack.

"He does not sound of himself, 'tis true, have you tried Kathrie Gretel's help?"

"No, not as yet, but will make no haste in seeking her help once I have found Marypat." Cornelius stated as he stuffed the last bit of his roll into his mouth.

"What are ye saying, is Marypat in harm?"

"'Tis not my fret of harm, but I am concerned that I did not find her in her room at the shack. Instead I have a note which leads me here to you." Cornelius stated eyeing Henry.

"Here, ye speak of the Blarney Stone?" Henry asked.

"Yes." Cornelius handed Henry the note and he read it.

"Would one know from whom this note was written?" Henry asked.

"My guess would be Kathrie Gretel as she was the one Marypat set here to see. But to this I may only assume." Cornelius replied.

"Well, if that is the case I have no record of her this turn, with plans to dine."

"Yes, that would be true as I do not believe that this note was for this turn but instead last eve." Cornelius stated.

Henry sat in his seat without an answer. He nervously rubbed his chin while avoiding any eye contact with Cornelius.

'What is it Henry? You know something don't you? "Cornelius urged.

"Sir, if only I could assist ye, but I am not . . . . able. . ." Henrys voice stated mechanically and then trailed off until he sat silent. His arms fell to his sides, his breathing seemed to stop, and his face went suddenly white. It was if something Cornelius had said had turned Henry's mind off.

"Henry?" Cornelius questioned as he watched his friends body go stiff. There was something strange going on, something strange indeed, but Cornelius had no way of knowing what it could be. He could only sit and watch unable to help.

"What is wrong? Henry?"

Just than a young Felden stuck his head into the room and asked shyly. "Is all well in here?"

"No." Cornelius answered sharply and with that, Henry dropped to the floor, stiff as a board.

"Uncle Henry!" The young Felden shouted, jumping to his uncle side. "What has happened to my uncle?"

Cornelius shook his head with great concern as he watched his friend lying out in front of him. "I do not know." He answered softly.

Tiger stood over Henry and smelled him. "He has breath, but a scent of a toxic flavor. Could it be the sugar buns, for me ate one as well." Tiger growled.

"No, tiger I do not believe so, Henry did not eat one." Cornelius answered.

Several moments passed as the two tried desperately to revive Henry. It took some moments before Henry regained the color in his cheeks and Cornelius observed that he was breathing better. Soon he was moving his eyes and attempting to speak.

But when he spoke he made no sense at all and it seemed to Cornelius that whatever bizarre going's on had affected Horatio, were also affecting Henry. There was only one thing he could do, and that was to seek the help of Kathrie Gretel. With only a moment's pause to pay for his cinnamon roll and excuse himself from the presents of Henry's nephew and the now delusional Henry, with a promise to return with aid for his ill and to collect the Grundle. Cornelius slipped out of the little room and back out on to the main road of Bolder Town with Horatio in hand and his mind on not only finding Marypat but now solving why everyone was acting so peculiar.

CHAPTER 5

The Ready Kathrie

The Ready Kathrie was a sight for sour eyes. Cornelius seemed more than a little relieved when he finally set foot inside the dark dusty old shop. Yet his relief turned to worry once more when Kathrie Gritty, greeted him with unease.

"What is it Gritty?" Cornelius asked not really wanting to know for fear it was more trouble.

"Leopold, has gone missing and left the shop open all night." Gritty answered as she moved a cauldron out of her way. "As you can see the shop is destroyed." And as she said the words, Cornelius realized the truth as his eyes witnessed the destruction for himself.

"It's as if a bust of anger rose from this very spot." She said pointing to the scorched wooden shelves and burnt debris scattered all about. "It will take at least a pass to restock these shelves with potions. Oh, this is so. . . . Horrid." She screamed.

Cornelius looked around in dread. It just seemed to be another setback, another question to answer, another problem to solve. Still he tried to go forward and asked Kathrie Gritty for help.

"Dear friend, I am sorry to see you so dismayed, and I would not wish to upset you anymore but I am in need of your remarkable talent." He said bowing his head.

Taken by the good Cornelius's compliment, Kathrie Gritty stopped her cleaning up of the mess in the store and stood up straight.

"Tisk, this is nothing. I shall fix it later. Come tell me your concern." She said showing him to the back room.

In the back room they were greeted by Kathrie Gretta and her oldest coven of three. They were all upset, they had seen the storeroom and were dizzy with rumor to whom had done it.

Gritty though was quick to quiet them so that Cornelius could speak. He filled them in on every detail of his morning, yet with every addition piece of information, Kathrie Gritty's face grew ever more disturbed. When he finished she shook her head in disbelief.

"So many things do not make sense; first, my sister did not write this note. We have not yet found the answer Marypat is in need of. As a matter of fact, Gretel never left her room last night. We are to meet this morrow with text to study, I have my compilations right there." She stated as she pointed to a stack of old leather-bound books.

"And mine are there." Added Kathrie Gretta pointing to her pile of books and notes.

"If that is so, then where is she?" Cornelius asked boldly.

The two sisters looked at each other.

"Is it possible your sister, found something last night, something that would solve the problem? Would she go out to meet Marypat without you both?"

"It is possible, but not likely. A Kathrieen works better in threes; beside she would never go to do a task like this, without our aid. No, she would not have gone without telling us." Kathrie Gretta said.

"So if she had not gone, where was she now?" Asked Cornelius

Instantly the two sisters jumped to their feet.

"To Gretel's room." They called out and without delay the group was heading down the narrow stairway that lead to Kathrie Gretel's private quarters.

Kathrie Gretta knocked on the door, but there was no answer.

Quickly she took out her wand and replied. "Vock to."

At once, the door opened and the large group rushed inside.

"Nothing is out of place, but still it seems peculiar to me, her bed has not been slept in, the books she was to study last eve are all still where they were when I left her, in fact by the look of them she hadn't even gotten any farther in them. This is same book I left her reading last eve." Kathrie Gretta said pointing to Magical mishaps, volume F. that sat open on the footstool.

There was nothing in the room to suggest foul play, yet Kathrie Gretel was missing.

"Where could she be?" Cornelius asked.

But both sisters had no answer.

"She's in here! She's been here all eve, won't even get me my milk." Came a very annoyed voice from the closet.

Kathrie Gritty rusted to the closet door and pulled it open. Inside stood the frozen body of her eldest sister Kathrie Gretel, and at her feet was Jack the talking coose.

"Well it's about moment, thought I would die of hunger, now who has my milk?" Jack said as he stretched out his back legs and shook the cramps out of each one.

"What happen here!" Kathrie Gritty shrieked at Jack.

"Get me some milk and I'll tell you what I know." Jack stated as he rubbed up against Cornelius knee and purred lightly.

"Tell me what you know and then you can have some milk." Kathrie Gretta quickly replied as she scooped up the coose by the neck and held him up to her face. "Talk Jack."

"All right, all right. It was Donovan." Jack cowardly said.

"Donovan? Why would he do this to his own mother?" Kathrie Gretta questioned.

"I don't know. I was a sleep in the closet, next thing I know; Donovan is stuffing a Kathrieen-icicle in with me. I do know he used a memory spell on her. But I swear that's all I know." Jack confessed.

"All right then, Hattie, get Jack some milk, but keep an eye on him." Kathrie Gretta said swinging the coose toward her daughter.

"What can we do for her?" Cornelius asked.

"Don't worry, he hasn't harmed her, it looks like a simple freeze, one of my girls could handle it." Kathrie Gretta said with confidence. "Come Hayley, you have a go."

Hayley stepped from the group. She was a skinny little thing with straight straw colored hair and big orange eyes. She looked nervous but her mother took her by the shoulders and guided her up to her aunt.

"Do your best dear, one can't learn without doing." Kathrie Gretta replied with a gentle tone.

With that Hayley raised up her wand. She moved it with a Dacular wave and whispered, "TEK WAY DO."

Instantly Kathrie Gretel awoke to find her niece standing in front of her, with her wand out stretched.

Confused at first, Kathrie Gretel's sisters were quick to fill her in.

"Donovan, my son did this? No! I do not recall anything." Kathrie Gretel whispered.

"There are many questions this turn, which we are left to answer." Cornelius stated as he stood at Kathrie Gretel's side. "Perhaps we should attempt to answer one." He continued, holding up the bag with Horatio in it.

"Yes, the Jinxie. Give him to me." Kathrie Gritty affirmed.

Cornelius handed Kathrie Gritty the bag, and she opened it to find Horatio ready to punch her. Surprised by his vigor, Kathrie Gritty shock the bag slightly in order to throw Horatio off balance and avoid his fist.

"Well in this state we can't do anything. We will need to chill him." Kathrie Gritty expressed confidently holding out her hands.

"Sisters!"

Kathrie Gretel and Kathrie Gretta stood then and held hands with their sister making a small circle with their bodies. Horatio, still in the bag hung from Kathrie Gritty's wrist. Kathrie Gritty and her sisters hummed, while they moved their hands forward, until all six hands and Horatio were in the center of the circle.

Together they called out. "QUANTOM BEE QEE!"

With that, Horatio fell silent, frozen, just as Kathrie Gretel had been in the closet.

Without a moment to waist the three Kathrieens, removed Horatio from the bag and laid him on Kathrie Gretel's soft bed. They did not wish to harm him only help him, so they made sure he was comfortable.

Once they had him placed properly, Kathrie Gretta called to her girls.

"I worry circle of three or six may not get the job done, but a coven of nine most definitely will." She explained to Cornelius.

"Hattie, Hayley, and Hazel come make six. Ingrid, Iniga, and Irene make thy coven nine."

The six young girls came quickly and encircled the three older Kathrieens. No one questioned their mothers call; each one seemed to know their place, their position. It was as if they had practiced as if they had done this before. And in truth they had, not for such a case, no indeed not, but they were Kathrieens and they were in training.

"Place the Halite." Kathrie Gretta called to her daughters. Hazel held up a large container, at the sight of it all six Kathrieens turned away from the elders and waited. Hazel poured the green crystal powder out of the container and on to the floor. Then she handed the container to her sister Ingrid, who continued to pour out the powder on the floor, till she handed the container to Iniga. They continued this until the container reached back to Hazel and there was a complete circle of Halite on the floor encircling the nine Kathrieens, the bed and Horatio.

"Cleansing." Kathrie Gretta then called and the girls in unison began to chant a blessing.

"Purify this space. Lift away any evil that may linger close. Allow us this space to free this member from his ghost."

Cornelius felt a gentle cool breeze fill the room as the Kathrieens chanted softly. He watched as it grew stronger with in the circle as their voices grew louder, until it whipped around them moving their hair and clothing violently. Then suddenly it rose above them, like a whirl wind and hovered there.

"Protection." Called Kathrie Gretta and again the young Kathrieens began to chant.

"GLAN KEE OM O E KEL FLIC-DREE HUM!"

With the protection incantation complete, Kathrie Gretel removed her wand from her pocket and then looked at each of her sisters. This was a very difficult spell, any interruption and it could back fire on the nine, causing each one the same curse as Horatio.

"I will need complete concentration and reassurance from you all. Are you ready?" Kathrie Gretel asked to which she was given a nod of yes from each one. With assurance from all, Kathrie Gretel proceeded. She placed the point of her wand on Horatio's right big toe and began.

"Power grand of evil might, I seek thou wisdom at this sight." Without breaking her stride, Kathrie Gretel move the wand tip from his toe to his out stretched hands that now laid above his head. "Grant this member a solemn plea, and cast thou curse away from thee. . ." Again she moved her wand tip, this moment to his left big toe and then back to the right, forming a triangle. She continued this action until she had recited the spell three times.

When she completed the last word, the bed began to shake and Horatio's tiny body spun around until out of his vest pocket, popped the silver token.

Instantly his eyes opened and he sat up. "Where am I?" he asked quite confused.

Kathrie Gritty reassured him that all was well, while Kathrie Gretta commanded her daughters to stand still and hold firm. The amulet was free and they needed to have control over it before they could break the seal of the Halite. The amulet was trapped within the Halite so long as their circle was not broken.

The three elder Kathrieens each swiftly removed a green velvet sack filled with saddle dust, from their waist ties and began dowsing the six younger Kathrieens with the contents. Then after dowsing themselves and Horatio, Kathrie Gretta ordered the girls to take hands. They did as Kathrie Gretel ordered and as they did the winds with a gathering spell was sung.

"Colee quee hesmor tee, amea emen wen jay a bree, comso fentee na re ket on bask. Mighty energy assembles here, amass great strength and power, collect, receive, and aid thee in this task." Then standing between her two sisters, with her one hand still holding high, Kathrie Gretta offered a glass vile with the other.

The winds from above swept down and around the nine, violently they swayed, yet the girls held firm. Slowly the winds pulled in tighter and tighter until they engulfed the glass vile in Kathrie Gretel's out stretched hand. With Kathrie Gritty and Kathrie Gretta's help, Kathrie Gretel corked the vile and the removal was complete. In the vile was a single silver token, now safely captured.

In Kathrie Gretel's stuffy warm bedroom stood nine wind whipped faces. Each was exhausted and worn, still their weariness didn't out weight their curiously for the now imprisoned amulet. Where it came from and how Horatio came to behold it? Were the most popular questions at hand.

"A fare young Colleen, gave it to me for assisting her with a lost necklace. Strange, I remember nothing after that. Marypat, she. . ." Horatio explained. His voice trailed off as he recalled the last fragments of his memory.

But before he could say another word, Cornelius interrupted. "Then you were with her last eve?"

"Yes, we were on our way to see . . . you at the Blarney Stone." He stated pointing at Kathrie Gretel.

Cornelius then explained that it was not Kathrie Gretel who had written the note. Instead she had spent the eve in a freeze thanks to Donovan.

"Donovan!" Horatio jumped to his feet. "I have never trusted Donavan, least of all around Marypat. Now all this makes sense, he wanted to meet with her alone, he couldn't afford for anyone to get in his way especially me. He has her. Donovan has kidnapped her."

"Now hold on, we don't know that for certain, but I think I know someone who might know the true, if only his mind was well."

Cornelius' thoughts went to Henry then. "Kathrie Gretel, we must now go to the Blarney Stone."

Nine tossed Kathrieens, a Jinxie and one frantic Balm made for quite a sight as the group marched through the main street of Boulder Town on the midday sweep. With the four elders leading the way and the six young Kathrieens following in a line one behind the next, they marched in to the Blarney Stone.

Henry was still where Cornelius had left him earlier that morn, in the breakfast room. He was now however sitting up in a chair and an older Lassie Felden was looking after him and Tiger curled up at his feet. When the group entered, Cornelius went straight to the nephew for an update on Henrys condition.

"How is he Fred?" Cornelius asked with great concern.

"He hasn't changed; he makes no sense at all." Henry's nephew Fred answered.

"I am sorry for that news, Henry is a dear friend. Come let the Kathrieens work, I must speak with you about last eve." Cornelius said as he and Fred stepped out of the breakfast room to allow the Kathrieens to help Henry and for Cornelius to have a quiet moment with Fred.

"Fred, did you work last eve?"

"No!" Fred answered quietly. "Uncle Henry, sent us all home. Had us close up early, It was very odd."

"Why is that?" Cornelius asked.

"The Blarney Stone, in all of its history, had never closed. But Uncle Henry said he had a private party and we were all to leave."

"Private party? Do you know who the private party was for?"

"No, Uncle Henry wouldn't say. All I know is he had been acting strange all turn. I don't want to say it, but I must, he was actually vile. As if he had been, corrupt by Ubil. Then this morrow, I find him on the ground giggling, acting silly as if he had been drinking ale. It was most unlike him. I tried to get him to go home and sleep it off, but he would not leave." Fred answered irately. "I tell you, Uncle Henry must be mad, acting so particular, running around screaming at everyone one moment and the next singing on his hands and knees while digging in the soil with his bare hands."

"Digs in the soil, what do you mean?" Cornelius asked.

"Here let me show you, he's practically destroyed the entrance way." Fred declared as he marched around the podium and halfway down the main hallway that lead to the private dinning coves.

There to one side was a heaping pile of damp soil and on the other was a hole, a large enough hole for someone to walk into.

"Horatio" Cornelius called and a moment later Horatio bounded out of the breakfast room and hopped onto the good Cornelius shoulders.

"Looks pretty bad in there, Fred, so sorry, But what can I do for ye doc." Horatio asked.

"Can you see where this leads?" Cornelius asked the Jinxie as he pointed to the hole.

"Sure." Horatio answered without much thought and off he bounced. A few moments later Fred and Cornelius heard Horatio gasp.

"What is it, are you all right?" Cornelius shouted into the hole.

"You gotta see this place." Horatio called back with delight.

Just then Kathrie Gretel and her sisters approached the pair staring into the dark hole.

"A Sherideen's Twindle way?" Gritty mentioned under her breath and her two sisters agreed with wide eyes.

Their worried faces had Cornelius questioning their response.

"What is a Twindle way?"

"It's an entrance into a Sherideens lair." Came the answer from one of the young Kathrieens that stood behind Kathrie Gritty.

"Why would a Sherideen's lair be here, in the Blarney Stone?" Fred asked with sarcasm.

There was silence in the group for a moment whiles the thought of such a thing here in the Blarney Stone, settled in their minds. For Kathrie Gretel it was looking as if her son had gone truly evil, everything was pointing at Donovan, everything. Though she could not allow herself to believe that is was his work, she would need more evidence.

"We should investigate." Kathrie Gritty said with uneasy in her voice.

"Yes! But first tell us, how Henry is doing." Cornelius asked.

"I'm afraid there is nothing we can do, I am sorry Fred. It seems your uncle is a victim of a mind grip." Kathrie Gretel said sadly, knowing in her heart that her son could not have done that to Henry. A mind grip was too cruel, too wicked. Donavan was not that kind of Sherideen, he was in love and foolish enough to use trickery perhaps but not Ubil enough to destroy a friend's mind. No there had to be another answer.

"Mind grip very nasty thing, out lawed ya know." Kathrie Gretta whispered.

"We have notified the council and they are sending their very best Torideen to investigate. He should be here within the sweep." Added Kathrie Gritty.

"Your aunt is with him now and she has requested your return." Kathrie Gretel added.

"I shall do that, but first I should like to see the lair." Fred answered bravely.

So off into the dark tunnel they went. Fred and the girls easily maneuvered through the winding passage. While Cornelius and the Kathrieens had more difficulty, just as Marypat had. Still they reached the end of it and entered the landing where Horatio greeted them with a smile.

"Incredible sight. AH?"

"Indeed" Cornelius answered, looking around at the four enormous archways carved from the blue lazurite.

Fred's face dropped as his eyes took in the detail of the lair. "They must have been here working for some moment, and we never knew."

"No!" Kathrie Gretel said with confidence as her hand ran down one side of an archway. "This was not made by hand, but by Magic."

"'Tis true." Both sisters agreed.

"It is well that we hurry our task here for these Sherideens illusions do not last long and I fear that this one will vanish with in the ray." Kathrie Gretel instructed.

With that, she pushed through the first curtain and entered the pitch-black room.

"Rum de la Mar" She called out. Her inter glow grow bright from her words and lit up the entire room. She could see then the pillar in the center of the room. She approached it and discovered the bowl of purified water held on the top of it. It was a visionary vat. One she was sure was used to not only to help Marypat free her grandfather, but also the one that trapped him. She in her heart did not want to see what had taken place here. But in her mind, she had to know, so she called out as the group entered the room.

"Sonto." (show me)

Instantly the walls came to life with the vision of the front room in Marypat's home. All was quite there.

She called again. "Rem domum, Sonto." (Deeds revealed, show me.)

Suddenly the visions on the walls blinked off and on several times before settling back with a clear picture of Marypat's family home. The group watched as the vision of Marypat's grandfather, Trevor approached the vat in the center of the room. He turned his head slightly as if he were listening carefully to something. Then he walked away out of sight. The vision blinked again and Trevor was back listening at the vat, this time though his eyes closed like heavy weights. But a moment later he shook off the sleepily look and stumbled out of sight. Again, the vision blinked and Trevor was again at the vat with his ear turned towards the vat. This time though his eyes never opened as he tried to walk away. Instead, he fell to the ground where he laid dead.

The vision never wavered it stayed locked on the lifeless body of Trevor. Moments passed as the group watched in horror the scenes of the outside world. Then they saw Lora, Marypat's mother enter the vision, her face amputated of emotion, her mouth screaming words they could not hear, but they understood there meaning.

Finally, they saw Marypat enter the vision. She knelt at her grandfather's side and pointed her wand at him. Then she jumped to her feet. Her arms flew wide, she tried many things, yet nothing worked. As they watched her, the vat of water, in the center of their room began to move. Slowly at first, like a small turning ripple, but then it grew until it rose out of the vat and into the vision.

The group watched as the whirlwind forced its way around the room in the vision causing an explosion of air to blow open the windows and turn off the light. They continued to watch as Marypat's grandfather was sucked into the whirlwind and thrown around until finally being sucked into the vat of purified water, there in their room.

One of the sisters gasped at the sight, while another uttered. "How can this be?" It was just too much to believe. The group was in shook as they continued to watch, the vision.

This time the vision showed Lora, silently staring at the vat. She had tears in her eyes. As she turned away from the vat, the vat again began to move. Slowly it stirred until it grew wild and fast and formed into a whirlwind. The whirlwind again forced its way out of the vat and into the vision. This time though it deposited Trevor safely into the vision and then disappeared.

With that, the visions stopped and the group stood in disbelief, stunned. The knowledge that someone from inside could manipulate the outside world was more than any of them could handle. And for Kathrie Gretel it was even more troubling as she believed it was her son, who had arranged it. It was bad enough, cursing Horatio, blowing up the shop, and locking his mother in a freeze, but now using a mind grip and tampering with the outside, these were criminal acts. Kathrie Gretel could take no more. She ran from the room and ducked under the second curtain hoping to find someplace to catch her breath. But what she found there upset her even farther.

The room was still set as it was the eve before. The dessert plates were still on the small yellow draped table, untouched. The wine glasses on the table in front of the settee. Half-melted candles were scatted throughout the room and the odor of candle wax still hung heavy in the air.

At once Kathrie Gretel headed to the table and discovered a small empty vile; she knew right away what it was. But she smelt it any way to be sure.

"Love potion # 2." She said.

"How do you know?" Ask Cornelius as he caught up to her beside the table. Horatio bounded up to the table at the same moment and listened in horror as Kathrie Gretel explained.

"It's my own potion." She stated as tears rolled down her face. "He used my potion." Suddenly the memories of the night before flooded her mind. It was as if the scent of the potion broke the spell on her memory, and it all came back to her. Every word he had said, every last detail. Yet it was all too much, and she began to sob.

Just then Hattie and Hayley entered the room and commanded the group to follow them. They did and the two girls lead the way into the last room of the lair, the laboratory. Horatio bounded up in front and watch as Hattie turned around to face the group.

"Watch." Said Hattie and she called "Sonto."

Suddenly the six mirrors came to life with the visions of Marypat. Each one posted Marypat in a different outfit just as they had the eve before.

Cornelius' face went white, there was his great-granddaughter before his eyes, but he could not touch her.

"What does this mean?"

"It's a dressing mirror, she must have changed in here." Hayley answered.

"But there is more." Hattie added. "Watch this, Sonto Amoy."

And with that four of the vision faded away leaving Marypat still dressed in two of the mirrors. As they watch one more faded away leaving Marypat standing happily wearing a long tan gown, with her hair pulled back in a delicate French knot. She stood in the mirror smiling, she turned around once and then all six mirrors flashed brightly with the same vision.

Kathrie Gretel collapsed into the overstuffed chairs and Fainted.

Kathrie Gritty quickly went to her side and revived her. When she opened her eyes, her lips quivered and her body shook as she spoke.

"They are wed!"

CHAPTER
6

Order of Tradition

The soothing sound of waves was broken suddenly as an echoing clang was heard in the distance. The clang rang four times and then stopped.

"What was that?" Marypat question her husband as she sipped her tea.

"That was the Observer from town, you remember we passed it when we came in." He answered in a reassuring voice.

"Yes! I should like to see the town sometime." Marypat remarked casually.

"We can make the trip after lunch, if the light stays strong." He smiled. Cimmevian Town had a history of dark clouds and stormy weather that plagued its harbor, but for some strange reason the sky

340

over the town this turn was bright and clear. It was a perfect turn for Marypat to visit the town.

So after their meal was complete, Donovan wrapped Marypat in a long brown cape and then took her on a short flight to town. Donovan set them down right in front of the tall stone Observer that sat directly in the center of town. Around them Marypat saw many Kathrieens, Sherideens and Ulldens, none of them paid her any mind, as she stood among them draped in brown.

"The observer was built around the age of the great migration to Cimmevian. A Sherideen named Spencer Wadsworth commissioned it in honor of the Ubil leader Bagree." Donavan mentioned as they toured the observer. "In the center of the twin crystal faces are identical black moonstones, given to Wadsworth by Bagree himself. If you look carefully on this side of the Observer you can still see Wadsworth signature and Bagree's imprint."

Marypat bent slightly at the waist and looked carefully where her husband instructed her. Her hand slipped over the impressions and as it did a shiver ran down her spin. Quickly she moved her hand away from the rock and stood up straight.

"Tell me about the areas decorated in difference colors." Marypat asked trying to move the subject away from the Observer.

Donavan smiled, and began to explain the Ubil ways. He told her about the four main elements of life, Air, Water, Rock and Fire. He explained that all members of the Green Isles believed in the Order of Traditions to which these elements were based.

"One cannot exist without all four. This is why there are four sections of the town, each section is host to one of the four elements. Each element has a Master Protector and a group of attendance. All are members of the Ubil sect. I am the Master Protector of Water." He declared as he showed her into the section of town known as Wells Rye.

The out cove of Wells Rye was constructed of blue marble and decorated with deep blue flags and banners. Inside the cove, the walls looked to Marypat to be an aquarium. She could see plant life and fish swimming, but when she touched the wall, the seen disappeared and when she took her hand away, it reappeared.

In the center of the cove was a fountain of clear water that sat on a narrow pillar. It bubbled gently upwards in a wide round basin and then ran over the lip of the basin and splashed on the large rocks and sand below.

"Hold your left hand in the water." Donovan commanded as he eased his bride closer to the fountain.

"I am interested to see which element you are naturally drawn too. If the water glows when you placed your hand in the water you are a protector of water."

Slowly Marypat's fingers entered the water and just as slowly, the water began to glow.

"How Exciting my wife, you are same element as I."

Donovan placed his left hand into the water as well. He took her hand in his and when he did the center of the fountain changed from a gentle bubble in to a high spraying shower that fell down around them in a rainbow of soft mist. It was a beautiful sight, one nether had ever seen before.

"What does this mean?" Marypat asked with delight.

"That we are meant for each other!" Donovan answered with a smile on his face. "But in truth I have never seen or heard of such a happening before. Not even during the rights of passage when all Water Protectors enter their hands into the water at the same time. Certainly this was not a bad thing; no it is a sign that all was right."

Delighted with the event, Marypat and Donovan excitedly exited Wells Rye on their way to Winds Port. Outside the cove they were greeted by a yellow-clocked Wardeen.

"Greetings Brother." The clocked member replied with a stranded voice. It was as if the words were difficult for him to speak and he had to use every effort to release them.

"Greetings to thee, I am most grateful to see thee and finally present to thee my enchanting bride!" Donovan announced with pride. "Marypat this is my esteemed friend, confrere nay brother, Ragnar. Ragnar this is. . ."

"Marypat of course, she is as breath taking as you described." Ragnar mentioned as he pulled his clock from around his head to relieve his long black hair and stunning blue eyes.

"Pleasure." Marypat replied with a bow of her head. He looked familiar to her, but she couldn't quite recall where she had seen him before. "Have we meet some . . ."

Again Ragnar interrupted, "No, dear!" His answer was curt and he quickly turned away from her and placed his arm around Donovan. "The Supreme Master must meet her at once; I shall arrange it for his eve. Bring her at dusk and we shall dine by the evening glow."

Donovan agreed and Ragnar disappeared from sight with a puff of smoke.

"Sorry about that, his likes to be dramatic." Donovan explained and they both laughed. "Shall we go in."

With a nod of her head, they set forth into the yellow cove of Wind, also known as air or breathe. This cove represented the very air one breaths. Inside, the walls looked like the sky, there were a few white clouds floating near on the ceiling and in the distance Marypat could see a single dark rain cloud. In the center of the cove was thick golden pillar with a vat of purified water resting on it. In the center of the vat, balancing like a top was a whirlwind, its delicate point danced on the water and moved only slightly on its course.

"What will happen if I place my hand in this one?" Marypat curiously asked.

"Nothing, see!" Donovan slipped his hand in and the whirlwind continued its course with no interference.

So Marypat followed Donovan and placed her hand into the whirlwind but when she did the whirlwind was knocked free from its base and filled the cove with an enormous gust of wind. The whirlwind swirled around her, growing as it sucked in the air from outside the cove.

Acting fast Donovan forced Marypat's hand away from the gold pillar, instantly the whirlwind stopped and all was calm.

"Why did it do that?" Marypat asked.

"It's not supposed to do that, unless you're a protector!" Donovan answered a bit stunned. "I've never seen anyone naturally drawn to more than one element." He said in astonishment.

After a moment he convinced his wife to move on to Red Chard, the cove decorated in red for fire. This cove was built of dark red marble with huge twisting veins of Smokey quarts running through the marble slabs. Inside, the walls looked as if they were a blaze; an inferno of brilliant thick flames shot up from the floor and licked the walls all the way to the ceiling. In the center of this cove was a small pit of fire, its flames grew to only Marypat's waist. Yet with all the fire around her Marypat felt no heat.

Once inside the cove, Donovan encouraged his wife to place her hand into the center of the flame.

Nervously she placed her fingertips into the flame in the center of the cove. The flames were not hot, they felt like whispers of air. So Marypat pushed forward until her entire hand was covered by flame. Immediately the docile flames flew to a height that hit the ceiling and fell backwards in a shower of sparks. It grew larger and hotter, its flame changing from red to blue.

Frighten Marypat withdrew her hand and throw herself into Donovan's arms.

"Why is this happening, I thought I should be drawn to only one element?"

"You, Marypat!" Donavan said, pulling Marypat's head gently away from his chest so that he could look her in her eyes. "Are very very special." Then he kissed her on the forehead before continuing. "We have one more element to check, now don't be frightened, these things that happen here in the coves are only specter's, they cannot harm you, I promise. Let us just see, if you hold the touch of all four."

"What will it prove if I do?"

"I don't know, but I do know the Supreme Master will, and when we dine with him this eve, I shall ask him." Donovan smiled.

Marypat agreed, even if it meant nothing, which in her heart she secretly hoped, she should still test the last element.

Hand in hand, they approached a moss-covered marble stone cove. Inside, the walls depicted every possible stone and mineral known to the members of the Green Isles. Granite, pewter, limestone, Agate, sandstone, obsidian just to name a few. Each hunk of rock fit into the wall like a puzzle, like a mosaic, like an intricate piece of art. Marypat was drawn to its design, the colors of the rocks flowed easily, beatify.

In the center of the cove was an enormous boulder of blue lazurite. Within the lazurite were tiny specks of pyrite and several cubes of light green Torbernite. In the center of the lazurite, slightly bend to one side, was a hexagonal shaped emerald that stood almost as tall as Marypat. It was a deep shade of green and she stared at it as if she had seen a ghost.

"What is it Marypat?" Donovan asked with concern. Marypat's face had gone strangely white and her jaw fell open slightly.

"It's. . . the emerald!" She stuttered, still staring at the enormous crystal in the lazurite. "It's like the one. . . this one!" She said holding her hands up and shaking them. "The one I. . . .fell into."

Tears filled her eyes as she tried to explain, but Donovan could not understand her. He did not know that his world of the Great Green Isles was like the one that sat in front of them now. This one was larger and had fewer stones in it, but it was cut from the same body of rock and Marypat found it a bit overwhelming.

She took a moment then and composed herself, the sooner she did the task the soon she could step free from the reminder of home. So, after the moment she moved forward and pressed her hand against the crystal. When she did, the cove lit up with an array of light beams that exploded outwards from her touch.

With the deed done, she removed her hand and walked out of the cove leaving Donovan to follow.

Meanwhile at the Pert a yellow clocked figure approaches the altar of the Supreme Master.

"Winds Port Protector, speak." The Supreme Master called aloud.

"Master, I bring you retched news of one who would plot against you and the very structure of this rite. He has brought forward with magic, unguarded, the one they call Marypat. The very one who destroyed our fallen Master, Gazpalding, the same one that has cursed us all with her careless deeds. Master, I gain no glee in my report, as it is with great distaste that I bring you this news." The yellow-clocked member pleaded.

"Who would brave such a treacherous deed, speak thou name!"

"'Tis Donovan, Protector of Wells Rye."

"No, you speak not the truth." The Supreme Master shouted as he stood.

"Master it is the truth; you may see for thou self." The figure proclaimed, he stepped to one side of the altar and approached the visionary vat. "He walks with her in the very city of Cimmerian."

"No!" The Supreme Master gasped, seeing for himself a vision of Donovan and Marypat walking along the cobble streets of Cimmerian.

"He has brought her back here to take your place, he plans to have the Maurieen dig up the bangle and force you out." The clock figure added.

"Why would he do this, when his era approaches?" Mumbled the Supreme Master as he fell back into his thrown.

The Supreme Master was a quiet ruler, after Gazpalding's failure and the passes of immeasurable Hisue that bombard the Ubil, Nicholas Northcliff had been a sensible chose for Supreme Master. Confident, composed and delicate when it came to dealing with the other groups of the isle. He had been the one that cooled the heads of many leaders, such as the Lachlanns and Feldens that wanted to destroy all of Cimmerian after the destruction of Gazpalding. He had been the one to bring calm back to the isle and settled the fears about the bangle. For him he had done all we could for his members and he was soon to step down, Donovan had been chosen, as his successor for Donavan was the son of Drake Gazpalding. So, all of this news made no sense to him at all.

"There is no need for such a plot."

"He grows tired of waiting, like his father he wants . . ."

"No! I will hear no more of this."

"Master, we cannot look the other way, he will surely kill you." The clocked figure whispered. "Allow me to handle it for you, you need not know a thing."

The Supreme Master sat for a moment and thought, he didn't like such brutal events, but he could not sit and allow Donovan to take over without defending himself. So he agreed.

"Do what you must, call me when the deed is done!' stated the Supreme Master. Then he stood and walked off the altar and disappeared from sight.

Orbital Receptacle

The silence of the muddy Twindle way grew noisy as the coven of nine, the Felden and Balm made their way out of the lair. Leaving Horatio behind still standing in front of the dressing mirror. No one noticed he was missing, no one realized his pain, his overwhelming feeling of failure. There was nothing he could do now, but he watched his Marypat spin in the mirror, spell bound by a love potion, that he could have prevented if had not been so gullible. His heart ached, he was destroyed inside, and he wiped quietly as the room grew dark and her vision faded.

Meanwhile Kathrie Gritty helped her sister Kathrie Gretel out of the opening and back up the slight embankment to the front of the restaurant while Fred and Cornelius quickened their pace and headed directly for the breakfast nock.

Once inside they found Henry sitting upright in a chair, while a very tall thin member dresses in a course purple robe stood beside him. The tall member had a long grayish white hair that fell well below the member's waist. Still longer was the members beard and mustache. He had a particularly worried look on his face as the Cornelius approached.

"Orida, 'tis grim this turn and there for difficult to greet thee warmly." Cornelius uttered with a sorrowful breath.

"Oh yes such corrupt circumstances to which bring us now together, my friend. Still to see thee well brings a taste of relieve to my eyes." Orida remarked.

The two old friends grabbed arms and held firm for a moment before releasing their grip.

"Tell me of the events that led us to this moment!" Orida inquired.

Cornelius did his best to fill Orida in on everything that had transpired, since Marypat's arrival. Orida listened intently and nodded in agreement. Once Cornelius completed his rendition of the turn's events, Orida made his disclosure.

"Two turns passed, as I watched my Oritor I noticed a gray cloud grow over the Flower River, at first I thought nothing of it. The Doodle Falls often clouds my Oritor, but after sometime, the cloud did not disperse. Later in the eve, the gray cloud turned black. I knew then, Ubil was at hand. Your information fulfills my many questions and leaves me still with others. My task here is done yet I should still like to see the vat that was found in the lair."

"What about Henry?" Fred demanded.

"Unfortunate creature, he is beyond care." Orida revealed coldly.

"No, ye must help him! I shall not allow ye to be so unmoved by his misfortune, ye will take him to Great Town, ye will find him care." Fred demanded.

"Be still ye Common folk, I shall not be spoken to with such heat. I meant no disrespect; I only gave ye the truth." Orida argued

Fred turned to his aunt and they hugged, it was devastating news to take, poor Henry would never be the same.

At the Vat in the lair, Horatio secretly watched as Orida inspected every detail. Orida watched the visions, and then he watched them again. He took a sample of the purified water and examined the pillar. There wasn't anything he didn't investigate.

But what he didn't notice was the small Jinxie who had hidden away in his cloak pocket and now sat determined to save his friend from the clutches of evil.

"I am still not convinced the one you call Donovan is the true culprit, I should like to take my evidence back to the council and there make my recommendation." Orida reported to the group as he exited the Twindle way and walked back to the breakfast room.

"In addition I feel it is imperative that, you Cornelius and Gretel accompany me, as your testimony is vital. Now. . ." He continued after facing Fred. "Having seen what I have seen in the lair and reviewing my thoughts on Henry, I feel that I must revoke my stand on his wellbeing and request that he too accompanies me back to Great Town."

Fred gave a nod and Orida announced. "We should leave immediately."

"Pardon my ignorance, Orida, but I feel that speed is essential and I am only a Balm with no means but my foot to make travel quickly, it would do you well to leave me and make haste." Cornelius humbly surmised.

"Make no worry, dear friend, in measures like these the council has tools for which to aid the righteous campaign." Assured Orida as he relied an orbital receptacle from under his clock.

"An Illegal device!" Kathrie Gritty gasped. Then she quickly gathered the circle of six.

"Girls cast your eyes upon its form, for one has never been seen nor will again."

The orbital was as large as a dinner platter and just as round. It was made of thick clear quartz crystal that thinned out slightly as it reached the edge. Around the edge of it was a ring of gold that wrapped all the way around it in a seamless form. Etched along its face were four sets of finger placements and on the reverse was the thumb. In the center of the Orbital was an oval shaped hole left empty for a purpose.

Orida held the orbital receptacle flat in his hand and then called to Kathrie Gretel and Cornelius.

"Ready thee right hand."

Cornelius and Kathrie Gretel reached out their hands and placed their fingers into the placements on the face of the orbital receptacle, and then they placed their thumbs on the bottom of the orbital in its place.

"Fred can see to Tiger until I can return?" Cornelius asked over his shoulder.

"Yes." Fred answered.

"Cornelius if you would be so kind as to raise Henry's." Orida asked softly of the balm.

Cornelius did as requested and placed Henrys limp hand on to the orbital receptacle and held it there as Orida continued.

"Please step back." Orida ordered the on lookers. There was silence in the room as he removed a stone from his ring and placed it in the hole at the center of the orbital. The stone was a golden yellow tiger's eye and it slipped in perfectly. Its marquise shape filled the space and began to hum. A moment later, the hum stopped and the four members disappeared for sight.

There was a bust of light and thrust of energy that throw the travelers on to a new floor. The orbital receptacle remained still hovering in midair as Orida recovered quickly and stood beside it. Cornelius and Kathrie Gretel also stood, leaving poor Henry where he had landed. They looked at each other as if to say, "Are you well." both nodded "yes" and then attended to Henry.

The place they had landed was dark and cold, but they soon realized that they were not alone.

"Good council I bring thee a report, these good members bring testimony. One I am sure will lead you to act." Orida declared.

"Let the Kathrie speak." Came a voice in the distance.

"I should speak, but not to a secret board. My son's life rest's in yours hands; I should want to know whose." Kathrie Gretel insisted.

With that, the auditorium was lighted and Kathrie Gretel could make out the faces of the members of the council.

"Very well." she began. She gave her testimony, explaining every detail, each one intimidating Donovan for the crime. When she finished tears were running down her face, in her mind, she had placed a noose around her sons' neck, she had pointed a dagger at his heart and left the council no other chose but to act.

The group was dismissed while the council decided on the root of action. Surely, they could not allow these deeds to go unpunished and the longer they waited the worse it looked to the members of Isle. The Regan was notified, and word then came that the council had authority to capture Donovan by any means possible.

The news was devastating to Kathrie Gretel, there was nothing she could do, but sit and wait, while the council arranged for the capture of her son.

The Pert

As the eve fell to darkness Donovan and Marypat soared above the Pert and glanced out at the world below. It was a remarkable view and a wonderful way to travel. Marypat was all smiles as they landed on the balcony of the Pert.

But suddenly her face changed as she stepped forward. It was like a wave of pain over took her and it was all she could do to keep from falling over.

"Marypat!" Donovan asked quite concerned as he noticed her sudden weakness.

"Donovan?" Marypat's question. Her eyes searched his. "Where am I?"

"We are at the Pert." Donovan said softly.

"What are we doing at the Pert?" She asked trying to keep her eyes open.

But before Donovan could answer her, an orange cloaked usher interrupted and instructed Donovan to enter the parlor.

"You may place your wife on the lounge." The orange-cloaked usher stated strangely and then he disappeared.

The word wife echoed in Marypat's ear. "Wife, whose wife?" But there came no answer. She was now lost as her mind faded from her own thoughts and turned to nothing, blank.

Donovan careful laid her down on the lounge. He kissed her softly on the mouth and whispered so only she could hear. "Let me make our apologizes and then I shall take you home."

He raised his head then and noticed a figure standing in the darkness.

"Uncle Leopold is that you? I thought you were working at my mother's shop, in Boulder Town?" Donovan asked strangely.

"One toils at a task, yah the task is complete, the maiden is at hand." Leopold said with a smile as he glazed at Marypat.

Donovan knit his brow at his uncle's response and inquired. "What do you mean by that?"

"Never mind him, Donovan. That will be all Leopold, go now." Ragnar stated as he made his presents known in the room.

"Very well master." Leopold said with a bow. A moment later, he was gone leaving Donovan and Marypat alone with Ragnar.

"I see that your wife is not feeling herself!" Ragnar mentioned as he approached the couple.

"Yes, it has come on suddenly, and I must apologize, but I'm afraid we cannot stay." Donovan replied as he stepped towards his friend.

"To bad really. . . "Ragnar said with a slippery tongue. "I had so hope to see her dig."

"What?" Donovan asked. His friend's words were so peculiar. Donovan was confused.

Ragnar smile a devilish grin as he slid in close to Marypat and whisper to her.

"Dig."

With that, her eyes opened and she proceeded to stand. Donovan flew to her side.

"Mary, are you all right?"

"Must dig!" She stated plainly, pushing Donovan to the side.

"Stop! What is going on here." Donovan shouted as his dear Marypat knelt on the ground and began digging in the very spot the bangle was buried.

Donovan watched in horror as Marypat move the Cinerin stone with her bare hands. A flash of memory struck him, of that moment when he had seen her do the very same thing so many passes ago, and he had done nothing to help her. He would not allow the same thing to pass, this time he would do something, anything to help her. He turned to Ragnar with anger in his eyes; he had to stop what was happening. He would not stand and watch this happen all over again.

"What have you done to her?"

"I have done nothing." Ragnar answered with an evil smirk.

"Then tell me what magic is this?" Donovan roared.

"Only the magic of your father. You still don't get it, do you? You really are a fool. You are so easy to manipulate." Ragnar laughed.

With his words, Ragnar turned a friend instantly to a foe. Donovan without thinking swung his fist at Ragnar. He wanted Ragnar to stop the spell on Marypat and if he had thought about his actions, he might have used another more successful means, but alas in his anger he choose his fist, a poor weapon against magic, and instead of knocking Ragnar out he only angered him.

"Ushers." Ragnar called as he flashed his hands in front of Donovan's face, causing Donovan to be flown backwards on to the floor beside Marypat. Instantly the room filled with orange robed Sherideens who grabbed Donovan before he could make any move to get away.

Ragnar approached the now restrained Donovan and looked him in the eye. His gaze was more evil then Donovan had even seen before. His lips formed a most vile grin and when he spoke, his voice was like venom, his breath like sulfur, and the words dripped from his lips like warm blood from a fresh kill.

"Did you really believe I would help you get her here, for you?" He laughed. "Why would I help the one Sherideen that has stood in my way and kept me from my rightful place as Supreme Master? No, I had you bring her here for me and soon I will hold all the power, I shall be the Supreme Master, and all will fear me." he laughed.

"Why you. . ." Donovan wailed as he fought to get away from the ushers.

"Now what to do about you!" Ragnar smirked as he stood up straight and patrolled the floor of the Pert. "Oh, I have thought long and hard about what to do with you and then it came to me how simple, how incredibly perfect. I would turn you over to the council, not only will they thank me, for turning over such a ruthless villain, one so wanted for his evil crimes but it will buy me the time I need to recover the bangle without fear of interception. They'll be so busy with you, they won't detect my work."

"What crimes? I have done nothing wrong." Donovan shouted at Ragnar.

"Oh really, well I recall that tampering with worlds has a very heavy penalty associated with it, I believe it is death by means of consumption." Ragnar stated calmly.

Donovan's anger grew as Ragnar continued his taunting.

"Yes, and there's the cost of a Mind Grip and possession of will, not to mention kidnapping, destruction of property, construction of a lair within city limits and freezing one's own mother."

Donovan squirmed. "But I didn't do all of that, you were the one that . . . I only set things right. . . besides what makes you think they will believe you?"

"Your Mother sits with the councilmen as we speak, she is convinced and has proof, that you are the one that is guilty. The balm is with her, he has also seen the evidence, you left behind. Besides, what of your hand? Hisue paid to one so innocent? They too will see it; it will be the one thing that seals your fate." Ragnar teased with delight.

Donovan closed his eyes in shame, it was true, the horrible wound he had received for giving Marypat the love potion, still pained him. And Even though he was behind the protection of the bangle the slash had grown. It now reached his shoulder and it had begun burning down his back. He had done something so horrible that not even the bangle could protect him. Still he had not done the things Ragnar accused him of and he fought to free himself and help Marypat.

"The council is prepared to arrest you, they will come after you, but I will hand you over easily. No need to fight, with you in their hands I can continue my excavating without interruption. Simple, I shall not make the same mistakes of your father!" His voice rose like a fiery burst.

Donovan had heard enough and with one huge gathering of strength, he exploded from his captures. Sending the orange robed ushers fling in all directions. Quickly he grabbed Marypat and pulled her out of the hole she knelt in. Then he swung his wand at Ragnar and shouted.

"Quantom Bee Qee." But the spell did not faze Ragnar.

Ragnar clapped his hands in applause. "Well done."

"Just let us go." Donovan shouted as he shielded the still weak Marypat.

"Oh, I can't do that, but I will let you say you're good byes." Ragnar laughed stomping his foot twice.

Instantly the Pert disappeared leaving Marypat and Donovan standing on a very narrow pillar that hung magically over what looked like the rocky rapids of Cliffdale. Donovan knew this place was not real it was a Confinement Chamber. One used to hold ones advisories. He also knew if he tried to fly or use magic here that it would not work. Ragnar had won, Donovan was trapped. Still the one thing he did have was Marypat, and if this was to be for only an instant then he wasn't going to waist it, by foolishly trying to escape.

"Marypat, darling, forgive me my desire, I never wanted to harm you, only to love you." He said with a most honest heart.

Marypat's eyes opened then and looked into Donovan's, the trance had vanished from her mind and she smiled. "Honesty of thy heart speaks to me in truth, and then mine can hold no regret for thou, only love."

With her words, Donovan's heart sank in his chest, if only the words she spoke were free of the love potion, but they were not. He sobbed, holding her in his arms. "I will free you, this will not be the end." he commanded. "Know that in your heart.. . ."

Marypat placed her finger on his lips and shook her head. "I understand that Ragnar wants the bangle and he wants to use me to get it. But I also know this is not your fault, this is not what you want." She paused for a moment as she looked in to his eyes. "Ragnar spoke of the council?"

"Yes!" Donovan answered surprised she had heard so much while under the trance.

"My great-grandfather is among them?"

"YES."

"Tell him, to know the truth one should read Legends and Tales."

"Legends and tales?" Donovan shock his head, perhaps the trance had injured Marypat's mind. It seemed like a strange thing to tell her great-grandfather but when she insisted he agreed. "Ok I will tell him."

"Good!" her lips fell silent then as tears welled up in her eyes. "I love you, Donovan." She said and then she reached upwards to kiss him, but before their lips could meet she disappeared from his sight.

"Marypat!" He shouted into the endless space of the Chamber. Unheard, unanswered and broken.

CHAPTER 9

The Capture of Donovan

A hush fell over the crowd, which had gathered below the steps of the Great Hall, as the official proclaimer declared the findings of the council.

"It was so found that the son of Kathrie Gretel and Sherideen Drake Gazpalding, fore named Donovan Drake Gazpalding, is guilty of the following crimes.. . ."

The proclaimer went on to list the crimes, each one bringing sounds of anguish from the crowd. No one more so than Kathrie Gretel, who seemed to fall ever farther apart with each word the announcer spoke.

"The afore named will be sought by any means so written by the counsel." This meant that the council had the rights, if Donovan resisted, to kill him.

Inside the auditorium, the council members were still gathered. There was a heavy debate as to the best way to insure Donovan's capture without harming Marypat or Donovan. Orida insisted that they allow Donovan the chance to turn himself in, as he felt there was more to it than Kathrie Gretel had accused. But others of the council argued that that would only alert him, and he might do something unthinkable to the maiden. The debt raged on with no resolution in sight.

As eve fell on the town, Orida felt that they might never agree in a proper stint. Defeated he gazed into his Oritor and watched as a gray cloud formed over the Pert.

"It is too late! Our inaction has allowed Donovan to move." Orida announced.

The council became frantic.

"What should we do?" They clamored."

Attack the Pert, call for a strike on the Pert!" Came the answers.

"No! Again, I urge you, to remain calm." Declared Orida.

Suddenly the Oritor began to bubble and spark. Orida hushed the crowd and turned to investigate.

"Quiet, everyone, please."

Suddenly the bubbling ceased and the water slowly went calm to relieve the vision of, Nicholas Northcliff. His voice rose out of the water and filled the ears of all who were close.

"Greetings members of the council, it is with deepest sorrow that I appear in your company this eve. It has come to my attention that you are seeking one of my members. Although I was not convinced of your accusations at first, events have occurred only within moments that have changed my position and I now find your concerns most forthcoming." Northcliff paused for a moment as he glazed to something at his side, shook his head once with a knit of his brow and then continued. "Usually we deal with our own in our own way, but in this case I felt that he should be turned over to you. Do with him what you want!"

With his last words clear and in anger Northcliff disappeared from the Oritor.

Almost instantly the Oritor began to shake and rock. The members of the council stood nervously and watched as a huge clear object rose out of the Oritor. Gradually it ascended until the entire capsule emerged and hovered over the water.

"It's Donovan!" Came a shriek from the back of the hall.

And indeed, inside the capsule, frozen like moss quartz was Donovan Gazpalding. The council cheered, the villain was captured, and all was well again.

The light pieced the crystal capsule and reflected off the vile creature captured with in. The town had long since gone to rest, relieved at his imprisonment. Their work was done. Donovan could do no more evil.

The only problem was he was not the complete solution, there was still Marypat, where was she, was she alright?

In the darkness, balled up like a kitten was one who could not bear to believe anything other than she was well and only needed, he, Horatio, to save her. He laid there in the darkness planning his rescue. But where was he to find her, for that he needed Donovan and there posed another problem how to get the information from him without setting him free? But Horatio didn't have long to ponder these questions for as he sat, someone else entered the shadows of the room and approached the capsule. Clocked in darkness the figure rounded the structure.

"Heat of flame, spark of light, builds such fire grand of might. Touch thy form but not thy flesh and melt away on thy rest." Sang the figure with expert form.

The spell ignited a burst of flames from the tip of the figures wand that licked the outer surface of the capsule. Eventually the solid substance holding Donovan melted away leaving him in a mound of slime, unconscious.

Horatio stood then and listen carefully as the dark figure continued to aid Donovan.

"TEK WAY DO!"

With that, Donovan began to move, sluggishly at first, but soon he awoke. Still hindered by the slumber spell, he was listless and unable to communicate. So, the figure tried again. "TEK WAY DO!"

Donovan sprang to life; his eyes went wide as he shouted. "Marypat!"

Horatio jumped at the sound of Marypat's name on Donovan's tongue. He had always disliked Donovan but at this moment, he wanted to kill him. Horatio had to control himself, he had to, in order to hear, and to get the information he needed to save her.

Donovan searched the face of the dark figure before he spoke. "Ragnar, has her, you must help me save her."

"Why would one believe an evil member as you?" Asked the clocked one.

"Ragnar said you would not believe me, he has planned it so the council will be satisfied with me as the enemy and they will not go after him. Even though he is the one who has done the crimes, I am accused of. Meanwhile she digs for the bangle again." Donovan revealed.

"Still I have no reason to believe you. Give me proof and I will do all I can to help you."

Donovan lowered his head. "I have no proof, I only have a message." He took a deep breath and let it out slowly. "Marypat told me to tell you this but it makes no sense, still she insisted. In order to see the truth one must read Legends and Tales."

Horatio bounced from the darkness and landed on the clocked figures shoulder. "Of course the book, we will know if he tells the truth by using the book."

"Horatio!" The clock figure announced with surprise. "How did you get here?"

"A Torideen coat has many large pockets, Cornelius." Horatio said with a grin.

It was enough to break the tension between the group and they laughed. For an instant, their hearts felt lighter, but it didn't last and just as quickly their thoughts turned back to Marypat.

"We must use the book then." Cornelius whispered, "But until I return, you Donovan must sleep." With that, he waved his wand and called "Quantum BEE QEE."

Donovan collapsed on to the floor, knocked out once more.

"I never knew you held such power!" Horatio remarked with admiration at the good Cornelius magical abilities.

"One should never flaunt one's capabilities!" Cornelius Recited in a most serious demeanor.

Horatio nodded in agreement, as he too held his ability to grow like a dandy a secret.

"Then yours shall remain intact." Horatio Affirmed with a nod.

The two allies gave each other a solemn wink, which told the other that they were in this together, they were a team, and they would not rest till Marypat was safe.

So together, they headed off towards the Maurieen Palace and the locker where magical items were kept under guard. They would need permission of course in order to use the book, but Horatio and Cornelius felt that that would not be difficult and it was not. Once Orida and Iola heard of their plan the foursome headed for the locker without delay.

Two ornately costumed guards stood in front of the large silver doors as the group approached.

"Fare eve, Exalted Grand Torideen." Announced the guards.

"Fare eve righteous members. May ye give way, a task is at hand."

The guards did not answer, instead they kicked their heels and turned around. Together they pulled open the grand door of the locker. Orida was the first to enter the darken room. He called out loud " Light" and the huge warehouse was a glow.

There were magical items of all forms stored with in the huge shelves of the locker. Most had been outlawed by the council while others had been confiscated for misuse, and still some were just fragments of spells gone wrong deemed unsafe for the general public. But none of these were much of a concern for the council, no these were just known senses, placed with in the locker to cause confusion, or a faux front. The true guarded items were kept in a secret concealed locker, only Orida knew how to open.

Orida swiftly guided the group down the long main aisle of the locker. His long purple clock drifted along behind him and seemed to float just above his heals. Cornelius followed him with Horatio riding in his breast pocket while in the rear was Iola, her step was not as speedy yet she managed to keep pace.

Orida turned right and continued his determined step. Then suddenly he stopped. He threw his arms upwards and sprung his body with force into the air. Instantly he disappeared into darkness.

Cornelius stood below and looked around but all he could see was the marble stone of the ceiling. Orida was gone.

"He'll be back. He's gone for it." Iola reassured Cornelius

The pair waited below and only a moment later, Orida reappeared with the glistening blue book entitled 'Legends and Tale, A Complete Account of the Most Legendary Events to Date.'

Horatio peeked out of Cornelius' pocket and inspected the bewitched book. It seemed like a life time had passed since he had last seen it, but then again he remember exactly what story he needed to enter, he knew where go and he couldn't get there fast enough.

CHAPTER
10

Battle at the Pert

There it laid Kathrie Penny's collection of legendary Realagraphs. The cover glowed slightly illuminating the dusty shelve were Orida had placed it. It was strange to think that this book held the answers they needed. This very book that had been the cattalos in Gazpalding capturing Marypat all those turns ago and now here they were expecting to use it to help her.

Orida pulled open the cover and laid it exposed. "Tell me the course." Orida asked of Horatio.

"The curse of the Sherideen heart, will bring you to the Dark Forest." Horatio answered as he stood in Cornelius' pocket and watched.

"Very well." Orida replied. He pulled back the pages until he arrived on the very story Horatio had requested. "Who among us shall go?"

Without a word Horatio popped out of Cornelius pocket and landed in the Realagraph, in a flash he was gone, heading in the direction of the Dark Forest.

"Brave soul!" Iola whispered and Orida agreed with a knob.

"No braver a member has ever lived, my wife."

Horatio moved swiftly through the thick grass until he entered the Dark Forest. Once there he hopped above the trees and then dropped to the forest floor, where the old smashed frame came into view. Rudy and Johnny G. had done quite a job of destroying the exit into the Pert and although it was not passable, it was still useful to Horatio, as he could see clearly into the Pert.

The sight he saw brought him to tears, it was true, and Donovan had told them the truth. Marypat was indeed a spellbound captive at the Pert again.

There just beyond the Realagraph was a scene from the past, only one thing was different, and that was Ragnar. Marypat was waist deep in the stone, her hands busy at work, while sanding over her was a tall yellow-clocked figure.

"That must be Ragnar!" Horatio said to himself as he watched from the Realagraph. Horatio did not know this Wardeen but he would not forget his face or the sound of his voice as he ordered Marypat to move more quickly.

"Faster, now Faster!" Ragnar commanded, waving his right hand over his left cuffed hand. There in Ragnar's hand Horatio could make out the spinning pin. The same pin that had once spell bound Marypat, was now in Ragnar's hand, holding her yet again by its power.

Certain now of Donovan innocents Horatio headed back through the pages of the book towards the exit.

His eyes were red and damp when he finally climbed out of the book and stood in front of the threesome.

"Donovan's tongue speaks the truth; our Marypat is again the unwilling servant of one who desires the bangle." Horatio uttered sadly. "Moment is short, her pace is steady, and his will is strong."

With Horatio's testimony on Donovan's behalf, the council moved quickly to drop all charges. Donovan was free and reunited with his Mother.

"I warned you, nothing good comes from the use of a love potion. Marypat now suffers at your hand." Kathrie Gretel maintained as she searched her son's body for signs of the Hisue but there were no scares, no redness, and no pain.

Donovan was shocked when his mother could not find anything. His hand was fine, his arm and shoulder showed no sign of the scare that had wrecked with such pain only a few sweeps pasted.

"How could this be?" he thought to himself. He remembered having pain when he was at the Pert, when Ragnar and he had fought. But then when he was with Marypat, he could not recall any pain. Then he remembered, "Yes", when they were alone, there in the confinement chamber, when he held her, the pain was gone, she had freed him from his pain.

Donavan's mind was deeply rooted in thoughts of Marypat, but his mother was not amused by her sons wondering ponder and quickly slapped him back to her words. "The council might have freed you, but I know what you have done, I know what you are guilty of."

Donovan did not argue with his mother, he knew she was right. He had brought this on himself and worst of all he had brought it on Marypat. If he had not been so consumed with bringing her here, having her, he would have never allured Ragnar to her abilities. It was his entire fault, he would take the blame, he would take his mother's shame, but not now. There was no period now. Now he had to move fast, he had to save Marypat.

The council had organized three squads, a troop of Andies and Kandies all foot soldiers, numbering over 10,000, a troop of Frandies, mostly infantry, numbering 5,000 and a troop of the Regan's special forces known as S.N.T.F. (Special Non-magical Task Force), numbering 200 of the Regan's finest, Hedlens, Wardeen's, Lachlanns and Feldens.

In truth, the council had little to do with organizing the invasion. The fact was once the council had informed the Regan of the situation, a stone was cast, and troops were instantly put in place and had been waiting. It was a scenario they were familiar with, every guard, every foot solider, from the lowest Kandie to the highest general knew the drill. The mission was clear, to Invade and hold the Pert. It had been practiced and rehearsed, discussed and debated. It had been that way ever since Bagree's initial attempt to rule the Isle.

The troops were ready. The Andies and Kandies were in place along the landing of Fire Beach, the Frandies had the mountain cliffs and the task of holding the Kert. Fifty of the S.N.T.F.'s were to back up the Andies and Kandies and 25 were left to sure up the Frandies while the remaining 125 S.N.T.F.'s had the grueling task of breaching the Pert.

Horatio and Donovan stood ready as well. Both determined to free Marypat, to save her and at the same time determined to do it without the other. Horatio still did not trust Donovan, although he knew Donovan would not hurt her, he still could not allow Donovan to be near her. Donovan had tricked her, bewitched her heart, and that was something Horatio could not allow to happen again. He would do whatever it took to keep her free from anyone who would harm her, especially Donovan.

When the word came and the troops began to move, Horatio turned to Cornelius. With a glance they both knew that this was it, it was the moment to go. Their moment to save Marypat and the Great Isle was at hand, they knew the mission could not fail, all was riding on them.

When Horatio turned back to Donovan, he was gone. He had disappeared from sight. This angered Horatio, instantly he became suspicions. What if it had all been a trick? What if he was indeed behind the plot? Thinking only of this, Horatio, quickly bounced to the front of the lines. He had to get to the Pert, he knew Donovan was there already.

And he was.

At the Pert, Marypat was deep within the Cinerin pit she had dug by hand, her movements were strange, like that of a blur. She moved rock after rock onto the edge of the opening and then returned to the pit to retrieve more. Ragnar stood waiting above her. His eyes danced as he watched her move. His hands anticipated their treasure, his thoughts wrapped in the bangles power.

Ragnar was so distracted by his own greed he never expected Donovan's charge.

A charge that came from out of nowhere, like a burst of hot wind, hitting its target and accomplishing Donovan's, well thought out plan.

The blow sent Ragnar flying across the Pert. He landed on his knees and quickly flipped back to his feet. Slightly stun Ragnar looked about the Pert to eye his enemy.

"Donovan?" expressed Ragnar in discussed. "I thought. ." he uttered while his right hand searched his pocket for his wand. But to his surprise Donovan, already held Ragnar's wand and was about to use it on him.

Suddenly a flash of blue light flew from the wand and Ragnar flipped again to miss its beam. Within moments Donovan had, Ragnar cornered but this fight was not over. Desperately Ragnar picked up an object from off of one of the tables, he rubbed it with his hand, and it turned into a knife. He waved it at Donovan and with a frantic thrust, he managed to hit the wand from Donavan's hand. As it hit the floor, it shattered into pieces.

"Is that all you have?" Ragnar laughed.

But it wasn't, and Donovan moved quickly to attack Ragnar again this stint with his own wand. The pair fought on, each taking a hit now and again, while Marypat uncovered the last bit of the bangle. She held it in her hands and gentle rubbed it clean. It began to glow before her eyes as she removed the last clump of dirt. With it free from the rock and clean of debris, she pulled it under her arm and climbed out of the pit. Once out she sat on the edge of the pit and held the bangle on her lap as the pair continued the fight.

Now bloody Donovan noticed Marypat's position and what she held. His eye movement drew Ragnar's attention and soon he too knew of her discovery. Now it was a fight to get the Bangle first, Donovan knew he had to keep Ragnar from the Bangle. If Ragnar could reach it first, all was lost. Donovan had to reach it.

Meanwhile just beyond the Pert the invasion had begun. The sound of crashing metal and fireworks echoed in the air, still Ragnar and Donovan paid it no mind as they continued their fight.

The power struggle was like a blast of streaming fire, whipping across the Pert. Donovan feared for Marypat's safety and tried one last desperate attempt to protect her and retrieve the bangle. His brave act sent him sailing backwards into the stonewall of the Pert with Marypat in hand.

He had to act quickly, Ragnar was on the move. With the bangle at Donovan's foot and Marypat in his arms, he wasn't sure what to do, but he had to do something. He had to protect Marypat and at the same time keep Ragnar from the bangle. Then it came to him, there was only one thing he could do. He pulled Marypat behind him and grabbed the bangle. Without a moments delay he slipped the bangle on his arm and snapped it closed.

"So the true Gazpalding is exposed." Ragnar cheered quickly trying to clear his stand with the new leader. "Brother! Together we shall control the Isle."

Donovan stood blood dripped from his brow; he was wounded in more places than he could count but still he had to fight on. With the bangle on, he had thought that all his pain and wounds would have been healed and that it might even clear Marypat of her spell, but it did not, it was as if the Bangle did not work. It was broken. With this belief, Donovan knew he had to remove the spell from Marypat, himself by destroying the pin that spun and spellbound her and Ragnar was the one that held it.

Donovan threw a blast at Ragnar sending him against the wall. Ragnar was held to the wall, he struggled to move free, but Donovan pinned him with his magic. Then Donovan moved in and removed the spinning pin from Ragnar's clutches.

The relief of finally holding the pin, distracted Donovan long enough to allow Ragnar to get free. Still for Donovan, the pin held more concern at that moment, so he let Ragnar free and stopped long enough to destroy the pin. Clapping his hands together, Donovan crushed the pin, instantly freeing Marypat's mind from the trance. Donovan's eye moved from his hands and caught sight of someone watching from the balcony. It was Horatio.

Horatio had seen what Donovan had done and for the first time trusted him with Marypat's life. Horatio could also see the delicate position Donovan was in at that moment. He could have allowed Ragnar to kill Donovan and then jump in himself and saved the day, but for that instant his decency got the better of him and he decided to help Donovan instead.

He bounced across the Pert distracting Ragnar long enough for Donovan to retrieve Horatio's sliver edged sword, which Horatio tossed to him from the side.

With it in hand, Donavan swung back at Ragnar hitting him on his arm. Ragnar quickly rolled away with a turn of his cloak. Donovan then moved again thrashing forward, this time though, he missed. As he did, Ragnar also moved forward and pressed his knife into Donovan's chest.

The pain ripped through Donovan's body causing him to react with his own thrust of vengeance. His thrash struck Ragnar at the neck, cutting through him, and coming out just below his arm on the opposite side of his body. The sight was gruesome. Ragnar was hacked in half while Donovan staggered beside Ragnar's bloody bits. Donovan then bent in Pain while blood flowed everywhere from his body.

At the sight, Horatio could tell Donovan was going to die. Quickly bounded out of the Pert and headed for the healers. He hated Donovan but he did not want his death to be on his hands. So he moved with vigor to save him.

Meanwhile, Donovan fell to his knees, his hands holding the knife in his chest.

"Donovan!".

"Marypat, is that you?" Donovan whispered faintly.

"Hold on, darling, I shall find you help!"

"No, stay with me, I need to tell you something. . . '" Donovan voice slipped off.

"I won't leave you!" Marypat responded with a reassuring smile. "I promise."

"Mary, I'm sorry, please forgive . . . ." Donovan tried to speak again.

Marypat held him gently in her arms, tears slipped from her eyes.

"No don't be sorry, I'm not!' She looked him in his eyes and he in hers.

In her eyes, he could see her clearly, there was no gloss of a spell, no trace of a potion, it was she and she alone speaking her heart.

"But I. . " He grunted in server pain.

"I love you!" She revealed her true heart to him.

Her words tore through him like a wave of joy, words he had wanted for so long to hear from her lips, now here they were a bittersweet reward. The price he had paid for them were much more than any other member would ever dreamed of paying, yet he laid there in her arms, near death itself, happy with the moment and satisfied with his future.

She leaned forward then and kissed him on the lips. It was a soft gentle kiss but it was enough to seal their love.

"Marypat," Donovan urged breathlessly. "You must leave the Great Isle and never return it is much too dangerous . . . Promise me . . ." He knew that there would be others who would want the bangle and they may come after her to get it. He couldn't risk her life again; he truly loved her and wanted her to be safe.

"But I won't leave you!" She answered calmly. "There is no danger now, Ragnar was dead. A master Kathrie is all you need; surely your wounds can be healed. All you must do is hold on darling."

"You must promise. . ." Donovan struggled to stay conscious, he was fading fast, and she pulled him closer to her as if to pull him back from the darkness of the beyond.

"No! Don't you dare leave me, after all this, you can't just give up, I won't let you!"

But Donavan lips fell silent, his eye closed and his head dropped back. He was gone. At that same instant, the bangle glowed and then it popped open and crashed to the floor beside.

Marypat pulled him closer to her and wept, her heart ached for him, it was more than she could bear. Her pain was so deep that she didn't even feel Cornelius lift her away from Donovan's bloody body or see Kathrie Gretel's reaction to her son's misfortune. She was still dazed by the events of the turn, too emotional to see anything more.

"Marypat, are you wounded." Cornelius asked as he held his great-granddaughter. Her clothes were covered in blood, but it was not hers, it was Donovan's.

Numb, Marypat didn't answer Cornelius; she only grabbed him tightly and cried.

The marrow came with silence. Cimmevian Town paused in a suppressed phase. The Ubil members caught for the most part innocent in an evil wed weaved by one of their own, Ragnar. With him dead, the rest of the Ubil members would have to pay for his greed. But for this moment they waited as the council decided their fate.

Meanwhile in the Maurieen Palace Marypat waited as well.

In the darkness, thick with dust and even heavier with sadness she stood with Cornelius at her side and Horatio on her shoulder. No words spoken, there was no need to speak, they had all their moment and it had been decided. Marypat should leave the Great Isle immediately and never return.

The council had expressed great concern over her staying. She was just too great a temptation for the Ubil, they could not afford another incident. No, there was no other way, she had to go. They had even taken possession of the Bangle. Orida had been put in charge of it, like the book, it would be under guard in his secret locker secure from the evil members of Cimmevian.

So, there was nothing more to be said, she would leave by Spit Cock to Doodle Falls and from Doodle Falls back to her home on the outside.

"'Tis not the way I wish to be remembered." Marypat remarked without emotion.

"One will remember you Marypat, but not for this, this was not your fault." Cornelius reassured her.

"Still I leave here an outcast, not even Iola will see me off." She sadly alleged.

"The council is still deciding what to do with Cimmevian Town, you know she must attend." Cornelius replied somberly. "She would be here if she could!'

Marypat lowered her head, she knew what she had implied about Iola was wrong, but she was hurting inside and wanted so badly to scream. She had been through so much, she had lost her grandfather, regained him, been kidnapped, tricked into marriage by Donovan only to fall in love with him and then loss him. Not to mention being enslaved by an evil Wardeen and after being saved was now being banished from the Great Isle for something she had no control over.

It just seemed so unfair. There were members Marypat wanted to see, like Kathrie Gretel. She had wanted to say goodbye, and Donovan. Dear Donovan, oh how she needed to pay her respects, he had been so brave, so fearless. He had fought to his death for her and now it seemed to her that she was running away without thanking him, honoring him. The thought of it brought fresh tears to her eyes, so she closed them and hide her face in her hands. She had to think of something else, she was after all going home, to her grandparents. Her grandfather was alive, that was something she could think of, something to hold on to and so she did. She turned her mind on going home, and the visions of her grandparents. She was just beginning to feel better when Iola buster throw the stillness.

"Marypat! Dear one, I could not allow you to go without my wish for ye safe travels." Iola Announced with a gracious flare.

New tears sprung from Marypat's eyes, it meant so much to her that Iola had come to say Good bye.

"Take this with you, dear and know I shall think of you throughout my age." Iola whispered in Marypat's ear as she pressed a small oval observer into her hand.

Marypat accepted the gift and smiled up at her friend. "Thank you; you don't know how much this means to me."

The two friends hugged, but their hug was abruptly interrupted when two white cloaked members burst past Cornelius and bounded into Iola.

"What is the meaning of this?" Iola commanded.

"The council requests a favor of the Maurieen?" One of the members divulged breathlessly.

"Well what is it?" Iola shouted.

"The request not of ye, Maurie Iola, but the Maurie Marypat." The second one mention shyly.

"Get on with it; she is to leave in moments!" Iola Demanded.

"The council has asked, and our study although not entirely precise, that is to say we do not have substantial evidence to confirm. . ." The first clocked member went on until Iola interrupted him.

"Get to it!"

"Yes, well we believe that Henry would do well on the outside, that is to say your world." The member babbled on.

"What are you saying?" Marypat asked.

"We want you to take Henry with you to your world; we believe that the mind grip will not affect him out there." Replied a familiar voice from behind the two white clocked members.

"Yes, that's it." One of the white clocked members stuttered as he stepped away to reveal Fred, the waiter, from the Blarney Stone with his uncle Henry under his arm.

"Please, Marypat, he has no life here in this condition. We want you. . ." Fred's voiced cracked and Marypat could see how hard it was for Fred to ask for such a thing. She also knew if she didn't Henry would surely die a slow painful death as his mind dripped away leaving him unable to substance life.

"Don't say another word. I shall take him with me." Marypat answered soberly and with that Cornelius grabbed Henry from Fred.

"Be well, dear Marypat." Fred said with a bow of his head then he disappeared from the dusty room.

"Are we ready now?" Lester questioned through the dusty air as he pulled on the straps of his navy blue pullovers. "Let's go, remember to stay within the drain, that's it everybody in."

Cornelius carried Henry on to the drain and held him up beside Marypat.

"Increase the spit by one." Called Lester over his shoulder to a wrangler, who stood on the upper deck of the receptacle. "Right then hold still." Then Lester stepped away from the group and headed up the ramp disappearing from their sight.

Iola gave one more good bye and Horatio ducked into Marypat's pocket just as the great door slid open and the strange cracking sounds began above them.

"Dom dee pat, hoc to."

With that came the now familiar sounds of heavy feet above them and the gentle sounding "Ho." A moment later came the huge slippery mass that flew through the air and hung above them. It hovered there long enough to form a consistent heap and then fell over them like a warm comforter. The goo slipped over them and dripped downwards to the drain and as it did, the group disappeared from Iola's sight.

Instantly the foursome reappeared on the banks of Doodle Falls. Before them lie the small bridge that was used as a platform for the flyers. There on the bridge was the Felden dressed in green just as he had been before, wet and miserable.

"Ye next?" he shouted at the group.

"Just Two" Cornelius answered the guide, than he turned to Marypat and hugged her. "Take care dear and remember my heart is with thee."

"I love you too, grandpa."

Horatio who had said nothing the entire morning now emerged from Marypat's pocket and hugged her neck. Then he bounced away to broken up to say anything.

The guide helped Henry to get in to place and then together the two flyers went into the falls and flew into the air. The sight from above was as grand as Marypat could recall, but her mind was not on the view but dealing with Henry once they hit the blue sky. But her worry was put to rest the instant the pair entered the open blue. Henry who had been without his mind was suddenly awake and was in control of himself. He glanced at Marypat though and questioned where he was.

"Where am I?"

It had been like waking up after a long sleep and having no idea what was going on.

"Just hold my hand and follow me, I'll explain later." Marypat shouted through the flowing water.

Henry did what he was told and a moment later they both stood sopping wet on the floor of the fount room of Marypat's family's home. The unusual vibration and sounds brought Lora and Trevor racing to the front room, where to their surprise stood their Marypat home again.

There was so much to explain, so much to tell, even Henry was surprised at everything that had happened. He could not recall any of it, yet his mind was fine.

"My Parents agreed to take Henry on, he could live with them. It would not be the life he was used to, but he would have a life, a home, and his mind. To that, he could ask no more. Henry has been happy with us. He still works at the house." Marypat explained to me.

I sat and watched Marypat as her eyes closed. I knew she had more to tell but she needed a moment to form the words. So, I waited. After a few minutes, she raised her head again and spoke.

"A few weeks later I discovered I was pregnant . . . . with Donovan's child. My Grandmother was so upset, well that was until she held Blaze in her arms then that all fell away. He is a wonderful child. I should like you to meet him as well as see the Crystal Isle; they are at my family's home just up the road. Would you have moment to come today?"

I glanced at the time it was just after noon we had been sitting at my house for almost five hours but it had seemed like only a few minutes.

"Yes." I answered and with that, we headed up the road to her family house.

PART 3

The RED ISLE

A Very Special Thanks to
Leslie Roberts
without his amazing help this story would not have an ending!

FOREWORD

That same afternoon I followed Marypat up to her Grandparents country home in upper Maryland. There was a short almost dwarf size man at the gate that greeted us with a broad smile and a strange Irish Jamaican accent. Marypat introduced the man as Henry.

"Henry, the Felden?" I asked. I could not believe it, he truly looked like one of the commoners I had seen in my dream and there he was standing before me. Part of me had been struggling with the thought that all of what Marypat had been telling me was just a story she had made up. I mean deeply in side of me I was hopeful it was not some false story but I also had to kind of protect myself from any foolishness leading me into an end result of someone's joke. So, I had been trying to keep my mind open to shield myself, but then this was the first sight that struck a chord in my whole vision.

"Yes, Henry has been with us for over 20 passes, haven't you Henry?"

"Yes, and I'm thankful for all ye have done for me." Henry said as he locked the gate behind us.

The house was an old wooden cottage nestled between several Otaheiti apple trees, wild ferns, and coffee plants. It seemed very peaceful and pleasant.

Once inside I was greeted by a tall broad-shouldered man with jet black hair and purple eyes. Instantly I knew he was Blaze but part of me was shocked at how old he was. In Marypat's story of her son he was only ten and this man had to be older than twenty-five.

"This is my son Blaze." Marypat revealed.

"It is truly an honor to meet you Blaze."

"My mother tells me you have had a dream about the Green Isle's. Is this true?" He asked as he showed me into the front room of the house. It was dark in the room, there were thick black curtains hanging over the windows and doorways.

"Yes." I answered.

"And you know there are more than the one we have?"

"Yes, fifty-five in total."

"Have you ever truly seen one or held one?"

"No, I have only seen them in my dream."

"Well a genuine emerald of the Whole has a precious crystal form which is a delicate reminder of its fragile existence. A human can hold such an emerald in the palm of his hand unaware of the magic it holds. Deep within lies it's meaning and it's true beauty." Blaze whispered. "Allow me now to reveal to you the Cluster known as the Great Isle."

With that the room was illuminated. There were large spotlights hitting the center of the room where a pillar stood holding a glass case. Within the case, delicately resting was the Paired Emerald stone from my dream. The glow from its body radiate towards me striking me in my memory and knocking me to my knees.

My brain weaved into my dream repeating the potion where I had seen this very Cluster. Inside me, I felt an overwhelming sensation of attainment. I had done it! I had found one and my dream, my vision; my haunting account was now proven, to be true. Reaching this moment was almost too much for me as I sat on the floor, holding my head and weeping with tears of relief. All of what Marypat had told me resonated as true and our reason for finding each other was being revealed to me as valid.

Blaze came to my side and helped me back to me feet.

"Are you ok?" He asked.

"Yes, the sight of the crystal has validated my quest, our quest, to put them back together and I see now that all of what your mother has told me is true. She has truly been inside."

"Yes, and so have I." Blaze imparted with his sparking purple eyes gazing down at me.

Instantly my brain was melded into his and his story opened to me.

CHAPTER
1

His Fall

The night sky was turning red when Blaze finally emerged from the bathroom. He peered around the door to make sure nether his mother or Grandmother was in sight. They were not, they were at that moment in the garden talking with Henry and laughing. Blaze could hear them so he made his move. He slipped out of the bathroom and down the hall. In the guest room, he put back on his jeans and his favorite blue t-shirt. The one with the skull and snakes submerged in fire in the middle of it. He then plunged into the closet and after a few minutes, he emerged with his backpack.

Throwing his pack onto his back, he moved down the hall towards his mother's old bedroom. Once there he ducked inside quickly, there was something he wanted, something he thought he might need, her opal tipped wand. It was lying on her dresser with an old leather-bound book, he grabbed up both and stuff them into it his backpack. Next, he went to his mother's nightstand where he found the tear shaped diamond his mother had told him about. It was on a thin gold chin, he knew it held magic as it had been formed from the Mist of Froymin on the Great Isle. He picked it up, hooked it around his neck and stuffed it inside his shirt. Then he ran back into the hall. He made his way to the kitchen where he picked up his sneakers. Then for a moment he stopped, and thought. It was not a thought about what he was doing, no instead he wanted to make sure he had thought of everything he would need. Then with one last glance and a grab over his shoulder, he pulled a box of pop tarts into his bag and disappeared into the darkness of the front room.

He flipped on the lights and there in front of him was the newly rejoined pair of Emeralds, the Great Isle and the Blue Isle. His eyes were transfixed on the huge green stones set in lazurite. He stepped up to it and smiled.

"If she won't tell me about it, I'll just find out about it myself." He declared.

Then he pulled on his shoes and slipped his backpack over his shoulders, freeing his hands. He reached forward and picked up the massive stones, they sparkled in the light and his eyes were drawn to them. However, peculiarly his eyes were not drawn to the eye of the Great Isle but to a large red Ruby that sat below the Blue-ish one and seemed to be broken just at the tip of it.

His glance grew ever deeper and then it happened. He could feel himself being pulled into the eye. Soon he was falling, falling and then thud. He landed on his back; he shouted instantly from the pain of landing on solid hard ground. Not to mention the fact he was wearing his heavily packed backpack, which caused him to bend in a most strange manner.

"OH, man that hurt." He said out loud as he grabbed at his body. His neck hurt and his bottom and he held both as he stood and looked around at his new surroundings.

The sky wasn't green as his mother had told him it would be. The sky he stood under was red. He had fallen into the eye of the Red Isle.

"Gee, I hope I can get to Doodle Falls from here." Blaze said aloud. But there was no one there around him to answer him.

"Hello, any little people out there?" he questioned as he searched around at the ground. He figured that there would be little members everywhere; they were there for his mother. Naturally, he would have no problem finding a helpful Etain or Pixie, more than willing to drop what they were doing to help him find his way. But to his surprise there wasn't even one.

"Hum. I guess I am on my own.," he said soberly and for a split second he thought that his idea to enter the red eye wasn't the best idea. Still he had and if he wanted to learn about the isle first hand, he would have to get moving, so he brushed himself off, pulled out his Walkman c.d. player, slipped on the headphones and looked around at his new surroundings.

"*Where to go?*" he thought as the music boomed in his head.

The sky was a burnt red with small puffs of thick black smoke rising to his left, from a huge reddish orange mound. The mound shot up high into the red sky and fell back to the ground with long slops. That direction north west was not passable, to the south west of him were red crystal mountains that seemed sharp and unmanageable as well. There was only one-way to go and that was east.

He walked along through the hot red soil. He could feel the heat of the island rising through his white Nike sneakers. The soles of his shoes were becoming soft and he began to wonder if they were melting. If they were, this could not be good and he needed to find somewhere to cool them down.

"Water." he explained as he spotted a pool of water on the horizon.

Nevertheless, as he ran he realized that the pool he saw was only a mirage. He continued to run and each time he thought he would reach the pool, the pool turned out to be dry red ground. With his hope nearly gone and his shoes almost a liquid mess, he tripped and slid into the hot soil.

The dusty red sand flew up and covered him. Barred by the parched soil, he wanted to cry.

"What have I done?"

He laid there wanting to give up, his skin now feeling the heat of the ground. It was like lying over a barbeque pit with the coals just right for cooking. He held his head and rubbed the dirt from his eyes. Then he looked around and thought to himself," well I can lay here and be cooked to death or I can get up and live."

However, before he could make the decision for himself, it was made for him. As he lay there, he felt a strange sensation on his leg, it was a little like a tickle but with a slight scratchier feel, it was lite but obvious. The sensations made Blaze jump to his feet and look frantically around for what had climb on to him. But there was nothing on the ground. Instead, his eyes went wide as he realized the thing had not been on him but in his pants.

Blaze stood there not wanting to move as the thing climbed higher inside his pants. Blaze began to sweat; the creature was just above his knee and still moving up. Blaze was not likening the position the creature was in and he panicked. He threw his leg into the air and shock it violently, but the creature did not fallout. Instead, it held on more firmly. Blaze could feel its craws growing tightly around his thigh and piercing his skin. Tiny jolts of pain darted through his thigh as the claws grew even tighter.

Blaze realized that shacking his leg was not going to make the creature let go. He had to think of something else. Jumping up and down he frantically searched around for an idea, was there a spell, a hex or incantation. Perhaps but the book and the wand were in his backpack and besides he did not have time to search through the book to find one. What could he do, nothing? He thought, so he ran. He ran with the creature gripped inside his pants, ripping at his flesh and shooting what seemed like electricity though his body. He ran with the heat of the isle melting his sneakers and burning his skin. He ran and ran, with all hope gone, he threw off his backpack, and headphones and then collapsed.

Blaze's lifeless body floated and gently rocked back and forth, as his mind knew he must be dead. His thoughts filled with a peaceful calm, he felt refreshed and cool. He opened eyes and looked up at the bright blue sky above him. He could smell the sea air and feel the salt water on his face.

"It must have been a dream." he said out loud. "It was all just a dream." He half laughed at himself for believing he had really fallen into the Red Isle and gotten into danger so quickly. His mind had been so cruel to create such jilt in him that it produced a nightmare and it had been a nightmare. Yet it was so real.

The only thing he could think of to explain where he was, was that he must have bumped his head at Lime Key and dreamt the whole thing, but there was one thing still nagging at him and that was the pain in his thigh.

He stood up. His eyes blinked and he rubbed the salt water from them. With his eyes clear finally he glanced about as a chill ran down his spine. He was not at Lime Key; he was not standing in the warm Caribbean Sea of Jamaica. He was standing on the shoreline of the Red Isle.

Panic hit him. It wasn't a dream, it was real. He had fallen onto the Red Isle, he had melted his new Nike sneakers, and there was a. . . . "AHHHHH" He shouted dancing in the waves as he realized that there was something still in his pants. Quickly he jumped on to the shore and unbuckled his belt; he unzipped his jeans and let them fall into the sand. As the jeans fell away the creature also dropped to the sand. Drowned it seemed from the plunge into the sea.

Blaze hopped away from the creature and inspected his wounds. There were six tinny red dots, three on each side of his thigh. They were not bleeding, they were just very red. The creature hadn't punched the skin, it had instead used its grip as some kind of shocking weapon. A weapon it probably used on its smaller victims to numb them. But Blaze was too large for it to numb, it had only caused pain and its own death in the end.

Blaze searched the horizon and found his backpack and cd player some yards back on shore. Where he must have thrown and dropped them when he was running in his blind panic. Blaze set out to get them. They were laying in red soil just beyond the white sand of the shore as he reached the red soil Blaze felt the heat of the isle again raising from the ground. He put his hands out in front of him as though he were warming his hands at a campfire. The heat was intense over the red soil but when he turned back to the white sand his hands cooled. It was an amazing discovery. He could survive the Red Isle if he stayed on the white sand. But he still had to retrieve his backpack, so he made a run for it and instantly as his body crossed into the red soil he felt like he was being cooked again. Without a moments delay he grabbed up his thing and dodged back to the coolness of the shore.

Once there he searched through, his bag and grabbed out a black plastic bag. He reached into the black bag and pulled out his swimsuit and put them on. Then he gathered up his wet jeans squeezed them out as best as he could and then rolled them up. He pushed them into the now empty scandal bag the swimsuit had been in, all crumpled up at the bottom for the bag. The same one his mother insisted he carry to put his swim suit in, just in case he went swimming somewhere. She didn't want him putting his wet suit into his bag and wetting up his books. As he stuffed the jeans into the plastic scandal bag he could hear his mother's voice reminding him to pack one.

"You never know, Blaze, they might have a pool. You don't want to be the only one not swimming, cause you didn't pack a suit, and put it in a scandal bag so if you do swim you can use the plastic bag to bring home the wet suit." she would shout. "Don't forget to put on sun screen, remember reapply, reapply, reapply." her voice echoed in his mind.

Blaze took in a deep breath. "Mom!" With all his thoughts and delusions of traveling to one of the Green Isles and all the wonderful adventures there, he had not once thought about what his mother would do when she discovered him missing. Nor did he ever expect to find himself on the wrong isle, with no known way home. He knew how to get home from the Great Isle but this was the Red Isle and it was certainly nothing like the stories his mother had told him. This isle was already proving hazardous and a mistake. He wished he had not been so quick to travel and had taken more care when staring into the eye, if only he had heeded his mother's words "never stare into the eye, or you will find yourself inside." He had stared into the eye, but the wrong eye, the eye of the red ruby, the Red Isle.

Now he wanted his mother. He thought of her as he pulled out the pink bottle of sunscreen. He squeezed some into his hand and rubbed it on his face; he stared up into the sky and tried to see beyond the crystal and into his grandmother's house. But he could not. After a long wait he finally lowered his head and sighed. He had to accept his fate. This was his problem, his alone and he had to make the best of it. He could think of it as hell or he could make it an adventure. His own adventure, no matter how different, how strange or how scary, this was his chance to explore the crystal world.

Determined he looked up and nodded. "This is it." he announce "no matter how it started out. How wrong, I will survive."

Then he went back to his backpack, stuffed the bottle of sunscreen back in and began to zip it up. From the corner of his eye, he caught sight of the creature that had climbed up his pants. It was lying on its back with its legs up. He went over to it and looked more closely at it. It was bright green with yellow and red striped along its back. It was the size of a very large garden lizard. It had a long-specked tail and three claws on each of the two short arms. Its large back legs were muscular and strong with three large claws and one small claw on each end.

Blaze thought it looked like a small t- recs and was excited to discover that there might be dinosaurs in this world. So, he quickly turned back to his backpack and search through it again until he pulled out a Ziplock bag filled with marbles. He poured the marbles into one of the side pockets of his backpack. Then carefully he lifted the lizard like creature and slipped it into the Ziplock, zipping it closed. He put the Ziplock back in to his backpack and then throw his pack on his back and started walking.

He did not know where he was going but he figured that somewhere along the beach he must find a town or village. Besides the shoreline seemed to be the only place he could travel. So, determined to go on he pulled his headphones back on his ears and set off on his adventure listening to the sounds of Rock and roll.

Back up at the house all seemed strangely quiet. The only sound was the hinge on the back door, straining, as Marypat pulled it open and stepped inside her Grandmother's house that sat nestled in the Blue Mountains of Jamaica. Her shoes clapped against the stale tile floor as she headed down the hall that led to the bathroom.

"Blaze it's time to go, come give your gram a kiss." She called sweetly.

When there was no reply or even a sound of movement from inside the bathroom, she called again. "Blaze, honey we have to go, you have school tomorrow." As she said the last word, she pushed open the bathroom door to discover there was no one inside.

"Blaze?" She called out again. Perhaps he went into the guest room to watch T.V. she thought so she stepped over to the other door and turned the nod. The room was dark and the T.V. was off.

"Blaze are you in there, come on honey we have to go?" But again there was no answer.

Marypat closed the door and headed back to the kitchen. Lora was just coming in the backdoor when Marypat reached the kitchen.

"What is it dear?" Lora questioned.

"Blaze." Marypat began to say, but before she could finish, her face went blank, then it turned white so white she felt as though she were going to collapse.

"What is it, Mary?" Lora asked, her eyes searched her Granddaughters' face, but all Marypat could do was stare straight ahead. "Mary, why are you staring like that? Why are the lights on in the front room? Did you leave them on?"

"No, it was not me."

"Well who did? Oh, no Mary you don't think. . . .no he wouldn't have done that, Oh Mary, don't worry yourself."

"But. . . he's. . . gone." Marypat's mouth could hardly form the words.

"He's not gone, come on we will find him." Lora reassured her granddaughter, patting her on the arm. The two women searched the house, Henry searched the garden and down by the river and finally when all other places had been checked, Marypat finally entered the front room. But to her horror she found the glass cabinet open and the emeralds laying on the floor at the base of the pillar.

Meanwhile inside the crystals, Blaze was strolling along the shore of the Red Isle. He had taken off his half-melted shoes and his white sport sox's. They now dangled from the side off his backpack and he was barefoot in the sand.

The sand was cool and silky almost healing compared to the deadly red-hot soil of the island. This he could live with, the cool sand, the refreshing water and the occasional shade from the trees and the dunes that now grew up alongside of the shoreline. Besides, he was making good time even though he had no idea what laid ahead of him.

Soon though he thought to take a break. He turned off his cd player and he sat down near the water's edge to eat one of the pop tarts he had brought with him. As he sat there, eating, it seemed to him that the view was quite similar to the view from Lime Key, and it made him think of home.

The waves crashed around him gently and bubbled as they rolled onto the sand, there were beautiful White Sea birds flying above him. It was just like home and for an instant, he closed his eyes and enjoyed the peace of the moment.

But suddenly the peace was gone and he fighting for his life again. The flock of white sea birds had spotted him and were diving after him, peaking at his hands and legs. Blaze kicked and waved his hand frantically. But the dive-bombing birds only came after him with more aggression. Twisting and jabbing they flung themselves at him, till blood began to flow from the wounds they had inflicted.

Having had more than enough Blaze got to his feet and ran toward the water. He dove in and the birds "squawked" in defeat. Not satisfied that he had escaped their clutches, some of the crazed birds hovered over the water, flapping their wings and kicking at the waves, still trying to reach him.

While the others flew back to the shore to consume their prize, the pop tarts. Dozens of birds came from nowhere, the beach was suddenly a frenzy of white wings, tiring and fighting for scrapes of the now designated chocolate tart.

Blaze watched in horror from the water as the birds began to rip at each other's feather. A Squeaking bird battle unfolded before him, several birds were bleeding and even more were missing clumps of feathers but none were interested in withdrawing. It seemed as if it would be a battle to the death.

Then suddenly there came a flash from behind the dune just beyond the birds. After the flash came an explosion of twinkling fire light that shoot straight into the mites of the battling birds. The fire light twirled and hissed, freighting the birds and causing them to quickly fly away, squalling horribly as they went.

Relived that birds had finally gone, Blaze emerged from the waves. He crawled back onto the shore with his half bloody limbs and collapsed. Although his body was exhausted, his mind was not, it was a fever of thoughts as to what or who had caused the fire works.

He wanted to rise from where he laid and investigate, but he found he had no strength. His arms and legs sopping wet from a mixture of blood and seawater would not move for him. It was as if heavy weights had been tied to his arms, stiffening and cramping them and they were getting worst every moment he laid there. So, all he could do was lay there helpless while the sounds of something approached him from behind the dune.

The crunch of sand just beside his right ear was last thing Blaze heard before his face was covered by a large black cloth and he was dragged away across the sand.

Note* If you want to know more about the Red Isle you can read <u>The True Tale of Fire Island </u> in the Legends and Tales.

CHAPTER
2

Marypat Return

With trembling hands, Marypat lifted the two large crystals and placed them back of the pastel in the center of the front room. Her worse fear had come to be. Blaze was within the crystal. For a moment she did nothing. She said nothing. She could only stand and stare at the crystals, while her mind raced.

Then without warning, she turned to her Grandmother, with her mind committed and her words affirmed.

"I'm going after him!"

Lora said nothing, while in her own mind she wanted to argue with Marypat. She wanted to shout at her, "It's too dangerous for you to return there. Don't you remember, they told you never to come back?" She wanted to shack her granddaughter and make her see that it was risky. But she said nothing. Instead, she remembered how she had felt when Marypat had fallen in to the eye for the first time. She recalled how frightened she was for her granddaughter. How much she wanted to jump in and help her granddaughter. But she also remembered her own inability to go after her. Tears filled her eyes and she felt the sting of coward-ness fill her again. She was so terrified of what lived within the crystals, but she also knew her granddaughter was not. She knew Marypat was not at all like her, and she believed in her granddaughter and knew that Marypat would do whatever it took to bring Blaze back. With that in mind, she also knew that she could not fight Marypat, she would not hold her back, and she would instead stand by and watch her granddaughter fall into peril once again.

"What will you need?" Lora asked bravely while tears streamed down her face.

"My wand, my book . . . and I need to change" She was wearing a sundress with little strappy sandals, which would not do.

"I have to travel a bit of a distance though a thickly over growth in the forest so I need a pair of sneakers and my watch." she answered.

"I'll get you a bag." Lora replied as she turned away from her granddaughter. She whipped her eyes and then set off towards the guest room. When she got there, she turned on the light and noticed that the closet door was ajar. This was strange to her, because no one ever used that closet; it was filled with old suitcases and junk from Trevor's Father, Walter's days in the Marines, his moth-eaten duffle bag, his uniforms and many other old military items. After a few seconds of thinking about all the things in the closet Lora's mouth dropped. "No" she gasped. "He wouldn't have taken that, would he?"

Horrified she ran to the closet and pulled it open. She grabbed for the long chain that dangled in fount of her and yanked it. The light went on. In the middle of the floor, dumped out were the remains of what use to be a neatly packed box of old army photos, letters, ribbons and of Course Walter's souvenir Japanese daggers. The daggers he himself had taken off a captured Japanese soldier back in November 1943 when the U.S. Marines advance on Betio Island during the battle of Tarawa. The same daggers that Lora, hated so passionately that she had insisted that her husband put them away, out of her sight.

Lora's eyes searched the debris, but the daggers were gone. She closed her eyes as fresh tears welled up in them. She knew that this couldn't be good. A weapon could be used for protection, yes, but more likely, it would be used to harm and if Blaze tried to use one of them, it was quite possible that the member Blaze was defending himself from, would have powers to take the dagger from him and possibly use it against him.

Lora shock her head in disbelief, it was too unreal. Like a terrible dream a dream, she wanted to end. But it wasn't a dream, it was all really happening and she had to try and be strong for Marypat. She could not run away, she had to go on.

She turned to step out of the closet but before she could take to steps Marypat was standing before her, dressed in jeans, a yellow polo shirt and sneakers. Her face was very serious as she spoke.

"He has taken the wand, the spell book and my diamond tear."

"He has taken your Grandfather Walter's Japanese war daggers, both of them." Lora added without emotion.

Marypat's head dropped and she began to sob. "What has he done?" Her bottom lip began to quiver and her hand shock.

Lora could see her granddaughter falling apart. It was as if her news was the last straw. It was all too much for both of them.

"He's made a very bad choice, that's true." Lora said. Her voice was strong and firm and she for once had found a strength she never knew she had. But she had to be, she had to pull Marypat out of the despair she saw growing in her eyes. "But that doesn't mean he does deserve our help."

Lora reached for Marypat chin and she gently raised her face until they were once again eye-to-eye.

"He needs you! You know that world; you know what they will do to him if they find him. You know what you have to do. Now stand up straight and go get my grandson." Lora said firmly.

Marypat's eyes grew intense as she listened to her grandmother words, she knew her grandmother was right, she knew who could help her find him and she knew what kind of danger Blaze would be in if anyone found out who he really was. She took in a long deep breath and then knobbed. "You are right, I better get moving."

Two women took one last look into each other's eyes before turning to leave the room. Lora crossed the threshold first but Marypat stopped and turned back towards the bed. There was something on the bed. She stepped over to it and bent down.

On the bed was Blaze's 9th grade math book, a pile of crumped up paper, a rubber band, a stripe of staples, a stapler, pencil shavings, two exercise books, a set of Motorola, Talk about fr50's and his organizer. It looked like Blaze had dumped out his backpack on to the bed, and left what he did not need. Her eyes glanced over the pile once again. This time she glared at the set of Talk abouts, it was the set she had given him for Christmas the year before.

Why had he left them?

A thought came to her and she scooped up both units and then headed to the fount room where her grandmother stood waiting for her. She tossed one of the walkabouts to her grandmother and instructed her to turn it on, she did the same and both turned on full charged and working.

"I don't know if they will work but it won't hurt to try." Marypat said with a nod. "Give me two hours to get to grandpa, and then turn yours on. With any luck they will work and I can update you every now and then."

Lora knobbed and stuffed the walkabout into her pocket. "Take care, and give this to my father." Lora said holding out a small round object.

Marypat took the object from her grandmother, then she stepped up to the pillar and the two women hugged.

"Be safe."

Was the last thing Marypat heard was her grandmother saying as she picked up the emerald and stared into the eye.

CHAPTER
3

Shan, Shanley and Shannon

The repulsive scent of burning sulfur filled Blaze's lungs. It burned his nose, his throat and his chest making him gage and cough, but it also broke through to his mind jilting him to consciousness. He awoke with a jerk, his body bounced and swayed as he tried desperately to focus on his surroundings. But that proved to be difficult for what he saw with his eyes made no sense to him what so ever and what made it even more difficult was the fact that he was tied to the ground, spread eagle.

Right above him affixed to the celling of what appeared to be a lime stone cave was a burning fire. The fire's smoke was most certainly the source of the sulfur odor. Strangely the smoke drifted down, directly pointed into his face. Each puff gently made its way towards him engulfing him as it passed.

On one wall of the cave and directly to Blaze's right, were three horizontal dug out spaces. Each space was the same length as the other and they were stacked one on top of the other. On the other wall were an old wooden table and three ricked looking chairs, three pots, a pan and six pairs of muddy boots. All were lined up neatly. On the far side of the cave and just beyond Blaze's feet was the strangest sight yet, there Blaze noticed three picks, three shovels, three buckets and three screens. But what made this sight so strange to him wasn't the picks, the shovels or the scenes. What was strange was the buckets. All three buckets stood on their handles, with the bucket end completely upside down. Blaze's mind still foggy, could not make sense of it. How could a bucket sit on its handle? And for that matter how could a fire hang from a ceiling. Then it came to him, he was not on the floor of the cave but he was the one on the ceiling.

With the knowledge that he was hanging upside down now clear in his mind, Blaze began to wobble uncontrollably. He wanted to pull himself free, but he soon realized that he was trapped. His arms and legs were tied firmly into two slings like straps that crossed over his body and supported him. Blaze stopped fighting and hung there. Was this going to his end? Was he going to be cooked and eaten by a strange creature, one his mother had never told him about? He grew angry, not at the strange creature who had done this to him, but at himself. What a fool he had been, why hadn't he listened to his mother? Why? The question bounced through his mind over and over again so loudly he didn't even hear the voices below him quarrelling over him.

"Him a thief, him after our luck!" one of the voices called out.

"Ye shouldn't have bought him here, Shanley, no good can come of it." Another voice said.

"But the poison was working too fast, there wasn't time to smoke the trortle moss there on the shore, I had no choice but to bring him here to our flame." the last one explained.

"Hold ye fists me brothers, him eye flitter so." announce the first.

There was a scurry of tiny feet and then Blaze opened his eyes to find three small green leprechauns like men staring up at him.

Somewhat stared, having been the first time he had ever seen a being on the Isle Blaze stumbled with a halfhearted greeting. " Hi. . .Top. . . of the mourning to ya?" He said thinking he should talk as people did on St. Patrick's Day.

He was relieved to find out his captures were leprechaun like, yet I had to remember which of the commoners were the ones with luck. Then it hit him these must be Feldens. His mother told him they were lucky and good-natured but they were always afraid others were trying to steal their luck, knowing they were Feldens Blaze knew they would not eat him or for that matter hurt him so long as he didn't trouble their luck. So, he smiled at them, hoping they would let him go if he looked harmless.

"OHHH." the three Feldens gasped.

"It's a trick, a Sherideens trick." The largest one squawked. "I told ye, him can't be trusted, ye should have left him out there to die."

"But brother, they would have eaten him alive and his eyes would hold the sight till he passes on. He can't live with that." The thinnest one pleaded.

"The weakest, Shanley, a shame for ye. Pap's would die another death, if he'd seem ye." The largest one shouted in disgust.

"Hello." Blaze tried to speak but the three Feldens continued to argue between themselves and not notice his calls.

The largest one continued "And now ye have us troubled with a Sherideen of all things and him probably already cursing us all."

Blaze's mind spun at the word Sherideen and he spoke aloud, "Did you say Sherideen? I'm not a Sherideen." but still the three paid him no attention and continued to argue.

"What will we do with him, Shan." The second and smallest Felden asked softly. "The smoking is nearly complete and his limbs will be of used to him again?"

"Yes, brother, can't we just let him go? Perhaps he won't harm us, if him knows we helped him." The thinnest one added.

"A Sherideen can't be trusted, brothers, remember what paps told us." The largest one maintained.

"Yes, brother, Sherideens do not belong here, they have no purpose but to steel." Both Feldens replied together.

"Besides remember the order of truce, so long as none of our members help the Sherideen here in." The largest one urged. "But since we helped him, all our members are doomed."

"How will they know?" complained the thinnest. "If we just let him go, no one has to know."

"He will tell them; don't you see it's a test." The largest one shouted so loud that nether brother had anything more to say.

In the silence, Blaze decided to try again to get their attention. "Hello, for your information I'm not a Sherideen, my mother is a Maurieen."

The three Feldens jumped, where eyes bugged nearly out of their sockets as they had forgotten that their captive was awake.

"I did not mean to startle you and I'm very glad to hear that it was you who saved me from those sea birds. ."

"They weren't sea birds!" The thinnest one interrupted. "They were blood seekers, highly aggressive; you should never have been out there without cover."

"That's enough brother, you speak as though he has no knowledge of the isle and I am sure he plays us for fools, is that not so?" The large one poked his fat green finger at Blaze.

"No, it's not so. I'm afraid I do not know this isle. My mother only told me about the Great Isle, but of course, she did not have this part of the Crystal when she came here. We only yesterday put the two back together. So, I would appreciate any help you could give me. . ."

Blaze was cut off short. "We cannot help you, it's against the truce."

"Yes, I heard you, but I'm telling you I am not a Sherideen. My mother is a Maurieen. That makes me a Torideen!" Blaze announced.

All three Feldens laughed out loud.

"Ye must be blind or ill in eye, for ye are no other than a Sherideen's fry." The large one danced around laughing so hard he fell over and laid on the ground still laughing.

The thin one stepped up to Blaze his face was filled with a huge toothless grin. "Forgive me brother, Shan, it has been very long that a laugh has filled him so. For that I thank thee. I am Shanley and this is my brother Shannon." Stanley explained as he pointed to his smaller brother.

"I am Blaze, form the outer world, beyond the eye. I have come here on an adventure, but I have not had much luck." Blaze said closing his eye's sadly.

Then suddenly Shan jumped from his place on the cave floor and ran over to Shanley and shock his fist at him. "Ye see brother he is after our luck, him said it for true."

"No." shouted Blaze. "That's not what I meant, please let me explain."

But Shan was not having any more of the Sherideens words. He wanted him silenced so he grabbed for his shovel and before either of his brothers could stop him, he had clubbed Blaze over the head, knocking him out cold.

The Cabin

There it sat the same old familiar green kettle post log cabin, nestled at the edge of the wood. Its moss-covered roof was a live with jingle toes of every color. Tinny wings and Kimmy flies were buzzes all around. It looked like dream a wonderful peaceful dream.

The cabin was a place where Marypat had always felt save and happy and now there it stood in fount of her, like a sanctuary. There was a fire going inside and Marypat knew she would find her great-grandfather working within. She stepped up to the door and knocked.

A moment later it creaked open and she caught a glimpse of Cornelius memorable face.

"Mary" he explained throwing open the door. His arms wrapped around her filling her with warmth, and for a moment emptying her mind of the dreadful news she knew she had to share with him.

"Great-grandfather, I have missed you so." She whispered the truth.

"And I ye, my dear." He said with a smile. "Come in, come in. We will toast your visit with an ale!"

Marypat ducked inside and quickly looked around. The house was exactly as she remembered it from the last time she had been there almost eleven years earlier. There was only one thing that seemed new and that was a dusty old painting of a pile of cauldrons. The painting was not hung on the wall instead it leaned against the wall as if Cornelius was planning to hang it sometime in the future.

Still she did not pay it any mind, choosing to follow her great-grandfather to the table, were to her surprise found Gillian and several high-ranking Frandies discussing the happenings of the last two turns.

"It's a sign the Ubil are ready to take back the bangle." The lieutenant shouted at Gillian.

"'Tis not!" Gillian roared as he gulped down a mug of ale. "Ubil members don't have the power to cause such a light, nor would they produce such joy in all members that they sing out in to the eve. No, I say it was more, delightfully more."

"Indeed, indeed, and as you can see with ye own eye, that one has come to tell us what." Cornelius explained to the group as he introduced his granddaughter. "You all remember my charge, though grown well, she has come to tell us of the news from outside the eye."

Marypat glared at her great-grandfather, what he was talking about, she knew no news from outside. The only thing she could think about was her son. She needed to find Blaze before it was too later.

"I don't know what you're talking about. . . "Then it came to her what they were recounting. The light from the two crystals being place back together, the rejoicing that she heard from within. They did not know, they did not know their world had been put back together. "Yes of course. . the second piece of the isle, Blaze. .I mean I found it." she said. She did not want to say too much about her son, with too many ears around. So, she smoothed over it by explaining that she had found it. "Your world is set right just as the Regan had fore-told."

The small group cheered and drank down their mugs of ale before biding each other a good eve and departing into the cracks and cupboards of the cabin. Gillian said his farewells and after a moment of strange whispering between Cornelius and himself, he slipped out of the door leaving Cornelius and Marypat standing in the kitchen alone.

"Tell me dear, the true meaning of your visit." Cornelius spoke softly as he guided her to the sofa where they both took a seat on the comfortable cushions.

"How do you. . . " she began.

"How do I know there is more?" he asked with a slight grin. "Because my dear, I know you. It must be something very serious to bring you back to a world that has wrongly held you accountable for the actions of the Ubil. Something so important you risk your own live to return. Am I correct?"

"Yes." Marypat whispered. She looked Cornelius in his eyes and spoke from her heart. "Cornelius, I have a son, his name is Blaze, he is the one that found the other half of the Green isle."

Cornelius grinned at Marypat, he was pleased to hear of his great great grandson. "Why that is fine news."

"There is more." She interrupted.

Cornelius face grew serious as he listen to Marypat describe what had taken place in the last two turns. When she was done Cornelius spoke softly.

"We must find the boy as quickly as possible. We shall seek Kathrie Gretel's advice as for the best course of action." He paused for a moment and stared at Marypat very seriously. "She will insist that we inform the council of everything you have told me. Without their consent. . ."

"I understand." Marypat injected. She understood full well what could happen to her if she was found on the isle without permission even now it was very dangerous. She had worried, when she first stepped inside the cabin that there were too many ears and eyes about. If one of the Frandies spoke about her outside the house, there would certainly be concerns. It was her best bet to get to the council as soon as possible and plead her case in fount of them.

"Gillian will return in the morrow. He has agreed to help in any way he can and I think it best if he travels with us to Boulder Town for security. You my dear will need a disguise, if any one spots you. . . . well, you understand how important it is you stay concealed."

"Yes, but what shall I wear?"

"Don't worry; I shall have something for you in the morn. Now excuse me while I have a word with the lieutenant. I must put them to orders at once before word leaks out." He explained, and then he rose and stepped over to a small crack in the wall where a slender figure jumped to a salute and stood ridged while Cornelius spoke commandingly to him.

Marypat took the moment alone to pull out her half of the walkabout set. She turned it on and listened while the static pulsed high and then low. She then squeezed the orange pad and began to speck.

"Grandmother can you hear me?" She asked feeling rather silly. She released the pad and listened for a reply. But all she heard was more static. She looked down at her watch, two hours had pasted since she and her grandmother agreed to try the walkabout. And according to her watch, her grandmother should have turned on the walkabout almost 4 minutes ago. "Perhaps the walkabout won't work." she thought to herself, "well there was no harm trying."

"Mary, click shsssss snap. . is that you. shhhhhhhhsssss" Came a voice over the walkabout. " shshshshshshs . . Well I hope you can sssssssss hear sssssshhh click, I don't even know how to use this tshshshshshs click."

"Grandmother I can hear you." Marypat replied excitedly.

"Click click shshshs Mary, where are you? click"

"I'm at Cornelius's cabin, he has agreed to help."

"Click Good click."

"We will go ask Kathrie Gretel to help tomorrow."

"When should I hear shshs click you again? click snap"

"Let's try again tomorrow same time, ok?"

"Click Ok, tomorrow 8:30 shshshs click."

"Right"

"Click shshsh Alright, take care, I love shshsh click click."

"I love you too mom."

SHHHHHHHHHHHH, was all Marypat heard after that. She stared down at the walkabout and slowly turned it off. She placed it back into her pocket and took a deep breath. It felt good to be able to talk to her grandmother. Never before had she been able to do that, it felt a bit strange, but it also was very comforting to hear her voice. When Marypat looked up she notice Cornelius staring at her.

"What magic is that?" He asked.

"Modern technology, not magic." She smiled up at him. "You would be surprised to see what they can do now."

"Indeed, it would be best not to show that to anyone." He said firmly.

Marypat agreed with a nod, feeling slightly scolded by his stern stare.

"Well some tea then before we head to our beds?" He asked more cheerfully.

Again, Marypat knobbed. She stood then and followed Cornelius back into the kitchen where he set to work on a pot of water to boil.

"So, where is Horatio on this fine eve?" Marypat asked expecting him any moment to jump to her side with a sack full of spiders.

"He no long resides here." Cornelius answered matter-of-fact-ly.

Marypat's chest fell. She felt an instant ach of lose. Horatio had left, he was gone? Why would he leave her? She sat down on one of the wobble old stools beside the kitchen counter and stared out the window. Her mind was lost in a flood of emotions that struck her cold in the heart. Horatio had left. But he hadn't left her, she had left him. Guilt now filled her mind. She had left him here all alone what had she expected him to do. Had she expected him to stay and wait for her. How ridiculous an expectation especially when she was told never to return. How could she ever have expected Horatio to wait here? She closed her eyes as tears welled up in them. Perhaps he found someone and he is happy. She knew in her heart she wouldn't have wanted him to wait. She would have wanted him to move on and find happiness.

Her next question to Cornelius came with a crack in her voice. "Do you know where he is?"

"Of course, I hear from him often." Cornelius proclaimed with a smile. "The council offered him a very good position. We'll see him when we get to Great Town."

Relief washed over her. She would see him. Her face beamed, her heart felt light. Like a young girl. How peculiar, she thought, she never expected to feel this way about Horatio. She missed him more than she was willing to admit to herself. She needed to see him, wanted to be near him and for the first time could not wait to get to the counsel at Great Town.

CHAPTER 5

A New Brother

A gentle breeze blow over the white shoreline of the Red Isle as three nervous members dragged a large object across the sand. Their movements were hurried as they fumbled and thrashed through the lose grains. Finally, they came to a large dune and flopped the object against it.

"Hurry brother, before him awakes." One of them shouted.

"Give me opportunity!" The largest one answered with anger as he dug at his vest and pulled out a small leather book. He opened it with one hand and flipped through it with the other while balancing something long and thin in the palm of his right hand. "I must find the right one."

"But brother, what of the Hisue? What if we have been wrong, what if Blaze is telling the truth, about the isles being put back together and all him want is to get to the Great Isle?" The thinnest one quivered.

"Be still, I cannot think with ye foolishness." growled the largest one.

"I agree with Shanley, what if the Sherideen is from the outer world and has no knowledge of our Isle. Him could be harmed even killed, and then what will be paid for leaving him here with no mind." The smallest of the three exclaimed.

"Do ye truly believe the evil tales of this member?" The largest one looked up for the book and seething turned his eyes on his brothers. "Do ye for one moment believe that one could fall from above? From a world beyond the eye?" He glared at Shanley and then at Shannon.

"And can ye imagine that him is the son of a Maurieen? That alone is impossible. Just look at his face, a Sherideen him is, a Sherideen him be. His words I tell ye are a trick, a lie, to fool us, so he can steal our luck." Shan's voice grew very serious as he continued. "Think about it brothers. Him say him wants only to travel to the Great Isle, but the Great Isle is no more. Ye know that to be fact, for more than 55 passes it has been fact." Shan went silent and his two brothers could only look at him with solemn eyes. What Shan said was true; they knew it to be so.

They could fight their brother no more and they stepped back while Shan raised the thin stick in his hand and began the spell.

"Silent spread to mind and will, delete the turns before this ill. Place instead a quiet thought of peace and calm here in brought." Shan finished the spell with the thin stick's point jabbing Blaze in his fore head.

With the spell complete, Blaze's eye's flow open and he gasped for breath. The three figures jump with fright and then stood frozen in place as they watched and waited for the Sherideen to retaliate. But all Blaze could do was throw his hands in front of him as if he was reaching for something and then he collapsed backwards into the sand dune.

"Quick." Shouted Shan as he stuffed the stick and the book into Blaze's backpack. "Go brothers before him comes too."

The two brothers ran from the dune, while Shan bent down close to Blaze's head and made sure that he was still breathing. He could not afford payment of Hisue for causing a death, knowing that would not be good. He listened carefully and heard for himself the steady laboring sound of breathing. Satisfied that Blaze was alive, Shan crammed the backpack into Blaze's lap and hurried off after his brothers.

Darkness grew around Blaze's body as he lay spread-out in the sand, his eyes were wide open but there was no glimpse of consciousness. Moments passed and then he began to stir. He lunged forward suddenly, and sat up. He was dizzy and confused. He glanced around at his dark surroundings with a strange look on his face. He recognized nothing, nothing except his backpack. He grabbed a hold of it, and held it tight, it was the only thing familiar to him and he did not want to lose it.

His mind raced, he could not make sense of where he was, was he dreaming. Nerves and aching he tried to stand, but to his surprise he was pushed back down by a large bony hand that grabbed him from behind.

"Blaze, brother, were have ye been, I've been looking for ye everywhere. Ye know ye shouldn't be out here in the open like this." Came an unfamiliar voice.

Blaze looked up and stared at the member standing now in front of him. He was a tall black-haired man, with huge purple eyes and a drawn white face. His face was so drawn and white that he looked almost like a skeleton. His body was thin and bony, though his long raggedy green rope hid most of him, his arms and face showed the truth. He was a man that was slowly wasting away.

Blaze did not recognize him. He looked at him strangely and tried to remember, but he had no memory of the tall boney black-haired man.

"Who are you?" Blaze asked innocently.

"Don't tell me don't recognize your own brother, Godfrey?" The man stated with his hands clench to his bone hips. "I can see you've been outside for too long, we better get ye home."

The boney man bent over and tried to take the backpack from Blaze but Blaze held onto it firmly. "Well alright then carry it; I was only trying to help."

Blaze stood and walked along with Godfrey through the darkness without saying a word. His mind was a flood of questions. He knew he didn't have a brother named Godfrey and he was sure that this place was not his home. But at the same time, he didn't know where he had come from or how he had gotten here. So, he followed the man in hopes of finding out.

After a short walk, the tall man bent below a large bush and disappeared. Blaze followed cautiously. He peered beneath the bush and realized the man was leading him into a limestone cave. At the entrance of the cave, was a pile of half chard wood and ashes. He stepped over the wood and continued on. Inside the cave, there were torches along the walls, lighting the emptiness. Blaze could see that the cave was spit in two by a crystal-clear stream that flowed through it and abruptly vanished into the right wall of the cave. Beyond the stream, Blaze could see two long table-like structures made out of raw timbre and what looked like drift wood. On one of the tables were earthy roots and leaves, on the other were what looked like polished rocks. Beside the tables were an old rusty cauldron and a pile of empty tin cans. There was little else in the cave.

"Did ye say something, Blaze, are ye delirious, brother?" The man asked sympathetically. "Perhaps we should eat; ye would feel better after ye have had something to warm the body."

The bony man strolled over to the pile of tin cans and shook the rusty cauldron from the pile. He took it over to the stream and filled it with water. Then he took the cauldron back toward the entrance of the cave and started a fire with the pile of wood there. Soon he was back, offering Blaze a tin of tea.

"Drink it up brother it is all we have till morning." Godfrey mentioned as he handed the hot tin can to Blaze. His eyes were tiered and Blaze could see he was sincere.

Blaze took the can with a nod and set it down beside him. "Thank-you, Godfrey." He said. "Perhaps I should let it cool a bit." It seemed too hot to drink right away and besides Blaze was more interested in looking in his backpack to see if he recognized anything.

He dug into it while Godfrey watched most interested. First, he pulled out the black scandal bag with his wet jeans and socks in it. He pulled out the jeans and laid them out to dry and flung the soxs beside them, then he continued diving back into the bag. Next out came the Ziplock with the lizard like creature in it. Blaze looked at it strangely and tossed it onto the cave floor. He shook his head, he didn't know where that came from but it was not important enough to stop the search so he continued digging in the bag.

He then pulled out an old leather book, a white box with bright letters on it, a round disk with several long strings hanging from it, a bright blue pouch, a strange gray object and a bright pink bottle.

There were several small objects at the bottom of the bag that Blaze ignored as he pushed his hand from side to side, but then he spotted something he had to look more closely at. It was his brown leather wallet. He quickly opened it up and glared at its components. There inside the wallet was a picture of him with his mother. They were standing on the beach and they were both in their swimsuits.

"Mom" He whispered.

Godfrey made no inquiry, he merely bent more closely to get a look at the object Blaze was holding.

Blaze flipped the photo over and in the next slop was a picture of his two cousins, 12-year-old Twin boys, Patrick and James, from his great-grandfather Trevor's side of the family. He had spent the summer with them in Florida and they had given him this picture of them. The next photo was a picture of him with his great-grandparents before his great-grandfather died. The last two photos were school pictures of his best friends, Louie and Niram. Behind the photos, Blaze found an old used phone card and his school ID. He pulled the ID out and looked at it closely. There was a photo of him on the left side of the laminated card and beside it typed out clearly was:

```
Hillel Academy High School
1997-1998 Identification Card
       for Blaze Sharp
         Third Form
  Blue House Sports Captain
```

Blaze stared at the card and then slowly slipped it back in to the wallet. He recognized it; he knew that that was where he went to school. But he didn't know where the school was. He continued through the wallet and discovered it had several bills in it that he too recognized a twenty dollar all green bill and about six one-dollar bills, these were American bills, the good stuff! He grinned.

"I remember these." Blaze nodded his head as his eyes for the first time glanced up to Godfrey who in return tried to look like he was not interested.

"And these!" Blaze said more surprised. He held up a red and blue bill and two powder blue bills. "These are Jamaica dollars!" He announced with a huge feeling of relief. He knew who he was and where he was from. He knew his mother's face and her name, but he still did not know where he was, how long he had been here and how he had gotten here. He turned to Godfrey then in hopes of finding an answer.

"You called me brother, why?" Blaze asked.

"We are bother's, how could ye. ."

Blaze cut him off. "We are not brothers; I do not have a bother!'

"Not a blood brother perhaps, but of the Sherideen brethren, you now have me." Godfrey stated confidently.

"You're a Sherideen?" Blaze asked strangely, his mind was a wave of doubt and confusion. If Godfrey was a Sherideen that meant he was not in Jamaica. Could he be in the crystal as he had wanted to be so badly, had he really done it, had he travel through the eye to the Great Isle? For a moment he felt excited and thrilled. His mind raced. The fall must have knocked him out. Godfrey must have found him and he is willing to help him. It was so great.

"Yes, and so are ye?" Godfrey mentioned gently.

"No! I am a son of a Maurieen, I am a Torideen." Blaze said half grinning.

Godfrey shook his head. "No, brother ye are a Sherideen, like me and if ye are willing, together we can get off of this eternal hell of an Isle." Godfrey's purple eyes flared red as he spoke the last few words.

Blaze stood. He suddenly felt that something was terribly wrong. His mind reeled with the word "Sherideen" as it flowed repeatedly in his thoughts. He grabbed his bag tightly to his chest and searched the cave with his eyes.

"What is this place?"

"This is the Red Isle, our prison." Godfrey answered.

"Prison?" Blaze asked still searching the cave. It occurred to him suddenly that a magical member like a Sherideen would certainly have more, than these mere objects. He recalled also something his mother had told him about Sherideens, Sherideens liked to live in the clouds. Why wasn't this one living in the clouds? Was he telling the truth, was this a prison?

"Yes, ye have been banished here, like me. But ye have many things with ye that can aid us in escaping. Work with me brother and we can be free." Godfrey said most convincingly.

Blaze thought for a moment, the Red Isle. He had never heard of the Red Isle. This was not where he wanted to be. He realized he needed to get to the Great Isle. From the Great Isle he knew how to get back home. He also realized he needed help, even if it were from a Sherideen. So, he accepted the Godfrey's proposal with one addition.

"I will help you get off the Red Isle, if you agree to take me to the Great Isle." He stated firmly.

Godfrey agreed easily, but in his own thoughts laughed at the young fool. The Great Isle no longer existed it had long since vanished, leaving a barren and dangerous sea in its place. Aware of this Godfrey agreed willing, knowing in the end he would be free of his prison, regardless of where they ended up, anywhere would be better than the Red Isle.

CHAPTER
6

Grundle Coose-lings

The morning light came early the next morn. Lora wanted her great-grandson to return home and she was even anxious for Marypat to get started. So, she flipped on the flood lights in the front room before there was even light outside in her world.

Marypat sensed the brightness and turned over in her bed. "Alright grandma, I get the message." She murmured to herself. "I'm getting up."

The sudden light outside Marypat's window did more than wake her up. It indicated a brawl between two very loud members. Their voices shot through the air and it entered Marypat's room with a boom.

"Ye worthless, pathetic beast." Roared the first voice.

"Ye are the weakling one." Bellowed the second.

Marypat's eye shot open. She scrambled out of bed and throw open the window. She expected to find two Lachlanns or at least two Frandies having it out but what she found surprised her and she had to take a step back. Before her stood two adolescent Grundles both as green as the moss that grew in the wood. Both with red flaming tipped ears, a single silver horn in the center of their heads and sparkling green eyes.

"Despicable!"

"Contemptible."

The two voices continued while Marypat stared in amazement. There was only one Grundle that Marypat knew could speak the tongue of the Members and that was Tiger. But these two were too young to be Tiger, he would be very old now, not frisky and energetic as these two.

"Now that's enough." Shouted Marypat through the window. "Now the two of you stop it."

"Tell him to give me back my Lofty Zort and I will." Complained the one on the right.

"Give it back, I eat it already." The one on the left licked his lips with a devilish glance. "You didn't want it anyway."

"Yes, I did."

"No, you didn't. If you wanted it, why did you drop it?" Questioned the one on the left.

"I dropped it because the light blinded me." The right one explained looking desperate. "And now that it is morn, I wouldn't be able to catch another until dusk."

"Well I see." Said Marypat. "I am very sorry to hear that the bright light has taken your hunting term away but if you would like I can get you some milk. That is if the two of you will stop fighting."

"Agreed." The two Grundles purred.

"Come to the door and I'll be out in a moment."

Before long Marypat emerged from the old wooden door of the cabin and was soon pouring milk into two very large saucers.

"There you are." She said. She couldn't resist the temptation to stroke their green fluffy fur and as she reached forward and scratched her fingers through the first ones neck it purred. Gently she scratch his head until the second one grew jealous and said so.

"My neck is more lovey then his."

"Oh really." Marypat said with a laugh "I suppose you would also like a scratch?"

"If you must." The second one purred.

So Marypat reached over to the second Grundle and scratched both until they were content.

"That was wonderful." The first one groaned as he stretched out at Marypat's foot. "Father always told us stories of when he had a scratch like that. Oh, we always thought him odd. Why would one want one? But now I see, he was right."

"Yes brother, very nice." The second one curled up next to the first and closed his eyes.

Marypat thought for a moment, it was possible, they looked just like him.

"Excuse me Grundles, what was your father's name?"

"We called him Grrra." The first one answered. And with that Marypat's hopes fell away.

"But brother, remember he said the Maurieen, who pranced in this house and gave him his tongue called him by a strange name, remember." The second one added.

"Oh, yes, she called him Tiger."

Marypat's heart flipped. Tiger, these were Tigers off spring. They could talk because she had feed their father the coose-gotta-tongue. It all made sense. She smiled to herself and asked.

"Where is your father this morn?"

"Oh, poor father, he has gone to sleep with the Pilly Pats." Answered the first.

"The what?" Asked Marypat.

"Yes, father was very old, two seasons ago, he went to sleep, never to raise again." The second one explained.

Marypat understood now, Tiger had died. Tears filled her eyes. So many things had changed and this one seemed so difficult to bare but she held her pain inside as she asked the two Grundles for their names.

"I am RRum and this is Grren." The first one answered.

"I am Marypat a very old friend of your father and I am very pleased to meet you both." She said patting them both on the head. "Perhaps we can have another scratch very soon?"

"Oh yes." The two Grundles purred in unison.

With that Marypat rose and entered the house. Cornelius was pouring himself a mug of tea and asked her if she would join him. She nodded yes and before long they were sitting together sharing breakfast.

"We shall leave as soon as Gillian arrives." Cornelius explained. "He said he would start out at first light, so he should be here soon."

And true to his word, less than a sweep later, Gillian was at the door ready for anything. He wore a dark gray tunic with leather fan trimming and a tall gray crown that was trim in black and blue leather and in the center of it was a bright blue gem. Over his shoulder he carried a black leather holster that held the sheath of a Hedlen crafted sword. In his one hand he carried a bed roll and in the other he held a green branch of Dagwood which he used to shield his eye from the bright light.

He entered the house and quickly was informed by Cornelius what needed to be done. Without hesitation, Gillian agreed.

"We shall leave at once." Cornelius announced and then stepped over to Marypat. He picked up an old black cloak and handed it to her.

"Put it on, keep yourself well covered until it is clear." He urged.

Marypat took the cloak and wrapped it around her shoulders. It fells over her gently, covering her full length. Then she pulled on the hood and turned to Cornelius.

"I'm ready."

He nodded in answer and then stepped over to the wall of the cabin. He stood in front of the old painting of rusty cauldrons and then called out one last time to the lieutenant.

"Keep a tight ship, and if anything changes, Ye know where to find me."

"Yes sir" came the reply and with that Cornelius bent down and climbed into the painting.

To Marypat's surprise the old dusty painting was a Realagraph. Marypat watched Cornelius disappear into the painting and then quickly followed.

The Change Begins

A dank musty odor rose up from the darkness that surrounds Blaze as he tried to sleep in the limestone cave. His body grew cold with a shiver and he pulled his still damp jeans over his legs. But it was no use, slumber was eluding him. All evening long he had tried desperately to sleep but the coldness, the stench and a strange throbbing in his chest kept him from it. Not to mention the fact that he had laid on solid rock and had only his back pack for a pillow.

It was no use he could not sleep. He sat up and stared into the darkness. Again, the throbbing in his chest stuck him and for a moment he sat stunned and unable to move. Soon the throbbing stopped and he thought to himself.

"Why am I so uncomfortable?"

But then it stuck him, he was hungry. He couldn't remember the last time he had eaten. He reached for his backpack and pulled out the box of pop tarts, he remembers seeing when he searched his bag earlier. He pulled out one of the foiled poaches and ripped it open. The package crackled as it opened, catching the attention of Godfrey, who sat up and watched through the darkness as Blaze ate the tart.

"What is that brother?" Asked Godfrey causally. Unlike Blaze, Godfrey could see perfectly in the dark in fact Sherideens preferred the damp darkness to warm sunlight.

Caught off guard Blaze answered, "Un this? It's a pop tart. Would you like one?"

"Pop tart?" Godfrey questioned. "I have never heard of such a thing, nor have I ever seen such a perfectly formed confection."

"I guess you could say it's like a pasty, it has a crust and a filling. This one has chocolate inside. You can have it if you want, I have more." Blaze said holding the tart out into the air. He couldn't see where Godfrey was but he reached out his arm in the direction of Godfrey's voice in hopes Godfrey could see it.

Godfrey's eyes traveled from Blazes out stretched hand to his face. He sensed the generosity of the gift Blaze offered. No one had ever offered him anything that didn't have a catch. Sherideens didn't operate that why. Even he expected something for helping Blaze.

"What would one want for it?" Godfrey asked with caution in his voice.

"Hun" Blaze responded. "I don't want anything, I just thought you might be as hungry as me. Listen it's yours if you want it, it's no skin off my teeth if you don't."

Godfrey found Blaze words strange but quickly took the offering from Blaze hand and began eating it. It was scrumptious. Godfrey had never tasted anything so wonderful. It was better than anything he could remember, better than his mother's Tangleberry pie, or Kathries Franny's Black Bottom Tort or even Miss Honey's Kox pear confections. He looked up at Blaze again and for an instant felt kindness wash over him as his evil Sherideen heart melted just a bit.

Godfrey watched as Blaze made his way to the mouth of the cave where it was brightly consumed with light. Blaze stood in the light with his eyes closed and he looked as if he was absorbing the warm of the light but then there was a strange noise.

"Crack." Blaze doubled over, grabbing his t- shirt. "Arrrr" He groaned in agony.

"Are you alright, is it the Feldens have returned?" Godfrey asked as came to Blazes' side.

As it was known Feldens and Sherideens had never liked one another. They had always been at odds even though they had many of the same traits. Neither trusted their own members, both were ready to fight at the mention of disagreement and both were highly skilled in war. Over the passes there had been many battles between them and it wasn't until the truce, 55 passes earlier, that they stopped fighting. It was a truce in which the Sherideens had vowed never to engage the Feldens if the Sherideens could use the Red Isle as an exile for cast out Sherideens who have been stripped of their powers. Knowing that no other members, except the Feldens could survive the Isles heat the Sherideens plan was to leave the cast out on the isle to die a most slow and horrible death. But the Feldens could break the truce if they helped an exiled Sherideen. Yet killing one would do nothing to affect the truce and that had been Godfrey's greatest fiery. He had no powers and little strength, thanks to the draining heat of the Isle. Add to that the little food he was able to gather made him an easily victim for the Feldens.

"What is it, brother." Godfrey asked as he nervously approached the cave entrance.

"My chest. . I can't breathe." Blaze uttered. He fell to his knees and held his chest.

Quickly Godfrey inspected Blaze's chest, but there was no wound, no sign that he had been struck by something. "I do not see the entry, where are ye hit?"

Blazes' face grew angry. He stared at Godfrey with an overwhelming wave of hate. His eyes flared red and sparks flew from his pulps, catching Godfrey off gaud and hurling him backwards.

Godfrey landed in the sand six hands away from Blaze. He sat there shaken for a moment and then grinned to himself. That instant it all came clear to him. Blaze was not an exiled Sherideen who had been stripped of his powers by the Chamber, like he had been.

No. Godfrey now knew Blaze had come from the outside world just as the Feldens had said. He was new to this world and best yet he was new to his powers. Thirteen passes worth of Sherideen painful magical growth was hitting Blaze dead on. Godfrey could sense the evil growing in Blaze; it was a power so great and strong, that it glowed an ominous wave of red sparks all around Blaze. It sprang his hair into spikes and flamed its tips with the look of fire. His skin went white and his shoulders and chest heaved outwards as his magical powers grew in him.

Godfrey imagined that Blazes' powers were stronger than even Gazpalding himself. And if it were so, Godfrey's reentry to the Great Isle would have a different outcome than he first expects. But in the same vein Godfrey knows he would have to gain Blazes trust and somehow cultivate Blaze's dependence on him.

With so much vile and wonderful thoughts running through Godfrey's mind it was difficult for him not to let his plan spill out to Blazes' ears. Yet with strength of compassion he never knew he had, he pulled himself up out of the sand and helped Blaze to his feet.

"I'm with thee, Blaze, let thy help thee." Godfrey whispered, supporting the laid with his bony frame. He led him back into the cave and brought him to a soft cot that was hidden in the far corner of the cave.

"Rest here, when ye are stronger I will take thee to the pier and we will inquire about passage to the Great Isle."

Blaze knobbed his head and then passed out cold. Godfrey laid him on the cot and then went to collect Blaze's things. How tempting it was to see the backpack unattended, but Godfrey knew if he wanted to gain Blaze's trust it would have to start now. So, he mustered up as much self-control as he could and left the bag at Blaze's feet unopened.

CHAPTER 8

News of a Grandmother

The rusted old cauldrons came to life as Marypat stood up. She was standing in a dusty storeroom with piles of cauldrons, straw baskets, and tin cans all around her. Cornelius stood in front of her waiting. She glanced at him for a moment and then turned back towards the painting she had just stepped out of, to see Gillian's large form emerge. But it was not a painting of cauldrons he stepped out of but a painting of Dr. McCarthy's old red sofa.

"No wonder the painting was sitting on the floor." Marypat said with a giggle. "When did you think up this one?"

"It wasn't my idea." He mentioned coldly. He then turned and stepped around a pile of boxes labeled, Timothy O Hara's fine drip cream. Marypat and Gillian followed him until he came to a small wooden door.

"Wait here." He said as he cracked open the door and peered out into the room beyond. He took a moment to look around and then turned his head back to his companions.

"Keep your hood tight around your face." He said to Marypat and then the three slipped out of the door. Quickly they walked along the long back isle of the Ready Kathrie. At the end of the isle Cornelius stopped. There were voices coming from the other side of the ancient shelve that were stacked with jiggers and vats. Marypat could tell that one of them was a voice she recognized. It was Kathrie Gritty. But the other two voices were Pattie and neither one of them seemed familiar.

"Dangerous creatures, dit nats" Kathrie Gritty mentioned.

"Especially if they never get livestock." Remarked one of the Pattie voices.

"I am sure that my sister's potion, here, will do the trick." Kathrie Gritty said confidently.

"How does one apply it?" Question a very deep voiced Pattie. His voice was scratchy and hoarse as though he were used to doing a lot of yelling and only spoke when he absolutely had to.

"It's very simply, get a cauldron, filled and boiling. Ye want it in a fast condition, really bubbling. Then just toss in the whole vile, with the cork off of course and the potion will do the rest. Now the directions are on the label, if ye forget. . . . ." Her voice trailed off as group began to leave the isle and Marypat could no longer hear her.

Cautiously Cornelius waited until the three members had moved to the front of the shop before motioning to his companions to follow him. They made their way along the back wall of the shop until they came to a large black door. Without hesitation Cornelius stretched his arm over the heavy locked door and whispered.

"Unlock do."

With that the door released its lock and slowly pressed open. The three companions slipped through the opening and found themselves in a work room that was set up for emergency's. It was somewhat dark in the room but Marypat could tell it was the same room Donovan had taken her to when she had broken her leg the first time she had ever been at the Ready Kathrie. It was also the first time she had met Donovan.

How long ago that was. How innocent they were then, how things had changed. Tears sprang to her eyes as she remembered Donovan's gentle voice, his touch and his horrible death.

She hadn't realize coming back here would stir up so much old pain but it had and she had to fight the urge to cry. She closed her eyes hard and reminded herself why she was here. *"Blaze."* She said to herself over and over, until Cornelius grabbed her arm and gently guided her on. They went down a hallway passed six or so rounded doorways and finally came to a spiral staircase that took them down below the Ready Kathrie.

The staircase ended on a floor of solid quartz crystal. Below her feet Marypat could make out the heads of lovely yellow flowers that were trapped within the quartz. She knew the quartz was the bedrock of the Flower River that flowed through Boulder Town. The sight of the boulders reminded her of Horatio, and the time they spent together along the Flower River. She would see him soon, and he would give her the strength she needed to go on. This made her smile and she raised up her head. She whipped the tears from her eyes and continued to follow Cornelius as he pulled open a narrow purple door and disappeared behind it. Once inside Cornelius called up a fire in the fireplace. Then he flicked his finger around the room until several candles lit around them, lighting up the darkness. On the right side of the room there were two comfortable purple sofas facing each other in front of the fire place. On the left were several high back chairs that formed a circle. Cornelius ushered Marypat and Gillian to the sofas and then turned to a small table that sat against the wall. On the table were nine tiny purple bells that stood in a line behind a long think dark green pad. He picked up the first bell in the line and shook it. Nothing happened, no sound came from it. But Cornelius seemed satisfied and placed the bell back on the table exactly where he had gotten it from. Then he went to join the others. But before he could sit down, the chairs on the other side of the room began to shake. They trembled violently and then went quiet. There in the stillness, Marypat could see a lone figure sitting in one of the high back chairs. The figure stood, brushed it's self-off and stepped towards them.

"Cornelius, is that you. I wasn't expecting you until . . . " The figures voice trailed off as she came into view of the three.

"Our greatest remorseful wise Kathrie." Gillian uttered with a bow.

"Yes, Gretel, we are sorry to interfere with your turn, but we are in great need of your assistance." Cornelius revealed as he stepped towards her.

"Shall we sit and speak?"

"Whom do you bring, cloaked from thy sight?" Kathrie Gretel interrupted. "I am not interested in small talk, I feel a change in the energy of this room, and I sense fear beneath the black cloak."

"Allow me to explain. . " Cornelius began, but again he was interrupted.

"Reveal yourself!" Gretel demanded in an angry tone. She pushed her way past Cornelius and stood in front of Marypat.

"Please, Gretel allow me. . " Cornelius pleaded.

"It's alright." Marypat whispered, pulling the cloak from around her face.

Kathrie Gretel gasped. "What have you done, Cornelius? How could you bring her here? You have endangered my coven."

"Please Gretel she needs your help. You are the only one who can help her." Cornelius begged.

"Help her?" Gretel shrieked, "After what she did to my son? He is dead because of her! Take her from my sight!" She turned away from Marypat and began to step back toward the high back chairs.

"No, please listen to me." Marypat exclaimed. She rushed forward and grabbed Kathrie Gretel's arm spinning her back towards her. Kathrie Gretel's face grew angry but Marypat continued. "I loved your son very much." Tears filled her eyes as she explained. "I loved him more then you will ever know. He held my heart and I his. I wish things had been different, and they might have been if Ragnar had not tricked him. You know this to be true, but what you do not know. . . " Marypat's voice went silent, she let go of Kathrie Gretel's arm and glanced at Cornelius for reassurance before beginning again.

"I have a son."

Kathrie Gretel's eye's lite up and her stern face soften as she listened intently to Marypat's words.

"He is your grandson." The two Lassies stood face to face. Both had tears washing down their faces. Their hands meet and held.

"What is his name?" Kathrie Gretel asked.

"Blaze." Marypat answered.

"That's a fine name. Tell me about him." Kathrie Gretel uttered as her voice cracked slightly.

"I want to tell you all about him, but first you must know that he is in danger, that is why I have come, I need your help. Will you help me?" Marypat pleaded.

"For my grandson . . .I will do anything!" Kathrie Gretel stated firmly.

There was silence in the dusty purple room, where Cornelius, Gillian and Marypat sat waiting. There had been waiting for more than a sweep and in all that time not a word had been spoken between them. Enough had been said just the sweep before and now they waited for Kathrie Gretel to settle things with her sisters so that she could travel with them to Great Town.

Marypat needed Kathrie Gretel to go with them to Great Town, she needed the council to grant her permission to search freely for her son, she also hoped that they would allow her to use the Oritor, and that it would be able to find him on the isle. But both of these requests had to be made by a member of the guild and Kathrie Gretel was a member.

Dr. Cornelius at one time had been a member of the guild but when Marypat had been cast out, he severed his ties with the guild. Arguing that the counsel was wrong and that the guild itself had no real powers, no real effect, no influence or clout over them. He stressed that their positions on the guild, were just a sham. Proven to be so when the guild, all of its 296 members strong voted unanimously for Marypat to stay and be schooled, and yet it was rejected by only two pathetic members of the council. Cornelius had felt that the counsel was to scared of her and instead of embracing her and training her for the good of the isle. They instead took a ill-mannered and reckless why out and in doing so left themselves wide open for what could very well occur if the Ubil members realize now that Blaze, son of Donovan, grandson of the mighty Gazpalding and son of the one with the touch of four was in within their reach.

The silence was finally broken when Kathrie Gretel pushed open the narrow purple door and hurried into the room. She rushed over to the table with the nine bells on in and stopped. She thought for a moment and then scribbled something down on the dark green pad that laid just in front of the bells. A moment later the pad lite up bright green and then Streaked off the pad into a puff of smoke.

"Right then, ready?" She asked, drawing her long velvet green cloak around her neck. "If we leave now we can be in Great Town by morning."

Marypat looked at her with surprise, it had taken them nearly three turns to reach Small Town the last time she travelled the Silky Flats. She couldn't imagine how they were going to move any faster than they had then, in less there was another Realagraph.

"How are. . . " Marypat's voice cracked.

Cornelius could see Marypat's confusion and turned to her with an explanation. "A lot has changed here, since your last visit my dear. Remember when we came a pone the black surface outside Small Town and we were picked up?"

"By a bus." Marypat recalled with a smile. It had been a most unusual ride through Small Town, but comfortable just the same.

"That's right, a bus only they call it a Tramp. Well that back surface is a road and it reaches all the way to Outbend now and as far south as Hapton beach. We can pick it up right outside of the shack." Cornelius explained.

"Yes, and it will be there within the sweep, so we better get moving." Added Kathrie Gretel as she urged the group out the narrow purple door.

The group made their way out of the tiny run-down Shack that looked exactly as Marypat remembered it. One by one they crossed the huge black surface, Cornelius called a road. Once across they turned and stood under the large dark green sign that stood to mark the Tramp stop. The sign was solid dark green color except for a flash of bright green light that flashed a cross every few moments. Below the sign was a small round table with the sign post driven throw the center of it. On the table was the same long thick dark green pad, that Marypat had seen on the table at Kathrie Gretel's. The same pad Kathrie Gretel had scribbled on and that had lite up a moment later.

Marypat looked at the pad, what was it? It was like a mouse pad, she used with her computer at home. But hers never lite up and streaked across the room, disappearing into a puff of smoke. As she watched and waited for the Tramp, the four were joined by several other members who were intending to take the Tramp as well.

The first group to join them was a pair of Lachlanns who seemed to be wrestling with a large crate. As soon as the Lachlanns put the crate down and tried to write on the green pad the crate shock and wiggled away from them. Over and over again the Lachlanns caught the crate and carry it back to the Tramp stop, just to have it wiggle away again. Exhausted the two Lachlanns finally managed to scribble something on the pad and before it streaked away, Marypat read what they wrote.

"One crate, cargo only, Port Fin." Then it streaked off the pad and disappeared into a puff of smoke just as the one Kathrie Gretel had written back at her house. Marypat figured it must be like instant messenger, but for the Tramp. Neat! She thought, turning away from the sign post finally satisfied with what it was.

Later a long wagon pulled up to the Tramp stop pulled by two handsome tan Sturn colts. At the reins was a tall Wardeen in a huge Stetson hat. With him were two small children, a young Wardeen and a Colleen. The last group to join them was a cluster of Pixies Lassies, all carrying enormous baskets filled with seeds. They were giggling and chatting to each other as if they were the only members around. Every once in a while, one of them would drop a seed and a flower would sprout up knocking one of them over and causing the whole group to burst out laughing.

Marypat watched them from under her cloak. They reminded her of Daisy and Rose. The two Flower Pixies that had helped her find her way that very first time she visited the isle. How innocent and naive she was then and how nice they had been to her. She could only hope that

Blaze had found members as well to help him. Her heart dropped in her chest and she ached to hold her son. Ached to know if he was O.K. Her mind was so filled with thoughts of her son she didn't even hear the loud sketching sound of the Tramp's brakes as it stopped before her.

"Here clear." Shouted the short Lachlann in the green plaid jacket. "This Streaked Tramp makes stops at Middleton, Goose Path, Small Town and Port Fin."

He flipped through the papers on his clip board and then shouted again.

"Reserve seating for Granger party of three with wagon and two heads to Middletown."

The Wardeen with the two-youngster stepped up pulling the Sturn colts by the reins. The Wardeen led the group to the back of the Tramp and slowly the group disappeared up the ramp, while the Lachlann continued to call his bookings.

"Cargo hold, one crate, Port Fin."

Marypat heard the words and smiled. The pad had been like an instant message to the Tramp conductor just as she had thought.

She watched as the two Lachlanns moved forward dragging the still struggling crate. They finally stepped up to the ramp where two other Feldens waited and then took the crate from them. The two Feldens easily lifted the crate and carried it on board while the Lachlanns stepped away and disappeared in the shack.

"Kathrie Gretel party of four to Port fin." Called the Lachlann.

Kathrie Gretel moved forward and the others followed, with Marypat trying very hard to keep covered by her hood. Marypat moved up the wrap and headed into darkness as she heard the Lachlann call out his last booking.

"Pixie convention to Goose Path." His voice trumpeted professionally and then turned angry.

"Hay stop that you Pixies, there will be none of that on my Tramp. Keep your seeds to yourself."

The familiar scent of livestock filled Marypat's nose as she made her way through the stables. In the stables she past the Wardeen with the children, they were busy tying down the wagon and seeing to the Sturn colts so she believed that they didn't see her pass.

Keeping herself covered she step from compartment to compartment until she came to the dinning cart where Cornelius ushered her into a seat. Gillian followed her in to the booth, his form and size would help conceal her as she sat beside the window. Kathrie Gretel sat across from Marypat and Cornelius across from Gillian.

"Any one with appetite?" Cornelius asked as he pushed menus towards the others.

Gillian was the first to answer. "One must never refuse an opportunity to replenish thy hollow!" He quickly opened the menu and looked it over.

Gretel nodded her head, she too would take the opportunity to eat.

"And ye, Patty?" His voice was soft and he winked at Marypat.

She looked at him strangely for a moment and then she realized what he was doing. They were after all in public and they needed to be very careful. So, he had called her Patty, never before had he called her Patty. He called her Mary for short sometimes everybody did. But never Patty. So, Patty it would be at least while they were undercover.

"No, thank-you." Marypat answered sadly. She had not the want for food. She looked out the window and noticed that they were moving through the wonderful grassland of Silky Flats it was a beautiful sight.

"Ye must keep up yearn vigor. One must not take sadness as ye bounty. No, my sister feed thy empty stomach with ample sustenance. A Loralac never fails their stomach." Gillian preached.

"Let me order something for ye. Ye may eat what ye can." Cornelius mentioned with a fatherly tone.

Marypat nodded yes and when the waitress came to their booth to take their order, Gillian a lone filled her pad. Marypat watched as the Lachlanns face went from an angry frown to a beaming smile. She remembered how happy Lachlanns were when you gave them a lot of work. By the time she had finished taking their orders she was giggly.

"Now that's an order, I dare say. Well done! And I'll have it out for ye in a blink." She announced.

The waitress hadn't turned away when the tall man in his Stetson approached their booth and exclaimed.

"Cornelius ye old boot, I thought that was you waiting at the Tramp stop. Good to see ye old friend."

"Why Ace, I haven't seen you in pass's. How are ye and ye father?" Cornelius asked, as he pressed his hand into Ace Granger's huge coarse hand.

"Me dad's great, still kicking, ye knew him, full of life. Oh, Cornelius these dem my kin, this is me son Johnny and dis pretty dove is me daughter Carmen. Sings like a bird she does. We came into town for Carmen to sing last eve at the Blarney Stone, she done so good they want her to come back. Figure she's got a profession already and she's only 15."

Ace rambled on like the proud father he was. While Marypat realized she knew him. She had met him and his father Lee, back when she first travel to Great Town, before there was a Tramp. They had camped out and when she didn't know how to unroll her log roll, it had been Ace who had opened it for her. She also remembered hearing his voice that morning in Kathrie Gretel's shop. He was looking at dit nat potion with Kathrie Gretel's sister Gritty.

"Can ye imagine my little baby girl, singing for all those members, she wasn't even nervous nor anything."

"Why that's great Ace!" Cornelius replied genuinely happy for the child.

"Why Kathrie Gretel is that you under that cloak? Why I was just in your shop this morn, ye sister Gritty sold my one of your dit nat potions." Ace's voice sort of trailed off as Kathrie Gretel was not acknowledging him. He then turned and looked at the other two members traveling with Cornelius then he bend down and whispered.

"Is all well?"

"Yes" Cornelius answered softly.

"I sense a great hardship, one that will end bitterly . ."

Cornelius interrupted him. "Let us hope it doesn't come to that."

"Yes indeed, but if it should, you would but need only to ask and my brother Wardeens and I . . . ."

Again Cornelius interrupted "I know Ace, your members have always fought on the side of good you are indeed a good friend, but I assure ye that all is well."

Ace glanced around at the three other companions at the table. Then he looked back at Cornelius.

"Take Tag with you, he will not hinder your travels, if you find a need, he will know how to contact me."

Cornelius nodded his head and Ace called out. "TAG! front and center."

A moment later a tiny voice rose from the floor of the Tramp. "Yes sir."

Ace quickly explained to Tag what he wanted him to do and then handed the Frandies to Cornelius.

The Frandies was dressed in a dark tan leather jacket with fringes that hung down from his arms. He wore black leather slacks with a dark tan set of fringe trimmed chaps. The pant legs covered the neck of his Jack boots but the front and heel were well exposed to show the intercut design on the leather as well as his spurs. On his head he wore a matching tan leather Stetson that covered his head well, exposing no hair. His face also had no hair making him look quite young. But he stood very formally as though well experienced at his job with Ace. Cornelius looked him over quite satisfied with the member and then set the Frandies on the table and said good bye to Ace.

"Safe travel." Ace replied.

"And to ye, Ace." Cornelius answered.

The two shock hands and then Ace and his two children head toward the back of the Tramp.

The conductor then announce Middletown just as the waitress began bring their food and before long the table was packed with platters and bowls.

"Your orders sir." Came the little voice from the table.

"Have ye had ye fill?" Cornelius asked the Frandies.

"NO!" The Frandies answered most shocked at the question.

"Well then eat well, we still have far to go and one never knows what lies ahead."

Cornelius responded as he stuffed his mouth with a fork full of huff.

A Lesson in Magic

The Felden village on the Red Isle was a bustling town of adorable shops, rustic cottages and stone structures. The main road through the town was made of bricks that had been formed from the red soil that covered the isle. Many of the shops were also made of bricks which added to the old-fashioned look of the settlement and helped to give the town its name. Ridley, from the red meadow.

The settlement actually formed a 'c ' shape, as it incorporated a large cove that provided shelter to many large cargo ships, as well as several fishing vessels. The cove also housed a long pier where many members of the isle lingered during the turn. It was too dangerous to venture onto the red soil of the Isle. So instead they stayed on the safety of the wooden pier that had been constructed many passes ago for just that purpose.

The Feldens needed the other member of the isle to keep their Isle flourishing. The Red Isle had many valuable resources like blood coal, diamonds and fish. Yet they could not grow food on the isle and it had proven even more difficult to raise livestock. Without trade with the other isle's, they were doomed. That was why the town had spent much of their resource to build an enormous pier, grander than any other known among the isle's.

The pier stretched the entire length of the cove and formed a gigantic arch on the land. It was lined with shops and Inns on the right and warehouses, a weight room and finical offices on the left. In the middle of the arch sat an enormous old clipper that looked as if it had been blown a shore and now rested on the edge of the pier blocking the entrance to town. But in fact, it was not a ship wreck. It was the piers ship house where information, tickets and travel logs were handled. Beyond the three massed clipper ship was a wide thoroughfare that overextended out into the water. In the center of the thoroughfare was a tall white lighthouse made of the finest birch. The lighthouse sat in the very center of the cove and gave light out to the sea. It was also the center of most of the visitor's attention. It was after all the highest structure on the pier and many members clambered there to get a view of the forbidding Isle. On the first floor of the lighthouse was a restaurant, called The Bait House. It's well weathered green cast iron tables and chairs spilled out onto the deck that surround the lighthouse, making room for many visitors. The second floor of the lighthouse, housed The Rusty Bucket, a bar that continued up and around the spiral staircase and ended just below the landing for the huge light fixture that made the light. All along the staircase there were places to sit, drink and enjoy the view.

On both sides of the lighthouse were several smaller docks that spread out perpendicular to the main thoroughfare. These smaller docks housed small fishing vessels and personal crafts.

In all the pier was a modern marvel for many members. Even to Blaze who had seem Kingston harbor and the huge Merchantman Ships that traveled there to him Ridley Pier was in did a sight.

"This place is something. It is awesome to see some modern convinces, after living in that cave." Blaze said.

The entrance to the pier, Blaze found ratter tiring. He was still suffering with tremendous pains in his chest, that weaken him severely. The steep winding wood deck that lead up to the Ship house nearly did him in and he found himself needing a rest. Still he pushed forward with Godfrey to the information window where he found a long wooden bench and collapsed.

The bench was below two bulletin boards stuffed with transport information, Etain moments, flyers, and colorful posters. Beside the bulletin boards was the information window, which was one of the ships original portholes cut along the bridge.

While Blaze had a rest, Godfrey stepped up to the window. He stood there for a moment before the Felden behind the porthole spotted him. He seemed bothered when Godfrey appeared before him.

"Good ark arr" The Felden stutter, his usually greeting caught in his throat. It was extremely rare for a Sherideen to make himself known on the Red Isle. He was used to seeing all sorts of members, Hedlens, Wardeens, Loralacs and even Whimples, but never a Sherideen, never in the light of a turn and most certainly never a pair. The Feldens eyes bulged slightly nervous as to what the Sherideen might want of him.

"I should like to book passage to the Great Isle." Godfrey replied in his most calm voice.

"Great Isle?" The Felden remarked with a laugh. "There has not been a transport to that Isle in passes, Don't ye know it's no more?"

"I am aware of the claim, but my comrade here, has word that the isle has returned." Godfrey mentioned soothingly.

"Blarney, ye comrade a seaman then, been out on the high seas and lived to tell of the isles return has he. Well then where's his vessel and why are you not using it to gets to the Great Isle?" the Felden mocked. "Beside isn't the Blue Isle the land ye members inhabit?"

Godfrey's body shook, his eyes strained and his mind raced as the words echoed in his thoughts. "The Blue Isle, The Blue isle." Oh, how horrible the thought of it was. He had forgotten all the pain and misfortune of that place, why did this Felden have to bring up the Blue Isle. Godfrey had to fight back the horror he felt and concentrate on the importance of his task. He shook his mind free and set his eye's back at the Felden inside the porthole.

"Yes, my members inhabit the Blue Isle, but we should like. . ."

The Felden interrupted. "YAh, yah the Great Isle ye told me, and I told you there aren't any vessel, ship nor Etie captain willing to risk his ship or his life on ye comrade's fantasy. The only why ye could get one willing is if ye bought the ship out right and owned it ye-self, then ye can do as ye please."

With that the Felden slammed the port hole closed and locked it. Godfrey turned to Blaze who had heard the whole conversation. His eye's flickered with evil and his voice pieced the air as he struggled to his feet and lunged towards the port hole.

"Let me show him. . ."

"No brother, ye must not, not here, not now." Godfrey lectured as he pressed Blaze back on to the bench. "At least not now."

"Did you not here him laugh at us? Did you not hear the mocking tone he used? Surely that is enough to call me crazy, but I am not. You must believe me, Godfrey, The isle is there I know it." Blaze pleaded with him.

"Yes, I told you before I believe you. Do not worry about my convictions." Godfrey assured Blaze. But his eye were not on Blaze but on the bulletin boards above Blaze's head.

"Ye heard only his contempt, I heard something different, I heard him tell of a way off this Isle."

"You did?" Questioned Blaze.

"Yes, brother, and I believe this is our answer." Godfrey reached forward and pulled one of the brightly painted posters off of the bulletin boards. He reread the title out loud while Blaze sat amazed.

"1,000 Pyrite's to the Conquering Eggazor!" Godfrey handed the poster to Blaze who took a hold of it and turned the bright picture so he could read it.

"What is an Eggazor?" He asked.

"They are creatures that hatch from crystal eggs, some are foul like, some are trortle like and some are Zort like. There are many variations. The Feldens use them for entertainment, as you can see by the poster." Godfrey's eyes glanced down at the horrible scene depicted on the poster. It was a drawing of a huge white foul peeking the eyes out of a large yellow reptile creature. "They fight them in an arena for sport. Dreadful and delightful all at the same moment."

"But where will we get one of these Eggazors?" Blaze voiced painfully.

"Why you carry one with ye, in a transparent case and one most rare and deadly I am sure, for a Pretty Jaw it is." He answered.

Blaze dug into his backpack and pulled out the zip lock with the dead lizard like creature in it. He shook it once and then handed it to Godfrey.

"Deadly? Try dead."

"True my brother but if we had a wand, it could be summoned to our cause." Godfrey revealed. "If only we had a wand!" His lips formed a vile grin as he pretended to think about where he could get one while at the same time hoped that Blaze would recall that he held such an instrument and he did. Blaze smiled to Godfrey.

"But I have a wand."

"What? You?" Godfrey acted surprised. "Then all our troubles are over, brother, bring forth the wand and I shall teach you how to summon the Pretty Jaw."

Blaze dug into his bag once more and pulled out the opal tipped wand. He handed it to Godfrey. But Godfrey refused to take it. Not because he didn't want to, and not because he was trying to show he could be trusted, but because he had no power to use it.

"No, brother, you must." Godfrey's face fell. He wanted so badly to use the wand and change his circumstance but he could not. He knew also that he could possible strip the wand of its power just by touching it. So, he was resigned to becoming Blazes instructor and with it, he also hoped to gain Blaze's trust.

"What do I do?" Blaze asked innocently.

"First we must find a more secure place." Godfrey uttered looking nervously around the ship house. Anyone could have seen them with the wand, and that he could not afford.

"Let us go back to the cave." Godfrey smiled to himself. He was surely looking forward to the things they could do with a wand. All his passes living in this damp, smelly cave, with no powers, no help, was to end if Blaze could prove he was half of what Godfrey saw in him.

With that the two Sherideens struggled back down the deck and headed towards the high dunes of the shore line.

The dank smell of the lime stone cave filled Blaze's nose as he stepped past the burn remains of the fire. He was excited and nervous all at the same time knowing his was just about to learn magic, real magic. That was why he had wanted to come to the isle, he wanted to know things, he yearned to know the things his mother wouldn't tell him. Now was his chance.

He turned to Godfrey electrified. The pain in his chest seemed to disappear as he held the wand in his hand. It was as if his Sherideen half was comforted by the object and craved using it.

"What do I do Godfrey?" Blaze pleaded. He hadn't even allowed Godfrey a moment in the cave and already he was anxious to get started.

Godfrey demonstrated three basic wand movements with a broken stick he picked up from the ground.

"Dacular! " Godfrey explained as bent his elbow close to his side and gave a single thrust of his wrist as if he were pointing at something. Blaze followed.

"Good, now try Archular." Again, Godfrey demonstrated the move. He held his stick at his waist height and slowly raised it over his head and down again to form an arch. Blaze imitated it perfectly.

"Now try Hextacular." Godfrey held his stick ahead of him and slowly formed a resting figure eight. Blaze again obeyed the movement well.

After a short while Godfrey stopped. "I am quite satisfied with your ease of wand movements. You seem quite natural with them but now

I should like to test your strength. The first trial is a simple Sherideen task. One every Sherideen must learn while a babe in arm."

"With a Archular movement, repeat after me. KENNOW UH TIWNDLE RE TOK."

Blaze repeated the spell and moved the wand just as Godfrey instructed.

A swirl of red light escaped from the wand. The force of the magic caught Blaze off guard pushing him slightly off balance. He had to grab the wand with both hands to control it as it pulsed with power. When the spell was complete Blaze felt his chest, pain decline a bit. It was strange it was almost like his body grew strength from him using his powers.

Looking up, Blaze found the cave was transformed. The cave walls disappeared behind white plaster, the lime stone floor became clay tiles and the ceiling arched with white beams that supported three wicker panned fans. There were two matching comfortable couches on either side of a round glass table. There was a dining room table filled with all of Blazes favorite foods and surrounded by matching chairs. Behind the dining room sit the wall unit was filled with a TV., a stereo system, and several pots with peace lily's in them. There was a stair case that led up to a very messy bed room and bath. It looked just like Blazes home in Kingston. The furniture, his bed and clothing all looked as if they had been sucked throw the eye and brought here for him.

Blaze smiled it was home, he was thrilled. He quickly ran to the table and began eating a slice of piping hot pepperoni pizza.

"You have passed the test of strength but for now, we must try and summon the Pretty Jaw. Bring the creature." Godfrey announce from the couch while he bit into an orange crusted meat pie.

Blaze did what he was told and brought the Ziplock with the lizard like creature in it. He didn't know where it had come from or why he had it, but they needed it so he didn't question anything.

He laid the Ziplock on the glass table and turned to Godfrey who had devoured his patty and was looking as if he wanted another.

"Use the wand Hextacular." He said, pulling himself up. He headed back to the table of food.

Blaze did.

"Now say ' A TEX RE FINX OM PREE." Godfrey lectured firmly. His fingers danced over the plates in front of him, while Blaze repeated.

"A TEX RE FINX OM PREE.

Godfrey finally selected a round tan morsel and held it up to his nose before continuing the instruction. "DOMPRAY OMEE AT KAN DO TEE."

Again, Blaze spoke the strange language. With the last word spoken the wand spit a single white spark towards the creature. A moment later the creature's chest heaved and then sank, it heaved again and then it opened its eyes. Frightened it sprang to its feet and glanced around it surroundings. Weak at first it stumbled inside the clear plastic bag and then dropped to its knees. It was dying again and Blaze quickly realized there was no oxygen in the plastic bag. So he vaulted over to the bag and snapped open the lock. Air filled the bag and the little creature was soon breathing strong. Slowly as it felt stronger it looked up at Blaze, the one that had saved him and stared at him.

Blaze smiled "He's gona be OK. Are you hungry fella?" Blaze asked as he waved a piece of pizza in the air. He placed it in the bag and the creature jumped on it ingesting it in one gulp.

Blaze was amazed, it liked pizza. "Want some more?' Blaze offered it more and soon the little Lizard was climbing out of the bag making purring sounds like a kitten.

Once the three were full and content they collapsed on to the couches. Blaze on one with his new pet curled up on his lap and Godfrey on the other. They talked about many things, but mostly Godfrey sat listening to Blaze retell his mother's adventures on the Great Isle. It was late when sleep finally hit them and none of them moved again until morrow.

CHAPTER
10

Lake of Whispers

The salty mist of the Great Falls billowed over the wooden railling of the Lady K. It's moist beads gently clung to the faces of the five companions as they stood staring at her awesome form. They were lost in their own thoughts as if the Lake of Whispers had taken on the effects of the Lake of Froymin that surrounded the Regan's castle. The mist was soothing and refreshing while it cleared their minds long enough for them to hear the whispers of their own hearts.

<u>What Cornelius heard</u>:

Cornelius as always heard the whisper in an easy gentle breath as it called to him with the same verse. "Ride safe in my water for you know, you live your life well . . . ." He expected the last line to be, "In happiness you go," as it always was but this time it was different. This time the last line changed and as he heard the words his mouth dropped. "Keep faith as you go."

The lake had given him advice. "Keep Faith. Keep faith." The words kept repeating themselves over and over again. He held them firm in his mind and vowed to the falls in his own whisper. "I shall."

<u>What the Kathrie Gretel heard:</u>

For Kathrie Gretel the whispers came up on her in a flash and sent her reeling into Cornelius who said nothing. He merely reached his arm around her and steady her at the rail.

"Lost love for which you ache must heal for thy grandson's sake." The whisper came in an angry tone. As Kathrie Gretel heard the words tears came to her eyes she knew she was holding on to pain that she had convinced herself was because of Marypat. She glazed over to her but said nothing. In her heart she knew she would try and change, she would try and embrace her daughter in law.

<u>What the Gillian heard:</u>

Beside Kathrie Gretel stood Gillian who was listening mindfully to the whispers that filled his ears. His eye strained blankly out into the mist, his face made no expression as he heard what he knew he would. "No truer eye can see thy heart or fate. Ye realize what lay's ahead this date. Ye does know, yet ye shall still go."

He closed his eye then as if to confirm that he did know what lie ahead of them. He understood what was to happen, but still his choice was to his honor. He opened his eye after only a moment and then walked away from the group. He would not linger at the rail it made no logical sense too. He had heard what the whisper had to say. There was nothing more he needed to hear so he went below to find his compartment and to get some much-needed sleep.

<u>What the Marypat heard:</u>

Meanwhile Marypat stood at the wooden rallying listening carefully while the whispers tinted her with the same phase over and over. It was the same phase she had heard the only other time she had traveled the Lake of Whispers. That first summer with Donovan.

"Steady be as steady go, Steady be as steady go!"

The whispers repeated it and repeated it as if it were stuck. Marypat lowered her head convinced that that was all the falls could read from her heart.

"Yes" she thought, "I am steady and I shall stay steady until I will find him!"

Kathrie Gretel saw Marypat's pain. She turned to her and both women hugged.

"We will locate him!" Kathrie Gretel affirmed in Marypat's ear.

Cornelius then wrapped his arms around the two women. The three-companion stood on the deck on the Lady "K" in an embrace that gave each of them strength.

"Come now, let us go below and find our rest." Cornelius said as he finally let them go.

Both women nodded and began to follow Cornelius out of the billowing mist. But as Marypat turned to walk away from the railing her mind was filled with a jarring whisper, unlike anything she had ever heard yet it was clear and intelligible.

"Steady be as steady go, when you find him you will know, that home and heart is one in the same, but do not look for it by name." Then the voice escaped her ear, leaving her miffed about its meaning. She shook her head and cleared her thoughts. What the whisper had said hadn't made any sense to her. Of course, she would know her own son, she would know him by any name and she of all people knew that home and heart were the same thing.

The whisper had been a waste of time and now wasn't important to her. It was all just a silly game. Wasn't it? No one really took what was said to them seriously. So Marypat decided not to waste any more time on the ridiculous sounds of the lake. She washed the refrain from her mind and marched off towards the stairs.

She stepped down on to the first step and noticed the activity below. On the docks the Lachlanns and Wardeens were still moving cargo abroad. Among the crates was the wiggling one that had traveled with them from Bolder Town. It was still fighting desperately to get away. Marypat watched as a huge burly Wardeen wrangled it up. He threw it over his shoulder, climbed over the entrance plank and took it below to the cargo hold.

With that Marypat joined Cornelius and Kathrie Gretel in the hallway. They were already saying their good nights, so Marypat added hers and then they all disappeared into their separate cabins. Marypat glanced at her watch, realizing the time she quickly pulled out her talk about. She turned it on and spoke.

"Mom are you there?" click hissst.

"Yes, have you found him." hisssss. Lora voice was hopeful but Marypat's news was not what she wanted to hear.

"No, hissst, we need an Oritor to see where he is. click, click. We are travelling to a place that has one." Marypat answered optimistically while knowing she was up against great odds in just having approval to look for Blaze let alone use the Oritor to find him. It was very possible that the council wouldn't help her and would instead insist that she leave. They had the power to remove her. It was all going to be very tricky.

"Tomorrow then, click, same time?" Lora voice seemed mournful.

"Yes, tomorrow and mom. . . " hisssst .Marypat went on, she could feel her grandmother giving up and she couldn't bear that. "I will find him." click.

"I know, be safe, I love you." hisst

"I love you too, Tomorrow."

Marypat then laid back on her tiny bed and listened to the world around her.

All the many noises, shouts and movements soon ended on the docks and the Lady K was under way. She moves effortlessly through the misty water, with her baring set on Great Town Harbor just on the other side of the lake. But it would be morning before the Lady K pulled in to port. The eve was young but the five companions were tired. It had been a very long day and the morrow most currently would prove to be even more exhausting.

The morrow opened with a flash of great light. It flooded the tiny cabin Marypat had slept in. Washing over her with a jolt. She jumped from her stillness and quickly put on her sneakers and cloak. While she did she found herself thinking about her grandmother outside the crystal. She wondered if her grandmother had just changed all the flood bulbs in the front room. It seemed so much brighter this morn, but in truth is was just that the mist was no long bellowing over the ship and smothering the light. The mist was long gone back at the falls, back at Port Fin. The Lady "K' was now approaching Great Town Harbor.

Marypat could see the brilliant spotless harbor from her porthole. It was a beautiful sight. She went up on deck where she found, Gillian and Tag watching the deck hands ready the ship for port.

"Have you seen Cornelius." Marypat asked Gillian softly.

"Yes, he is arranging our transportation to the Palace." He answered in a gentle tone.

Tag was sitting on Gillian's left should, glanced down at the cloaked figure beside him. His voice was sharp but low as he made his declaration.

"Silent lip thou carry thy burden, yet know this fare one, ye are not alone on thy quest and one need not speak of discretion or thou custody."

Marypat's eyes searched the tiny face of the Frandies. His words were insincere and she understood their meaning. He didn't know nor would he ask what the secret was. He would however protect her. It was a gallant statement and Marypat respected it. She reached her hand up to him and shook his hand. Nothing more was said between them.

The three companions merely stood on the deck of the Lady 'K' and watched as the Wardeens tied down the ship and began removing the cargo.

While Marypat watched she noticed the crate that had traveled with them from Boulder Town being dragged out onto the polished dock.

The same huge strong Wardeen was holding the crate steady while three lovely Kathrieens all dressed in bright yellow tunics fussed over him.

"What's your name, buck?" The first Kathrieen cooed into his ear as she curled a lock of his long brown hair in her finger.

"Trista, control yourself!" The second Kathrieen bellowed. She pushed the first one aside and tossed her long curly hair over her shoulders before approaching the handsome Wardeen.

"He's all mine, I saw him first." Her voice was soothing and the Wardeen seemed mesmerized by the second Kathrieen. Even Marypat couldn't take her eyes off the stunning figure now standing eye to eye with the Wardeen. She had magnificent blue eyes that sparkled like the most perfect diamond. Her skin was milk white and her lips were rosy. She was just about to kiss the Wardeen on his lips and complete her spell, when the first Kathrieen grabbed a handful of her gorgeous long blonde hair and yanked her backwards across the dock.

With that the third Kathrieen interfered with a shoot from her wand to both of their heads. Instantly the two identical twin sisters were bound together by their long blond hair. The spell the third sister had put on them had caused their hair to be braided into one. Immediately the two sisters fell silent while the third one took control.

"Trista, Trixie, you are aware of our purpose here?" The third Kathrieen said as she stepped up to them. She looked just like them except she had dark brown hair and green eyes.

"Yes, Trini." The two replied as they struggled to be free of the other.

"Then allow this member to proceed with our parcel. Trixie, remove the amora-more charm." Trini commanded.

Trixie waved her hand towards the Wardeen with a most unhappy glance back towards her brown-haired sister. Instantly the girls' hair was released and the Wardeen stood up straight. He shook his head and rubbed his eyes. He didn't seem to be unset as he went back to work.

"Where to?" He asked the long brown haired Kathrieen, who smiled at him shyly and pointed to the awaiting carriage.

He strapped the crate onto the back of the carriage and then helped the three Kathrieen into it. Trini was the last to step into the carriage but before he let her hand go, he pulled it to his lips and softly kissed it. Trini blushed red while the two blonde Kathrieen roared angrily at her.

"Trini, how could you!"

A moment later the carriage pulled away. A moment later Marypat was being told it was time to go. On the dock two grand sliver carriages had pulled up where the three Kathrieens had just been and they were the carriages Cornelius had arranged to take them to the Maurieen Palace.

Meeting of the Council

T he sight of the Maurieen Palace was like a vision, sculpted magnificently into the countryside and nested among the soft foliage. Its sight was breathtaking and it was just as Marypat had remembered it with its brilliant silver towers caped in dark purple. It's five lilac buildings accented and trimmer in the same rich purple and its high arched entranceway made from crystal amethyst.

She smiled as they approached the entrance, it was like going home. This was where she belonged, these were her members. She felt their energy in her heart, her soul and her entire body. She knew that they, the Maurieens and Torideens, would no matter what, support her. The dread and worry that had filled her over what the council would reply was washed from her thoughts. She felted invigorated. With new found strength she stood and stepped out of the carriage.

Marypat glanced around from under her cloak expecting to see the young Colleens dressed in their pretty purple greeting dresses. But this turn they were not there to greet her. Instead Cornelius ushered her quickly through the entrance arch and into the wide-open mirrored lobby. Once there he assorted her to the far left of the lobby entrance and ducked behind the long crimson drape that hung there. Behind the curtain was a very small room. All of its walls were draped in the same crimson fabric. The only other thing in the room were four small wooden stools which Cornelius was quick to offer Marypat a seat on one.

"Stay here, we will return soon." He said sharply. He didn't mean to sound angry and Marypat understood the pressure he was now under, with her at hand. So, she did not confront him instead she did as she was told and sat down. "Gillian, Tag, stay here. . . " His voice trailed off as he made eye contact with the Loralac. ". . . You understand, what I ask?"

Gillian knobbed, he understood very well what his friend needed from him. He had known the moment she arrived at Cornelius door, two turns past. He among all of them understood why he was there. He was to protect her, and he would protect her with his life.

Tag also agreed and took his position across from Marypat on one of the stools. Sword in hand he stood his ground, while Gillian took up his post at the curtains entrance. He allowed only his eye to be outwards, the rest of his form was hidden by the long crimson curtain. From there he could see the entire lobby and he watched as Kathrie Gretel and Cornelius disappeared down a hallway on the far right of the lobby.

The moments appeared to tick by and it seemed like several sweeps had passed but in reality, it had only been a half a sweep when someone approached the curtain and asked to enter.

"I seek thy permission to proceed within." Came a masculine voice from beyond the curtain.

Tag jumped nervously from the sound and ready himself.

Gillian's right arm clenched his sword tightly and spoke.

"What business have thee?"

"Noble Gillian, do you not recognize thou own steward, Horatio?" Answered the voice softly.

Marypat jumped to her feet. "It's Horatio." A smile burst to her lips and she sprang towards the curtain. But Tag grabbed at her cloak and yanked her back. His tiny form didn't hold her for long but it was enough to stop her.

"Do you not recall the purpose you are here? Your son. Showing yourself now will not help." Tag pleaded.

Marypat lowered her head and sat back down on the stool. A moment later Gillian turned his face towards Marypat. He seemed most unhappy with his actions. He knew of the deep friendship, Marypat had with Horatio but he also knew he had to deny his entry. They could not take the chance; the cost was too great.

While Marypat sat waiting on her small wood stool, another sat waiting just across the wind-swept field that stretched the length of the back country of the Maurieen Palace. In fact, this member sat perched high above the palace with a clear view of its splendor. But in their eye, they did not find strength, no, to them the palace had always symbolized a failure. A miserable Sherideen disaster.

"Why master do ye let it tear at ye so. Shield thou eyes from its terrors glare and think not of ye brethren's fate." An orange cloaked figure pleaded.

"Leave me Verrill, I am weak from thee quelling." The figure declared wavering the other away. He stood then and stepped away from the balcony edge of the Pert. His long copper robe dragged behind him as he stood to his copper high back throne and throw himself into it as if he were tired of it. He slumped into a relaxed position in the chair and then shouted to a second Orange robed Sherideen. " Send me news from abroad."

"Yes master." Answered another member and he ran behind the copper curtain and brought forth a dry Oritor. Quickly he arranged it and filled it with purified water. He held his hand over it and it began to swirl and pitch.

"I see a great change, master." The Sherideen said with great surprise. "The isle. . yes.. It is the blue isle, it has returned."

The copper cloaked Sherideen gave out a great laugh. "Handrew, thank ye a laugh is well in need."

"No, master I do not jest, it is here among the waters of my gaze. Come and set eyes upon its glory!'

The copper figure stood and stepped over to the Oritor. He glanced down into its clear blue water and saw for himself that the long-lost isle had indeed returned to its rightful place.

"My brother, we must send a party to welcome them home."

"Yes, master Leopold!' Handrew remarked softly, "But master there is something else that I see . . ."

"What is it Handrew, tell me."

"A speck of golden fleck, see it there." Handrew pointed into the vat of water.

"Where, I don't see anything. Ye must be seeing things." Leopold shouted.

"It is there just above the Palace. It dances there like a tiny sprite, a glow for an instant and then unseen."

"What does it mean?"

"I do not know, never have I seen such a display, perhaps. . . it is a warning?"

"Indeed." Leopold uttered solemnly, all had been quite still since Ragnar's attempt to take over the position as Supreme Master Sherideen. But his failure and the fact the bangle no longer rested in the Pert had given the Ubil reason not to cause problems on the isle. They were no longer protected by the bangles power to absorb Hisue, leaving all of its members vulnerable to enormous pain and injury do to their actions. Life for the Ubil had become dismal, punitive and simply unbearable for most. Many Sherideens had left Cimmevian Town, there was no reason for them to stay, because it no longer protected them. There were so few Sherideens still within the confines of the Cinerin Mt's that there was no one of value left to rule the Pert.

Leopold Norwood, Kathrie Gretel's only birth brother, had taken the position for his own personal gain. Leopold was not a strong Sherideen. He had never amounted to more than an aid in his element. He had been passed over in previous openings for the position of Winds

Port's Master Protector. It was only because he was Gazpalding's brother in law that he had even had any position at all. But with no one of any true worth to hold the position, it fell into his lap and he couldn't resist the status.

In the eyes of the counsel Leopold Norwood had been a great leader, curbing the evil activity, suppressing the offensive moment to take over the isle and simply ruling his members with a firm and controlling hand. But in truth he just didn't have the ability to come up with a plan, let alone the fact that no one would follow him, even if he had one.

So, he sat at the Pert ruling an empty court, dreaming of the glory turns gone by and wishing for a sign that things were going to change.

"Perhaps this is the sign I have been waiting for!" He thought to himself. He was still gazing in to the water of the Oritor when Verrill came running up the stairs from the Kert.

"Supreme Master, Supreme Master, there is news ye must hear at once." Verrill shouted. He stood before Leopold and bowed. "My sisters, Trista, Trixie and Trini have come to make confirmation of what they have learned."

"Very well, bring them forward." Leopold announced. He walked away from the Oritor, with his mind still fixed on the shiny object in the water. He didn't even notice the Kathrieen emerge from the stairway and approach him.

The three-lovely young Kathrieen dressed in matching yellow, stepped forward and bowed.

Trini spoke. "Master please forgive our abrupt interference, but we have news from our father, who has been traveling in Finster."

"Go on, what is it." Leopold spat, he was bored already with them and he wanted to go back to studying the shine thing over the palace.

"Yes." Trini repeated as she bowed again. "Oh well, our father sent us this crate, within is a beast with the tongue of a Vaster. . ."

"So, what!" Leopold screamed as he threw himself into his copper high back chair. "Ye interrupt my survey, for a beast who has taken the potion coose-gotta-tongue? 'Tis not illegal ye know!"

"Yes my master. . but. . 'tis not that . . my father lay claim that this coose speaks of one fare Maurieen that ye may indeed be interested in."

"A Maurieen, I have no need for a Maurieen." He bellowed, "Why do ye bother me so?" He covered his face with his hands. "I am tired leave me."

Handrew who was standing beside Leopold was dumb founded by his master's response. Had he forgotten about the Maurieen who had taken from them their personal bangle and changed their lives. Handrew wasn't so eager to rush the Kathries away he wanted to hear everything they had to say so he quickly jumped forward and moved them and Verrill, out of ear shot of Leopold. Once he thought they were safe he turned to the Kathrieens and asked them to continue.

Trini looked and Handrew curiously. "Why do ye want to hear when the master does not?"

"He is a fool in a master's robe. I cannot tell ye how difficult it is to serve one so useless." He commented harshly. He glanced at Verrill and Verrill nodded in agreement.

"Fool is too kind, his more truthfully a moron." Verrill added.

"Word from ye father, Master Hyatt Radley, is mention enough that it is worth an ear. Please tell of his claim." Handrew insisted.

"Let the coose speak, sister, father said it would if thou hands are gentle." Trixie voiced as she smiled at Handrew.

"Very well." Trini replied.

Verrill opened the crate and untied the burlap sack that held the beast. A bright green Grundle's head shot out of the bag, its mouth tied shout and its horn broken into a nub. It blinked its bright green eyes and twisted its flame tipped ears as it glanced from member to member. He was scared and Andrew could see that if he didn't earn the coose confidence he would never learn his secret.

"It alright, I want to let you go." Handrew said gently. He slid his hand forward and allowed the big Grundle to smell his hand. Once the Grundle accepted the sent, Handrew slid his hand over the coose head and scratched him softly until he heard the coose begin to purr. With that he slid off the gag and allowed the coose to shack his head.

"Thank ye member, it has been no joy in this box though at first I found it fascinating, it has proven itself not." The Grundle said.

"I'm sorry ye had the misfortune, still before I let ye go, can thee tell me of a Maurieen known to thee?" Handrew asked.

"'Tis only one Maurieen I have ever had the decency of meeting. A fare and good Maurieen she is and as my father would agree, no finer a scratcher she be." The Grundle mentioned with a purr.

"Does thee know the name of this Maurieen?" Asked Verrill as it hit him who the Grundle might be speaking of.

"Marypat, she said her title be, and I discovered she was my father's pet. The one who gave him cause to speak, Oh the joy to know she has returned to us." The Grundle purred loudly.

Handrew stood up and stared at Verrill with a vile grin. "Is she, the one?"

"But they banished her, how. ." Verrill stuttered.

"Do not ask, brother. This is like a tantalizing crumb, not wanted by the Great Master, but desired by the roaches." The five grinned at each other.

"How will we find her?" Trixie asked twisting her hair in her figures nervously.

"I believe I already know where she is, she is at the palace as we speak. We must watch and wait until she is vulnerable then we will act. We will save her and force her to return the bangle. With the bangle we can restore the Ubil powers. In the meanwhile, we must organize what members we have left, inform them of our secret plan. We must trust that all of them will be willing to act. Go now and meet me later at the cove of elements." Explained Handrew.

"It is moment, bring her forward." Came a familiar voice from the other side of the crimson drape.

"We haven't a moment to waste."

Gillian drew back the curtain and knobbed to Tag, who jumped from his place on the stool and urged Marypat forward. Outside Marypat found Cornelius. His eyes were tied but he seemed full of energy as he waved the group on. He darted back across the lobby and down along narrow corridor lined with mirrors. When they came to the end of the corridor it opened into a large mirrored room. The room was circular. It had six mirrored doors each spaced evenly from the next and each one guarded by a council guard.

The mirrors gave the illusion that there were hundreds of guards in the room. Marypat found it more than nerve racking as she followed Cornelius up to the 4th door from the right. She feared that if they discovered her, that they would arrest her. So, she pulled her cloak tightly around her face and stuck close to Gillian. But the guard never even looked at her. His eyes never waved from their stare far above the group's head. Instead he stepped aside easily allowing the four companions to pass through the door.

On the other side of the door was another long narrow corridor. This time though the walls were crystal clear and it seemed to slop downwards gradually until they entered a second large round room. In this room there was a single wooden table with a bright red vase on it, in the center. The walls were draped in dark purple silk and on the walls near to the floor where dozens of painting. There was a painting of a table leg, a painting of fresh green grass, and several paintings of chairs. Not one of them was fit for a gallery but Marypat suspected that this was no gallery of art, but instead a gallery of Realagraphs. Which Cornelius proved right when he stepped through a painting of an old broken chair.

The group quickly followed and found themselves in a third-round room. This room was small and had only three Realagraphs on its walls. One was a painting of a large clay pot with huge red kitty tails stuffed in it, one was a painting of desk and the last was the one they had just step through, a painting of an old wooden table with a bright red vase on it.

Again, Marypat was urged to move on and she was quickly taken through the long black curtain, they covered the entrance to the small room. On the other side of this curtain Marypat saw for the first time the enormous round council chambers.

Within the chambers, Kathrie Gretel was waiting for them. She signed to Cornelius and he gently maneuvered the group to a long bench, that sat along the back wall. Marypat took her seat on a fluffy yellow pillow and glanced around the room. It was dark and there were few members milling about but she could still make out the layout.

The Chamber seemed to be like a large arena with benches lining the walls. The benches were broken into four bleachers like structures. The main one took up one third of the chamber and had only two lines of seating. The other three bleachers were smaller than the first but were equal in size to each other and had four lines of seating. The lines of seating were topped with comfortable pillows and cushions all of different colors and sizes. In front of each group of bleachers was a podium and in front of the podiums, in the center of the room where the four elements of tradition. The elements each had their own diamond shaped pedestal and sat down in a well, out of the way.

While Marypat studied the chamber, several members of the council began to enter and take their seats on the main bleachers. Cornelius stooped over Marypat then and whispered a description of each member.

"The Gulden is Hazel, she's been with the council only a pass of two. She sounds willing to help."

Marypat sat and said nothing. She nodded her head as he went on.

"Moiré O'Neal, representative of the Feldens. She doesn't trust anyone, but that's her nature. Remember if we can earn her trust, we can sway her, vote. Those two are, Kipp Gee of the Kandies and Andies, and Egan of the Frandies. They're with us. No Kandie or Frandies I have ever met would fear a good fight. It's the Ulldens and the Lachlann that will give us the most trouble, they dispute that you are of fraud. Constance Regan, sister to the Ruling Regan is on the Head Council. See her there." Cornelius pointed to a short dark-haired Lassie Lachlann who was talking to Moiré O'Neal. Marypat knobbed her head while Cornelius continued.

"The pretty Lassies is Maurie Louise, you met her once she was a Greeter here. Remember?"

Again, Marypat knobbed. She did remember her.

"Any way I get the impression she liked you, but as Colleens go they prefer to avoid confrontation. So, we need to still win her vote. Now that's Tantan of the Whimples, Warwick of the Loralac and Ullus of the Ulldens, they are also with us I hear as well as Orida, who you know and Cobb Axel of the Wardeens."

Suddenly a fluff of blue flew in from behind the black curtain, leaving two Teenys struggling with the drape. Gillian noticing the struggle and quickly pulled open the curtain to reveal two small members. He bowed to them slightly and they huffed angrily at him.

"Did you see her?" They asked him.

He nodded yes and they huffed again.

"And they claim we are sister!" Shouted one of the Teenys as she straighten her long fluffy pink dress. "The way she goes on, you would think she was the Regan!"

The other Teeny beside her agreed with a nob.

Gillian said nothing. He just stood there tall holding back the drape and waiting for the two Teenys to move away from its grasp.

While Cornelius continued his introduction "The blue blur is Peep Joy, wood Etain, she could go either way. The two Teenys in the drape are Blossom Bud a Pixie and Clover Samuels a Daxie. Both older members they are sure to vote against. They always vote with the Regan. That leaves Hildegard Lamont, Hedlen, an easy no and Rowan Lazarus, the only Sherideen on the counsel. There's no telling how he will vote. But I don't see either of them yet. And they won't start until all are seated, so we can relax for the. . . oh wait that's Rowan there."

An utterly tall thin, dark haired Sherideen stepped up to the bleachers and stopped beside Constance. He shock her hand and she giggled slightly as he made conversation with her.

"I didn't know Ubil was allowed on the council?" Tag asked from beside Marypat. She had wondered the same thing but was afraid of speaking out loud.

"True, but he is not Ubil. He's a Sherideen that never took his Sherite Extolel. Apparently, his mother a Kathrieen by the name Edna had him blessed at the Cascades instead and in doing so, he has not the powers of a Sherideen but that of a Wardeen. I had heard that something had happened to his father, I'm not sure what, but I do know that his mother was adamant that Rowan, not join the Tribune. So instead he is a member of the counsel, hardnosed I hear. As you can see he's with the Regan's sister, I can imagine we won't win him easily."

Marypat knobbed again.

There was a commotion on the other side of the chamber. It came from behind another long black curtain. Several gasps, a smash and a shriek. The noise brought Gillian and Tag to their feet. In an instant they were ready to protect Marypat at all cost.

The Colleen on the counsel, Maurie Louise, had first turned her attention to the drape as everyone had but quickly Marypat found her glance back on Gillian's tall form. Her face frown as Gillian grabbed the handle of his sword and stood in a defense position. Marypat noticed as well that the Colleen was looking at her with a most serious glare. This made Marypat's thoughts race as to what the Colleen might do.

Beside the Colleen was Warwick a Loralac. The Colleen turned to him and squeezed his arm. He glanced down at her and then at Gillian.

"All is well sister, he is my Cousin Gillian of Finster. Ye will soon learn of his intention, and they are of good." He assured the Colleen.

The Colleen then glanced away allowing Marypat to breathe again.

The commotion behind the curtain calmed and Gillian sat down still on edge as he waited for the members to come from behind the curtain. Soon the member revealed themselves. But it was not what Cornelius or Kathrie Gretel had expected or wanted. The Chief Counselor Sanborn Regan had travelled to out Bend on the break and insisted that the Regan, Quinton Randolph Regan the three, himself attend the proceedings.

Dread filling Cornelius, there was no hope. With the Regan himself leading the council they were sure to fail.

Moments later Sanborn stood and called all attending to sit and be well.

"Good turn, brothers and sisters of the isle, I am rightfully pleased to have my brother Quinton with the counsel this turn. Let us greet him well." Sanborn declared.

There was an unfamiliar roar as the members sitting in the three smaller bleaches echoed forth a greeting. To which the Regan bowed slightly.

"Let us move to the matter at hand, Kathrie Gretel, a member of the Een guild has a quarter sweep, Kathrie Gretel are you prepared to take the podium?"

"Yes." Kathrie Gretel answered from the podium that stood directly across from the council.

"You may proceed." Voiced Sanborn. Sanborn took his seat beside Quinton as Kathrie Gretel began.

"Good turn to all. It is with great regret that I appear before ye and ask for thy aid." Her voice saved for a moment as she thought about her next statement. She knew it would not be easy for her to say or for the council to hear. It might even end the proceeding and she had misgivings about the wording. Causally she continued, " Two turns ago a Pattie child fell to isle and is now lost."

Kathrie Gretel held her breath expecting the council to attack her. But only a few of them began to speak among themselves the rest sat dumb from shock. They knew of only one other member who had fallen to the isle and she had been banished more than 10 passes earlier.

"The child is endanger of discovery, if he is found by the wrong hands, the isle too will be. . ."

As she spoke the council members murmur became so great that Kathrie Gretel had to stop.

"Get to it Kathrieen." Shouted the Hedlen Hildegard Lamont. Hildegard's voice was a terrible shriek. Her hands were shaking and her face turned red. She was in a panic and it was apparent that she knew already the outcome of her questions. " Ye dance around the true point, why should we fear for the isle? Who is this child? Tell me the truth Kathrieen. Who do you protect there?"

Hildegard jumped to her feet and pointed at Marypat as she sat on her yellow pillow cloaked in black. "Who is that? Tell us now."

Rowan the tall Sherideen gently reached forward and held Hildegard's shaking shoulders. He whispered something in her ear and she slowly sat back down beside him. Then he spoke.

"Ye may proceed.

Kathrie Gretel nodded her head and searched the other councilmember's eyes for anyone else that might jump forward as she tried to continue.

"It is true I protect the member cloaked in black, but I do this not to hide anything from you. I will reveal to ye the identity. But first I must make clear to ye that this member didn't want to come here, but had to come. To protect the Isle. The Isle is in great danger if we do not find the child."

"Why?" Shouted Hildegard nervously. "Who is the child?"

"The child I speak of is this members child." Kathrie Gretel revealed.

With that Moiré O'Neal and Constance Regan jumped to their feet. "Show us who you protect, show us now." The two Lassies whaled.

"Enough, sister take your seat." Quinton demanded as he stepped forward and approached the podium. Moiré and Constance took their seats but continued to stare in Marypat's direction.

"Ye say this member has come to protect the isle?" Quinton asked calmly.

"Yes." Kathrie Gretel answered.

"Then why does she fear to show us her face?" Quinton asked diplomatically.

"Because she is not wanted here, there are those among ye that fear her."

"Why is she unwanted Kathrie Gretel?" Quinton continued.

"She was banished from the isle." With Kathrie Gretel's words the three Commoners began to fuss again.

"I see, and for her to come here now, is certain death for her. But still she comes. She must believe the situation to be very serious for her to risk her life." Quinton speculated.

"Yes."

"Tell me, why?" Quinton asked softly.

"The child is the son of Donovan Gazpalding."

The entire chamber went silent, there wasn't a sound.

"The child is then a Sherideen?" Quinton continued.

"We believe he is." Answered Kathrie Gretel.

"Has he been washed, and blessed." Became a nervous voice from behind Quinton. It was Rowan the Sherideen and he now looked more nervous than any in the council.

"No." Answered Kathrie Gretel.

Rowan stepped forward. "He is new to isle?"

"Yes."

"Then he would be new to his powers also." Timidly Rowan walked up to Quinton. He whispered to the Regan and both members grew solemn. After a moment Quinton turned back to Kathrie Gretel and asked.

"This is uneasy news, but still it doesn't give cause for the council to approve of this member coming here and fathomer for us to help her."

Kathrie Gretel was shocked at their response declaring the son of Gazpalding would warrant their help. Her face went flush and she stood there un able to move.

"Let us move on then." Sanborn replied. "The next order of business."

Marypat had hoped that the council would help her without her having to reveal the true worry she carried about her son. But now she would have to come clean, she would have to tell them everything. She jumped forward and reached Kathrie Gretel just as she stepped away from the podium.

"Please Kathrie Gretel there is more I must tell them. Please ask to speak again."

Without hesitating Kathrie Gretel turned back to the podium and spoke aloud.

"Good council, I must ask to speak . ."

"Your quarter sweep is spent." Sanborn answered unmoved by the request.

"Then I beg each guild to render for me." Kathrie Gretel turned to the members of the other guilds.

Within moments she heard their replies.

"I Forrest of the Jinxie's relinquish my quarter sweep."

"I Grace of the wood Etains relinquish my quarter sweep."

"I Kennard of the Dandys relinquish my quarter sweep."

"I Baldric of the mighty Ulldens relinquish my quarter sweep."

All around her the other guilds were relinquishing their moments in front of the counsel for her. They were behind her, she could feel their energy fill the room and with a new strength she turned back to face Sanborn and made a second request.

"With your permission I shall proceed."

Sanborn could say nothing; the guilds had given her the floor. He had to allow her to speak.

"Good council, the member before you now must reveal something of importance, will you allow her to do so.?" Kathrie Gretel's voice echoed through the room.

Quinton waved his hand and Marypat stepped forward. She walked to the edge of the pit that held the four elements and then proceeded down the three narrow steps to the base. Once her feet hit the white tile floor the pit began to raise until it was fully extended above the floor of the chamber.

Marypat walked to the center of the floor and laid out her hands in front of her. She then turned to the first element, air. She placed her hand into the small whirlwind that balanced on the vat of purified water. The whirlwind sparkled at first and then began to glow. Gently she balanced it on her hand as the glowing warmth filled her body. Carefully she removed the whirlwind from the vat and then stepped over to the next element, water. The pillar had a miniature water fall suspended in the center of it. With her other hand she slipped her fingers into the flowing water. Instantly the water reacted and shot into the air, falling back on her like a blue mist. Holding the water in one hand and the wind in the other the council chambers suddenly filled with a flurry of distressed voices. No member before had been naturally drawn to more than one element. There was only the old prophesy that spoke of one holding the touch of all four. But that was a legend it had never happened.

Now before them Marypat stood holding two. She placed her hands together forcing the water to mix with air. The combination caused her inner glow to change to a radiant green color and the mist to swirl around her. With her hands free she stepped over to the element, Fire. On that pillar was a blazing red glowing fire, she placed her hand into in. Instantly the soft mist turned violent, crashing lightning grew out of nowhere and the soft green glow of her body turned to a fire red. With her hand she carried the flame back to her chest and laid the flame upon it. With a flash she now stood before them engulfed in flames. Blasting like nothing they had ever seen before, Marypat stepped over to the final pillar and held both hands out to the crystal that laid there in the center. She picked it up and held it. As she did she burst into a shower of bright, intense light.

The room filled with panicked voices bellowing from the sight of such increasable power. But not one member moved, they sat transfixed as they watcher horrid. Slowly Marypat drifted forward while her feet lifted above the floor. She hovered just in front of the council and spoke her finally words.

"See what power mine possess? " Marypat's voice rose in an angry tone and filled the chambers with an eerie chill. "The vision in the Vista's eye was clear beyond a doubt, that one shall come, born not of the isle. He shall walk among us as any one might, yet he is unknowing the power in his touch and given this, his choice is yet his own. Waver he many between the good and bad but this point is but true, given to the evil ways the isle is doomed."

"Be guarded and beware of such a member who many step across thou path. A member drawn to all the elements and Holds the Touch of Four." She went on. "Do not turn thou back on him, as ye did me. For this power I do hold.. . " Her eyes flared forward towards the members of the council. "Is within him, 10-fold."

Her flaming body hovered above the council for a moment longer. While Cornelius and Gillian slipped ahead of her.

Cornelius spoke to her an easy tone. "Let them go now, Mary, give them to me."

Gillian raised his hands and catch her lifeless body just in time as she let the powers of the elements leave her and enter Cornelius. Easily Cornelius slipped each element back on to their rightful pillars and then followed Gillian back to the bleachers where they had been sitting.

Anxiously Sanborn stood, his voice cracked as he tried to take control of the proceeding. But there was such a commotion that arouse that he had to call to his brother Quinton to silence the room.

"Silence NOW!" demanded Quinton. "The council must take a vote, we need silent to proceed. If the guilds cannot silence themselves they will be asked to leave."

A hush fell on the chamber and with-it Sanborn took to his feet in front of the podium and called for a vote.

"The call will be, Yay, we will, nay we will not help locate the Child." His voice was stun.

"Feldens representative Moiré O'Neal?"

"Nay."

"Lachlann representative Constance Regan?"

"Nay."

"Hedlen representative Hildegard Lamont?"

"Nay."

"Daxies and Naxies representative Clover Samuels?"

"Yay"

"Yay? I'm sorry, Clover I didn't hear you correctly, did I?"

"The Daxies and Naxies vote yay!" He said clearly.

Stunted Sanborn, tried to recover but stuttered as he continued to called out the representative. "Pixies and. .?"

"Yay."

Sanborn's face dropped, it was obvious that he was upset by the answers of Yay.

"Etains and Laddies?"

"Yay"

"Ulldens?"

"Yay."

"Torideens and Maurieens?"

"YAY!"

"YAY!"

"Loralacs?"

"yay"

"Whimples?"

"Yay"

"Frandies and Krysdies?"

"YAY"

"Kandies and Andies?"

"YAY"

"Guldens?"

"YAY"

"Sherideens and Kathrieens"

"Yay"

"Yay"

"Colleens and Wardeens"

"YAY"

"Yay!"

With the last council members vote complete. Sanborn stood behind the podium dumbfounded. He was lost in thoughts of denial. He did not wish to help Marypat, he had hoped that once the council had voted "Nay" that they would arrest her and her companions. But the vote had been Yay. Yes, they wanted to find the boy and Sanborn did not know what to do. He stared out at the guilds, with sweat dripping from his brow and said nothing.

"What is the vote?" Cry someone from one of the guilds. "Let us hear the tally."

Sanborn didn't answer, he fumbled through his stack of papers which he did not complete when the vote was called. But he didn't have to answer for the entire room knew the tally. Even Quinton knew. He too did not like the outcome of the vote but he also knew that something had to be done, someone had to speak and if his brother Sanborn had not the strength then he the Regan would have to.

"Three nay to twelve yay." Quinton answered loudly so all could hear. The room went silent as they watched their leader stand and remove Sanborn from the podium so that he could address them.

"The vote is clear that most of the representatives of the council trust that the Maurieen is telling us the truth and with this vote I must then allow her to travel freely to search for her son. The only question left then, Kathrie Gretel, is how the counsel can aid thee?"

Constance gasps and turned to Moiré. Both listened in horror as the Regan extended an open request.

"My good Regan," Kathrie Gretel expressed with relief. "Our request is but small. We require the use of the Oritor."

"A quite reasonable appeal." Quinton replied with a nod of his head. His short stern body then turned to his left as he continued "Orida can it be prepared within the sweep?" he asked.

The tall form of Orida Nnon Frothper the 3rd stood and bowed. His voice was strong as he revealed. "Yes Regan, it stands ready."

"Very well then, we shall meet in the Observatory in one sweep, Constance, Moiré and Hildegard you will be excused from the proceedings. All other members of the council will be expected to attend. I shall now call this meeting of the council closed until after the reading of the Oritor."

With that the room back into conversation and movement. Some members dodging out of the Council Hall and behind the long curtains, some sat fixed to their seats engulfed in deep discussion about what had just occurred. There were some like Constance and Moiré that were horrified. Their voices seemed the shriek and tremble as they recount the sweep. But most were not terrified. Most were compassionate and genuinely concerned. Many stopped and spoke to Cornelius and Kathrie Gretel. They passed on words of wisdom, wishes of welcome and blessings of visions and speed.

Finally, Orida approached Cornelius. They spoke for a moment and then the group followed him out of the Council Hall. They head back through the curtain and in to the painting of the old table with the red pot on it.

The Observatory

The observatory was already filled to capacity when Orida entered with Cornelius and party in toe. The Moderately sized room was a hexagon shape. All eight walls were heavily draped in navy blue curtains. While the ceiling seemed to be open to a never wavering evening sky. The floor of the room slopped gently downwards until it reached the center where it evened out to a flat surface. On the flat surface sat the only one purpose of the observatory and that was to accommodate the Oritor. The Oritor was positioned directly in the center of the room on a stone pillar. It measured Eight hands across and was large enough to reveal the entire Great Isle in one reading.

Wasting not a moment Orida approached the Oritor. Sanborn and Quinton were already positioned beside the large vat. They watched as Orida laid his hands out above it and spoke softly, "Vic Son Free."

The vat of purified water vibrated gently and then went still again. Orida turned to Quinton and nodded.

"It is ready!"

"Come near all and see as the child is revealed to me." Quinton called out.

The crowd of members moved in closely around the Oritor. Everyone wanted to witness the findings.

Orida bent down to Marypat, his voice was a whisper as he instructed her. "Bring forth ye wand and place only it's tip within the liquid."

"Can ye not use yours?" Marypat asked faintly.

"'Tis best if thou who yearn, a mother's bond 'tis stronger than any other. Besides the Predom Excel has the power to eliminate any false hopes." He answered with concern in his voice.

Marypat's eyes filled with fresh tears and she stared hopelessly into Orida's stern face.

"The boy travels with my wand." She revealed painfully.

Orida closed his eyes it was clear to Marypat that he was not pleased with the added news. It was certainly bad enough that the grandson of the evil Gazpalding, a new and powerful Sherideen was lost and could be manipulated by evil. But now he even had the unauthorized use of the Predom Excell, the most powerful wand ever constructed in all the isle. It's mixture of Seppentinite and Torbernite, both petrified and mingled held the illumine magical feather of a Sandchurt and the spiritual essence of hollowed Ones. The Predom Excell was no simple wand it had been created for Marypat with her own possessions as a gift of thanks from the Regan, Stanhope the 2nd, Quinton's father. It had even been topped with a blue fire opal, Marypat's power gem.

The Lachlann that crafted it, Rayburn Hurst feared its force and pure power. He had warned the council of it, though at that interval no one took the warning seriously, Orida now worried it had fallen into the wrong hands. He opened his eyes and looked down at Marypat. His lips pulled tight as he spoke again to her.

"Take mine."

Marypat took the thin wooden wand from Orinda's out stretched hand and place the tip of it into the vat of water.

"Use a Granular motion, three times to wide while repeating, Hail Sec to Mor Gran, Blaze, Toman. Then remove the wand." Orida instructed her.

She did as she was told and as soon as the wand tip slipped out of the liquid the entire Great Isle came into focus in the Oritor. Quickly Orida, Sanborn and Quinton searched the isles reflection but there was no indication of the one they had called to locate. They could not find the boy.

"Call again" Quinton urged Orida.

Orida took the wand from Marypat and called out "hail Sec to Mor Gran, Blaze, Blaze Toman!"

But still there was no glimpse of the boy.

"What does this mean?" Marypat question nervously. She was certain her son was here. She had thought that it was going to be so easy, they would see where he was and she would just go and collect him. But now they couldn't see him with the Oritor. Was it not powerful enough, was Blaze unreadable?

"Is it not strong enough?"

"Yes, I believe it is, but it can read only the Great Isle." Orida attempted while he still studied the vat of water. "Are ye certain of his intention to travel, here?"

Marypat stood without an answer for Orida.

"Perhaps he has ventured elsewhere!" A strong masculine voice added from over Marypat's shoulder. She did not recognize the tall handsome Dandy that stood over her. He had fare yellow skin and bright blue eyes. His hair and beard were dark gray, both were neatly trimmed to show off his distinguished dandy ears. He was indeed respected among the council it showed in his confidence and voice as he continued to speak freely. "The isle is now complete is it not? Did thee not tell of its reclaim just last eve?"

"Yes" Orida confirmed "But I do not see how that is important at this junction."

"Don't thee?" Question the Dandy. "I am told by one of knowledge that this child from the outer world is the one that brought us our missing isle's. It was at his hands that our world is now one again. Is this not true?" He asked Marypat.

"Yes, he was the one that found the second half." She made known.

"Then I believe he has ventured beyond our view, he has but many an isle to choose and we must make visible more than our own land of the Great Isle!' The Dandy declared with a firm tone.

"'Tis True, the Kennard speaks with a wise tongue." Quinton mentioned.

"Orida can thee make known the rest of the isle's?"

"No, my Regan, this Oritor eye, sees only the Great isle. One would need the power of the Vista to see all of the lands." Orida conveyed.

There was silence among the crowd until the Kennard spoke again.

"Then we must travel to the vista." He said looking confidently at Quinton.

"That is the rightful path, but am I to believe Kennard that Ye are willing to hold position on this venture?" The Regan asked strangely.

"Yes, I am willing. The importance of this, child's well-being and the well-being of our isle lays precisely to my position, therefore I make my application."

"Very well then, I shall leave you in command, Right Honorable Kennard. Make ready ye plan and all entry will be available."

Marypat glanced from face to face, had she heard them correctly. Was this perfect stranger willing to help her find her son, was he taking control and had he opened the door for her to travel anywhere she needed to find her son.

She looked up at him and he smiled at her. His face was gentle and calming.

"Do not fear, Maurieen, we shall find young Blaze and all will be well."

In his face she found peace, his voice relaxing, confident and for the first time since she had left her grandmother's side she felt at ease.

The Regan dismissed the group and instructed the Kennard to move swiftly. With that the crowd dispersed and Marypat was ushered into a small room beside the observatory. Iola was there and she greeted Marypat with a hug.

"All will be well, sister." She assured Marypat. "Orida tells me, the Kennard plans to move within the sweep and we haven't but this moment to speak. So, I am hurried to welcome ye, but know that given proper space I would have wished ye to stay."

"I know, and I thank-you." Marypat answered "Iola, would ye please do me a favor?"

"I would, what might ye need?"

"I had hoped to see Horatio, but the moments are not. ."

"Of course, my dear. Do not say another word, I will see him . . ."

But that was all that was said between the two, for they were abruptly interrupted by the Kennard, Cornelius and Kathrie Gretel.

"We must go." The Kennard stated. His large form was nearly two times that of Marypat, shadowing her as he approached.

"Be well." Iola called to Marypat as the group escorted her down the narrow hall.

A few moments later they were in the Spit cock Receptacle at the palace.

Gillian and Tag were waiting with what looked like supplies. Cornelius and Kathrie Gretel quickly took their place next to Gillian while Marypat questioned where they were going.

"To the Vista. Remember the tale, The Caves of Ebon?" Answered Cornelius in a soft reassuring voice.

Marypat nodded her head yes as she watched the Kennard. He was busy speaking to one of the Cock-Spit controllers. His face was firm while the short round Lachlann dressed in Navy-blue overalls looked confused and then ran off suddenly.

Cornelius was uninterested in the Lachlanns confusion and continued his explanation. "Well, the vista is the secret treasure of the Caves. But I'm afraid that the Spit cock will not get us entirely to the Vista itself. No, the Spit cock will only get us part of the way. We will have to travel by foot the rest, hence the supplies." He went on while Marypat continued to watch the Kennard as he marched back and forth awaiting the return of the controller.

"I have never been there myself but Gillian has a brother who has been a protector there for many passes."

"Yes, and I should think best that he should do most of the negotiations. Dealing with that sort is most difficult, I assure you." Kathrie Gretel added nervously.

"What is thy meaning?" Gillian interrupted.

"No harm, Gillian. I just mean that Loralacs understand each other. The protectors are your members. It is best that ye do what needs to be done." Kathrie Gretel retorted.

There was a loud bang above their heads abruptly cutting off all conversation. Marypat recognized the sound and realized that the huge cock was in place. The controller returned then. He quickly repeating the destination to the Kennard and ran towards the group ushering them closer. Satisfied the Kennard joined the party and stood beside Cornelius who was back to explaining the Vista.

"Thinking on I must remind thee of the three questions, my dear." he was saying while the Controller hollered over him.

"Party of 6 Vasters, 1 Teeny to Emerald Pass."

"Do you recall the test?" Cornelius was asking Marypat, but Marypat wasn't listening to Cornelius. Her mind was busy trying to recount the members of the party. She had only counted five Vasters and one Teeny. Why had the Lachlann called for six?

"I believe that you my dear will need to answer the three questions in order for ye to use the vista..." Cornelius went on, his voice was just a buzz in Marypat's ear as she watched the controller recount the members of the party.

"Where is the sixth?" He shouted at the group.

But only the Kennard understood the pause and answered unnerved. "He is delayed but will soon arrive."

"We have no moment to wait, the cock is set." The controller hissed in a panic.

"Ye do not understand the repercussions of a mistake in quantity. Ye Vasters have no understanding of science of spit or the dangers involved here!"

"Make no mention, for I do understand the danger, honorable Lachlann." Replied the calming voice of a tall clocked shadow that appeared behind the frantic controller. "Now, prepare the spit, for all are set."

With that the clocked figure stepped forward and joined the group standing on the drain. He stood just in front of Marypat with his back to her while the controller ran off shouting.

"Stay within the drainage area, ready the spit!"

The wooden balcony just ahead of them began to vibrate and rattle.

"Dom dee pat." A voice called.

Then Marypat could hear the giant footsteps on the balcony above her. They scratched the wooden floor as they came toward her.

"Hoc to." The same voice called out.

And then came the "HO", the slippery thick sound of the "ho." Marypat looked up and watched the milked substance fly above her and then hover just above them all. It hung there for a moment while it formed a perfect circle. Then it fell on them with a heavy gush, covering every spec with its warm, wet goo. Slowly it slipped over them until it touched the drain and they all disappeared.

Marypat felt the ground below her change. The firm feel of the drain was replaced with the soft bounce of dry fallen needles from the Blue fur pine and the thick growth of trortle moss that now laid below her feet. She was standing in a thick grove of Orange Prickly Chestnut trees and Blue Fur pine that were surrounded by Henmax Plants well blossomed in bright yellow, at the foot of the Emerald Mountains.

Standing there she felt a gentle breeze blow across her face and the scent of the Orange Prickly Chestnut mixed with Henmax fill the air. She opened her eyes and saw for the first time the magnificent sight of Emerald Pass. The pass was a huge archway cut into the side of the Emerald Mountains. It seemed an easy venture but she quickly reminded of the dangers ahead by Kathrie Gretel who seemed all too familiar with its sight.

"Don't let this clear, clean archway fool ye, Marypat, the turns ahead are no less then perilous." She mentioned as she pushed passed her and entered the archway. Marypat followed and soon found that the moss-covered ground died off under the arch and exposed a slippery crystal base.

"Watch ye footing, Maurieen, there are razor edged cliffs ahead that are not readily seen by the eye." The clocked figure remarked as he strolled pass her leaving her alone to follow the group.

After several sweeps the group seemed to slow and Marypat finally caught up. Only to find the reason for their delay was a very narrow ledge that span an abyss. Gillian with Tag, Cornelius and Kathrie Gretel were already across. The cloaked stranger was still straggling the gap when Marypat approached. She watched as he easily maneuvered though the opening and with one last vault he landed on the other side. As he landed his cloak fell away revealing his face. It was the Sherideen, Rowan from the council. How strange Marypat thought it was that he should come along. But even more peculiar was that he was hiding himself from her. But why?

Her thoughts were interrupted by the Kennard who had instructed her to go.

"Slide your foot along the edge and use the rope line as a guide for your hands." His voice was firm but at the same time it filled her with confidence. She stepped up to the ledge, grabbed the rope and slowly started across. But half way through her right foot slipped free and she stumbled. She grabbed tightly to the rope and tried to pull herself back to the ledge but it was no use she had not the strength to pull her own weight back up. Horrified at the sight Cornelius called to the Kennard who without thinking flung himself towards her and scooped her up in one of his powerful arms. With a second lung he propelled them both forward, landing them beside Kathrie Gretel, who was still hiding her eyes from freight.

"Oh, Mary dear." Kathrie Gretel cried out. She grabbed a hold of Marypat and sighed. "For an instant I thought I was going to lose you to the eternal abyss and that is more than I can endure." Kathrie Gretel's emotions were laid out on her flesh and she could not control herself.

Something was painfully wrong with Kathrie Gretel. Never before had she loss control of her emotions. She had always been so strong, so steadfast, but now she was a basket case, sobbing and crying at the slightest emotional change.

The Kennard and Marypat stood up while Cornelius helped Kathrie Gretel to her feet. "All is well, Gretel, all is well."

Cornelius held Kathrie Gretel there for a moment while she composed herself then the group moved on. Before long they stood before the second abyss. This one was twice as long as the first and again it was Marypat that proved to have the most trouble with it. Before she even placed one foot on the rouged edge she had turned back and protested to the Kennard.

"I can't do this, it's just too hard, I can't." She sobbed. She was so frightened she couldn't move. "Why can't we just use magic to get there?"

The Kennard bent down to her and held her arm. "One cannot travel to Ebon with magic, one must travel by one's own foot, and ye must do this, for it is ye own son we hasten to find. He needs ye to do this."

His voice was firm but calm. Again, he filled her with confidence, but this time when she stepped out he went with her and stayed with her every step of the way. Together they navigated the narrow ledge of the abyss and climbed to the safety of the pass.

There would be two more open pits for the group to maneuver throw before they rested for the eve. But finally, they did.

They set up camp on a stretch of the crystal pass that was scared by others who had travelled the same way. There were remains of previous campers and traces of a fire pit burned into the green emerald ground. It was a sight used but it had not been used in a very long stint.

When Marypat finally was able to relax she realized she was physically and emotionally exhausted. All she wanted was to sleep, but before she could do that she knew her grandmother would be anxious for news, so she sat near the fire and pulled out the Talk about. She turned it on and called to her grandmother but there was no answer. It was still early and Marypat assumed that Lora had not turned her on yet. So Marypat set the Talk about down beside her and waited while she nibbled on a piece of dried hoof.

"What is that?" Questioned Rowan who was sitting near her and had watched her call out into it.

"Mortal Magic." Marypat answered with a smile. "It is the instrument I use to speak to my grandmother in the outside world."

"Fascinating, is it a spell?" He questioned.

"No, there is no spell, this works on radio waves. We call it a Walkie Talkie. Out there everyone has some form of a communication device. Something like this, or a pager or a telephone, there is even phones you can travel with I think they call them car phones. But only the wealthy have those. Anyway, out there you can call up anyone if you have their telephone number. Although this doesn't need a telephone number, I don't know why I even mentioned phones." She said nervously making conversation. She really didn't know what to say to him, he made her nervous. She still didn't know much about him, and why he had concealed himself all turn but now suddenly wanted to talk to her.

"A number, does everyone have a number?" His voice was a curious whisper.

"Well when you buy a telephone, they give you one. But you're not born with it or anything " She answered shyly.

"I see, does ye youngster have a number?"

"No. This is his, he should have had it on him, he left it behind but then again it only works at a certain distance so it may not have even worked here for me to reach him." She sighed as she rubbed her eye.

"Ye son is a Sherideen, of this you are certain?"

"I am not certain, but I can tell you that he has the look of his father and although he is a mindful child he has that temper I have seen in Donovan."

"And ye say he has not been bathed at the purified waters of the Cascades?"

"No, this is the first his foot has traveled here."

"Then what I tell you, now, pains me to do so this ye must understand for it is not my intention to cause ye distress, but instead to make ye aware of the truth." His words were stranded and he moved closer to her as he continued. " I fear I have no choice but to confide in you. The turns of a Sherideen are painful turns, but understand that they are bearable to most young. This pain I speak of is a growing pain a hardening of heart and soul. Relief comes only when evil is done and magic flows from within. But in this benefit the Sherideen is bound to evil and flourishes in evil. This is why all Sherideen become Ubil. Now. . . ye son, Blaze if he is indeed as ye fear a Sherideen and not born of this land. He will undergo a change but it will not be a turn by turn change as I have lived. . . No, he will experience a far greater pain." Rowan grabbed Marypat's arm and examined her eyes with compassion. "A pain so intense that the only relief will be pure evil."

His voice echoed in the evening air and tears filled Marypat's eyes.

"Are you saying there is no hope?"

"No, what I am saying is that we must act quickly. The evil inside him will fester and grow beyond any power that has come before. We must secure him with haste and present him before the Sanctifier's of the Cascades. It is our only hope that the pure waters can wash him clean of the Ubil stench."

Tears rolled down Marypat's face as she looked deep into Rowan's eyes.

"I appreciate your honesty, but tell me why I should trust ye, when ye hide yourself from me."

"My dear, I do not cloak mine self from ye but from the guardians of Ebon, they do not take to Sherideens in their land. It is my wish to help thee, and bring my brethren to the good, but if the guardians see me they may devour my flesh and spew me forth into the sea."

"This risk you take for my son?" Marypat's eyes were gentle on Rowan's face as she comprehended the danger he faced on this quest.

"I take this risk for the good of all members, I sense a change is near. Do you not feel it sister?" Rowan's eye turned the Kathrie Gretel who had been listening all along.

"Yes." her lips quivered and fresh tears flowed from her eyes.

"It is the great change, the change that will finally brake the Sherideen cured heart. I recognize it three turns ago, but this very turn I knew it was so when I learned of your son. The son of a Maurieen and a Sherideen, only this Newling could have the pure power to brake the curse. But in order for this to occur we must get him to the Cascades before he is called to his Sherite Extolel." Rowan's replied with honesty.

"That's where I know your name, you weren't there." Marypat declared.

Rowan stared at her and shock his head.

"The turn Donovan was called to his, your name Rowan was called, but you never came forward. Your name was washed away. They washed it from their post, their hearts and their lineage. But still you want to free them from their curse? You still want to help them?"

All went silent then. There was an uncommon stillness that was broken by Lora voice as she called over the Talk about.

"Mary, are you there?"

Marypat retrieved the Talk about and spoke into it.

"Yes, grandmother." Marypat said as she stood and strolled away from the group. She spook to her grandmother in private and then returned to the group a few moments later. She put away the Talk about and then she sat back down on her log roll. No one was talking so she closed her eyes and fell to sleep. So much had happened and her brain was full. So full it bleeds into her dreams and she was soon engulfed in visions.

Her brain opened to a dream were above her floating in the Crystal Mountain was Donovan. His arms were held out to her and she tried to reach him but he was just out of range. After a few attempts he turned his back to her and floated away.

"Don't go." She shouted from her sleep. "Don't go!"

But Donovan's vision disappeared and soon there was a bright light in her eyes and the feel of sand under her feet. She was at the beach; the sun was bright and she was searching for something in the surf. Suddenly Blaze appeared from nowhere. His eyes shot red flames at her and he laughed. Then he ran passed her and she tried to follow but he too disappeared and she was left standing in darkness.

"Come back come back!" She shouted out loud but the vision of Blaze didn't return. Instead she was pelted by small red spiders that bounded up and down on their threads. She shrieked and ran until something grabbed her and held her tightly. She bawled again and cry "Horatio, help me, Horatio."

Tears ran down her face as she struggled to get free, but when she looked up to see what was holding her, she saw Horatio's boyish face.

"Horatio, oh Horatio, where have you been, I need you." She sobbed.

Her arms grabbed the vision of Horatio around the neck and she kissed him. The vision kissed her back and at last she was calm. All was right in Horatio's arms. Horatio was with her and he would save her.

She opened her eyes from the dream, she could still feel his arms around her. But when she looked up it wasn't Horatio's face that she saw, it was the Kennard. His mighty arms did indeed hold her. They held her so tightly that passion was not their aim. No, he held her for fear as they stood at the very edge of a great abyss and it was all the Kennard could do to keep them both from falling in.

He had followed her in her restless sleepwalking and had grabbed her just in time before she fell into the open space and now he had to calm her freight as she realized where they were.

"Do not panic, easy ye wait for me and we can step back." He whispered softly in her ear.

She did as she was told and allowed the weight of her body to fall onto his massive form. Easily he maneuvered them backwards and after several steps they were once again on solid crystal. Marypat removed her arms from around his neck and stood wearily in front of him.

"Thank you!" she uttered. Her heart was aching and she was made to feel worse with the embarrassment she felt for having endangered them both.

"No weep. It is my task to protect ye!" The Kennard answered.

Marypat looked up at him with a question look on her face. She thought he was there as a member of council. He was there to protect the council's best interest not her. Her mind filled with so many thoughts, thoughts of her son, thoughts of Horatio and now thoughts of why the Kennard was there to protect her. It was all so much to think about. So much she didn't respond to his comment instead she turned away from him and began walking back to camp.

"I mean no added suffering but I must ask ye a question." The Kennard mentioned as he followed Marypat back towards the camp.

Marypat made no attempt to deter him, she was still lost in her own thoughts so the Kennard continued.

"Ye mentioned the name Horatio."

Marypat stopped in her tracks, the word Horatio echoed in her ears. *How did the Kennard know Horatio's name, had she spoken his name out loud?*

"Horatio is my dearest friend, never a day. . . a turn goes by that I do not think about him and how things might have been different. . . . . Whenever I have needed him, in the past, he was always there . . . for me." She revealed.

"Ye are of need for him now?" The Kennard asked.

Marypat lowered her gaze and spoke from her heart. "As my guard, Ye have filled his shoes on many of occasions recently, and for that I thank you. But Horatio is more than a protector, he restores my hope and he rebuilds my strength."

Marypat's words made the Kennard smile slightly but he quickly removed it from his lips, before he asked. "Why is he not here with ye then."

"It has been many passes since I was last here. A long stretch for which I was told never to return. I am certain he never anticipated seeing me again. Knowing this he had to move on. I could not expect him after so much space that he could still. .. . . . feel beholding to me.. . . . . Though more than anything I am beholding to him."

Marypat then turned away from the Kennard and strolled back to the camp. She laid down on her roll beside Kathrie Gretel and tried to go back to sleep.

Thunder cracked in the evening sky as four hooded members swept pass the huge stone observer that stood in the center of Cimmevian Town. They ducked through an archway blanketed in Red, where they were met by six other hooded members who seemed pleased at their arrival.

"Brethren is it true, has the Maurieen returned?" Asked one of the new hooded members.

"Yes, see here for thy self, she travels to the Caves of Ebon as we speak." The orange cloaked member divulged as he pointed to the vat in the center of the cove.

"But, brother how will we capture her as Kathrie Trixie has foretold to us? Sherideens cannot travel there."

"'Tis true, but one does not travel to the Vista for length. She will soon have to tread forward. That is when we shall take her. We must be patient, brothers and sister the moment will soon be ours." The orange clocked member announced. "Extend the good word and stand ready, I will contact you when it is the moment to act."

"Salute Protector Handrew, Salute thy voice and deed. We shall advance thy plan and multiply thou followers." Cheered a green hooded member.

"Salute the Master Handrew!" The group Hailed.

CHAPTER
13

Eggazor Championship

The pier in the town of Ridley was bustling with activity. There was an excitement in the air that flowed over into every aspect of life on the pier.

The Eggazor Championship was being held that very turn and there were many in town looking forward to it. A 1,000-pyrite award was to be played to the winner. Members had come from a far to participate as well as view the spectral. The games had been a tradition on the Red Isle for over a 1,000 passes. Stared by Jacob Miszner as a way to study the various Eggazors he had unknowingly unleashed on the isle. The practice had slowly formed into a sport.

The town's activity to showcase the event was not lacking for thrills. There were Feldens riding unicycles on wires that hung the full length of the pier. Every so often they would stop and shot a water projectile at an un-expecting member and then quickly rode off showering all below them with tiny paper eggs. The boardwalk was decorated with large colorful egg-shaped bulbs that sprayed out colorful sparks and every so often whistled and spun shooting the sparks in a circular pattern. There were even Etains dressing all in red and caring long ribbons in each of their hands that floated around flapping the ribbons behind them. Many of the shop keepers had brought their wares out on to the boardwalk for easy viewing and there were small venders every few feet selling a variety of food and snacks.

There was so much activity that no one noticed the two well-dressed Sherideens that were strolling down the wooden pier on their way towards the enormous warehouse known as "the Rink".

It was the rink that many members were on their way too, for that was the place where the competition was to take place. It was a massive structure, with more than ten floors. Four of which were under ground, the remaining stood before Blaze and Godfrey as they marched up the giant wood stairway and entered the building.

Inside Blaze was amazed to find an almost hollow structure. There before him was a simple balcony and nothing else. To his right a door and his left a stairway that leads down. But beyond the balcony there seemed to be nothing just a wide-open area.

On the balcony though was a small table and two short thin Feldens who were busy making notes on their clip boards when he and Godfrey approached.

"We shall like to apply." Godfrey expressed with confidence.

"Apply, oh yes good good." Cheered the older of the two Feldens. He was thin with a very heavy beard and mustache that was almost entirely gray. He had bright green eyes that seemed to welcome them until he looked up at their faces.

"Oh, no no no, this can't be. Sherideens no, against the rules it be."

Blaze slid forward and whispered just loud enough for the two Feldens ears to catch his verse. "Vic son hocus dom me nom." His wand pulsed slightly from under his cloak.

"We shall like to apply." Godfrey conveyed again this time with a Feldens voice.

"Name and beast please." The old Feldens said as if he had no memory of Sherideens standing before him.

"Blaze Sharp with a Pretty Jaw." Answered Blaze in a mono toned voice, he didn't want to break the spell on the Feldens so he spoke gently.

"Pretty Jaw? There has never been a Pretty Jaw on record as being captured. Are you sure that is your beast?" Replied the younger Felden with an edge of curiosity.

Blaze pulled back his cloak and revealed the lizard that was clinging to his vest.

"His name is P. J. Care to pet him?" Blaze mentioned as he stroked the creatures scaly back.

Both Feldens were speechless. After a moment the older Felden composed himself and uttered, "The application is one pie-it."

Blaze glanced at Godfrey and Godfrey shock his head. " I had no idea there was a fee to enter. I have no coins."

Blaze thought fast and without much choice pulled out his wallet and unzipped his coin purse.

"I am afraid I am not for here and my currency is not that of a pie-it, but perhaps you will accept this?" Blaze pulled out two Jamaican one-dollar coins and laid them out on the wooden table.

The younger of the two Felden picked one up and inspected it.

"I have never seen such a unique coin, where did you say it hails from?"

"The city of Kingston." Blaze answered.

"Such fine craftsmanship, it is well minted. Look Alexander it holds thy name."

The older Felden picked up the second coin and studied it closely. After a moment he pulled it away from his eye and grinned at Blaze.

"Yes, this is my Great-Great-Grandfather. The nation hero of Kingston Port on Keel Key. I recognize his face. We will take your currency." He pocketed the two coins and then handed Godfrey a slip of paper with a schedule written on it.

"Do not be late, a late entry into the cell will create an instant defeat. For now, take the stairs down to the second level give them this ticket." The younger Felden handed Blaze a small hard piece of paper with something scribbled on it. "And wait till you are called to your first cell. Games begin on the sweep, so I suggest you head down right away."

The younger Felden then stood and placed his hand towards Blaze. "Good luck, brother Felden, I will be pulling for your Pretty Jaw." He said proudly.

Blaze shook his hand and then followed Godfrey down the long narrow stairs that led to the nine other leaves of the Rink.

On the second level they had just enough of a period to hand their ticket to a round Lassie Felden when a bell rang to call in for the next opponent. The Lassie Felden pointed them to enter cell number 208 and then she ran off with another contestant.

Godfrey opened the door of the cell and entered the arena. Blaze followed and was surprised to see above him several other cells all arranged in the open space of the warehouse. He had not seen the arenas from the balcony on the tenth floor where they had registered because all of the arenas were hanging below. There were eight cells per floor with viewing posts every third floor. The cells themselves were clear toped balconies with transparent barriers around each one to prevent the Eggazors from escaping, while still allowing a clear view of the action for the spectators. The cells floors were lined with red padding and each one had a large white circle in the center. A thick black mark around the circle indicated the out of bounds.

Inside their arena they found a Felden waiting nervously with a yellow lizard like creature. It was bigger than P.J. and seemed well trained. Blaze for the first time wondered if one turn would be enough training for his Eggazor to win even one event. But he was soon put to ease when P.J. aggressively attacked the larger yellow creature and was called victor.

The next several challenges were so simply won, that Blaze thought the competition would be a cakewalk. It was not until P.J.'s ninth challenge that he actually went up against a creature that could possible beat him. They went six rounds before the black lizard tripped out of bounds and the challenge was called with P.J. as victor.

P.J. had two more events before the final bell rang which called him and a Lightning Foot to the ultimate challenge. The creatures weren't even given time to rest. They were set to fight in the largest of the arena's, number 405.

The Arena Cell number 405, moved slowly away from the wall of the warehouse until it was in clear view of all the viewing posts of the 6th, 9th and 10th floors. It rested in the center of the rank while spectators packed the viewing areas and clamored for their choice.

The bell rang. The Lightning Foot took off darting P.J. with his thin fingers and ripping at his skin. But P.J. was not even fazed by its attempts to harm him. He just stood there and waited for Blaze to give him the sign to attack and when he did P.J. attacked zapping the Lightning Foot over and over until it could take no more. After that Blaze squeezed his hand into a fist. P.J. understood and snapped one arm forward grasping the Lightning Foot around the throat. He held him off the mat and waited there while the creature squirmed. Blaze signaled again and P.J. followed by tossing the Lightning Foot out of bounds.

With that the bell rang and P.J. was hailed the victor.

With prize money in hand Blaze and Godfrey made for the end of the pier where they had heard they could purchase a craft from a Wardeen named One Eyed Andy.

One Eyed Andy was a crusty old sea dog with matted black hair that surrounded his face and head. He had only one eye as his name suggested. He had lost the eye during a brutal conflict between him and a Pirate known as Magee. Magee and his Wardeens had tried to take Andy's ship, the Cordella by force late one night, far out at sea but they were met with their own deaths. When Andy and his faithful crew stopped their pursuit. Unfortunately, not before Andy was cut in the face by Magee. Magee had damaged Andy's left eye so severely it had to be removed. Later on, Pelican Isle a Good Natured Kathrie gave him a blue lapis to take its place. The lapis eye enabled him perfect vision on the eve sea. Still even after all he had been through One Eyed

Andy was a mild tempered Wardeen who didn't mind doing business with Sherideens, so there was no need for Godfrey and Blaze to use a visionary spell or so they thought.

Blaze and Godfrey found One Eyed Andy at the Rusty Bucket, sitting up along the spiral staircase of the lighthouse, baptizing his throat with a gully of ale.

"Yo's been publishing such outlandish lies. Me Treasured old Jewel is not for sale, me rather ye cut off me good peg than let ye take my Cordella." One eyed Andy billowed as he swayed on his stool inside the Rusty Bucket.

On Eyed Andy stood and wobbled forward. He pointed his finger at Godfrey, squinting his one good eye as if he was sizing him up. "Ye looks of Magee, would thee like to die like em?" He spat with his dagger ready.

Godfrey stepped back, his frail body would be easily crushed by the Wardeen of his size, who now stood before him full height and weight.

"Why not good fellow. . " Godfrey uttered still trying to move away from the suspended hulking form of One Eyed Andy. The light house structure gave little room for Godfrey to move so it seemed to Blaze that he had no other choice but to act.

Blaze jumped forward, pushed himself between the two Patties and flashed their new-found wealth. Surprised and delighted One Eyed Andy stepped back and eyed the sparkling coins.

"Well why didn't ye say that in the first place, mine ears are always willing to hear when there's Verts involved." One Eyed Andy smiled slightly as he swaggered back to his seat. He sat and downed the remains of his ale before turning his good eye to Blaze.

"Open ye trap, lad, ya done bait the hook, na don't tease it at me." He billowed.

Blaze slipped into one of the rod iron chairs that set around the small wooden table on the slight platform of the lighthouse. He pulled himself up close and whispered to One Eyed Andy.

"Take us to the Great Isle and . ."

But before Blaze could finish One Eyed Andy was already laughing out loud.

"The Great Isle wah haha wah. The lad wants to go to the ha ha ha ." He slapped the table and stomped his foot on the wooden floor. "HA HA HA."

He laughed on for a while until Blaze stood up and said. "We were told ye won't afraid of anything. I see now they were wrong." Blaze made a look as if he was going to leave when One Eyed Andy shot to his feet and grabbed Blaze's arm.

"Those are fighting words, lad." One Eyed Andy growled.

"Perhaps, if I were looking for a fight, but I am only interested in buying passes to the Great Isle. What do you have to lose? I'll pay you whether the Isle is there or not. Ye win either way." Blaze stated firming as he looked One Eyed Andy dead in the eye. He showed no sign of coward-ness or fear and One-eyed Andy respected that.

He released Blaze's arm and sat back down, he waved his hand for Blaze to do the same and then he asked.

"What makes ye think it's there, it's been missing going on 50 passes. Many a good sailor has tried to find it and lost everything in that ill-mannered sea where it once held ta."

"I know because I put it back." Blaze stated confidently.

One Eyed Andy grinned and almost let out a laugh but he was quickly cut off as Blaze leaned forward suddenly and mentioned.

"Laugh if you will but ye will never know unless ye take my wager and prove me wrong."

"Wager?"

"Yes." Blaze answered.

"Right, then a wager it is." One Eyed Andy grinned. "250 pie-it each for ye passage and the same if the land ain't there."

"Right, and if it is, ye will give us back our passage fee!" Blaze added.

"Agreed!" One Eyed Andy announced, forcing his hand towards Blaze who stood up suddenly and shook the Wardeens hand.

"Agreed."

The Cordella was an awesome sight. Midnight blue from bow to stern, her form blended into the sea. The hull was crafted from the finest Blue Fur Pine. The keel of the ship was wide and cut deep into the harbor. Four stories sat below her decks filled with wares and goods. The schooner measured, 1,800 common hands long and 90 wide. With two masts that held sails that varied slightly in shades of blue. Starting with the base of the main sail in navy all the way up to the top of the sail in a powder blue. One might have missed the Cordella on the sea and most certainly on the horizon. It was just what One Eyed Andy desired when he painted her so, soon after that troubled eve at sea when Magee attacked. One Eyed Andy was certain that if Magee had not spotted his bright orange sail that eve, he would not have attacked her. So, convinced he was of this, that he decided to create an illusion with the ship by painting the entire ship blue and binding it with the obligation of his nagging wife Cordella herself.

"Don't be bringing those filthy Sherideens into my hull." Shouted a voice from above Blaze's head as he approached the ship.

He looked up but saw no one, only the ship's bow with its detailed carved Lassie figurehead that protruded forward over the water. The wood of the figurehead seemed different from the ship's wood, it was lighter somehow. The caved dress the figurehead wore seemed alive as it swayed gently in the breeze. The carved lace of its sleeves and form fitting corset bounded with the action of the ship. Her face, neck, hands and chest were painted a pale white with a little light pink in the cheeks and her hair was a golden yellow. They were the only things on the ship not painted blue and Blaze found the figurehead most unique.

"Shut ye hole, ye old hag, these them be me employers. With pie-it a plenty. Make ready, we sail within the sweep." One Eyed Andy shouted over his shoulder in to the air.

Blaze found One Eyed Andy's shouts in the air strange but then there came an even stranger reply that nearly knocked him on his rear.

"Andrew Wilfred Harding, don't ye shout at me like that." The same shrieking voice echoed above Blaze's head but this time Blaze saw where it was coming from. His eye's opened wide as the figurehead's mouth opened and shut. Her eyes flamed a heated yellow and her faced turned towards Blaze.

"What are you looking at? If I had the use of me hands I cast ye into the sea, ye worthless Sherideen." The figurehead shouted at Blaze.

Blaze stepped back nearly tripping over a rope that laid behind him on the wooden pier. Quickly he chased after Godfrey who was already on the deck of the ship awaiting the cast off.

Godfrey himself had the feeling that he was in a dream. For so long he had hoped and dreamed of leaving this dreadful Red Isle and now here he was free at last and sailing for home.

CHAPTER 14

Guardians of the Vista

T here it was after two grueling turns of travel the Slick Down. The solid slippery form that would bring them to the base of the Ebony Valley. Below her, Marypat could see the dark shards of the valley floor. All that stood in her way was the long narrow twisting channel of the Slick Down that lay before her.

Gillian with Tag went first with Gillian calling as he went to his brother, Langston. Cornelius and Kathrie Gretel slide down together followed by Rowan well covered by his cloak, then it was Marypat's turn.

Marypat sat down on the Slick Downs slippery slide like surface sat and hesitated.

"An ease of thy bottom will aid in speed." The Kennard instructed but it wasn't that Marypat didn't know what to do. It was instead a sliver of denial that the vista would even help her find her son. All this travelling could be for nothing. Not knowing why, she hesitate the Kennard merely sat down beside her and took her with him as he pushed off.

"An ease, did I not say." he mentioned as they slipped along the slippery surface together.

The Slick Down was a mystically place that seemed to sparkle as Marypat slid through the cavern like slide. Soon they came to the bottom where the ground was covered with thick broken shards. A crystal Souldale and her colt were just beyond where Marypat and the Kennard landed, neither seemed disturbed by the sudden appearance of two members. The Souldales just continued to graze on the rich black shards. Marypat watched as the young Souldale followed its mother. She had never seen one so close. How fascinating they were. Marypat could tell that the colt was still very young because its body was still clear, only it's huffs and ankles were rich emerald green and its tail were sliver. Just like it's mother, but the mother body was a solid emerald green and her clear horn glowed white with maturity.

Suddenly the peaceful moment was broken as Marypat realized the group was waiting for her.

"We must keep moving, the Vista is this way." Gillian urged in a whisper. "I have not seen Langston and the other protectors are just beyond the bend, we must proceed with an eye of caution."

The group moved swiftly through the thick shards. Gillian all the while scanned the huge Mountains for signs of the protectors. He worried that he would not find his brother in time and that one of the others would first.

They reached the bend; the cave of the Vista was now in sight. It was just a quick dash ahead of them. The open cave lay on the other side of an open field of shards, 150 common hands wide. It was so close, so near. Still there was one thing preventing the group from entering, the protectors. There in the clear green crystal mountains were the

Protectors. Their forms like great sculptures caved deep in the stone, ten times the actual life size, they stood still guarding the cave mouth.

Gillian stopped the group and cautiously peered around the bend. There were three protectors carved into the stone, Langston was not among them. Gillian's heart fell. He knew their chances of entering the cove was not good but he had to put it to the group.

"Langston is not present, do we wait, or do we proceed?" He asked.

"Do ye recognize those present? Would any be of service?" The Kennard asked as he too peered around the bend.

"Edmund and Javier here to the right, might hear thou argument, but cousin Blanford on the left, should not give them time to hear. He has no patients with the living. It might do us well to wait for Langston." Gillian whispered.

"WAIT? COWARD'S!" Came a billowing voice from behind them.

"TO ADVANCE WOULD AT LEAST SHOW STRENGTH OF CHARACTER!" Came a second deafening voice.

"YES BROTHER, BEHOLD THE SHAME OF OUR BROTHERS WEAK TONGUE!" The first voice roared.

The group look back the way they had come. They glanced up into the slippery sides of the mountain, back towards the voices and there carved in the mountain were two more protectors. Both towered over the group. Their massive forms were richly adorned with solid gold strapped that formed an armor. Each Loralac seemed dressed for battle, ready to strike with their golden swords or their jewel tipped daggers. But these protectors did not need their weapons in Ebon, their power and strength over the living was immense.

"Brother Alastair, Brother Litton." Gillian greeted with authority.

"IT IS TOO LATE FOR THAT!" Came another billowing voice from the direction of the caves. Alastair and Litton's loud voices had awakened the three guarding the Vista. Now the group was surrounded.

Gillian fell silent they had heard him speak with weakness. He had no respect in their eye, it was no use in him negotiating. The Kennard realized the position and quickly moved the focus to him.

"Respect Honorable Loralacs of Ebon. We are here on a quest for the Regan!' The Kennard declared.

"THE REGAN HAS NO POWER HERE, WHY WOULD HE SEND YOU?" Countered Alastair.

"The isle is endanger, the Vista is the only. . ."

"WAIT!" Interrupted Blanford, "I SMELL THE STENCH OF THE SHERIDEEN BROOD". His eye narrowed as he smelled the air. When without warning he swooped his mighty arm forward and scooped up Rowan who was still hiding under his thick black cloak. The Crystal Protector then throw Rowan into his mouth and spit him high into the air. Rowan tumble helplessly. He tried to right himself and after a moment he managed to take flight in his our course. He flew back to where the group stood and shouted to the Kennard all the while dogging the angered fists of Blanford.

"I shall wait for ye at Raye Point, be well." Rowan declared. He dogged one last pass of Branford's mighty fist and then flew away over the mountain.

"WHAT SCENE MY EYE SURVEYS?" Came a powerful voice from a sixth Protector. This protector had just cleared the enormous mountain peak far above the Vista. He stood head and shoulders taller than the rest and his costume was more richly adorned than any of the others. He was a commanding presents and the five other protectors moved to attention at the sound of his voice.

"SPEAK BLANFORD, FOR MINE EYE SEES YE HAND IN THIS."

"PRINCIPAL LANGSTON, A FORBIDDEN WAS DISCOVERED AMONG THE TRAVELERS. YE OWN BROTHER, GILLIAN AND KATHRIE GRETEL BROUGHT HIM A FOOT. A TUMBLE, MINE DUTY YE EYE SURVEYED." Blanford reported in a coarse tone.

"WELL DONE, COUSIN." The Principal Protector Langston stated as he took his eye off of the Blanford and shifted his sight to the group of travelers. His eye quickly found it's mark. Gillian. "IT PAINS THEE, BROTHER GILLIAN, A FORBIDDEN?"

Langston shook his head slightly as he gazed over the other travelers. "NOT ONLY DO YOU ALLOW A SHERIDEENS IN EBON BUT NOW TO CAST MINE EYE UPON THEE SO SOON AFTER

THY LAST VISIT. YE KATHRIEEN, I SHALL NOT SPEAK OF PROMISES NOW BROKEN."

Kathrie Gretel began to shake as he bent over her.

"YE KNOW THE CONSCIENCES OF THY POSITION?" Langston asked.

Kathrie Gretel shock her head, yes.

"WHEN LET IT BE DONE." Langston expressed in discuss. He waved a signal at two of the other protectors, Edmund and Blanford. Who instantly swung forward and scooped up Kathrie Gretel and Gillian. Both were swallowed whole, neither screamed or even resisted.

Marypat shrieked in horror as she watched her two friends be swallowed whole before her. She fell to the ground and sobbed. It was all her fault they had come and now they were gone. Her tears soon changed to anger as she listened to the Principal Protector Langston as he demanded an explanation of their trust passing. The anger welled up in her so great she could not help her rage. Desperately she tried to control herself. She needed to grab hold of something, soothing that could keep her from exploding. But all she could reach was the shard cover ground. Her hand grabbed fistful of razor shape shards that sliced at her skin. The pain flooded her senses like a torch and with it all the elements were present. The tears on her face, water. The air around her, breath. The shards in her hands, stone and the anger inside her, fire.

Her body jolted forward exploding in a bright red fire, her hair rose above her like a liquid flame and her eye flared with a flash of the inferno within.

The protectors gasped at the sight, never before had magic been able to be seen in Ebon. Ebon was a place where magic was void. It was the reason all member had to use their own well to get there. It was why the Spit cock couldn't reach there. And why they couldn't fly there. No spells, no incantations could work.

The protectors grew cautious and stepped back slightly into the mountains. Their outlines were just faint lines along the slops. They stood there silent as they watched her rise up from the ground and project her voice into the vast valley of Ebon.

"These ye have cast away, bravely guild me on my quest to find my son. For they understand that the welfare of the isle is more important than their own lives. So, I say to ye. . . be guarded and beware for I hold the Touch of four and lost within the isle is mine son, the member for told by the Vista itself. Born not of the isle. He walk's unknowing the power in his touch and given this, his choice is yet his own. Ye must waver not, for the stint grows near when he will choose between the good and evil. Without guidance he will give into his Sherideen heart and embrace the Ubil ways. If he does the isle is doomed. " Her voice vibrated through the valley.

After hearing Marypat, Langston moved forward until it chest protruded out of the Mountain. Then he spoke. "YE TRAVEL TO THE VISTA FOR IT TO SEE A CHILD?"

"YES" Marypat answered flaming brighter.

"IS THIS YE ONLY REQUEST?"

"NO, I WISH TO HAVE MY COMPANIONS BACK!" Her anger sparked from her like tiny embers. Her eye's flashed blue as their stare burned Langston's stone chest.

"WILL THAT THEN BE ALL YE ASK?"

"YES"

"THEN LET IT BE, YE MAY ENTER THE CAVE NOW AND QUESTION THE VISTA. IF WHAT YE CLAIM IS SO THE VISTA WILL KNOW AND YE COMPANIONS WILL BE RETURNED BUT IF WHAT YE CLAIM IS NOT SO I WILL SWALLOW YE!" Langston conveyed convincingly.

"LET IT BE." Marypat retorted as she allowed herself to drift back down to the shard covered floor of the valley. Her bloody hands allowed the shards they held to drop free and instantly her flaming body subsided leaving her drained. Cornelius ran to her side and held her.

"Mary are you al-right." He asked, examining her blood drenched hands.

"Yes. Now let's get to the Vista." She answered.

The four remaining companions hurried across the open space of the valley. While the six protectors watched from their places in the mountains. Their forms now at attention, their face's empty, their eyes shut. There was no resisting, no argument.

The entrance to the cave was dark. There was a strange musty odor in the air, but Marypat didn't stop to notice. Her attention was elsewhere. Quickly she entered the opening with Cornelius, Tag and the Kennard following close behind. The Kennard's inner glow gave Marypat and Cornelius just enough light to see their way in to the grim cave. Before long they were deep within the cavern where they were halted by two protectors carved in the cave wall.

Their massive forms stood the full height of the cave, but they were not even half the height of the protectors in the valley. Never the less they were powerful looking and intimidating.

"Halt thy foot and hold steady thy pace, for thou has entered a most honorable place." The two stone carvings rhymed together.

Marypat stopped and turned to face the carving on the right. "Good morrow, honorable protectors."

She began but the protectors had no time for small talk.

"Three puzzles lay before ye wait, give good thought ye answer state. But heed my word this solemn plea and hence forth use but one eye to see."

As they completed the words, Marypat noticed that the cave's floor lite up with an enormous glowing radiance that devoured the darkness of the empty cave. The crystal floor then changed and formed a row of four large tiles. On the tiles carved deeply were the four elements of tradition. Water, Air, Fire, and Stone.

Marypat having read her copy of Legends and Tales, the caves of Ebon, anticipated that she would have to answer three questions. She seemed ready to proceed, but was thrown, when the first question asked of her was not the same question she remembered from the story.

"Choice once and there place the element of one here in cased." The protectors sang out loud.

"What? That's not fair. That's not the question, it's something like all importance of thou race!" Marypat shrieked.

The protectors smiled and replied. "One needs change in thou verse, for we are not ill willed or cursed."

Marypat turned her worried face to Cornelius who tried to step forward to help but the stone guardian was quick to stop him by grabbing his shoulder.

"Silence to those who follow the maid, or we will be forced to allow all to fade." the protectors announced.

Cornelius stepped back and the stone protector removed his grasp as Marypat watched desperately needing guidance.

"You're on your own Mary." Cornelius rendered.

She turned back toward the tiles. Her face showed the stress of the moment. "Can you repeat the question?" She asked as her mind raced to figure out the answer.

"Choice once and there place the element of one here in cased." The protectors sang out loud again.

"Here in cased." She repeated in her mind. *"One here in cased. Who is here in cased? The protectors are in cased but I don't know what element they are and for all I know it could be all four elements. The answer in the Legends and Tales was a trick answer it was all four. May-by it's all four for this one too."*

"Oh, I don't know, this isn't fair how am I supposed to know this?" She shouted out loud. She was growing angry, she needed to see her son and this was just too silly a thing to go through. She felt like she was losing control.

"Ye must relax and not think so hard." The Kennard whispered softly but the protector heard him and lunged forward with his stone hand. He grabbed the Kennard around the mouth silencing him.

Marypat was horrid by the protectors action, she wanted to scream but she knew she had to control herself and do as the Kennard advised. She closed her eyes and took a deep breath. Then she thought calmly. *"The element of one here in cased."* She looked at the stone protector that was holding the Kennard. His massive arm was solid stone. Her mind came alive like a bolt of energy. *"It's Stone, their incased in stone."*

Quickly she hopped forward and landed squarely on the tile with the stone symbol on it. But as she landed a wave of anxiety stuck her. What if she had guest wrong. She lowered her head as she waited for the stone protectors to render the solution but neither spoke instead they waved their hands at the floor erasing the four elements of tradition.

Marypat raised her head and realized she must have gotten the answer correct. She stood then silent and watched as below her a tapestry of symbols appeared floating in the crystal floor. The same symbols used in name tapestry's. Marypat recalled the one she had bought in Great Town when she was a young girl. It had the names Cornelius, Marypat, Tiger, Donovan and Horatio wavered into a beautiful pattern. Some of the symbols she saw below her she recognized from her tapestry and she hoped that they would ask her for one she knew. Quietly she stood and waited for the stone protectors to begin.

"A tapestry of life unfolds, and with it the bead a Sherideen holds." The protectors sang.

Marypat's eyes went wide. She didn't know what bead was meant for a Sherideen to hold. She searched the floating symbols, there was a heart. No, she thought a Sherideen wouldn't hold a heart, their heart is evil. Then she looked at the star, the diamond, the flower, the butterfly, the clover, the eye, the leaf, the pear and the ribbon. All not for a Sherideen she decided. She eliminated all the ones she could until she was left with the circle, the tear and the square. Quickly she tried to think what they meant but she could not. If only she had studied them before. But she hadn't and now she would have to go with what she could remember. Trying to buy time she asks the stone protectors to repeat the question but when she did, the stone protectors grew annoyed with her and instead of repeating the question they removed a part of the crystal floor behind her, leaving her standing on the edge of a great abyss with no other choice but to step forward.

"Think" she shouted in her mind as tears welled in her eyes. She was so frightened she could hardly think. She could not remember ever seeing the symbol of the circle or the square. She did not know what they meant. She did however remember seeing the tear someplace, but where, she couldn't recall. *"Where have I seen the tear?"* Then it stuck her as she felt a tear drop from her cheek. Her tear shaped diamond from the lake of Froymin, it was the symbol of sorrow.

"Of course, that explained why Bagree's bangle had tear shaped diamonds on it." She replied out loud. "It's the tear."

She jumped forward and landed on the tear and as she did the floating symbols held firm. She glanced up at the stone protectors who again said nothing. They waved their hands at the floor and the symbols disappeared. Then they turned slightly away from her and waved their hands again at the ground as they sang.

"Place ye stand with two answers well, yet one still holds for ye to tell. Give this answer wrong this turn and ye shall stay in Ebon Burn but if ye answer well this one, the Vista's view is ye have won."

With that the floor moved violently. The open abyss behind Marypat closed allowing Cornelius, Tag and the Kennard to reach Marypat's side. Together the four watched as the crystal floor just beyond them fell and reformed into four identical crystal pillars.

Marypat knew what to do, this part she was sure must be the same as the legend. This they couldn't change. She stepped up and stood tall as she awaited the protector's instructions.

"Four are placed in thy keep, and set are they in thy peace." They sang.

Without a moment's delay Marypat set off towards the first pillar and called out "Water." With that a clear stream of water shot out of the pillar and ran onto the crystal floor of the cave. Careful not to touch the water Marypat moved on to the second pillar and called out. "Air" With that a small whirlwind formed on the base of the pillar and twirled insistently. Again, Marypat carefully moved on to the third base where she called out "Fire." Instantly a brilliant fire bellowed out of the top of the pillar. Satisfied she moved on to the final pillar and called out stone. A moment passed and then two emeralds pressed against each other appeared on the pillar.

The stone craved protectors smiled and then bowed to Marypat. She had completed the final test and they were pleased. They sang out one last time.

"Water rise and hold thy base,
strength thy form hold thy place.

Breath fill thy body with thy might
give substance to heed thy sight
fire run thy length to see
and lighten thy shadows that may impede.
Stone, casted from the isle here be
allow the vista an eye on thee."

The protector's voices filled the cave and with each additional verse the elements acted accordingly. First the water flowed from its base and forcefully collected on the floor in the center of the pillars. It rose up forming a base that continued to hold it shape as the protected called for the breath. With that verse the air in the cave seemed to go thin and a small twister formed on top of the water base. Then the protectors called for fire. Instantly a spark of flame shot from its crystal base and struck the whirlwind on the top of the water base. The fire and the air turned inwards forming a tumbling shape above the water pillar. Then the protectors called for the stone and with that a tiny shard of crystal slipped off the Emerald on the base and floated into the tumbling shape still twisting above the water pillar. The instant the shard struck the shape the vista formed. The Vista's Eye blinked twice as the four complains watched in amazement.

"What do I do?" Marypat whispered to Cornelius.

"Go look in to the eye." He answered softly.

Marypat moved forward. She glanced at the stone protectors who now stood silent. They did nothing to stop her so she continued until she stood precisely in front of the eye.

"I wish to see my son, Blaze." Marypat declared.

The air around her suddenly moved swirling gently throw her hair creating an undertone.

"*He is the one. The one in the eye. He is the one.*" The murmur hummed.

Marypat glanced around but there was no one else in the cave.

"Did you hear that?" She asked her companions.

They all three nodded yes, they had heard the strange whisper too.

"Look in the eye, can you see him?" The Kennard asked.

Marypat stood on her tippy toes and glared into the open eye of the Vista. She could make out the Great Isles Southern Coast and she reported what she saw to the others as the Vista revealed more.

"I see the beaches of Hapton, now the port, a ship called the Cordella. He is on the ship, he is alive, he is alive." Marypat's voice rejoiced for the moment and then went nervous once more.

"He looks . . . ill. . his face . . . so pale. . . .. and. . . .he travels with two Sherideens, . . .one is old . . . and thin the other covered by a cloak. I do not know them. They are leaving the ship together, where are they going? Show me where they are going?" Marypat asked the Vista. But this the Vista could not answer. It did not know but what it did know was clear as Marypat continued to look into the Vista.

"One shall come, born not of the isle. He shall walk among us as any one might, yet he is unknowing the power in his touch and given this, his choice is yet his own. Waver he many between the good and bad but this point is but true, given to the evil ways the isle is doomed." The faint undertone grew into an angry tone. *"He is here, he has come, he walks among us, the protégée is done."*

With that Marypat's eyes went wide as the visions in the Vista change drastically.

"I see fire, blood, a war . . . . a terrible war. . . . . Blaze. . . . NO!" Marypat streaked and then dropped to the cave floor, "NO, NO, Tell me this has not happened, tell me. Oh!" She cried and moaned.

"The son of Donovan must not choose the way of the Ubil." The mur mur whisper passed their ears again. *"Or this will be the isle's end."*

The Kennard fell beside Marypat and scooped her into his arms as a whirlwind engulfed them and Marypat realized she now had touched the Vista. All four elements were in her power once more and she became the Vista. All the visions of the isle came to her in a flood. Her eyes glowed projecting the visions that overwhelmed her on to the cave walls like a movie. Cornelius and Tag stepped back horrid and confused as they watched the gruesome display unfold on the walls. Meanwhile the Kennard sat frozen holding Marypat as her body fluctuated between solid and liquid.

Even the stone protectors looked stunned. They slowly moved away from the group toward the cave mouth. Where they stood nervously calling to their brother Loralacs.

"Cornelius you must help her." Came a strange voice from deep within the crystal wall. Cornelius franticly turned to face the voice but there was no one there.

"Who said that?" He asked in a shout.

"One who cares. Pull her free of the water and ye will break the Vista's hold. Ye must hurry, Cornelius, or it will kill her." The voice filled the cave.

Cornelius did as he was instructed, he lunged forward and grabbed Marypat's arm. A spark of fire electrocuted Cornelius, filling him with an enormous amount of pain. His hair flue straight up and turned orange, his body tingled, but with his mind focused he pulled with all his might and freed Marypat and the Kennard from the vista.

Stunned the three companions laid on the floor of the cave lifeless and drained. While Tag stood over them unable to revive them.

Note* *The Caves of Ebon* and *Crystal Souldale* *can be found in the legends and Tales.*

An Old Friends Help

The journey across the Hapton Straits was an exhausting one. The Cordella was indeed a jewel of the sea traveling well and sure throw thundering waves that towered over her bow and crashed relentlessly upon her. Still within her bows she lacked the comforts one needed for a moments rest and instead her passengers and crew had only one choice and that was to hold on for the ride.

And if it wasn't bad enough that the ride was harassing, but poor Blaze had to suffer the ghastly influence of change. His body was plagued with pain that ripped throw his body. Forcing him into moments of uncontrollable fits.

By the time they reached the mouth of the Coose, Godfrey had had enough of the young Sherideen. Blaze was too much trouble; besides he had gotten what he had wanted from the lad. He was free from the Red Isle. Free to go and do as he wanted.

Godfrey owed Blaze nothing. The only thing he had promised the lad was to get him to the Great Isle and he had fulfilled that. The Cordella was docked at Hapton port on the Great Isle.

One Eyed Andy had almost ripped his head off when the Isle had come into sight that morrow, and he cursed the turn he had accepted the Sherideens bargain.

But now with his pockets full of the shiny Verts, Godfrey departed the ship. With no remorse or regret he left Blaze behind near death and penniless deep within Cordella's smoldering bowels.

In the town Godfrey found a lively old tavern filled with Kathrieens, Sherideens and Wardeens and for the first time in 40 passages he felt at ease. No one noticed him or turned to shun him. He was just one of the crowds. Excited he went inside and ordered a filling meal of spider soup with whip cream and a jigger of aged Jay berry juice.

He was for a Sherideen happy and content. Nothing could have made the eve any better. He sat back in his Tinkwood chair and watched was the huge curtain that had been draped across the back of the tavern was pulled open to reveal a stage.

"Evening one and all." A thin Wardeen laughed as he stepped on to the stage and bowed. "If ye know me not, I Dad's the herald for this evening's performance." He laughed again at the audience with a big toothless grim.

"Let me bring out to ye first a sweet little group of Colleens, triplets me call the dancing pretty toes." He threw his hands in the air and the audience clapped their hands. "Little Jessie, Katelyn and Hailey J."

Three little Colleens all dressed in pink flowered dresses cross the stage. They danced a routine that was impeccable. Before long they were finished and Dad's took the stage again.

"Darlings, weren't they?" He shouted over the applause. "Up next is a blissful rendition of one of my favorite tones, Paradise, song by our very own Sara Dream cookie and accompanied on piano by Courtney Penn."

The crowd clapped harder and then went silent as the beautiful long-haired Colleen began to sing. Her perfect voice filled the tavern and left not one dry eye. When she finished the audience jumped to their feet clapping in a thunder. Even Godfrey was moved by her pleasurable voice.

Next came Christopher Harpo and his assistant Lauren Von Braigh, with their knife throwing spectacle. They were followed by Matt, and his six Hair Long Retrievers and his two Prairie Hounds doing aerobics. None of the performances were of much interest to Godfrey, who after watching them he decided to pay his bill and leave but as he stood to go, Dad's voice rang throw his ears with a familiar name, "Geraldo the Great."

"Could it be?" Godfrey questioned himself. *"My old friend, Geraldo Medora."* His eyes shifted to the stage as a short disorganized Sherideen took his position under the bright lights. Godfrey watched the pathetic Sherideen while he stumbled through his routine. The tricks he did were basic slight of the hand and nothing more. But the crowd didn't seem to mind they clapped just the same. When he was done Godfrey approached him.

"Geraldo Medora, is that ye?" Godfrey asked with a bright smile.

"Yes!" The shorter Sherideen answered most annoyed. "I don't give autograph's."

"Well I didn't want one, ER, I only wanted to say hello to someone I thought was an old friend." Godfrey fumed over the shorter Sherideen in a heated whisper. "I had no idea ye would turn out so lofty a Sherideen as to snub a brother in exile."

Godfrey's eyes radiated with spit as he watched the shorted Sherideen turn his tired face up to him. Geraldo's eyes widened as he realized who was standing before him. His voice waved as he spoke. "Godfrey, brother. . .how. . . when. . I mean to say is really ye?"

"Yes" Godfrey answered almost with a grin.

"But how are you here? Oh, Yes, the isles are as one again, poor Linus' mishap repaired. A joy in itself, but still ye were banished by Gazpalding to the Red Isle. No Sherideen could have survived the chamber and the heat of the isle?" Geraldo asked.

"But 'tis true, it is I." Godfrey answered quietly. He did not wish to be over heard, for fear that word would reach the Pert that he had returned. Surely Gazpalding would not wish to see him and he might do worse to him if he knew he had escaped the Red Isle. But at the same time Godfrey needed to know how freely he could proceed so he confronted Geraldo. "Now brother speck to me of our master, Gazpalding. Tell me must I fear my foot on this Isle?"

"Brother, you do not know of much, sit I shall recall the happening of the isle" Geraldo excitedly informed his old friend. The two Sherideens sat down at a small round table in plain view. While the stage filled with Etains that danced with two long haired Colleens dressed as flowers.

"Our master Gazpalding met with a terrible death many passes ago." He began as Godfrey listened and grinned to himself. Godfrey was thrilled to hear that Gazpalding was no more and he could be free to venture forth on the isle. Yet he sat and listened as Geraldo continued "A vindictive and cunning Maurieen, who had fallen from the eye, freed Bagree's bangle from the Cinerin stone. Then she tricked Gazpalding into wearing Bagree's bangle, once he had she pulled it from him, leaving him filled with vile Hisue that ate away at him and turned him in to liquid puss."

Godfrey's chin fell, he had never heard of anyone falling from the eye and now he had heard of it happening twice. This Maurie and Blaze, the Sherideen he had left in a desperate shape on the Cordella. Not only that but no one had ever had the power to remove the Bangle from the Cinerin stone before. So, he questioned Geraldo.

"What do ye mean, a Maurieen fell from the eye and freed the bangle?"

"Strange I know, but I was the one who discovered her. She ruined my act one eve at the Blarney Stone. When she picked up the piece of Cinerin stone and held it like it was nothing. Those around her said she had fallen from the world above, the mystical world the weak sodded for and ran to when our members controlled the isles." Geraldo said with an anger tone. "Still she came again. Many passes later. This time brother Ragnar who had tried to take the Place of Gazpalding's son, Donovan was the fool she destroyed. The encounter resulted in the council recovering the bangle and abolishing the Ubil's only protection from the balance."

Godfrey sat quiet for a moment trying to let everything Geraldo told he, sink into his brain. Then he asked Geraldo two vital questions. "Who holds position at the Kert as we speak?"

"Brother Leopold Norwood. Though he holds no great power. Most of the truly strong Ubil have left Cimmevian Town."

"This Maurieen did she have a name?"

"A most vile name if I ever heard one, they called her Marypat. The name burns my lips." Geraldo said with a spit to the floor. "All Ubil members shall never forget the repulsive sound of her name."

Godfrey repeated the name to himself. Then it hit him, it was the same name the young Sherideen had used for his mother's name. *"Marypat." Could it be? Could the Sherideen be the son of the powerful Maurieen, Geraldo was speaking of? And if he was did he also hold the powers of his mother.* The possibility was like electricity to Godfrey's blood. He could hardly contain himself as he thought of what he could do with Blaze as his advisory.

But suddenly it hit him, he had left Blaze on the Cordella. In the most horrible state. What if the Cordella had left already with Blaze still on board? Godfrey's joy fell away and without warning he stood up knocking over the table.

"What is it old master, have I said something troubling?" Geraldo asked pulling on Godfrey's cloak.

"No!' Godfrey stammered nervously pulling himself free from Geraldo's grasp.. "I must go now."

"May I aid thee?" Geraldo asked enquiringly. "You are weak, allow me to help ."

"Yes. help." Godfrey agreed. He would need help removing the lad from the ship and caring him to the Pert single handedly would be next to impossible. So, he agreed to Geraldo's help. "Come brother your help is greatly needed."

Together the two Sherideens headed out of the tavern and back down to the pier where the Cordella was still docked. Godfrey sighed with relief at her sight and actually quicken his pace until he came to her side.

"Oh no ya don't, I won't take on any more of ye wrenched Sherideens aboard me ship." hollered the wooden figure head on the front of the ship.

"Clamp ye hole, ye old wrench." Bellowed One Eye from the deck of the ship. He had been emptying his pipe, tapping it gently on the side rail as the two Sherideens approached. "Thought ye had left me waited with the affected one." He said pointedly to Godfrey.

"Forgive my rude disappearance, I had need of assistance." Godfrey answered knobbing to Geraldo who responded with a gantlet bow towards the captain. "We will see to the young one and ye will be rid of our sight." Godfrey continued.

The mention of the young one perked Geraldo interest. He knew there was something big that Godfrey was withholding but he never thought that it might be a newling.

In the hold deepness bellow the deck they found Blaze in a heap. He was unconscious and very near death. Geraldo was shock at the condition of the young Sherideen. But he said nothing as Godfrey pulled the lifeless member over and began to lift him.

"Take his other arm." Godfrey instructed. Geraldo did as he was told and soon the two Sherideens were caring Blaze from the under belly of the Cordella and out into the cool air of the Hapton.

As they stepped out onto the open deck of the Cordella, One Eyed stopped them abruptly. "If one was approached and his pocket empty, one's lip might just fall open." He mentioned casually.

Godfrey turned sharply towards the caption, he understood what he was implying. "How full would one's pocket need to be, for such a lip to remain shut?" He asked bitterly.

"500 pit-it, would bolt it tight." One Eyed answered with a slit grin on his face.

Godfrey said nothing, he merely stuffed One Eyed hand into his cloak and removed the pouch containing the coins. Then he tossed them to the captain.

Pleased the captain stepped out of their way and bowed slightly as they passed and stepped onto the gang plank.

"'Tis a pleasure doing business with ye."

The three Sherideens shuffled their way off the pier and slowly made their way back into the town. Godfrey's mind raced. He hadn't planned to be tied down with an invalid. He had to rethink his reentry onto the Great isle. He needed to find someplace to hide the lad and he needed a moment to gather his thoughts.

"We must find someplace to . . . " Godfrey began.

"This way, ye can stay in my Twindle way." Geraldo said pushing the twosome to the left and down a dark alley. They walked along only three paces when Geraldo came to a stop in front of a large rusty dented drum that stood waist high. It was leaning against the wooden building with its labels half way turned away from the group. But Godfrey could make out the words J and J's energy drink, the drink that gives you zip.

Geraldo wasted no time. He placed Blaze in Godfrey's hands and turned back to the drum cursing under his breath.

"Dem, think is drum for dem trash. I always having to clear me path." He complained as he pulled the bits of waste out of the drum that had been piled in it. Once he had thrown out all the real garbage he turned back to Godfrey and frowned. "It's not a palace but it'll do."

Then he ran his fingers around the lip of the drum and with that it spilt open revealing a steep staircase that led deep down into the ground. Geraldo took hold of Blaze again and the two Sherideens struggled together down the stairs of the Twindle Way pulling younger Blaze with them. Once inside the large metal drum swung closed be hide them with a crack that shook the stairs and caused several pieces of mud and dirt to jilt free from the walls. The stairs were muddy but firm and before long they were at the bottom of them and facing a long narrow corridor. The corridor was filled with bits and pieces of old wooden crates that formed the support beams and arches. Godfrey could make out several familiar products as he pushed onwards through the corridor like, Himan's ale, Ohara's drip cream in bars, Anton's peppermint tongue toffee, Jimbum's own medical sprout soil solution and Cargill's liquid "Vigor." It seemed odd to Godfrey that Geraldo's Twindle Way would be made up of such things. Twindle Ways were usually, muddy yes but beyond the mud they were actually sound and well-constructed using the best materials available. After all a Sherideens magic would cover any imperfections even if one had had to use such inferior materials. So why was Geraldo's Twindle Way in such bad condition. Godfrey had not a clue but he ignored it for the moment and continued down the corridor until they came to a huge open hall lite up by three fire places.

The fire places were spread out each one on a different side of the hall. And they were built out of what looked the finest cut gray/blue marble each one a perfect match of the next. The mantle pieces were carved in beautiful detail with diamond back fling hawks standing ready a top of each. The floor of the room was also constructed of a fine gray marble, and it was obvious that at one time the hall had been a magnificent show place.

But now the hall was a show place for trash. On the walls of the hall were bits of wrappers, newspapers and tin cans. The trash was like a living wall paper moving and covering almost ever speck of space. Every so often another piece of litter would drift into the hall and fill in an empty space. There were wrappers from every known product produced on the isle and Godfrey was shocked to as he entered and glanced around at the walls.

Geraldo though said nothing, he had grown use to his strange wall paper and didn't notice Godfrey's reaction to the surging trash, instead he manipulated the groups path and armed for the large pit in the center of the room. The large pit was filled with over stuffed burnt yellow pillows. They were dusty and well-worn but it seemed the perfect place to dump Blaze and so that just what they did leaving him in a heap.

"What should we do with him now, brother. Surely he is in dire need of a healer." Geraldo commented as he climbed out of the pit.

"Yes, I need him well. He cannot travel in this condition. We must find one who will heal him and at the same time I must plan carefully my return to Cimmevian." He said as he stepped over to one of the large fire places and leaded against the gray blue tile.

Geraldo looked up at Godfrey and prosed. "Brother tell me of ye plan and I shall be your faithful servant."

Godfrey knew he could trust his old colleague. He knew he could because they had both been cast out by their own members.

They had both been stripped of their titles, their connections and their powers. Godfrey had endured the worse. He had been stripped of his powers by the chamber and now had no magic at all. While Geraldo had lost only the strength of his powers. It was why his Twindle Way accepted trash for its supports. He had not the strength in his powers to make it seen any other way. It was also why he made his living doing only simple magic tricks. He had no more power than an average Wardeen yet he had always dreamed of the moment he would return to the Pert and take back his rightful position and powers. Just as Godfrey dreamed.

The two Sherideens grinned at each other both wanting revenge for their exile from the Ubil. Both desiring a triumphant return to the Pert and their members. So together they devised a plan. They would seek a healer for Blaze and then with his powers they would take control of the Pert and rule Cimmevian Town.

Note* If you want to read the story <u>The Quake at Thorny Pass,</u> it is in Legends and Tales.

The Sentry

The stone protectors appeared around the group of four and prodded them to their feet.

"Ye must leave this place and never return, the Vista has given all ye may learn. Go now and we shall return to ye, the companions to whom we agreed."

Weak the four companions stood up and held onto each other for support. They stumbled towards the caves mouth but were stopped by Langston who held up his hand and commanded.

"LET THE SENTRY REMOVE THY COMPANY."

"YES." The other protectors agreed and turned back towards the place on the stone wall where Cornelius had heard the voice. The voice that had told him what to do to help Marypat.

The group searched the crystal wall with their eyes and watched as the form of a normal sized Vaster member appeared in the stone. To Marypat's surprise she recognized the form.

"Donovan!" She squealed jumping to the crystal wall. Her face met his stone carved equal.

"How?" She asked as she raised her hand to touch his caved cheek but as her figures touched the stone they slipped smoothly into the solid rock as if it wasn't there. Surprised she pulled her hand back and glanced into Donovan's eyes.

"Don't be afraid, you have the power of Stone, remember." He whispered to her. He took her hand and gentle pulled her into the Emerald Mountain. Once inside she found herself standing in front of her husband's natural form. Powerful repressed emotions stuck her and she couldn't help but throw herself into his arms. He too was filled with emotions and took her into his arms more willing than she knew.

"I don't understand, how did you get here, I thought you were dead."

"I am." He answered honestly.

Shocked at his answer, Marypat pulled away from him. "Dead, but you. ."

"But I look a live? Yes. In here, within the stone, my essence is preserved."

"How?"

"My mother and Gillian the Loralac, brought me here soon after it happened. She made a bargain with the protectors." His voice went silent as he moved towards Marypat and held her hand. He pulled it to his lips and kissed it softly.

"I loved you and I never meant to hurt you, this you must know."

"I do, Donovan, and I hold no ill towards you, this I need you to know. I would have been yours, with a free heart, if you would have waited." Her voice was gentle as she continued. "My love for you needed not a spell, it needed only interval for which to grow."

"Yes, I know this now I was a fool. . "His voice trailed off but then he lifted his chin with confidence as he continued. "The Vista, it spoke of your son."

"Our son, his name is Blaze." Marypat interrupted with a smile.

Donovan smiled. "That is a fine strong name for my son. This news fills me with joy but in this same moment I understand how imparities it is for you to find him and keep him from choosing the Ubil way. There is not a moment to waist, if what the Vista shows is true, that Blaze travels with a Sherideen."

The Kennard and Cornelius nodded.

"I must get you throw the mountain then with haste. What place would suit ye best?" Donovan asked still holding Marypat's hand.

"Raye Point. Rowan awaits us there." Cornelius answered.

"Very well then, stay close and follow me." Donovan said as he waved his hand at the wall of crystal stone that stood between himself and Cornelius. The wall split like jelly, just wide enough for Cornelius, Tag and the Kennard to fit throw. They entered the crack and followed behind Marypat and Donovan as they strolled together hand in hand.

The pace through the mountain was an easy one, and Donovan took the opportunity to clear his conscience with Marypat. Marypat in turn told Donovan about his son. By the time they reached Raye Point, Donovan was all caught up with the knowledge of his son.

When they reached Raye Point, Rowan was indeed waiting for them. He didn't seem the least bit surprised to find the group appear to him from inside the mountain. He did however seem shocked when Donovan came into view on the side of the mountain and opened the surface to allow Cornelius, Tag and the Kennard step free of its form. Before Donovan closed the opening two more members flowed from the opening and landed on the needle covered ground beside Rowan. They were Kathrie Gretel and Gillian both looking startled. Rowan helped them to their feet and then approached the mountain where Donovan still stood with Marypat within the crystal stone. They were saying their good-byes when Rowan approached and called to Donovan.

"Brother Sherideen, a protector?" Rowan asked with surprise.

"Yes, brother and who might thee be?" Donovan responded.

"I am Rowan Lazarus." Rowan answered.

"He sits on the council and he has agreed to help find our son." Marypat said in Rowans defense. She could feel Donovan's doubt in trusting a Sherideen and she thought she better try to smooth the waters between them before something happened.

Donovan's eyes turned back to Marypat. "Do ye trust him?"

Mary nodded her head 'yes"

"Very well then. I must get back to the Vista, but I will watch over Blaze from there. Take this crystal shard, if I have news I will appear to you within its face." He said handing her the dark green emerald shard. Then he bowed forward and kissed her softly on the mouth. When she opened her eyes, Donovan was gone.

Sadly, Marypat stepped from the mountain. She was weak. Her emotions spent but she hides this from Rowan as she walked away from him and approached Kathrie Gretel.

Kathrie Gretel caught Marypat's sad eyes.

"Why didn't you tell me?" Marypat uttered.

"Would it have changed anything?"

"Yes!" Marypat replied. She had so much she needed to know but Cornelius over heard the Lassies and broke in before she could ask them.

"We don't have occasion for this, the boy travels with Sherideens on Hapton soil. We must leave right away, to stop them." He said with authority.

"We must reach the Cascades before the eve, the trail through Raye Raye Forest is too torturous without the dawn and the light will soon be spent." The Kennard interjected.

"Why the Cascades? When there is an easier span over the Darling River at Kidd crossing." Tag interrupted as he listened from Gillian's shoulder.

"Yes, 'tis true, but the Hedlens, Baldric and Colb will meet us at the Cascades, they have with them the means to transport us to the Haptons without delay" Rowan explained.

Marypat stood listening to the group. She wanted to tell them not to worry about the light, she could easily ask her grandmother the leave on the light. But when she tried to speak she was to exhausted. She knew she needed to get to her son but at that moment her body gave up and she collapsed on the ground. The Kennard ran to her side and scooped her into his arms.

"Mary are ye alright?"

Marypat's mind was so drained she could not respond. She could hear him calling to her but she could not react. Her eyes slipped closed and she was dreaming.

It was a bright beautiful day and she was running on the beach at Lime Key, in Jamaica. The water was licking the shore and she could feel its coolness on her toes. She smiled as she heard a familiar voice behind her calling to her. She turned around and there standing behind her was Horatio. He was smiling at her and said.

"Rest now we shall travel when ye are able."

Outside of her dream Marypat's companions agreed halfheartedly to stop and rest. They were taking a chance by stopping now. Blaze and the Sherideens could get away. But at the same time, they could not travel with Marypat in such a weak state. They needed her to be strong. The entire group needed to be strong. They had just been through hell and they all needed a chance to rest. So, it was decided that they would camp under the trees at Raye Point and start off early the next morrow for the Cascades and the awaiting Hedlens.

Meanwhile at the Pert a shadowy figure slipped out from behind the huge copper curtains and disappeared down the stairs that led to the Kert. At the Kert he was met by a crowd of cloaked Ubil members eager to hear his words.

"'Tis the moment. Her company rests at Raye Point, kill whom stands against ye but remember do not harm the Maurieen. It is the Maurieen to whom our future relays." the figure whispered.

With that the crowd became excited.

"Quite or ye shall disrupt my chance at surprise." The clocked figure hushed them. "Go now, but hasten thou step until ye receive my sign that the Pert is ours."

The crowd of Ubil Members hurried through the Kert and headed in the direction of Raye Point, leaving the shadowy figure standing beside an orange clocked member.

"Come Verrill, 'tis the junction of change." The shadowy figure remarked before disappearing back up the stairs to the Pert.

A Yellow Glow

In the Haptons a soft feathery yellow glow was drifting throw the muddy corridor of Geraldo's Twindle Way. It gently bounced along until it came to the large warm hall. Once inside it drifted up to the trash cover ceiling and took a good look around. A fire was burning in the middle fireplace while the other two were smoldering. Their smoking embers were all that remained of the blazing fire.

In the center of the room, unconscious was a young member lying face down. Beside him sat an old skinny skeleton like Sherideen, talking to a younger plumper Sherideen. Both seemed unaware of the small yellow ball of fluff drifting high above them and both jumped with surprise when a single high-pitched bell ran twice just over their heads.

"What the. . . " Godfrey shouted jumping to his feet.

"No worry, brother. . It's the Kathrieen we sent for Edith Ting." Geraldo explained.

Geraldo stepped forward and glanced up at the tiny fluff ball. "It is ye, Edith?"

The yellow fluff drifted down until it hovered just at eye level with Geraldo. Then in a flash of yellow light the puff ball disappeared and standing in its place was a young beautiful Kathrie caring a wooden frame.

"Good morrow." She replied with a curtsy. The little Kathrie was dressed in a fluffy yellow dress that fell just to her knees. She wore white stocking and white sparking leather shoes that came to a sharp point at the toe. She had jet black hair that she wore pulled up into two high ponytails that sat on the top of her head. The ponytails were held together by two yellow Etains that were chained to the ponytails. Her face was beaming with joy, she could hardly contain. She smiled broadly up at Geraldo before continuing.

"I'm afraid Mother has been called off to the Pert on urgent matters and she has left Me. . " She curtsied again. "Ella. . in charge of the office. How can I help ye?"

Godfrey wasn't amused. "Is this some kind of joke." He turned on Geraldo. "Do ye find this amusing."

Ella was offended and quickly jumped to defend her qualifications.

"I assure ye Master Sherideen I am indeed well qualified to aid ye. I have been schooled since birth and I have attended two in-depth passes at Logan's Academy for Kathries, for which I achieved high honors in all subjects on the GXC. " Ella declared with an air of anger. Her entire body blinked pink then and she raised her hand to her head and flicked one of the tiny Etains twice until she glowed yellow again.

"Furthermore." She continued." My mother would never allow me to take charge of her accounts if I had not been able to prove my abilities under pressure and that I have, as a matter of fact, by working this entire last pass at Great Town's infirmary." She blinked pink again and this time when she flicked the little Etain she turned her anger on her.

"I told you not to do that, if ye turn pink again I'll feed ye to Auntie Edna." She screeched. Her eyes turned red and for a moment all could see the true evil in the young Kathrie. How sweetly it was camouflaged by the yellow lace and fluff, but in truth it was just a disguised.

"Well then." Godfrey began." Now that we have that out of the way, I am Godfrey and this is my . . . Son. He is in great pain. It seems that he has had a delayed reaction to his Sherideen growth. It appears it has hit him all at once."

"Poor dear, I never heard of such a thing. Has he had his Sherite Extolel?" she asked sweetly.

"No and as a matter of fact that is where we are heading, but as ye can see the lad can't travel like this." Godfrey mentioned in his most fatherly voice.

"Oh, no he must not travel like this, it will only make it worse." Ella remarked calmly.

"Have ye encouraged him to . . . ye know.. .kill something," she implied with her eyebrows lifted. "Sometimes a simple evil act can relieve the pain, the Hisue one pain is far less than the pain of change."

"Oh yes, I agree, but as ye can see we can't even wake him. He has not the strength left to control his own wand." Godfrey explained.

"I see, yes it's gone on too far." She thought for a moment and then placed down the small wooden frame she was caring under her arm. She placed it on one of the tables beside the burning fireplace and then turned back to Godfrey. "I shall consult with my sisters."

Godfrey and Geraldo watched as the Kathrie opened the two-sided frame to reveal what looked like two mirrors but when Ella pressed her face up to the glass there was no refection.

Ella raised her hand to one side of the glass frame and tapped on it.

"Edda, Edina are ye there? Sisters." She called out.

Suddenly both sides reflected a perfect replica of Kathrie. Yet one was blue and the other green. The three girls chatted softly to one another while Godfrey and Geraldo stood quietly waiting. After a moment or so Ella turned to the two Sherideens and spoke.

"My sisters and I believe that a strong pain reliever is advised but we also want to give him something for vitality. Give him a little zip, it might encourage him to use his magic and that might evade much of the paralyzing pain he is experiencing. Therefore, eventually eliminating the need for the pain reliever."

Godfrey glanced at Geraldo and Geraldo nodded his head. "It sounded good to me." Geraldo said.

So, Godfrey gave his ok and the three Kathries set off to work making the potion.

"I'll need a cauldron of five hands or more." Ella said to Geraldo who quickly returned with one.

"Hang it over the fire." She instructed him then she turned to her sister and asked "What's next?"

Edda the one dressed in green pulled out a large leather book and read from it out loud while Edina, the one dressed in blue seemed to disappear from sight leaving her mirror open.

"Prepare a cauldron of five hands or more, drip in one cattle can of Andree oil remember don't pour." Edda read.

Suddenly Edina reappeared on her side with a cattle can full of Andree oil. She handed it through the mirror. Ella took it from her sister and stepped over to the cauldron. Slowly she added the oil to the cauldron as it sparked and spit with each additional drop.

Edina disappeared from sight and in her place was the head of a gray white striped house coose. The coose glanced through the glass, then it pressed its nose against it until its surface gave way and allowed the coose to climb through. The Kathries didn't notice as the coose made itself comfortable in front of the mirrors, purring happily while it cleaned its face.

Edda read on. "Add two handfuls of Saddle Dust to cool then scrap with a spatula heap in a pool."

Ella stepped back to the mirror as Edina offered one heaping handful of Saddle Dust. Ella accepted it and tossed it in the cauldron, quickly she returned to the mirror and again Edina was ready with the second handful of dust. Ella quickly tossed in the second handful and then set off to stir the pot.

Meanwhile a second gray and white striped coose pressed her face into the empty glass where the blue sister had been and she too pushed against the glass until she was able to jump through. Upon landing on the other side though the second coose startled the first one who then popped the second in the nose with her paw and then jumped to the floor. The first coose then strolled around the hall while Edda continued reading.

"Slowly add one jigger of Sage Moss Water, mix evenly and allow the pot to get hotter."

Ella accepted the jigger of Sage Moss Water from her sister and then went back to the cauldron. She slowly added the water as she did bright purple sparkles filled the room. Slowly the sparkles subsided and Ella waited while the cauldron slowly began to boil.

"Boil well, a quarter sweep will do then add one drop of Henmax dew. Stir round one last moment fill vial, take one and ye will be fine."

Once the potion had boiled well enough Ella stepped back to the mirror and notice the sleeping coose coiled up on the table. Edina was not yet in her mirror so Ella turned to Edda who was just putting down the leather book when she too noticed the coose.

At the same time the girls reported. "Edina, ye left your glass open again. Auntie Edna has escaped."

The cooses ear perked up just a bit but beyond that it showed no sign of concern. Edina on the other hand returned to the glass and pushed through the last ingredient for the potion. Her hair was a mess and one of her blue Etains had escaped.

"Next moment I get to read the potion. I always have to run to get the component. Do you know where mum keeps the Henmax dew? It's all the way up it the rafters I tell ye. I nearly broke my neck retrieving it and all ye care about is Auntie Edna."

"Well dear sister I have a potion for a broken neck." Edda commented coolly.

Edina was not amused with her sister comment, so she stormed away leaving her glass open.

Edda stepped over to Edina's side and pushed Edina's glass shut. "She's so moody lately. By the way did you need a vile?"

"Yes, give me a few. I want to give the father enough potions for the trip." Ella replied as she scratched the half sleeping coose on the neck.

Edda passed a handful of small vials though the glass to Ella who placed them down beside the Henmax dew. Then Ella curled up the purring coose and handed her back through the glass.

Ella stepped over to the potion and added the last element, the Henmax dew. It foamed up the instant the dew hit the solution. It frothed for a few moments and then the frothily bubbles popped liked a pot of corn. When it subsided, the potion was done. Ella poured out the gooey green contains of the cauldron into the small vials her sister had given her and then turned to Godfrey.

"He will need to take this one right away and I 'll help ye to administer it. But keep these handy." She said handing him five extra vials.

"Ye should watch him closely, and never let him get this bad again. Once he on his feet, try and encourage him to use his magic, that will take the edge off the pain and it might just be enough that he would not need another douse of the pain reducer. But if it doesn't give him one vial every 4 sweeps. The five vials should be enough to allow ye to get to the Pert and direct his Sherite Extolel. Once he's been called the pain will stop and he won't need the pain reducer anymore."

Godfrey accepted the vials and stuffed them away in his cloak.

"Very well then let's have him over." Ella instructed.

Geraldo and Godfrey jumped into the pit and turned Blaze over for the young Kathrie. He was still out cold; his eyes were closed tight and his face was the palest of white. But upon her first glace of him, Ella was enamored. Slowly she moved towards him, she knelt down in the pit of fluffy pillows beside him and studied his fine face. She had seen his look before. His features were distinctly different than his father's, she thought. To her he looked more like the Noble Gazpalding lineage. With their highly distinctive widow's peak, delicate shaped nose and wide jaw. Ella looked up at Godfrey and said. "He has not the look of ye."

"Yes, I know he takes up for his mother's side."

"Oh!" Ella replied, that made sense the mother must be a Gazpalding, but it did not quench her remarks. "Then we must get him well so he can take his rightful place at the Pert. All will be well again, with a

Gazpalding in power. My family and all the Ubil can return home to Cimmevian." She beamed.

Godfrey stood silent he was shocked by Ella's comments. Why would she think Blaze was a Gazpalding, the Sherideen family he hated more than any one? He had never thought that Blazes look was that of Gazpalding but as he looked on the lad at that moment he too saw the likeness to that of his old master.

"No, could it be?" Godfrey thought to himself as his mind became absorbed in questions. *"The son the Maurie, Marypat and the son of Gazpalding?* " Suddenly his hate for the Gazpalding line changed as he grasped the true path he held with Blaze. It was almost too good to be true. The members at the Pert would have to hand over power to a Gazpalding. There would be no need for surprise, no need to fight. It was Blaze's place, he was the rightful heir. Godfrey grinned a most evil grin.

Meanwhile Ella was busy trying to press the green gooey liquid in to Blazes mouth. As she did she continued to unknowingly reveal to Godfrey important information about the Pert.

"Well now I understand why ye are in such a rush to get him well and to the Pert. With that vile Marypat returning to the isle, he will want to witness for himself her demise. But ye already knew that's why mother was called to the Pert so urgently. Seems Handrew Koke has had enough of Leopold Norwood's reluctant leadership. I mean when they found out the Maurieen had returned Leopold did nothing. Can ye believe that? Our one opportunity to kill the wretch that has poisoned our way of life and he ignores it. Well I can tell ye that there are many of us who see it quite differently. Mother says it's the sign they have been waiting for. It's the moment of change. So she has gone to be a part of the vile Maurieens capture. Mother said they would have her in confinement by morrow." She grinned evilly. " Perhaps by eve of the morrow I can shed these distasteful garments and return to the comfort of my robe. Oh, wait till my sisters hear." She declared. She finished administering the potion and then jumped to her feet. She bounced over to the mirrors and tapped the glass.

Godfrey again was surprised by the young Kathie's words. His mind was numb, he wanted to stop the Kathrie from telling her sisters but he didn't react fast enough. It was too late and beside Blaze was waking up. His arms were grabbing at Godfrey for support and it took all of Godfrey's attention.

"Sisters come quick I have news to tell ye."

The two sisters appeared once again and Ella explained that the young Sherideen was the nephew of the late great Drake Gazpalding. The two young Kathries gasped in delight.

"OHHH, is it true, let us set eyes on him for ourselves. So, we too may be filled with hope."

It was as if their words brought strength to Blaze's legs. For as they spoke, he stood up strong and looked around.

"Where am I?" Blaze asked still hold onto Godfrey.

His husky voice made the Kathries swoon.

"Oh, he so sultry." Melted Edina as she tried desperately to fix back her hair. She had recaptured to blue Etain and had her almost back into place on the top of her head but the little Etain kept kicking the hoop out of Edina's finger and flashing purple every time she was successful. Finally, Edina gave up and tossed the Etain to the side leaving the right side of her head covered in her long black hair.

"Oh, he looks just like Gazpalding! A dream to the eyes" Edda sighed.

Blaze looked at the Kathries with a confused look on his face.

"Do not be alarmed gorgeous, ye are among friends." Reported Ella cheerfully. "I am Ella and these are my sisters, Edda and Edina." The yellow Kathrie said with a giggle. "My word what an interesting blouse ye wear, the art work is most clever."

Blaze said nothing his mind was spinning and he seemed exhausted. The pain was gone but it was as if he needed to sleep, even though that was all he had been doing for the pass two turns. He rubbed his eyes and swayed slightly.

"Don't worry sweetie. The pain reducer works faster than the vigor. Ye will soon fill with life ye will see." Ella calmly replied.

She smiled up at Blaze and he looked down at her, just then the vigor kicked in and his eyes sparked with tiny orange embers. His body flashed with energy and he felt great.

Ella smiled a broad smile. "What did I tell ye? Well I see my work here is done. That will be 30 pie-it please." She announced holding out her hand to Godfrey.

Godfrey paid her and with that she danced over to the mirrors and giggled to her sister. "Look sister our first wages."

The sister giggled merrily as Ella passed them each their coins. Then she closed the frame and snapped her fingers. Instantly she turned into a soft yellow fluffy ball again and began drifting back towards the entrance of the Twindle Way but before she disappeared from their sight she called out one last time.

"Call on us any mourn or eve, we're pleased to be the Kathries ye need!" And with that she was gone.

Battle in the Bush

Eve had set and the darkness was thick around the small group of exhausted travelers. Their only means of light was that of their glow. Which three of the travelers had none? Still the remaining four cast enough of a glow to illuminate frames among the dense forest floor.

The group lied together in a brake of the Blue Fur Pine and Henmax plants, where the ground was covered in soft Trortle moss and pine needles. Among the plants humming in unison were Howie Beetles. Their hum at times were deafening but for the small group they seemed not to notice as they slipped off to sleep.

The seven travelers slept unaware that their small glimmer in the huge Raye Raye forest had led a herd of Ubil straight to them and now they were surrounded by a massive gathering that was preparing to attack. The Ubil stood waiting for a sign. The sign that said Handrew had control of the Pert and they could resume their task.

Suddenly the Howie Beetles went silent in the thicket. The stillness awoke Rowan with a start. He sensed something was wrong. He reached for his wand and gently nudged Tag who was passed out on a patch of bright green Trortle moss.

"Warn the others, quietly, we are not alone." Rowan whispered to the Frandies.

Tag hopped to his feet but before he could reach his companions, a flare was shot into the air far in the distance at the Pert. It was the sight that the Ubil members had been waiting for. The Pert was Handrew's and the Ubil now had his blessing to attack and capture Marypat.

Rowan spun to his feet twirling his wand over his head and quickly called out "Mem bree a me!"

The sparks from his wand shot out in a circle that enclosed the small group in a bubble, protecting them from the on slot of evil spells that were being sent towards them. But with each new strike the bubble wavered and Rowan knew it would not hold for long. It would however give him the interval he needed to awaken the others.

With an array of sparkles flashing all around, the group awoke and quickly organized their defense. Kathrie Gretel, Cornelius and Rowan readied their wands. Gillian, Tag and the Kennard prepared their swords and daggers while Marypat desperately searched for the crystal Donovan had given her. With it she could have all the elements of Tradition and she could defend herself with her powers.

Finally, she discovered it in her bag and grabbed it up, tightly gasping it in her left hand. Her mind raced, she needed a spell, she needed to know how to channel her powers. But she had never been trained to, she had never been taught. For an instant hopelessness filled her. She knew she was to be of no use to the small brave members of her company. She knew they would fight to the death for her and she could be no help to them. Her heart fell and tears filled her eyes. As they did her body tingled with power and she began to glow blue. All but one of the elements were present, air, stone and her tears as water.

Only fire was missing but still she could feel the energy of the elements within her and she did not know how to control them.

The Kennard noticed her then and stepped to her side. "Do not relinquish hope, Marypat, we will defend ye."

"I have no doubt you will, but it is I who has not the knowledge. I don't even know a simple spell to help with." She complained.

Kathrie Gretel turned to her slightly while still keeping her eyes set on the advancing Ubil beyond the bubble and said. "Use a Dacular movement, thrust ye hand forward and call out DOM ME A GRON."

Marypat nodded and said the words to herself again and again. Until she felt confident.

Three more flashes hit the bubble and it was enough to break the spell. The bubble broke and the small company was revived. Instantly the battle began. Sparks flew from Kathrie Gretel's wand striking one of the cloaked figures and sending him hurling into the air. Cornelius and Rowan fended off one entire side as they worked together spraying the attackers with an array of colorful spells. The Kennard and Tag ran forward with their swords and slashed through the bushes, killing several Ubil while Gillian stood with sword ready just beyond Marypat and Kathrie Gretel. He was her last line of defense. He was not to move and he did not waver even when they were bombarded with incoming spells.

Kathrie Gretel managed to fend off most of the spells while Marypat tried to assist. Her first attempt was a complete failure. Her intention was to hit a green clocked Sherideen standing beside a tall Blue Fur Pine. But her aim was off and she struck the tree with her gesture and it cracked the tree in half fling the top half of the Blue Fur Pine back into the forest. Undeterred she tried again while the green clocked Sherideen sent his reply towards her, sticking her painfully in the leg. Anger filled her then and that was the last element she needed. Her body burst into flames, her hands glowed with fire as she send her second attempted towards the same Sherideen.

"Dom me a gron." She bellowed.

"Whack!" The spell flow forward striking the Sherideen burst him into flames and disintegrated right before Marypat's eyes.

A horrible clamor arose from the tree line as the remaining Ubil realized the powers of their opponent. Several Ubil members retreated, but most grew infuriated. Their firry united the Ubil members on the second line of attack giving them the strength to overpower the right flank. Together they moved forward spreading a heavy array of spells that struck Cornelius and Rowan. Both were sent hurling throw the air.

With Cornelius and Rowan out of the way the Ubil members were able to advance. They preceded forward striking Kathrie Gretel off guard and freezing her with her wand still pointed forward.

Gillian then moved with his sword swinging towards the advancing Ubil, desperate to protect Marypat and Marypat continued calling out "Dom me a gron." Missing most of her marks but trying none the less.

Gillian's mighty attempt was no match for the unending flow of Ubil. He was over run. Down they pulled his body until he laid face down in the moss, dead. Marypat was horrified.

"Gillian no" as she swung madly tossing fire balls in all directions walloping three of the Ubil's and sending them to their knees

Marypat's voice echoed through the evening air, sticking the Kennard's ears and sending shivers down his spin. He was fighting for his own life just beyond the tree line and there was nothing he could do to help Marypat or Gillian. He jumped to his right, to try and see where her voice had come from but as he took his eyes off of his appointed he was struck with a powerful blow that knocked him out cold.

Tag alone watched in horror as the Kennard fell. He had no choice but to remain hidden while the Ubil moved in on Marypat.

"Detain her." Came the command and with that Marypat was driven to the ground knocking the crystal out of her hand and rendering her uncaused. Her body laid there with a slight shimmer of a blue glow that slowly faded. With her powers gone the Sherideens quickly tied her hands and feet with bonding rope, a strong magical rope that incapacitated her from using her powers.

Then they draped her in a black cloth and flew away with her in the direction of the Pert. Leaving others die where they lied.

Tag hoped from his hiding place as the last Sherideen took flight. He ran to Gillian his friend, he was dead. There was nothing he could do for him. He lowered his head in sorrow for his friend and then sudden there was a noise behind him. He sprung to his feet, whipped out his dagger and ready himself to avenge Gillian's death.

"Put it away Tag, it's only me and Rowan." Cornelius uttered as he and Rowan stumbled back into the bloody clearing. They had seen for themselves the Sherideens fly off with their prize, draped in black but they were too far away to do anything to help.

"Do we just give up?" Tag shouted angrily.

"NO, we go after them." Came a weary voice from the Henmax bush. It was the Kennard. He was still sitting on the ground, his head had blood running down the side of it but he was determined to get her back.

"Yes, we must go after them, but we must first notify the council." Rowan insisted as he inspected Kathrie Gretel and prepared to release her from her curse.

"That would waste a precious stretch. We must leave immediately." The Kennard voiced.

Cornelius didn't bother arguing with his companions instead he went over to Gillian's side and knelt. He placed his hand on the back of his dear friend and whispered softly. Only Tag could hear the pain and devotion of his voice. Only Tag heard his pleading words.

"Bless the spirit of this mighty champion, known for his worth deeds. An honorable friend, warrior and brother. Guide his soul to his rightful place among the heroes of the stone. Keep him there in your place of homage, that he might never fade." Cornelius bent his head in sorrow.

Tag looked up at the crystal mountain and gasped. He stepped backwards and tripped landing in Cornelius hands. Cornelius noticed Tags expression and glanced over to see what had him so shocked. There in the stone were all eight of the mighty Loralacs. They were standing precisely the height of a normal size Loralac. They had not their tremendous carved forms but their natural appearance. They were lined up at attention and on Langston's order they marched forward in two columns. As they moved out from the Crystal Mountain the mountain moved out with them. They marched onwards until they came to Gillian's body. Then they stopped and Javier called.

"Brother we welcome ye to our clan."

Cornelius rose grabbing Tag as he stepped away from Gillian lifeless body.

They watched as the eight Loralac began moving forward again. The mountain stretched with them as they moved along both sides of Gillian. Their march continued until Gillian was completely enclosed by the emerald Mountain. Then the eight Loralacs bent down and picked up their brother. Each one having a hand on him. Then they turned towards the mountain and marched back within, disappearing from sight.

Tag turned back to his companions only to realize they had all witnessed the Loralacs claim Gillian's body. Kathrie Gretel was unfrozen and in tears having just realized what had happen while she was frozen. Rowan and the Kennard had stopped arguing. They had decided to head to the Cascades as they had originally planned. From the Cascades Rowan could head to the counsel and inform them of what had happen to Marypat and at the same time the Kennard could head to the Pert.

They would leave right away. They would have to travel by eve, it would be a tricky path but there was no other way.

At the Pert the scene was one of claim. There had not been even one spark that transpired during the takeover. In fact, Leopold simply removed his robe and handed it to Handrew upon his first mention of position. Leopold was not one for conflict. He had no desire to fight for the title. He could just as easily step aside and allow Handrew the post. For Leopold holding the position of Supreme Master was no reason to die. So, he stepped down and took his new post as Master Protector of Windsport. He even went as far as to send the signal for Handrew that the Pert was claimed.

Then the three Sherideens, Handrew, Verrill and Leopold waited and watched the evening sky for their followers to return with their spoils. Hardy a sweep pasted and then there in the sky came a strange shape. As it grew closer it was obvious the band had been success. Marypat was their prisoner and before long the Pert was a buzz of activity. Sherideens and Kathries who had not been a part of the assault, saw the group returning and run to the Pert to see for themselves the wicked one known as Marypat.

The gathering crowd cheered as the returning blood socked Sherideens and Kathries landed on the solid flooring of the Pert. Quickly Marypat was swept up and taken to the Ramp. She was tied with her arms over her head and her feet were pulled and stretched down the full length of the ramp. The bounding rope was then treaded through the rollers at either end and cranked until they were tight. She laid there unconscious while the mob grew with excitement.

"Kill the demon!" The multitude roared.

"Ripe her limbs from her!" Chatted a group from Stone as they shook their fists in the air.

"Crush her bones!" Cheered several from Red Chard.

The energy of crowd grew to a dangerous level and Handrew found himself surround by a surging horde of irrational blood thirsty Ubil who couldn't see beyond killing his new prize. He had plans for her, plans that would return the Ubil to greatness. He needed Marypat alive, not necessarily well, but alive. He could not afford for the masses to take control of her so he had to do something and he had to do it quickly.

To Cimmevian Town

Meanwhile deep below the rustic clay of the Haptons the three Sherideens had discovered that the young Kathries had left one of their cooses behind. Geraldo was busy trying to contact them while Blaze sat listening to Godfrey explain that they were on the Great Isle and how he had gotten to Geraldo's Twindle Way.

"You were very ill on the journey me lad, I did all I could do to keep you comfortable." Godfrey lied. "Then once we arrived I rushed to get ye help. Geraldo was so kind to allow us to enter into his lair and contact a healer."

"The yellow Kathrie?" Blaze asked. As he watched the gray coose curl up on Godfrey's lap and begin purring so loud it filled the hall.

"Yes, her name is Ella." Geraldo added reassuringly as he stroke the purring coose.

"She spoke of my mother returning to the isle." Blaze's voice trailed off as he realized that his mother had followed him and now she was in danger because of him.

"She called her vile and a wretch. Will they kill her?" Blazes question was more painful to utter than anything he had ever needed an answer to. He feared Godfrey's reply.

But it was Geraldo who responded to his words. He jumped to his feet, his eyes were wide and he pointed his finger at Blaze as he accosted him.

"Ye a Sherideen, are the son of that Creature? I had no idea that this lad was the child of the feared Maurieen." His face flared red with anger.

Blaze sat confused not knowing how to respond.

"Retreat brother." Godfrey stated unmoved by Geraldo's show of anger and he continued to stroke the coose. "The lad is a Sherideen, he is one of us, look at him. He is our mate. Did not the Kathrie Ella say he had the look of Gazpalding himself? Well?"

"Yes, she did. . ."Geraldo relinquished. "The lad is no doubt a Sherideen but how? If his mother is the evil Maurieen how is it possible for her son to be a Sherideen?"

Geraldo's hands then began to shake and he turned away from them and quickly counted on his figures. "11" he said as he turned back to Blaze.

"What is the number of your Birthrite?" Gerald asked.

"Do you mean how old am I?" Blaze asked.

"Yes."

"I'm 13."

Geraldo nodded "Ye father is Donovan Gazpalding."

The hall fell silent as Blaze took in the claim.

"No, they were only friends." Blaze replied stunned. He could not make sense of Geraldo's claim. His mother didn't like Donovan, not that way.

"Perhaps but I know for a fact that they were married, just before Donovan died and the council banished her from the isle." Geraldo said with confidence.

"Married. . .to Donovan. . .banished, she was . .. " Blaze couldn't take it. The guilt was too much, tears welled up in his eyes and as they did his body began to glow. Blaze could feel an enormous wave of energy encircle him and it grew with the anger he felt for Geraldo's words towards his mother.

Geraldo stepped back away from the lad and Godfrey followed after dropping the coose to the floor.

"Ye need to calm down." Godfrey nervously lectured the young Sherideen. He sensed the enormous power building within Blaze. The same power he sensed back on Fire Isle, and didn't need the young Sherideen losing control now. Godfrey needed to reassure Blaze that he was going to help him, and he would do anything, say anything to earn the lads trust. He was even willing to help save Marypat if it meant Blaze would follow him. His only problem now was convincing Geraldo of the advantages of helping the lad.

"Go along with me, he is the answer to us retrieving our powers. Don't be stupid!" Godfrey whispered to Geraldo then he turned back to Blaze.

"Do not fret Blaze, we are your adversary's." Godfrey assured Blaze.

Geraldo net his brow in disagreement but Godfrey was quick to elbow him.

"Just think about, if you are Donovan Gazpalding's son, then you are the heir to the position of Supreme Master. No Sherideen can refuse your post, no Sherideen can go against ye and ye alone can quash the plans to harm your mother."

"The Pert will be yours, not one Ubil can deny ye. Your mother will be safe. Please allow us to help ye." Godfrey pleaded.

"Why? Why would ye help me, ye are Ubil, are ye not?" Blaze flashed as his body radiated a bright orange.

"Yes, we are but many passes ago we were wronged by the members of Ubil and it would give us great pleasure to return to the Pert and reclaim our positions." Godfrey confessed.

The gray coose perked up her ears and listened intensely while the two Sherideens continued.

"How were you wronged." Blaze asked.

"I was sent to the Red Isle to die a very slow and painful death, do ye not recall our prison there. Is ye mind so unwell that it doesn't remember the heat of that place." Anger grew in Godfrey as he defended his plight.

When he finished the grey coose stood and glazed up at Godfrey. Her eyes blinked with a sad look, then she rubbed up against his leg and meowed.

Blaze lowered his head. "Yes, I do remember you telling me you had been banished to the Red Isle and I do recall you tell me you had no powers that they had been stripped from you. I am sorry you have been very helpful to me even when I was at my weakest, you could have left me to suffer and die but instead you have done so much for me. You have indeed proven yourself to me, I do trust you and thank you."

Blaze then stepping closer to Godfrey and reached out his hand. "Brother, what is your plan then, on how we will enter the Pert?"

The two shook hands and then Godfrey smiled. He had done it. He had earned Blazes trust.

"Well, let me tell ye. . . ." Godfrey began as he moved the two Sherideens over to the long dining table and sat down. Together they laid their plan on how best to take command of the Pert. They spoke together for almost a sweep until they were interrupted by a familiar yellow fluffy ball.

The ball drifted in from high above and came to rest just beside the table where they sat. In a flash the yellow ball disappeared and, in its place, stood the young Kathrie caring her wooden frame.

"Well I see the young master is feeling better and might I say it's a very good thing too. Why I just heard from mum and she say that the evil Maurieen is in custody at the Pert this moment." The young Kathrie almost giggled with her excitement.

Blaze on the other hand did everything he could to control himself. He wanted to throttle the young Kathrie for calling his mother evil.

"And let me say it's a good thing I got your call when I did, a moment later and I wouldn't have heard." She added.

"Why is that?" Asked Godfrey as he stepped away from the table and bent over to scoop up the gray coose.

The young Kathries eyes went wide and her face filled with a most peculiar grin.

"Why? Everyone is heading to the Pert this eve, to set eyes, for themselves, on the repulsive one." she remarked with a smirk.

Then she tried to grab hold of the coose but the coose curled its head back on Godfrey and purred. "That's odd Auntie E never talks to anyone." She babbled on. "Ever since her husband disappeared, she's been intolerable with everyone."

Ella's words about his mother struck Blaze hard and anger flared inside him. His outer glow flashed red and the tips of his hair burst upwards with flames. Geraldo noticed the change in the lad and grabbed his arm.

"Easy there, we don't want to ruin our plans." he whispered to Blaze.

At the same time Ella's words about the coose hit Godfrey dead on and he had to inquire more about the coose.

"What happen to her husband?" Godfrey asked as a strange numbness filled his chest. He knew it was possible that the coose he held in his hands could have been a Kathrieen at one time. It was common for a coose to be the host to the soul of a Kathrieen but was it possible that he knew this one? Was it possible it was his wife, Edie? He had to know.

"Oh, we're not allowed to talk about it. It's the family disgrace. All I can say is that Mum has done all she could over the last 30 passes to prove she had nothing to do with the disaster on the Blue Isle. While Auntie Edie's choice to renounce the Ubil and support her husband." She discloses in a whisper.

"How did she end up like this?" He asked.

"She renounced her own membership, what else could mum do?" Ella voiced aloud. Ella became annoyed with him and stomped over to the table and put down her frame.

Godfrey curled the purring coose in his hands. He raised her to his face and looked in to its eyes. "Edie?" He whispered to the coose.

The coose seemed to blink in agreement. A heaviness filled Godfrey then as he gazed into Edie's eyes and saw his wife looking back at him.

"Oh, the misery I have plagued upon ye." Godfrey uttered quietly, then he held the coose to his neck. He could feel her purring and somehow that made everything alright at least for the moment. He wished he could repay his wife for her faith in him, and for her loyalty even after he was gone. Still at that moment he couldn't take the chance of relieve himself to the young Kathries, he could not allow them to find out who he really was. For he had been the reason for the family's disgrace. He had been the one who had tried to clear the Blue Isle of the Smithsonite, 35 passages earlier. He had been the one banished to the Red Isle. Leaving his wife alone to face the discrimination of all the Ubil. But for now, too much was at stack for him and he knew all he could do was hold her, scratch her and promise to avenge her soul.

Meanwhile Blaze was trying with all his will to relax. Ella words were still echoing in his head and he had to do everything he could to not allow her words to anger him. Slowly he gained control and his body cooled to a yellow glow. He opened his eyes again. When he did he noticed that the Kathrie had placed down her frame and was talking to her sisters again, both sisters were dressed in hooded clocks. Their hairs were down and the cheerful faces were gone.

"Pass Auntie E through and let's get moving." The green cloaked sister shouted.

"I bet we're missing everything! If it wasn't for Auntie E we'd be there already." The blue one expressed.

Godfrey listened to the Kathrieens while he helped Ella, push the coose back though the mirror and then he asked.

"The Pert is several turns travel from here, how are you able to arrive there this eve?"

The three Kathrieens turned to Godfrey in shock, as if a terrible secret had been revealed. But then the yellow Kathrie turned back to her sisters and calmly replied. "No harm sisters they are our brethren."

Both sisters agreed with a nob and Ella explained. "Mum has a Realagraph of the observer in the center of Cimmevian Town. It was painted by Spencer Wadsworth himself." She grinned proudly.

Godfrey gave the Kathrieen a look that said he was impressed. Which only made the Kathrieen smile even larger.

"Would ye like to see it?" She asked.

"Ella! Mum wouldn't be pleased!" The two sisters cried angrily from inside the frame.

"Hush sisters." Ella whirled around to face them. "They are our brethren, besides the young one needs to get to his Sherite Extolel forth with and why should they miss all the fun, sister think about it, should we leave them here while the rest of the Ubil members celebrate this eve?"

Both sisters could not deny Ella's words. It would be wrong to leave them so Ella invited the three Sherideens to travel with her back to her coven where her sisters waited for her.

On the other side of Hapton town, far from the odor of the decrepit port laid the neatly assembled community of Hapton's Beach Resort Village. The village was an extension of the finery and detail of the old Hapton's Plantation House. The house that still stood in the field of Haps Palms that grew on the peninsula. The old house was a model for the rest of the village. Each home was built with its own uniqueness whether it had a different color or layout but they all still embarrassed the old style of wood work with sculpted trimmed accents, etched pillars, arched entrances and wide balcony's that encircled the homes. Every element crafted from the finest martials.

The streets of the village were lite by a series of lanterns set ablaze on top of trotter pillars that lined both sides of the street. Each pillar was exactly 6 hands high, hexagonal in shape and connected to the next with a thick metal chain. The lanterns were also hexagonal in shape and fit the pillars perfectly. Their clear glass sides were held together with a metal frame that came together at the top to form an eight-sided cone and handle.

The light from the pillars illuminated the village and allowed the three Sherideens a clear view of the homes and perfectly manicured lawns. There was not a spec of trash anywhere. There was not a rock or pebble out of place. In fact, there was not a flaw, not a blemish on any of the homes that lined the street.

The group strolled along passing eight brightly colored homes. On the ninth Ella motioned to the group to stop. She then waved her hand at the thick metal chain draped between the two trotter pillars that sat directly in front of house #9. The thick chain disappeared allowing the group to enter the path that led up to the house.

House # 9 was no different from the rest of the homes on the street. The lawn was immaculate. Bright green mugs grass was trimmed and edged flawlessly. The flower beds draped around the large yellow plantation house with matching yellow mims and Christy toes. Even the stone carved path and steppes mimicked the other houses and it was seemed odd to Godfrey that a coven of Kathrieens, Ubil Kathrieens no less would live in such a pretty place.

Still he followed the young Kathrie into the dainty home. Inside the house it was sterile, it looked unlived in. It was unnatural, but just as he began to question his decision to follow the Kathrieen, the young Kathrie reveled the true entrance to her family's coven home.

"Think, blink, wink." called the Kathrie out loud.

Suddenly the large empty wall before them faded away revealing a concealed archway and tunnel carved out of thick yellow halite. The opaque halite glistened at them as the young Kathrie motioned for them to enter. They did and once inside she called out, "Trick, thick, blink." Her words caused the wall to recover the entrance and seal them within.

The group followed the tunnel which quickly turned into stairs that spiraled down deep under the ground.

Moments later the group found themselves in a small round room with a single round mirrored table in the center of it. The walls of the room were covered with unframed paintings and mirrors. There were so many of them that they hang one on top of the other with hardly any space between them. On the far side of the room close to the floor was the only framed painting. The painting was of an old dusty kitchen. It didn't seem to be a piece of art work worth framing but an instant later Ella's two sisters emerged from it. They were both dressed in long cloaks. Edda in green and Edina in blue.

Edda tossed Ella a long yellow cloak as she hurried over to the mirrored table in the center of the room.

"I thought ye would never arrive! We are going to miss everything!" She cracked.

"Oh, relax sister, ye are turning purple. 'Tis not ye best color." Ella giggled.

Edda frowned at her sister and then spit. "Well at least I don't turn Pink!"

Both sisters stared angrily at each other while Edina took control.

"We'll never get there if we don't set the draw." Edina lectured. She stepped up to the mirrored table and glanced into the refection. There on the table was the reflection of all the paintings and mirrors in the room. Quickly she sought out the painting of the Stone Observer. She pointed to it on the tabletop. Instantly the paintings and mirrors that hung on the walls moved and flipped until her selection was in place behind the frame where the painting of the old kitchen had been only a moment before.

"Shall we!" Edina mentioned to her sister who were still arguing. The two Kathrieens stopped quarreling long enough to step into the Realagraph. But once through Edda sent Ella a spark to her head which caused Ella's entire body to flash continually between pink and yellow.

Edina shook her head and turned back to the three Sherideens. "I must apologize for my younger sisters, but if ye follow me I take ye to the Pert."

The three Sherideens agreed to follow Edina. Then they pulled on their long black cloaks. Blaze paused for a moment, he placed down his back pack and unzipped the front pocket. Carefully he slipped his hand into the tight pocket and pulled out the two Japanese daggers from his great-grandfather's days in the war.

Blaze passed one of the daggers to Godfrey, who in turn looked at him in surprise. He had had no idea that the lad carried such a remarkable weapon and he was sure he had seen everything, Blaze had in his bag. He could not imagine where Blaze had acquired it and not only was he surprised the lad had such a weapon but he was shocked that Blaze had willingly handed him it.

"Just in case." Blaze remarked as he placed the second dagger in his belt.

Godfrey nodded in agreement and then cautiously stepped towards the Realagraph. Godfrey still worried that his return might cause them trouble, but he hoped that the excitement of the capture of Marypat might over shine their entrance. At least for the moment.

The reflective Realagraph hung on a corner of a shop near the Stone cove, that overlook the Great Observer. Godfrey was the first of the three Sherideens through and even with his anxiety about what lie ahead, it still felt so good to finally step back on Cimmevian soil. He stood up and looked around while he waited for his companions to follow.

Blaze was the next one through and from where he stood, Godfrey could see the expression of awe grow on the lad's face.

"'Tis a sight to behold." Godfrey affirmed.

And it was, a dark eerie sight. The sky was cracked with red flickers, the air thick with the odor of rotting flesh and the ground covered in soot. Still for some strange reason it felt refreshing to Blaze. It was as if for the first time he could breath. His lungs filled with the stifling stench and at the same moment he was filled with energy. His eyes sparked, his fingertips surged and every hair on his head flashed. The feeling was sensational.

Geraldo joined them after he stepped through the Realagraph. Behind him following unnoticed was Aunt Edie, the coose. She slipped through the Realagraph and hide behind Godfrey. Then without any more delay the group headed off towards the Kert, where they could finally climb the steep steps to the Pert.

The ancient carved steps were filled with Ubil members trying to push their way up to the Pert. Godfrey, Geraldo, Blaze and the three Kathrieens could only stand at the every back of the crowd and listen as the voices in front of them surged with a force of shared evil.

Blaze could feel the intensity growing. He could hear their chanting and calls for death of the Maurieen. Blazes mind flashed with a vision that he was too late. His heart sank, grief filled him as he realized what his foolish adventure had cost him. It had cost him his mother's life.

He stood on the marble stairs and covered his face, tears rolled from his eyes. He could not control his misery. Then suddenly Ella grabbed his arm and spoke with a gasp.

"Young master ye radiate with a might unknown to me."

Blaze opened his eyes and glanced down at Ella's shocked face. Then he noticed that he was not standing on the stone steps beside her but hovering above her and glowing a most sorrowful hue of blue. The realization of his position instantly broke the spell and sent him plunging to a hard landing on the marble steps.

Upon landing on the dusty steps, his hands which took most of the impact, were covered with soot and dirt. The dirt instantly reacted with him and the tears still on his face causing him to begin to glow a bright orange.

Godfrey rushed towards Blaze and grabbed him with both hands. "Brother, thou must control thy self or ye will ruin our plan."

Blaze's body shook, he was trying to take control of himself but could not. "Help me brother." Blaze whispered, the pain of the change was encircling him again.

"The pain reliever." Ella suggested as she moved towards Godfrey and removed a vile from his cloak. "Drink this." She calmly replied as she placed the vile to Blaze's lips.

He drank the green goo and then collapsed. A moment later he was back on his feet and looking like a new lad.

"Wow, that stuff is better than mountain dew!" He said with a grin.

Godfrey released his hold on Blaze and the group turned their attention back on reaching the Pert. But just as they began to push their way up, there came an ominous voice from far above them.

"Enough! Restrain thou tongue and heed mine word!" Roared the voice.

The voice filled the air and stifled all that heard it.

"That is Handrew Koke?" Godfrey asked.

"I believe it 'tis." Geraldo answered.

"Brothers and sisters, I understand your eagerness to eliminate the Maurieen, but one does not butcher the stinger who retrieves the delicious honey from the hive. NO!" The voice echoed. "We must use this opportunity to retrieve our most precious honey, our bangle." With his words the crowd roared with delight.

"Allow me ye patients and I will in turn regain for all, the Ubils way of life."

The crowd cheered again.

"Go now and permit me to set forth my plan to remove Bagree's Bangle from the locker at the Maurieen's Palace."

The enormous crowd thundered with excitement. For too long they had been ruled by weakness, forces existed hidden while their bangle sat in the locker of the Maurieen Palace unused. Finally, they had a leader willing to recover it and fight for them.

Slowly the crowd dissipated until there were very few members still lingering around the Pert. Even the young Kathries had run off to find their mother leaving Blaze, Godfrey and Geraldo alone on the marble steps.

The threesome made their way up the stairs. There before them was the Pert. The strange place Blaze had only heard about from his mother. How odd it seemed to him to actually be there to feel the energy of it, to experience the power of it for himself.

Blaze stood on the marble patio and looked around, there was no sign of his mother. The only things he could see were the huge marble pillars that stood along the back of the Pert draped with heavy copper colored curtains. The Pert itself was empty except for the copper chair and there were still a few members standing about on the balcony but none of them looked to be of any importance.

Geraldo who had moved ahead of the group motioned to him from beside an opening in the huge copper curtains. Blaze joined him and peered through the opening. The sight on the other side struck him sick. His mother was laid out on what looked like a torture device from the medieval period and beside her stood two orange cloaked members. The orange cloaked Sherideens seemed angry.

"Let me try, ye have not enough of her blood." One of them shouted as he pulled the wand from the other and jabbed Marypat in the neck were an open wound dripped blood.

Blaze watched horrified, he wanted to exploded. His hair flashed with fire and his eyes sparked. He wanted to rush in and kill the two Sherideens, he would do anything to save his mother.

"No, not now, Handrew has a powerful protection spell around her. I can feel its power." Godfrey said pressing the palm of his hand forward. "We must leave her now and rethink our plan of attack."

Blaze reached forward slowly and felt the electric sparks from the spell. He turned back towards Godfrey and spoke in a whisper. "I can't leave her like this."

"Ye must, it is not safe here." Godfrey urged.

As he spoke they heard one of the orange cloaked members shout.

"Grette re hemper ta in ale, hep ye fen hep gwe onee." Then a shot flow from the end of his wand and struck the other orange cloaked member in the face. The second member dropped to the marble floor and quivered.

"Well? Did it work?" The second questioned the first

The first one shook his head. "NO! The master won't be pleased, we must find a way to copy her, or we will never be able to retrieve the bangle."

"Try again, brother, this stint uses a locket of her hair." The second said as he rose to his feet again.

"Yes?" The first one agreed. He then moved towards Marypat and grabbed a handful of hair and said the spell but again it did not change the second Sherideen to look like Marypat.

The two Sherideens continued to try while Godfrey, Geraldo and Blaze moved out of sight. Auntie Edie darted behind one of the thick copper curtains and then reappeared beside Godfrey, still unnoticed by the group.

She listened curiously as they spoke in whispers.

"What are they doing to her?" Blaze asked.

"They are trying to copy her. I believe once they have copied her, they will attempt to enter the Maurieen Palace and remove the bangle."

"Our plans to take control of the Pert is not going as we have planned. The capture of your mother Marypat has created a very delicate situation especially now that we know she is being held under a protection spell and we are not able to reach her. We will need many more members on their side to break the spell." Godfrey reported with a frown.

Godfrey's face grew blank as he struggled to come up with a new plan. All the while Blaze himself was thinking things through.

"Do you think they will kill her?" Blaze asked bravely. It was the one most important issue to him. If he could have a chance that they would not then he could attempt his idea.

"NO, they need her alive in order to get the bangle. As long as she is alive they can copy her and hold her copy." Godfrey admitted.

"You say all Handrew wants is the bangle?" Blaze asked as a glimmer of hope stuck him.

"All, is such a small word for the magnitude of the chore." Geraldo commented as he to pondered their position.

"Tell me Godfrey, if we held position of the bangle wouldn't we hold all the cards?" Blaze asked.

"What cards? We are not playing cards." Geraldo answered.

"Hush, brother, let Blaze speak." Godfrey voiced pushing Geraldo to one side.

"You said the Bangle was now in the locker at Maurieen Palace, right?" Blaze asked eagerly.

"Yes!" Godfrey answered.

"Then I think I know how we can get the bangle before them, but we must hurry." Blaze said with a grin as his eyes searched the walls of Pert.

"How?" Godfrey and Geraldo asked.

"My mother told me about a Realagraph of an Enchanted Forest that once hung here in the Pert. It was pretty well mashed up, but if we can find it, I know I can get the bangle." Blaze reveled as he slowly emerged from their hiding place so he could search the other walls.

But Geraldo grabbed him back.

"Wait, I know of only one Realagraph of an Enchanted Forest that hung here at the Pert." Geraldo began his eyes went wide as he revealed what he remembered. "It was painted by Kathrie Penny and it was a Realagraph into a Legends and Tales book used to trick your mother. . . . ."

"Yes, that's the one. Do ye know where it is now?" Blaze interrupted.

Blaze's eyes studied Geraldo while he waited for his reply.

Geraldo 's head dropped and his mind drifted back to the turns that followed Gazpalding's tragic end. There had been so much turmoil, so many changes but that painting had been left as a horrible reminder of Gazpalding's failure. A tragic souvenir to scorn those who had aided him then. It had been such a painful memento that after it had been used a second time it had been placed deep in the bowels of the Pert. Geraldo could not believe that that cursed battered painting would be used once again. He raised his face to Blaze and utter.

"Yes, I will take ye to it."

CHAPTER
20

The Ancient Tunnels
Help the Task to
Find the Bangle

longside of the huge vain of Cinerin Stone, that made up
the impassable ridge of the Cinerin Mountain range, was an
ancient buildup of limestone, marble and rich red clay. This
mixture is what naturally covered the immense vain of Cinerin Stone
and the valley of Cimmevian Town. It is in these soft rocks and soil
that the Ubil build their Twindle Ways, tunnels and homes. Magically
burrowing deep within the mountain avoiding the Cinerin as they

proceed. It is also here that the Pert itself had access to the soft easy soil that bordered the Cinerin vain. This access allowed the Ubil to construct two enormous tunnels.

The first and nearest tunnel to the group was also the largest. It was just beyond where the two-orange cloaked Sherideens stood with Marypat. It had been commissioned by Gazpalding to house the new Grand Meeting Room, Lecture Hall, laboratories, library, apprentice study salons, dormitory, kitchen, cafeteria, Masters and Supreme Master's residences and bed chambers. This tunnel was the most current construction and was heavily populated.

The second and smaller tunnel was cut into the mountain just outside the balcony of the Pert. It was the older version of tunnels used by the Ubil. It had been commissioned by Bagree him-self after he had gain power as the first Supreme Master of all the evil members in the Cimmevian Valley. Before this period of massive cooperative construction, the members used a primordial system of tunnels and coves that once threaded their way up from the base of the valley and opened out on to the balcony on the Pert. Bagree used the already existing insignificant tunnels and expanded them to create his empire.

During Bagree's regain the tunnel system was used for many things including a dungeon, a Library, a study salon and Dormitories. Later during Gazpalding regain the ancient tunnels were abandoned except for use as storage. The very purpose that Geraldo recalled. Deep below the new Lecture hall was the olden Masters Chamber used now as a store room. It had been in that room the mashed up Realagraph had been hung, after Ragnar had met with his tragic end just 11 passages ago. Geraldo himself had moved the painting, placing it above the old fire place that still torched up when a member approached.

To get to the storage room would be an easy venture if the group had been able to enter the newer tunnel. But since it was blocked by the Sherideens over Marypat, the group would have to enter the older section of tunnels and undertake the trek through the ancient muddy system that stretch blow the Pert.

The older section was for the most part abandoned and the small group had no problem reaching the entrance. Quickly they dodged through the small archway and down the long corridor to the lobby. The lobby was dingy gray, but one could see the exquisitely carved walls, high ceilings and pillars that at one period would have made the lobby an impressive sight.

Once inside the lobby Geraldo swiftly turned into the vestibule. The others followed and they were soon pushing their way through the large wooden doors of the Old Meal Hall. The hall was dark but in the distance, there was a light that gave the group enough reflection for them to easily maneuver round all the long tables and benches left piled there.

The light was coming from the current Laundry chamber. The only place they had to pass where members would be. Cautiously Geraldo peered into the chamber. The room was filled with steam. The steam was coming from a row of enormous metal pots that were boiling on the top of the massive stoves in the center of the kitchen. Beyond the boiling pots were shelves and bins filled with fabric that were folded perfectly. The room reeked of sulfur but it did not slow Geraldo, he entered pushing his way throw the old swing doors that hung at the chambers entrance. He stepped in to the room and glanced around. He saw no one but just as he was about to motion for Blaze to follow, he was blind-sided by an enormous bundle of dirty sheets.

The weight of the bundle knocked him to his knees, stunning him for a moment. When he tried to get to his feet he was struck again and again until he was covered with bundles of sheets and cloaks. The others watched in horror, unable to help, as he was surrounded by Ulldens.

"Bloody good!" Shouted the largest Ullden. His voice boomed, filling the air while his enormous form cast an eerie shadow across the room.

Godfrey moved Blaze back into the darkness of the Old Meal Hall. Quietly they watched through the crack in the old swing doors as the Ulldens grabbed at Geraldo. Both ready their daggers as they stood and watched.

The Ulldens common size forms forcefully waded through the bundles tossing the bundles aside. The Ulldens wore only simple pantaloons with a long white apron. Their dark gray chests were bare and so were their huge hairy feet.

"Cursed Sherideen. 'Tis no place for ye." Another Ullden bellowed from the other side of the chamber.

"Remove him. Bring him to me!"

Geraldo was helpless. He could do nothing but lie there while their thick gray hands grabbed at him and pulled him to the feet to the largest Ullden. The largest Ullden bent over slightly, his eyes flashed red as he faced Geraldo. His large fat face dripped with sweat and his arms and chest heaved as he spoke.

"Ye should never stand under the shaft especially when it's open. The weight has killed many a member. Ye are fortunate this turn. Now gather ye self and be gone from my sight or I shall cook ye in a bath of under garments." The Ulldens voice echoed through the huge chamber. The other Ulldens stood around him and burst out laughing.

"Tusk! he believes ye, look at his face." One of the Ulldens roared with laughter.

"'Tis true, he is frightened of ye!" Another Ullden chuckled.

The largest Ullden could control himself no more and he too erupted with laughter.

"Did ye see how easily he dropped?"

"His expression of fear was the best!"

"And him a Sherideen, afraid of us!"

The group of Ulldens hollered with hilarity. While Godfrey and Blaze continued to watch through the crack in the door. They did not know what to do to help their companion. They needed a plain, but before they could act another Ullden enterer the chamber. This Ullden was not laughing, this Ullden was quite serious and she revealed herself to the other Ulldens with a clap of her hands.

"Clack" Her hands slapped together. The Pattie Ulldens immediately stopped laughing and looked in the direction of the sound.

"Clear these parcels straight away, or I will boil ye!" She roared at them.

Instantly the Pattie Ulldens went back to work dragging the bundles of laundry away, leaving Geraldo alone with the Lassie Ullden.

Geraldo struggled to his feet and turned to the Ullden.

"My apologies madam." Geraldo said. He was certain she would report him and he would soon be surrounded by loyal Sherideens to Handrew. So, he stood before her and lowered his head.

The Ullden shock her head in disgust and then huffed away. "Why do they always have to get lost in my chambers?"

Surprised and relieved that the Ullden was not suspicions of him, Geraldo waited until the Ullden left the laundry chamber before heading back to the swing doors where Godfrey and Blaze stood.

Then together the three Sherideens entered the laundry chamber. The Ulldens, busy at work made no notice of the group as they rushed through the large hot room and slipped down the old tunnel entrance that led to the ancient passageways below the Pert. The ancient tunnels reeked even worst of mold, the stench filled Blaze's nose, making him sneeze. Each sneeze caused the top of his head to burst into flames. Troubling him at first but after a while the flame from his hair gave him the light he needed to see down the long narrow and muddy tunnel.

Along the way they passed the ancient Kitchen cove, that was filled with old rusty cauldrons and broken cauldrons. They passed several dark Twindle Ways, small archways and curtained coves. The tunnel seemed to go on forever but finally they came to an old Peters Pine door set in a solid marble frame and arch. The door and archway completely sealed off the tunnel.

Blaze studied the door and observed a crest elaborately engraved in the wood. He placed his hand on the door and allowed his finger to trace the crest. It looked so familiar to him yet he had never seen it before.

The crest had two Damascus swords each with one tear in its handle. One sword was on the Dexter side and the other on the Sinister side both meaning Leader. At the base of the crest was a ribbon of determination and in the chief position was a pointer crown meaning fearless. The crown held four tears for a total of six tears shapes on the crest, representing advanced knowledge. In the very center of the shield, taking up the base, navel and honor point was the flames of power, fueled by the strength of wood.

Blaze slipped his hand over the flame and as he did the flames for an instant came to life and the door popped open. Blaze jumped back in surprise and looked at Geraldo who also looked surprised.

"I've never seen it do that before." Geraldo uttered.

"Whose crest is it?" Blaze asked.

"Bagree's, this is his old Twindle Way, held together to this turn by primordial magic." Geraldo answered as he pushed open the stiff door. Its hinges were rusted but it opened for Geraldo just the same with an eerily screech.

The three Sherideens pushed passed the wooden door and as they entered the cluttered room, the primitive fire place burst into flame. Within a few moments it was a glow, lighting the entire space. Everything was just as Geraldo had recalled, nothing it seems had been touched.

He looked up over the now brightly burning fire place and retrieved the familiar battered wood frame. With Godfrey's help they laid the painting on the dusty floor and tried to bend the frame back into place. But it would not budge more than a bit. Upset Godfrey through his hands into the air.

"It's no use, we can't move it." He bellowed.

"We cannot give up now, this is the only way. Look if both of you pull at the same moment. I think I can wiggle through." Blaze assured him.

"It's worth a try." Geraldo agreed.

So together the two Sherideens pulled apart the bent wooden frame until there was enough space for Blaze to slip into the Realagraph. Once inside Blaze dropped to the forest floor, cutting his face on a jagged corner of the frame as he fell. He landed on the thick underbrush of the forest, smeared the blood from his cheek and looked around.

"Look for the cabin on the far side of the forest, the exit Realagraph should be near there." Geraldo stated nervously.

Blaze knobbed and then took off running into the forest. The forest was dark and eerie but he knew there wasn't anything to fear in the dark forest. The evil Sherideen from the tale had been real, Kathrie Penny had never painted the Sherideen in the tale. Gazpalding had wanted it that way. Therefore, there was no evil Sherideen in the book and no evil characters to fear.

Blaze continued to run until the forest suddenly ended and before him laid a vast open prairie.

"The house must be near." He said to himself and sure enough just beyond a tiny hill sat the Kathrieens cottage. It was nestled sweetly in a field of wild flowers just as his mother had described. Blaze knew the exit must be near. He looked carefully around in front of the cottage but saw nothing. For a moment he thought that the council must have removed the page from the book. But if that was the case then the cottage itself would not be there before him. So, he moved away from the cottage and began searching the field of wild flowers. After all, as he remembered, Horatio had had a problem with the flowers when he first stepped into the book. With that in mind Blaze widened his search and soon came upon an odd rectangle shape hovering in the sky. Carefully he reached for it and discovered that it was a huge sheet of canvas.

"This must be it." He said to himself. Without even thinking Blaze ran at the canvas and hit it with all of his strength.

"Thud."

The canvas gave way and the entire book fell over, tossing Blaze out onto the huge shelve where the book had been stored. The shelf was high above the floor of the locker and Blaze found himself to be like a speck in the enormous space of the locker. There were rows and rows of endless wooden shelves, some towering far above him.

He stood there for a moment and wondered how he would ever find the bangle in the vastness of the locker. He had no idea where to start or even how to get down from where he was. If only he knew a spell or incantation that would bring the Bangle to him. Then it came to him, he had a spell book and a wand. So, without another moment of thought he threw down his backpack and zipped it open. The book was an easy find and he soon had it out. He sat on the edge of the self and laid the book out on his lap.

"The Green Isle Patrimony Edition of Incantation's and Spells." He read out loud.

"Simple spells, Changing spell, Levitation, could be useful if I need to get down from here. . . . Repair, copy, Fire, return. Return Spell? To return an object to its original place. Oh no that won't do. Let's see. . . Broom spell, disappearing spell, no, wand work, no. . . . Spells for the Master, summon spell, interval spell, Weather spells, rain. . . wind. . sea. . Repel spell, that's a good one, Dom me a gron, I have to remember that one. . .. Unlock spell. . . Retrieve Spell. Retrieve Spell? That looks good. Let's see . . use the wand in a Cecular movement and say, Dom me a sue. . come here. . ok. . now where's my wand?"

Blaze grabbed his bag and searched through it, panic hit him as he thought he had lost it but then way at the bottom of the bag he found it. He pulled it out as a wave or relief washed over him. The opal tip glistened as he held it and he felt a surge of energy pulse from it.

Blaze held the wand out in front of him and tried to remember the wand movements that Godfrey had showed him back on the Red Isle.

"Cecular, round? It'll have to be a big circle to work in this place."

With his grandest movement he turned his arm over his head making a complete circle as he called out. "Dom me a sue." But nothing happened.

"Rats" He said frustrated with himself. He had forgotten what Godfrey had taught him.

"Clear your mind, think only of the spell, think only of the desired outcome."

He took a deep breath, cleared his mind and pictured the bangle in his mind. Then he called the spell again. "Dom me a sue." As the last word left his lips the bangle appeared in his lap. Half surprised and half excited that the spell had worked, he shouted with delight.

"Cool!"

Satisfied with himself, he jumped to his feet and packed up the book, wand and bangle. Then he jumped back into the book and ran off in the direction of the dark forest.

A Meeting

The trek through the Raye Raye forest was not an easy one for the five tired companions. The dense wilderness was rarely if ever used by travelers. Therefore, there weren't any paths or even a slit worn trail, there was no route or course to follow. They had only their wits to guide them through the towering trees and waist high undergrowth.

The forest consisted mostly of enormous Orange Prickle Chestnut Trees bathed in Joey buttons and massive Blue Fur Trees covered in Trortle moss and lilac colored wild Ever Lyn's. The floor of the forest was most certainly a wilderness of overgrown Henmax plants, razor shape Frazer ferns, poisonous Robert Anders Purple Horned Fronds, and Clinging Mea Moores. Not to mention the non-threating plant growth and dozens of insects that buzzed around franticly when the ground was disturbed.

It was hazardous to say the least and there was nothing Kathrie Gretel wanted more then to use her magic abilities and get out of there. But there was nothing around her that she could use. To levitate herself she needed Etain Dust, which she had none. To return home she needed a cauldron of 8 hands and a potion, again she didn't have. To fly she needs her broom and that she left at home. Her only hope was to find a Haley May Green Birch tree, the very wood used in making bloom handles and again that seemed unlikely as the forest she stood in had only Blue Furs and Orange Prickle Chestnuts.

Still she walked along following closely behind Cornelius while studying the dense dark thicket hoping to find just one lost and forgotten Haley May. Then to her surprise the forest opened to a gentle slope of Jennie Pops. The low slithering vine had chocked the area of other plants and taken over the clearing leaving an easy path for the group to maneuver through. With each step the group made, the Jennie Pop, flower exploited with a pop. The pop sent a small white seed into the air and before long the air around them was filled with tiny fibrous seeds.

Kathrie Gretel grew annoyed at the tiny tickling seeds. She drew out her wand and zapped the air. "Dom me a gron," she replied. Her wand flashed, sending all the petite white seeds sailing high into the air. It also lite up the entire clearing, giving Kathrie Gretel an unforgettable sight. There to their left just beyond a row of Jingle Toes was a grove of Haley May Green birch. Kathrie Gretel's jaw dropped. If she hadn't been annoyed by the Jennie pops, she would never have seen the Haley Mays. She shook her head and grabbed at Cornelius.

"Look." she laughed. But the others didn't see the grove and had no reason to get excited.

Kathrie Gretel held up her wand and shouted " Luminous sue mar." Her wand flashed again and lit up the clearing once more. "Look through there. There are Haley Mays over there."

Cornelius instantly understood what Kathrie Gretel was implying, While the Kennard, Tag and Rowan seemed unconcerned by her discovery.

Kathrie Gretel shocked her head again this time in disgust. "The Haley May Green Birch is used in making brooms. Now I can make each of us a broom to fly on." Her voice sounded relieved.

Moments later they each held a branch of the Haley May Green Birch tree.

"Pick it clean, unnecessary twigs and leaves can make your ride unbalanced." Kathrie Gretel instructed. Then one by one they presented their branch to Kathrie Gretel for her to enchant.

"Place your hands firmly around the bark and repeat after me." She commanded "Zen blue dree, part hem se."

After all, four brooms were enchanted the group set off into the air. They were still some distance from the cascades but the brooms would indeed quicken their pace.

Meanwhile back at the Pert Geraldo showed Godfrey and Blaze the remains of an old tunnel that connected Bagree Twindle Way to the new section of the Pert. The tunnel had once connected Bagree Twindle Way to a powerful Kathrieens cove hidden deep within the mountain. But when the new section was built the tunnel was cut off and all that remained was a short piece of passageway that now connected Bagree's quarters to a secrete closer inside the New Grand Lecture hall.

It was there that the three Sherideens finally emerged from the ancient tunnels and reentered the main level of the Pert. Cautiously they stepped out of the dark tunnel. Geraldo leading the way. He alone knew where the latch was that opened the secret panel.

"Click." it opened easily.

Godfrey peered out from the secret opening and found the hall filled with Handrew's supporters. Undetected they slipped out of the closer and mixed in with the other cloaked members. They found it quite easy to blend in and before long they were out of the hall and crossing the Grand New Lobby.

They were determined to make it to the podium, where they knew Handrew would be waiting. They had intended to use the bangle to barter for Marypat's release. Godfrey believes the plan was weak and he had wanted Blaze to use the bangle himself, but Blaze chose not to.

Blaze had heard from his mother what had happen to Gazpalding when it had been taken off of him. She told him about the wicked way he swelled and boiled. Blaze had no wish to die that way, he did not want to put such evil so close to him. It was bad enough he had to carry it in his back pack, he did not want to put it on.

"Well I thought ye lost." Came a cheerfully friendly voice from across the main lobby. It was Ella and she was standing outside the entrance to the Supreme Master's Chambers." I suppose ye have seen her, ah. . . Young nephew of Gazpalding?" She giggled. "Now that ye have, ye should want to speck to the new master. Yes?"

Blaze knobbed his head yes.

"Well he is below in his chambers, making plans as we speak to eliminate the council. I am certain he will want to see ye and know he has the support of Gazpalding's heir." She revealed with a grin.

Blaze looked over to Godfrey who nodded in agreement. It certainly would be easier to confront Handrew in the confinement of the chambers. There would more than likely be few members there with him and perhaps an easier negotiation could take place. Even though he was against Blazes position on the bangle, Godfrey hoped to still gain control of it himself, once they had negotiated the Maurieens release. After all he wasn't afraid of using it himself.

So, with a gentle nob to Ella, Godfrey led the way into the elaborate marble passageway that leads down into the main room of the Supreme Masters Chambers. The chamber was seal off by a hulking pewter door. Two orange clocked members stood on guard in front of the door and as the group approached the guards stepped forward.

"Hold thi foot, brothers. The master is in conference."

"May we wait!" Godfrey asked boldly.

"Indeed" Answered the guard. Godfrey turned back to Blaze and whisper in his ear. "Make ready your wand keeps it close and do not reveal it unless we need to."

Blaze nodded his head and did as he was told. He retrieves his wand from his bag and tucked it into the sleeve of his cloak. A few moments passed and then the huge pewter doors swung open. Four hooded members stepped out. The first was from a Stone, his long black cloak had flames of Green raising up from the hem and sleeve. The flames flickers and glowed as if they were real. The second was from Red Chard, his had Blood red flames. The third was from Winds Port, his cloak had a golden yellow flame. The last was from Well's Rye, his robe had blue flames.

Godfrey knew these were the Master protectors. They had been with the new Supreme Master. Probably affirming their commitment to him. This meant he was now alone in his chambers and it was the best situation for them.

"Ye may advance brothers." The guard announced, stepping out of the way.

The three Sherideens moved passed the pewter doors and entered the long marble corridor. The walls of the corridor were polished smooth and they seemed the glow as the group passed.

Soon they came to a second set of Pewter doors, where two more orange cloaked guards stood.

One of the guards stepped forward as they approached. He pulled back his hood and revived his face to Godfrey. Godfrey recognized the member, he was Kyle Frig from Winds Port. He was one of the members who had been at the Pert when Godfrey had been given the chamber. This member knew of Godfrey's shame, he had witnessed it first hand and now he stood between him and the new Supreme Master. Godfrey stopped cool in his tracks, his mind went wild with fear. *Would Kyle recognize him? Did he still hold resentment for him because of the scandal at Thorny Pass?* Godfrey could do nothing more than lower his head and hope Kyle would not recognize him.

"The master is eager to have words, brothers Godfrey and Geraldo" Kyle Frig stated without emotion." He waits for ye within."

Kyle's words ring in both Godfrey's and Geraldo's ears. They had been discovered. Geraldo turned to run back up the tunnel but as he began to move his arm was ceased from behind. He looked back over his shoulder and saw the four Master Protectors had doubled back to prevent their escape.

Blaze meanwhile looked confused. Things were not going as he had hoped.

Godfrey swallowed hard and then stepped through the open pewter doors. The main room of the Masters Chambers was well lite by two opposing fire places. The one on the right, was crafted in the trunk of a fire birch tree. The enormous tree stood within the wall, its roots protrude out into the room. While its branches stretched along the ceiling. The trunk was partially dug out and in its place was a burning fire over which a cauldron was hung.

The fire place on the left was built from twain Shag bark trees, connected by their top branches. Their roots also extended out into the room and their stub like branches reached high in to the ceiling. Between them sat a raging fire.

In the center of the room was a pit separated into three cushioned seating areas. Beyond the pit was a huge mirror used for visions and in front of it was a vat of water. Beside the vat stood the Supreme Master, Handrew Koke, draped in copper with two of his loyal followers, Fredrick Predwick and Max Milton.

The Supreme Master was watching the vision in the mirror. The vision was Godfrey entering his chamber.

The supreme master grinned and then turned away from the mirror.

"I had thought Mine eyes fooled, but now I see they were not." He cheerfully exclaimed. He stepped away from the mirror and walked over to the pit in the center of the room. "Come my brothers, sit. I am pleased to receive ye." He said gesturing to Godfrey to take a seat in the pit. He then stepped down the few steps that led into the pit and sat down on a copper cover cushion before continuing.

"Brother Fredrick bring forth some Warm Sweet Wine. Brother Geraldo please come and sit, bring ye ward along for I must set eyes upon him."

Nervously the three Sherideens enter the pit and sat down. Blaze fingered his wand, waiting for Godfrey to give him the sign to use it. But Godfrey didn't wish to start a fight quite yet. Instead he wanted to know, Handrew's position on his return. He also wanted to know how powerful Handrew was. Beside they had the bangle in their position as a last resort, he figured he could use it himself. He didn't need the lad after that but still that was a last resort and for the moment he wanted to hear what Handrew had to say.

"Godfrey ye strength of will is most impressive, how did ye ever escape the deceitfulness of the Red Isle?" Handrew asked as though he truly wanted to know but before Godfrey could answer Handrew turned to Geraldo and began question him. "What is the name of ye companion, have I had the pleasure? He is a Sherideen, is he not?"

"No master ye have . . . " Geraldo was cut off.

"He is not a Sherideen?" Handrew interrupted, sitting straight up in his seat.

"Yes, Master he is a Sherideen, but you have not met him, we have just brought him to prepare for his Sherite Extolel." Godfrey quickly explained.

"Oh yes, 'Tis near the moment." Handrew answered as he sat back in his seat.

Fredrick stepped down in to the pit, then and handed him a metal cup. Handrew accepted it and drank some. "MMM, Sweet Nicks, makes the sweetest wine, wouldn't ye agree? I suppose it's been quite some moment for ye, ah Godfrey?"

Godfrey accepted a cup from Fredrick he pretended to take a sip and then set it down.

"Yes, a long moment. It is Delicious, it's better than I remember."

Blaze and Geraldo each took a cup and drank some. Blaze chocked on it.

"Yuck! It tastes worse than warm beer." Blaze gaged as whispered to Geraldo. He quickly set the cup down and gazed at Geraldo who was trying to squeeze the very last drop out of his cup. Blaze nudged him and then offered him his own. Geraldo switched cups and drank down the second cup with a grin.

Boldly Godfrey began questioning Handrew. " I have missed much over the last 35 passes. Much has changed. Geraldo has told me of this Maurieen ye have captured. He has told me how she has troubled our kind before. Tell me master, what are ye plans and how many we assist ye?"

"Ye kindness is much to grand, Brother. My plans are simple, now that ye have come to me." Handrew remarked with a grin.

Handrew stood and snapped his fingers, in a flash the two daggers floated out of Godfrey's and Blazes belts, landing on the floor at Handrew's feet. The wand popped from Blazes sleeve and his back pack rose off his back. Blaze struggled with the pack. Grabbing it with all his might but soon it had Blaze several feet in the air. It twisted him back and forth but Blaze would not let go.

Geraldo tried to help Blaze but he and Godfrey were grabbed from behind and held while Blaze dangled above clinging to the bag.

"Unhand it now young one and I shall let ye live." Handrew claimed with a frown. He never liked doing the dirty work. But if he wanted what was inside the bag he had to do it himself. He could effort to let any other Sherideen touch it.

Blaze grabbed even tighter to the bag. Handrew grew annoyed. He had had enough. With a slight movement of his wand he sent Blaze crashing into the wall.

"Thud"

Blaze lost his grip on the bag and he fell smashing his head on the ground. Tears of pain filled his eyes and anger filled his body. Yet he laid there unable to move. Meanwhile the bag flow to Handrew, who quickly seized it.

"Did ye really think ye could come into my chambers unnoticed?" He said to Godfrey. "Ye are the most pathetic Sherideen ever, ye aren't even worth killing."

Then he turned away from them and pushed his hand into the bag. His hand felt the cold melt of the Bangle and he grinned to himself. "I knew it, I knew ye had it. I knew it the moment I saw the second speck of gold, dancing in the vat. First over the Pert, then over the palace and just now back here at the Pert. I don't know how ye did it, Godfrey, I never knew ye had such resources but my Brother I am glad ye have no sense for power." Handrew laughed.

Handrew raised his hand out of the bag and revealed the bangle to the room. It sparkled in the firelight and everyone in the room gasped at its sight. The four Master Protectors who were standing behind Godfrey and Geraldo stepped back away from them. They had had no idea that the bangle had been in the bag, nor did they know all that Handrew knew. They were in awe of their Master and they stood ready to obey.

"Wait!" Shouted Blaze as he watched Handrew begin to put the bangle on. Blaze was frantic to make one last attempt to save his mother. The rage in side him grew, feeding the element of fire. His hand grasped the ground, his fingers digging into the clay soil charging the element of stone. The tears of his face fueling the element of water and his lungs filled with the element of air. All four Elements were present and for the first time Blaze filled with all the powers of the isle.

Godfrey trembled he had felt the young Sherideens power before but this time it was far beyond what he had ever seem. Blaze was rising above the ground. He sucked the very energy from the room. His body glowed and flashed with sparks. His hair raged like an inferno and his hand surged with flames. The air around him swirled like a whirlwind and he was growing stronger with each moment.

Handrew stumbled backwards, his eyes filled with the awesome sight of the lad. Never before had he ever seen anyone with so much power. What he could do with power like that, he thought. Fear filled him then, but he was not willing to give up his bangle. He held it close to him and shouted at the lad. "What do ye want?"

"Release the Maurieen and allow me to leave with my brethren Godfrey and Geraldo, and ye may have the bangle." Blaze's voice roared through the room.

"Fine whatever. Fredrick bring me the Maurieen." Handrew bawled. He wasn't concerned about the Maurieen anymore, anyway. He didn't need her and surely now that he had the bangle he would have as much power if not more than the lad. So, he agreed, pulling the bangle on to his left arm. He couldn't figure out what they would want with her, except to get the bangle but they had gotten without her. It didn't make sense he had seem the golden fleck in the vat go from the Pert to the Maurieen Palace and back to the Pert. They didn't need the Maurieen to get the Bangle. They had gotten it without her. Still it angered him that they would try and fool him to get his prize.

But as he clipped it shut he realized it wasn't working. His mind panicked he had been fooled, it was a fake. He unclipped the bangle and threw it at Blaze. His face filled with anger. His eyes sparked. "It's a fake, ye tricked me." Handrew wailed. He pulled out his wand again and threw an enormous spell at Blaze. The spell sends Blaze fling backwards against the wall.

Blaze didn't know how to focus his power and he was an easy target. Handrew took notice of that as he observed how easily his spell struck Blaze.

Blaze on the other hand sat on the floor dazed but not hurt. His body still surging with power while his mind flashed with Handrew's words. "It's a fake. A fake." Blaze knew it wasn't a fake, he rubbed his head and thought. *"How could it be a fake."* He had gotten it himself from the locker at the Maurieen Palace. Then it occurred to him that the council might have taken its power from it before storing in away. He picked it up and looked at it. The pyrite bangle was dull but it still glowed when the light hit it. Blaze turned it in his hand. There were six prongs in a line on the one side. Instantly he noticed that one of the tear shaped diamonds was missing. Where had he seen one of those before. His brain hurt and he couldn't remember.

Suddenly his thoughts were interrupted as Fredrick bounded into the room dragging Marypat. "Master, I bring ye the Maurieen." He announced.

"Bring her to me." Handrew ordered. His face was filled with hate and revenge. He swung round and grabbed up one of the daggers. Fredrick carried Marypat down into the pit and Blaze watched in horror as Handrew approached her.

Godfrey at the same time struggled to get away, but the guard held him even tighter. He tried to Call to Blaze "Blaze get .." But again, the guard stopped him by grabbing him around his mouth. There was nothing he could do but stand and watch as Handrew moved in on Marypat.

"Is this what ye came for?" Handrew shouted. Grabbing up the head of Marypat.

"Ye thought ye could come here and trick me into giving ye the Maurieen, well ye were wrong, she's mine." Handrew hollered while he held the dagger to her throat.

Blaze's mind still whirled with confusion over the bangle and at the same time he couldn't bear to see Handrew hurt his mother. He had to do something. He had to act before it was too late. Then it hit him. He knew where he had seen the diamond before. It was like his mother's diamond. He grabbed his chest and reached for the necklace. The small tear shaped diamond shimmered as he held it up. Quickly he slipped the diamond into the empty prang on the Bangle. The instant the diamond touched the metal the bangle began to glow. It started to hum and everyone in the hall turned to Blaze who was now standing.

Handrew turned his eyes went wide as he stared at the bangle he had tossed away only a moment before. "No, it's a fake." he shouted "How can that be?"

"Let the Maurieen go." Blaze said holding the bangle out in his hands.

"No, hand me the Bangle." Handrew demanded.

"Let her go or I'll put on the bangle." Blaze threatened. He didn't want to put it on, but for his mother's sake he would do anything.

"Give me the bangle or I'll kill her." The blade of the dagger slide into Marypat's throat and blood sprayed from the wound.

Blaze freaked, his mother was being murder in front of him and it was all his fault. There was only one thing he could do. So, without another thought Blaze slipped the bangle on and clipped it closed.

The bangle vibrated as it recognized its place on Blaze's arm and began to accept Hisue. His form surged with its power. He rose above the ground, with his torso bending backwards. The bangle corrected every imperfection on Blaze's body. It repaired the scratch on his face, he had just gotten when he slipped into the Realagraph. It healed the many scratches on his arms and legs he had gotten from the sea birds on Red Isle. It even healed the enormous five-year-old scare on his thigh. The one he had gotten when he fell of his bed and hit his dresser. The heat from the bangle filled every part of his body while the members in the hall stood and watched.

Handrew watched too. He removed his hand from Marypat's throat and dropped the dragger. He realized he had only a moment to act. That very moment in fact. It was the precise moment that Blaze was the most vulnerable and he seized it. He pulled out his wand, pointed at Blaze and ran towards him shouting.

"Atee om ree, om wen jay,om kole hert rut-in re hem-op trol." His voice filled the hall and everyone present witnessed what Handrew did next.

Handrew drove with his wand out stretched. He stuck Blaze in his chest with his wand as it flickered green. The wand sunk deep into Blaze, disappearing from sight, sucking Handrew along with it. The force of Handrew's body entering Blaze own, caused Blaze's form to shake and then drop.

The entire hall of spectators could not believe what they had seen. The guards stepped back towards the pewter doors. They dropped their hole on Godfrey and Geraldo. They were uncertain of what had happened to their master and a mixture of panic and excitement filled them as they watched the lad struggle back to his feet.

Blaze stood up, his entire body glowed a brilliant white. His hair flicked with a strange hue of flames, so intense it was blinding. A smile came over his face and he threw his hands into the air.

"The power is so awesome." Blaze's mouth boomed. The sound vibrated through the hall and up the tunnels. Even the members waiting in the lecture hall heard him speak. But it was not Blaze who spoke. It was Handrew's voice they heard, and it was Handrew, now, who controlled the powerful radiating figure of the young Sherideen Blaze.

Maurieen Palace is Under Attack

Handrew stretched his hands and moved them deliberately as he slowly gained capability of all his new powers. Easily he moved in on Godfrey and Geraldo. He used them for practice throwing them from one side of the room to the other. Before long he had mastered his form and was ready to move on.

"To the Palace?" His voice echoed through the Pert. The guards throw opened the pewter doors and Blaze's body drifted through. In the Main lobby he was joined by his followers who were stunned to find their new master in a new form. But no one questioned it, they all stood ready to follow, ready to obey.

"Call to arms we attack the Palace on the sweep!" His voice boomed again.

Excitedly the Ubil members follow him out onto the patio of the Pert from there he sails out into the evening sky. He turned back to face his members and spoke.

"This eve we take back what is rightfully ours." His followers cheered. "And the isle will fear us once more." His body flickered and the thousands of loyal Ubil members rushed forward to see their leader's enormous power. They roared with excitement, finally they had a leader they could follow. Finally, they could return to the great dominance of the past. Their cheers filled the air.

"Let us remove the council from their posts and burn it to the ground." He beckoned.

"Burn them." The crowd chanted.

Blaze's body ignited in flames of red and the crowd whet wild. "To the palace." He commended and suddenly the evening sky was crammed with flying Ubil. Within a sweep Blaze and his followers were descending on the Maurieen Palace.

The energy around Blaze ripped through the sky creating a trail of flames. The flames engulfed him as he landed on the principal balcony. He through has hands forward and the ball of flames that surrounded him flew forward demolishing all the glass windows, wooden frame work and sterling silver walls that made up the entrance into the lobby of the Maurieen Palace. There was nothing left to block his entry.

The sudden invasion sent the members within the Maurieen Palace to panic and run. Blaze's form enjoyed the look of terror on the faces of the simple Colleens and Wardeens as they ran away from him, fleeing the lobby. He moved forward with his loyal followers close behind. Flames whirled off of his body striking anything that might burn. Once inside he pushed forward an enormous fire ball. The fire ball crashed into the Triptoephant water fall that stood in the center of the lobby. The entire structure exploded into rubble.

Blaze's form laughed to himself, it was almost too easy.

"Sped out, destroy everything and everyone, leave no one alive." He commanded.

With the Supreme Masters approval, the Ubil Sherideens and Kathrieens spread-out in the palace. They struck through the weak defenses posted at the wings of the palace and in no time the palace fell into their hands.

The evening sky over the serene waters of the Cascades was suddenly populated by flying bloom handles carrying four worn-out travels. The travers set down on the Cascades island and were greeted by two officially dressed Hedlens.

"Kennard." they saluted. "We are at ye service." They announced together. They were dressed in matching green uniforms. Their shirt vest buttoned down the front in two rows that started at their shoulders. Their pants matched the Kennard, foliage green with gold stripes.

"At easy " The Kennard order.

"We must act quickly." Rowan voiced to the Hedlens. He knew each Hedlen carried only one orbital receptacle and if the Kennard was to use one to go after Marypat at the Pert. That would leave one member without a ride. Unless one member was willing to go with the Kennard. It was his feeling that informing the council of Marypat's kidnap was far more important than risking capture at the Pert. So, he did not intent to assist the Kennard in any way. "We must get back to the palace and inform the council at once that. ."

He stopped dead in midsentence. His eyes filled with disbelieve as everyone around him filled with the same dread as they faced west and realized the Maurieen Palace was in flames and under attack.

Back at the Pert the halls were deserted. No one was there to witness the gray and white striped coose run out of the Lecture hall. It scampered across the lobby and disappeared down the marble tunnel that leads to the master's chambers. Both sets of huge pewter doors were left open and the coose past them with easy. Finally, she came to a halt just inside the second set of doors.

She looked around then and spotted what she was looking for. It was Godfrey and he was unconscious beside Geraldo. They had been left in the Supreme Masters Chambers unconscious, battered and beaten but alive. The Supreme Master seemed not to worry about leaving them and the Maurieen behind unguarded. He gave no command, left no orders on what to do with them and so the three laid in the chamber unrestrained.

Quickly the coose ran to Godfrey's side and pressed her nose against his. A tiny spark stuck him and his eye flitter open. The coose purred and Godfrey smiled as he opened his eyes to see Edie standing in front of him.

Weary at first, it took Godfrey a moment to regain his strength. But soon he was on his feet and at Geraldo's side.

"What should we do brother he possesses the lad?" Geraldo asked.

Godfrey had no wish to be a hero. He wanted to run away, leave the Pert and find some quiet place to hide and live out his life undisturbed. But something kept coming back to him, something he could not forget it was something Blaze said, *"Allow me to leave with my Brethren."* The words resonated in his brain. He held his head as the words floated back to him.

"Allow me to leave with my brethren."

Mixed with emotions he gave in and turned to Geraldo and stated. "We must do all we can to help him!"

Geraldo was shocked it was not in a Sherideens nature to risk themselves for another or to care. But in truth they both had grown to like the lad. Blaze was honorable and trustworthy. Two words that rarely described a Sherideen but in Blaze's case he was no ordinary Sherideen

So, they both agreed to help rescue Blaze.

"What should we do first?" Geraldo asked.

"We must awaken the Maurieen." Godfrey stated as he stepped over to Marypat's side.

"Find the wand, brother, while I prepare an incantation."

Geraldo scurried off in the direction he last recalled seeing the wand and soon returned to Godfrey with it in hand.

"Ye must say the verse, I have no magic." Godfrey admitted sadly.

But Edie, the coose pushed her way between them knocking the wand from Geraldo's hand. It tumbled to the ground striking the coose on the head.

Instantly the coose ignited into a bright orange glow. Godfrey and Geraldo jumped back as the coose disappeared and Kathrie Edie materialized in its place. Kathrie Edie knelt there completely naked. She had only her long black and gray hair to cover her.

She gazed up at her husband, her huge yellow eyes and eye brows remained slanted like that of a coose. Her skin also remained striped, but the fur and tail were gone. To Godfrey she still looked as young and beautiful as he remembered. She had not aged a turn. Astonished Godfrey knelt beside her and quickly rapped her in his cloak. Their eyes met and they kissed.

"I knew ye would return to me. I knew ye would come back and break my sister's embeastment curse on me." She cried.

"Why would ye sister do that?" Geraldo asked in shock.

"Perhaps later I can explain it all to ye, but for now I believe the Isle is in need of our attention." Kathrie Edie expressed calmly. "This Maurieen, she is the one my nieces speak of?"

"Yes. She is the young Sherideens Mother." Godfrey revealed.

"Then she is as powerful as the lad?" Kathrie Edie asked.

"We believe she is." Godfrey answered.

"She alone can stop him!" Geraldo added.

"Good, then we must hurry I fear there is little time to spare." Kathrie Edie affirmed. She bent down and picked up the wand. Then she stood and approached Marypat, who was still out cold on the copper colored cushions of the pit. Her hands and feet were tied with the bonding rope and Kathrie Edie pulled them off and through them to the side. She raised the wand and used a Dacular movement while calling out.

"RA TON DO PON RE."

A stickling blue ray of light emitted from the wand rushed forward and covered Marypat. Suddenly she was awake, confused and on guard.

Last Response Position

The waters of the Cascades rushed passed Rowans feet as he stood at the edge of the falls and drank in the horror. The sight was beyond words and his mind was cluttered with possibilities. He was not sure what he should do or what plan of action should be taken. He was not prepared to deal with this and in his relief, he did not have to.

The Kennard on the other hand took charge. He sent the first Hedlen, Baldric with Tag, Cornelius and Kathrie Gretel to organize the troops in what the Kennard called 'Last Response position.' Leavening the second Hedlen Cobb, to take himself and Rowan to Maurieen Palace to check out firsthand the devastation.

In a flash the first Hedlen disappeared, with Cornelius and Kathrie Gretel holding on to the orbital receptacle. Tag was stuffed into Cornelius pocket and they were gone before Rowan could object to the Kennard's plan.

The group reappeared in Middleton City on the silky flats just before dawn. All was quiet but that soon would change as Tag jumped from Cornelius pocket and ran towards the cities bell tower.

"Do not hast, I will accomplish my mark." Tag declared with a glace over his shoulder to Cornelius.

And with that the Hedlen, Baldric, released the nob and the group disappeared again from sight.

Tag on the other hand dogged a pile of manure and then sprinted up the stone steps that lead to the tower. In the tower he found a sleeping Wardeen lend against the riggings for the huge copper bell. Tag hopped onto his knee and shouted.

"Attention, Ringer, I Tag of Granger have orders from the Kennard."

The Wardeen jumped to his feet, knocking Tag to the stone floor.

"What are ye orders." The Wardeen asked half asleep.

"The call is Last response position." Tag replied breathlessly.

"No, not that?" The Wardeen shrieked as he went to the riggings and strengthened the coil.

"Yes, the Maurieen Palace is under attack by Ubil." Tag informed him.

Quickly the Wardeen reached high into the coils and with all his might pulled on them until the bell ring through the air.

"Bong, bong, bong" Swiftly he sentenced the bell, holding them for a pause. Then he pulled them again with all his might, letting them ring again. "Bong, bong, bong." Again, he held them for a length before allowing them to ring a third time.

"Bong. bong, bong." It was the sign that all was not well. Three bells, meant all members were to come at once the city square. All messengers were to be prepared to move. All transport was to be made available and every willing hand was to stand ready.

Moments later the square was full of ready hands waiting their orders. The mayor, who was still dressed in his evening clothing, was stumping up the stone steps to the tower. His face was serious and his hands were shaking.

"Who called three bells." He shouted.

"I sir." Tag announced from the floor of the tower.

"A Frandies?" The mayor bawled. He seemed very annoyed with the Frandies.

"Yes, sir, I have just come from the Kennard who instructed me to use, Last Response Position." Tag relayed confidently.

The mayor stood in shook. Last Response position, was code for the worst-case scenario. He rubbed his brow with the back of his hand and turned away from the Frandies.

"Sir " Tag called as he climbed to the open arch of the tower. "We must send out the messengers right away, the palace will not stand through the dawn."

"Right." The mayor stuttered with a blank look on his face.

"Sir the Messenger stand ready, ye must send them now." Tag insisted.

The mayor nodded his head in agreement but did nothing.

"Sir may I address them?" Tag asked nervously.

"Very good, then." The mayor uttered then he left the tower and headed back to his bed.

Tag looked up at the Wardeen and both members shook their heads. They couldn't understand the mayor's actions, but still there was no time to sit and wonder. So, Tag took off down the stone steps and a moment later stood before the messengers and all the members ready to fight, prepared to address them.

In front of Tag stood 1000 spear ready Kandies and Andies and Andies, marked with the Kingdoms symbol of messenger. Each one knowing their target and duty. Each one standing willing and eager.

"Haste not cousins, the Kennard has ordered Last Response position. Go now and inform your post, may ye travels be swift." Tag announced and with his command the Kandies and Andies and Andies vanished from his sight. Then he turned the vast members who stood ready to defend the Isle from the Ubil.

"Make ready the Fight, Maurieen Palace is under fire!" With that the massive members ran to gather weapons supplies, while Tag and the Wardeen organized their path to the palace.

Meanwhile at the Regan's palace on Mystic Island the Hedlen, Baldric and his company appeared in the Regan's receiving room. Cornelius released the orbital and gave the signal for the Hedlen to go ahead with Kathrie Gretel to Out Bend.

Cornelius rushed to the Regan's side, but the Regan was already in conference with his brother, Sanborn. Sanborn had only a moment before stepped from the Spit cock receptacle and escaping the horror of the palace.

The two Lachlann's welcomed Cornelius to the meeting. Cornelius quickly filled them in and informed them that the Kennard was himself at the palace. He was to survey the situation and then retreat to Kats Clearing at the base of the Raye Raye Forest. He would wait there for the Regan's orders and recruits.

Pleased with what Cornelius had to add the Regan immediately order troops sent to Kats Clearing.

At Out Bend Kathrie Gretel was met with sarcasm by the young Lachlann in charge. But once a clear order from the Regan himself was received by Spit cock the atmosphere changed and soon they too were sending troops to Kat's Clearing.

At the Maurieen Palace the second Hedlen, Colb, the Kennard and Rowan appeared in the council room. The room was deserted and demolished there were burns on the floor. The curtains and pillows were ripped apart, their guts thrown about. The elements of tradition in the center of the chamber were all knock over, their pillars smashed. Even the councilman seats where Rowan himself had sat only a few turns ago, had been blown apart. But what was most disturbing to the three was the dead bodies they found lying all around the room.

The bleachers were filled with dead Colleens, Wardeens, Hedlens, Feldens and Lachlanns. All members who could not disappear or fly away. They were massacred in a flash. No chance to defend themselves.

The Kennard and the Hedlen quickly searched the bleachers for someone alive but it seemed all were lost. Rowan searched the counselor's seats and found Orida Nnon Frothper dead. He closed Orida's eyes and then called to the Kennard who rushed to his good friend side. But there was nothing that could be done, Orida was gone. Rowan moved on to find Cobb Axel, Warwick, Hazel and Moiré O'Neal all dead. They were all gone. It seemed only the members who could vanish or fly had any chance at all. But just as Rowan was about to give up, the Hedlen, Colb called to him.

"She's breathing."

Rowan ran to the Hedlen and looked down at the member, it was Constance Regan. Rowan bent down to her and scooped her into his arms.

"Connie, darling you're alive."

Her eye fluttered. She was barely holding on.

"We need to find her a healer." Rowan whimpered.

"Use the orbital. It will be the fastest. . .way." The Kennard ordered before bending down and passed Rowan the round disk.

"What about ye and the Hedlen." Rowan asked in surprise.

"I must continue here, I must know what we are dealing with in order to defeat it. The Hedlen may travel with ye and then return for me when Constance is safe." The Kennard stated bravely.

Rowan agreed and in less than a moment they disappeared from the Kennard's sight.

The Kennard made his way towards the Gallery. He hoped to use the Realagraphs in the gallery to enter the Maurieen Palace. He pulled back the remains of the crimson curtains and stepped in the room. The old table was knocked over and the red vase was smashed on the floor. Two of the paintings were missing and the only one that remained was the one to the Maurieen Palace. Relieved the Kennard stretched his leg and began climbing into the Realagraph. When he heard someone mournfully cry out.

"Don't go!"

The Kennard stepped back into the gallery and looked around the small room. But there was no one there.

"Who said that?" He asked.

"I did." Answered Hildegard Lamont as she reappeared in the corner of the room. Her face was scared with tears and she was still shacking. "I only got away because they couldn't see me."

"Ye were smart. But please tell me who couldn't see ye?"

"The Ubil they fly with fire on their heels. Their leader glows with a brilliance that blinds. Many of us tried to escape, but the Ubil burned the Realagraphs to prevent troops from getting in. They left only the one to the Maurieen Palace so they could get back there. But back in the Palace it is worse than here." She sobbed. "So, I came back here."

The Kennard patted her head. "It's alright, stay hidden here and I will soon return to take ye out."

"No. If ye go to the palace ye will not return." She shouted.

"Why do ye say that?" He asked.

"Because." She paused soberly. "Their leader wears Bagree's Bangle."

The words hit the Kennard like a cold burst. He did not expect the Ubil to control the bangle that quickly. He could not understand how they had come to have it. He shook his head and gathered his strength. Even with Hildegard's information he still had to see for himself the evil at the palace. So, he climbed into the Realagraph and stepped out into the Gallery at Maurieen Palace.

In the huge gallery at the Maurieen Palace, all the paintings were on the floor in a pile. Only the one to the council chambers still hung up on the wall. The Kennard stood up and looked around. Two guards laid dead their blood in a pool beside their bodies. The Kennard pulled out his sword and started up the clear glass tunnel at the entrance of the gallery. Without hesitation he stepped through the mirrored door and out in to the circular mirrored room. Two more guards laid dead on the floor.

With his sword ready he cautiously entered the reception hall of the Palace. Before he could even turn the corner out of the mirrored hall, he heard several horrifying screams. The voice sounded like that of a Colleen and she was in terrible pain. The Kennard rushed towards the sound and soon found a young Colleen standing between two young Sherideens. The Sherideens were taking turns practicing their spells on the her.

"Dom a may." One of the Sherideens dressed in green shouted as he flung his wand in the Colleens direction. A flash of green light flew from his wand striking the Colleen in the knee.

"Drate to low." The same Sherideen yelled while the Colleen sobbed with pain. The Colleens body seemed to be under a spell that held her in place. The only thing she could move was her head. The Kennard watched in horror as the second one prepared his spell.

"Dom a may." The second Sherideen dressed in red called flinging his wand towards the Colleen. A flash of yellow exploded on the young Colleen's arms and both Sherideens began laughing.

Suddenly to the right of them came another horrible sound. The commotion caught their attention and they went off running towards the noise allowing the Kennard an opportunity to free the Colleen.

"Thank-you." She sobbed gratefully.

"Do you know where their Master is?" The Kennard asked in a whisper.

"He must be in the grand dining room, that's where all the noise is coming from." She answered before running out the front entrance of the palace.

The Kennard quickly darted toward the Grand Dining Room. He knelt behind one of the huge Triptoephant that graced the entrance. From there he could hear very little of what was going on inside, he had to get closer. Without hesitation the Kennard set his sword in the crack of the Triptoephant hind leg and instantly shrank down from his dandy size. Out of his dandy size and back to a Teeny, he could slip in to the room unnoticed and listen to the Ubil master.

The grand dining room looked as if it had been prepared for a glorious celebration. The tables were set with red and white table cloths, baskets of el Carmena Granda's and mim's laid in their centers while streamer of red swirled out of the flowers and whirled in the air. There were two banquet tables lined with food and decorated with confetti. Even the dance floor had been surrounded by pots of delicate mims and streamers of red.

In deed the members now using the room were celebrating. They were celebrating their success. They had taken over the palace and destroyed the council. They had done what they set out to do and now they were rejoicing. In the center of the dance floor they had pulled together a make sift thrown and there sitting in it was Blaze's form as a young Master.

The Kennard hoped in closer and found a place to hide while he listened to the Master speak.

"I am bored of this place. Perhaps this palace isn't the finest." The young Master announced.

"The palace at Out Bend I hear is very large and wondrous." A Kathrie with long black hair mentioned to him.

"Mystic Island is very nice beside the falls." Replied an orange cloaked Sherideen.

"Why not both? We could take them both by morning." The young Master said sitting in his thrown.

The group laughed out loud.

"And then the isle will be yours Master Handrew." The Kathrie added.

The young Master stood then.

"To the Spit cock!" The young Master announced. He went to take a step forward, but his right foot gave out and he stumbled. The orange clocked Sherideen caught him before he fell and held him up.

"Master what is it?" The Kathrie shrieked.

"This form is growing weak, Blaze's being is fighting me. I must rest." The young master cried out. With that the Sherideen placed him back on the throne. "Allow me a sweep and then we will take the Regan's Palace at Mystic Island."

The Kennard had heard enough to make his report. Quickly he bounced out of the Grand Dining Room. He ducked behind the Triptoephant statue. There he grew to his Dandy size and recovered his sword. Then he headed back to the council chambers to meet the Hedlen, Colb.

The Touch

The light of morn came sudden and bright. It reduced the look of flames burning at the palace and made clear the devastation. Smoke poured from the remains and for several dimensions around the grounds laid its ruble. Behind the destruction of the Palace, just beyond it's back gate lay Kat's clearing. Its lust green gentle slops were for the most part silent, except for the occasional "slop!"

The sound was soft and it echoed only within the clearing. Once it past a tide of willing soldiers would appear in its place and they would move out to join the other members. The waiting members numbered more than one hundred thousand. Each ready to act for the good of the Isle and all now sat waiting with the Quinton, Sanborn Regan, Cornelius, Rowan and Kathrie Gretel.

Before long the clearing was overly full of members prepared to die for their Regan and the peace of the isle. All they needed was their orders from the Kennard which came when he appeared with the Hedlen, Hildegard Lamont who had been stranded in the council room.

The Kennard quickly filled in the Regan and explained how they need to move in now before the Ubil made their advance on the Regan's palace and now while the evil master was weak.

With the Regan's approval of the Kennard's plan, he gave the order for the troops to make ready their attack. Word was sent to Small Town for the Wardeens to advance to the palace.

All of the practice situations, and training war games were now worth their weight. All the turns used in training and planning for just such an event was now paying off. The Wardeens, Feldens, Frandies. Kandies and Andies from the Haptons up to Grassy Point were now gathering in Small Town. In Small Town they would Spit cock to the front gates of the palace. While the Hedlens, Lachlanns, Ulldens, and Laddies from Outbend, up to Le bog and across from Marwood to Beacon point, were now gathered at Kat's point.

The war was under way.

At the Pert, Marypat was just coming to.

"There ye are, do not fret, I am Edie I wish to help ye." Kathrie Edie said softly as not to frighten the Maurieen.

"Where am I?" Marypat asked.

The kind Kathrie Edie explained to Marypat all that had occurred and Marypat sat up in disbelief.

"Handrew possess my son? How can I stop him?" Marypat ask Edie.

Marypat hoped there was a simple spell she could use to get Handrew out of her son's body.

"I don't know, ye son has great power and he wears Bagree's bangle."

The bangle did not concern Marypat. She knew that the bangle was missing a stone from its prong. She had taken it, herself. After all it was her tear from the mist of the river Froymin. She had had the stone put in a necklace, in the very necklace her son had taken with her. So, if he used that diamond to make the bangle work, the bangle would accept her touch.

What did concern her was Handrew. Handrew would not care if he damaged Blaze's body. He would do anything to protect himself even at the expense of Blaze. Marypat on the other hand did not want to injure her son and his life was too big of a price for her to pay. She didn't know what to do all she knew is she had to try.

"I will need a crystal, one of the isles and a wand." She said.

Kathrie Edie handed her the wand she held and Marypat looked at it strangely. Tears filled her eyes she recognized it. It was her Predom Excel, her wand.

The wand slipped into the palm of her hand. The cold Torbernite mingled with Seppentinite felt perfectly comfortable in her palm, as if it were a part of her. She squeezed it tightly. Instantly her body surged from the cool blue aura into an instance orange.

She looked up at Kathrie Edie and said. "It looks like I won't need the crystal after all."

Kathrie Edie, Godfrey and Geraldo, stepped away from her. They could see the power building in the Maurieen and they did not want to get in her way.

Marypat took in a deep breath as she did the air in the room grew thin. The air swelled around her and lifted her. Three of the elements came to life within her, they were at her command, and all she was lacking was her element of fire. She knew that the element of fire would grow the moment she saw the palace. She knew the emotion of rage would bring fire into strength. She needed only to wait.

"Thank -you, all of you. I must go now and try and save my son." Marypat said softly as she knew she could now fly.

Kathrie Edie bravely approached Marypat. She placed her hands above Marypat's head and recited an Incantation.

"WEN JAY NO BREE POE, LOX COLL ME APON RE. Strength and power do not go, great might stay with thee." Then she lowered her hands. "Be well, sister."

"And ye." Marypat answered before flying out of the chamber.

A moment later Marypat was drifting across the sky heading for the palace, below her she could see the Regan's forces descending on the Maurieen Palace. She knew she had to hurry. The Regan's forces would not know that Blaze was an innocent. They would not care. They would kill the lad to get to Handrew no matter what happened to Blaze. She was the only hope Blaze had to survive she had to get there first. The thoughts filled her head and at the same time filled her heart with rage. Igniting within her the last element she needed. Her body surged with red flames, bursting across the sky like an enormous ball of energy. The troops below ceased their movement for a moment, half in shock, the other half in fear as she passed above them. They stood and watched as she descended towards the place, while three lonely members followed on brooms from the Pert.

"More Ubil." Cried one of the Hedlens from below.

Marypat heard them and quickly turned back to the masses and shouted, "I am a Maurie, I have come to stop the conflict, do not heed my passage and leave those who follow me in good care."

Cornelius was among the troop and he quickly made himself visible to her. "Marypat he is in the Grand Dining Room, the Kennard has him cornered."

With that information Marypat started back on her path towards the palace with the Grand Dining Room as her focal point. Outside the dining room Marypat found the Kennard with a troop of Lachlann, Wardeens and Frandies secured behind the remains of the Grand Triptoephant that only a sweep before stood tall on either side of the entrance. When she approached, the troops stood back in awe at the sight of her glowing form.

"She has the powers of the other, we're surrounded." One of the Wardeens shrieked

"No! She is with us." Commanded the Kennard.

"Tell me what ye know." Marypat ordered the Kennard and he filled her in as she peered into the hall. The tables were turned over and all the flowers, streamers and ribbons were scattered through the room.

"The young master is within, he is surrounded by his faithful. We have tried to overtake them but we cannot move forward. The Bangle protects all those near him only those who were outside the hall have we been able to intercept." The Kennard informed her.

"I will remove the bangle, but ye must promise to leave the master to me, I do not want the lad harmed." Marypat urged.

"It is Handrew we want, Maurie. Remove him from the lad and ye may have the lad." The Kennard answered with a bit of irritation.

Marypat needed a moment to compose herself. All she had to do was touch the bangle and it would open to her touch. She knew using magic against it wouldn't work, but she also knew she needed magic to protect herself from the Ubil followers who now surrounded her son. She also feared what would happen once the bangle was opened, Gazpalding had swollen into a mass of pus and then melted away. What if the same happened to Blaze? But then she remembered that Donovan had worn the bangle, it had opened freely for him. Perhaps it does not affect those who are good. It all was just too much to think about, it was going to be tricky.

Nervous but determined Marypat rose up from behind the barricade and slowly drifted forward. She entered the dining room. Her body glowed enlightening the entire room. Instantly she was struck from every side with streams of sparkles. Spell after spell was directed at her, but each and every one was adsorbed into her aura. Nothing slowed her advance. Before long she stood in front of her son's form. Blaze's eyes bulged at the sight of the Maurieen.

"Step free of the lad and I shall not harm ye." Marypat demanded.

Blaze's form just laughed at her.

"Do not annoy me." She persisted.

"Annoy ye, oh no, I wouldn't dream of it." Blaze's form continued to laugh. Several of his followers surround her. Again, she felt her body vibrate as spells were dispatched in her direction. But none had the power to harm her.

Irritated by the on slop of sparks Marypat was absorbing, she spun around with her wand pointing out. Quickly she struck every Ubil with one of the only spells she knew.

"Dom me a gron." She called out sending all the Ubil members sailing back away from her. In the same instant she slipped her wand into her pocket with one hand and dried her tears with her other. Her body cold to a soft yellow hue. Then she took a deep breath and allowed herself to relax.

She gave one last exhale and permitted all the elements to leaving her. Her body dropped and, in that instant, she forced herself forward and touch the bangle. Instantly the bangle unlocked and she removed it from Blazes arm.

She curled the bangle under her body and dropped it to the floor.

Blazes' form grew angry with the Maurieen but it did not swell and fester to that Marypat was relived.

He rolled up his fist and waved it at her. His power picked Marypat up and flung her into the ceiling. She had to fight to keep hold of the bangle as her body was slammed against a beam. Within his grasp Marypat managed to take hold of her wand once more and with it she soon returned to her bright red glow.

Her powers ripped through his grip on her and she was soon free.

"I have the bangle." She shouted as she sailed out of the entrance of the Grand Dining Room and past the Kennard. She knew that having possession of the bangle was only half of the fight. She needed to get the bangle out of the area so that the Ubil members couldn't be protected by its power. With the knowledge that Marypat had the bangle, the Kennard gave the order to attack and the battle began. Hundreds of Frandies swarmed forward covering the floor of the dining room. While four hundred Lachlann, Wardeens and Hedlens followed close behind. Swords clashed, daggers thrust forward, all the while stunning spells whirled through the air.

Meanwhile Blaze's form surged with anger. The rage grew in his heart and the element of fire was fed. A fresh wave of power filled him and he charged after Marypat. Their glowing bodies raced out of the palace and into the open sky above the principal balcony.

Blaze's form shot a wave of furry towards Marypat's back. It hit her and she turned around in surprise. Her surprise was not that he hit her with a spell but that it wasn't all that powerful. She studied him carefully as he threw another ball of furry her way. Easily she dodged it, which only made him more angry. The weakness of his power opened her thoughts to the fact that he had only two of the elements creating his power. She was using all four. If she could hold him off long enough she might be able to reduce his strength and then with one good zap she might be able to separated Handrew for his sons' body. But how big of a zip might she need to use, and would it damage Blaze, could it harm her son? He was being harmed enough as it was. Possession spells always harmed the possessed. Wasn't he hurt enough she couldn't bear to hurt him anymore. Her mind drifted to poor Henry, how horrible it was for him when his mind was striped. How lucky he was though that the outside world was not affected by the magic used here and out there he was normal again.

"Outside?' She said to herself. That was it. If she could take Blaze to the outside world, Handrew could no longer possess him. It could break the spell.

Without even thinking about her own safety, Marypat throw herself at Blaze and grab a hold of him. Blaze struggled wrapping his arms around her and beating Marypat violently in her face and shoulders. Still she hung on to him with all her might. Then she forced herself to raise, faster and faster she forced the two bodies to ascent into the sky.

Below them the troops stood in astonishment. No member had ever flow as high or as fast. Cornelius, Kathrie Gretel, Godfrey, Geraldo and Kathrie Edie all watched as Marypat soared upwards pushing the possessed Sherideen higher and higher in to the open sky. Then suddenly the green sky fell away and they were soaring in the blue air of the outside world. Instantly the spell was broken. Blaze's body flashed white and Marypat lost her grip on him. Sparks flew from his nose and ears and then Handrew was vomited out of his mouth. Handrew tumbled through the air and quickly fell back into the eye of the emerald.

Blaze's body immediately collapsed. He was unconscious and he too was falling back into the eye.

Marypat out of the eye was powerless. She could do nothing but allow herself to fall back within the eye and hope she could regain her powers once back inside. As she fell she watched the blue sky turn green once more. Then she grabbed her wand and took a deep breath, her body began to glow a bright yellow and it was enough for her to regain control of her flight. Quickly, she spotted Blazes lifeless body falling back towards the ground. Proximately she sored to him and grabbed him turning him safely in her arms and then landing near the principal balcony.

Handrew during his fall also regained some of his powers once inside the emerald. It was enough for him to steer himself away from the troops, but the Regan never hesitated. He ordered his troops to follow him and arrest him.

Inside the palace the Kennard and his men were still in the heat of battle. But once the Ubil heard the cheers coming from the troops outside they knew their master must be dead. Fearing the worst, the Ubil fled leaving behind their dead and injured.

The tranquil principle balcony with its pink marble stone floor in the shape of the peaceful design was a disaster. How odd, the symbol of peace laid at their feet while all around them a war had been raged. Still it was where Marypat had landed as it was to be the true sign of what was to come that there would again be peace for them.

Marypat's feet touched the marble and instantly she was surrounded. Cornelius and Kathrie Gretel were the first to reach her. The Regan, Rowan and the Kennard followed closely behind while Godfrey, Geraldo and Kathrie Edie approached cautiously.

Marypat laid Blaze down on the marble and stepped back to allow his grandparents to have a look at him. Cornelius knelt beside him and began apprising his condition.

Blaze was still unconscious but he was alive and Marypat was finally able to breath. She wasn't sure what she should do next. She didn't know what the Regan would do to him or her after all the destruction at the palace. But what she did know is that she had to call her grandmother and let her know he was alive.

Kathrie Gretel had Marypat's back pack and willingly she handed it back to her. The two women smiled at each other. Both were relieved the boy was alive.

Marypat Quickly dug in the bag, but her concentration was broken when she heard the Regan shout.

"Sherideens arrest them!" He bellowed as he pointed nervously at Geraldo and Godfrey.

"No!" Marypat jumped as she realized who he was pointing at.

"They are not Ubil, they helped me escape and they are the ones who protected my son."

There was sentence on the balcony as those present did nothing but watch the three slowly approach.

"Do you know them?" Marypat asked Kathrie Gretel.

"Yes, I recognized them they are the last three members I would have ever expected to see this turn." Kathrie Gretel answered.

"Why is that?"

"That first one is Geraldo Medora a low skilled, no talented preforming magician. Do you remember he was the magician that night we had dinner at the Blarney Stone?"

Marypat knobbed, 'yes'. She remembered angering the magician that eve but she did not know that this was the same man.

"The Kathrie is a very old friend of mine. She is a good-natured Master Kathrie, her name is Edie Cummings Lazarus. Her sister told me she died some 30 passes ago and the Sherideen is her husband, Godfrey Lazarus. The same Sherideen, my husband Drake Gazpalding, had banished to the Red Isle more than 50 passes ago."

Marypat stood in shook at Kathries Gretel's knowledge of the three members who had helped her to escape the Pert.

"Geraldo, Edie, Godfrey Lazarus, Thank you!" Kathrie Gretel welcomed the three.

"Gretel old friend, 'tis good to set eyes on ye." Kathrie Edie replied with a smile.

"And on ye, I had thought ye dead, by your sister's report. Where have ye been?" Kathrie Gretel inquired.

"'Tis a tale of anguish." Kathrie Edie began. "When Godfrey had been banished by my own members, I refused to allow my son to become one of them."

As she spoke Rowan stepped forward. Tears filled his eyes as he listened to his grandmother's words.

"My sister Edna and I took him to the Cascades and washed him of his ties to the Ubil. After that Edith cursed us with an embeastment torment and both of us have been house cooses ever since." She lowered her eyes and Godfrey put his arm around her.

"The curse was broken when I found her again." Godfrey replied quietly.

There was sentence in the group as Rowan stepped forward and Kathrie Edie took in the sight of her son. "Rowan, my beautiful son."

The two hugged and Kathrie Edie quickly introduced Rowan to his father. The newly reunited family stepped off the balcony together unhampered while Marypat went back to trying to calling her grandmother.

"sssssshhhhhhh. Mom are you there." Marypat called.

"sssshhh rrrrr pop Marypat is that you?" Lora shouted into the Talk about.

"I've been so worried, sssshhh I've left the phone on hoping you would call. Is everything alright?"

"Yes, grandmother, I have him." Marypat answered.

"Then come home now, I want you out of there. sssshhhhh ."Lora yelled back.

Marypat didn't want to tell her grandmother that Blaze was unconscious or about what had happened. But under the situation Marypat and Blaze could not leave quite yet. She had to think of something to tell her grandmother so she wouldn't worry. "Soon come, grandmother we just have to settle something first."

"I want you home now." Lora added angry.

"I'll call you back in a little while and let you know when we are coming."

Marypat stated calmly then she clicked off the walkabout and stuffed it into her bag. Before Marypat had a chance to release the walkabout the air, was filled with torturous screams. She turned to find Blaze awake and in horrible pain.

Godfrey heard the shrieks too and ran to Blaze's side. He pulled out one of the vials of green goo and handed it to Cornelius.

"This will easy his growing pains, but he needs to have his Sherite Extolel, to stop them completely." Godfrey divulged.

"No father." Rowan stated as he stood above his new-found father. "He needs the Cascades." Rowans words reverberated like the truth of the ages and all those around agreed they needed to get him to the Cascades.

But it was not their choice to make, it was Blaze that had to make the choice himself. So after administering the vial, they waited for Blaze to gain his own mind before asking him the vital question of his life's path.

"Blaze you must make a vital decision, the entire Isle awaits your course. Will your life's path be of good or of Ubil?" Rowan asked.

Blaze reached his hand out to his mother who crumbled into his arms and held him. They energy instantly blended together and they rose above the crowd of members who had collected on the Principle Balcony.

"Mother, I am so sorry. I never wanted to bring you pain, I only wanted to see this place for myself. Your story of this place was so . . .arrrr. . . arr." Blaze tried to speak to his mother as they hovered above the crowd. But he was suddenly struck with more pain it was as if the potion in the vial was already wearing off and it would not be of any more help to him. He needed to act, he needed to make his choice as Rowan had suggested.

"Blaze, all is fine do not worry about me, what you need to do and you need to do it NOW is choice son, choice will you be of goodness or of evil!" Marypat shouted at her son as his body weaken in her arms and they began to drop.

Blaze with his last bit of strength shouted for all to hear. "I choice for GOODNESS." With that his body collapsed in Marypat's arms and she had to struggle to hold him as she landed beside Rowan and Cornelius.

The sky of the marrow radiated with a glow of shimmering rainbows. The mist of the Cascades rose and mingled with their brilliance. Causing a spectacle of color that danced in the air around the cascades.

The members present all stood on the blue sandy beach of the Lazurite island. There was Marypat, Cornelius, Kathrie Gretel, The Kennard, The Regan, Godfrey, Kathrie Edie, Rowan, Constance and

Geraldo. All stood silently and watched as the eight brightly colored robed Sanctifiers took hold of Blaze and entered the freezing cold waters of the Darling River. Blazes body flinched with pain but soon calmed as the waters cooled him.

Slowly the Sanctifiers floated him out onto the rippling waters. Their hands undressed him as the High Sanctifier robed in white called out from the beach.

"Son of a Maurieen from here on Hail, Solemn spirit appear unveiled, hear thou word, press clear redeem, wash pure, soul now clean. . ."

The words of the Sanctifier pulsated through the group and everyone noticed a sudden change in the air. It was like stillness, as though all of life stood still except for those at the cascades. Even the high Sanctifier noticed the change and he stopped with the ceremony and glanced around nervously.

The water of the river stopped and stood still the air around them ceased to move. The mist from the river evaporated and the rainbows disappeared.

Then from the north came a mystical sound. It was soft at first but then it grew stronger as it mixed with the voices from the Lake of Whispers. The voice sounded familiar to Marypat. It was the same voice she heard at the Vista and it filled her beings with a chill.

"He has chosen the goodness, he has chosen the goodness." It echoed over and over again. The wind picked up as the words grew louder around them. The Emerald Mountains shock and rocked. The small group looked up into the mountains and saw the Guardians of the Vista looking down on them at the cascades. Donovan was among them and Marypat could see he was proud of his son.

The voice continued to grow stronger with the strength of the wind. It turned in and picked up Blaze from the water. It held him above the Sanctifiers and rotated him around in a circle. The water turned bright yellow and, in a flash, rose up and consumed him. Marypat frantic on shore ran towards the whirlpool of water. But a wall of water swiped towards her and kept her from proceeding. She watched in a panic as her son was drowning in the water and the voice continued to call out.

"He has chosen the goodness, he has chosen the goodness . . .A new breed created and a heart cured of its curse, Torsheen ye shall ever be, by name, step forward new member, receive thy claim."

With that a bright light stuck Blaze in the chest. His body arched backwards in pain. His flaming hair flashed white and his eyes flared yellow after a moment all went still around Blaze. From his chest rose a blue mist, it swirled out of him and then brock into hundreds of sparks that flew out in all directions. One of the sparks sailed towards Godfrey and stuck him in the chest, sending him to his knees. One hit Geraldo and he too fell to his knees. Another struck Rowan, who gasped as it struck him. Then from all three a yellow mist escaped from their chests. All around the Great Isle and in all the lands of the Isle's Sherideens were struck with the blue spark of removal. The curse of the Sherideen heart was broken.

The water instantly fell still, the winds died down and the voice went quiet. Gently the whirling water set Blaze down in the hands of the Sanctifiers who brought him back to the beach and his mother's arms. His eyes fluttered open, he was alive. She smiled at him and he smiled back, as he did one glowing goodness diamond appeared on his neck like that of his mothers.

"I'm so sorry mom, I don't know what I was thinking." He whispered.

"I told you, it's ok, everything is ok now." She answered as she studied her sons face and neck. He had changed. His hair no longer flashed with flames, it now was back to its sand brown color. His eyes no longer sparked red, they too were back to their rusty brown hue and his neck held the diamond of goodness like that of the Maurieen line. He was no longer a Sherideen, he was now a Torsheen. A new breed and new member to the isle.

CHAPTER
25

Enrolled

B
ack at the Maurie Palace all was still in shambles but several good natured Kathries had come together with their covens in hopes of pulling together their strengths in repairing the Palace. Kathrie Gretel and Kathrie Edie volunteered to help while Marypat sought out Iola and Horatio.

It was a solemn meeting for the Maurieen who hugged and cried as Orida Nnon Frothper, Iola's husband was removed from council chambers. The dead numbered 342 in all, Horatio had not been among them. Iola assured Marypat that Horatio was alive and that lessened Marypat's pain. But still Marypat couldn't help but feel responsible for Orida's death.

"If only. . . " She sobbed.

"A heavy heart will drown one's soul. We must not look upon this moment and remember only this, we must hold on to who he was and how much he gave to us." Iola uttered.

Her words were wise but Marypat still felt guilt and Iola saw it in her eyes.

"Let it pass from ye mind and soul. Guilt is not on ye hands my sister, but on a larger fist and I will not rest until the wrongs that have been done to ye are undone." Her words were sharp and direct. With her husband's death she now had the strength to stand up and voice her opinion to what was left of the council and that was just what she did later that turn when the Regan called a meeting of the remaining members of the council.

The Regan resided over nine of the original 15 councilman who had survived the attack and were able to attend. Their decisions were swift and finally. Taking only a sweep to complete. In the end Marypat and Blaze were called to stand before them for the reading of their findings.

The council chambers had been rebuilt but the stench of death still lingered in the air as Marypat and Blaze stepped up to the podium beside Iola. The Regan stood and stepped up to his perch before addressing the small gathering of members.

"It is found by the council that Blaze Gazpalding . . . " The Regan began.

The name Gazpalding shot shivers up Marypat's spin.

"Was not at fault for the devastation and deaths here in this turn, therefore it is the findings of this council that he be immediately enrolled in one of the three approved priory academy's here on the isle. Once enrolled he will be instructed in the Order of Tradition and guided in the way of the good. At the same moment it is found by this council that his mother Marypat . . ."

Marypat cringed, she was fearful that they were going to order that she be separated from her son. That she was to be banished again, but this time it would be too difficult she would have to leave her son behind and that was just too much. She could not leave her son. She would not leave her son.

"Be enrolled at the Maurieen method Instituted for adults, here at the Maurie Palace." The Regan concluded.

The words rang in her ears and Marypat couldn't believe them. They wanted her to stay and learn. Finally, they wanted her to stay. Marypat hugged Iola and thanked her. Marypat knew it had been Iola whom had insisted that the council embrace them and so they did.

The Regan then added. "As for Bagree Gazpalding's Bangle I must insist that it be returned to the only place where it cannot be used to destroy and that is back into the Cinerin Stone at the Pert. The Kennard, Godfrey and Rowan Lazarus have agreed to see that the bangle is replaced within the stone this very eve."

He stepped forward then and held his hands out to Blaze.

"We have at our door a new member and new breed, we must embrace this new membership denoted as Torsheen. Together our world will be stronger for it. To this I give my command for this membership to be added to the book of nations." He proclaimed.

Marypat was pleased with the findings of the council. But she still had a very big problem a head of her and that was what to tell her grandmother. She wanted to stay, she wanted her son to learn how to use his powers. It was just, now, how to convince her grandmother that what they were doing was safe.

And then it came to her. She grabbed Blazes hand, told Cornelius they would meet him for dinner and then she grabbed a hold of a crystal shard. Both Marypat and Blaze began to glow and hover above the ground. Marypat turned to Blaze and asked.

"Ready?"

Blaze nodded his head and smiled as they both went sailing into the clouds. Up, up, up they went until the green sky turned blue. Then they both jumped into the front room of the house in Jamaica.

Lora ran to them.

"Your back." She shouted hugging them both. "I've been so worried!"

"Yes, we are back, but not for long." Marypat laughed.

Then she scooped up her grandmother and all three of them dropped back into the eye of the emerald. Lora streaked with fear as they fell without powers but soon Marypat regained her glow and she was flying the group safety landed back at the Maurieen Palace where Cornelius was still standing and watching them.

"Well done, Mary," he laughed "Seems ye are getting the hang of it finally."

Marypat introduced her grandmother to Cornelius, her father. Cornelius was overwhelmed to hold his own daughter in his arms again and the joy in Lora's face was beyond any happiness Marypat had ever seen in her grandmother's eyes. Before long the group strolled off towards the newly restructured Grand Dining Room. Where the Kennard, Kathrie Gretel, Kathrie Edna, Godfrey, Geraldo and Iola sat waiting for them. It was a period to remember those lost in the great battle, but it was also a stint to celebrate.

Marypat for the first time in very long time was completely happy. She sat down beside the Kennard and looked in his eyes. He had just returned from the Pert where he and Rowan had placed the bangle deep within the old open crater in the Cinerin stone. The stone had accepted the bangle and then the mountain shock and closed in on it once more. It had been an exhausting turn and it showed in his eyes as he shared a moment with Marypat.

His glace seemed different than that of the Kennard, there was something in his eyes. She was not sure what it was but it seemed very familiar to her. She looked at him again and he smiled. The Kennard had never smiled at her before. She looked closer and there he was.

The words came flowing back to her. "Steady be as steady go, when you find him you will know, that home and heart is one in the same, but do not look for him by name."

Tears filled her eyes and she whispered to the Kennard.

"Horatio?"

He smiled back at her.

"Why didn't you tell who you were? I've needed you so much." She asked honestly.

"I could not allow my emotions to get in the way of my duties." He disclosed.

"And now, do your duties end?" She inquired as she reached for his hand.

He smiled again at her as he accepted her hand in his. "This duty shall never end."

The bliss between them was soon ended as Blaze bounced between them and grinned.

"Mother it is time we move forward." Blaze's voice broke the moment and the vision fell away opening my eyes back to the front room of Marypat's grandparents' home in Upper Maryland, Jamaica.

"Now that you know your dream is true what should we do next?" Marypat asked me as I reclaimed my own thoughts and tried to focus again on this world.

Here I was, I had seen a true crystal of the Green Isles. I was completely overwhelmed that it was all real, while all this time I thought my vision was a dream and now I knew that Marypat and I have been brought together somehow in order to help the crystals. Our greatest concern was remarkably the same, we NEED to get them back together we do not know how but we must.

PART
4

Cornelius' Story

An explanation of man's place in life.

For
Isabelle and Irving Brown

Grandparents loved and missed beyond words.

FOREWORD

After coming to grips with the fact that Marypat and I were on the same path to bring the Whole of the Green Isle back together it became my focus to gather as much information from her and her family as possible, in hopes of finding our next step.

"Your Great-grandfather said he received this Crystal in Ireland?" I asked

"Yes, Cork I believe."

"And he didn't know how it got here in Jamaica; did you ever ask your Grandmother how it got here?"

"I believe she said she brought it here, after she got married to my grandfather."

"Is that all you know?"

"Grandma said there were four individual Crystals and when Great Grandfather went missing, grandma and her three sisters each took one." Marypat added.

"Do you know the sisters? If we can contact them maybe we can start by getting these four together."

"No, I believe they are all died." Answered Marypat sadly.

"Well where is your Grandmother, maybe she knows where their families are and they have them."

Marypat looked up at Blaze with an odd face to which Blaze replied.

"Yes mother, she is, I took her down just before you arrived."

"Took her down? Down the hill?" I asked thinking he meant he took her down the Mountain road into Kingston to go shopping and we would have to wait till she came home to talk to her but Blaze just laughed at my question.

"No, not down the hill, down into the eye."

His answer shocked me for a second, but then I realized they could travel within at any time they wanted they had a power to fly once inside and it must be an amazing thing for Lora to visit her father when she wanted with the help of her Great grandson.

"Are you prepared for this?" Blaze smiled at me as he reached his hand forward towards me.

"Prepared for what?"

"To travel beyond the eye?" He laughed.

"The first time is a stunning fall, but at least you will not have to worry about the landing, Blaze will see you down." Marypat explained.

My mind and body stood in complete astonishment. I never expected to be taken within and now I stood on the edge of the eye gazing into the world I had dreamed of my entire life.

With the strength and guidance of Blaze, I took my first fall through the eye. The vision of the glowing green hued world filled me with awe as we sailed effortlessly to the ground. When we landed, I was surprised to discover we were just outside the door of an old wooden cabin just as Marypat had described to me.

The lush green ambiance reminded me of Jamaica and it felt like home.

As I was taking in the beauty of the surroundings Blaze and Marypat knocked on the cabin door and before I knew it a man was standing in the door way greeting the pair. When his face came clearly into view I stumbled slightly for his appearance was that of my own father. His bright blue eyes, round face, gray lengthy hair combed over the top of his head and gentle smile brought my dream back into light. The man before me was truly of my family and I had to hold back my want to call him, "Dad."

"Great Grandpa this is my friend and she has agreed to help me in our quest to put the isles back together." Marypat introduced me.

Cornelius approached me with open arms and welcomed me into his home. Inside I met Lora, Marypat's grandmother who was sitting with three teenage looking members, Mary, Patricia and John. Instantly I assumed they were Blaze's children but as it turned out they were Marypat's children with her second Husband, Horatio. All three glowed with an inner light that I had never witnessed before and according to Lora they were born within the isle and had not been outside of the eye.

As for Blaze he had never married nor had children, his life's ambition had been to keep peace within the isles and save the Sherideens from their cursed hearts. A job that he knew would increase once the isles were rejoined, as it is his being that generates the force that breaks the curse upon the Sherideens heart. His presents on each isle would need to happen in order for each Sherideen to be touched by his cleansing aura. But as it stands he cannot move forward with his work until the isle are put back together therefore his focus had become towards his mothers and mine aspiration.

After meeting everyone Blaze took the children outside while Lora, Cornelius, Marypat and myself sat down so I could ask my list of questions.

There were many obvious questions we needed answers to but there were also several not so obvious questions I wanted answers to, to help me see the entire story.

"Cornelius, Marypat tells me you received the crystals from your father. Can you tell me what year that was and why you received them when you didn't know anything about them?'

"Well from what my mother told me back when I was a small child, she was my father's second wife. His first wife Linda died in 1873 after giving birth to twin boys. They had seven children, I think. Then in 1877 my father married my mother, I was born in 1879. My mother left my father before I was born. I believe something happened at their house, an attack of some kind in which several family members were killed including my father's younger brother Michael. My mother couldn't take the stress of what my father's family was hiding so she left. My father told me later on his death bed that at that point when she left, the family cut her off from any link to them. He said he did it to protect me but in doing so I knew nothing about the crystals until he handed them to me and begged me to protect them." Cornelius explained with an upset look.

"Why did he give them to you, he had two older sons, right? What happened to them?" I asked.

"My father had five sons including me. The eldest Patrick was to be the inheritor but he died in his twenties and didn't have a family. So, his second son Justin and his line became the inheritors. Justin had two sons and a daughter. Justin's oldest son Leroy then had a son Mark and one daughter Lin or Linda. Anyway, it was this great grandson of my father that was to take hold of the crystals but you see this was the issue they had gone to Dublin May 31, 1941 and were killed in a German bombing raid that struck Dublin killing twenty-eight people and destroyed over 20 homes. At this point in my father's life he was one hundred and three years old and I believe this happening pretty much weakened him to his end. So, you see at that moment he had no one else to rely on, I was his only living Pattie relative so he had to call on me to come and take possession of the crystals. I promised him I would protect them and he told me it wouldn't be long before someone from Bantry would come to meet me and help me. They would explain what I had to do and pass to me the family history but unfortunately that never happen for me. My Father died June 13,1941. That night and I left the next morning with the crystals and returned home two days later. It was the day before Lora's wedding. Do you remember that day Lora?"

"Yes, father I do, you were very upset when you returned home. I remember you telling us four girls that we needed to keep the crystals safe. They were so amazing beautiful, I remember looking at them with such amazement, but father you never told us that your father had died why didn't you tell us?"

"I didn't want to upset your special day, I was going to tell you all after but that night after your wedding I was stupid. I took out one of the crystals, this one we are now in and looked into it so intensely, I ended up falling inside. I was so wrong to have done so." Cornelius confessed with a voice of shame.

His voice filled my ears, my mind and my presence. It was as if I had been transported into his being and transported back to the moment he had fallen within.

CHAPTER 1

Cornelius' Fall

Mesmerized by the beauty of the crystal Cornelius' eyes couldn't pull away from its hold. The exuberance of the form grasped him pulling his entire body into its eye and dropping him within. As his body fell he could feel an intensity of vigor fill him and he began to fly. At first, he thought he was dreaming. A dream of flying through a vision of the heavens but then he could feel a breeze blow across his face and instantly he realized he was not in a dream but he was really flying.

When the realization hit him, it throws him off his gliding course and sent him tumbling over and over in a crazy state in which he could not recover from or correct himself. His tumbling sent him forcefully downward towards the ground within. His body twisted and turned causing his form to be bent in an odd way. As he reached the ground his head and back smashed into the terrain. Every bone in his body was shattered and he was unable to move.

The pain was unbearable and it sent him wailing uncontrollably as he laid there among some very tall moist grass powerless.

Nearby on a ridge of trees was a troop of Frandies who overheard Cornelius' cry's and came to his side. As they neared Cornelius he could hear their footsteps and their voices as the leader called out to the others.

"Halt."

Cornelius could tell the group was of military principles. It was war time in Europe and was surely reassuring to hear the sound of solders as they would know what to do for him as well as have medical men with them. Unfortunately, Cornelius could not see them, he was blind, his eyes were filled with blood, and his only concern was that the group was not of ally forces but instead were that of the enemy. The Germans after all had just bombed Dublin a few days earlier killing his nephew and his family.

"What is this?" Questioned one of the military beings that stood beside Cornelius broken body.

"Looks like a Wardeen beaten beyond fistful power, it might be of Ubil." Another voice answered.

"It might and if it is, we cannot help or we too shall be slaughtered."

"Awww www, please help me sir, please I beg you my body has been crushed from a fall or possibly an explosion. I need your help, I have no manner to get up on my own and I assure you I am not of the Nazi force." Cornelius begged the strange voices that he was certain now were not German; they sounded English with a slight French influence.

While he begged for help he tried to conceive what had really happen to him and where he actually laid. It took him a while to comprehend what had happened to him, only moments before he was standing in his own home and now he was outside lying in a field of grass and rocks. It was possible that there had been another bombing like that in Dublin. The explosion could have injured his head and made him feel as if he had been flying while the blast sent him outside of his home and we worried his family had been injured as well.

"Who did this to yee?"

"I do not know, please I will give you anything I have if you will help me and my family, I promise anything." Cornelius pleaded as his body began to swell and his head initiated his racing heartbeat with a pounding drum beat that made it difficult for him to speak. The sound created a panic within him as he worried what was going to happen to him and his family.

"Anything?"

"Yes!" Cornelius confirmed.

With Cornelius confirmation that he would promise anything, the troop began to whisper between themselves all the while Cornelius laid there among the tall grass as is swayed in the breeze. The edges of the grass and rocks were sharp like knives and each time it moved and collided with Cornelius skin it cut him and increased his pain. He could barely wait any longer for help he was losing his fight internally to stay conscious.

"I am Lieutenant JohnJohn. My troop has agreed to aid yee at our utmost capability if yee agree to be at our loyalty."

"Yes of course I will agree, your help will grant you my undying loyalty." Cornelius pledged unknowing that his word of agreement would become the path of his future.

It was within, extremely rare for a vaster to be indebted to a Teeny. In most case of the two species coming in contact with each other, it was the Teeny that was indebted to the vaster for the Vasters kindness and willingness to protect and allow the teeny breed to take up shelter among the Vasters home, property and business. Therefore, the sight of a Vaster willing to imbed their devotion in to a troop of Frandies was tremendously beneficial to the Frandies, so much so they could not pass it up. So, the troop agreed to help the broken Wardeen, and do all they could to save him.

"I shall send forth a trek of runners to call forth a healer meanwhile the rest of my troop will attempt to move yee out of this Weeping Grabby grass." Lieutenant JohnJohn explained.

With that Cornelius felt a thousand of little hands grasping at his body from all around him. At first it was shocking but as he began to move away from the sharp slashing blades of grass he began to settle down. The movement seemed slow but steady and after several moments of what seemed like level ground and bearable progress the gestures of the tiny hands changed drastically and suddenly Cornelius was being pulled and shuffled in an excruciating method. The pain of the movement was so horrible that he could not hold back his agony.

"Stop! I can't go any farther." Cornelius panted.

"Well we have yee out of the Weeping Grabby Grass and the terrain here is quite rocky. We had hoped to get yee just over there, to the patch of meadow beside the forest. Where it will be cool and comfortable to lay there while we wait for the healer. If yee can bear a few more lengths otherwise yee will have to lay here among the boulders." Lieutenant JohnJohn said.

Cornelius could feel the rocks below his body as the tinny hands set him down.

"Alright then, do as you must and I will try my best to keep my sorrows to myself." Cornelius expressed in a fragmented tone.

With that the tinny hands raised his body back up and began to move him again. Over and over ripping pain shot through his body until he could take no more and he passed out.

CHAPTER
2

The Cabin

W ithin the dim light of an enclosure, Cornelius struggled to open his aching dry eyes. He blinked them several times before he could hold them open and take in the vision of his surroundings. The faint light revealed paneled walls, a high celling, a table, and the frame of a bed in which he was in. His body laid out upon its soft comfortable structures with its velvety sheets, fluffy pillow and smooth mattress. His mind drifted to the thoughts that he must be in a bedroom, though it didn't look like his own bedroom he believed that it must be his and that his vision was playing tricks on him.

He recalled that he had had thoughts that he had fallen in a field of tall grass and had been in severe pain and yet as he laid there in that moment he felt no pain and he was obviously not outside. Baffled by his thoughts and memories he tried to sit up and when he did an enormous amount of extreme pain shot through his body overwhelming him and hurling him back into the bed.

"There now, best yee stay still for my treatment will take a few more turns to heal your inners and we have not yet been able to acquire a willing member to repair thou bones." Through his pain Cornelius heard a strong voice with a tone of a professional medical person, one who seemed used to dealing with injured people.

"Is this a doctor?" Cornelius asked himself believing it must it.

"I am so thankful for your help, doctor, I am also a general Practitioner in Galway. My Christen name is Cornelius." Cornelius uttered respectfully expecting the very tall man with his back to him to understand him.

Cornelius also expected that he was still in Ireland. He was not sure how his falling would put him anywhere other than somewhere near to his own home and Family. After all he had been standing in his office in the front of his home when he had been struck with the vision of himself falling and yet looking at his surroundings he was very hesitant about where he was or how he had gotten here.

"Pleasure to meet yee Cornelius. I am Gillian of the Cave Breed Loralacs. I am not of an official practitioner or post, I'm afraid but I am a basic Balm, this is why we will need an accomplished Kathrieen in order to complete your healing process. The first and most important point was to aid yee in surviving. When I reached yee four turns ago yee were near death. Yee body was shattered within and your blood was seeping through your pours. I had no choice but to concentrate on healing yee blood tracks and focusing on yee organs, my specialty by the way. Unfortunately, though, because of the intensity needed to repair your internal body I had not the stint to send for or organize one to repair your bones. But now that you have recovered to this point and awakened, I believe we can move forward in acquiring a Kathrieen." Gillian explained as he stood over Cornelius and blinked his one eye.

The sight of a one eyed individual nearly frightened Cornelius to the position where he couldn't speck. But then it struck him that it was wartime and it was possible the man had been severally wounded in the war with a horrible facial wound that one of his eyes had to be removed. With this thought Cornelius tried not to allow the sight of the man's face to trouble his chance to communicate with him and learn about where he was and how he had gotten here.

"Can you tell me where I am?" Cornelius asked.

"Well the Frandies troop that found yee told me they discovered yee at Weeping Grabby Grass Terrain a few lengths from here. Do you know of this point?"

"No." Cornelius answered as he thought back about the troop of little hands that had helped him. How strange it was that a military troop had had such an unusual method of moving their injured but there again it was wartime and being able to move the wounded under barbwire and other traps was a critical necessity in which he thought the government had developed a new technique.

"Well Weeping Grabby Grass Terrain rests at the edge of Finster Forest where the Forest reaches a ridge of the Emerald Mountain." Gillian described.

Cornelius had never heard of any of the placed Gillian mentioned and because of that he continued to ask questions.

"Are these places in Ireland?"

"I do not know of Ireland; this Isle is the Great Isle of the Pair Mountains grouping. For many passes this isle and its three sister isle groupings, The Golden Mountains, The Pyrite Mountains and the Holy Mountains have been separated from the Whole of the Green Isles. Then four turns ago the Great Isle became separated from the other three isles, for which we now stand alone. Perhaps you have fallen from one of them and that is why you do not know this land."

Cornelius's mind flashed with distress as the words of Gillian brought him to realize where he truly was. He had entered one of the four crystals his father had just asked him to protect. He had had no idea that what his father had given him had actually been a world of its own and the duty his father had passed to him was actually imperative. Broken inside that he had betrayed his father's request Cornelius looked up to Gillian and spoke with a daunting voice.

"No! I have not fallen from one of the other crystals. I have fallen from the world above. I was to be your clusters protector and now I have failed you. I must get back to them, I am the last Pattie of my father's line. I must get back my daughters will not know what to do nor will they have the strength to protect them."

Gillian's face drifted backwards away from Cornelius with a look of complete shock.

"Outside?"

"Yes, the world outside."

"I have heard that there was possibly an outside world but I have never seen anyone who has actually been out there. I have always questioned if it was real, but it has always been what the philosophers claim to be how and why our lands and Isles have been lost at stints and returned at others." Gillian clarified.

"Well I can tell you that the world out there truly does exists and if I do not return the isles may be in danger of being destroyed."

"Destroyed?"

"Yes, my father told me there are people out there who wish to possess these crystals to obtain their magic. At the time I thought he was mad, I believe that people would want them for their value. The crystals after all are the most stunning gems my world has ever seen. I could see someone wanting to make jewelry out of them and that alone would destroy them but not for magic. Now that I have been here I understand why it is important not to allow them to be destroyed, there is truly life within and I now must return to my world to see that this world is safe."

"I believe yee are correct. I shall do all I can to aid thee. I shall find us a Kathrieen to repair yee bones meanwhile yee will remain here in this cabin the Frandies have built for yee." With that Gillian left the room, leaving Cornelius alone in the dark.

A moment later the door to the bed room opened and several tiny flashing lights dashed across the floor and then moved to the end of his bed. When Cornelius looked to the end of his bed he was stunned to see five tiny men dresses in military like clothing. Each man stood less than a foot tall and glowed with a yellow hue.

"Yee are truly awake, sir!" One of the tinny men said with glee.

"Would thee care for some food, we have prepared a fresh pot of Potash, if yee think yee can handle it?" Another of the tinny men added.

"I a. . ." Cornelius stuttered as his eyes focused in on the men that were now marching up from the end of his bed. He was more shocked at the sight of these small men than he was of Gillian and his one eye. The one-eyed tall man was more easily acceptable to his brain than a group of men who were smaller than a newborn baby.

"I'm Lieutenant JohnJohn, glad to see yee looking better, is there anything we can get yee. Sir?"

"You're the men that saved me?" Cornelius asked as it came to light in his wits that the tinny hands that had lifted him out of the Weeping Grabby Grass were truly that of little hands and not of a new military method of moving the wounded.

"Well we can't take credit for saving yee, Gillian should have that acclaim. We are merely the ones entrusted with your care. As you can see we have constructed for yee this modest Cabin for which is yours, for as long as you can bear to use it. We have done all we can to make yee comfortable as well. I can only hope that we have met your requirements." Lieutenant JohnJohn expressed.

"You indeed have far exceeded my needs, I cannot thank you enough."

"Well, good then, again if you are in need of anything please let us know, we are at yee service."

"I could try some food."

"Fine, then . . . sergeant Pen see to it that Master Corn receives a Vaster portion of fare."

"Yes sir!" One of the tinny men shouted before jumping off the bed and running out the door.

"Master Corn? Is that to be me? My name is Doctor Cornelius McCarthy." Cornelius asked with a soft tone. He didn't wish to upset his caregiver after all without him, he would not be as comfortable as he was or looking forward to a meal.

"Please accept my apologies I had been in the room when yee had your conversation with Gillian and I thought yee said yee name was such."

Cornelius laughed. "Well that's fair, I just thought you were going to want to call me, Corn."

The four small men began to laugh as well and before Cornelius realized it he was feeling so comfortable among the Teenys, it's as if he had always been with them and he was at home.

CHAPTER 3

The Kathrie

The next morning Lieutenant JohnJohn and three of his troop members entered Cornelius's bedroom and quickly worked to awaken him.

"General Gillian has acquired a registered Kathrie of Mending strength, quite rare she be, but just what thou bone shall require to repair them to cured. She is at the front door as we speak and has only one sweep to see to yee needs. So, we need yee to be attending." Lieutenant JohnJohn conveyed eagerly.

"Yes, of course." Cornelius said with excitement. Finally, he was to have his bones looked after. He knew it would be several weeks before his body would be mended and he could possibly stand, but at least he was now going to be on a track to recovery.

A few moments passed and Cornelius could hear a large amount of activity taking place outside his bedroom door. First there was the sound of a large metal object being dropped on the floor and then there was the sound of water flowing out and splashing against something with a hollow echo. Then after several moments his bedroom door was pulled open and there standing in its openness was a lovely young maiden that Cornelius estimated was around 12 years old.

The young maiden was dressed in a dull green ankle length dress with long sleeves and a high collared neck. Over the dress she wore a lime green apron trimmed with white lace and splattered with yellow slim. Her face was pale while with high cheek bones, soft orange eyes and long wavy brown hair.

"Good marrow dear Wardeen. I am Gretel. My sisters and I are here to aid you with the healing of your bones but before we began may I enter your chamber and examine your form?" She asked in a gentle voice as she stood in the doorway of his bedroom.

Cornelius was slightly surprised that a young woman had been brought to help him. He questioned in his mind why Gillian would have not brought a person with more experience, but before he could make any sense of it, Gretel asked again.

"Pardon me sir, may I enter?"

"Yes." Cornelius replied.

"Thank you, sir." She said as she entered the room and floated over to the end of the bed. She placed her hand on his left foot and then gently slide her hand down to his ankle and then up to his right knee. When she reached his knee, she removed her hand from his leg and then touched his left hand. Her fingers creased the back of his hand delicately moving along his bone structure until she reached his wrist. When she reached his wrist she then took both of her hands and grabbed his forearm and held it for a moment before moving her hands up to his shoulder. She continued her examination over to his right side and then along his ribs. When she was done she faced Cornelius with a look of sincerity before speaking.

"Both of your feet and ankles are undamaged unfortunately they and your right elbow are the only portions of your bone structure that has not been damaged. The rest of your body has endured a server impact causing both of your femurs and humorous bones to have experienced a comminuted fracture. Your Radius, ulna, carpals metacarpals, patella's, cranium and several of your ribs seem to have undergone simple fractures while your clavicle and vertebrae have both experienced a transverse fracture. The most serious of your injury is that of your pelvis, your left elbow and your sternum, they have each suffered compound fractures. These three areas will be the most difficult to repair but let us start by repairing the others first." Gretel reported.

Cornelius eyes went wide as his mind thought through what the young women had said. She was obviously more intelligent than he had expected her to be and with her report, Cornelius accepted her advice and allowed her to do her treatment.

"Sisters I will need you now." Gretel called.

A few moments later two more young women stepped into Cornelius room. Both looked like Gretel, the only difference between them was their clothing. One wore a blue dress with short sleeves and a bonnet while the other wore a purple skirt with a white shirt that was embroidered with pink flowers around its neck.

"This is my sister Gritty." Gretel said introducing the young woman in the blue.

"And this is my sister Gretta. We will need to move you now so please hold still, do not fight our rise or you may damage yourself even farther."

"I will do my best not to fight you." Cornelius said.

The three girls then encircled Cornelius with one on his right side, one on his left and the last at his feet. Then they reached their hands out pointing their hands at each other creating a triangle.

"Few bree atee see, hol grif re." The three young Lassies called together and with that Cornelius slowly drifted above the bed and levitated.

"Few bree atee see, hol grif re . . . .Set greem." They called out.

This time Cornelius floating body began to move forward towards the door. He drifted out of the bed room and into the living room of his cabin. In the living room on the floor was a large metal box that the girls maneuvered Cornelius hovering body over.

"Few bree atee see, hol grif re. . . . Dom me a gron."

Slowly Cornelius body drifting down into the metal box that was filling with a yellow goo and tiny white worm like creatures. The solution was creamily and warm and once Cornelius' body was completely in dredged in the solution he was overcome with sensation of serenity and he pleasantly fell to sleep.

The scent of fresh peppermint and lemon drifted into air. The vapors filled Cornelius nostrils and slowly began to stimulate his state of mind. Sluggishly his eyes began to open and he was waking up.

The last thing he had remembered his body was being laid into a bathe of warm goo and now his body was dry and laying on his bed on his left side. He was in no pain and yet when glanced down at his left elbow he noticed it was in a very strange grip like device that was smothered in what looked like the same yellow goo that had been in the metal box.

"What is that?" He asked himself and without thinking he reached over to touch it with his right hand and when he did, he realized his arm, shoulder and hand were completely healed. He looked at his hand in complete surprise.

"How can this be? How long have I been asleep?"

"Four sweeps, I am afraid. I had hoped that one sweep would have been enough but as you can probably tell those three areas we spoke of as the most difficult to repair have been our delay." Gretel answered from his bed side.

In Cornelius mind he didn't know what a sweep was, he suspected that he had been asleep for four weeks or even longer. Just looking at his hand and arm, and how perfectly they were healed he knew he would have had to be healing between six to eight weeks.

"That long?"

"Yes, it has been a long morrow but at least you will not miss your midturn meal. That I promise. Now once we have removed the grips, we will see how well you can stand, if you can stand on your own, my job here is done. Are you prepared for the removal? It may sting a bit."

"It has only been a few hours, it isn't even moment for lunch?" Confused Cornelius agreed to allow Gretel to proceed with the removal of the grips. The one on his elbow slipped off with little pain and he was shocked at how painless it was for him to bend it. Then she moved to his back where she detached two more devices and wiped his skin clean of the goo. When she was done she called to her sisters and the three girls again lifted Cornelius off the bed but this time they placed him in a standing position. Slowly they positioned his feet onto the floor and with a gentle ease they allowed him to take control of his body.

Still a bit weak Cornelius fluctuated slightly but overall was able to stand and incredibly was able to walk.

"I can't believe this, you are amazing. How can I ever thank you, or pay you for this? What do I owe you?" Cornelius stuttered as he stepped forward wanting to hug the young women in an unbelievable urge of appreciation.

"You owe us nothing, General Gillian of the Cave Breed Loralacs has already taken care of your bill. Perhaps you should speak with him. He is in the kitchen with your Lieutenant." Gritty answered.

"Well if there is anything I can do for you ladies please let me know, I am indebted to you."

Gretel stepped towards Cornelius and laid out her hand to him. Cornelius accepted it and kissed it. When he looked up from her hand their eyes met and for the first time he was over taken by the young woman's simple beauty. She reminded him so much of his daughters and he wanted to get back to them.

"Again, thank you, I can't express to you how much I value what you have done for me and for this isle. Now that I am fixed I can return to my world and see to it that this world is protected and safe. All I need now is to find a way out. Do you know of a way out?"

"What do you mean a way out?" Gritty asked.

"I am from the outside world. I fell into the crystal and as you had seen the fall nearly killed me but now that I am healed I can go back to my post of protecting this world. I just need to find a way out."

The three Kathrieens looked at one another and frightfully shook their heads.

"No, no you cannot leave!" The Kathrieens said in unison.

"Why not!"

"Is there magic in your world?" Gretel asked still holding Cornelius hand.

"No, not like what you have here."

"Then what we have done for you here, to heal you will drop away as you exit the eye. Your body will crumble and you will die an excruciatingly painful death." Gretel revealed.

"So you see .. . . . I had no choice I had to stay within. It was not long after this the Isle went completely dark and I was lost in darkness, and my mind was lost. Luckily, I had made friends with Gillian who helped me to adopt to this world and of course the troop of Frandies I had become indebted too. Without them I surely would not have survived." Cornelius explained to the group gathered in his living room.

What Next?

"Oh Dad." Lora said as she held her father's hand and consoled him while I continued to ask my Questions.

"So, you received the crystals in Ireland. How did this one find its way to Jamaica?" I asked.

"That was me, when father went missing we girls, my sisters and I, thought someone had come after father and we needed to hide and protect the crystals as father had just told us the day before. So, we each took one." Lora explained.

"You did." Cornelius said with a slight sad look.

"Yes, father remember my husband was from Jamaica and we were to move to Jamaica after the wedding. I brought this one to Jamaica and in less than a year after we had arrived, it went missing. I thought it had been stolen. I was extremely upset that I had failed you father especially after Mora called me a week later to tell me a man from Bantry had come to see them and that they needed to know how he could met with me in Jamaica but I had to confess that mine was lost."

"So, your sisters did have the other three crystals, do they have family that we could call? If we can get these four back together that would be our first big step in righting this." I asked.

"All my sisters have passed away and only Mora had a daughter, Patricia. She still lives in Ireland, I can call her." Lora said as she reached for her cell phone.

Lora pressed a contact number and a moment later we could hear a women's voice on the other end of the phone.

"Ello."

"Patricia this is Auntie Lora."

"Oh, nice to hear from you, how are you doing?"

"Fine, fine, thank you, how about you?"

"Good thank you."

"Patricia can I ask you a very important question?"

"Of course, Auntie Lora you can ask me anything. What is it?"

"When your mother passed away did she leave you anything unusual that had been from your grandfather?"

"I don't understand, what do you mean unusual?"

"Some kind of a rock or crystal?"

"No, the only rocks my mother ever talked about that had anything to do with her father were not given to me."

"Do you know what happened to them?"

"No Auntie Lora I don't. Why are you asking?"

"I'm just having a moment of thought about your grandfather that's all. The last time I saw him he had some beautiful rocks that he showed us girls and it made me think that your mother might have given one to you and it would just be nice to see one again."

"Oh yes that's right yours went missing, I remember my mother saying something about that, but my mother never actually had one."

"What do you mean? I know when I left Ireland each of my sisters had one, including your mother."

"I don't really know about that, all I do know is what mom would talk about when she was very ill and delirious."

"And what was that?"

"She would constantly talk about the day grandpa went missing. She was so upset she could not believe he was gone. She would talk about looking for him and all that remained were these crystals. The beautiful crystals, the crystals of the Green Isle she would call them. She would just go on and on about these things and when I asked her where they were she would hold my mouth and tell me to keep quiet or they would come from St. Finbarr and silence me. We were not to talk about them it was a family secret."

"Oh, my yes I suppose it is. I guess we shouldn't speck about them anymore then. I am sorry to have troubled you about them."

"No worry Auntie, I think Mother was just making it all up, she was after all very ill."

"Well thank you for your time, Patricia, nice chatting with you."

"You too, give my best to the family. Good bye."

"Bye dear."

With that I turned to Cornelius.

"St. Finbarr that's a Catholic church in Bantry, right? The same town your father said someone would come from to help with the crystals and the same town in my dream."

"Yes!" Cornelius answered as he stood up and looked at me firmly. "It is, the very town."

"What does that mean, is that our next step?" Marypat asked.

"Yes, Marypat, we are off to Bantry, Ireland."

Printed and bound by PG in the USA